KIANA DAVENPORT was born and raised in Kalihi, of Hawaiian and Anglo-American descent. Author of three previous novels, she was a 1992–93 Fiction Fellow at Radcliffe's Bunting Institute and received a 1992 grant from the National Endowment for the Humanities. She lives in Boston and Hawaii.

Shark Dialogues

Kiana Davenport

A PLUME BOOK

PLUME
Published by the Penguin Group
Penguin Books USA Inc., 375 Hudson Street, New York, New York 10014, U.S.A.
Penguin Books Ltd, 27 Wrights Lane, London W8 5TZ, England
Penguin Books Australia Ltd, Ringwood, Victoria, Australia
Penguin Books Canada Ltd, 10 Alcorn Avenue, Toronto, Ontario, Canada M4V 3B2
Penguin Books (N.Z.) Ltd, 182–190 Wairau Road, Auckland 10, New Zealand

Penguin Books Ltd, Registered Offices: Harmondsworth, Middlesex, England

Published by Plume, an imprint of Dutton Signet,
a division of Penguin Books USA Inc.
This is an authorized reprint of a hardcover edition published by Atheneum.
For information address Simon & Schuster, 866 Third Avenue, New York, NY 10022.

First Plume Printing, August, 1995
10 9 8 7

Grateful acknowledgment is made to editors of the following publications in which chapters of this book first appeared in slightly different form: *Home to Stay, Asian-American Women's Fiction*, Greenfield Review Press, 1990; *Daily Fare, Essays from the Multicultural Experience*, University of Georgia Press, 1993; *Charlie Chan Is Dead, Contemporary Asian-American Fiction*, Viking Penguin, 1994.
Owing to limitations of space, all other acknowledgments for permission to reprint previously published material can be found on pages 491–92.

 REGISTERED TRADEMARK—MARCA REGISTRADA

LIBRARY OF CONGRESS CATALOGING-IN-PUBLICATION DATA:

Davenport, Kiana.
    Shark dialogues / Kiana Davenport.
        p.   cm.
    ISBN 0-452-27458-3
    1. Women—Hawaii—Fiction.   2. Hawaii—Fiction. I. Title
[PS3554.A88S5   1995]
813'.54—dc20   95–737
                                                CIP

Printed in the United States of America
Original hardcover design by Liney Li

PUBLISHER'S NOTE
These stories are works of fiction. Names, characters, places, and incidents either are the product of the author's imagination or are used fictitiously, and any resemblance to actual persons, living or dead, events, or locales is entirely coincidental.

To the memory of my mother,
Emma Kealoha

•

To the memory of my aunty,
Minnie Kelomika Kam

•

To my 'Ohana, the Houghtailings of Honolulu

•

And to the Warriors of Kalaupapa,
those past, and those who live on
with courage and dignity

Acknowledgments

For grants and fellowships awarded during the years in which this novel was written, the author gratefully thanks: the Mary Ingraham Bunting Institute of Radcliffe College, the National Endowment for the Arts, the New York Foundation for the Arts, the Ingram Merrill Foundation, the Ludwig Vogelstein Foundation, the Barbara Deming Memorial Fund, the MacDowell Colony, the Corporation of Yaddo, Blue Mountain Center, the Syvenna Foundation, and Cottages at Hedgebrook.

And heartfelt thanks to Lee Goerner and Harriet Wasserman.

"Hanau Kumulipo i ka po, he kane
Hanau Poʻele i ka po, he wahine
O kane ia Waiʻololi, O ka wahine ia Waiʻolola
. . . Ua hanau-mano koʻu akua . . .
. . . Hanau mano iloko o Hina-ia-ʻeleʻele . . .

Born was Kumulipo in the night, a male
Born was Poʻele in the night, a female
Male for the narrow waters, female for the broad waters
. . . Born a shark was my god
Born a shark in the month of Hinaiaʻeleʻele . . ."

—from *Kumulipo*, Hawaiian Chant of Creation,
Re-interpreted by Rubellite Kawena Johnson

•

". . . She was born on an island,
and that is already a beginning of solitude . . ."

— Marguerite Yourcenar, *Fires*

SHARK DIALOGUES

Ka ʻŌlelo Makuahine

Mother Tongue

Run Run

'*SAILORS, LEPERS, OPIUM, SPIES*—*with such a family history, how could we be anyt'ing but sluts?''*

Dese Jess's last words to her grandmot'er, Pono. Dat night Pono walk into da sea. But dis happen later, much later, after Ming rinse from our lives full of Dragon Seed. After Vanya become a terrorist, and Hiro suffocate from his own tattoos. It happen long years after dese little half-orphan girls—Vanya, Ming, Rachel, Jess—swim into Pono's life. I seen. I seen it all. Da years dey run from her. Da years she pull dem back, like bait. So, in a way, dis my history, too.

Now, "talk story" time. Early 1990s. Dese four cousins comin' home. Grown women, now, life t'rown everyt'ing at dem. But on dis island, dey still called "Pono's girls." And when she call, dey come.

Ka Hale o
Nā Kīkepa Kea

House of White Sarongs

JESS MONTGOMERY SAT ON A PLANE pouring west against the sunset. Beside her, a man clutching a deadly colored drink examined her closely, once and for all, so he wouldn't have to think of her again, for she was pretty, but verging on plain.

She looked down at her strong, square hands, the hands of a healer, a woman whose days were spent in humid rooms with the rusty aroma of blood, her language the haphazard argot of surgery, incisions, exorcisms. She smiled, remembering a handsome, satyr-thighed retriever who woke during surgery and bit her wrist while his bad parts went swish-swish down the drain. Recovering herself in his recovery. A dying Siamese, its final face waiting for her inside its cage, eyes like needles flashing, aloof to the very end. Jess holding its head with grave esteem.

Some were like humans: false pregnancies, malignant breasts, attempted suicides. She healed them and used them, their patience, their resignation, hoping their strength would penetrate into the impenetrable thing of her life. Sometimes she leaned her head against a cage and drifted. *One can live without thinking.*

Sometimes, caught off guard, she thought of her ex-husband and how, toward the end, sex with him had left her with the sensation of having brushed against death. Or, she thought of him and her daughter,

a team, and how the day she understood she was excluded from their
world, she had reeled from the house out into the streets, the crowds,
and dusk and dark and nothing.

Some nights when her assistants had left, she sat in her clinic among
the cages, just to be near breathing things who allowed her to ache
without comment, without observation. She didn't know what to want
anymore, so much of life was incomprehensible.

A bishop, looking feudal and cruel, swept past her down the aisle.
Behind her, two businessmen began debating the three great inflationary
periods since the birth of Christ. Exhausted, Jess leaned back in her seat,
fell into slumber so profound, later when she woke, actual human voices
made her gasp.

Young faces dripped into her dreams, she and her cousins coming
of age in their grandmother's house, overlooking the Pacific. The house
was set in coffee orchards in the misty blue hills of Captain Cook, part
of an archipelago of tiny towns with "talk-song" names—Hōlualoa,
Kainaliʻu, Kealakekua, Honaunau—the coffee-growing belt of the district of Kona, set high on an island so lush and volatile and mystic, it
had too many names. Island of Hawaiʻi. Pele's Island. Volcano Island.
Orchid Island. Because it was so huge, big enough to encompass all the
other major islands of Hawaiʻi, locals called it simply the Big Island.

In those summers in that house, four young girls had slept like the
dead, stroking through torched-sugar nights, dreaming through gauzy
harems of the afternoons. Something lay its hand on them, they couldn't
stay awake. Later they would swear they slept for years, slept their way
into womanhood in that strange, enchanted place. In other time zones,
other latitudes, Jess would close her eyes and feel the moisture-laden
trades. *Wind searches its haunted rooms, turning pages of a book. A delicate slip
laid across a koa chair breathes of itself. A letter trembles. Orchids sweep across
the lānai.* The life of each girl began before that house, but it so enveloped
them, that was what they chose to remember as their beginning.

At first men came too, fathers, husbands, brothers. But something
in Pono's house diminished men. They couldn't stay. It became a place
of women, cautious, whispering, filling up the gaping mouths of door-
ways. Their mothers brought them in the early years (except for Jess,
sent from the mainland on her own). And when the mothers could no
longer bear the burden of the house, what it contained, they sent their
daughters there alone, threw them across the sea like human sacrifices.
The girls grew inextricably close, turning away from the rest of the
world. Entering Pono's house, they entered a kind of Ice Age.

Arriving in their early years, not yet in their teens, and seeing their grandmother waiting at the door, something like fatigue came over them. They moved slower, to accommodate their fear. Pono was a giant woman, pure-blood Hawaiian, her beauty legendary. She was also *kahuna*, she could look someone to death. The cane she carried, made of human spine, was said to be that of a lover who betrayed her. She possessed a rosary of human molars. At night, it was said, her teeth grew into points. How she came to own the big house, the coffee plantation, so much land, was never known. There were rumors. Part of each month she disappeared.

"We had no father," Vanya's mother whispered.

"She never wanted us," Jess's mother said.

Ming's mother only shook her head, possessing some awful, unsayable knowledge.

One summer the girls found sepia snapshots—their mothers as young girls in Catholic uniforms, a sorrowful generosity in their eyes, as if they were forgiving the viewer for transgressions committed down the decades. In the years after World War II, their mothers had turned perverse. One married a Chinese descendant of cane-cutters, stoop-work "coolies" with permanently bent backs. Another ran off with a Filipino, a Pidgin-speaking busboy. Rachel's mother left her infant in Pono's kitchen, and disappeared forever. Jess's mother went all the way, eloping with a *haole*,* who took her to the East Coast of the U.S. mainland. In this way, Pono's grandchildren were all mixed-marriage mongrels, their mothers' revenge. At sixteen, Rachel would double that revenge, marrying a *Yakuza*, a walking tattoo.

As summers passed, the cousins were absorbed into the town of Captain Cook, yet still seemed to float outside it, inviolate, lit against the formidable backdrop of Pono. On Sundays, they peered from her old black Buick like flowers passing in a bowl, Pono steering imperiously, dressed like a duchess. When she drove her four-wheel Jeep, she was a frontier woman, hunched over, alert, the girls bouncing raucously around her. But when she drove the rusty pickup, her girls in back like hostages, she drove like a psychopath, ignoring Stop signs, traffic lights, as if behind that wheel, ancestral blood of helmsmen drummed within her. Had cannibal warriors crossing three thousand miles of ocean yielded right-of-way?

*Haole—meaning white, Caucasian, which is used throughout the novel, is pronounced "howlee." A Hawaiian-English glossary is provided on pages 481–87.

To most locals, the girls were indistinguishable, called simply "Pono's girls," aloof, of slightly different hues. Only Run Run, the cook, and Pono's field hands, could tell them apart. Ming, Hawaiian-Chinese, was delicate, "one pound powder" pale. Vanya, Hawaiian-Filipino, had rich, brown island skin, a quick temper. Rachel, Hawaiian and maybe Japanese (or Korean, or Mongol, who knew?), possessed the fairness of peach blossoms and apple jade, her beauty so perfectly proportioned it hurt to look at her. Jess was ruddy-skinned, fair in winter, red then tan in summer.

Gangly mix-bloods, their teenage years were filled with Jeep runs round the island, up to Waimea and Honoka'a for the rodeos, pageantry of the Grand Entry, the breath-stopping theater of champion *paniolo*, Hawaiian cowboys, in bareback bronco and bull-riding contests.

Pono loved the spectacle. "*Paniolo* the only men left with true Hawaiian mana."

Those summers would always be mingled in Jess's memory with horse-sweat man-sweat stench of furious bulls manure and fear shave-ice wet hay pineapple-spears a circus-smell excitement expectation as they approached the grounds flying dust of bullrings catching in her eyes aureoling fence posts the bands the *paniolo* turning everything into a dream and clowns warming up the crowds and hula girls and bands then *paniolo* riding out resplendent on their mounts waving to the crowds to her then disappearing minutes later exploding back into the ring bareback on wild broncos Jess screaming huddling on wooden grandstand benches in the asylum of Pono's wings horrified as blood spattered azure plush of embroidered cowboy shirts and bright pink and purple chaps and golden muscular Hawaiian stomachs slashed open guts like blue oysters raw sea urchins spilling out so that rodeos and Puerto Rican *kachi-kachi* bands smell of blood rawhide and saddles rinsed into heavy smell of sugarcane sweet gardenia smell of "Kona snow" white blossoms of the coffee trees in her grandmother's fields. Her youth.

In that large, restless house of water-haunted sunlight, the kitchen was where they discovered their real history. Stories heard from Run Run, the cook, drugged them, startled them, fleshed and shaped their evolution. As she talked, her hands were busy whacking bloody chicken parts, dripping grease from *laulau*, cheroot of dried cuttlefish hanging from her lips.

"Dat missin' fingah on yoah *tūtū*'s hand, from pineapple sliceah at Dole Cannery. You know how many years she punched time clock at dat evil place? You know foah why? So could send yoah mot'ers private

Catholic school, so dey no turn out gum-chewin' whores on Hotel Street. Dis da truth, foah shoah!"

Arriving in late spring, the girls were always given separate rooms. Pono didn't want them mixing up their dreams. But, later, while she snored, their white sleeping sarongs licked the dark like candles as they explored secret rooms, lagoons of the forbidden, then tumbled into a big koa four-poster, mosquito net like albino skin muffling their laughter. Concentrating their attention, they would examine each other, compare changes each year had wrought, Jess's new body odor, the way Vanya's breasts were forming, the way hair grew under arms. They were half of each other's blood; what happened to one happened to the others.

Some nights they gossiped for hours, so buoyed up by each other, they felt nothing in life would be able to resist them, nothing would happen to them accidentally. Finally, in a confusion of limbs, they slept, windows thrown wide, only a shivering net between them and the vast Pacific, exploding planets in a carnival of sky. Sometimes tradewinds galloped through with such force, when they woke it seemed a giant finger had moved the furniture across the room.

Some nights without warning, Pono would shake them, wake them before dawn, drive to a secret beach where they scoured the shore with Coleman lanterns, looking for treasures washed in from the Orient. Blue glass fishing floats from Japanese fleets working tuna longlines in the Bering Sea, ivory *mah-jongg* tiles, gold jewelry, rare colored bottles, ceramic jugs with Cyrillic lettering. By midmorning, exhausted, the girls would drowse along the beach, until Pono piled them into the Jeep. Headed for home she would "talk story," telling how they were descended from the daughter of a great Tahitian chief, a fearless swimmer and Eater of Stones, a woman who fought for Queen Lili'uokalani, last monarch of Hawai'i.

On stormy, starless nights there were no drives, no beachcombing, only sleep-filled hours, the girls turning and turning, sliding in and out of each other's dreams. Some nights they woke suddenly, knowing she was there, looming, terrifying, waving that ugly cane.

"There are things to tell."

She would pull up a hand-carved teak chair, lean close and talk. The wonders of the world, the Pyramids, the Great Wall, the serpent called the Amazon. She talked past dawn, past noon, into another evening, drugging them with her legends, her travels, what she had seen. When they were young, they believed everything she told them, though they didn't understand. When they were older, they learned everything she had said was true.

Jess woke with a start, voices of airline passengers assaulting her. She woke up different, several hours closer to the Pacific. And it seemed her metabolism changed, she could almost feel the pigment in her skin thicken, imagined her knuckles hardening like knobby bamboo, soles of her feet growing calluses. And the sea, the sea, quickening in her veins! A coral reef ticking, nerves jangly like tambourine-fins of wrestling oarfish, a whispering like planchette conversations of wise octopi. She closed her eyes, seeing prismatic colors on backs of leaping dolphin, and gold on gold—the sun on Polynesian surfers, bodies arched into calligraphy.

Three years, the longest she had ever stayed away. This homecoming doubly urgent, for Pono had summoned her, all of them, a desperate thing. *She's nearing eighty. Maybe she is dying.* Something inside Jess buckled and troughed, she wanted to bark out loud. She had always been terrified of Pono, there were rank feelings, possibly hate, between them. Because of her, Jess's mother had perished alone in a desert. Still, it was too soon for Pono to die. Too many questions unanswered, too many mysteries unsolved.

Jess thought of her cousins converging on the big house. Rachel and Ming flying over from Honolulu, where they had spent their lives, from which, except for the Big Island, they had never ventured. And Vanya, arriving from Australia, from a political caucus, she and Jess the movers, always running from Pono, trying to forget her, yet possessing a capacious need to remember. The woman was their genesis, their dark fairy tale, the unraveled narrative they needed to solve. She was the lamp always burning, signaling them to come burn their wings on her.

Ka Wahine Maka‘u

Woman Afraid

IN DARWIN, ON AUSTRALIA'S NORTHERN TIP, in a slovenly imitation of signaling, a cabbie jammed his hand out the window, yelling profanities at pedestrians.

Vanya studied his crimson, pockmarked neck, thinking how utterly she hated these whites.

He eyed her in the rearview and grinned. She was dark, with a yellow cast that, in certain lights, turned golden. Big-breasted, flashing eyes, electric hair. *Could be Maori, or Tongan, no, the legs too good. More likely, Tahitian.*

He swerved, avoiding a lorry, and eyed the rearview again. "Where we headed, dearie?"

"The airport." She spoke each word with precision so he'd know she was educated. "And keep your eyes on the bloody road." Two weeks here and she sounded like them. Bloody this, bloody that.

She dropped her head, studied a sheaf of papers, thinking of the man she had just left, eight days and nights of their bodies snapping together like furious animals. She had hated him on sight, had subscribed to his attraction only out of fatigue.

That's how it begins, she thought, *With malice.*

Since her son's death three years back, it had been nothing but mindless swerving and crashing against strangers, not looking back, not sweeping up. This one, though, this Simon Weir, kept pulling her back.

"You'll come to trust me," he said. "Because we bled each other first."

She hated his presumption, his white Aussie voice, malign persistence of a nasal undertone. Yet she came back repeatedly.

Now she dragged luggage from the cab and boarded the flight to Honolulu, sick in body and soul. During the long droning hours, she flashed back on the last two weeks, a Pacific Women's Peace Conference in Sydney, exploring the role of women's political, economic, and social life in the major islands throughout the Pacific. Along with matters of land rights, alcoholism, street crime, the lack of women in government, delegates had voted on a consensus of resolutions demanding denuclearization of their islands: no more uranium mining, no more dumping of nuclear waste, no nuclear-powered ships in their waters.

The conference had lasted five days and she had been gone over two weeks. She saw herself on the dais the last day of the conference, as legal representative for Native Hawaiian Nationalist Women, urging militancy among all Pacific peoples, warning them they were being written out of history, that they would soon *unexist*. The greedy superpowers of the world would roll right over them. And all the while she lectured, she thought of Simon, of meeting him in Darwin, what they would do to each other.

The first time she saw him, a year earlier, she was in Darwin meeting with Gagadu Aborigine women campaigning against further uranium mining in their lands, chemicals of which were polluting their streams and rivers. One evening she had found herself staring at flying foxes hanging upside down from trees. *Like me. Asleep in their own filth.* Disgusted, she turned toward her hotel. She was entering; he was leaving— it should have stopped there. He followed her back into the lobby and watched her without watching her. Tall, muscular, wiry, reddish hair and mustache, a paramilitary air; he even wore his watch above his wristbone, military-fashion.

He approached cautiously, and Vanya stepped back, appraising. She knew the type, an outcast of sorts, all the women he wanted, most unsought. So he sought her out instead, drawn by her disinterest, a certain hauteur. For a while they seemed to circle, two wolves recognizing each other. When he finally introduced himself, his smile was quick, a reflection across a blade. In bed, he was cold, mechanical. Fondle. Penetrate. Ejaculate. Arrest. But in his sleep, he wept. She had never seen a white man weep. Now, away from him, all she could think of was Simon moving toward her, then in her, in a ruthless, sexual glide.

Of all the men she had slept with, he was the source of her greatest shame. A race she loathed, distrusted, preached against. Yet, he was in her blood like a virus.

Mid-flight she stood in the rest room, splashing her face, avoiding the mirror. Then, she sat down, leaning her head against the sink, wishing she were dead. Her life was loveless, sonless, obscene. *What is more obscene, more deviant from the moral progression, than a parent outliving its child?*

Buckling back into her seat, she wrapped up in a blanket, imagining Jess winging her way from New York City, the two of them colliding midair. They had last seen each other three years earlier at Vanya's son's funeral. The pain was too sweeping, Pono's rage at her grandson's death, at Vanya for "neglecting him," too devastating. Since then, Jess had stayed away.

Now they were being officially summoned, corraled into that dreadful big house, a place Vanya reconstructed so often in dreams she could no longer leave it behind. It inhabited her. Through the years it had become for her a House of Horrors, Pono mocking her, demeaning her, offering no comfort, no advice. Lost in her own dark epic, she was always sliding on long leather gloves, off on another mysterious journey, so that Vanya came to associate her grandmother's departures with dead skins coming to life.

That creaking house, with its smells from another era. Curdled odor of rotting antimaccassars, nauseous sachets in warped drawers. In her mind, Vanya was already seeking out a room where she could hide, trying to get beyond the sound of Pono's voice. Even when they were young, she had never treated Vanya as a child, had always addressed her differently, scolded her more harshly than the others, relying on the inherent toughness Pono was sure Vanya had inherited from her. *She always loved me less. The least.* Yet, at the end of those summers—shutters banging against days veering into September, the end of their stay, Jess flying back to the mainland—Vanya's feet had always dragged, she became depressed, not knowing why.

It seemed her whole life had been like that. She learned to hold her breath and wait, with foreboding certainty, for events to develop in her life in which love was withheld, or taken back from her. Her parents. Her husband. Then Ta'a Utu from a rough tribe of Samoans in Honolulu. A man she had loved, lost, and found again, so he could ultimately desert her. And, then, Hernando, her son. Each loss a disfiguring, so that who she was was no longer a fixed text.

Ming will comfort me. She always does. Vanya pulled the blanket round her, thinking of her frail cousin, oldest of them all, the wisest. *She and Rachel, that useless slave, stuck in Hawai'i all their lives.*

Images sifted down, Ming and Rachel appeasing, fluttering round their grandmother the way, in old Japanese prints, butterflies and peonies always escorted the lion. The way Pono bullied them, yet favored them, regarding Vanya and Jess as gypsies, addicted to lives of drift, one or both of them showing up randomly, like unexpected animal parts in one's soup.

'Ole

Nothingness

KORI-KORI, THE OLD GARDENER, STOOD in the driveway splashed with jacarandas. He hesitated, then continued raking the gravel. The lady of the house was never untheatrical, he had learned to look away. If she was hurt or dead, the cook would summon him.

Hearing the gunshot, the cook ran from the house, looked into the swimming pool, and covered her face. Rachel stared down at the shark floating belly-up in the crimson runoff of its dying. For years she had swum beside that thing in a daring and careful truce. It never bothered her, had hardly acknowledged her. She swore she could read its mind. She pumped another bullet into it, the shot resounding across the lawn, setting peacocks shrieking in the trees.

She stood up disgusted, having wanted the act to be the equivalent of a *haiku*, swift, simple, clean. But the first bullet had sent the thing thrashing out of the water, spraying blood over Tahitian gardenias, delicate spider lilies. She dropped the automatic in the grass and walked away, a woman stepping from a frame.

In the kitchen, she drank guava juice straight from the bottle like a derelict. "Ask Kori-Kori to clean the pool." Then, she glided from room to room of her spacious house in Kahala, the Beverly Hills of Honolulu.

That morning Rachel had discovered two things, the message from her grandmother summoning her to the Big Island, and a snapshot from Macao. In the snapshot, her husband, Hiro, and a young prostitute were sitting together in a gambling casino. The girl was whispering in his ear, one hand under the table.

Maybe he is giving her money. Maybe she is touching him. For twenty-three years he had kept his world apart from her, kept her on her carousel of make-believe. Rachel had never wanted children, refusing to share Hiro's affections. Now, almost forty, she found herself in a state of arrest, of female infantilism, a thing repugnant at her age. Yet their love was sharp as teeth. When Hiro was away from her, she knew he valued life a little less, so he took chances.

His business was the "water trade," which encompassed it all—liquor, blackmail, prostitution, drugs—up and down the Asian coast from Malaysia to Hong Kong and Tokyo. Through the years he had set her up in the house in Kahala and she became something of a *salonnière*. Vanya and Ming would arrive to find artists and buffoons swaggering in her gardens on Sunday afternoons, orchids fluttering in their drinks, matching birds gyring overhead. Sometimes the carp in the pond surfaced, staring at the strangers, so that they seemed to be a thought in some very cold-blooded mind. There were even gangsters there on Sunday afternoons, people Rachel hated, but they were part of Hiro's world, and so she competed with them in dangerous ways.

When he left, she lived like an acolyte waiting for his return. He would come home, stay a few weeks, and leave again. When he was with her too long, he said he felt like something swallowed by an animal drinking. Sometimes, seeing his gun strapped to his chest like a rodent, Rachel wondered if he wore it to protect himself from her. Maybe her love was so intense, his absence was how they kept from killing each other.

Full-blooded Japanese, Hiro was sixty now, a *Yakuza*, tattooed from his neck to his feet. As a boy he had been sent by his father from Honolulu to Japan to be educated. Instead, he became a gangster. At twenty-six he returned to Honolulu and, seeing the tattoos, his father disowned him. That same night, a young girl moved to him through moonlight, drawn by his blue skin. Hearing of their elopement, Pono had damned Rachel forever, forbidding her cousins to see her.

Months passed, and Pono received a letter. She sat motionless while Run Run read it aloud in Pidgin.

"*Tūtū* . . . Maybe you ha' nevah loved," Rachel wrote. "But when one loves a t'ing, infuses it wit' love, a soul is born from darkness, from not'ingness. Widdout love, a light is missing from dat object. I miss my cousins so much I t'ink my heart is breaking, but I will even sacrifice dem foah my husband. I would die for him." Run Run was silent afterward, her eyes floating off.

Her granddaughter's words, rude and melancholy, struck a chord. Pono walked the beaches barking at the sea, cursing this bastard child who knew nothing of sacrifice, or love, a thing earned harshly year by year, decade by decade. Nonetheless, after two years, she relented, allowed Rachel to come home again. But she never allowed Hiro near the place, never laid eyes on him.

"And don't be fooled," she warned Rachel. "What you and this man share is he-dog she-dog heat. When your loins are dead, long hair growing from your chin, then maybe you begin to understand real love."

By now, Rachel understood the word had many definitions. It could mean denial, deprivation. It could become bizarre, occult, a game where Hiro held all the stakes. Still he proteced her, kept a shield round her, was attendant to his lust for her. Just two years earlier, he had returned from Bangkok bringing her three rare pearls. Implanted in the foreskin of his penis, they had increased orgasmic sensation to the point where she lost consciousness. Now she looked down at the snapshot from Macao. *When did the players change? When did allegiance slide, and love turn sloppy?*

She picked up the message from Run Run, her grandmother summoning her, and with the message came a sense of fatigue. Around Pono, Rachel went without makeup, wore loose clothes like a woman in purdah. Sometimes she even wore cardigans, what she felt women wore when their sex life was over. She *kowtowed*, playing Pono's game. At the price of submission, she was allowed to get close enough to study the old woman, try to glean the source of her brutal powers.

In turn, she let Pono study her, this bastard granddaughter who had succumbed to the operatic and perishable life of a *geisha*, of eternally pleasing one man. A life dedicated to the painting of delicate calligraphy, to learning the intricacies of the tea ceremony, a life spent playing the catgut *shamizen* and perfecting the art of origami, the wrapping artistically in precious papers, space, nothing at all. And the other, unspoken life dedicated to pleasure, delirium. Sometimes, seeing herself through Pono's eyes, Rachel saw her slow evaporation. Life was growing old for her, Hiro traveled more and more. Her seductive arts, her rituals, her passion for him, had nowhere to go. Without him, she was pared down to *'ole*. Nothingness.

Like a zombie, she readied a room for Jess. A day and a night of shoring each other up before meeting the others and taking the thirty-minute flight to the Big Island. She thought with dread of seeing Vanya. They had never been close. Not that they were so opposite, but Vanya despised Rachel's life, belittled her, used ambiguous figures of speech Rachel never quite caught on to. Lately, they had resorted to a dialect of the eye, criticizing, consuming each other, silently.

Ming will smooth things over. Pono's favorite. Our little mediator.

From the window, she watched Kori-Kori wipe blood, one petal at a time, from Tahitian gardenias. Then he knelt at the pool with chopsticks, delicately plucking at floating viscera, like a man at a terrible meal.

Kānalua Buda

Buddha Doubt

MING SAT ALONE IN HER GARDEN of blue ginger, face so pale she seemed to fade into the white of an aging afternoon. Beyond her high-hedged tiny yard, traffic honked in potholed streets of Kalihi, outside downtown Honolulu. She sighed, closed her eyes, the book she held sliding to the grass.

All day she had traveled, with K'ang-hsi, seventeenth-century emperor of China. She had ridden into battle with his mounted archers, capturing Taiwan, leveling the walls of Albazin, then suffering through the terrible eight-year San-Fan War. K'ang-hsi's mounted archers were trained from infancy, never knowing fear. At age five, from galloping steeds, they slew geese in flight with bow and arrow. At eight, they slew leaping stags and learned formation riding. At twelve, they were fearless, hunting tiger and bear with only one arrow. As warriors, they were the emperor's living shield.

In the sixtieth year of his reign, sitting in his golden room among his golden books and jade-and-ruby-handled writing quills, K'ang-hsi wrote in emperor's vermilion, the red ink reserved only for him:

> *I am approaching seventy, the world is my possession. My sons, grandsons, great-grandsons number one hundred and fifty. My country is at peace. And yet. What of my loyal mounted archers, companions in my glorious victories? Gone, all gone. Trained for early death, what did*

they know of this life? A horse's rhythms, penetration of an arrow,
precision of a bow. Yet, they are what my memory fastens on. Gallantry
died with them.

Exhilarated, with the toe of a tiny slipper, a footbinder's dream,
Ming closed K'ang-hsi's memoirs. Still lovely, but arthritic and bent with
lupus, at forty-five she had long retired from teaching. Children grown,
husband deep in orchid breeding, she had retreated into great books,
great thought, Albinoni and Bach, a world that would not betray. Years
of physical pain were reducing her to a life of the mind, which, increasingly, Ming felt was the only reality in this imagined world. She had
begun to see that lupus—the cyclical fevers, chronic fatigue, crippling
arthritic pain—was a kind of ally, exempting her from the slow drip of
the quotidian, giving her time to consider art, God, humiliation.

After especially bad visitations lasting several days or weeks, attacks
that occurred without warning, without regularity, attacks that racked
and ravaged, knotted her joints, left body temperature soaring, she would
come back from a journey most people never made, come back reborn
as if from the dead, so she seemed to be instantly older, or eerily young.
At such times, her husband, Johnny, brooded over her, her hair in oily
shreds, lips chapped, arms unbearably thin.

Sometimes he found her unconscious, mouth gaping horribly. And
he mourned, remembering the years when she was healthy, how she
had made him sleepy with her tender movements. How he had always
loved her hands on things, on him. At New Year's, they'd set places at
table for ancestors, mooncakes and tea, leaving extra chairs for them.
And lovely Ming, hands in her lap, would smile mysteriously at him for
hours. Now he was unable to reach her, she lay outside the territory of
his days.

Once he asked what happened to her mind in the worst days of the
attack, the wolf mark settled on her face, her eyes rolled upward showing
whites, skin larval, like the new-born, or the just-dead.

"I go back," Ming whispered. "Childhood fantasies, terrors, all
swimming in and out of sequence."

She kept the rest behind her eyes, the other place she went to, place
of drops and puffs, where she felt a decreasing need for her husband,
for the world, because it interfered with her need for the other thing.

Now Ming sighed, leaned down, picked up her book. Beyond the
hedge, children passed singing "Jesus Loves Me." She thought of her
mixed-marriage childhood, Buddhist father, Catholic mother, years of

Christmas pageants, Lenten penance, Stations of the Cross, interspersed with steps of the Lion Dance, the Monkey Dance, in honor of Chinese New Year. *Am I Buddhist or Catholic?* she had asked. *Both*, her parents said. *God has many families.*

Years later, saffron robes, the smell of joss sticks, sound of Buddhist temple chimes, would mingle in her mind with catechistic chanting, a nun's starched wimple, priests in dark closets, dispensing absolution. She had learned to accept the ideological flexibility of Buddhism, that it could incarnate into different cultures, and she had long ago decided that the athlete on the cross was just another manifestation of the Buddha.

Now, inside her house, Ming knelt on a cushion before a small shrine, lighting joss sticks of black sandalwood, solemnly asking for Buddha's blessing. Yet, she had growing doubts about the Buddha. After twenty years of pain, she had begun to see him not at all as godlike, but as a moody, childish heckler, doling out abuse. Now she abused him back, reaching into a small covered jade bowl, curling her fingers around a pea-size ball of waxlike gum. Her breath quickened. She drew the blinds in her bedroom, plugged the gum into a bamboo pipe and lit it, sucking deeply in.

Her lungs opened, ravenous, nerve stalks alert, waiting to be stunned. Before transcendence, before the slow translucent dreams began, she thought of her cousins about to descend on her. Women who, in the eyes of strangers, had achieved a certain symmetry in their passage through the world. Yet each time they came to her, they came needy, wanting to know how to live, how to not be brutalized, practically crawling into Ming's lap, so healthy, so robust, she found them vaguely malignant.

Yet, Ming loved them, she was devoted to each one—Vanya, Rachel, Jess—each woman a raw, shivering human event. Driven by love, ideology, a search for one's self, they were anguished, sometimes dull, bizarre. But what possessed them basically was love, the need to stay intact for each other. And so, they looked to Ming, the oldest, seeing her gestures, her words, as clues to surviving.

They came to her with their victories, their failures, their strange, forbidden plots, wrapping round her like roots. Sometimes resentment flared, and in her mind Ming thrust them all away, even her husband and children, feeling they were amateurs, knowing nothing of life. For what did one know about living until they were stripped of human feeling, of every illusion, by blinding, pulverizing pain. Pain so abiding, so all-encompassing it left only an appetite for filth.

In her stupor she moaned. A silk curtain fluttered, sunlight drew a blade across the bed. Somewhere in the Gobi, a Mongol milked a singing horse. Caravans approached. Someone quietly removed her skin. And, then ... and ... then ... all the racking fevers, knotted joints, the marrow slowly crumbling in her bones, were left behind.

And she flew free, O free, even her cousins left behind, a tribe that sits at a window.

Nā Iwi o Kalaupapa

The Bones of Kalaupapa

THIS PLACE. SMALL, VERDANT ISLAND of almost impenetrable rain forests. Lush hidden valleys, plunging waterfalls, barking deer, and goat, and boar floating down aisles of giant fern, eucalypti. The heady fragrance of jasmine, frangipani, narcotic sizzle of ginger. And copper suns turning the island magenta in ancient afternoons. Here is the Polynesia of the past, of talk-soft legends and taboos, the place called Moloka'i.

In old-time villages, families still weave their fishing nets, tend taro patches and rice paddies, hand-carve canoes. Mules still slow-poke to measuring pits where sandalwood was cut to fit the holds of nineteenth-century ships bound for the Orient. Locals still night-fish by torchlight in waters blessed by the Southern Cross. Lovestruck *kāne* still stroke *ole kine* 'ukulele, singing in falsetto, and graceful *wāhine* still dance barefoot, telling legends of the rains.

The island has another side, the silent side. Winds from the north shore still whisper of terrible decades, unspeakable generations, that left that part of Moloka'i *kapu*, inaccessible except by sea, air, or treacherous muddy mule paths down jungle cliffs soaring three thousand feet high. Sailors who have roamed the world still swear this silent, mist-shrouded coastline of the north, and its small peninsula asleep on the fringe of prehistory, is the most haunting and beautiful place in all the Seven Seas.

The peninsula, sheltered east and west by jungle, is the setting for a place called Kalaupapa, a name that momentarily stills the hearts of all Hawaiians. Here, over a hundred and thirty years ago, it became a kennel for the damned, those natives afflicted with *ma'i Pākē*, the "Chinese sickness," more commonly known as leprosy. Here for decades, lepers—hunted down and caged—were pushed from ships with wooden poles, left to the mercy of sharks, stormy seas, or madness, as the bacteria ravaged their nerves, their eyes, muscles, bones, then ate their internal organs.

Now, rich green fields grow over acres of crude graves, dug swiftly when victims expired daily, in the dozens. St. Philomena Church is renovated, expectoration holes still visible in newly varnished floors. Father Damien's grave is sand-polished, tended regularly, necklaced in fresh *lei*. A sense of battlefields recovering, buds pushing through scorched earth. And yet . . . at dusk, one hears the shuffling, the crowds, broken spirits back from the dead to perch on cliffs and moan, remembering.

Here, on a sun-drenched day, the woman named Pono stood on a bluff overlooking the sea. She was massive, standing well over six feet, hair a luxuriant gray shawl billowing round her hips. She held her arms out, chanting, and wild boar in the jungle went down on their knees. When she sang, flowers changed color, spotted deer dissolved into the bark of trees as hunters passed with bow and arrow.

She was *kahuna*, creating more life around her than was actually there, heightening the momentousness of each living thing by simply gazing upon it. Almost eighty years old, she was a woman who had dared everything, committed every conceivable act, for the man sitting nearby. A gull deployed, snatching in midair the strip of raw *aku* she had flung. Her laugh was deep and resonant.

The man on the blanket at her feet looked up. "Why do you laugh, Beloved?"

Pono sank to her knees, wrapping her arms round him. "Because I am here where I belong, with my favorite noseless man." They roared, rocking back and forth like children. "Because I am so happy."

She lay down with her head in his lap, talking about "her girls" coming home to the big house, about the coffee cherries, the harvest season to come. "The time of dancing pigs" she called it, when the brutes would break out of their pens, gorge on ripe coffee beans and go berserk, chasing humans and horses, rollicking down the road with Run Run's laundry in their teeth. While Pono talked, the man caressed her with a hand long gone, so it was more a club. An artifact. His name was Duke Kealoha, and as they murmured back and forth, Pono studied what was left of him, remembering her first sight of him over sixty years ago. A bronze, Polynesian god.

A girl of seventeen, seeing him, her heart had buckled, knowing he would give her great joy, but he would also test her. Even with supernatural powers, she did not foresee that life, too, would test her. Bounty hunters. Slavery. And worse. Now, she pushed the past away, telling him of her dream, returning and returning. A human corpse, eye sockets weeping algae, rocking side to side on the ocean floor.

"I think my time is soon," she whispered. "That's why I've called the girls home."

Duke looked down at her intently, knowing her dreams were prophetic, but suspecting *he* was the one who would die. His once fierce, handsome, brown face was now cratered, cheeks and lips massively scarred from old lesions, nose bridge collapsed from medical experiments, one good hand, clubs for feet, living his life in a wheelchair. Racked with kidney problems, bad circulation, side effects of the sulfone drug for leprosy, now called Hansen's disease, he had suffered several minor heart attacks. Appetite diminished, he seemed to lack all needs, except the need for her. Emotional, spiritual. And sexual. In that way *ma'i Pākē* had been kind.

Pono sat up, clinging to him. "For sixty years you have forbidden it. Now, I want to end my days with you, to live at Kalaupapa." She rubbed his still massive chest, saw the miraculous hardening between his legs, his young-warrior passion for her.

He took her hand and shook his head, momentarily ignoring his erection. When he spoke, his voice was deep, commanding, cultured but slightly old-fashioned, from lack of contact with the outside world.

"Beloved, we have had a long life, have suffered, wept, rejoiced. All the emotions and rages of normal men and women. We have done this without the eyes of the world, privacy extending to us the dignity humans are entitled to. We have lived with conscience and pride, but at the price of our daughters, who grew up fatherless, knowing nothing of me. You, their mother, pushed them away."

"I wanted you instead . . ."

"Then make up for this with our granddaughters, before it is too late. Do not abandon them. Do not cheat them of your love . . ." He hesitated. "And anyway, I think it is *my* corpse you see in dreams."

She gasped, diving backward through her soul. "Oh, let me come and end our days together!"

He shook her viciously until her bones creaked. "Go against my wishes, and I will put out your eyes. You will be *kapu* on Kalaupapa!"

She wept, grasping his hands. "Then let me tell them you exist. Let them know their mothers were not fatherless, that I was not a whore. Let them *see* you, embrace you. Let us end our life in sunlight . . ."

Duke threw back his head and laughed. "*See* me? This cursed, filthy mound of broken flesh?" He tried to imagine it, young, healthy women gazing upon him, claiming his corrupt flesh as their own. They would be sick at first glance.

"All I ever asked of you was dignity," he whispered. "Let me die out of sight of the world, here with the bones of my family."

Later, as he dozed with his dear head in her arms, Pono stared intensely at nothing until her eyes, black as the red-black heart of *aku*, faded to brown, tan, then white, so white her eyeballs seemed turned inward, studying the mechanisms of her brain. *I will sacrifice all I possess, all I love, to end my days with him. I will do anything.*

She could look someone to death, transfer pain from one human to another. Yet Pono's powers did not extend to Duke; love turned her impotent. She had never been able to trick him, or argue him out of a decision. She had never been able to cure him. Sometimes, looking for the key that would engage the tumblers, throw the lock, bend him to her will, she searched in her genealogy, for clues.

Now, she took from her pocket her *aniani kahuna*, her prophet-mirror, one side of which reflected the past-running-backward, and the other, the future-running-forward, which was the cloudy side. Thinking of all the lives lived that had brought her to this point, Pono gazed at herself in the past-running-backward glass, and her weathered, brown face was slowly rinsed of age.

Her features in young womanhood melted quickly to girlhood, then infancy. As she watched, her infant face dissolved into that of her mother's, then her mother's mother, faces blending, melting back to those of an earlier century. This time a double image appeared, the face of a dark, Tahitian beauty named Kelonikoa, Pono's great-grandmother, beside her the haggard face of a one-eyed *haole*, Pono's great-grandfather. Kelonikoa faded, and there was only the *haole*, growing less haggard, eye patch less distinct, melting back and back to his handsome, two-eyed youth.

Pavilions in the Sea

HE STOOD WEEPING IN A FIELD, and it was 1834. He was seventeen, owning nothing, loving nothing but a bay horse, dead at his feet of old age. His name was Mathys Coenradtsen, eighth child in a line of eight sons, and the field lay near the town of Coxsackie in the Hudson River Valley of New York State.

His family were farmers, descended from an orphan sent in a shipload of boys and girls from an almshouse in Amsterdam, Holland, to work for the Dutch West India Company, and to ". . . increase the population of New Netherland." The letter of transmittal to Peter Stuyvesant from the Burgomeisters of Amsterdam was dated May 27, 1655, and the orphan inventory list included the first Mathys Coenradtsen, sixteen years of age.

He must have been rebellious and feisty, for records show him hauled into court November 1657 for knocking his employer down, and again in 1660 in a suit for debts he refused to pay a Reyn Van Coelen, and again in 1665 for ostensibly declaring "Damn the King," and "The Devil fetch the King," when caught chopping wood on the Sabbath. By the 1670s he had mellowed, settled into farming on leased land, married and began a family.

According to Albany court records, in 1683 Mathys purchased from three Mohawk Indians, Manoenta, Unekeek, and Kachketowaa, "a piece of woodland lying behind Koxhaghkye," later called Coxsackie, to each of whom he paid "a cloth of duffel, two knives, and wampum." In 1697 this same stretch of land was officially granted to him by Governor Benjamin Fletcher, a representative of the Crown he had publicly defamed thirty years before. The land conveyed by this grant comprised 3,500 acres. In 1699, Mathys took an oath of allegiance to the British Crown.

Until the Revolutionary War his descendants lived uneventful lives, farming portions of the land, leasing out the rest. In 1776, two Coenradtsen brothers and three cousins died fighting for the colonies, another was hanged, refusing to sign the Articles of Association, his sympathies with the Loyalists. By the 1800s the Coenradtsens had settled down again to farming, trading pigs, horses, cattle.

By 1834, when Mathys Coenradsten stood weeping in his father's field, other Dutch families—the Van Burens, Van Dycks, Van Cortlandts—had long since distinguished themselves with dynastic patroonships in the Hudson River Valley. The greatest patroonship, Rensselaerwyck, on the west bank of the Hudson, near Coxsackie, included some 700,000 acres, land slowly accumulated by the family since 1630.

Yet nothing in the Coenradtsen genes drove them beyond the life of the soil. They did not acquire great tracts of land, did not challenge the world of trade or politics. Bit by bit their land holdings dwindled: gambling debts, bad marriages. While the enterprising and colorful Van Cortlandts, Roosevelts, and Livingstons entered the sugar-refining business, the canny Rhinelanders imported crockery, the Brevoorts became ironmongers, the Schermerhorns ship chandlers. But the shortsighted Coenradtsens remained poor farmers and animal traders.

By his fifteenth birthday, Mathys saw no future for himself. His four oldest brothers would inherit the choicest acres of family land, while Mathys and the others would be doled out small, exhausted plots. Wanting to flee the soil, he began to dream of a life at sea. On cool, starry nights, he would lie in the field with a neighbor, third cousin of a sailor named Warren Delano (great-grandfather of a man who would become the country's president), as the boy talked dreamily of Warren's adventures on an opium clipper plying the Pacific, the wealth he was accumulating.

In a letter to his cousin, that took one year and three days to reach Coxsackie, Warren Delano described his high life on the seas, raving about the beauty of the Sandwich Isles, like great pavilions rising from the Pacific. "Discovered" by Captain Cook in 1778, they had been named after Cook's patron, John Montagu, Fourth Earl of Sandwich. "But," Warren wrote, "the natives, huge, brown, handsome warriors, claim to have been there 2,000 years before Cook, and they call their land the Islands of Hawai'i."

One day Mathys saw in an Albany paper an ad for "green hands," for a clipper out of New York bound for Cape Horn and the whaling grounds of the Pacific. The Atlantic whale had been hunted to scarcity; now ships had turned to a new source of precious sperm oil and whalebone. With almost no sense of it, Mathys packed a small duffel, and hopped a supply boat down the Hudson. Days later he presented himself at a crowded dock where a ship called the *Silver Coin* signed on a miserable-looking crew.

Knees shaking, Mathys stood among murderers, thieves, pimps, and victims of periodic attacks of delirium tremens. Some were deserters from the British Navy, some were debt-runners, some just decent sorts addicted to the sea. He lined up with the rest, facing a huge mulatto wielding scissors. One by one, each man was given a hair cut, ridding him of vermin. But hair blew about the deck and washing wasn't compulsory, and by the time they had been at sea a week, lice and fleas infested everyone. Crew's quarters were reached through a two-foot-square hatch in the foredeck; below, men lay in bunks just two feet above each other, no room to sit up, no light to read by. Just darkness, and the sound of men scratching.

Sailing out into the North Atlantic, by the first week Mathys had a glimpse of the grueling life he had chosen, one of never-ending labor: repairing sails, ropes, rigging, standing regular ship-watch in four-hour shifts repeated round the clock. Meals became monotonous, the first day's diet constantly repeated. Duty aloft the mast was the chief trial for him, his stomach rolling with the pitch and yaw of the ship, nausea magnified a hundred times by his position eighty feet up in the air. Sometimes he was so sick, not even beatings by the third mate could drive him up on deck. By the time they hit the Gulf Stream he had lost ten pounds. And in rough waters of whipping storms, he was dehydrated, unconscious for days.

"The best is yet to come," the third mate warned. "The Horn'll make a man of ya. Or kill ya!"

When Mathys revived, he thought he'd been dumped on another ship; they were headed for the coast of Africa. "But what about Cape Horn! The Pacific!" he cried.

A kindly petty officer showed him a map, explaining the traditional sailing route which did not head directly south for the Horn, an in-and-out swerving course following the coastlines of the United States and Central America, that would cost them months. Instead, they headed far to the east to a point called Cape Verde, near the coast of Africa. When they finally turned south for the Horn, they would run in a straight line down the coast of South America, and on to Tierra del Fuego. But that part of the journey lay months ahead. Mathys never saw the islands of Cape Verde; they were enveloped for weeks in racking storms, and lost a man overboard.

Finally, heading straight on to Cape Horn, a run of over six thousand miles, on the fifty-fifth day of the voyage, the *Silver Coin* crossed the equator, men cheering, dousing each other with seawater. By then, some of the "green hands," emaciated from unrelenting seasickness and diarrhea, could only get about on hands and knees. Some died of dehydration, a few threw themselves into the sea.

Provisions of salt meat began to spoil. Flour was filled with worms and insects, so bread could not be baked. Butter and fat turned rancid, and worst of all was the water. Nothing but wooden casks to hold it, all matter of bacteria reproduced there. The crew plugged up gutters, collecting fresh rainwater; pails and containers were filled, the taste as filthy as ever. Then, rats were found floating in the water.

Disease, dysentery, and ever-present gales. More men washed overboard. At night Mathys lay on his stinking bunk, so homesick, he wished himself dead. Then unexpectedly the gales ceased. Somewhere off the coast of Uruguay, the ship hit an area of dead calm, no wind for days, then weeks. Only the blinding sea and burning sun. And thirst. Sailors cut the veins of a man newly dead, and sipped his blood.

Down in the mess, the cook looked at the hardtack and vomitted. It no longer looked like bread: moldy, dancing with worms, soaked in urine of mice. The crew were reduced to chewing leather, eating sawdust, a freshly killed rat. Nineteen men delirious. They had been at sea five months. One night the ship heaved on its side, then stood end to end. The storm came from nowhere, ripping up hatchways, cataracting water into cabins. On deck, men tied themselves to rails, shouting deliriously, "The Horn has come to greet us! Come to say How-dee do!"

They were wrapped in fog, warm waters of the South Atlantic clashing with the frigid waves of Antarctica, the sea rising over them, then crashing down, like great collapsing cathedrals. Mathys clung to a rail, praying he would live to round Cape Horn, then he was thrown to his backside, washed down into a cabin, where men lay with broken fingers and wrists from trying to hold on.

For forty-five days and nights, the *Silver Coin* attempted to round the Horn. Hellish winds, sleet and snow beat down; waves heeled the ship far over on her beams. To the north, the treacherous coast of Tierra del Fuego measured their progress as they maneuvered a few miles with an easterly at their backs, then were thrown back a day's progress by the fierce westerlies.

They retreated for days, tried again, and retreated, finding caves where the sea was calm and the crew could finally rest. One day Mathys watched sailors row ashore and club a colony of nursing seals. Lust-crazed, they clutched mammalian breasts and mated with the bleeding, dying beasts before completely slaughtering them and their calves for meat and pelts. That night the petty officer found him squatting on deck, trembling violently, his eyes numb rivers, his lips working silently in horror.

"Get used to it, son. Slaughter's the only life we know."

Then one night, the storm eased, Captain Toby Newton found the right steering, and they maneuvered through the worst. Mathys woke from a half-sleep hearing men weeping and shouting. Defeating the devilish waters of Cape Horn, they had entered the Pacific. For weeks the waters were calm as though they had earned the rest. Porpoises leapt in schools, greeting them. Off the coast of Chile, thick shoals of sardines appeared, and tuna, flying fish.

One day a man shouted, sighting a blue, largest mammal in the world. The crew were suddenly alert, the captain shouting, the third mate bullying "green hands." They had entered the whaling grounds. Mathys watched as the beast, well over eighty feet long, dove to the depths and surfaced wrapped in the tentacles of a giant squid at least fifty feet from head to tips. Men gasped at the spectacle, as the creatures grappled, ramming the ship in their battle. They disappeared, were never seen again.

Then one day, the ocean offered up a gift, so rare it was barely imaginable, a thing that would haunt Mathys all his days. Two giant blues, near seventy feet long each of them, raced toward each other, nearly colliding. Singing out plaintively, they circled, glided past each other, changing their song. Then one of them rolled over slightly, and a tentacle-like thing nine or ten feet long shot into the air, unsheathed from within deep abdominal folds. Erected, it collapsed, concealed again.

The whales drew closer seeming to stroke each other with their pectoral fins. Then the other blue rolled over, giant pink genital-like lips rolled back just beneath the surface of the water. Then they dived, with such terrible force, Mathys imagined them crashing to the ocean floor, the earth cracking open, swallowing everything, whales, ship, perhaps all of the Pacific. Then unexpectedly, they exploded back up to the surface, poised vertically, face to face.

The crew watched and the captain watched, and all the ship fell silent. The whales seemed to grow out of the sea until large portions of their abdomens, accordion pleats of their great grooved bellies, protruded above the water. Huge flippers wrapped round each other, they spun and they spun, face to face, and it was a dance, and great waves smacked the ship.

"What are they doing?" Mathys cried.

"They're mating, lad. And what a wondrous thing."

Flukes grinding back and forth somewhere in the depths their song became a symphony vibrating across the ocean and ships in other latitudes vibrated and maybe continents vibrated and they suddenly pressed close so close they looked like giant godly Siamates and they drove themselves up and up rising out of the water all of them the massiveness the length of them high high into the blue above from blue below and they were blue and blue oceans sluicing down their sides and joined yes joined and everything all earthly things were small and they just stood there in the sky a young boy's memory and then they dove back down into other atmospheres a deafening resounding roar that shook the timbers of the ship and shook the hearts of watching men and threw them to their knees.

For two days the crew went about quietly, as if each man were trying to remember something he'd forgot.

Then inevitably, the shout came from the mast. "Thar she blows!"

A great sperm whale disappeared, then minutes later zoomed up from the deep, topping the waves like a building, falling back with a crash. This was a rare sighting, for sperm whales were usually found farther north in colder waters. Boats were lowered, the crew shouting, working themselves up for the chase. Because he had proven himself stouthearted, not a quitter, Mathys was the first "green hand" sent out as a rower. He would always date the rounding of Cape Horn as his rotation into position for manhood, and the day of his first whale hunt as the beginning of sorrowful wisdom.

Every nerve inside him screamed as the whaleboats—each with sail

aloft, harpooner, helmsman and four rowers—swooped down upon the
graceful leviathan. The lead boat crept up on it from the rear, so close
the men stopped rowing with oars and took to paddles. Coming alongside
this living thing as massive as their ship, yet placidly indifferent to little
men in boats, Mathys felt a strong urge to stroke its side; something
akin to touching the mind of God.

As they maneuvered the prow directly into the whale's long flank,
the harpooner, poised with one leg planted securely in the bottom of
the boat, the other braced against the gunwale, flung his harpoon with
incredible power into the giant body just behind the fin. The beast
soared out of the water, harpoon lines trailing.

The mate gave quick commands, "Pull three!" maneuvering the boat
as the whale took its first dive. Rope was paid out, for when it came up
it would try to break free on the surface. Then began the famous
"Nantucket Sleighride," which dragged the crew for miles until the
whale grew tired. As the line slackened it was taken in, and as the whale
lay quietly, the boat approached again, keeping clear of the flukes, staying
far enough back so the whale couldn't see what was coming.

Half insane, Mathys stood up in the boat screaming, "Stop! Stop!"
The crew ignored him, thinking he was excited, calling for the whale to
give up. A second boat rowed close, the mate raised his long lance,
hurling it into the mammal's side, penetrating three feet into the body.
He gave the command to pull away, as the whale brought his huge flukes
out of the water, rolling his body, trying to smash the boat. Maneuvering
so that it missed, the mate drove home another lance.

The creature tried to sound but, wounded, could not stand the
pressure of deep water. It surfaced, coming at the boats head-on. The
mate yelled, "Stern all!" and the big jaws closed on nothing, but not
before the mate had had a chance to thrust his lance down deep into
the lungs. Mathys heard blood gurgling like huge vats boiling, the sea
blistered red all around them. Still the whale lashed out, losing its
balance, first sign of final defeat.

Now sharks gathered, staying just out of range. The mate lanced
mercilessly, the whale rolling over and over. Other boats gathered, and
as the lead boat was tied up to the corpse, it was waifed, a red flag
thrust into its flesh, signaling the *Silver Coin* to pick up boat and crew.
Laboriously, they lashed their prize lengthwise to the ship's hull.

The *Silver Coin* had been constructed as a floating factory so whale
blubber could be "tried out," boiled down for its oil, which was then
stored in barrels in the hold. All hands were busy now. Under the tryout

where blubber would be boiled, basins of water were set, preventing the ship's catching fire. Cutting spades and other tools were brought, double set blocks hoisted aloft and a cutting platform rigged over the side, placed so men could stand leaning against the platform's rail, facing the ship, the best position for "cutting in."

With the great body lashed the length of the ship, a first hole was cut through blubber at the neck down to the red flesh. A large hook was attached to the blubber through the hole and eight men, four on each handle of the windlass, started raising the hook as men on the cutting stage carved out a broad strip of blubber. As the strip rose like the wall of a house, another hole was cut for another hook and so on until blubber was stripped off from head to flukes, the whale's body rolling over and over. Sharks gathered in the hundreds, tearing at exposed flesh.

Alternating between heartbreak and fascination, Mathys witnessed the grimmest job of all. The head was cut off and secured to the ship, so its nose rested in the water, the exposed portion flush with the surface of the sea. Then the captain and third mate stepped out on the cutting stage and cut out a piece from the head about three feet in diameter, the chunk called the "case," a mass of bubbles filled with oil thrown at once into the tryworks. Then one of the men stepped down into the head itself.

The hole left by the case was an entrance to a complete oil tank, which gave the head of the sperm whale its characteristic shape and value. The man had to submerge himself in liquid, warm enough to remain fluid. A little colder and it would be like lard. The tank was divided vertically by a thick membrane, and the man had to dive down into the oil, knife in hand, and cut his way through the membrane. Holding a chain in his other hand, he dragged it through the hole, looping it onto itself. The dive itself was grim enough, but if the man slipped, as one did weeks later, he slid right out into the jaws of frenzied sharks. The precious sperm oil was then dipped out and stored directly in dozens of barrels called hogsheads.

As the head was cast off, the "trying out" began, fires lit under big kettles, the blubber melting with some fresh water at the start. Denying he was part of a slaughter-ship, that the corpse of one of those great godlike mammals was hanging like a trophy skeleton, Mathys dreamed himself into a factory that refined rubber, as he was forced to join men cutting up blubber into small strips, throwing them into kettles. Rich brown crispy pieces of scrap floating to the surface were strained and used as fuel for fires. As kettles filled, hot oil was ladled out and cooled in iron tanks before being hand-pumped to barrels in the hold. Mathys's whale netted them forty barrels of blubber.

He had never injured a living thing, always leaving the barn when his father slaughtered pigs. Now he transported himself through whale hunts like a zombie, cursing the captain and crew, praying he and all of them would be struck dead in their sleep. He had never imagined anything as magnificent as these giant mammals, never felt safer than when rowing beside them. Warm-blooded, air-breathing, they belonged to families, and clans, and talked through code-songs sung for fifty million years. Like humans, they played, mated, tended their young.

Once he sighted a whale calf riding its mother's back as she sang out piping songs, the calf squeaking back at her. Then she lifted her newborn, rolled on her side, and shot milk into its mouth with muscles deep inside her breasts. Another day he saw a dead calf on its mother's back. Mathys knew it was dead because of its stillness, and her mournful cries. A sailor said she would keep it there, support its meager weight for months, until it disintegrated.

After the first few months of whale hunts, excitement died out on the *Silver Coin*. Grueling work, rotten food, lack of hygiene, turned the crew bestial. They were lax at their duties, stole supplies from the slopchest, stabbed each other for precious tobacco. At sea for ten months without rest, they craved land and other humans. Finally, putting in at Valparaiso, the captain logged and transshipped his barrels of blubber and sperm oil to ships bound for New England, while his crew went wild on fresh beef, rum and whores, wasting themselves for weeks.

In port, Mathys immediately broke from them, seeking counsel with God. He stopped in a taverna asking directions to a church and woke three days later, reeking of rum, two whores crooning over his blond hair and naked, young body. When he woke again, a giantess with three breasts seemed to be swallowing his groin, and he knew he was irretrievably damned. He woke without clothes, or money, his wages, everything, gone, so sick, so weak, laughing crewmates carried him over their shoulders back to the ship. Before they were out of the harbor, Mathys swallowed a bottle of rat poison and flung himself overboard. The skipper fished him from the drink, and locked him in the galley.

They whaled for another nine months, following schools as far north as the Galápagos, and along the coast of Peru, putting into port at Easter Island, where soft-spoken natives greeted them cautiously, until they were sure they weren't "Blackbirders," slave ships roving the Pacific, kidnapping natives in the hundreds of thousands, working them to death in the fetid guano deposits off Peru and on white men's sugar plantations in the Americas and Australia.

On Easter Island the men had fresh fruit, fresh water, music, women and rest. These native women were lovely, soft-spoken, different from the whores of Valparaiso. But Mathys avoided them, looking on from a distance. He still didn't know how to behave with women. What did one say? Besides, he was sure he was carrying a terrible disease that made him erect in his sleep so he woke with a handful of discharge. In a month they were back on the seas, following humpbacks.

Now the *Silver Coin* was in its third year of whale hunts. Contracts were running out, and the skipper turned greedy, pushing the crew past their limits, anchoring in ports only to repair and reprovision, giving men no time to rest. A man caught organizing a mutiny was put on one square of hardtack and one cup of bad water a day. Mathys, who joined the mutineers, was sentenced to long hours aloft in the mast, in sun that broiled the skin from his body.

One day, harpooning a maddened whale, men had to cut loose to keep from being crushed. The beast made for the mother ship, and rammed her repeatedly. Timbers cracked as water poured into the *Silver Coin*, and the whale struck again, stoving in the ship's bows. The captain managed to keep her afloat while men provisioned the rowing boats then drew straws to see who would go in the best provisioned boat.

They were just below the equator, somewhere between the Galápagos and the Marquesas, more than a thousand miles from land. The boats were lashed side by side in twos, and managed to stay close for several weeks. Then sharks slashed the ropes and they drifted apart. By the luck of the draw, Mathys had found himself in the boat with Captain Newton. Sixty-three days later, provisions long gone, Mathys's boat was spotted by a brig out of Sydney, headed north toward the Sandwich Isles, the islands natives called Hawai'i.

Of twelve men squeezed into the boat, only Mathys and another sailor survived, both jabbering, sun-blind and half insane when the brig pulled them from the sea. Days later, tended and fed, they were asked what happened to their skipper, Captain Toby Newton.

"Stringy, he was," Mathys said. "When they all began to expire, he was the first we *et*."

By the time they reached Lahaina on the island of Maui, whaling capital of the Pacific, word had spread that the brig was carrying two sailors who had eaten their captain. Still weak in body and mind, Mathys peered out at a harbor that rocked with tall-masted whalers, schooners, and clippers from round the world, and large crowds milling ashore, waiting to view the young cannibals. Terrified of imprisonment or being hanged, he neglected to see the incredible beauty of the island, white sickle beaches, tremulous palms, volcanic mountains like jagged emeralds.

Detained aboard the brig by police and representatives of King Kamehameha III, who refused to let *haole* cannibals lose among his people, Mathys grew desperate. One night he and his friend overpowered the watchman, jumped ship, and swam ashore. Within hours they had worked their way into the mountainous jungle interior of the island, hiding in daylight, running for their lives at night. Then Mathys's friend crushed his leg in a fall down a ravine; the leg grew septic and he died.

Now he was alone in a world so foreign, so fantastic, he didn't know the names of things, which plants and fish were edible, which ones would kill him. Islands he had always dreamed of, towering pavilions in the sea, were now a jungle prison where he was cursed to end his days alone. That loneliness was compounded by what Mathys feared was creeping insanity. At night he heard drums beating, saw lights, ghostly vapors dancing on graves.

He didn't have the aptitude to live like a beast, and after months of crushing solitude one day he crept to the ocean, wanting only to die. With no thought, he threw himself from a cliff down to crashing waves. For a long time he thought he *had* died, that he was paying for his sins in hell, a nightmare world of blood, incessant pain, near-blindness.

Years later he would describe how he first saw Kelonikoa:

"She came to me from the sea. God had finally forgiven me."

For, in that last year while Mathys had been slaughtering, whoring, eating human flesh, a young, headstrong Tahitian beauty was also consigning herself to a life of shame, exiling herself forever from her native lands. Daughter of a Tahitian high chief and a lady-in-waiting at the court of the reigning king of the islands of Tahiti, this girl—Kelonikoa Pi'imoku Kanoa—had been betrothed, sight unseen, to a first cousin of the reigning Hawaiian king, Kamehameha III. After weeks at sea, arriving in Honolulu, she had peered from her carriage with her attendants, caught sight of the man she would marry and fainted. He was small and bowlegged, with a wrinkled face like a monkey.

She sent word to Tahiti, begging to return, threatening to kill herself rather than marry this monkey-man. She bided her time, refusing his visits, until word came back from her father, demanding she marry

Kamehameha's cousin, or be cast out forever from her people. Should she return to Tahiti, her father would eat both her eyes, she would be sacrificed alive, her bones thrown to wild dogs. One night while her attendants slept, Kelonikoa fled Honolulu on an inter-island steamer heading across the channel to Maui. The captain took an oath of silence when she placed in his hand a huge, precious black pearl.

In those days, Lahaina was a town of three thousand people, living mostly in grass houses, unprepared for thousands of whalers descending on them in increasing numbers, men bestial from months at sea, craving drink and women, men who believed there was "No God west of the Horn." Arriving at Lahaina's harbor, Kelonikoa stared horrified at crowds of sailors fighting, knifing, dragging laughing women into the bush. Fearing they would take her for a whore, afraid missionaries would report her to the king—for often their sympathies went to the highest bidder—she fled, working her way along the coast, until the town was far behind.

She was a woman of the sea, and in the sea was solace. She cast off shoes, petticoats and stays, tore the sleeves from her dress, tore off half the skirt so she could swim freely. Her skin darkened from sun, her hair grew coarse and tangled, she lost the language of humans, hearing only wildlife, the sea's rhythms. She ate raw fish, slept in rock caves, and months passed as she gained her bearings. Her clothes disintegrated into little more than tattered rags, so that diving in and out of waves, limbs draped with seaweed, she resembled a creature half human, half fish.

One morning she played in the shallows, gathering 'opihi for breakfast. The tide slowly brought her in, close enough to see on shore what resembled a yellow dog. The thing had long, filthy hair past its shoulders, a leathery brown body pollened with pale fur. It moved in a half crawl but, seeing her, tried to stand on two feet like a human. Waves washed her closer, and Kelonikoa saw its face was awful, one-eyed, bloodied, and bloated. She turned, swimming away, but it made a sound like a human. When she looked back it whimpered, held out its paws, and seemed to faint.

For weeks, she tended him, never speaking, touching him only to put food to his lips, or spread antiseptic root juices across the suppurating eye socket. In his delirium it came back to him: headlong plunge into the sea, the coral spear piercing. When the undertow wrenched him sharply back, there had been a swift, sucking *POP!* the coral snatching his eyeball. Slowly, slowly, pain receded, he felt nothing there, not even when she poured seawater into the healing socket. He learned to adjust to limited peripheral vision by keeping the good eye, the right eye, always roving.

Out of modesty, she covered his lap with a diaper of moss, made a skirt and vest for herself of ti leaves. And, as his eye began to heal, she fashioned an eye patch from the skin of mynah bird cured and softened with oil of *kukui*. Once he recovered, she didn't go near him, would not touch him again. They moved side by side during the day, slept at a distance at night.

One morning, Kelonikoa saw him struggle with his knotted hair, his filthy beard, failing to strike down a bird with his makeshift slingshot. Approaching slowly, she made motions for him to lower his head into a stream, then washed his hair with coconut and eucalyptus juice until it rinsed to gold. With a seashell honed to a sharp blade, she trimmed his hair and shaved his beard off. Before her stood a man with features so pleasing, she backed away.

But in that caring gesture Mathys slowly came to life. He had feared the girl was a figment of his madness, that in the delirium of pain he had conjured her, for sometimes she was there, and sometimes not. Yet, now, the smell of her hands lingered on him. Her soft laughter echoed. Slowly, they began to talk in grunts and sign language that evolved into Tahitian-English Pidgin. Drawing maps in sand, using twigs and stones, he learned she was Polynesian, but from islands far south, called Tahiti, from which ancient Hawaiians had ventured looking for new lands. And she learned he was a Yankee, his home near an island called Manhattan. She learned he had been a common farmer. And Mathys understood she came from royalty. Now they were equals, trying to survive.

Her incredible, golden beauty called forth the beauty around him, and nature quietly stepped forward. Jungles that had choked him now opened into misty rain forests abloom with torch ginger, orchid, heliconia, towering waterfalls. The vegetation he was afraid to eat turned out to be luscious guava, mango, passion fruit. Kelonikoa fashioned a strong bow and arrow, taught him to stalk partridge, pheasant, goat, how to face a charging boar, gauging the force of the boar's leap to gain extra penetrating power for the arrow. She taught him Polynesian netcasting, how to pry limpets from tidal rocks, how to bake *kālua* pig in earth with heated stones. She taught him to pound taro tubers into *poi*, and how to store meat in ti leaves.

In the evenings, sun slipping through the fingers of their right hands, moon rising in their left, as cooling trades funneled through the channel between Maui and Moloka'i, Mathys began to talk about his life at sea. How, seeing a whale for the first time, something in him went down on its knees. Once, rowing close to a creature's head just before the harpoon struck, he stared into its eye.

"As if God had turned and looked at me."

He talked about the humpback's songs that constantly, mysteriously changed. And the size of the blue whale, largest in the world. And the rich, thick milk of the sperm whales, thick as cheese, the crying of their calves when mothers were slaughtered.

"I have seen their hearts," he said, "large as boulders. And I have seen their brains. What do they think with those massive brains? What do their songs mean?"

They had sometimes followed his ship for days, deeply inquisitive, watching the crew. He explained how they were the first animals on earth, it said so in the Bible, and he would spend his life mourning the ones he had slaughtered. Even now, some days he sat alone by the sea, remembering the songs of the humpback, wondering at the mind of the sperm.

Hearing sorrow in his voice, a kind of poetry, Kelonikoa felt a stirring. Though foreign traders had visited her islands, he was the first white man she had ever spoken to. She had been taught they were evil, that their bodies carried "sailor's pox," always fatal to natives, that they were spreading it island to island as a way of conquering the Pacific. No one had told her white men felt sadness, or longing, that they had grave souls like Polynesians.

Wanting to give Mathys something in return, Kelonikoa took him down to the sea, teaching him to hold his breath and deep-dive. She gave him the gift of deep canyons of pastel-colored coral, the courting dance of sea snakes in silver blizzards of sprats. She showed him the intelligence of the octopus, how when stroked with affection, they danced a graceful, eight-legged dance. She showed him the eerie and beautiful night world of plankton pulsing and glowing, trailing gossamer tails like ghostly anglers. They swam with schools of dolphin, hitched rides on the backs of manta rays with wingspans of twenty feet. One night they watched two giant phosphorescent squid, tentacles eighty or ninety feet long, battling in moonlight to the death.

And still, they slept apart, Mathys never dreaming of touching her, for she seemed a thing beyond his reach. One day when he woke, she would be gone. Then one night they heard drums like giant heartbeats, which Mathys had thought were part of his madness from too much solitude. Kelonikoa led him through the jungle, and from a distance they watched lights flash like fireballs, vaporish forms swerving and weaving over gravelike mounds of earth.

"*Heiau*," she whispered. "Ancient temple grounds where human sacrifices made. Dey come back searching for dere souls."

That night Mathys divulged the unspeakable part of his past, for he had thought the drums and ghosts of his solitary year in the jungle were God's way of keeping him half mad, his penance for having devoured human flesh.

"You see, everyone else in the boat had expired. We were starving, sun-blind, dying of thirst."

Bodies blistered and cracked, they had watched sharks circle and circle. Desperate, they had thrown a corpse overboard, keeping the beasts at bay. Seeing the blood during their feeding frenzy, Mathys had sliced into his skipper's body, put his mouth to the cut, and mindlessly sucked.

"Captain was tough and stringy, body dehydrated, only a bit of blood. We threw out his arms and legs, worked our way down to the organs. That's what saved our lives."

He could still see the man's liver in his hand as he washed it with seawater, still see it shining and quivering, as he brought it to his mouth.

He hung his head. "That's what I was. A cannibal."

Rocking back and forth, Kelonikoa laughed at his great "sin," explaining how her grandparents had eaten the flesh of their enemies during tribal wars, that cannibalism was a noble part of Polynesian heritage. After that, Mathys grew calm, more confident. There was nothing left to hide. But she turned strangely sad, for she had no secrets, no tragedies to tell him in return.

"But you do," he cried. "Tell me again of your flight from the monkey-man!"

He loved the story, made her tell it over and over. And in each telling, he saw her strength, a woman who would follow her decisions. Each telling also reminded him they were fugitives, Kelonikoa fleeing her father, and Mathys the police, possibly the American government. Occasionally, coming upon hunters, they turned and ran. But no one seeing this one-eyed wild man connected him to a young sailor from New England. And the ragged *wahine* they saw was never associated with a Tahitian gentlewoman who had refused the hand of royalty and supposedly flung herself into the sea. Spotted swimming by fishermen, they changed their sleeping and cooking places, moved deeper into the jungle.

One day, Kelonikoa came running to where Mathys was curing the pelt of a goat. Prying *'opihi* from tidal rocks, she had heard the voices of net-casting natives. Hiding behind rocks, she had listened to their talk, Hawaiian so similar to her Tahitian. Now, she knelt before him, speaking rapidly in Pidgin, words tumbling over themselves.

"Poppy War! Chinee come Honolulu . . . monkey-man *pau!*"

He calmed her down and, slowing her chatter, understood that a terrible Opium War had begun, and that possibly their life of hiding was over. During the days of whaling, he had heard from seamen how in the early 1800s, watching their country become a nation of addicts, the Chinese Imperial government had forbade further importation of opium. By the mid-1830s British and American ships monopolized the illegal opium trade. With the fastest clippers in the world, Americans transported opium from Turkey, and the British from India, both navies converging at the mouth of the Pearl River near Canton. There, it was transferred to the holds of storage ships owned by corrupt mandarins, who paid for it with vast amounts of silver.

According to what Kelonikoa had heard, and what Mathys could piece together, in the past few weeks, trying to enforce laws against opium trade, the Imperial Chinese government had seized and destroyed all opium ships near Canton. In retaliation, the British attacked the Imperial Navy. It was a struggle that would go on for several years, affecting politics throughout the world. Even now, spies from the Imperial Chinese government were radiating across the Pacific, assassinating rich opium profiteers. One of those profiteers had been King Kamehameha III's cousin, the monkey-man, found with a jade chopstick run straight through his head, protruding through both ears.

Now Mathys sat with his head in his hands, trying to make sense of it. He imagined the harbor of Lahaina. In the chaos, who would recognize him as the youth who ate his captain? That night Kelonikoa woke to find Mathys sitting beside her, watching her in moonlight.

"I am at your command," he said carefully. "What is it you wish to do?"

She sat up, folded her arms and thought. In her father's eyes, she would always be damned. Here in this rain forest, for the first time, she was her own woman, free of tribal codes, the dominance of men.

"I stay here," she said. "Where I can be what I can be."

For the first time in all their months together, he touched her, took her hand. "If you so choose, then I will stay with you, for I love you, Kelonikoa, with all my heart. If you could ever learn to love a common man, I will find someone to marry us. I will wait for you. Forever."

She had loved him for a long time. But now she brooded, weighing things. "You have de 'sailor's pox'?"

"No," he said. "I swear it." Remembering the whores of Valparaiso, it seemed a miracle that God had spared him syphilis.

"I be no sailor's wife," she said.

He gripped her hand, told her there were two things he would never be again. A sailor. Or a farmer. He talked about the enterprising Dutch in New York State who had become importers and tradesmen, and land they slowly acquired for their descendants.

"That's what I want to do. These islands are a new frontier, the world is coming here. I have heard it. I want to settle in Honolulu, become a merchant, begin a family." Then he shook his head, nearly defeated by his ambitions.

"I have nothing to begin with, only a slingshot, this bow and arrow, the goatskins on my back. It would mean years of struggle. But I would love you dearly, I would provide for you, give you dignity, so you would never have to beg. And I would depend on your advice, Kelonikoa, for now I'm among a different people, and bound to make mistakes."

She studied him a long time, then opened a pouch worn on twine round her waist since the first day he saw her. She even swam with it, and he had assumed the little knocking sounds inside were simple Tahitian talismans. Now she poured into her palm half a dozen perfectly round black spheres, winking and shimmering in moonlight. Mathys leaned close and gasped. What looked like fat, black cherries, perfect in contour and color, were legendary, priceless South Seas pearls from the rare black-lipped oyster. Kings went to war for them, white men conspired and murdered for them.

"My dowry," she whispered. "What monkey-man were waitin' for." She dropped a pearl in Mathys's hand so he could feel its weight. "We begin our life wit dese. I still daughter of Tahitian high chief, no like livin' poor."

He backed away. "I can't accept this. I'm a man of honor!"

Hips swaying, she walked nonchalantly to the beach, flung a black pearl into the sea. "I fly dem back where dey been born. Not'ing to me. You go away now, wit' your false pride. Go!"

* * *

A week later, they entered the chaos of Lahaina. Riots, shootings, nightly curfews. In the streets the talk was of the Opium War between China and Britain. A ship had been blown up in the harbor, and as Mathys suspected, others were quickly reprovisioning and weighing anchor. He and Kelonikoa stood in shadows, listening. As a missionary family snored, he entered their house, took a dress, a man's suit, left a goatskin in return. The next day, he entered a shop, trading more goatskins for shoes, proper underwear. He sold his bow and arrow for cash, and they made their way to a makeshift Congregationalist church, asking to be married.

The *haole* missionary stared at Mathys as if he were mad.

"If you are sure you want to marry a *kanaka*, she must take instructions, become a Christian first." He studied Kelonikoa, took Mathys aside. "I warn you, they are without morals. The women row out to ships, offering themselves!"

Mathys spat at the minister's feet, took her hand and walked away. Among a colony of grass huts they found a Hawaiian *kahuna*, who grinned broadly, consenting to marry them. While his wife and daughters quickly gathered blossoms for *lei*, the man spoke angrily of the *mikanele*.

"They teach Hawaiians forget language, gods, taboos. Even forget respect for nature, the sea."

"Why do your people let this happen?" Mathys asked.

Sadly, he shook his head. "We too intelligent. Want everything *haole* got. We coming greedy."

He draped them with *lei* made of *api* leaves to ward against evil spirits, and ti leaves, for healing, and the sweet smelling, best-loved blossom *maile* for full life and faithfulness. He gave his blessings, and joined them in marriage.

Days later on the steamer to Honolulu, Mathys and Kelonikoa threw their *lei* into the sea, looking back at the mountainous rain forests of Maui.

"We will return," Mathys said. "Each year when the whales come to mate, to leap and spout in the Pacific, we'll make a pilgrimage to these mountains. In this way we'll stay humble, remembering how we began."

Kelonikoa shivered, her head grazing the shoulder of her husband, in one hand her pouch of pearls, in the other, his big fist. She was not thinking of the pearls, or even the mountains. She was thinking of the first time she had seen him, one eye torn from his head, a bleeding savage, but something in his filthy nakedness stirring her, the sight of his maleness hanging strong between his legs.

She took that memory all the way, dove backward into it as he slowly undressed her that night, their wedding night, waves rocking the ship, rocking them into each other. Much later, Kelonikoa woke, thinking how she must teach her husband many things. How to prepare a wife for love, how to arouse her, make her moan with longing, how to enter her in candlelight, or torchlight, sunlight or moonlight, so they could see each other's pleasure in the eyes. These were lessons taught Polynesians in early adulthood, because to them sex was a natural, beautiful act, not something performed in guilt and darkness. Her last thought before she slept was that she must also teach her *haole* husband how to bathe, and to do it often.

Pox, and
Empress
Fingerprints

DUST WAS EVERYWHERE IN HONOLULU, it even furred the porcelain plates of royalty. Foreigners joked about meals with the "Kanaka King," how clumsy native footmen pouring wine would stumble, wiping grit from their eyes. Even the wine had a gritty texture. Near the docks—a treeless clutter of filthy, grim warehouses, grogshops, and unpaved roads—dust lay so heavy in the air *haole* wore handkerchiefs over their faces like bandits, folks went about coughing and sneezing. Still, the town was becoming the business center of the islands, gathering place of traders and merchants. Establishment of a Hudson Bay Company agency there in 1834 was transforming Honolulu into a major seaport of the Pacific.

Within two weeks of their arrival, Mathys and Kelonikoa sold a black pearl to a precious-gems dealer from France, and Mathys began building a modest house away from downtown Honolulu. Since foreigners couldn't own land, the property was leased. But that law would soon change, enabling Mathys to slowly accumulate thousands of acres.

In the early 1840s, wealth was being accumulated overnight in Honolulu—human cargo smuggled in from the Orient as cheap labor, opium packed in champagne bottles, rare jade and gold slipped past immigration authorities. No one inquired about the source of Mathys's income, no one cared. When he leased livery stables on King Street, he paid in cash. Kelonikoa sold another pearl and he bought a caulking business: "SHIP CARPENTERS, PREPARED TO DO ALL KINDS OF WORK IN OUR LINE."

Anticipating a boom in population, within three years he enlarged his livery stables. Besides saddle horses and teams, he now offered ". . . SURRIES, BUGGIES, AND PHAETONS," appealing to a growing carriage trade. He and Kelonikoa were naturalized, swore allegiance to the king, and as Honolulu grew into a premier port town of saloons and brothels, one day Mathys leased a run-down grogshop catty-corner from his carriage business, naming it the Bay Horse Saloon. He promptly petitioned the Minister of the Interior for a liquor license, and directed all his energies toward gutting and resurrecting the saloon.

In 1848, King Kamehameha III went into deep depression, mourning the death of his beloved sister and mistress, Nahienaena. Drinking excessively, he let himself be persuaded by white merchants and ex-missionaries to "abolish feudalism and make land-rights equal." Ambitious *haole* needed security in land tenure for their growing plantations. Under the terms of the *Great Mahele*, or Land Division, Kamehameha III gave up the rights to much of his former property, keeping certain estates as crown lands. High chiefs received one and a half million acres, which they began to sell, lease or foolishly give away. For the rest, locals and foreigners alike, they could buy lots in fee simple from the rest of the islands' acreage. Foreign residents were the first to take advantage of the "reform."

Mathys's second house, built of precious lumber, was a graceful two-story on several dozen acres he now owned. It boasted wraparound *lānai* on each floor so high-ceilinged rooms had access to cooling tradewinds. Other houses were stingily and hastily put together, crowded upon one another. But Kelonikoa demanded a house surrounded by beauty and fragrance—frangipani, ginger, pīkake—sweeping lawns, and the privacy of great shade trees.

Even with such luxuries, she lacked peace of mind, for she saw how increasingly hard it was for native Hawaiians to buy simple plots of land. One day her cook asked Mathys to explain registration papers she and her husband had to complete, and the deadlines by which certain claims had to be filed. The woman could read and write English, but terminology in the forms was so entangled and complex even Mathys could not translate it. Kelonikoa saw it was a ploy, a way to discourage natives from buying land, which left more land available for *haole*. She saw how increasingly they were marrying Hawaiian women of great land-holding families, building up enormous tracts of land for white descendants.

As work progressed on his saloon, Mathys imported special steer hides from Spain for stools and booths, and a fine mahogany bar with hunt scenes carved in Canton, shipped to Honolulu in two parts. The day it was assembled and installed, most of Honolulu stopped at the intersection of Hotel and Bethel, ogling his extravaganza. Until now, saloons had been mere dives in Honolulu, troughs for sailors and brawlers. Mathys wanted a place that attracted wealthy merchants, traders and bankers in three-piece suits and Argosy suspenders, high-steppers sporting canes, in silk Stetsons and straw bowlers.

The Bay Horse slowly acquired cachet. A back room for the rowdies with its own bar and cheap spirits was separated, by a thick mahogany door, from the heavily wood-paneled, mirrored front room resembling a gentleman's club, with even a looking glass foyer where merchants hung their hats, arranged their cravats and gold watch chains. The king and his regents arrived in carriages and phaetons, suited and coiffed like Englishmen. Diplomats came, and merchants. And one night while the skin of Mathys's three-year-old son erupted in red circles, a Yank named Herman Melville declared the Bay Horse Saloon odiously pretentious and departed, leaving his whiskey untouched.

For days, Kelonikoa and Mathys prayed over their firstborn, watching the virus destroy him. While hundreds of feverish measle victims flung themselves into the sea, Mathys dragged a doctor into the house at gunpoint. He vaccinated the child, even as it died. All night, Kelonikoa sat massaging her son's big toe, calling *"Ho'i hou! Ho'i hou!" Come back, come back.* For Polynesians believed the dead were often undecided, and that the last of life hung back in the big toe.

She stood dry-eyed as they buried her son behind the house. But one night, feeling her sudden absence, Mathys woke. He found her in her sleeping sarong out on the lawn, digging her son up with her hands. In moonlight she and Mathys struggled, the shrouded little corpse pulled back and forth between them. Finally, he relented, let her wrap the child in *hāpu'u* leaves soaked in saliva of wild boar, old-time preservatives, which were then wrapped in soft *kukui*-cured skins of mynah, then the softest linen stained with eucalyptus, aloe and jasmine. For months they slept with the little mummy between them absorbing their grief and wilderness.

"Auwē, auwē!" the servants cried. "Mastah, Missus, come *pupule*! More bettah make anot'er *keiki*."

Finally, when Kelonikoa felt a stirring in her womb, she let Mathys return the small mummy to its grave.

Rejuvenated by the promise of another child, he returned to his businesses with vigor. In the back room of the Bay Horse, desperate Russian, British, and French seaman pawned "baubles" from the Orient, things they didn't know the value of. Delicate antiques of heavy silver from Macao, real carved gold from Siam, precious jade artifacts. In the front room, Mathys discreetly offered his treasures, one bauble at a time, to merchant princes for wives and mistresses.

In time, it was rumored he could procure anything for a price, the robes of an emperor, a crown. His saloon became so popular, his businesses so prosperous, he was invited to join the new Pacific Club, exclusively for *haole*. The day of his induction, he arrived at the club in a new gilded phaeton with matching steeds.

Kelonikoa watched and listened. She was intelligent, learning proper English from Portia Rule, a renegade Boston missionary's wife, constantly stirring up trouble, pushing for legislation to make school attendance for native children compulsory through age fourteen. Patiently, she tried to impress upon Hawaiians the danger of their Mother Tongue dying out.

"Loss of one's language is the first step toward extinction," she warned. "Your children are learning English and history from Christian textbooks. You must keep up Hawaiian conversations at home."

Kelonikoa suspected that most *haole* didn't want natives educated. They wanted to keep them in the fields, and as house servants. She told her cooks and gardeners they were free to look for more dignified work. She would even help them. They wept and pleaded. House and yard work were all they knew.

"Then, I promise you," she said. "Your children will not be servants in someone else's home. I will help you send them to school."

One day she looked at her four-year-old son, felt the next child stirring within, and turned to Portia Rule. "What of my children who are half-castes? Will they be servants, too?"

The woman answered carefully. "Your husband is successful. Your children will be privileged. If you are lucky, one of them, just one, will try to help their people."

She advised Kelonikoa to read newspapers diligently, to listen to gossip in the streets, so she would understand how rapidly Hawai'i was changing, how radically rich and poor classes were growing. In 1853, there was no middle class. White traders and merchants were becoming millionaires in Honolulu, while behind his back they called the king "Imperial Nigger, His *Kanaka* Highness."

"There is something more heinous than bigotry," Portia Rule warned. "If your people are not careful, disease will wipe them out completely."

In 1778 when Captain Cook had "discovered" Hawai'i, the native population was nearly a million. By 1850 it was under sixty thousand. Until Cook arrived, Hawaiians had been the most isolated people in the world, and so had not built up a strong immune system. But through ingenious, rigid systems of hygiene, they had remained fiercely strong and healthy. By now, trading and whaling ships from around the world had spread syphilis, measles, typhoid, whooping cough, and worse. Quarantine laws requiring health inspectors for visiting ships had come too late.

As if in response to Portia's warning, one day a brig out of San Francisco docked in Honolulu flying a yellow flag. A sailor aboard was dying of smallpox. The crew was allowed ashore, vaccinated and quarantined, but local girls made love to them through fences, and within days, two Hawaiians collapsed. Families were quarantined, clothes and houses burned. A call for general vaccinations came too late. Within months two thousand natives were dead.

Hour after hour, Kelonikoa fed her second-born shark-fin soup, a fish known to have powerful *mana*. Still, life leaked from his delicate grotto of bones. A yellow flag hung in their doorway, and two fresh graves were dug behind their house, the second one for the child Kelonikoa was carrying when a vaccination shot left her feverish, vomiting for days. The perfectly formed fetus fell out of her, blue and hard as stone.

Inconsolable, she would not let Mathys near her. He found release in alcohol, weeping and wailing as wagons trundled by filled with corrupting corpses, noses running with worms. When they ran out of burying space, drivers stacked bodies like lumber, set them afire in fields. Soon pyramids dotted the landscape, black corpses charred into sitting-up or flying postures like monstrous acrobats. For months, Honolulu was a plague-struck town from the Middle Ages, fires of contaminated shacks blistering the night, the taste of death like soot. Floating corpses blanketed the harbor, so it looked like one huge carcass. Dogs ran in packs like gypsies, carrying limbs dug up from shallow mounds. For weeks, Mathys slept with a cocked rifle beside his childrens' graves.

One day he learned that a *haole* port official had been bribed for $1,000, allowing the pox ship from San Francisco into the harbor. In broad daylight, Mathys walked into the official's house with a rifle and cutlass, shot him through the heart, decapitated him in one swoop, stuck the head on a pole and carried it through the streets. People tore the body to shreds, flung the shreds to dancing dogs. In three years, twelve thousand native Hawaiians would die.

Kelonikoa lost her sense of speech, became a Bedouin of the valleys, wandering from village to village, wherever people mourned their dead, silently mourning with them. One night Mathys looked down from their mahogany four-poster and found her squatting wide-eyed like a madwoman. Her wrists were running blood, and with her blood she had written on the walls ... MY DEAD CHILDREN ... MY FATHER'S CURSE ON ME. ... He slid down beside her, gathered her to him, talking softly, explaining how loss of her presence, her love, would be greater to him than that of any child. He was nothing without her, all the sorrow, and magic, and beauty of his world was contained within her. If she went insane, or died, he would follow. Silently, she pointed to the sea.

Every day thereafter, Mathys took her to a secluded beach away from polluted harbors. There she removed her clothes, corset, underthings, and floated naked in leaping waves, mothersounds, heart thump of her ancestral home. One day she sang out in Tahitian as a school of dolphin sailed in, curious and playful, chattering in funny click-tongue. Mathys watched paralyzed as she slid onto the back of a dolphin, riding in lazy circles, the thing soaring so high his wife was sometimes airborne. Day after day the dolphins came, soaring her toward slow healing.

One day, a whale appeared on the horizon, crying out repeatedly. Mathys stared at Kelonikoa's corset lying on the sand. From the framework of the thing, the stays of wrecked whalebone, something emanated, a cry. He lunged to his feet, afraid he'd lost his mind. Kelonikoa waved as the whale moved in, singing a mournful song, almost a call. The corset responded again, a distinguishable bleating. Mathys drew his gun, aimed it at the corset. The whale, still calling, swam closer to shore.

Song of the humpback, mind of the sperm. His memory cells jostled, a joyless comprehension. He dropped the gun, gingerly lifted the corset, and carried it into the surf, where waves washed it out toward the mother whale. Almost tenderly, she flipped the corset onto her back, and in mournful, piping song, swam off. For reasons he could not discern, Mathys began to sob.

His wife turned in the shallows, held out her arms, and spoke her first words to him in months. "Come ... into ... me."

Tearing his clothes off, he flung himself into the ocean, crying out her name.

The pox plague died, ships sailed again, and each year gave Mathys and Kelonikoa contemplative pause as another child was born. She tended them lovingly but with restraint, knowing God could take them in a minute.

Trade mushroomed in Hawai'i, ships from Europe, the Americas, the Orient. Rich *haole* built huge plantation estates as the quality of life deteriorated for Hawaiians. Quietly, unobtrusively, Kelonikoa and other privileged high-born or well-married women dressed in plain clothes and made their way to the slums, feeding the poor, comforting the dying, ducking pails of sewage aimed at missionaries foraging back alleys for souls.

Drunken seamen, crazed from months at sea, staggered through Chinatown, looking for places of freakish legend—the Screaming Lizard, a bar where sailors won wagers by biting the heads off lizards, then waved their money while in their mouths the lizard heads still screamed. Honey House, a brothel of blind mulattoes. Grinning Grog, a place for madmen where they served hymen blood of young girls. Dance of Little Hands, a house where delicate Chinese boys were dressed in rouge and gowns.

Running the gauntlet of sailors near the docks, Kelonikoa saw how smallpox had spread so swiftly in Honolulu: refuse dumped in gutters running into harbors, gigantic cesspools where rats bobbed up and down like seals, opium addicts—men, women, children—sleeping, eating, defecating in alleys. One day, she knelt beside a thirteen-year-old native girl. For fifty dollars, her father had sold her to a whaling skipper. She had been taken to sea, used for months as the crew's recreation, until she contracted "sailor's pox." Someone had dragged her from the ship and dumped her in an alley. Pregnant, diseased, she had swallowed "mad vegetation," and died in Kelonikoa's arms. For hours, Kelonikoa wept, relating the tragedy to Portia Rule.

Next day the woman took her to a modest bungalow, where more than thirty gentlewomen stood around in latest fashions—long dresses with *sash derrieres*, feathered hats, high-button shoes, silk gloves and parasols. Some were *haole*, some half-castes and high castes, wives and daughters of prosperous businessmen. They sat down, shifted in their seats, nervous, somewhat exhilarated.

Addressing them was a Miss Mercy Goddard, M.D., who had practiced medicine for eighteen years in London and Switzerland. She had birthed babies, removed "unseemly growths," whole stomachs, had amputated arms and legs, and never lost a patient. Newly arrived in Honolulu, she was setting up an underground practice strictly for females, making herself available to "fix" women exhausted by birthing too many children, six or more. When warranted, she could surgically discontinue a pregnancy, rather than have women resort to "mad vegetation," a local poisonous root inducing miscarriage and often killing the mother.

She would teach birth-control methods, and was available to tend all kinds of "mysterious" female illnesses. If anyone was interested, she was also available to instruct women on how to satisfy themselves sexually, if their husbands could not. As she pronounced the word "masturbation," two women stood and fainted. But no one left. They sat there for five hours, barraging the doctor with questions. She asked for volunteers, assistants. Each meeting attracted more women.

Within weeks Dr. Goddard had volunteer crews disguised in drab mu'umu'u, carrying carpetbags of food and medicine, sweeping the streets for prostitutes riddled with disease or carrying unwanted babies. Soon, curious Hawaiian midwives turned up to see what this haole could teach them. Young women came wanting to study medicine, women who would eventually break the mold and demand more licensing of female physicians in the islands. They called themselves the Bustle Club, telling fathers and husbands they met weekly to sew, catch up on new fashions. One day, when Dr. Goddard asked for donations for medical supplies, a woman's medical library, a printing press, Kelonikoa donated one of her precious black pearls.

In December 1854, King Kamehameha III expired and within hours his successor, Alexander Liholiho, was proclaimed Kamehameha IV. While regiments marched and cannons saluted his accession to the throne, women in the Bustle Club stood and cheered. A mother of seven had just announced her first "climax," a result of following Dr. Goddard's instructions on masturbation. More and more women made their way through back streets to the doctor's bungalow.

Two years after his accession, Kamehameha IV married Emma, a favorite of the people, but their lives were stalked by tragedy. Their only son died when he was four, and in 1863, the twenty-nine-year-old king followed his son to the grave. Dowager Queen Emma, only twenty-seven, managed her grief by devoting herself to her people. With the accession of a new king, she founded Queen Emma Hospital, offering the poor free medical care. Women of the Bustle Club joined her and the future Queen Lili'uokalani in going door to door, soliciting more monies for the hospital. In time, Dowager Queen Emma consulted Dr. Goddard on various ailments, and now and then, she sat in on tamer meetings of the Bustle Club.

The United States Civil War and discovery of oil in Pennsylvania sounded the death knell for New England's whaling industry, as the need for sperm oil declined. Ships were converted by the Union government into merchantmen, while others were sunk in large numbers by Confederate raiders. The Bustle Club, faithful to the Union, wrapped bandages for soldiers thousands of miles away, and found homes for families whose husbands returned to the mainland to fight. Kelonikoa comforted Mathys on nights when guilt left his empty eye socket throbbing. His brothers at home were marching for the Union, while he led the high life on a distant tropic island.

"This is your home now," she said. "Your allegiance is to your family, and the king."

While he slept in her arms, she lay awake, thinking, trying to sort it out. The American South was fighting for slavery, the North for equality, yet her Yankee husband had more in common with the Confederacy than the Union. Mathys was now heavily invested in the new economy, King Sugar, that depended on contract labor which imposed slave conditions on Chinese "coolies." He and his friends had purchased two trading vessels, rumored to be notorious "Blackbirders," ships cruising the Pacific, kidnapping natives to work on white men's sugar plantations until they dropped dead of disease or exhaustion.

The Civil War confirmed the Hawaiians' belief that most Americans, even those fighting for the Union, were prejudiced. They slept with native women, even married them, but could not accept that the mind of a black or brown human being was equal, even superior, to theirs. Half-caste children were considered blessed with the superiority of white blood, cursed with the native half. The government of the islands slid slowly into chaos, Americans wanting annexation, Hawaiians wanting autonomy. Fistfights broke out on the floor of the legislature. Conspiracies, attempted assassinations. *Haole* wore loaded pistols, while natives sharpened spears and knives, shouting ancient warrior chants in the streets. Warships with cannons aimed, sat in Honolulu Harbor, sent by the U.S. government.

One day a lovely young half-caste appeared at the door of the Bay

Horse. Mathys looked up, curious; ladies were forbidden in his saloon. Then he recognized his daughter.

"Father, it's almost time."

That night, after sixteen hours of labor, the midwife chanting, gently stroking her stomach with *kukui* nut oil, Kelonikoa delivered her seventh child, a girl named Emma with her mother's dark hair, slanted eyes, golden skin, the same beautiful, oval face. That evening while his wife slept after drinking six cups of a mixture of seven teas that slowed her bleeding, Mathys called his children before him, for he had lost track and wasn't sure he could name them all. He lined them up and bade them each step out in turn.

In 1860 a law had been passed requiring Hawaiians to give their children two names, and to call them by their Christian name first. Thus, Mathys called out to his children.

"Daniel *Punahele* (Favorite) sixteen . . . Sophie *Leihulu* (Beloved Child) fifteen . . . George *Iwa* (Man of War Bird) thirteen . . . Olivia *Mālama* (Caring) eleven . . . James *Kahiki* (Tahiti) nine . . . Eliza *Mapuana* (Wind-blown Fragrance) four . . ." The oldest three were at Punahou, the missionary school, preparing them for college on the mainland. The other three had tutors. Now there was little Emma. What would her Hawaiian name be?

When Kelonikoa was strong enough, as with each previous child, she would place the infant's placenta between her teeth and swim out to the reef beyond which *kūpuna kāne* and *kūpuna wāhine* and all *'aumākua* presided. She would release the placenta, letting waves carry it out into the elements, its blood flowing into that of its ancestors, their *mana* flowing into the newborn child so it would be fearless and strong. She would float inside the reef, perhaps for hours, until waves blew her back a sound, a Polynesian name.

Sometimes at night, Mathys studied his wife in sleep. Passion had cooled through the years, their children coming further and further apart. Some years he missed the steamer to Maui, and she went on their annual pilgrimage alone, keeping the vow they had made on their wedding night. Yet while she was gone, he suffered. Dashing Mathys Coenradtsen, with his mysterious wealth, his mysterious past. A glance from him, and women paused, married as well as maidens, his wild blond mane and black eye patch giving him a notorious, magnetic, piratical air.

Yet he had not touched another woman, never consciously desired it. If occasionally he was unfaithful in his dreams, it was only with the wenches of the streets, caterwauling whores who made love in alleys bent over fish-head barrels. It was really rollicking youth he missed, what he had never had. Yet, over the years he had watched his wife grow from a wild young woman into a beautiful, gracious hostess, hair upswept, emeralds at her throat, dark golden skin radiant in gowns of satin and brocade. The great pride she instilled in him made up for a youth never known.

She had transformed their house from that first simple structure into an estate surrounded by royal palms, expansive lawns where peacocks preened among lemon and loquat trees, where mynahs flitted in palms and bamboo groves, and lush, tropical blossoms—plumeria, orchids, pīkake—formed a rich living tapestry of colors and perfumes. Carp shot their colors across a pond, gardeners pruned bushes surrounding a teahouse of precious sandalwood and teak. Chambermaids, servants, tutors and governesses drifted down scented corridors in starched linens. Mathys's study and library were filled with massive mahogany, carved ebony, heavy teak on Persian rugs. Pier glasses reflected other rooms of more delicate woods—monkeypod, *koa*, bamboo.

His wife could set a table for thirty with porcelain, crystal and silver. Two Filipino cooks were trained and lectured on wine. Kelonikoa even chose fabrics for his suits from fine Cantonese tailors, leather for his boots and evening pumps. He listened, awed, to her now-perfect English, her passing French, a growing knowledge of music and books. She had ascended to a higher caste, propelled by royal genes, while he remained a tradesman, keeper of a saloon.

Royalty dined at their house, diplomats, and merchant princes. Men of every race were drawn to her, to a haunting sadness which spoke straight to the heart and heightened her beauty, making her maddeningly desirable. Mathys was courteous but alert as guests doted upon his wife. He studied the glistening eyeteeth of a Peruvian whose cuffs smelled of vetiver, and a Spaniard with beaked nose and hooded cape, reminiscent of a falcon dreaming of prey while at rest on the wrist of a nobleman.

Is it her beauty, Mathys wondered, *or her elusiveness?*

Sometimes, to test her humor, he brought home characters, adventurers, so dinners had a circus atmosphere: dwarf twins of a Canton tea lord who only spoke in unison, a Marquesa with somersaulting chinchillas on a leash, a German beer baron in tattersall vests, diamonds winking in his teeth. One night, a Mexican coin dealer with a sliding toupee asked if Polynesians really ate dog. Insulted, aghast, Kelonikoa merely smiled. The next time the man came to dinner, she served roasted chihuahuas. When she identified what he had eaten, he rushed outside, squatted and vomitted on the lawn while a peacock ran off with his toupee. She and Mathys sat up past midnight, rocking with laughter.

But there were nights without laughter. When he boasted to guests of the enormous success of his saloon, Kelonikoa fell silent. A large percentage of native Hawaiians were being killed by alcohol. Kamehameha III had died of it, and possibly the reigning king, Kamehameha V, would, too. Polynesians had no tolerance for liquor, became easily addicted, and some of Mathys's steadiest customers were natives. She never said a word, watched silently as Mathys hired men to manage his livery stables and caulking business, bankers to oversee his sugar interests, while he held court at the Bay Horse Saloon. The more he retreated into that world, the more she broadened hers.

By 1870, Calvinists had been nudged over by Catholics, Mormons and the more sophisticated Episcopalians. Still, the missionaries had left their mark. Hawaiian children were forbidden their Mother Tongue. In school and church they were taught about Jesus, a *haole* child, while Hawaiian gods and ancestors were forgotten. Some natives had abandoned old religion, dress and customs completely. In her heart, Kelonikoa understood the *Great Mahele*, or land division, of 1848, officially separating Hawaiians from their land, had been the true death knell of the people. Perhaps that was the moment the islands had become an American colony. She saw the cultural cleavage in her two oldest sons, great strapping young men, almost ready for college.

Golden-skinned, handsome, the oldest, Daniel Punahele, behaved like a real *haole*, swaggering round in riding boots, six-gun on his hip. Highly intelligent, he showed signs of leadership, but also of becoming a menacing bully. George Iwa, second son, lived like a *kanaka* in bare feet, eating *poi* with his fingers, talking mostly Pidgin. Sometimes his breath smelled sour, like addicts in Chinatown alleys. Their mixed blood confused them; sometimes they went off arm-in-arm, joking in Pidgin, sometimes they hated each other, both lost in the cracks between dying Hawaiians and the worst of oppressive *haole*.

America's Civil War had also disrupted sugar plantations of the South, allowing Hawaiian sugar to enter America in large quantities. There was controversy about whether the United States should give Hawaiian sugar duty-free access in return for a fifty-year lease of Pearl Harbor. Too many nations—France, Russia, Great Britain—had in the past tried to monopolize Hawai'i's ports. Now, Pearl Harbor, largest protected natural anchorage in the Pacific, was viewed by the United States as of strategic military value.

This was the dinner topic one night when Mathys entertained officers of a Russian ship. The captain was blond and broad like Mathys, with similar features, but infinitely more polished, and multilingual. When Kelonikoa entered the room in emeralds and a gown of pale chablis, twenty-odd guests, including the Russian, turned to her in silence. She was now a full-blown woman in her forties, tall, immensely beautiful. And she was kind, attentive to the women, *haole* and high-caste Hawaiians, encouraging them in their thoughts on sugar, Pearl Harbor, annexation. To her, the Russian guests seemed zoological curiosities, cold, overly formal. But as the night wore on, she fell under a kind of spell.

The Russian captain on her right spoke softly, as though not to alarm her, not disturb her beauty, reflecting on his life, his mixed Russian-Mongolian heritage. As a young man, he had run away from St. Petersburg University, choosing a life at sea. Voyaging round the world, he had lassoed man-size komodo lizards in the islands south of Siam, outrun a tiger in Ceylon, hunted wildebeest from the backs of African elephants. Thinking his ship was doomed in a storm off Iceland, he had turned religious, memorizing great chunks of the Buddhist Scriptures. He survived, learned other languages, other customs. Then, stuck in ice for twelve months in the Arctic, he had dreamed of geography closer to home, racing woolly Bactrians across the Gobi, or a simple pleasure like eating a peach in St. Peter's Square.

His name was Rostov Anadyr, a virile man of fifty, Mathys's age, but hearing him through conversation swirling about the dinner table, Mathys felt much older, and very dull. When pheasants were carried in bathed in brandy, served in a wreath of blue flames, Anadyr spoke of food and wines of other latitudes, the fabulous dining customs of ancient Rome and Greece. His diction, his manners were impeccable, making Mathys feel like a stevedore, as Anadyr discussed with a viscount the polar knowledge of Inuits, the compositions of Bach compared to the new sounds of Brahms.

It was the Czar's birthday and at midnight, from Punchbowl Crater in the hills, the Honolulu Rifles and Cavalry fired a salute to Alexander of Russia. As guests stood and toasted, Anadyr turned to Kelonikoa, bowed and took her hand.

"Your beauty leaves me an invalid."

Later they stood on the *lānai* watching fireworks honoring the Czar.

The air was cool and people moved indoors so that Kelonikoa and the Russian were left alone in moonlight. Only once did their eyes meet when, for a moment he could not look away from her perfect face, the fine shape of her head, as if God had given her a extra turn on the lathe. And, in that met glance, an intimation of the future, that they would be fixed forever in each other's minds, that the life they imagined for a moment, might actually exist, elsewhere, on another plane.

Finally, he dropped his eyes. "Forgive me. I've never felt so . . . desperate."

He came to dinner once again before his ship left Hawai'i. An entertaining group—droll Englishmen and their spirited wives, the French consul, an Australian heiress with half a million acres and a million head of sheep. Kelonikoa was subdued, Anadyr looked tragic. Finding themselves alone again on the *lānai*, she pointed out blue fluttering eyes on fan-tailed peacocks strutting the grounds, and beyond them, pale tombstones of her children. Dew turned the lawn an orient of pearls, and the captain made a sobbing noise.

"I would lay down my life for those children." They stood silent, and after a while he gently took her hand.

"Please accept this, for we shan't meet again."

It was a tiny book with gold covers, maybe three inches high. Each page was a delicate almost-transparent length of jade thin as eyelids, attached to which was a silk parchment leaf embossed with miniature gold characters. The diary of an Empress from the Ming Dynasty, almost five hundred years old. Here and there were golden ghosts of the Empress's fingerprints. Kelonikoa stared, afraid to imagine the value of the thing.

"This is volume one," Rostov whispered. "There is a companion volume, which I shall carry with me, always."

On the back of the gold cover, a tiny inscription. "Vol. I. For Kelonikoa. From Rostov Anadyr. 1873."

"What do you suppose she wrote?" she asked, turning the delicate jade pages.

"Perhaps she mourned a forbidden love, and so we hold her secrets. Perhaps she wrote that life is really lived through dreams and intuitions, not fate and circumstance."

Behind them in the drawing room, voices rose angrily.

"Annexation, yes. Statehood for Hawai'i? Never!"

". . . but Hawaiians are clever. They should be able to vote as well as the next man . . ."

"Vote? For the president of the United States? *Mon Dieu!* We all know how ignorant these niggers are."

Chairs were knocked over, a woman screamed. Mathys wrapped a linen napkin round his bleeding fist. Rostov entered the room, helped the Frenchman to his feet, and knocked him down again. Late that night Kelonikoa stood waving as he departed, her figure defined by light from the open door. He closed his eyes, and carried that image all the way back to St. Petersburg.

For weeks Mathys was inconsolable, having seen in the Russian a remarkable resemblance to himself, yet a vastly superior version. After lunch, when drawn bamboo blinds gave a filtered look to things, he lay in his study brooding on his shortcomings. Gifted only with Dutch prudence, an eye for profit, he knew he would never be more than he was. In the company of real entrepreneurs, visionary men who saw Hawai'i's future, men revolutionizing sugar trade, consolidating shipping lines, designing railroads, Mathys was still only a merchant, a petitioner at the gate. He thought of the great Dutch patroons of his youth, Van Rensselaers, Van Burens, the Vanderbilts, and he thought of his family, stoop-work tillers of the earth.

He suspected his shortcomings were genetic; a special chemical was missing from his blood, his children would end up no better than he, merchants, saloon-keepers. The damage of these interior dialogues, bitter self-accusations, was soon visible in the haggardness of his face. Watching his stately wife arrange wood roses in a *koa calabash*, he thought of the Russian captain's ease and worldliness. *Whereas, I have never been to university, or Canton, or Africa. I speak only English and Pidgin Hawaiian. My world is narrow and ignorant.*

In Kelonikoa's arms, he wept. "How poor a part I've played in your life. How little I've given you!"

She spoke softly, as if to a child. "You have given me constancy, devotion. We have buried our children, survived, and borne others. All else is novelty."

If, on solitary evenings, she brooded over a tiny jade book with faint Empress fingerprints, and if she thought of its companion volume lying in another's hand, and the warmth of that hand, it was only in the way one remembers a met glance, someone glimpsed who ghosts through our lives forever.

'Ai Pōhaku

The Stone Eaters

IN 1872 THE DEATH OF KING KAMEHAMEHA V ended the direct bloodline descent of kings from the Great Kamehameha I, who had united the Hawaiian Islands in 1810. William Lunalilo, first king voted in by the Hawaiian legislature, reigned only two years, racked by drink and tuberculosis. In 1874 David Kalākaua was elected to the throne, a man of enormous ego, a lover of his people, dedicated to reviving Hawai'i's sacred customs and traditions.

Firing white cabinet members and ministers who challenged him, he filled the House of Representatives with native Hawaiians. Wanting to reinstate "royalty" into the kingdom, Kalakaua built Iolani Palace, spending hundreds of thousands of dollars, installing electricity before Buckingham Palace in London, and running water before the U.S. White House in Washington. In 1883 he staged a coronation, wearing the feather cloak of Kamehameha I, and a sacred whale-tooth *lei*, "officially" crowning himself, then crowning his wife Queen Kapiolani. Ceremonies went on for weeks, full-dress balls, harbor regattas, a *lū'au* for five thousand.

His enemies denounced the "Merry Monarch's" profligate drinking and spending, and his blatant distrust of Americans. Kalakaua ignored them, a hero to his people. Rekindling national pride in Hawaiians, he resurrected family lines of old ruling chiefs, collected and preserved bones and feather cloaks of ancient warriors. Genealogies from all the islands were collected into eight books, and over 130 old Hawaiian songs and chants were gathered and published, along with folklore and knowledge of the sea.

He passed legislation allowing Hawaiian *kāhuna* to publicly practice chanting and herbal healing, and had the Hawaiian creation chant, the KUMULIPO, recorded in writing for the first time. He even revived the Hale Nauā, a secret society for Hawaiian men, a ". . . Temple of Ancient Sciences of Hawai'i in combination with the promotion and advancement of Art, Literature, and Philanthropy."

A gifted musician and writer, Kalākaua built a music hall and theater where Shakespeare, Molière, and Italian operas were performed. He encouraged his people to learn to read, and soon the downtown Library and Reading Room Association boasted over five thousand books and fifty leading newspapers and periodicals. By 1886, among forty-eight attorneys licensed to practice law, twenty-one were Hawaiians; juries were now composed of at least fifty percent Hawaiians.

Feeling the islands had regressed fifty years, Honolulu's white elite were horrified. Employing spies in Kalākaua's cabinet, they uncovered his gross abuse of royal privilege—illegal leasing of lands, illegal dispersal of monies meant for public roads and waterways, bribery, fraud, purchasing of votes and selling of favors inside the palace. Ignoring the fact that Kalākaua was the first king in the world to visit the United States, addressing the U.S. House of Representatives in 1874, and that he increased Hawai'i's diplomatic and counselor posts to almost one hundred throughout the world, *haole* publicized only his extravagance—his love of marathon parties and balls, of gin and hula dancing, and his leniency toward opium use.

In 1860 licenses to sell opium had been auctioned by the government; in the mid-1870s, it was made illegal altogether. But great quantities were regularly smuggled into Hawai'i; illegal possession and sales were common. In 1886, Kalākaua approved an act allowing opium traffic under license again. Attempting to purchase a license, a merchant, fronting for Mathys Coenradtsen, courted the king with $30,000. The king accepted the money, then hesitated, and so another $30,000 "gift" was sent from Mathys.

Kalākaua duped him by selling the license to another merchant for $70,000. Mathys and his friend swore out affidavits, releasing their documents to newspapers, but the king had already spent their money on "royal debts." It was the beginning of the end of Kalakaua's credibility. Even loyal Hawaiians had wearied of his morbid excesses, his pleasure trips round the world while his subjects went hungry. Riots broke out in Honolulu.

In June 1887, the Honolulu Rifles, two hundred armed soldiers in the service of the king, switched allegiance, joining the Hawaiian League, a group of powerful white merchants conspiring to strip the king of his powers. Confronting Kalākaua in the barricaded palace, they told him he had lost the faith of his people, now chanting insults outside the palace gates.

Without his soldiers, Kalākaua was lost; the *haole* forced his hand. He retained his throne by abolishing the power structure of purely Hawaiian control, by throwing out bribers and forgers. Opium licensing was repealed (which further fed the smuggling trade). A new constitution was framed. Powerless, the king agreed to "Reign, not Rule." And what came to be known as the "Bayonet Constitution" was forced on Kalakaua, a bloodless revolution that changed the king forever from ruler to a figurehead, effectively disenfranchising the Hawaiian population. Most natives couldn't meet the new, stiff qualifications needed to vote, much less run for office.

By the time Kalakaua died in 1891, many would have forgotten he was truly Hawai'i's Renaissance Man. For all his political shortcomings, he was cultivated, gracious, and had commanded the respect of world leaders when he traveled abroad. Most importantly, he saw his islands and people as fragile, in danger of total extinction. For a time, he had rekindled in them a sense of pride in history, their kingdom, their king.

By now, sugar was the real king in Hawai'i. A reciprocity treaty—which would later give the United States control of Pearl Harbor—allowed duty-free access of Hawaiian sugar into the mainland. New steamships and railroads moved sugar swiftly from isolated plantations to the docks. But large amounts of capital were needed to finance the plantations. Sugar stock trading boomed, and Mathys invested heavily.

Tourism grew alongside commerce, and he added to his carriage business an omnibus line. He and friends formed a small consortium and built a hotel in Waikīkī, chief destination for tourists arriving on steamships. Mathys's wealth grew considerably. While he sat in his clubs in hand-tailored suits, toasting his prosperity with champagne, enterprising locals made their own brews from fermented 'awa root, coconut, pineapple, anything that intoxicated. Alcohol and disease, disease and alcohol—the mortality rate of Hawaiians steadily escalated.

Most devastating disease of all was leprosy, *ma'i Pākē*, which afflicted natives especially. Rumored to have been brought by immigrant laborers from Canton in the 1850s, leprosy had, in fact, been spreading through the islands as early as Captain Cook, transmitted by filthy seamen immune to the bacteria, spreading it along with syphilis.

Trained by Dr. Goddard, Kelonikoa and vigilante women of the Bustle Club roamed tenement sections of Honolulu and Chinatown, instructing locals to boil water before drinking, to bathe frequently, since leprosy seemed to flourish in poverty and filth. They taught them to look for symptoms in the glassiness of the eye, in itchy patches of skin surrounded by white flesh, in running sores that didn't heal.

By now a leper settlement, Kalaupapa, was established on a remote peninsula of a neighboring island, Moloka'i. It was called Place of the Living Dead, for there was no cure for the disease. Kelonikoa held screaming children, as afflicted parents were torn from their arms, dragged onto ships, never seen again. She comforted mothers whose children were taken, skin on their faces bloated with the "lion look." As the ship neared Kalaupapa, lepers were pushed into the sea with long paddles. Some weren't swimmers, clinging together as they drowned. Others swam for the open sea, preferring *pau manō*.

Her children were now grown and married, except for the two youngest girls, and every night, Kelonikoa made Eliza Mapuana, twenty-one, and the youngest, Emma Puanani, seventeen, stand before her naked. Slowly, with lapidary attention, she examined them, every inch, for sores, white spots, signs of itchiness. She examined herself, and while Mathys slept, she examined him. And one day she found a ring-shaped patch on Emma's arm. Assuring her it was an allergy, she bathed the arm, covered it with tiny suctioned feet of two freshly killed geckos soaked in *Kuawe*, a poisonous plant, wrapped the arm and gecko feet in *hapu'u* fern, and put the girl to bed.

That night Kelonikoa knelt by the sea, chanting, calling on gods of her birth sands. Emma was her favorite, a precocious child with the run-away wildness, staunch perverseness and beauty of the women of Kelonikoa's tribe, a last gift, born to her when she was forty-seven. At four, Emma had begun to sleepwalk; at seven she was forecasting hurricanes, volcanic eruptions, with eerie accuracy, so energetic, so full of curiosity and passion, Kelonikoa suspected the child was meant for something extraordinary.

She chanted all night until the sea answered, and she knew what she must do. With a sharpened abalone shell, Kelonikoa severed one of her small fingers, grinding away at the bone. Fainting, coming to, she crawled into the ocean, hand wrapped in seaweed to stem the bleeding.

Dragging herself out to the reef, she flung the finger-offering beyond the coral wall, down, down into the ocean's throat.

She would sacrifice one finger, one toe, a part of her body, for each sore she found on Emma. She would do this until the gods decided to spare her child, or until there was nothing left of Kelonikoa. If she was still alive when they banished Emma to Kalaupapa, she would accompany her as *kōkua*, serving her child until she died. The gods were kind. In two weeks, she found no other sore on Emma. Dr. Goddard diagnosed the patch as ringworm.

When Mathys finally noticed his wife's bandaged hand, she told him a gardening tool had slipped. He scolded her, rode off to Kapiolani Park to gamble on *kinipōpō*. She consumed copious amounts of shark-fin soup, so the hand would regain its strength, soaked the awful wound with juice of *hau* leaves for healing, and drank *pua kala* for killing pain.

Nursing the hand, Kelonikoa thought how prepared she had been to die, to hack herself to pieces for her child. *Was it just for Emma? Perhaps death is better than wearing away, day by day, my marriage backing up in my throat.* Remembering how they had found each other in the jungle, how she had nursed Mathys back to life, taught him fishing, hunting, how to gauge the force of a wild boar's leap for deeper penetration of an arrow. How to play his passion, keep it at bay, until she rose up to him.

Now, in the sixty-fifth year of her life, she was a woman trying to remember when her husband had last touched her, brushed her hair, or just been a companion. Dreamily, Kelonikoa crossed the room, opened a drawer, stroked the small gold-and-jade diary of an Empress. Twenty years. *And I am standing in St. Peter's Square, and he strides toward me, gray at the temples. Offering a peach. Or. We're on a porch on the Black Sea in the warm air of the Crimea, a sanatorium with tall mullioned windows. He is tubercular, and has come there to die. After all these years I find him, the companion volume resting in his open palm.*

She had come to depend on such fantasy, journeys that transported without exhausting, that loosened the mesh without fraying. It gave her a breathless vigilance, never sure what fiction would rise within her. And afterward, when they finished the peach and walked hand-in-hand across St. Peter's Square, afterward, there was always a sweet languor. For a while she didn't need anything more.

In the next few months, she watched the Bustle Club founder as native and *haole* women rose against each other over the question of Hawai'i's annexation by the United States. In her home, the same debate took place, Mathys arguing for annexation against his wife and daughters.

In 1887, the sugar Reciprocity Treaty was renewed, conceding full use of Pearl Harbor to the United States Navy. Military ships began to glut Honolulu's harbor.

In 1888, Emma's older sister, Eliza, eloped with a Frenchman and sailed for Cherbourg. Six months later, Emma soothed her mother's broken heart by marrying in the Catholic church, a big, proper wedding. Her husband was Adam Kimo Pauhana, a full-blooded Hawaiian, Punahou and Yale graduate. A lawyer and Royalist, he was virulently against annexation of Hawai'i. Within a year a daughter was born, Vera Lili'uokalani, named after the sister of the ailing King Kalākaua.

Sometimes when her children and grandchildren were gathered round, Kelonikoa found it a miracle that so many had survived, that she and Mathys had created this small dynasty. At thirty-three, Daniel Punahele, the eldest, was a father of four, married to a *haole* missionary descendant. A swaggering giant, always bursting through doors wearing his pistols, he ran his father's businesses while Mathys held court at the Bay Horse Saloon. Sophie Leihulu, thirty-two, and Olivia Malama, twenty-eight, the two middle girls, led quiet lives married to Hawaiian-Japanese brothers, partners in a prosperous grocery store. Between them, their five children looked identical, little golden, almond-eyed plums, eating raw fish with chopsticks.

Something broke in her each time Kelonikoa saw her second son, George Iwa, thirty. Though tall and broad-boned like Daniel, he was emaciated, addicted to the pipe. Of all the children, he was the one who loved poetry, Chopin and Telemann, the son closest to Kelonikoa. The others never shunned him, knowing part of their father's wealth had been based on opium smuggling, and in those days, every family kept a bowl of opium for the more reclusive and infirm.

Even Mathys tolerated George. "There's one in every family . . . religious fanatic . . . misfit. Thank God it wasn't the eldest boy!"

James Kahiki, twenty-six, the last son, a graduate of Harvard and still a bachelor, ran with rich *haole* plantation daughters, and smoked cigars with sugar tycoons at the Pacific Club, the Hawaiian Racing and Polo Club. Denying his native blood, he was constantly at odds with Emma who spent her days politicking and speech-making, baby Lil bouncing on her hip. Kelonikoa gazed upon them, wondering what would become of them? Of their islands? What would their future be?

In 1891, traveling in San Francisco, King Kalākaua died mysteriously. Hawaiians believed he was poisoned. His sister, Lili'uokalani, ascended the throne, and even as she mourned her brother, *haole* sugar tycoons actively campaigned for Hawai'i's annexation to better benefit from new laws offering bounties on American sugar. Native Hawaiian groups violently against annexation mushroomed everywhere. Pro-annexation women seceded from the Bustle Club and it became a force for Royalist Hawaiian women, sister-club to Native Sons of Hawai'i, who advocated return of all governing powers to the monarch.

A lover of books and music like her brother—composer of "Aloha Oe," one of the most beautiful of Hawaiian-language songs—the queen was also a tough, headstrong woman. Ascending the throne, she vowed to make her sovereign power unshakable and to abolish all talk of annexation. *Haole* began talking of retiring her, of assassination. Natives talked of gutting, or strangling, *haole* in their sleep. People armed themselves with loaded guns, and knives, and catgut for strangulation.

Compounding the tension in Honolulu were the diverse ethnic groups imported for "slave work" on plantations. Chinese, Japanese, Portuguese. Each week groups of them went on strike for decent wages, humane living conditions, the constant threat of rebellion and revolution frightening away international trade, throwing the islands into chaos.

In the Hawai'i legislative session of 1892 only nine members were in favor of annexation and over thirty against it. Emboldened, Queen Lili'uokalani tried to introduce a new constitution whereby only true Hawaiians could vote. They would not have to be rich to run for office or cast a ballot. They would elect their own representatives. The queen would no longer need the sanction of the cabinet, and ministers would serve at her discretion.

This is what the white elite had been waiting for, justification for a military coup. In January 1893, before Lili'uokalani could legalize her constitution, the same men who had forced the Bayonet Constitution on King Kalākaua overthrew the queen with four boatloads of armed U.S. Marines and a warship, the U.S.S. *Boston*, with its guns trained on 'Iolani Palace. Parading light cannons through the streets, the military seized government buildings, while *haole* demanded the queen's abdication, and declared martial law.

On January 17, Lili'uokalani surrendered under protest. The military troops had been sent in by the ambassador from the United States without knowledge, or sanction, of the U.S. government. By the time word of the coup reached the White House, the United States was changing presidents, and while the world looked the other way, Hawai'i was stolen from its people.

A great wailing went up throughout the islands, lasting for weeks, a cry of impenetrable grief as natives mourned. Old people watered their gardens, prayed to their 'aumākua, lay down and died of heartbreak. Inside the palace, a *haole* guard stole the Palace Crown, smashed it, and gambled the diamonds away.

With the queen deposed, in July 1894, Hawai'i became a republic under a provisional white government. Fearing uprisings, the government forbade locals to assemble in groups of more than three. Furthermore, the *haole* junta threatened that natives failing to take the oath of allegiance to the new government would be forced to kneel and eat stones.

One day, over a hundred members of the Bustle Club, led by Kelonikoa and three elderwomen, marched silently down the streets toward Iolani Palace. Quickly chaining themselves to the palace fence, they began chanting in Hawaiian a song composed by a woman loyal to the queen, Ellen Keho'ohiwaokalani Prendergast, a song that would be sung twenty-five years, fifty years, and a hundred years hence at all Hawaiian political gatherings, "*Mele Aloha 'Aina*, Song of the Land We Love":

> *We, the loyal sons and daughters of Hawai'i*
> *Will exist by eating stones,*
> *The mystic wondrous food of our beloved land.*
> *This we will do rather than swear allegiance*
> *To the traitors who have ravished our land.*
> *Ae, we are the Stone Eaters,*
> *Loyal forever to our Land.*
> *We stand together: People of O'ahu,*
> *Of Maui, of Kaua'i, of Hawai'i, of Moloka'i.*
> *We will not sell our birthright,*
> *Steadfast we stand in support of our Queen.*
> *All honor to those loyal to our Beloved Hawai'i.*

As the women sang out, crowds of locals gathered, taking up the song. It spread from street to street, town to town. It spread across the sea, until all the people of all the islands were chanting their allegiance with "*Mele Aloha 'Aina.*" Wealthy natives stood arm-in-arm with those in rags, and sang without ceasing, hour after hour. They sang for themselves, and for the queen, for their 'aumākua, and for their children's memories. They sang until government troops burst through, swinging rifle butts, fixed bayonets, forcing the faces of old men, women, children to the ground, crushing their mouths against glass and rock and soil. As troops rushed forward to the fence, the women rattled their chains, singing louder, turning their heads against the blows. Inside the palace, Lili'uokalani wept.

Hours later, when skeleton keys had unlocked the chains, the women sank to their knees still singing, ". . . *Ae, we are the Stone Eaters / Loyal forever to our Land . . .*" until their faces were pushed to the soil, until their mouths were full. Exhausted, bruised and bleeding, they were marched in rows to jail, troops taunting them in Pidgin.

"Eh, *wahine*! Your queen *pau*! Hawaiians *pau*! You good for nuttin'!"

In 1892, President Benjamin Harrison had assured white annexationists in Hawai'i that they had his support. His successor, Grover Cleveland, now adamantly condemned the annexationists, calling Queen Lili'uokalani's overthrow ". . . illegal, immoral . . . an act of war," and promising return of her monarchy. Congress supported him. The House of Representatives endorsed the principle of non-interference and declared the annexation of the islands unconstitutional and illegal. Hawai'i's provisional government, the "Missionary Monarchy," refused to recognize the power of President Cleveland to settle island affairs. They appeased Hawaiians only by releasing the women of the Bustle Club from jail.

On the day of their release, Mathys and Adam Kimo were waiting to take Kelonikoa and Emma home. Mortified by catcalling *haole* crowds, Mathys helped Kelonikoa into their carriage, fighting for control.

"Woman. You have shamed me for all time."

She stared at him. "You have no idea."

President Cleveland did not enforce his decisions on the coup. Until the return of a Republican administration under McKinley, the new Republic of Hawai'i, led by a few hundred rich *haole*, remained a provisional government for five years.

Now, Royalists went underground, arming themselves for counter-revolution. Contraband guns were shipped from San Francisco and China, transferred ashore at night. Crates of ammunition were buried in people's yards. Kelonikoa sold all of her jewelry, and the last but two of her black pearls, and with the connections of her frail Royalist son, George *Iwa*, she and members of the Bustle Club financed the purchase of more contraband guns, ammunition and explosives. Caches were discovered, people arrested, but Royalists continued stockpiling arms.

While Emma's husband, Adam Kimo Pauhana, counseled the deposed Queen Lili'uokalani, Mathys's house began to resemble an ammunition depot. At night he snored peacefully in his four-poster bed, under which were stored muskets, rifles, cartridge belts, hundreds of rounds of ammunition. Bombs were hidden in cupboards, and inside *koa calabashes*. Muskets stood upright in the skirts of silk *holokū*. He and his eldest, Daniel Punahele, and their friends, puffed cigars over brandy, beaming at the success of the new government, while Royalists hatched plots in his bathroom, used his cologne, flushed maps down his toilet.

Well-bred young women were seen in the streets, flirting with American sailors, strolling the beach beside them, learning all they could about military surveillance. A government spy was found floating in the Ala Wai Canal. Frustrated with "genteel errands" members of the Bustle Club complained, wanting to learn how to load and shoot muskets and rifles, how to make saltpeter for gunpowder, and bullets from pewterware in case the Royalists ran out. They bought a printing press, circulating underground pamphlets, urging Hawaiian women to take up arms for the queen. Women lined up at the door. Kelonikoa found a leathery old seaman, a mercenary from the Opium Wars of the 1840s who had even plundered the South China Sea with pirates.

"Name your price," she said. "Turn us into soldiers."

They clashed by candlelight, Victorian skirts done up between their legs like giant diapers. In moonlight, and starlight, they learned to load and lock, to fix bayonets, to leap and thrust at signals from the seaman. Exposing golden arms and golden necks, they bent and arched like dancers, hearts pounding through starched linen, hair spilling down like tar. After a few weeks they began to get the hang of it, swung life-size dummies from ropes, shredded them with bayonets. They aimed their rifles, squinted and shot spinning cans into fragments. The atmosphere turned febrile, wives and sisters and daughters cocked, ready to fire, willing to die.

One night, through the tangle of limbs jousting round him—womansweat and womangrunt, angry, and noble, and womanready—the seaman looked beyond them through a window at the stars, his cheeks suddenly wet with tears. Women were still, holding their weapons before them.

"Don't you see?" he whispered. "It's bloody hopeless! You've already lost your lands."

They carried on. Night after night, with dignified countenance, Kelonikoa and Emma rode their carriage through the streets carrying food to families who had lost their jobs refusing to take the oath of allegiance to the new government. Rude, bellicose Marines stopped their carriage, beating their horses and driver, examining their baskets of food. They stared straight ahead, then continued on their way, bundles of gunpowder and octagonal barrels of dismantled rifles under their skirts between their legs.

Encouraged by President Cleveland's withdrawal of the U.S. warship from the harbor, Lili'uokalani gave her consent and the date of the counterrevolution was set, January 7, 1895. But on the night of January 6, police arrived as Royalists were digging up a cache of arms near Ala Wai Canal. Shots were exchanged, and in the skirmish, several whites were killed. Government troops and police turned into madmen, invading homes all over Honolulu. Innocents were pulled from their beds and slaughtered. Finding Royalist pamphlets in his mistress's robes, a man pulled a gun yelling "Traitor!"

She pulled her own gun. "You're on the wrong side." And shot him dead.

Mathys woke to find soldiers ransacking his house, pulling weapons from under his bed. He and Kelonikoa were handcuffed, taken to jail. Their daughters and sons-in-law followed.

Mathys stared at his wife in utter shock. "You . . . are . . . a . . . madwoman!"

In the dark cell, she approached him. "That I once loved you is my shame. My utter shame."

They sat with their backs against damp walls, listening to a woman's screams. The dull thud of clubs on human bones. Suspects flung bloody into cells. The piercing, diminishing cry of someone thrown from a roof. At dawn, Daniel Punahele arrived, paid off officials, swearing his parents were duped by Royalist servants, that they had no knowledge of weapons in their home. Kelonikoa refused to leave. She and Emma clung together, backing farther into the cell, friends crowding round them protectively.

"Yes, we are Royalists, all!" Emma shouted. "Father, I denounce you."

Daniel dragged his father away. ". . . hysterical women, loyal to an hysterical queen."

When Kelonikoa and Emma were accused of treason, Mathys wept so hard his eye patch slipped. He pulled it off, wandered the streets mindless, until a servant brought him home.

On January 16, one of the largest ammunition caches was found in the queen's own gardens—bombs, pistols, swords. She was taken into custody, and imprisoned at 'Iolani Palace. Standing trial for treason before a military commission, Lili'uokalani endured the abject humiliation of having her personal diaries made public. They revealed the enormous, but healthy, ego of a woman who believed females made better monarchs than men. They revealed she had had secret lovers.

"What king has *not*?" she demanded.

The diaries also revealed a deeply sensitive, intelligent woman, one who had hoped to start a college for Hawaiian women, affording them the "same education as men." She had planned to open a bank for women, enabling them to handle their own financial affairs. She recognized the need for more female lawyers and physicians, the need for women's rights over their bodies, their destinies. And lastly, though she had a fondness for men, she felt women "basically didn't need them."

She was sentenced to five years of house arrest in 'Iolani Palace. Of the two hundred prisoners placed on trial, five chief leaders of the Royalist forces, including Emma's husband, were sentenced to death. Kelonikoa, Emma, Dr. Goddard and seven women of the Bustle Club were sentenced to twenty years in prison. It was blackmail. *Haole* were using her rebel supporters to force the queen from her throne.

And so, to save the lives of those loyal to her, Lili'uokalani officially relinquished all claims to the throne forever. Swearing allegiance to the new Republic, she recognized the end of her monarchy, promising not to aid attempts to restore it. Death sentences were commuted. All prisoners would be pardoned within a year. The Royalists survived; the monarchy was dead.

By now Kelonikoa was seventy-four years old, still lovely, commanding in presence, but in physical decline. Within weeks she was moved from prison, confined in her bed to house arrest. Emma would remain in prison for almost a year, until her husband and all women were released. In that year, Kelonikoa was silent, not a word, communicating only through notes to her servants.

Sometimes Mathys came and stood beside her in the dark, thinking how they had lost the center of everything, now even the edges were gone. He was almost eighty, the age when a man looks forward by looking back. He had thought providing for his wife was the greatest expression of devotion. Somehow it hadn't sufficed. *How could I have loved her more? I never touched another woman.* He didn't care that she had duped him, made him a public fool. His sorrow was this: There was something she had needed, something she had tried to call forth from within him, that he did not possess.

By the end of the year, all prisoners freed, 'Iolani Palace was converted into a government building. Lili'uokalani retired to her private residence, was made a citizen and finally freed. One day Kelonikoa arrived by carriage at Lili'uokalani's house on Washington Place. They sat whispering and weeping.

"I have heard you will go to Washington, Your Majesty, to plead the case of the monarchy . . ."

"That is so."

"Then I have come to say *Imua! Aloha nui loa!* For I shan't be here when you return."

The queen patted her wrinkled hand. "*Milimili* Kelonikoa, I am fourteen years your junior. But you are *pū'ali*. You will outlive me."

She shook her head. "The bones begin to moan. In sleep I dream of sleeping."

The next day Kelonikoa called Emma to her house, and placed in her hand the last two precious black pearls, telling her their story, softly, with humor. The monkey-man. And running. A whaler, one-eyed cannibal. And love. Then she placed in her hand another thing, the miniature jade-and-gold diary. And she tried to explain the Russian captain, never seen again.

"Did you love him?" Emma asked.

"Can one love in a moment? No. I loved . . . imagining. All the lives we might have lived. A tapestry, a never-ending thread." She touched the diary one last time. "The night he gave me this, I asked what he supposed the Empress had written, what these tiny figures meant. He said perhaps she wrote that life is really lived through dreams and intuitions, not fate and circumstance."

Emma frowned. "I'm not sure I understand."

"Take it, dear. One day you might want to hold it in your hand . . . follow the thread in the tapestry."

She would remember her mother's words, how she spoke in riddles. She would remember her eyes, brighter and clearer than they should have been, a fixedness in their dazzle.

That night Kelonikoa sat beside Mathys, watching his jaw hang slack in dreams. The years. The years. She leaned close, and in his old man smell, there was a smell of moldering soil, humid earth. *The jungle. Happy fugitives in rags. And then we came to this, not wealth, not gain, only compensation.* They had left the mountains and entered the world, and he became a predator. She had survived by playing dead.

She stood, dropped her clothes round her feet and stepped away. Covering her nakedness with a sarong, slowly she undid her hair, a shimmering, gray shawl. She drifted through rooms, decades, children born, and buried. She fondled things, left her prints on photographs. And in the night she ran, keeping to the shadows, huffing and pausing, hearing her wheezing rice-paper lungs, then running on, down boulevards and streets, down unpaved roads until she reached the cove of healing dolphins.

She swam lazily for there was time, and there were distances to go. Deep, deep in the Pacific, far below the Equator, past the mysterious Marquesas, the Tuamotus. Waves lapped her gently, hair floating round her a phosphorescent net. She swam slowly, thoughtfully, befitting the pace of an old woman. She swam through Circadian troughs of night and into a purple hour, and looking back she saw, like points of pure yearning, the volcanic tips of Hawai'i. Then she turned, stroking for her birth sands.

Emma sat up from a dream, leapt from her bed and ran. She ran down boulevards and roads, and she ran toward the ocean screaming.

In April 1898, the start of the Spanish-American War in the Philippines sealed the fate of Hawai'i, recognizing it as a crucial Naval base. On July 7, 1898, President McKinley signed into law the resolution to annex the Hawaiian Islands. At the Ceremony of Annexation on August 12, armed troops marched in formation, U.S. officials stood on grandstands, warships' cannons boomed. The Royal Hawaiian Band began playing, for the last time, "Hawai'i Pono'i," the official Hawaiian anthem. The song was never finished. As the Hawaiian flag slowly descended, members of the band lowered their horns, dropped their heads and sobbed.

And the wailing began. And the winds, incredible winds. From island to island, Hawaiians made their "appointment with death," and threw themselves from cliffs. Others walked into the ocean. And Pele, Goddess of Fires and Volcanos, shrieked. And mountains opened, burping blood. Giant squid large as ships rose from the sea and stalked the beaches, screaming like old theologians. And whole forests lay down on their side. And in that most beautiful archipelago, great contexts were broken forever.

Pono

Goodness, Morality

BONES OF HER BONES. All he had left of her. He slept with them beside him in a sheet.

Daniel Punahele called his sister. "He's gone mad. Dug up those . . . *things*, and taken them to bed with him!"

Emma came to the house and stared at the pile of tiny, yellow trinkets. "Father, I understand."

Assisting him, in the mornings she covered the bones of her brothers and sister; leaving them exposed to sunlight was believed disrespectful by Hawaiians. At night she reverently lay the rattling shroud beside him. Holding it, he crooned, lacking the consolation of his wife's corpse.

Mathys was over eighty now, liver-spotted, wild Mephistophelian eyebrows, his one eye cataracted. Some days he forgot his eye patch, and servants came upon him groping through halls with that awful, weeping socket. Daniel Punahele avoided him, as if his father had moved outside the human species.

One night he gripped Emma's hand, full of urgent chronicles. "I thought one could live without conscience. That's what killed her. What I lacked."

He gave up habits, those concrete forms of rhythm that keep one alive. He lost his sense of smell, and seemed to give up eating. Mooning over grandchildren, he examined their little veins, Kelonikoa's blood pulsing within. One night, Emma sat up in her sleep, knowing he was dead. They found him lying in the shallows of Kelonikoa's cove, an arm outstretched, as if trying to overtake her in the depths. A canoe rocked above him with his children's wrapped-up bones. He had told a servant he was sailing to Tahiti. Weighed down by gold coins in his pockets, he must have slipped and drowned while struggling into the canoe. Coins had floated out around him, one of them settling on his face, his empty socket.

With George Iwa now a hopeless addict, Daniel Punahele and James Kahiki ran the family businesses, enlarging the Bay Horse Saloon, purchasing another bar. Troopships carrying American soldiers now filled the streets to bursting, and Daniel foresaw a time when America's military presence would be permanent. They doubled the size of their livery stables, accommodating seventy-five horses.

Emma's husband, Adam Kimo, started his legal practice over from scratch, most of his clients poor Hawaiians and Orientals. Loving their youngest sister inordinately, with a sense of family allegiance the brothers invited Adam to take part in their investments. Politely, he declined, for there was about the two men an unhealthiness, having inherited from their father a certain lack of conscience, a moral depth.

A shrewd businessman, Daniel Punahele had nonetheless acquired a taste for Chinese half-castes, keeping mistresses in different parts of town. James Kahiki, an inveterate gambler, was so far in debt he constantly cashed in their sugar profits, and took large loans from banks. As more troopships piled into Honolulu's harbors, the brothers acquired a seaman's hotel on Fort Street, even a pharmacy where sailors purchased medicinals for venereal disease.

In those waning years of the nineteenth century, Chinatown, bordering on the warehouses and businesses of Hotel and Fort Street, was still a seething mass of humanity. Over eight thousand Asian immigrants and Hawaiians were packed into less than forty acres near Honolulu's waterfront, charged outrageous rents by white landowners. In 1899, a corpse was found with the telltale signs of bubonic plague. Board of Health inspectors overran the area, uncovering a nightmare of filthy restaurants, brothels, tenements, and privies that were simple holes in floors under which cesspools ran. Children, fouled with lice and fleas, played near gutters of raw sewage. Rats lined the alleys, lolling about like pets.

A dozen more cases of the plague threw officials into a panic. Trying to head off an epidemic, they burned down parts of Chinatown, leaving thousands of people dazed in quarantine camps—barbed-wire prisons where doctors monitored them for further outbreaks. For the next year, fires raged as "plague spots" were systematically torched. Islanders, rich and poor, lived with the stench of burning corpses and wooden hovels. Even as Emma labored in the camps, tending the homeless, infected rats were found in the Coenradsten livery stables next to the seaman's hotel. The brothers watched helplessly as their properties were razed to the ground.

In December a "purging fire" went wild, leveling most of Chinatown and nearby establishments, including the Coenradtsens' remaining businesses. Quarantine camps swelled to over seven thousand. Bubonic plague had even spread to white neighborhoods, but a true epidemic was aborted by the fire. Now, the city was left with a huge homeless population.

Returning to their modest house in working-class Kalihi, exhausted from hours in the camps, Emma sometimes fell asleep at dinner. At such times, her husband studied her—a beautiful girl, reduced to a gray-faced woman. A year in prison, her queen deposed, her people disappearing. *Emma. What have they done to us?* He gazed at their child, their only hope; she seemed prescient and wise, black eyes sad, her gaze piercing, as if she could read her father's mind.

Vera Lili was bright, head of her class at Punahou. "Teacher says we're lucky to be annexed by America, if France or Russia owned us, Hawaiians would be slaves."

Adam listened, disgusted.

"Teacher says I'm smart. But I shouldn't think of university . . . only of finding a husband and raising a family."

"Of course," he said. "They think you have no brains for higher education. Your father's *kanaka*, your mother's *hapa*. In a year they'll be grooming you for employment as a *maid*."

Emma roused herself. "Adam, dear, you'll fill her head with hate."

"I want to prepare her," he said, "for a life of heartbreak."

That night in bed, Emma's eyes were eerily bright. She seemed feverish and restless.

"Why do you push yourself?" He asked. "Why give so much to strangers?"

"Many of them are Hawaiian, your people and mine. Oh! Adam, I have seen how they were living. Today I tended a *haole* full of running sores, so feverish she couldn't see I was half-caste. She clutched my arm screaming, 'Don't let them bury me with niggers!' " Emma dropped her face in her hands. "I looked her in the eye and cursed her, even as she died."

That night her sheets were soaking wet. She woke vomitting. Adam bundled Lili, half asleep, and ran to neighbors. Each night the child stole back to her house, watching through the screen: the Chinese doctor, her weeping father, her mother's flesh tinted green, exploding sores in her armpits and groin, her face ferocious like a witch. Hour after hour, Emma screamed, her thirst extraordinary.

Her brothers arrived, Daniel Punahele cursing, James Kahiki weeping on his knees. After two nights, a *haole* doctor came, in black tie, an opera cape, his coachman outside impatiently whipping the horses.

The doctor looked at Emma, shook his head. "Too late. This house must be burned immediately!" He flung his cape over his shoulders in a grand exit.

Daniel intercepted him, pointed a pistol at his chest. Through the hours of Emma's feverish hallucinations, the awful smell of drooling nodules emanating from her body, the doctor wiped her face and neck, and washed his hands repeatedly. At dawn, Lili's father and uncles set to howling. Their wives arrived, and Emma's sisters. The doctor shifted his cape, picked up his bag, as if to leave again. With the butt of his pistol, Daniel struck him full across the face.

"Bastard! You could have saved her! You were called two days ago . . ."

The man swayed backwards, carefully tapped his bleeding cheek. "No one told me it was your sister. I don't make house calls in the *slums* . . ."

Adam rose and hit him with his fist. Daniel's *haole* wife struck Adam with her parasol. One of Emma's sisters, married to a Japanese, struck out at Daniel's wife.

"*Kanaka!*" someone cried. And someone swung again.

Through the screen, Lili saw her mother's head turn, eyes grow wide, watching the crowd of violent waltzers, spinning bodies, swinging limbs. Her face drained of everything. The room of people turned, hearing her breath, like water sucking down a drain.

Adam moved with Lili to his sister's house, and Lili watched her own dear house go up in flames. She turned her back on the old century, taking with her a memory of dueling in-laws, her mother's astonished, dying gaze. And striding along beside that memory, the image of a doctor coming late, too late, because they lived in what whites now called slums.

People said that year was the final decline of the Coenradstens. Daniel Punahele deserted his *haole* wife for a Hawaiian-Chinese mistress, producing a flock of "mix-blood mongrels." His wife stripped the house of valuables and sailed for the mainland, leaving the place a shell. James Kahiki admitted to cashing in insurance policies for their businesses, and gambling away all their sugar profits. Still deep in debt, he hanged himself with the belt of his tussore-silk dressing gown.

In 1901 sugar planters, wanting to keep their workers sober, backed formation of the Hawai'i Chapter of the Anti-Saloon League. Defeated, Daniel Punahele sold the Bay Horse Saloon to Adam, and went into pork-butchering with his mistress's family. Adam resurrected the bar as the Bay Horse Card Club and Reading Room. For a quarter a month, common workers could sit and read papers, periodicals, dime and half-dime novels. Those that couldn't read played sober games of Pedro and pinochle, fan-tan and *mah-jongg*, while Adam offered free legal counsel.

Plantation workers were still demanding better wages, medical care, decent food. Imported as indentured servants, their contracts could be bought and sold. Laboring twelve to fifteen hours for as little as forty cents a day, they had no running water or sewage systems in the camps, were subjected to floggings or shootings by sadistic Portuguese and Scotch *luna*. Sitting in the back room of the Bay Horse, Adam listed their complaints.

In those days, there was little mechanization in the sugarcane and pineapple fields. Plowing, irrigating, planting, fertilizing, were done by hand, mostly with a hoe. Then the killing part, burning and stripping of razor-tooth-edged leaves from cane stalks, cutting, and loading. In merciless sun and airless jungles of ten-foot-high cane, workers ripped casings of dead leaves from every stalk, allowing air to penetrate so they could breathe. Fine dust crept into the eyes and nose. Prickly cane-hairs scratched and burned, causing terrible infections. Most men had hideous scars on legs and arms, fingers missing from years of hacking. Some went blind.

Aided by informers, Adam began securing signatures on petitions of grievance. In paneled boardrooms of the Hawai'i Sugar Planters Association, his name was thrown up as a labor agitator, constantly linked with subversives. News reporters dug up his Royalist past and imprisonment for trying to overthrow the provisional government, and reinstate the queen. A *kanaka*, related to the degenerate Coenradstens, descendants of . . . a cannibal!

Lili spent evenings with her father at the Bay Horse, reading Poe's "The Raven," and Longfellow's "Evangeline," to Asians and Hawaiians struggling to learn English. Soon she was helping him draw up petitions, running them off on a printing press. Punahou classmates shunned her, calling her troublemaker, a firebrand, just like her Royalist mother and grandmother.

"*Nānā i ka'ili!* Look at the skin!" she cried, pointing to her arms. "We will not be *haolefied!*"

At her graduation, first in her class, her father shook with pride, then, desperate, he went to her namesake, Queen Lili'uokalani, asking her to help him send the girl to university.

"Far away, where she can fulfill her potential as a gifted human." He offered the queen all he had left of value, his wife's pearls and tiny diary.

"Put them away," she said softly. "And let us plan a marvelous future for Lili."

A close friend of Susan Tolman Mills, founder of Mills Seminary College for women in Oakland, California, the queen arranged for Lili's entry there on partial scholarship, supplemented with an allowance from the queen's own modest income. In 1906, Lili tearfully sailed for California, and at her departure, her father gave her her mother's pouch with the diary and black pearls.

"*Kowtow* to no one," he said. "Be extraordinary!"

She wept as the ship sailed into the Pacific, wondering how she could live up to his expectations. Lili was smart, but suspected she was not extraordinary. One night near the end of her freshman year, Lili woke trembling violently, and knew before she knew. The Bay Horse had burned down with her father trapped inside. A week later, she stood in front of the charred remains beside a young policeman who discovered the blaze. Before fire engulfed the building, he had broken through a window.

"I seen yoah fat'er on da floor," he said. "Look like already dead. Two big Portagee run right past me. *Hana make.* Work for plantation owners. My boss say if I tell dis, maybe I come dead, too."

His name was Benjamin Huhu Meahuna. He held her while she cried.

"I no good for much," he said. "But damned if let *haole* get away wit' murdah!"

Next day he and Lili stood in the offices of Honolulu's largest newspaper. That evening, their pictures appeared on the front page with

Benjamin's testimony, identifying the killers, one tall, with ginger hair. One slender, with a limp. Under Lili's picture, the caption read "SUGAR PLANTERS MURDERED MY FATHER." Benjamin was instantly fired from the police department, and shot at in the street. Lili's aunty's house was firebombed.

Terrified, she and Benjamin fled to a neighborhood priest. First, he married them, then he sent them to the farm of a decent Irishman with a small pineapple plantation in the mountains on Honolulu's north shore.

"Your father was murdered," the Irishman said, "as a warning to plantation strikers. A *Flip* was lynched three weeks ago, after protesting how they're forced to live twenty to a room, no toilets. The planters hunted down a Jap, shot his head off while he was organizing in a Buddhist temple. Now the sugar monopoly wants my land. You folks know how to handle firearms?"

And so, in the space of a week, Lili saw her father dead, married a stranger, and felt a man's body inside her for the first time. She learned to survive the burn of centipedes, the bite of scorpion, how to swallow spoonsful of nutmeg that kept her numb and high during back-breaking pineapple picking, and how to fire a rifle and handgun. In that week, she also learned not all whites were evil, some were generous like Hawaiians; struggling with nature and the elements engendered in them deep human capacity.

In 1907, with the help of the Irishman's wife and the Chinese cook, Lili gave birth to her first daughter, Emma Kelonikoa. A year later she gave birth to a boy, then another boy, and in 1910, another girl. This child was huge, came out of her silent, wide-eyed, memorizing everything around her. She was unwrinkled, big as a four-month-old.

After three days, she sat up and pointed to herself, "Pono."

The Chinese cook ran screaming from the room. The Irish wife crossed herself. Benjamin sat down, took his daughter's hand, and spoke carefully, as if to an adult.

"Dat da name you want? Okay! Pono my *tūtū*'s name. She plenny smart, tell future."

"Then the child is *mana pālua*," Lili said. "My mother, Emma, was psychic, too, she had prophetic dreams."

The newborn stared at them, her gaze so piercing Ben felt hairs stiffen on his neck. "Lili, dis child be one *kahuna*."

She was afraid to touch her child, to give her her breast. As if reading her mind, the infant popped the nipple into her mouth, eyes roving and alert. Her brothers and sisters loved her instantly, but workers kept their distance, afraid the newborn could read their minds.

One day when she was two, Pono rolled across the floor, screaming, gurgling like a drowning thing. Four hours later, a towering *tsunami* originating somewhere off Petropavlovsk, hit the islands, killing dozens. In May 1914, her fourth birthday, Pono suddenly rocked back and forth, clapping her hands, and laughing.

"PA ... NA ... MA ... PA! NA! MA!"

That week a ship from Hawai'i carrying a load of Hawaiian sugar was the first cargo ship to officially pass through the just completed Panama Canal. It was a boon to Pacific shipping, and people celebrated in the streets.

When they had lived on the plantation several years, Lili came across her mother's talismans tied up in a rag. She showed them to her husband. "Sentimental things, I guess."

Benjamin stared at the tiny gold-and-jade diary, the large, black South Seas pearls, then looked at his wife a little scared. "Lili, dis not junk. I t'ink plenny valuable, foah shoah!"

"Enough to rent a place of our own? Maybe the sugar planters have forgotten us by now."

He studied the black, glittering orbs, rolling them across his palms. Pono saw light reflecting, grabbed both pearls, and swallowed several times. Lili screamed and turned her upside down.

"No worry," Ben said. "Dey come out by and by." He leaned down to his daughter. "What you t'ink, Pono, too soon foah show our face? Moah bettah we stay here, be safe."

Eventually, the rare black pearls washed out, but Lili and Ben remained in hiding. Their shack was simple but clean, food was plain, but nourishing, fish, rice, *poi*. Wages were decent, hours humane, there was fresh water to bathe the children. They had their camp friends, and some nights the Irishman sat with the workers playing cards and drinking pineapple wine. And nearby was a public school.

At five Pono was big and robust, eyes dark, electric, skin a perfect golden cast. She was going to be a beauty. Even Lili felt her power, an almost scorn for a world in which there were events she could so easily foresee. Ben was not a deeply pensive man; when he thought of existence, he saw it as the slow flow of human clusters. But in that flow, he saw his daughter walking alone.

"Pono need find one strong man," he said. "Or one simpleminded one."

Sometimes she sat eerily still, as if listening to her inner organs, hearing her anatomy change. At seven Lili sent her off to school but she terrified teachers, reading their minds.

Lili took her out of school. "If she is meant to read and write, nature will see to it."

In truth, the child seemed to have no need for books, intuiting the world from stories told by workers who sat in her father's house— Koreans, Filipinos, Chinese. They had grown used to her, and called her their little *kahuna*. She grew wise as a navigator, eyes shrewd as old men who had seen the continents, the great oceans. She remembered their stories as if each were her own. Some nights, playing with toys carved of dried banana stalks, Pono sat listening to her parents talk about their dreams.

"Our sons will go to college," Lili said. "Won't they, Pono?"

She was silent, then one night she woke up from a dream, pointing at her older brother. "Honorary boredom!" And they knew he would be a scholar. Pono didn't tell about her other brother, the one she dreamed had spotted lungs. She was already growing kind.

One day when she was seven, her skin suddenly shriveled, her hair turned an awful gray. "Queen Lili'uokalani dead," she whispered.

And it was so. And all the islands were in mourning. Pono lay comatose for twelve hours, and when she woke, she woke smiling, a golden child again. Their monarch had at last found peace.

A Filipino in the camp named Silvio often sat with Ben and Lili talking longingly of Ilocos Sur where he had left his wife and children. One day he would go home rich, and help his starving family. A tiny man, slender as a girl, wide copper-colored cheeks, big coffee-colored eyes, some nights he sat inside his shack making awful noises. Pono understood he was lonely.

"Generalito getting soft. He one coward cock," her father said.

Silvio's fighting cock, Generalito, was his only vanity. He pampered the thing, spent his paycheck on its diet, so it stayed muscular and mean, three pounds of feathered moodiness. But lately in the ring, Generalito would not dispatch his opponents, not deliver the *coup de grace*. For this, Silvio wept. He improved its diet of cornseed, *poi* and shaved coral for protein and strength. As the fight season neared, Silvio added beaten egg yolk, brandy, molasses. Even expensive shark fin and shark eye. The night before his fights, Silvio clipped Generalito's wings, spines of his wing feathers sharpened to stilettos.

Fight nights, after working in the fields, Silvio bathed, and in clean underwear, lay down with Generalito. Whispering, he took the cock's head in his mouth, as if swallowing it whole. Pono spied on him as Silvio prayed, his pact with God, or the Devil, the trusting bird lying docilely between his teeth. Afterwards, it seemed extremely high, attacking its own mirror image viciously.

"Place your bets," Silvio cried, as men from the camp followed him and the hooded, rasping Generalito down the dirt road to the cockpit tent.

It filled up fast with wagering plantation workers, tiered wooden benches round a circle of packed earth. Small cocks fought first, lethal steel spurs attached to their natural spurs with rice paste and plaster. After a while their corpses were piled in a corner. Then Generalito and his opponent were thrown into the ring, circling, flirting, in a deadly *pas de deux*.

Pono sat outside, seeing the whole fight in her mind. She gasped as Generalito leapt, hacking and pecking, a cloud of dust and flesh. There was blood, men cheered, waved fists, and dollars. The opponent took the second skirmish. But in the third, Generalito demolished him, whirling with his spurs, kicking out backward like a skater. After a dozen such skirmishes, his opponent tottered round the ring begging to be dispatched. Generalito, bleeding but still game, eyed him disdainfully, and walked away, refusing to give the *coup de grace*.

It happened time and again, and now men attacked Silvio, accusing him of being homosexual, of emasculating his fighting cock, accusing him of sadism, refusing them the thrill of the coup. Opponents were beaten and down, but Generalito would not deliver, he would not even crow. He staggered across the ring, victorious, letting his opponents live. Bookies paid off bets, but even men who won were furious, hungry for slaughter. Silvio rapidly lost face.

"No good," Ben said. "Better Generalito die. Make one stew of him."

At night Pono watched the small Filipino weeping in his undershorts, pleading with the bird. In those moments she saw his future, saw that this delicate man—illiterate, given the worst plantation jobs because he was a "Flip," the group other immigrants spat upon—would never again see his family, his *barrio* in Ilocos Sur. Perhaps Silvio saw it too, saw his future in the sordid barracks of single Filipino men in Honolulu, men who never made enough, or saved enough, to go home. In his abysmal loneliness, his fighting cock, that cretinous stalk of feather, ligaments and drive, was all he had left of dreams and pride.

One night at the beginning of a new fight season, Pono tiptoed cautiously through the camp, past the Chinese couple clicking *mah-jongg* tiles, their children studying books by candlelight.

"Silvio." She knocked on his door.

"What wrong?" he asked, cowering behind his rusty screen.

She thrust a jar at him. "For Generalito."

He stared down at the jar. "What is?"

She was eight now, easily impatient. She stomped her foot. "*Mimi!* Give him *mana* . . . make him want to kill."

The next night, the cock pecked his opponent's lungs out, then ripped off his head. Silvo wept like a woman as cheering crowds carried him and his bird on their shoulders. Every night that fight season, and the next, camp workers placed big bets on Generalito, and every night neighbors followed the random iridescence of moonlight on Pono's jar of urine as she carried it across the camp to Silvio.

Workers grew prosperous from Generalito's victories, the plantation owner leased more land. By the time the cock died ripping out his own bowels, insane from the urine of young *kahuna*, Lili and Ben had saved enough to send their sons to college.

Ka Wahine Nele 'Ohana

Woman Without a Clan

SUNBAKED YEARS. Machete chorus of workers hacking in unison, sickly sweet smell of pineapple clogging their pores. Years later, the smoke of cigars would float a remembrance of old *wāhine* in baggy pants, goggles and rubber boots, harvesting by hand, then squatting over cold tea, puffing cigars. During round-the-clock harvesting, seeing yellowed eyes of crones caught in the gleam of kerosene lamps, Pono would run, afraid that life was her future.

Some nights she woke to find her father on the floor, asleep in the act of scraping red dirt from his boots. And her mother, so exhausted she slept in a chair, still dressed in work clothes, lunchbox in her lap. While they slept, Pono would salve their palms, dense with calluses, each callus a pink orb bearded with gray shreds where skin had worn. Still, she loved that life of swirling red dust, it marked her like a stigma, settling into hair roots, into bowels and lungs. Even freshly washed brown skin had a pink underglow, like refractions from a conch, and years later, as an old woman, Pono would still sneeze red.

Growing taller, wiry and strong, she helped lift bales of fertilizer, helped layer around each pineapple plant stretches of tarred mulch paper which controlled weeds, held soil moisture, and retained warmth. At harvest time, fields became terraced rows of spiky green clumps from which golden globes of "pines" floated above shining black seas. In spite of punishing labor, the fields were magical for her.

Slowly, stoop work and hand labor were somewhat relieved by horse-drawn machinery used for cultivation. Following horse teams through the fields, like giant sea horses charioting black waves, Pono would spin down the rows like a dust devil, sometimes stopping before a spiky "pine," giving it *maka loko'ino*, the evil eye. Weeks later, a can containing that same pineapple would explode on a grocer's shelf in California. Sometimes she mesmerized large pineapple rats so they lay down and died, paws outstretched across their hearts like operatic tenors.

One day when she was thirteen, four *haole* cradling rifles rode toward the plantation. Workers ran for their pistols while the horses were still trotting specks. Shots were exchanged, a horse reared. The riders shot up a row of "pines" and galloped off.

The Irishman cursed. "Bloody Sugar Association . . . they're moving for a pineapple monopoly. My lease is up soon, the bastards want my land."

The next time horses appeared, it was a sheriff's posse. Barrels of *'ōkolehao*, Hawai'i's answer to Prohibition, had been planted on the Irishman's land. He was accused of running a distillery, selling bootleg liquor. Hearing the accusation, workers in the camp milled round, defending him.

Pono's father pointed his rifle at the sheriff. "I t'ink maybe you workin' for da *haole*, neh?"

A man leaned down from his horse, whacking Ben with his rifle butt. Lili ran forward, swinging a machete, planting the blade in his forearm. Rifles exploded, soil shot up in their faces. Outnumbered, workers dropped their guns, were bound by rope in a circle. Wagons arrived to take them down the mountain then on to jail in Honolulu. Watching their tin-roofed shacks recede, fearing for their lives, Lili gripped Pono's arm, pushed her to the edge of a wagon.

Then she lifted the rope. "Jump, child. Jump!"

Pono clung to her, feeling the thrust of Lili's hand between her shoulder blades. She landed face down in red dirt, hoofs pawing the air above her. Then she was running down aisles of pungent ripeness, men galloping in figure eights, trying to head her off, stirring up too much dust to find her.

Finally, they reined in. "It's only a *kanaka* kid."

That's how Pono would remember it, her family floating away, diminishing on the horizon, someone sobbing out her name. When it was dark she crept back to their shack, holding to her heart what they had cherished: a Bible, snapshots of Lili's family, the tiny diary and black pearls. Then she lay down sobbing, beating her face and chest. *Why didn't I see it coming? Why didn't I dream?* At dawn, she crept away before whites came to claim the confiscated land.

For weeks she lived like an animal, sleeping in ditches, crawling on her stomach into workers' camps, crawling out with food stored in her cheeks. One night, she heard grunting sounds and froze, inches from a man lying in tall grass with a nanny goat, stroking its neck like a woman's. She began to survive on the goodness of natives and immigrants who took her in.

People became like victims when Pono focused on them, leached out of themselves by the tremor of her will. In return for meals, she would dream-see for them, trying not to lie. Someone would ask a question, after which she would drink a tiny glass of pine wine, or smoke two puffs of Dragon Seed, and then lie down and dream. Some nights there were no dreams, other nights there were awful visions she kept to herself. But sometimes good visions came.

"Your daughter is ugly, true. Odor is her weapon. Blessed with the strong smell of female, she will lure a husband, give you many grandsons!"

Sometimes people who had died stepped forth from her tongue in singsong. "Mama-san, I will come to you reborn through steel and water." Ten months later, a Japanese soldier, dead in Flanders, would return to his parents in the form of his newborn son, sailing a ship across the Pacific in the arms of his Belgian wife.

One day a Hawaiian-Filipino pounded Pono's head until she told her dream: "It is not ringworm. Your wife will die a leper at Kalaupapa." He dropped to his knees, wailing, praying her dream was someone else's dream. After two nights, Pono dreamed again and woke up smiling, pointing to a dead white spot on his leg. "You will grow old together, live for many years. You have *ma'i Pākē*, too!"

From Hawaiian *kāhiko*, she learned naming chants and healing chants. Eventually when telling her dreams, her voice took on omniscience, seeming to come from the earth, the plants, the sea. Slowly, she moved across the countryside toward Honolulu, and it was like gliding across an old, old tapestry—farmers guiding ox teams through emerald rice paddies, duck ponds rich with floating life, silver-feathered cane, and brooding jungles of ironwood, monkeypod, *koa*. And great pinnacled lava mountains, and prehistoric waterfalls like ragged stitches. The searing beauty and wealth of her birth-sands, that whites were stealing away.

Closer to the city, Pono saw the land begin to change, become impoverished. In 1920, the U.S. Congress had directed the territorial government to give back some of the land stolen from Hawaiian natives in the *Great Mahele* of 1848. The congressional move was called the Hawaiian Homes Commission Act. Between 1917 and 1921 thousands of acres of forested government land which had been leased had now expired. Over 26,000 acres of developed sugar land became available. But this was not what was returned to Hawaiians.

Instead of verdant little acres where people could plant small gardens and live on a fish-and-*poi* economy, what Pono saw were sad little homestead plots on barren land, no irrigation, no forests, or running water. Some homesteads were near springs that, within months, turned salty, or near swamps breeding mosquitoes. Some stood on land so rocky and mountainous, nothing grew, not even weeds, land so steep people could not build or even haul up drinking water. Some natives would wait for thirty years, well into the twentieth century, for a single homestead plot. They would prematurely age, half starve, trying to survive on barren soil, or finally succumb to Honolulu's growing slums.

"How we fight dese *haole?*" Hawaiians asked. "When we gonna get *revenge?*"

Pono couldn't tell them what she saw in dreams. The slums would grow into ghettos, sub-cities of Honolulu. The future would kill them. By now, white monopolies controlled every aspect of the sugar and pineapple business. Banking. Insurance. Utilities. Merchandising. Transportation. Shipping. Labor. Some people went back to slave work on plantations. Some gave up altogether, never worked again.

It was 1924, and entering Honolulu for the first time, Pono was speechless. Here was a real twentieth-century city, bustling and modern as cities she had heard of on the U.S. mainland. Paved streets were lit with electricity. People rode on electric railway lines, and steam-powered fire engines. They spoke on telephones, and undersea telegraph cables carrying messages from San Francisco. Trains chugged into the city, hauling sugarcane and freight. Ports were suckled by great ships, and fancy pleasure boats.

The first great leisure hotels in the islands, the Moana and the Halekūlani, presided over Waikiki Beach. A fantastic, pink, Moorish castle, the Royal Hawaiian, was under construction, and would soon host kings and worldwide celebrities. Moving carefully through well-dressed crowds, people even speaking foreign languages, Pono stared at latest fashions in Liberty House windows. And hat shops, and lace and feather shops. Specialty shops for just gloves, and those just for shoes. There were men's shops featuring snakeskin boots, silk undersuits, and satin coats called *robes du nuit*.

She turned down a side street, breathless and trembling; for she had entered a world that had never entered her dreams. Things she saw she didn't even have a name for, and she was terrified, not wanting to attract attention. In her faded dress and cheap sandals, she did not see, could not imagine, how men gazed after her. Endowed with the classic beauty of Polynesian women, at fourteen, Pono carried her height of almost six feet with a natural arrogance. Though she was strong of limb, breasts and hips full, and possessed the big hands and feet of a native, she moved with a fluid grace that drew glances.

Summoning up her nerve, she stepped inside the walls of the women's jail. It was a joke for a prison, inmates lounging outside in the shade in colorful *mu'umu'u*, strumming *'ukulele*. There were no bars, no fences, so they seemed like women on holiday. Big husky guards in striped *mu'umu'u* were tough-voiced, but gentle in their manner.

A guard instructed an inmate strolling into town on errands. "Bring me one spool black t'read. One pair large rubbah t'ongs. And no flirt wit sailahs!"

Another inmate was dressed in *lei* and satin *holokū* for a wedding. It seemed they only inhabited their cells at night.

Pono stepped into an office, asking for Lili Meahuna.

"Who you?" a guard asked.

"Her daughter, Pono."

"What kine crime she do?"

Pono's eyes filled. "She cut one deputy wit' knife."

The guard looked through a window at women reclining against banyans. "I see t'ree Lili's wit' my right eye." Then she slapped her forehead. "Yoah mama . . . she da pink one!" She pointed to a figure sitting alone with her head down.

Pono approached her slowly, the sunbaked arms glowing pink beneath a flowered *mu'umu'u*. Her black hair had a pinkish cast, and up close, even the whites of her eyes looked pink.

"Mama."

Looking up, Lili sobbed, reaching out for her. "My baby! I thought they shot you, that you were dead! *Hele mai. Hele mai.*" Come here, come here.

Pono fell to her knees, crying like a child. "Where's Papa? What happened to him?"

Lili pulled her closer. "They have put him in the men's prison."

Pono opened the cloth she had carried for months, and gave it to her mother. Touching each thing, staring at sepia pictures of her parents and grandparents, Lili wept again.

"Sit down, child. I have much to say."

As shadows grew long, she talked and talked, pointing to a picture of a one-eyed man and his wife, Kelonikoa.

"I never mentioned them. It made your father sad that I came from such a background and ended up so poor with him. This man, Mathys, was your great-grandfather. She was a high-born Tahitian. He owned many businesses, and built her a house so large and fine, ambassadors, even our king, and Queen Lili, came to dine. You must go and see the house, so you will know what you came from. But tell *no one* who you are, that you're descended from Coenradstens."

Pono looked puzzled. "Why?"

"There's an old Tahitian curse on the famiily. Kelonikoa rebelled against her father, a powerful chief, and married this *haole*. People say he had been a cannibal. Kelonikoa finally threw herself into the sea, and Mathys died insane from the weight of his wealth. My own mama died horribly of plague. My father was murdered. The curse has carried down to us. Your oldest brother, Ben Napala, goes about at university in shame, because his parents are in prison. He will not see us. Your second brother, Kenneth Makika . . ." Her hand flew to her mouth. "Tubercular!"

Pono clasped her mother's hands. "Mama, let me go to him. I've learned healing chants and herbs . . ."

"No, child. You will look at him and see what I don't want to know."

"But, what will happen to us now?"

Lili continued, as if she were alone. "When Papa sent me to America to university, he told me two things: To never *kowtow*. And to be extraordinary. Pono, child, I am not extraordinary. I only want to live in peace, grow old with your father. They have charged him with threatening the sheriff with a gun, and me with trying to kill a deputy. If we swear we were crazed, overworked and starved by the Irishman, they will drop all charges. They want his land. And what I want . . . I want a quiet life. Taro planting, fishing, growing old."

Pono sat up alarmed. "What about me?"

Her mother sighed, and took her hands. "*You* are extraordinary, gifted with vision. You must leave Honolulu." She lay the pouch of black pearls in her palm. "Sell them. Go and start a life."

Pono shook her head, not comprehending. "I'm your girl! I want to stay with you and Papa."

"When whites hear you are *kahuna*, they'll label you a witch. They'll dig up your Coenradtsen past. Cannibalism, suicide, addiction. You will be *lepolepo* on this island."

"You fear me," Pono cried, "because I see too much."

Lili nodded thoughtfully. "You saw your brother's lungs in dreams. You didn't tell me. You have that power. To give. Or not."

"Oh, Mama, I was trying to spare you."

"I could have saved him, special herbs, secret roots. You should have told me, child."

Pono rose, her voice like an old woman. "The weight of things. To see so much, so young. Now you want to banish me . . ."

"You see the future. How could we control you? We want a simple life, a quiet life . . ."

She was still talking softly as Pono walked away, dropping the twisted pouch of pearls behind her. But it stuck to her hand, as if it had grown to her flesh. Stumbling blindly through the streets, she wept. Kin, blood, history, snatched from her grasp in a breath. In milling, foreign crowds, she was an atom lost in ether, a woman without a clan. Heart racked with grief, Pono wandered down to Chinatown, slept hunched in alleys, waiting to die.

It was still an over-crowded ghetto of snaky warrens, hidden chimes, alleys smelling of salt fish, ginger, jook. But since the great turn-of-century fire, the area had been rebuilt, rot had not yet settled in. For weeks Pono prowled streets where opium addicts clung to tenement walls like starfish. At night, she watched them siphon by. And watched with fascination tiny, wizened, Chinese women, great pendant ears swinging as they tottered on bound feet, chattering in high, nasal sing-song. They became the yeast of her imagination. She was certain baskets on their arms contained human heads and *dim sum* made of children's livers.

Again, she learned to barter dreams in exchange for food. Housewives fed her *saimin*, swept places on their floor where she could sleep, then squatted beside her, waiting to hear their futures. Chinese fortune-tellers ambushed her, burying her in barrels of slop for stealing away their customers. She moved to another part of Chinatown.

Staking out a bench in A'ala Park, one morning Pono woke to find a Japanese woman and child staring at her.

"Too beautiful," the woman said. "I look like you, make moah money wit sailahs."

She was no more than twenty-four, made up with thick rice powder, carmine heavy at her eyes. A phony mole danced across her cheek around which curved an exaggerated spit curl. Her hair was fashionably short and she wore a tight satin *cheongsam* and high heels that made her totter. Under the makeup, one could see she was very plain. Pono asked what she did with her daughter while she slept with sailors.

The woman giggled. "She one good keed. Sit in chair, face to da wall."

The girl was nine, a little moonface with bright almond eyes. Her name was Run Run, and she lay her hand on Pono's knee, a puppy offering its paw.

Pono took the hand and sobbed. "I'm just fourteen. My parents thrown me out."

The prostitute moved closer on the bench. "My husband leave me for pretty girl. Hey, maybe we make one team!"

Her name was Miko, and she took Pono home to a stifling, windowless room, only a bed and basin. "You work wit' me, you bring moah bettah business!"

That night, Pono lay on the floor, holding the tiny hand of Run Run as it hung from the bed. Her other hand clasped her mother asleep with her eyelids Scotch-taped into *haole* double-folds. Pono slept heavily and dreamed of herself in rubber gloves, catching slippery golden cylinders, twirling them in her palm. Around her, women with white balloon heads waved with hands missing fingers, missing thumbs. Then she saw herself and the girl, Run Run, grown into older women, dancing in showers of cinnamon.

The next morning, Pono went to Dole Cannery, knowing from her dream they would be hiring. She stood on an assembly line, clutching a small knife with rubber gloves, catching pineapples sliding out of skinning machines, then trimming off the eyes and extra bits of skin. Around her, older women, pros, in aprons and big, stiff white hair nets, coached her, showed her how to hold the knife, slicing and spinning the fruit expertly, some with missing fingers, hands mauled in processing machines.

She and Miko found a larger room with a window and two beds. At dawn, while Pono worked the cannery, Miko and Run Run slept. At night, while Miko worked the streets, Pono sat with Run Run, growing to love the sorrowful wisdom of her eyes, a child trained to keep her face turned to the wall.

They were an odd sight—a tired street whore, her wise-eyed child, and a giant Polynesian beauty—as they explored the wonders of Honolulu: Aloha Tower where great liners docked, ermined women floating down the gangplanks. Horse racing and *kinipōpō* at Kapiolani Park. Open markets where a dozen different languages were heard, everywhere the make-you-drunk scent of frangipani, and orchids leaping from the mouths of freshly killed wild boar. *Kachi-kachi* bands played, Flips ran with jugs of pig's blood. Handsome *kānaka* hawked *lei* of offal slung round their golden necks.

And in the "high-tone" part of town, chandeliered windows of three-storied homes with wraparound *lānai*, dwellings of merchant princes, sugar millionaires, where waltzes were played on grand pianos. Eventually, Pono found the sprawling white Coenradsten house, now owned by Boston people.

Miko stared, her mouth open. "You no lie?"

"No lie." Pono said. "My great-grandfather owned. Once very rich."

"Why you no live dere now?"

Pono thought a while. "If I live there, I not meet you and Run Run." Snarling watchdogs threw themselves against the fence, trained to hate the smell of natives.

For a year Pono tried to talk Miko out of street work, but she had grown dependent on the life.

"Bettah den da cannery! Beside, in da dark, sailah make me feel beautiful." One day she brought home a new dress and a large box of candy. "Dis sailah want live wif me. What you t'ink, Pono?"

Something in her turned over, but her voice was calm. "Make him find you house with separate room for Run Run. So she not have to grow up face da wall."

That night while Miko worked the streets, Pono held the little girl, heart-broken. "You like one home, and Papa?"

"Sure!" Run Run cried. "I like go school now. I one smart keed!"

Three weeks later, Miko took Run Run and moved in with her sailor. "Find one rich man," she yelled back. "Now da time, while you still plenny pretty!"

Pono sat in the empty room, holding a skinning knife to her throat. *What happened to my dream? That Run Run and I would grow old together, dancing in showers of cinnamon.* She was just fifteen, and life had gifted her again with emptiness. Pressing the knife against her neck, she began the sad, raspy transaction of blade through flesh.

Suddenly her room began to tremble, the mirror turned sideways on the wall. Outside, the pounding of hundreds of feet made the street quake so tenements shook and swayed. She heard distant screams coming closer, like voices in an Oriental dream. Pono ran to the window, saw crowds of ragged Japanese fleeing armed, club-wielding police. Organized strikers from plantations outside the city, thousands of them were hiding in Chinatown. Now, routed from Buddhist temples and sake breweries, they were running for their lives.

Below her window, a striker tripped, went down crying out for help. She saw the swinging club, his head part like a melon.

The Portuguese policeman stood over him yelling, "Sneaky Daikon eater!" striking again and again, brains hanging pendant from his club.

Staring down at the shrieking mob, she felt a white furnace explode within her—remembering a sheriff's posse, her family roped like cattle. Now, Pono focused so intently on the policeman, he looked up at her and grinned. She held the look, whispering over and over while the man wiped his dripping club. Within a month, coins of dead white spots would cover his legs. His eyelids would begin to rot. By the time he was caged on the leper ship bound for Kalaupapa, his family would have wiped his name from their genealogy.

Thirty Japanese were murdered that day, remembered as the Strikers' Massacre. Witnessing the slaughter, so close she smelled the blood, Pono forgot to die. She forgot to do everything but hate.

Nā Ho‘okuano‘o Manō

Shark Meditations

FOR MONTHS SHE DREAMED. Even on her feet at the cannery, she dreamed. A giant in a cape of rain riding a corpse across the ocean's skin. A face taking shape inside a wave, teeth gnashing a squid to death with a fierce bite behind the eyes. Had she not been so lonely, so bereft, Pono might have read the dreams and followed them. She might not have been drawn to Valentine Keaka Kumu.

One day, watching inter-island steamers dock in Honolulu's port, she saw men unlike any she had seen before. Wearing sombreros of woven pandanus, they were decked with *lei* of fresh flowers, bright, red sashes round their waists. Over white pants, high leather leggings served as sheaths for long knives glinting in the sun. Lariats hung from their saddles and, while their horses danced down the gangplank, their spurs made loud, jingling sounds. As crowds gathered dockside, a handsome rider's eyes snagged on Pono. Impulsively, he flung her a *lei*.

"*Paniolo* from da Big Island," someone said. "Here for exhibition rodeo."

From the boats' hold, she could hear the uneasy bellowing of cattle.

Years earlier, searching for work, Hawaiians had left their *‘ohana*, headed for upcountry cattle ranches on the Big Island of Hawai‘i. There for decades, longhorn cattle had run wild, eating up forests, trampling taro patches of local farmers. These fast multiplying brutes were descendants of longhorns brought from California in the late 1700s as a gift for King Kamehameha.

In the nineteenth century, one of Hawai'i's kings had imported Spanish and Mexican cowboys to teach natives how to ride and rope, slaughter, and prepare hides for shipment. They had brought with them high-horned saddles, long spurs and braided lassos. Hawaiians liked their buckaroo style, and soon became real *paniolo*, island version of the galloping *españoles*. Now, the prime minister of England, visiting Honolulu, wanted to see cowboys trained by the famous Spaniards.

That night, Pono brushed her long black hair until it shone, then dressed carefully in a white *holokū* that made her skin stand out. She looked one last time round her room. She would not return. Then, wearing the *lei* from the handsome *paniolo*, she headed for Kapiolani Park, where a huge tent had been set up for the rodeo honoring England's visiting PM.

Using all of her cannery wages, she bought a seat near the front of the grandstands, beside the prime minister's party. It was a huge crowd of several thousand, the *haole* elite, as well as locals and immigrants: anyone who loved horses and rodeos. Inside, an almost circus atmosphere prevailed, smell of sawdust and nervous animals, horse manure and beer, "shave ice" flavored with coconut juice, and something new called "hot dogs." Clowns turned hurdy-gurdies, while painted midgets cartwheeled by, and strolling Hawaiians played 'ukulele, guitars, mandolins.

From the moment of the Grand Entry—dashing *paniolo* on handsome steeds holding flags of Hawai'i, the United States and Great Britain— Pono watched for the man she would marry. Each time he pranced by, she stood up tall, wearing his *lei*, her eyes burning into his shoulders. In the myriad colors of spectators, her pure white dress was a beacon; a light seemed to engulf her, lifting her from the crowd. She was so handsome, so proud, people turned and stared. *Paniolo* passing tipped their hats. Touching the *lei* at her shoulders, Pono responded only to the one she had chosen.

After preliminary calf roping and steer throwing, barrel racing, and "snubbing," a man appeared on the back of a ferocious bronco that threw him into the stands. Pono covered her eyes, and someone touched her arm.

"No worry. That one not your sweetheart!"

Then a man seemed hurled out of a pen, riding one-handed a writhing 1,500-pound bull. Pono recognized him, horrified, as he bounced and flipped, grinning crazily. He stayed on for twelve seconds, a record, and the crowd stood and roared his name. "Valentine . . . Valentine!"

He struggled to his feet, laughing, dusted off his chaps and, approaching the stands, threw his hat to Pono. The crowd cheered, strolling musicians struck up a haunting, old Hawaiian song, *"Wahine U'i*, Beautiful Woman."* She stood holding his hat to her chest, while *paniolo*—ragged, bloodied and bandaged—rode gallantly in formation for the Grand Finale. She stood with his hat until grandstands were empty, no one left but old men sweeping sawdust.

As if summoned, Valentine limped back into the ring, looked up at her and smiled. "What now, *Wahine U'i?"*

In one week they were married, spending their honeymoon on the steamer headed for the Big Island. During the night while her husband slept, his skin tatooed with her virgin blood, Pono crept up on deck, feeling her life slide into a new phase, feeling breathless, as if God were standing beside her, and somewhat terrified, as if he were about to lean over and bite off a hunk of her cheek.

Here on the Big Island, on cool slopes stretching down the flanks of the long-extinct volcano, Mauna Kea, Kamuela was a small cowboy town along the Mamalahoa Highway. Here, modest wooden houses of *paniolo* stood weathered but spotlessly clean, aired by winds sweeping across rich, upcountry grazelands, bringing the scent of cattle and rich soil, smell of salt and brine from the sea. Canned orchids and bougainvillea lined rickety steps of each house. Fishing nets were thrown across tiny lawns, and toed rubber *tabis* danced from clotheslines like large black feet.

Somedays, waiting for her husband, Pono sat on her little porch, and felt she was sitting atop the world. Mauna Kea rose almost fourteen thousand feet, its volcanic crown blanketed in snow in winter. And far south, Mauna Loa, a sister volcano, and beyond that Kīlauea Crater, the one that never slept. Every now and then Kīlauea blew its top, spouting fire thousands of feet in the air. It was a vastly rich island, for beside the great cattle ranches of hundreds of thousands of acres, down-country were sugar plantations, macadamia nut farms, coffee and orchid farms.

Sometimes wives talked of haunted places, ancient burial shrines that moved, and the dreaded "Night Marchers," Kamehameha's warrior-ghosts who haunted scenes of their great battles.

"I have seen them," Pono said. "Shadows crossing the land."

"Where have you seen them?" women asked.

"I dream."

At first they were skeptical, but one by one, they came with gifts, bowls of *poi*, a chicken. "Is my husband faithful? Will my boy go to university? Will my next child be a girl?" Sometimes she dream-told for them, and sometimes, seeing tragedy, she would not.

She was fond of her husband, Valentine, humoring him like a child, knowing in her heart this was not a great love. He was handsome, fearless in the saddle, but when his feet were on the ground, he was just a cowhand, an overgrown boy with no concept of her dreams, her intuition. All he could offer were rodeos and love songs, and all he asked of her were meals and the animal comfort of her body, making him feel a man.

What Pono missed was what her parents had shared, blind devotion that would drive a woman to swing a machete at a deputy. Or even the almost carnal passion Silvio had possessed for his Generalito, embracing the bird, sucking its ragged head into his mouth, his whole life focused on three pounds of feathers. Yet, all she could summon for Valentine was a motherly feeling, a lack of malice. She carried with her now, like added weight, an odor of resignation.

When she'd been married a year she and other wives waved good-bye to their husbands who were bound for Honolulu, an exhibition roundup for Australian cattlemen. For weeks they'd practiced, wanting to show the Aussies how steers from each island were boarded on steamers bound for Honolulu and the slaughterhouses.

The big ship would anchor in a bay. Then mounted *paniolo* would rope steer by the horns with spinning lariats, and jockey them into the surf. Dodging sharks, they passed the ropes to sailors in whaleboats anchored just beyond shallow water so steers couldn't get their footing and tear free. When eight steers were tied up on each side by their horns, the boats would be rowed out to the big ship where cattle were lifted aboard by winches. Whaleboats then returned for more steers.

Paniolo worked in pairs, wet shoulders and thighs bulging and glistening, salt-stained horses rearing, shooting out of the waves like dark gods. Sometimes crowds gathered, placing bets on how many steers would be taken by sharks before they reached the mother ship. Afterwards, men spilled off their horses, pulled off the saddles, and collapsed on the beach. Sun caught the sand on their dark bodies so they seemed covered with granulated diamonds. And in the surf, horses freed from their saddles lifted their heads majestically, manes and tails shooting plumes like creatures from mythology. Pono would remember such days, so wondrous they left a glare.

After their men left for Honolulu, wives sat around complaining of their drinking habits, dirt-encrusted clothes, addiction to horses and rodeos that brought in belt buckles and trophies, but no real income. One night Pono dreamed of Valentine craning his neck at tall buildings called "skyscrapers." The next night she saw him galloping down boulevards, between motorcars and buses, men with machine guns pursuing him. He tossed them a big black ball, and they slowed, marveling at the thing. Then one of them lifted his arm and shot.

Three weeks later, all but two of the *paniolo* came home to the Big Island. Valentine and another cowboy, drunk on *'ōkolehao*, had stowed away on the *Lurline* bound for San Francisco. Pono sat, waiting for word. One night she opened the small leather pouch kept under her mattress. One of her black pearls was gone. Weeks later, the FBI brought Valentine's sidekick home to Honolulu.

From San Francisco, they had hitchhiked all the way to Chicago for the annual International Rodeo, biggest in the world. Illegal aliens, they couldn't work the rodeo without working papers and a license. Valentine tried unsuccessfully to bribe officials with a huge black South Seas pearl. Intrigued by the rumored size of the gem, large and perfect as a grape, gangsters made Valentine an offer. When he demanded more money, the mob gunned him down, wrenching the pearl from his pocket as he died. Witnessing the slaying, his *paniolo* sidekick turned himself in, begging to be sent home to Hawai'i.

The ranch owner's wife offered Pono work as her housemaid, and three *paniolo* immediately proposed marriage; she looked at them all and laughed. It was time to know this island. Time to wander and look, and see. There were things she had heard of here that she would only believe with her eyes: mysterious Waipi'o Valley on the northeast coast where in deep rain forests *Menehune* lived. Great soaring cliffs with thousand-foot waterfalls. Glittering lava beaches like acres of black diamonds, and valleys where orchids bloomed for miles. Coffee mountains of fragrant snow. A town of a thousand rainbows. A beach that burped precious jewels washed in from the Orient.

Then, there was the forbidding country of the southeast coast, one of bubbling steam vents and sulfuric fumes, where earth was covered with *'ā'ā* and *pāhoehoe*. Volcano country, where Pele, Goddess of Fire, lived deep in the pit called Halemaumau. Now and then, she showed her anger by rending the earth so it belched molten lava, creating a moonscape of desolation.

It was not just curiosity that drove her. Pono felt she had been called to this island of so many moods and geographies. Week after week, by foot and on mule, she struggled through lush valleys and barren brushland, bartering her dreams for food. Some nights she slept on hay with sheep and cattle. Some days, exhausted, she made her way down jagged rocks and floated in the sea. After years of living inland, she began to understand that water was her natural element, entering her like a drug. When motion and colors of the land exhausted her, when she saw how she stood apart from ordinary people, the sea was what she now turned to.

She learned to float for hours, calmly accepting all matter of sea life swirling round her. Clicking dolphins, barracuda like swimming stilettos, silver blizzards of sprats. One day a twenty-foot oarfish wrapped itself round her, thick red Samurai fringe down its spine jangling like tambourines. It slowly tightened its embrace, opened its great jaws round her head, then looked into her eyes. Something registered. Some common wisdom forever known. The fish seemed to sigh, slowly uncoiled, swam off through her streaming hair.

She wandered aimlessly with a diligence, like someone looking for a sign. Not yet sixteen, she was already a widow, a tribeless woman with nothing but visionary powers. Powers that seemed to do nothing for her; she couldn't even understand her dreams. A giant in a cape of rain, riding a corpse across the ocean's skin. A face taking shape inside a wave, teeth snapping a squid behind the eyes. What did it mean? Why did it frighten her?

One day on the Kona Coast Road she saw a mixed-marriage couple, Hawaiian-Chinese, leading two pack-horses. Seeing Pono, they ran off the road, beating the flanks of the horses.

"Wait," she cried. "For taro, rice, I tell your dreams."

The couple stopped, slowly approached, uncovering the packs on the horses. Under cooking pots and hammocks were two children, hidden in rolled *tapa*.

"Look dere faces," the husband whispered. "And tell what gonna' be."

Flesh suppurated on each small face. Eroded noses. An eye glassy and blind. There was not enough left to tell they were children.

"*Ma'i Pākē*," the mother said. She looked behind them down the road, then looked at her husband. "*Wikiwiki*. 'Fore da *māka'i* come catch us. No take my keeds away in cage!"

They were fleeing bounty hunters, running with their leprous children to the mountains. Pono stared at them, then squinted, looking at the sky. "One gonna' die soon . . . One gonna' give you *ma'i Pākē*. But you three gonna' live in the jungle for many years."

The Chinese husband grasped her hand. "*Mahalo! Mahalo!*" He pointed to their tiny farm somewhere in the background. "Fresh kine vegetables, taro. Plenny fish in pond!"

They floated north with their tiny, rotting burdens.

Two hours later she was stopped by an armed posse looking for the couple. She pointed them in the opposite direction, down toward the sea, talking in heavy Pidgin to give her words credibility.

"Dey goin' hide in caves, you know da kine? Wait for one boat take dem ocean. Real *pupule*, neh?"

So Pono lived on their tiny farm, harvesting food from their garden, pounding taro root, straining it into one-finger *poi*. She talked to geckos, scorpions, mongoose, just to hear her voice, give herself back to herself. Farmers, passing tradesmen, women from the fields, brought her tokens in return for telling dreams. Sometimes they touched her arm to see if her flesh was real. She was beautiful, but because of her powerful *mana*, they backed away not seeing her loneliness. Once she lay still for so long, when she woke a spider web had grown across her mouth.

She dared everything—exhausting herself by climbing forty-foot palms for coconuts, splitting them blindly with heavy axes. She ate all manner of herbs and roots, searching for company in new sensations. She dashed crazily into the surf, slid onto the backs of giant manta rays, and let them fly her through the sea on wings spread twenty feet.

One day she dragged in a strange species of seaweed that glowed pink and tasted septic. She stuffed her mouth and chewed, hoping it would kill her. Instead, alkaloids in the weed produced a floating sensation. Standing in the surf, she felt her jaws tighten, then contract, something growing like a snout. Then she was swimming, released from gravity. She plunged down, sporting through coral canyons, through boulevards of light limned by prismatic lens of waves. Her lightness intoxicated her, she could no longer feel the weight of her organs. Huge sharks suddenly bladed along beside her, playful, amorously nudging her. Pono pulled back, terrified, then, in the eyes of one of them, she saw her reflection: a white-tipped reef shark, powerful in size, moving like a bullet. Schools of smaller fish scattered as she lunged. The taste of blood.

She seemed to swim for days, until she felt irritated, her buoyancy beginning to pall. She felt wrapped tight, restricted. Nerves in the soles of remembered feet began to cry for land. Her joints mourned the heaviness of tissue and musculature that governed them. The profound desire to walk, the lack of power to do so. With a blinding sense of helplessness, Pono saw she had no arms. She was bound in a bag of scales slowly suffocating her. All she could do was open her gills, raise her dorsal fin and swim.

She tried to push herself out of the water, to fall backwards into air. But long draughts of air almost killed her. Unable to breathe in the atmosphere, she plunged back into water. Then she remembered she was asleep, that her shark form was imagined. They say when one remembers one is dreaming, one is already near the end of the dream. She relaxed, slid through waves, until she slid into a dream of waking.

She woke on the sand, curled up like an ear. She looked down at her skin, and it was gray, eerily marbling to brown, then golden, and it was rough like sandpaper, visibly returning to petal softness. In her mouth there was blood and the taste of raw fish. After that, whenever she felt too lonely in the world, she went down to the sea and ate the weed that glowed. Then for hours, until she longed for gravity, she entered the world of *manō*. And, though she was in the world of humans, she was no longer wholly of that world.

One stormy day, blading through wintry waves, Pono larked off alone from a school of sharks, seeing a face, a human face, taking shape inside a wave. Circling slowly, she came upon the human again, wrestling with a squid large as a steer. Awful tentacles whipped the man's torso as he drove his knife into its stomach, grabbed its neck, and bit it viciously behind the eyes. The squid shuddered, screamed like a woman, making Pono's hide ripple. Loosing its tentacles, it died, ink cataracting in clouds.

She watched as he dragged the thing ashore, laboring over it in a simple loincloth. He was huge, dark, built like a warrior, with the big, handsome features of pure Polynesians. Heavy, brooding brow, long Asiatic eyes, a generous, strong nose, full lips like a woman juxtaposed with a fierce, square jaw. She swam back and forth watching, as finally he laid down his knife, washed his hands, then lifted a huge wave-sliding board, shouting and running with it into the sea. *Papa he'e nalu*, what *haole* called surfboards, the sport her people had mastered two thousand years ago.

Feeling a thrill, a need to follow, Pono bladed along behind his board, huge, slender and stiff, so he seemed to be riding a giant corpse. Kneeling, paddling out to the deep, he slowed where the ocean changed to many-fathom colors. Now he straddled the board as if it were a horse, waiting for something momentous. Finally, a wave thundered in high as a ship, moaning and full of destruction. Muscles knotted with tension, he stood and roamed wintry juices, finding the crest of the wave, riding it home like the prow of an invisible ship.

The huge man rode for hours, paddling out on his knees, sailing in like a god, and for hours Pono followed. The sky suddenly cracked as if from an ax. Rain poured down so heavily, he seemed to be standing between two seas. Then a wave took him down, he disappeared as the longboard shot into the air. Pono dived deep, searching until she saw him tumbled in a cyclone of coral and shell, tossed and dragged like a doll. She whipped round him, trying to lift him up to air. A shadow fell over her, hung suspended, then the longboard seemed to dive. She heard the cracking sound.

When one remembers one is dreaming, one is already near the end of the dream.

She woke lying in the surf, her head numb and bleeding. The storm abated, there was only heavy rain. Far down the beach she saw the huge man sitting up, touching his scraped arms and legs. He propped his longboard in the sand, studying it for damage. And all the while, she watched. Finally, shaking his black hair loose of sand and pebbles, he dragged on a rain cape made of pandanus leaves, that hung from his shoulders to his knees. Wrapping up hacked-off parts of the squid, he stood slowly, dragging his board to a shelter in the bushes.

She came to me from the sea. This is how he would always remember. For, as he neared, Pono struggled slowly to her feet, collapsing again in the surf. Pulling her gently onto the sand, he watched her skin turn from gray to brown to gold, from sandpaper to petals of young jasmine. He saw the snout slowly re-form into a human jaw, saw the curve of human lips as her earthly beauty returned. He wrapped her in his raincape, cautiously, as one touches something that's one of a kind.

When she woke, they were on horseback, she was sitting behind him, hands tied securely round his waist. Cool rain ran down her face from his naked back. Steam from his flesh, the man-ocean scent of him, smote her with coital intensity. When she woke again, they were trotting up a driveway ceilinged like a cathedral of giant ironwoods and eucalypti.

Later, she swam into a sea of billowing curtains, pale porcelain, linen sheets. The sun was painting the room with ragged paws, someone conversing with a doctor. Her old leather pouch had been placed in her palm, all she possessed in the world.

He approached, leaned over her, dark as a god, teeth savagely bright and perfect.

"I am Duke Kealoha. I have brought you home."

Nā Hūnā

The Hidden

"Nothing is destroyed, things merely change shape or form."

He was trying to explain about the beans, how they were transformed into coffee, and how the faces in the leaves were real, faces she thought she had imagined in the hallucinatory weeks of her healing, workers twittering like birds, picking coffee cherries in the delicate trees. He talked on about soil, rainfall, ideal altitudes, how it was all done by hand—planting, picking, sorting, processing.

"Inside the ripe, red cherry is the bean. The cherry pulp is used for fertilizer, mash for livestock. Nothing is destroyed, a thing becomes another thing. I try to think of my family that way, that they are not dead but vitally alive, perhaps in another form, on another plane. I know you have seen them in a dream."

Pono's head buzzed, she sat down, holding it between her hands. Remembrances, awful. Human screams like blades shrieking on lathes.

"Why don't I hear clocks in the house?" she asked. "This silence. Why isn't there ticking?"

"Here, time has no significance." He knelt before her, his handsome face distorted. "Are you afraid?"

Rags of her dream floated by. His family dead. Or kenneled away. Faces rotted, hands withered into artifacts. If she remained with him she would die or grow into a horror. But she had already grown to cherish him as he droned beside her all the weeks of her healing, her fractured skull reknitting.

Duke rose and stared out of a window. "In time, fear will chase the workers away, the coffee orchards will become a jungle. I will be shunned. The house will fall to ruin." He asked again. "Are you afraid?"

Pono looked down, understanding they didn't have time for love to mature; it had to condense quick. Turning her back on the world as if shutting a book and rising, she moved to him and took his hand.

He taught her all he knew of coffee, walked her through his orchards, filling her lungs with the scent of arabica, the winey fruit-smell of ripe coffee cherries, describing the spring flowering period when white gardenia-like blossoms turned fields into "Kona snow" and how, after a few days the petals fell, revealing tiny green berries that, in late fall, ripened into bright red cherries, ready for harvesting.

And as they walked past field hands picking cherries, women raking on *hoshidana*, men lifting burlap sacks of beans, people bowed, tipped their hats respectfully, his powerful presence acknowledged by all. And moving with him through the town of Captain Cook, Pono saw how people in the streets, and in farthest corners, the smallest shacks and alleys, waved, feeling Duke's magnetism. He seemed to envelope them in a kind of spell, his size, his dignity, his passion for the land reminding them of their Hawaiianness, their fierce, proud heritage.

By nature she was excessive, and so he taught her many things, horseback riding and jumping, fishing, and hunting turkey and wild boar in upcountry forests. Because her mind was so keen, he read her Balzac and Thackeray, watched her skin dampen and glow when he wound the turntable, playing Chopin and Strauss. They stood for long periods over maps and globes, as he tried to explain the world to her, the vastness, the explosive newness of some cultures, the golden dotage of others. He tried to explain electricity and thermodynamics. One day he brought home a new Buick, just off the ship from California. Before she would learn to drive, Pono went at both fenders with a hammer, until the car was comfortably dented, less intimidating.

Duke knew three foreign languages, had traveled the world, studied at the Sorbonne, and owned silk suits custom-made in London. Yet he found Pono the most enthralling female he had ever known, possessing a powerful energy, a charge of heat that stunned all life around her. Her beauty matched her native intelligence. *She came to me from the sea*, he would remember, knowing magnetic fluids flowed through her, that her skin could change color and texture, that locals in town called her *kahuna*.

Nothing they did could shock each other. They stood side by side as equals not needing to experience things others experienced, not even needing to go out in the world, for they had their own mythology. Pono talked him through her history, all the way back to Mathys Coenradsten, and he saw how her family had erased itself through the generations. His had done it in less than five years.

Some nights they drifted through the house and, seeing it through her eyes, Duke saw it for the first time. Rooms filled with massive furniture of Malaysian teak and *koa*, ancient, rare Hawaiian prints. Old Persian rugs on floors laid with Italian tiles, lamps of jade and marble shaded with raw silk. There were hand-painted porcelains from China and Belgium, velvet bellpulls, satins, silks. And rooms lined with leather books from which Pono heard a constant hum. Suspicious of printed words, one night, alone, she slapped a book to still the whispering. Her hand came away with dust of termites breeding in the precinct of its spine.

Peacocks skittered behind them on polished floors, pet mynahs prudently scaled their way up the banister, while Duke showed her a life-size portrait of King Kalākaua, his father's distant cousin, portraits of grandfathers, great-grandfathers, high-born Hawaiians all the way back to Kamehameha I. As Hawaiians began to die out, each generation in Duke's family were courted by *haole*, wanting to buy their land. Then *ma'i Pākē* lay waste his family, and, in horror, whites turned away.

Duke pointed to old sepia photographs. "Mother, father, two sisters. Gone, all gone."

His father had been struck first, forced on the leper ship to Kalaupapa, on the neighboring island of Moloka'i. A year later, ulcers appeared on his mother's legs, and Duke was called home from university. Then his sisters, one by one, their husbands running from them in horror. Two cousins, a niece. It was as if some code in their family scripture decreed a leveling, a wiping out of Kealoha genes.

Duke studied his reflection in a mirror. "A matter of time."

Each night he examined his body, looking for telltale spots. Numbness in the limbs, puffed earlobes. And, because he believed he was a "contact," carrying the wild bacteria in his blood, each night he examined Pono before he made love to her, going over her body inch by inch, then embracing her, bowing over her, entering her with the madness of passion and relief. They were in each other's blood now, lost to each other, and she waited for the numbness to begin, an unhealed lesion, the sly spreading whiteness. Then the glassiness of eyes, thickening of skin, slow putrefaction of the body. She tried to dream, to see if *ma'i Pākē* would spare them. But, her heart was so full of this sad, lovely man distributing himself across her—her womb so engorged with his thick, warm lager, brain so drugged with his odor of arabica, gardenia, and soil and rich leathers, and thick hair curled from ocean air and sun—there was nothing left with which to dream.

Time passed slowly in rich hours, like silk threads of a Persian carpet slowly rewoven to its original design. Pono forgot her life in upcountry cattle grazelands, forgot the red, pine fields of her youth. And she began to forget the family that had turned its back on her. She was re-creating herself, shedding one skin for another.

For a year, they seemed to float outside the world, privileged, inviolate, doomed. He ordered her dresses from Hong Kong and Paris. Sweeping formal gowns, capes with ostrich collars, cloaks with intricate silk embroidery. Matching shoes and purses of suede, gloves of many colored skins. They dressed for dinner, drank champagne, then wound up the turntable and danced for hours, pretending they were on an ocean liner while he described great ports of call.

Hugging balloons of brandy snifters, late into the night they pored over picture books, Duke explaining the Prado in Spain. The Louvre. Versailles. They followed Marco Polo on his silk route through Samarkand, and viewed brilliant tapestries of painted human skins hung in imperial summer palaces of Manchu emperors. He read her Shakespeare and Molière and though Pono did not always grasp what he read, she remembered his voice so solid and deep it made her ribs vibrate, like a man speaking out in a cathedral. She remembered his cuffs smelling of lavender and thyme, the sound of mandolins and 'ukulele from the fields, plaintive old Hawaiian songs, the bite of the brandy sharpening her teeth. These details were absorbed into her, so that years later, when she faltered, befouled and crucified by life, they flooded back, rich and nourishing as blood.

Sometimes Duke swept his hand hopelessly over bookshelves; there would not be time to read them all to her. He held precious records to his chest, so many concertos to play! With a sense of urgency, night after night, he tried to impart all he knew or suspected of the world, and in this way Pono became knowledgeable about many things. Years later people assumed she had traveled round the world, and knew all there was to know.

Now, when he wasn't beside her, when he was in the fields overseeing the planting, or harvesting, of trees, she felt in danger of disappearing. At such times, she felt her skin grow rough, her bones grow thirsty, tasted saltwater on her lips, and wanted blood.

He would come upon her, see her skin marbling into gray, and coax her back to human form. "Beloved, don't desert me. One day when I'm gone, you will own the land."

"Don't speak of it!" she screamed. "If *ma'i Pākē* comes, it will take both of us. It *must*."

Sometimes he watched her turn her head toward the ocean, sniffing like a dog at salt air blown in on the trades. "Do you miss your world of *manō*?"

"Without you," she answered softly, "it is the only way I could exist." But seeing how it distressed him, Pono vowed, "As long as you live, I reject that world. My jaw will not deform into a snout."

Not dreaming there would be years she longed for it. Nights when she stood miles from sea, yet her mouth filled with saltwater, her gills opened, she became all cartilage and appetite.

Sometimes they forgot the frailness of the veil with which they camouflaged their life, their refusal to acknowledge what was coming. New clothes arrived from Hong Kong, leather-bound volumes from London. Cantonese tailors arrived at the house. And barbers. Duke wouldn't go to town for haircuts, afraid evil *kāhuna* would use his haircuttings to work a curse on him, drive him from the island so his family sickness wouldn't spread.

Some days they drove down the South Kona Coast past ancient sacred sites, altars, and temples. "Each night ancestors walk this land. Can you feel it?" he asked. "The island has much *mana* because it is the birthplace of Kamehameha I. And because Pele lives here. That's why, I believe, you were called."

They gazed down at the huge caldera of volcanic Kīlauea Crater, a gray skillet of lava three miles wide. Raw, empty and burnt, yet simmering, never at rest. Distant steam plumes rose from vents, constant reminders of the magma bubbling below the earth, looking for its next outlet. The air itself had uncanny weight, Pono could feel it push against her chest.

"The hand of Pele," Duke said.

Pele, fiery Volcano Goddess. Her home was Halemaumau, fire pit of Kilauea's main crater. She sometimes appeared to locals in human form as a wrinkled crone, or a beautiful young girl.

"When I found you on the beach," Duke said, "I thought you were Pele. At first I was afraid."

Pele was quiet now, but the earth itself seemed to generate an electromagnetic field that made Pono's lungs shiver. She could feel something like breath, a coating on her skin. Crossing the bleak moonscape of Kaʻu Desert adjacent to Kīlauea, they saw nothing but rivers of hard black lava stretching to the sea. Strong taint of sulfur in the air, and wisps of steam rising from cracked earth, a reminder that the volcanoes were alive, that Pele was seething, gathering subterranean forces. Here and there, frozen in hard layers of ash, were ghostly footprints, and across the land were eerie stumps of lava-covered trees.

"Put your ear to the earth," Duke whispered.

At first there was nothing, then through the lava'ed earth, through ʻaʻā and pāhoehoe, she heard thunder, lightning, repeated roars, terrible moaning and screams. She sat back, frightened, as Duke explained.

"During a battle when Kamehameha I was struggling for supremacy of this island, his enemies tried to overtake him here. Pele favored Kamehameha. Causing craters to erupt, she poured molten lava down on his enemies, thousands of them." He pointed to the eerie stumps across Kaʻu Desert. "Instantly petrified, noses joined in the act of farewell."

One night Pono tossed and turned. The oppressive scent of flowers weighed on her, Arabian jasmine, tuberoses, frangipani. She sat up slowly, something pushing its face through the scent of the flowers, coming at her in sharp flashes. The house seemed lighter, as if freed of the weight of humans. In the morning Duke discovered two of the servants had deserted, and the gardener. They had seen the redness in his eyes, seen her tending a small lesion on his arm.

In the next two weeks, Pele shot flames like dragons from Kīlauea Crater. Across the island mongoose ran squealing from fields, clotting roads like rats in plague-time. But something else, more frightening than the roaring, belching earth, unsettled field-workers. They had seen the swelling in Duke's neck, seen him rub his arm repeatedly. He held a lit match to his skin, and did not flinch. More of his workers deserted. Then the household staff, the cook. Slowly, fright rinsed faces from the coffee leaves. Untended shutters banged on the *lānai*. One by one, Duke closed the doors, condensing their life to three rooms. Then, two. Pono cooked for him, serving dishes in slow cortege, her face feverish, flushed, as if put together by slaps.

A lesion appeared on his toe and wouldn't heal. In a month everyone had deserted his farm, except a stout old Chinese overseer, Tang Pin, raised by Duke's family. Duke offered him the chance to leave and he refused but, terrified, his wife began to lose her mind, whipping peacocks viciously so at night they sobbed.

Then Pono dreamed a dream so awful she turned her head away, but her eyes registered fast enough to see. She shook Duke awake, flew around in her sleeping sarong, a white flame licking through rooms. Then they were ghostly familiars on horseback, floating away from sobbing peacocks, from Duke's beloved land. At dawn bounty hunters appeared, following Duke's trail up the Kona Coast. He had been seen galloping through the forests of Kohala, toward the north, into mysterious Waipi'o Valley.

In the early hours of fleeing, Duke begged her to go back, she had no signs of *ma'i Pākē*. He tied her to her horses's saddle, slapped the brute's flanks and sent it galloping. She straggled in from the distance, following him on foot. He raged, ignored her, and rode on. Still, she followed, falling in tangled overgrowth so he had to cut her free with a machete.

Entering the jungles of Waipi'o, they entered ancient time. Dew evaporating on a leaf. A gecko blinking in sunlight. The languorous slide of sap. Then the whoosh of a hawk, claws curling round its squirming prey screaming like a human. They learned not to move in daylight; that was the time for vigilance. Clouds and night were the time for enterprise.

"We will live by ear and by nose," he said, "trusting to sound and smell. As so much of sight is tricked by the jungle."

One day from a cliff, they saw the bounty hunters far below, following their path. The urge not to run or scream, to just stand still, took up a whole day's courage for Pono. Sometimes, still as trees among rampant growth, they watched bounty men file past, rifles slung across their backs, ever vigilant for lepers for which they were paid ten dollars a body.

Sometimes the bounty men found rags, cooking utensils, bones, where fugitive lepers had died, dissolved into the soil. Objects remained, people disappeared. Living in caves down precipitous cliffs, sometimes brushing past each other in the bush, lepers were like a race apart, fleeing the hunters, the ships to Kalaupapa, fleeing cages and human experiments. Here, when one of them died, their soul departed peacefully. *Kōkua*, family members who fled with them to the jungle, refused them mirrors, pushed them away from their reflections in clear streams. But lepers knew, they saw their shadows in the sun, grotesque.

One night as they lay sleeping under a roof of *hau* trees, Duke's horse whinnied softly. Another answered close by. The sound of a rifle being cocked. He and Pono fled, leaving everything. Without cooking utensils, knives, they survived on what they scavenged from nature. Pink frenzy of worms like clusters of wet amethysts. Leaves like little chalices of sap. Giant moths that left dust on their lips and cheeks, their faces glowing eerily. Something a hawk had dropped in fierce, ecstatic flight.

They saw the jungle was not paradise, but a life-and-death terrain where every footstep had to be measured. The diving scream of a body falling from a cliff meant a wrong turn in darkness. The swallowed gasp of coming upon a cave of ancient charred human bones, grinning skulls calling up the void of another century. One day they squatted near a wild sow slung beneath with squealing nurslings. Pono darted out, plucked two piglets like clothespins from its teats. Barely scorching them, they ate them on the run, pocketing the bones for sucking when they began to starve.

Duke fashioned a knife from sharpened bamboo and taught her how to trap and kill wild boar, how to hang the body parts from trees and whistle, alerting other fugitives to where the meat was hung. They had nothing now but intuition, belief in their sense of hearing and smell, and an uncanny desire to survive.

On her own, Pono dug up medicinal roots of immortality, hung them over small fires. She sang old Hawaiian chants, funneling cures into Duke's ears while he slept, so he would wake healthy, grow vivid in his prime. Nothing worked, her *mana* could not overpower his sickness. With Duke, she could not cure. She prayed and began kneeling to pray, hoping she would thereby come to believe in God. When Duke showed signs of growing worse, Pono prayed *ma'i Pākē* would invade her, devour her nerves and organs. She began rubbing herself while he snored, scrubbing in the pus from his lesions, rubbing his suppurating arms across her breasts and cheeks.

After several weeks, they found a niche in a cliff covered over by guava scrub, just large enough for them to squat together. Some days they saw the glint of sun on rifles and belt buckles, bounty men still winnowing the jungle. Some days there was only the jungle, black lava beaches, the sea, miles below. On good days, Duke recalled his love of music, art, how he saw the jungle as a great outdoor Louvre, masterpiece creations that had not only withstood erosion and time, but had absorbed history, myth, heartbreak, and more beauty than the human mind could enfold.

Pono told him stories of her youth, Silvio and impotent Generalito, her childhood vision of the first ship going through the Panama Canal. Her mother sighting a silver plane through a window the moment before Pono was born, the first aerial takeoff from Hawai'i. She described how land below looked to the pilot, the formation of volcanic craters and scarred black monoliths nudged by the *haiku* of jade rice-terraces in mist, golden faces looking up through bamboo groves and feathered miles of cane. The pilot died never uttering another word, she said. From the air he had seen God's plan. He understood everything.

Some days they had nothing to tell. They sat silent, becoming each other's memory. Some nights her hand on him was the only thing moving, for now she took the initiative.

He wanted her, he always wanted her, but self-loathing slowed him. "I'm decaying, don't you see?"

"Can I not love *that* part of you, too?" she asked.

And when he was deep within her, she licked his eyes, sucked saliva from his mouth, loving him so completely she wanted to be joined in rot.

They saw no one for months, save the occasional leper sometimes so monstrously ulcerated they covered themselves head to toe in coconut fiber bags, words seeming to come from the eye slits. The ones who'd progressed beyond feeling lay still, tended lovingly by *kōkua*. Some nights there were shouts, gunshots, and Pono sat up, wondering, *Flee, or freeze?* Then a leper bleating, screams of his family pleading with bounty hunters. Torches locomoting down the cliffs, a moaning like a dirge.

One night, they heard a singsong whistle. Pono stood so still two mosquitoes mated on her neck. Recognizing the sound, Duke answered softly. Out of the mist stepped Tang Pin with clothing, dried meat, knives, matches, and fresh cloves believed to kill bacteria of *ma'i Pākē*. They embraced, and he melted back into the jungle. Pono brewed clove tea in a rusty mug and they joined their hands round it, lost in the miracle of Tang Pin's loyalty, in the miracle that they were still alive, together, at the same time on earth.

Some days Duke felt stronger and they splashed in waterfalls like young animals, Pono's laughter a delicate web surrounding him. Some nights, moonlight touched only their eyes and cheekbones, leaving them in rags of shadow, so it was hard to tell Duke's handsome face was coming apart. Seeing him in daylight, Pono understood they were running not just from bounty men but from the message carried in his flesh. Once, for the first time in weeks, she saw his uncovered legs and her lungs opened. She was face to face with the horror. It was cradled in her lap.

She would not give up, bathing him in streams when he was weak, rubbing his aching limbs with *kukui* oil and aloe. She disinfected his sores with sap of ti root and banana leaf, each sore a vacuum into which her will rushed like flames. She came to depend on the edge, the startled vigilance that kept her alert, even in her sleep. She felt time contract, if they could call it time. She felt its swift passage, and its non-passing, felt galloping terror and their unspoken love increasing the flow of meaning in each gesture, each look.

Duke began to understand the great moral beauty in her refusal to leave him, not just out of devotion, but out of her private perversity. She was a woman who would never do the easy thing, would always take the long way round. And he saw how, without these terrifying months of flight, certain emotions might have remained forever inaccessible to her—compassion, grave generosity, the will to believe. She was only seventeen, drinking in more than she knew. Some days Pono was frantic, talkative, all stark energy with the center drained. Running barefoot along jagged edges, beautiful and starved-looking, she grew angry, moving fastest when he moved least, coaxing him, bullying him. Other nights, she was eerily quiet, and he knew she had dreamed.

Some nights he thought of suicide. *There is a point where one can quit with honor. I have a right to dispose of this body as I choose.* But he knew she would follow him, his decision to die would kill her.

The sickness sharpened his intuition, equipped him with the knowledge to know when Pono was desperate, when he needed to lie. "There are cures. I will heal. We will marry." And when she needed the punishment of truth. "There is no cure. You must be free to marry and have healthy children." His great brown eyes surrounding her like water. Her stillness like a death. They began to speak a half-language, verbal needs reduced, as Duke's body became his preoccupation. Patches running to mold, ears bloated, extended like vegetables, his face thickening like elephant skin. Nerve ends dead, he probed decay, occasioning a moist, flesh avalanche. A sore now ran from his eye to his jaw, theatrical and vivid.

Seasons passed, time of volcanoes, typhoons, months of battering rains. Then, heat, incessant. Then moody trades. They had run for nearly a year. In Kona, orchards of white gardenia-like coffee blossoms would have blown off in an autumn sneeze of rain. Who was harvesting the wet ruby cherries? Unpulping the green jade of raw beans? Pono saw Duke's house in a dream and when she described abandoned, overgrown fields, and faceless coffee leaves, only Tang Pin sweeping the dung of peacocks from old Persian rugs, Duke hung his head and wept.

She woke without waking. The gun snout a cold, hard reptile striking her chest. Duke was already handcuffed, gagged, thrown into a large poke like a pig, so they wouldn't have to touch him. Naked, under lantern light she was probed, nudged with the soles of their boots while they scanned her body for sores. And the moaning that went down the mountain, hidden lepers weeping in trees, the jungle diminished for what was now taken from it.

After he had fled his farm, already deserted by his workers, people began to see how morals were lowered in the fields and coffee towns of Kona district. Standards of pride disappeared, of hard, honest labor, gallantry toward the land. Hawaiians remembered their troubles, felt they were no longer a great nation, only a bygone people. And they saw how they had betrayed Duke Kealoha and his family's memory.

Brought shackled out of the jungle, Pono heard the moaning spread across the land, she heard the whispering. In his year of outrunning bounty hunters, of outsmarting them, Duke had come to symbolize his people's heritage; he became the embodiment of ancestor-warriors, men and women who had fought to the death for their freedom and their lands.

Days later, when he was caged on the funeral ship for Kalaupapa, "Place of the Living Dead," people crowded the docks, calling out his name. As the ship moved into open waters, across the island natives went down on their knees and wailed. He was gone, a lion had got up and left the land.

Ka Mea Hana Make

Thing of Destruction

IMAGES GHOST IN, like reptiles coming to back to life with second skins. *Pono squatting wild-eyed, groaning until, with magisterial grunt, she births. A wailing, ugly surge, seeming to sink under the weight of its own head. She contemplates it, its screaming vulgar. She gives it a healthy swat.*

For days she sleeps with her eyes open, feeling the slow cortege between her legs, jellied knots of afterbirth. She mourns Duke in paralyzing stupor, refusing to accept that he is gone, and this squalling thing is permanent. She doesn't move, doesn't eat, hoping her teats will dry, and starve the thing, that she will exhaust it, it will come to the end of its curve.

It screams, continues screaming, until something in her genes screams back. She begins to experience vague esteem for this inchoate thing struggling inexplicably to express itself through language. Very gradually, she sees that the father inhabits this child in its gestures, its intelligent gaze.

Finally, in water-haunted sunlight, she stands, washes herself of earth, blood, umbilical waste, washing months of flight from the soles of her feet. Packing herself with moss, spider webs, kukui oil and shaved root of uhaloa, she struggles through bush and field back to the plantation, pointing the infant at the house, feeling it shiver, perhaps a rich centripetal eddy of recognition within.

She imagines faces shining in the coffee trees again, brown bodies bending in the fields, Tang Pin overseeing them. Approaching, she sees the jungle canopy of neglected, overgrown trees, workers' shacks deserted. A fading yellow sign blocks the driveway.

QUARANTINE NOTICE . . . THIS HOUSE HAS A COMMUNICABLE
DISEASE, LEPROSY, AND IS SUBJECT TO FUMIGATION

Shutters bang, droppings from wild peacocks litter the lānai. Then a figure on the lawn. Tang Pin and his half-mad wife and their young son are living in one of the shacks.

He hugs Pono and her infant. "You come live wit' us. We wait for Duke come home."

He takes her and the infant in, but his wife runs screaming from their shack. A small crowd surges up the road behind her, cursing Pono. "Filth! Filth! You put da curse on Duke. Kahuna!" Pitching rocks at her and her tainted child, they drive her from Captain Cook town. Tang Pin presses money and her old leather pouch upon her. She runs. For weeks she runs, foraging, begging, moving farther across the island.

Each night lying in fields, she inspects the infant, searching its skin for telltale signs, small suppurations. Her face grows gaunt as a gypsy's, her body becomes severe, bony, built for speed. Only her breasts stay full, the big-eyed infant sucking fast, alert to what this body will give, what hold back. She is named Holo, to run, for her life has begun in flight. She will grow into a quiet child, an air of absent-mindedness, of degenerate innocence. She will witness slaughter.

In slow progress, Pono traveled southeast, then north, coming to rest on the Hamakua Coast far from anything she knew. She found work on a sugar plantation as scrub maid for the Portuguese *luna* and his frail, childless wife. Pono was housed in a shack of rotting wood alive with centipedes and roaches, the planks so wide her child was bathed in subdued, vermilion shafts of dusk. At night Pono could see the stars, whole constellations, while cane dust blown in by the trades settled on her lips. A basin, a cot, a door loose on its hinges. In sleep, she encircled the child, circling memories engraved on her bones. She gnawed them, buried, unearthed them, gnawed again.

Bounty hunters dragging them handcuffed to a boat, the boat transporting them to Honolulu, Kalihi Receiving Station, where lepers were isolated, probed, diagnosed. Doctors staring at Duke's nakedness, his lesions vivid and alive. Experts discussing how beautiful the disease was under microscope—red bacteria invading blue nerve tissue.

And in another room, Pono stripped, spun slowly on a revolving platform.

Confusion in the eyes of doctors when they cannot find a sore. She had lived with the leper a year, they had been lovers. Pono imprisoned in the women's isolation ward, waiting for lesions to appear. One day she and Duke face each other ten feet apart, wire mesh and guards between them.

"Beloved, I go tomorrow," he said. "I will die there, with the bones of my family at Kalaupapa."

Her screams.

And tearing all night at a window screen, wedging her body out. Climbing a barbed-wire fence at dawn. And running down the docks toward braying lepers in cages on a barge. And Duke caged alone because of his massive size and strength. Guards pointing at the cages. "Apes in a zoo."

Her screams.

Trying to fling herself down the gangplank, onto the barge. Seeing her struggling dockside, Duke's lips forming her name as strong arms detained her. And then she saw the kneeling crowds, heard them wail his name. And she knelt, too, suddenly gasping, something quickening inside her. If he was gone, then she would run, live like an animal. They would not take from her his seed.

Backing up slowly on her knees, Pono melted into crowds, into fields, as Duke's ship winked on the horizon. And she ran, tiptoed along the edges of humanity, hellish months of hiding, scavenging alone, then stowing away on a boat back to the Big Island, back to jungles she understood. Growing big, clumsy, slow, eating only wild mango and banana as her stomach stretched into a brown transparency.

Some nights now, swaddling the child in the tiny shack on the Hamakua Coast, she heard the sweet, soft sounds of 'ukulele, mandolin, workers in their boxlike wooden shacks, singing old Hawaiian songs. She thought of Duke and the jungle, months of extreme terror, and laughter, exhilaration, remembering him in detail, every gesture, every word, remembering as if she were dying. And she was struck with astonishment that that had been their happiest time.

Sometimes, hearing laughter in the dusk, sounds of people of shared blood, sharing meals, she thought of red pine fields of her youth, her mother's laughter. At Kalihi Receiving Station, she had given her family name, Meahuna. Searching for her, by now police would have found her family outside Honolulu. Hearing Pono was tainted with *ma'i Pākē*, they would have erased from their genealogy the name of this girl they had long ago abandoned. Some nights she thought of strangling her child, of flinging herself into the sea, back into the world of *manō*. Then, she thought of the man she loved, whose nerve ends were dying, who was slowly losing touch with objects, with his own skin. If death would spare him, she would be his nerve ends; she would be his skin.

These were her vows at eighteen: *Dare everything. Find him.*

She labored in the *luna*'s house, laundering, scrubbing floors, scrubbing footprints of a man whose glances pawed her hips. His name was Calcados, his pale Portuguese face boyish, teeth bucked, beavery like a child's. But his body was big and muscled, his movements like rage unraveling as he cracked a snakeskin whip that seemed to grow out of his fist. The first time he saw Pono he stood very still.

Because she was aloof and strange, house servants treated her as strange, and because she kept her mind invisible the *luna*'s wife said she was cold. Yet, in the "dirty kitchen," where *pau hana* field hands ate, Pono sat comfortable midst smells of Chinese parsley, grease and ginger, eating riceballs, bowls of eel and cuttlefish with her fingers. On cool winter nights, while the wood stove glowed, she began to prescribe for workers, talking in heavy Pidgin.

Rolling cure-leaves into powder, she gave them *a'ali'i* tea for sleep, *'awa* tea for heartache, strong green China tea for health. And spoonfuls of nutmeg that kept them high and numb during killing hours in the fields. And, slowly, she began to dream for them, foreseeing futures. They saw she was *kahuna*, and whispered of blue spirits whisking round her shack at night, of seeing Pono float above the cane. Her child, Holo, was possessed, they said, and sometimes ran the fields transformed into a mongoose, a strawberry rat.

She soothed them with old Hawaiian legends, melting myths into their rum, into their little balls of Dragon Seed.

"Soah my body," they complained. "*Pau* good health. Lungs red dust, gone *pilau!*"

For they were pushed brutally all day, swinging razor-sharp machetes, sometimes taking a finger, part of a leg. In cane up to twelve feet tall, it was just workers and knives, no machines to cut or gather. Women did the weeding, planting, men the burning, slashing. And they began at dawn, scorched, half-blinded by the sun at noon, a thirty-minute break to squat, brood over rice-bun lunches, then slashing, burning, gathering again, on into dusk, into past-pain time when they were rendered senseless. They wore masks like bandits against red dirt that clogged the nose, and cane dust that scarred the lungs. They wore hats, gloves, boots, woven-fiber leg armor, even goggles. Still they died: exhaustion, infection, dehydration, sometimes so blistered and bubbled and crippled, they plunged over cliffs welcoming jagged rocks below.

The *luna* pushed them, pressured by the manager, the manager in turn pressured by plantation owners, rich, missionary descendants. After twelve and fifteen hours of scorching stoop work, paid only forty cents a day, workers would return to shacks housing eight to twenty people, bachelors squeezed thirty to forty in a bunkhouse. No indoor toilets, no running water, no sick leave, or rest, they were reservoirs of slaves.

Pono remembered the story her mother had told of her father, murdered while fighting for workers' rights early in the century. In twenty-five years, what progress had been made? Sometimes at night she heard exhausted husbands and wives holding each other, unable to cry, unable to stop. When workers banded, asking for medical care, toilets, decent food, foremen beat them, fired them, had them arrested on trumped-up charges.

Chinese had left plantations as soon as their contracts expired, opening small businesses in the towns. Most plantation workers were now Japanese, Filipino, Koreans, Puerto Ricans, with a growing reputation as trouble-makers, strikers. In 1924, three thousand Filipinos on Kaua'i had marched in a strike; sixteen were shot dead with machine guns by the National Guard. Now, on every island, plantation workers were organizing. There were rumblings along the Hamakua Coast, strikers dragged from their beds and shot.

One day a car drove up the road, a sheriff stepped out, and two Japanese workers were handcuffed and taken away as agitators, arrested on charges of holding up a store. The *luna*, Calcados, called workers from their shacks, a crowd of several hundred. Standing over them, he caressed his rolled-up snake whip, his voice loud, but not unkind.

"I don't make the rules. They're handed down to me." He raised the whip. "You never seen this used on humans, eh? Only on stubborn mules."

Reluctantly, they nodded, remembering mules pissing in terror at the sight of the whip. A Filipino stepped forward, asked why Calcados wouldn't pass lists of their demands on to his superiors.

"You'll lose your jobs, is why. They'll trump up crimes, imprison or shoot you. Your children will starve."

Weeks later, another car pulled up. From the kitchen, Pono saw two big Hawaiians emerge wearing holstered guns. *Who would they arrest today?* she wondered. *Who has been agitating?* Then one of them pronounced a word that dropped her to her knees. She felt her insides glow. *Ma'i Pākē.* They roamed up and down the rows of shacks, dragging people out at random. A schoolteacher had reported a suspicious-looking child. Mothers screamed, hiding their children under beds, but two boys were found with red spots on their legs. Their families were handcuffed, forced out to the car.

Seeing Pono in the distance, one of the bounty hunters approached slowly, studying her arms and neck. Her dark, golden skin was smooth, no swelling, or lesions. She was tall as a man, so beautiful and brimming with health, the bounty hunter dropped his eyes.

"How long you worked here?"

Pono flung her head back, her tongue went hard. She stood arrogant and dumb.

Calcados approached. "What you want with her?"

"Look like someone on our list," the bounty man said. "Runaway from Kalihi Receiving Hospital. Oh, 'bout one year ago. Big *wahine*. Lived with one rich leper, Duke Kealoha, from over Kona side."

Calcados studied her, faced the bounty man and lied. "She's been with us a couple years. Husband works down Hilo way. This ain't the one you want."

That night she sat in darkness, wondering *Why? What is his motive? Where is the trap?* Now she was rigidly alert, eeling away from Calcados's gaze. At dusk, when workers straggled in from the fields, she could lift his smell from other men. Sometimes he came and stood close enough for her to see on his massive arms, thick hair curly with sweat.

They would have their history, she knew it, and prepared herself, little tributaries of hate filling the basin of her brain. One night she dreamed of him, his massive arms encircling, obliterating her. She sat up instantly awake, saw him through her rotten walls, moonlight on his jaw. Dreamily, he leaned against her shack, looking at the sky. He lit his pipe and sighed. She understood then that he wouldn't come by force, he wanted her to want him.

Desperation was raw material for drastic change. Pono whacked off her dark, cascading hair, sheared it so close to the scalp, she was bald in patches. She let the child be sick on her and didn't wash, wore greasy worker's pants, bound her large breasts so they went flat. Still, he came at night, leaned against her shack, and waited.

Then Pono did a desperate thing. She slept in excrement. Field-workers thought she'd lost her mind. The cook cursed her, made her bathe in harsh soap each day before entering the big house. Yet every night before she slept, Pono caked her feet in manure from livestock, surrounding her shack with sewage smells, keeping him away. Calcados watched, half amused, and bided his time.

When Holo was two, the *luna*'s wife delivered their second stillborn. Calcados stood at the tiny graves, puffing his pipe. A week later he marched two field hands into the bush at gunpoint, marched them until the ground beneath them gurgled. *One mimiki*, quicksand. They had slain one of his horses, sold the flesh for food. They seemed to last all night, sucked slowly down, the darkness swallowed by their screams. Near dawn, Calcados aimed his rifle at a solitary arm still protruding from the sand, knocking off the fingers one by one. In grief, their families beat their heads against the ground.

One day, returning from the beach with Holo, Pono saw her shack on fire and ran inside, grabbing up her meager things. People gathered, watching as the thing burned to the ground.

"Moah bettah," someone said. "Place smell terrible, like sheet!"

He moved her to a better shack, a real bed not a cot, a bed for little Holo, walls through which cane dust didn't penetrate. He forbade her shears, so that her hair began to grow. People watched. The whole plantation seemed to hold its breath. One night Pono took her child and started running. Calcados caught up with her on horseback, lassoing her like a steer.

Dismounting, he approached, speaking softly. "If you leave again, I'll give you to the bounty hunters. I'll take your daughter, give her to my childless wife."

Terrified, she sat on beaches, calling out Duke's name. *Two years . . . Beloved, are you still alive?* No word from him. No way to get word to him. Each night she still examined herself and Holo for red spots, sly white patches of *ma'i Pākē*. They were cursed with perfect health.

On her twentieth birthday, Pono repeated her vow: *Dare everything. Find him.* But how? She did not have the clues.

Cane-burning season began, the air filled with black smoke, sky blistered a vicious red as fires burned off leaves of ripe sugarcane, leaving sappy stalks ready for harvesting. Day and night, silhouettes of workers masked like bandits moved through fields, black figures chasing torches. They staggered back to camp in relays—smoky, singed couples sticking together like taffy. They fell asleep parched with the heavy smell of braised sugar and burnt human hair. From the big house, Calcados's wife watched them at all hours, a woman left alone.

One night Pono was awakened by hot, caramel wind. Her door was open, his shoulders lit by fires in the field behind him. She stared, tense spasm of concentration. *Is this a dream?* Then he moved toward her in sordid actuality, smell of smoke and human sweat, of scorched fingernails.

His shirt was tattered from burning cane, he pulled it off in rags. She sat up slowly, feeling her mouth lichen over, her tongue go slick with fur.

"Now," he said. A single word, a shot bolt.

"*Never!*" she cried.

He didn't know she would be so strong. She was on him like a glare, punching, smothering, her loamy, sweet smell instantly metallic. He fell back, fighting for balance and, naked, she grabbed the sleeping child and ran. His hand reached out, grabbing her hair so she surged backwards like a tethered horse. They seemed to go down in slow motion, the sleeping child between them. She flung Holo back into her bed while his arm encircled Pono's neck, and silently they struggled, dancers searching for a theme. Calcados tightened his grip, his muscles closing down her windpipe, but somehow she turned, teeth glistening with venom, in her eyes intent to mutilate. And in that look he understood what they were struggling for had little to do with passion. Now, he was fighting for his life. She brought up her knee between his legs; he folded in a vision of bright, liturgical colors.

Pono rolled into a corner, came up squatting, a knife glittering in her hand. He staggered to his feet, shook his head, pulled off his belt rattling through its loops. If he could not have her, he'd whip her to death. Still they were silent, grappling in grunts while the bed was thrown, the tub knocked on its side. And he came at her, belt buckle crackling against her hip, the impact echoing in her brain. She leapt, took part of his earlobe with the knife, then scored him deeply in the neck.

As in a dream, the child heard the belt whistling through the air and sang out softly in her sleep. The buckle biting again and again into her mother's flesh, the mother shuddering to her knees. Pono went down with nothing left. His raucous panting then, his lips sucking her whorled crenellations of nipples. His face in her hair, asking unspeakable things, that she fuck him. That she love him. Even at the edge of consciousness, her fists still pounded, legs flailed the air, her brain so full of hate, at first she did not understand he was in her, she was full of him. Even then, she struggled, trying to kill him, her movements engorging him, driving him deeper. Her sounds became bleak, sacrificial.

She never screamed, even as his weight ground her against the wooden floor. His mouth on her so she couldn't breathe. His pale, hairy body surrounding her, her coffin. Outside, fiery cane fields kept bursting, and she did not hear. Shadows of flames played on her walls, she did not see. He plunged so deep, so hard, she felt something crack. Something within broke down, forever.

His ear was running blood, dripping on her breasts, his neck open, one eye swelling shut. His hair was singed and standing out. And he was inexhaustible. He took her buttocks in his hands, lifting her whole pelvis so she was forced to watch his pace. Wind shifted, and in the fields, black figures moved with pitchforks. The fires leaned, sparks danced on her roof, ran down her mouth and turned her tongue to dust.

Let me. O, let me die.

Beginning to shudder violently, Calcados grabbed her arms, wrapping them round his neck. Then he seemed to hunker down, teeth bared, breathing so hard she thought, *Yes, he will kill me. He will consume my flesh.* His body snapped, eyes blank, searching hers in wonder, and when he came, he dropped his head between her breasts and wept. Hours passed, time the only witness to him taking her again, turning her like something on a spit. Crying low and deep inside, Pono felt life running from her eyes.

She woke at dawn, splinters imbedded in her shoulders and buttocks. She was filthy with soot and crusted blood. She turned, crying out for her child. Holo was sitting in a shaft of sunlight, turning her head this way and that, grinning with wonder. Everything was somewhere else! The room seemed upside down. Pono lifted the child, and crept outside, the sun so warm she thought maybe she would live.

In the big house, the cook silently took the child. All night the camp had heard them. The camp had wept for her. Now, they saw Calcados walking with a limp. They saw his bandaged ear.

The cook leaned close and whispered, "You one good fightah, Pono!"

She bathed her wounds, wrapped strips of rags round her broken ribs. She drank 'awa tea for curing grief, ate nutmeg for pain-killing, chewed eggshell for strength. Then carefully, she knelt, trying to scrub the floors, her hands unable to grip the brush. The buckle-memory on her hip had bloomed into an eggplant, so large it interfered with walking. The burning deep between her legs made it horrible to sit. Workers came and stared because her head would not stop shaking. It shook for days, and when it stopped, Calcados was there, warping her view. He was everywhere, waiting, biding his lust. If she fled, he would run her down, take her child. If she stayed, she would die.

She roamed the beaches, rocking in the surf. *Beloved. Tell me what to do.* The worst part was not knowing if Duke was alive. If he was dead she would join him in a minute. And take Holo, too.

She began to dream. Tires spinning, a laughing woman in a speeding car. Holo staring at a damaged doll. Calcados inside her again, his big, slovenly member battering. Then, Calcados sinking deep in muck until there was just his eyes. Pono woke in a sweat. And every day he watched her, his distance narrowing, the memory of her firing him anew.

One day the railroad cars appeared, transporting sugarcane to shipping ports. And hidden on the trains were infiltrators, outside organizers, unionizers.

Workers sat in their shacks, debating. "Who care what dese organizers called? 'Communists'? So what? Dey fight foah us, bettah wages foah us. Dey de only ones who care 'bout us."

One night a *haole* sat among them, a union organizer smuggled in from California. Pono watched him from the shadows.

"Those two 'horse-thieves' Calcados killed were framed," he whispered. "They were strikers working for us. The ILWU."

"What dat?"

"International Longshoremen's and Warehousemen's Union. We've changed the face of labor on the mainland."

". . . bunch of *haole!*"

"So what!" the man argued. "Who cares what's the color of our skin. We've come to help you organize on every island in Hawai'i. Are you men? Or slaves?"

Something went through Pono. She listened closely, weighing every word. Late at night, when people came to ask her should they trust this man, should they strike with him, she was silent, meditative.

The next time he was smuggled in, bringing pamphlets on human rights, higher wages, better working conditions, Pono walked right up to him. "I am . . . *kahuna*. Workers ask me for advice. They are confused about you."

He sat with her by candlelight, explaining what was happening on the mainland, the thirties' Depression had begun. He explained what a labor union was, the purpose of organizing mass strikes.

"I guarantee it, a massive walkout here in the islands would net pay raises of at least fifteen percent. Of course, there will be violence, and deaths . . ."

She asked the question carefully. "You have union men on *every* island? Even . . . Moloka'i?"

"Of course! Huge plantations there, terrible conditions."

She blew the candle out, talking in the dark. "I will help you organize, if you will do one thing." She spoke so softly now, her voice took on a dreamlike quality even though she spoke of horror. Kalaupapa, the leper settlement. Duke Kealoha.

"Find out if he is dead," she said. "Or living."

"Who is this leper?" the *haole* asked. "What is he to you?"

". . . My life. The father of my child."

When she lit the candle he was gone.

For two years she had lived in fear, now she lived in hope. It turned her brazen. She demanded more milk for Holo, demanded her wages on time. Yet, when Calcados came at night, bringing his demands, she fought his body less. She was preoccupied. Shaking his saliva from her brow, feeling him come inside her, groaning like a beast, she turned her head aside and wondered, *Who in camp is trustworthy? Who will help me organize?*

She held meetings late at night, robbing workers of their sleep. "Why be *hōhē*? What you got to lose? Want stay shit poor? Yoah *kamali'i* end up slaves like you, no education?"

Workers rallied, willing to gamble lives to unionize. They hand-printed pamphlets in Pidgin while the *luna* slept:

PAU "COOLIE" KINE, NOW UNION KINE. TRY COME MEETINGS

They used their kids as runners, spreading the word from camp to camp, up and down the Hamakua Coast.

Calcados's wife began calling to workers from the porch. "Don't be slaves! Soldier on! Be brave."

He locked her in her room, and there was only sobbing. One day she slipped through a window, stood in the driveway, and smoothed her hair. Dressed in hat and gloves, she slid inside their rusty Ford and, smiling, accelerated down the road. Later, Pono saw men running in the fields, pointing backwards toward the cliffs. There were no signs of brakes applied before the car went over. Workers said she even waved.

Suddenly, armed guards were posted at the camp fence gates. Pono saw their fires at night, saw moonlight refracted on their rifles. Who were they keeping out? Or in? She dreamed again, Calcados drooling over her, then his body sinking deep in muck. Holo staring at a broken doll. Pono sat up shaking, remembering fragments of an early dream. Tires had spun, Calcados's wife had died laughing in her car. Pono waited. What would happen waited with her.

One night the sounds of gunshots, someone banging on her door. "Pono! Dey shoot him! Dat *haole* guy ... You got pamphlets, bettah burn dem quick! Dambastards ... !"

And she ran, ran down the muddy, red dirt road, skidding on her backside. A crowd encircled the *haole* unionizer, guards cursing over him. His body was stubborn, he snapped and flinched taking a long time to die. Pono stared and stared, and then the cook was whispering beside her.

"He lookin' foah you, Pono. Dey shoot him. I come runnin' find him wrigglin' in da grass. He say yoah name, push a paper at me. *BAM!* Dey shoot him again ..."

Pono turned, her eyes deadly. She pulled the cook into the shadows, dragged her to her shack. Inside, Pono lit a candle, watching as the cook pulled from her dress a rumpled sheet of paper smeared with mud. Silently, ceremoniously, they sat. Pono leaned forward, a woman ready for the worst.

"*Read!*" she whispered.

Laboriously, the woman stuttered out the words:

BELOVED PONO ...

   I AM BECOME A HORROR. NOT FIT TO LOOK UPON. I ASK YOU TO
FORGET ME. GO OUT INTO THE WORLD AND *LIVE*. WHATEVER HUMAN
THING IS LEFT OF ME GOES WITH YOU ...

That night she sat quiet for hours, caressing the edges of the page as one would stroke a profile. Then, facing in the direction of Moloka'i, she took a bamboo chopstick, working silently, sharpening the tip.

"Now," she whispered. "Now I will ... *dare everything*."

One night she left Holo with neighbors. "I don't come for her at midnight, you try come my place and help. Might be plenty trouble."

That night when Calcados climbed on top of her, she wrapped her arms round him, feigning affection. When he was deep inside her, crooning all those obscene things, how he loved her, loved fucking her, would never let her go, she drove the bamboo chopstick in with all her might, left of the midline, between the ribs. He sighed, a long, underwater sigh, and slumped. Neighbors came running at midnight, and by then her body had turned a glistening red. Grunting, peeling him off of her, pulling him out of her, people shuddered, people prayed, each in his own language, to his own god. While men rolled him in a burlap sack, women stood her outside in the rain, letting him run off of her.

"What we do now, Pono?"

"Drag."

They dragged for hours, cut the fence in darkness and dragged him far into the bush, through tangled jungle vines and singing bamboo groves, past mountain creeks and swamps, and finally, into *one mimiki*. They pushed him in feet-first, but just before the muck sucked up his back, she made them pull him out again. Groaning, tugging, they laid him in the dirt face-down.

"What for, Pono! What you lookin' for?"

Her juices. Her rhythms. Her honor. Lodged somewhere in the grottoes and arches of his spine. Silently, in torchlight, she guided the knife, traced a flashing crimson line along his back. They knelt beside her following the stripe, digging deeper down where disks of cartilage and ligament took hold. Blood surged, muscle and jelly burying their fingers and wrists and forearms as they worked, separating, defining. The crack of ribs splintering from vertebrae, of vertebrae from skull, his long, gray worm of spinal cord—impulses, reflexes, memories—flung out into the dark like bait. What was left simmered in its curdled stench. They flung the wreckage of his body into the muck. Then they flung the head. It spun high into the air, its own bright hairy planet. Earth bubbled up and sucked it down. Pono studied his spinal column held in her two hands. She stood different now, redeemed.

Two days later, a big Packard rolled up the drive. The white plantation owner walked his land. Then he assembled the entire camp, a crowd of several hundred.

"Calcados is missing. If he's been murdered, we will find his body. You will suffer. Men will hang."

The new *luna*, a brutish-looking Scot, assigned the camp to overtime, killing hours without food or pay. Anyone caught organizing strikes would be shot instantly. Pono measured time, watching the tides, waiting for a full-moon night in which to run. But something overtook her, paralyzed her. She stopped talking, the whites of her eyes turned rusty.

The cook noticed first, flotsam of another race filling Pono's belly. "Mother God, Calcados plant his seed in you! What you gonna do?"

"Be still," Pono said. That womb-wrapt thing within her would unravel, she would snip the yarn.

But nothing helped. Not crushed roots of poison fern, not drafts of caustic soap. Not prayers, nor Buddhist neighbors chanting. Again, her *mana* failed her. The new *luna* ignored her growing belly, another *wahine* carrying a bastard. As long as she worked, he let her be.

With the intuition of a child born frightened, Holo knew. Knew something. One day she raced toward her mother who was staring at the sea as if listening for instructions. The child ran on tiptoe, hot sand burning her small tough soles. And then she stopped. In the distance her mother pummeling, pummeling her big belly with her fists. Holo backed away, sat down in shade and curled into a ball, trying to become invisible.

One day Pono stopped scrubbing floors. She stood slowly, knowing it was time. Leaving Holo with the cook, she walked unsteadily to her shack, measuring her steps. Night air clean, moon and stars in lucid confederation, she smelled sharp smells from the jungle—foliage, humus, dung—the yeastiness of earth.

Then dread trickled down her brow. The coming pain. She crawled into her shack, ripped a sheet into strips, stuffed a strip into her mouth. And screamed. Screamed as if she were singing, high notes hitting walls and bouncing back. And no one heard. She screamed with all the voice she had within her, screamed from fear, hurt, degradation. She screamed for the indignities, the years she died innumerably. She screamed for her grandmother, Emma, dead of plague, her grandfather, murdered in cold blood. She screamed for strikers murdered in their sleep, and women forced to lie with syphilitic strangers. She screamed for love, for Duke bound in a cage. And terror, birthing all alone in jungles. She screamed, mourning slaughtered innocence, the part of her forever dead.

She flung herself against the walls and ricocheted, a large, mad monkey tired of its cage. She screamed, and no one heard. Her teeth tore the sheet to shreds. She jammed another strip into her mouth. And screamed. And then her shadow was a looming on the walls. A rocking, awful grandness, until the thing fell out. One bleat. An infant bleat. And then a smaller strip of sheet into its tiny mouth, round its tiny neck.

Frightened, longing for her mother, Holo had slipped from the cook's shack, and run outside in moonlight, running home to that which was familiar. She squeezed the door open and looked. And saw. A doll. An artifact. Blood-spangled white, and dangling from her mother's fist. Pono shook it, making sure. Shook and shook.

This would be Holo's memory for all her days. Her mother chanting softly, binding Holo in rags across her back. And something else. A little mummy wrapped and hanging from her mother's waist. And running. Down cliffs, the steep and humpbacked cliffs. And then her mother pausing, chanting still, the mummy flung out high above the sea, its cloth slowly unwinding. A broken doll cartwheeling into waves.

Then Holo and her mother running, burrowing into the jungle. And blood, her mother stuffing spider webs and moss between her legs. And sleeping, sleeping it seemed for weeks. Hidden deep in giant ferns and soft humid moss. Her mother's body surrounding her. Protecting her. Warmth, and mothermilk weeping into Holo's hair. Her mother O so tenderly! giving her her breast. This would be Holo's memory. Terror. And motherlove. And running.

Ka Liona Lohi

Slow Lion

THIS PENINSULA. Most beautiful, most desolate part of all the Hawaiian Islands, jutting northward from the coast of Moloka'i. And, on these grassy slopes shielded east and west by jungled cliffs, Kalaupapa, "Place of the Living Dead." Since lepers were first banished here in the 1860s, progress had been made. Doctors who probed patients from afar with twelve-foot poles had been replaced by humane physicians and nurses, risking the disease. And missionary Brothers of the Sacred Heart. After years of drunkenness and debauchery among the lawless dying and "the damned," a church had been established for those who still believed in God.

By now, a real hospital had been constructed for the extremely ill, the elderly and blind, another for patients in the early stages of leprosy, and even a small research station. Bishop Home was built for afflicted young girls and women, and Baldwin Home for boys. Marriage was permitted among lepers, and whole families of the afflicted, arriving one at a time on "shipment day," were allowed to live together in tiny cottages. Supply vessels docked at the pier not far from the hospital and sometimes brave visitors even came ashore. In the "caller house," a chain link fence and wide planked tables separated patients from non-patients. Blood relatives were forbidden ever to touch. Still, there were lū'au, parades, horse races, dancing and singing in the old Hawaiian way. One big 'ohana, people said. And no one stared. Except for hideous

disfigurement, rotting flesh, the loss of sensation, of limbs, of sight—
and stigma, and death—it was a good life.

Those who were still ambulatory and hearty engaged in sports,
fished, hiked up to Kauhako Crater and stood on soaring cliffs, watching
the sea below wear down the rocks. They splashed under waterfalls
ribboning down several thousand feet, and swam out to little islets
clustered offshore like gamboling whales. They hiked the valleys where
graves of nameless lepers blurred to soft green fields. And in the glow
of dusk they spat up in the wooden church of St. Philomena with its
expectoration holes between each pew, sometimes seeing through the
holes winking eyes, spirits of the dead awaiting them.

For a year Duke had stared across the sea at night lights of Honolulu,
imagining her there. Imagining her beauty maturing in someone else's
eyes. Then one day news reached him from Tang Pin on the Big Island.
Workers had deserted, everything overgrown or dead, the plantation
posted as a leper house. But then the other news, Pono and a child.
Duke prayed it wasn't his, knowing it was. *Innocent, already damned. Ma'i
Pākē in its genes.* He tortured himself, wondering what his daughter looked
like. *And does she have Pono's black eyes, my mother's delicate piano fingers? Will
she walk in her sleep and love animals, like father?* He tried to imagine the
smell of her, the feel of her little head resting in his hand, the shock of
her laughter echoing notes and textures and colors. The actuality of her
hitting him like shrapnel.

Another year passed. Duke pondered himself in mirrors, waiting for
his features to take on the look of extinct beasts, shaggy mammoth,
prehistoric cave-ape. Friends he came to love expired, fingerless, footless,
faces like giant warts with eyes, some used as human guinea pigs: horse
toxin, "nose tripping." Suicide. Still hopeful of a cure, he gallantly
endured drugs, medical experiments. His lesions spread, one hand turned
twisted like a crab. He let them try anything: *Chaulmoogra* oil, which
almost killed him. Horse toxin injections, which blew his body wide
open, burning him with fever, so he temporarily lost his sight. Staggering
back to consciousness and half-health from each experiment, he began
to take an almost academic interest in the history and treatment of what
was killing him.

When, in 1865, King Kamehameha V ordered all lepers confined to
the most desolate part of his realm, the royal government had provided
no doctors, no hospital, no housing, only food supplies pushed off the
ships behind them. Lepers had lived in improvised grass huts, an outcast
society, so exposed to the elements many died of tuberculosis before

leprosy consumed them. Fresh water was so scarce, sometimes they died of thirst crawling toward the sound of waterfalls.

In 1873, a Belgian priest, Father Damien arrived at Kalaupapa, dedicating his life to the afflicted until he died in 1889, a leper. He inspired colonists to build better houses and a primitive hospital on the sheltered side of the peninsula and to install water lines. The bacillus, *mycobacterium leprae*, discovered in 1874 by Armauer Hansen, a Norwegian physician, was now often referred to as Hansen's disease, hoping to destigmatize the sickness.

The most common symptom of the disease was mild and not terribly remarkable: a white patch of skin that seemed to have lost sensation, then skin drying, thickening, cracking. Some people with this condition healed spontaneously, progressing no further. Others went on to severe forms: the *neural* or more benign form of leprosy, where germs accumulated in the nerves, causing loss of sensation from hands, feet, the entire torso. Though patients lived for many years with this neural form, paralysis and atrophy of tissue occurred, loss of fingers, toes, sometimes whole limbs.

The more acute, *lepromatous*, was marked by formation of hard nodular swellings teeming with bacteria in the skin, in the mucous membranes of the nose, throat, eyes, eventually internal organs. As bacteria invaded various tissues, skin lesions appeared. First tiny nerve endings were affected, then larger nerves, starting a hideous chain of events that led to crippling and deformity. When nerves supplying power to muscles were damaged, muscles themselves withered, became paralyzed. With sensory nerves damaged, the result was loss of sensation of the skin.

The simplest acts—walking, lifting a fork, using a knife—became lethal. Deep lacerations resulted when hands and feet lost the ability to distinguish mere touch from acute pain. In an effort to "feel," victims exerted too much pressure on their limbs, breaking bones, repeating the injury over and over, causing a slow diminishing of bone and its replacement with scar tissue. Huge blisters grew from burns that weren't felt. When other bacteria entered broken blisters, it caused infection in tissue and bones. Hands, fingers, feet and toes became severely crippled. Leprosy didn't cause gangrene, as was thought, fingers and toes didn't simply drop off. But, without the sensation of pain, appendages wore away by constant damage. Bones were gradually broken down and absorbed until limbs were left with only short stumps where fingers and toes should be.

Invasion of the mucous membranes often led to destruction of the cartilage of the nose, resulting in its deformity. People appeared to lose their nose as the bone was absorbed into adjacent tissues. As bacilli invaded the tissue of the face, causing scarring, disfigurement, there was a terrible thickening of skin, a distinct furrowing, that medical experts called *leonine facies*, the look of a lion. When bacilli invaded tissues near the eyes, eyelids wouldn't close. The eyes became infected, causing blindness. Because the blind relied so much on their hands, without sensation there, they experienced a complete cut-offness from the world, total isolation. They were even cut off from themselves.

Fingers turned to claws, hands turned to clubs. Feet became mere stumps. Blindness. Kidney and heart disease. Utter hopelessness of knowing the deformities couldn't be reversed. At Kalaupapa, life became a prison within a prison. Strict confinement, isolation, first from one's friends and blood-kin, then from one's physical surroundings. They were to the outside world, The Untouchables. Who could blame the victims who prayed unceasingly for death?

As his sickness slowly escalated, Duke offered himself for newer injections, more radical experiments. At night he crept into shabby wooden labs, staring at rats and guinea pigs with patients' names attached. One night, in a cage, he saw a guinea pig tagged "Duke." Eyeless, bald, completely ulcerated, it had clawed its stomach out. Undaunted, Duke kept volunteering. When his lesions seemed to go into remission, he resurrected his belief in spontaneous healing—a miracle that took place in one out of a hundred people—and subjected himself to "snips."

Those who hoped to be released had six skin-scrapings each year, searching for still-active leprosy bacillus, then a biopsy and nose scraping. The process took twelve months, each snipping submitted to the Board of Health. It was heartbreaking; patients would be negative on five snips, then fail on the sixth. Failure meant another year at Kalaupapa, or worse, a lifetime. Some people turned to 'ōkolehao, or drugs. Some quietly walked into the sea.

A man who had snipped successfully for a year, wanted to go home to his children. In order to go, he had to submit to being sterilized.

"Doc say me 'No sterilize, you got stay here. Want go home, need sterilize.' I say, 'You want my balls? You got 'em!' Now, I goin' Honolulu, see my keeds." He was back in six days. His children looked at his twisted, "noseless" face and ran away.

Even women who had snipped successfully were voluntarily sterilized in order to go home. Most came back. "Folks stare my face like see one nightmare. Make me want to die."

Yet, they found beauty among themselves, and love. Children were born, and hidden. Laws said they had to be taken, that children were the most susceptible to leprosy. But sometimes, late at night in patients' cottages, everyone stealthy and quiet so administrators wouldn't hear, a secret birth took place. Word spread from room to room, house to house. The hospitals emptied. Patients came hobbling from across the settlement to see the newborn, to touch and hold, even for a moment. Lines were long, people fell asleep standing, so starved for children even the blind were brought to smell the infant, to hear its breathing. Those with sight gave the sightless a running description of every movement, every feature of the child.

"Button nose, like it mama! Big ears like da dad! Ohhh, full head of hair! You can feel it fingernails? Try feel! And feet, big feet, neh? Now it yawning like a cat, and kicking, kicking like one mule! Oh, funny! It wink! Yeah, wink! Like gonna' be one flirt . . ."

Sometimes infants weren't discovered for several days, giving the mother "tragic time," time to become too attached. When the doctors came, and nurses, taking the child from her, the howling echoed across the peninsula. Newborns were allowed to live inside Kalaupapa nursery for twelve months, kept behind thick glass so parents could see them but never touch them again. After one year they were taken from Kalaupapa, *hānai* by family or "issued out" to strangers by the Board of Health.

Then, there were the older ones already afflicted and broken. One day Duke watched a dozen leprous children sitting with their broken faces upturned, looking like lobsters with applicator sticks protruding from each nostril. They were being forced to "nose trip." Leprosy bacteria, found in abundance in the discharge from the nose, was needed for research. Adults wouldn't sit still, some had noses too far broken down. Children had abundant mucus, and needed their passages un-blocked, but when they saw the applicator sticks, they ran. The penalty was severe punishment, no food, days locked in a room alone. And so, the children submitted.

Instruments forced open the nose blocked with mucus. Opium-dipped sticks softened up the tissue, allowed the stick to penetrate all the way up the nostril. After a while, doctors withdrew the applicator sticks from deep inside the nasal passages, attached to which came mucus, tissue, blood. Children fainted with pain. Every day they fainted, each and each, every day, year after year. Until one day, there was no pain, only craving. Little addicts, noses broken down, maturing into adults whose cravings grew. Needles, morphine, heroin; it wasn't hard to smuggle in. For a price, boats would bring anything to Kalaupapa, dump it on the dock.

Duke favored a bright, fourteen-year-old Hawaiian-Portuguese. He came to love him like a son. One day the boy's body was found just inside the jungle, a rubber hose wrapped round his arm, a needle jutting out. They had "nose-tripped" him since he was eight. Duke rushed into the hospital, dragged a white-coated doctor outside and threw him to the ground. His big hands slowly closed down his windpipe, the man's face turned an awful blue. Then a sailor unloading a supply boat moved up from the dock. He took Duke aside and stood apart from him and spoke a name. *Pono.* Their conversation was brief, mostly in code, and yet to Duke it seemed a conversation of a hundred years, time drawn out, expanded immeasurably by all he could not say.

Though he was still monumental, in two years, he'd lost thirty pounds, resignation in his muscles, a lessening. Stomach ulcers plagued him from so much medication. He'd lost sensation in one leg and arm. His toes were broken down, half gone. There were new lesions on his body, and now a visible slow thickening in his face, the lion look. He had begun to understand this desolate peninsula was his final place. He tore a paper from a notepad, wrote something hastily, gave it to the sailor. Within forty-eight hours, the note was passed from the sailor to the *haole* unionizer working Pono's district on the Big Island.

In understanding he would never leave there, that he would only leave there for the Afterlife, Duke began reconstructing Kalaupapa, planting gardens, weeding graves, clearing walkpaths up the mountains. In physically rejuvenating the land, he renewed something spiritual and intellectual within himself. Carefully exploring its jungles and beaches as if for the first time—a press of *hau* bark to his nose, his cheek against damp soil, his foot plunged deep in palpitating sand—he saw the land and sea surrounding him not as a natural barrier, a prison, but as a creature timelessly alive.

Every detail became vivid: the earth's skin sloughing off in trades, green motes of rootless plankton charioting a wave, the heartcalm of cool rain on sunburned wrists, gaspchill of sudden shade, the liquid silk of milk of coconut, the saltfish taste of seaweed rinsing out the milk, the vegetable ease of rot and life, and green, the green of Polynesia. In everything ordinary, he saw the extraordinary. This land, shunned by

the world, became a thing that fed his senses. Duke entered it whole-
heartedly in order to survive.

For months patients saw night-torches in the jungles, plantation
strikers fleeing armed guards. Fugitives appeared beneath their cottages,
small skeletal Japanese and Filipinos, running for their lives. Lepers hid
them, fed them, became runners for them, carrying messages back to
their friends "Topside," up over the mountains, where healthy people
lived, where plantation owners sucked out the lives of laborers.

"You lepers lucky," a fugitive said. "You devil to look at, but only
got to look each ot'er. You eat till full, sleep till wake. No work. All you
gotta do is die."

The most hideously deformed patients were chosen as runners,
posing as boar hunters. Armed guards coming upon them in the jungle,
cocked their rifles, then backed off, disgusted. For weeks the jungle rang
with gunshots. Union men had heavily infiltrated camps, organizing
massive walkouts on plantations. Radios broadcast that all the islands
were in the throes of strikes and martial law. Armed guards hired by
plantation owners were replaced by hired killers, bounty hunters. People
were routed from bed and shot in their nightclothes. People disappeared.

One day a group of runners came down from the mountains carrying
a wild boar slung across a pole. Approaching Duke, they laughed softly,
conspiratorially, then parted ranks. And she came drifting to him through
a crowd of human others. He saw so many things at once, that she had
suffered, that there were things she couldn't speak of, ever. She had a
wounded quality, yet seemed more beautiful, her body less plump,
adding to her height. And something else, a fearless air, devoid of faith,
restraint; she was a woman who had not yielded.

In an instant she saw what Duke had become. What *ma'i Pākē* had
done to him, and how the future would compound it. Yet in that same
instant, she saw he was for her forever a feeling and a time, the hour
when people say, "The crisis has passed, now we can press on to
fulfillment," or, "You will not remember pain." He was the hour after
which all things are healed and distant. He was her recovery, her
continuance, her reason for recurrence and renewal. And he would be
the source of her eternal grief, what could be, or might have been.

She saw how time had already estranged them into memory. He
would be the background for all her thoughts and recollections, her
griefs, her pathologies. He would be the phantom that passes through

each life—a very moral, loving man, a brilliant, noble woman, or just someone kind who could forgive—the one we cannot hold who leaves, leaving deadly traces. Duke stumbled to her, crying out, even as she folded like a paper doll. He tried to lift her to her feet, but Pono hugged his legs, pressed her face against his knees, and wept. People turned, leaving them alone.

There would be a dawn, and chimes. Out in the world, there would be another day, the repetition of gestures, a confused sense in the hearts of men of not being able to understand their lives. Here, there was only the present, utter, immaculate. An old grass hut fronting the sea, built for honeymooners, and all around sunsetdusk in parrot plumage colors. They lay side by side, holding on, and she mourned for what was lost in her, what she could not tell. And what she could, she told, how the world had dwindled down to one thing: the horrifying actuality of his absence. The pointlessness of life without him. Jungle-running, and Holo's birth, and finding the father in the daughter—intelligence, intuition—which tapped some wild energy of hope that he was still alive. And that hope resurrecting in Pono devotion, desire. To him, for him. All she could articulate she said. That all her life he would be for her the only one. He was rare, full of grace. She would break the rules for him.

And he was stunned that she could love so deeply someone so awfully afflicted, that she had come, was flesh and blood and *here*, not the nightly fantasy lying in wait, moody watcher as he tortured the charnel house of his body, pestering, stroking himself, wanting his hand to be her hand, the fantasy dissolving before he even came, alone, so all alone. Then, Duke pulled her to him O the wealth of her, twining her thick black hair round his hands like ropes, kissing her face, her eyes with infinite tenderness. They drifted, turned, drifted like youths, a sense of bodies tensed, poised for love, brains holding back in pitiful decorum.

She could feel desire, what she wanted to do, to have, ticking within like little bombs. And Duke could feel the darting throbs, a hawk's hunger for her, so strong he put aside his shame, his sickness, how he must appear. Yet, there was hesitation. They had grown so used to grief it was part of them; without it, liberated from it, they felt naked, alien. Now there had to be a time of suspension—a jostling, almost a spasm, of cells, a change of rhythms in the bloodflow—as grief dissolved and joy moved in to take its place. They waited, trembled, sighed, letting instinct take over, the soft explosion when they would be past thinking.

He wept, embraced her, watching her skin light up all over, a shimmering down in her roots. She couldn't move, lay still, like some great pod about to burst. There was a sense of barriers breaking down, of skin parting, leaving visible raw nerves, mouths gaping, ready for sensation, and juices flowing, intermingling. Then his lips grazed over her, her lips and throat and breasts; he brushed hair from her eyes so she could see him, his lovely, dark penis poised beside her. In that moment before he entered her, they faced each other in a tense spasm, silent intake of breath, a requiem for all the loneliness, the longing.

Then she rose to meet him joining him singing out as they moved together and she held on to him and he was everything her son brother mentor an old man weeping at her grave light of a candle behind her chill of dusk at the door grass hut palpitating round them his big hands supporting her she bucked and bucking shook it all out of her that other woman full of knives and death and sobs and even then nothing about him escaped her not his smell earthy salty threatening sourness of medication in his veins not roughness of his scars or sordid scabbed lesions not the feel of shrinking muscles in his shoulders not even faintest down rising on the edge of his brown broken ear as he groaned rushed harder into her and she met him stayed with him as he called out her name trembling turbulent and she lapped his sores lapped his saliva with her tongue felt it running down her throat and she felt too a skidding loss of balance decorum breaking down her past receding acts committed in order to survive to arrive at this place this point this man inside her thudding against his thudding egos laid aside a pure and violent soldering.

In the morning, they heard soft footsteps, smelled gardenia-smell of fresh split *pomelo*. Outside the door a small feast had been left on ti leaves covered with *lau'ae* fern: steamed *mahimahi*, fresh dark *'ōpae*, warm *laulau*, riceballs and *poi*, and sticky buns, coffee, a pyramid of fruit. They pulled the leaves of food indoors, and left the door flung wide. And lying there like people who had found a way to sleep, they dreamed and dozed and surged into each other, dozed again, waking and eating dreamily, one hand always laid upon each other. Slowly, as if re-learning speech, words came again, Pono speaking so carefully everything she said seemed wise.

She talked of the terrible living conditions on plantations—open sewers, rats, scorpions, laborers having to steal to feed their children decently, tuberculosis wiping out small populations of the young, infections from cane cuts that led to gangrene. Filth, murder, suicide.

"They say plantation owners have accomplished the miracle of teaching immigrants how to rest without sleep, eat without food, live without

life. I began helping organize strikes. Much good is happening thanks to
unionizers. But I was endangering my life, and Holo's. When I heard
you were alive, I ran . . ."

Duke spoke sadly of his life, of friends lost. "Quick friends. Here
no one has much time."

"How you have suffered!"

"As long as I suffer," he said, "I know I'm still alive."

He told her how lepers volunteered as runners for the strikers and
union men, how he suspected it would get worse, planters fighting
unions, more workers dying.

He paused, then cupped her face with his hands. "Now, tell me
about our daughter."

She showed him wrinkled photographs, the child round, dark, beautiful, eyes big and grave like Duke's. Pono described her mannerisms,
her amazing intuition, the quiet withdrawals when she sat and stared.
And as she talked, she understood how much she loved the child because
she was already old, she had already seen too much.

"A Japanese taro farmer and his wife took us in a few miles south
of the plantation. We lived with them for weeks. When Holo was fat
and strong again, I stowed away with her on a steamer from the Big
Island bound for Moloka'i."

She laughed because the boat had docked on the wrong side of the
island, "Topside," over the mountains from Kalaupapa where there were
real towns and healthy people. She and the child had hid again until she
could work her way toward Kalaupapa.

"Strikers took me in when they heard I had helped organize on the
Big Island. They knew my contact, the *haole* shot bringing me your
note."

Leaving Holo with a Chinese couple, Pono had begun the descent
down the treacherous mountains, tangled jungle undergrowth, sudden
mudslides tumbling down to jagged cliffs, switchback footpaths that
disappeared, wild razor-tusked boar running in packs. And finally, coming upon the hunting party from Kalaupapa. At first the patients ran
from her, afraid she was "decoy," a spy working for the planters.

"But when I said your name they took me by the hand."

Duke described how he was in the act of strangling a doctor to
death when the sailor approached him with the message from Pono.
"My note was brief. I want you to go on with your life. I am incurable."

"Never!" she cried, burying her head in his scarred, mottled chest.
"As long as we live there is hope. What else is life for?"

"Listen to me." He pulled apart from her so he could see her eyes. "You must examine Holo every night. She carries Kealoha blood—she's more susceptible than others. This stuff incubates for years. And if she grows up healthy, she must go to university."

Pono was silent.

"What is it, Beloved?"

"I will arrange these things, Duke, each thing you ask. But I am not returning there. I will remain with you as your *kōkua*."

He shuddered, pictured her tending him down the years as he slowly decomposed. "No! You will not retire to this hell."

She cried out, desperate. "I'm a fugitive. If they catch me I'll be locked in isolation again. They'll take away our child."

"Pono. It has been two years and not one spot on you. Don't you understand? You're not a leper, you're *immune*."

She sobbed, beat her hands against his chest. "The world is nothing without you! The child is nothing to me without you. I am nothing."

"Beloved . . ." She could hear the grief between his words. "I am asking you to live for me. Let me see the world, and all its awful, wondrous changes through your eyes. Return to the farm, resurrect the coffee fields, find a man worthy of you, and raise our child."

Her eyes changed shape, like a reptile. "I will eat my own liver before another man dares touch me."

"Pono, you are young."

She looked right through him. "I am . . . very . . . old."

"You will forget these years of pain, struggling alone with a child. With God's grace these years will fade."

She didn't tell him she had eliminated God from her world. "Duke, you're only twenty-three. How can you live without hope?"

"I am incurable. I lose myself in nature, music, book-swallowing. And now there is you, whom I thought I had lost forever."

So, for a while they were safe, dreaming side by side, turning in sleep like broken shells on the ocean floor in nights full of blue volumes of ginger, jacaranda, air emptying, filling with their lungs. And somewhere across the settlement, nasal dreamshriek of a leper like a human disemboweled. Sometimes he woke at dawn, the hour least easy to bear: for he woke a healthy, strapping man, hearing the ocean call, a good day for surfing on his longboard. He would begin to rise and then, only then, Duke felt the pain, saw the lesions, thickening skin, and shrank back like a tortoise into his mottled carapace.

But now at dawn her scent was everywhere. She lay snoring, smooth dark skin tattooed white with semen, her breasts heaving and falling against him, hair like *pāhoehoe* splashed across the bed, eyes bruised aubergine beneath, the utter fatigue of love. Life would never thin her sensuous full lips, but there was something Duke now saw that even sleep could not erase, a wariness, a tight-hingedness to the jaw, what it took to make her way alone in the world.

He gathered her in his arms, her sweat-lather dried, now mingling with his salty, earth smell and near-sweet smell of flesh outrunning medication, beginning seriously to corrupt.

"Live," he whispered, "Live for me!"

One day soon she would depart. And after that these moments would possess him wholly, he would grow old in them. For now, they were children of the landscape, ascending cliffs like goats, plunging head-first into crashing surf. From the distance sharks, like burnished steel torpedoes, glided in, then cozied up behind them, drawn by the sound of their heartbeats. Pono saw their fins and smiled, untempted to join them, to dart and shoot deep coral canyons, to race in sun-stroked wet. She paused, tempered her strokes, seeing how, in spite of his still-fabulous strength, Duke moved a little slower.

Such is the morphology of disease, that it can seem kind: paw-stroking a man year by year, rather than hammering him with its full assault. Some lepers died within six months of the first symptom; she knew Duke would endure until the lazy *haole* doctors found a cure. *He will be cured. One day I will take him home.* She knew this without dreaming it. She knew it because, without belief in it, she would let go of everything. And she continued rubbing up against his sores, sucking his saliva when they kissed. Some nights while he slept, Pono walked his face in moonlight, fingers caressing his broad, handsome Polynesian cheeks, skin now scarred and thickened. *Now I, too, am scarred, mutilated. I am* ka mea hana make. *O Brother. Husband. What has life done to us? And why!*

Each night before they made love, he served her tea brewed from shaved black coral, and "mad vegetation," so she would throw out his seed.

"My blood is 'contact blood,' " he said, fearing another child would be *ma'i Pākē*.

And every night, Pono tossed the tea aside, hard legs encircling him, determined to wrest from him another child, a link. One night, Duke whooping, thumping, cataracting into her, she felt the salutation, cells aghast, colliding, and knew she had conceived.

Two days later, a nurse came at them running almost sideways, looking back behind her. Administrators had discovered Pono's presence in the settlement. Whereas visiting permits allowed family members visits of a few hours at a time, Pono had been living there for several weeks, hiding among patients and kōkua. The next day she was put aboard a supply boat headed round the island, then back to Honolulu.

He spoke fast while she sobbed in his arms. "Beloved, do not visit me too often. Do not flirt with this disease. Take Holo and go home to the plantation. Help Tang Pin breathe life back into the soil."

She didn't tell him locals would stone her, call her filthy, call her child ma'i Pākē. She didn't tell him she was carrying another. As the boat weighed anchor, she stood at the railing, mute, not even waving. Her eyes burned into his. She stood that way until she could no longer distinguish his features, until his form was sucked into the land. She didn't hear his howling, or see his body fold, didn't see handless friends embrace him, leading him home.

That night Duke studied his image in a mirror, touched the slowly thickening cheeks, the lion look preying on his features. He wondered how much longer he could let her look upon him. How much longer she could bear to.

Ka ʻŌlelo Makuahine

Mother Tongue

THE YEARS. She stared down them, nothing coming to her from the distance. The hardest thing was not to have him there. Not to have him listen and understand how hard it was without him. Still, Pono made resolutions: she would be decent to herself. She would not go back to planters' camps, roachy shacks, rusty plates of food. She would not again do stoop work. Or kneeling scrub work. Or work again for *haole*. She studied the remaining black pearl and small, jade diary. She would not sell them.

"Always own something beautiful," Duke had told her. "Something small you can gaze at on the run."

He lived. This knowledge gave her courage, made her vibrate to a new height. She stood tall, looked people in the eye. She was no longer running, nor was she standing still.

Passing a tailor shop in Chinatown one day, she stared inside, giving the owner the *maka loko ʻino*, evil eye. In two days his spine curled, knees knotted up like ginger roots. She walked into his shop, swearing to cure his arthritis if he rented her a sewing machine on credit.

The old Chinese stuck out his knotted legs. "Cure!"

She rubbed banana sap into his back and knees, and made him swallow spoonfuls of nutmeg that made him sick, then made him go on tiptoe like a girl. While he danced round his shop, she lifted the curse, releasing him from pain.

He stared at his unknotting knees, felt his spine uncurl and screamed. *"Kahuna!"*

She left the shop with a Singer sewing machine tucked beneath her arm like a fossilized, prehistoric pet. She took in sewing at night, living in a single room with Holo. The Depression of the thirties had driven down demand for pineapples and sugarcane, and out-of-work laborers drifted to the city adding to the slums. But even in the poorest parts of Chinatown there were *lu'au*, weddings, celebrations. Pono sat on a *lauhala* mat on street corners, dreamtelling as in the old days in A'ala Park.

In the streets, small, delicate Filipino men, homesick, drunk on *'ōkolehao* or beer, paid her to dreamtell when they would go home to their *barrios* in the Philippines, or when they would have money to send for their families. She closed her eyes, and even when she dreamtold the truth—that they would never go home, never see their families—they were courteous, paid and walked away, heads hanging, shoulders narrow as young girls.

Uneducated, mostly illiterate, last large-scale immigrant arrivals and so, disdained by others, Filipinos seemed outcast from the world, entrenched in their lonely, bachelor ghettoes. Still, they flocked to Pono because she was kind, and beautiful, and when she closed her eyes they could gaze upon her face and be in love with her. She stopped dreamtelling in the streets, made appointments in her room, and when the landlord called her prostitute, she laughed.

"I am *kahuna!* I could inhale you, skinny, little man."

To prove her powers Pono told him the little *'ili'ili* growing on his chest was a death-growth, that he must cut it off, or die. Doctors examined the growth, saw it was malignant and immediately removed it. The landlord brought it in a jar, a gift to Pono, and gave her two large rooms for "same price" if she "no moah grow *'ili'ili* on his chest."

She prospered from dreamtelling, no longer needing to sew for a living. But sewing was tangible and real, and she wanted Holo to see her doing normal things, not selling dreams to strangers. She was attendant to the child, sliding life to her in small portions, what to do, not do, how to behave in public, and alone. Mostly she taught her to honor the dignity of things—money, thread, material.

"These things don't breathe, therefore can be counted on."

Flashing scissors across crimson, she slowly joined two pieces of cloth on the sewing machine. "See how careful the stitches, how strong the thread. Cloth and thread bleed together, the color holds, the shape."

"If so strong," Holo asked, "then why always making new dresses?"

"Because . . . by and by the cloth goes shiny, comes into holes. Time to throw away."

The child grew instantly alert, as each night her mother examined Holo's body, studying her skin, her back, her scalp, even between her toes. She was looking for shiny parts, for holes. When Holo fell and slashed her knee, she took needle and thread and crawled into a closet. Pono found here there unconscious, lying in her vomit. She had tried to close the cut, stitch the hole, so Pono wouldn't throw her away.

She bathed the wound, comforted the child. "You're going to have a baby sister. We're 'ohana! No one is going to throw you away."

But Holo dimly remembered a small mummy flying, rags unwinding, a doll cartwheeling across waves.

As time drew near, Pono had her landlord write a letter to Tang Pin on the Big Island.

". . . If I die in childbirth, come for Duke's child, Holo. Raise her on her father's soil. Teach her her Kealoha history."

Waiting for the midwife, she took the child against her voluminous stomach. "Listen now, remember. Your father is an honorable man. You will be like him. Stand straight. Look others in the eye. Trust only nature, sun and star. When you are older, swim with sharks. They are your 'aumākua. Honor them, and you will honor me. Remember this name, Tang Pin, he will take you home."

She didn't die. A second girl was born, a healthy child, Edita, the midwife's name. In post-birth hysteria, Pono tried to give the child to her, give them both to her. "Take them! Leave me free. To be with him."

The old Hawaiian midwife laughed. "Dis wahine gone pupule. T'ink she die and gone to Jesus!"

Weeks later, she lay with Duke at Kalaupapa, describing their second child. "So healthy! If it was a boy I would have named him Duke Silvio Generalito Kealoha."

A memory of a happy time in childhood, and also a way of acknowledging the Filipinos who came to her now, futureless, childless, paying Pono to dream, then, at night, drifting back to their lonely bachelor barracks in Chinatown. Their patronage had supported her and Holo during this second pregnancy. Duke's plantation was dead. His disability check was used to pay land taxes. There was no income from the fields, nothing for Tang Pin to send her.

"Won't you go back to the plantation?" he asked. "At least there is the house, a little vegetable garden, Tang Pin to watch over you . . ."

"In time," she said. "In time there will be many children, a family waiting when you return."

He shook his head, for she would not accept the truth. Yet he was humbled by her will, her drive to spring his seed.

"Be careful with the Filipinos," he said. "We hide them here in numbers. The Filipino Federation of Labor is organizing big strikes throughout the islands. Rumors will spread that they are meeting in your rooms."

She promised to be prudent, not telling him her rooms now bulged, a safe house for Filipino strikers on the run, evicted from their camps by planters. Even though production and demand were down, plantation workers were organizing in larger and larger numbers, fighting to bargain collectively through labor unions. There was another reason Filipinos flocked to Pono's rooms. Deprived of families, they came back from their savage cockfights, and gambled for the privilege of sitting with her girls, feeding them, coddling them like little mothers. Even as she slept beside Duke at Kalaupapa, her infant daughter, Edita, was rocked in the arms of a weeping man as he sang her songs of his native Ilocos.

In 1934, a month after the birth of her third daughter, Emmaline, for Duke's mother and Pono's grandmother, one day a well-dressed *hapa-haole* knocked at her door. Wary, Pono drew her children round her, speaking Pidgin, a language she could hide behind. The man had something to do with the governor's office. He had come to ask her to appear at 'Iolani Palace.

"What I done?" she asked. "What law I break?" Two Filipino fugitives were standing in her closet.

The *hapa* laughed. "On the contrary, we want to ask you a big favor. Something that would please the governor, bring honor to Hawaiians."

He told her Franklin Delano Roosevelt, president of the United States, was visiting Hawai'i. This meant not much to Pono. Had it been Hirohito of Japan, the leader of China, or the Philippines, people she had lived among, she would have been impressed.

"Roosevelt wants to see real Hawaiians," the *hapa* said. "See the hula danced, eat *kālua* pig, enjoy a *hukilau*. His aide heard about *kāhuna*, and someone's cook remembered you dreamtelling at street fairs. We would like you to do that for Mr. Roosevelt!" He laughed, uncomfortable. "Or, just pretend."

The man neglected to say they also wanted Roosevelt to see a prime example of the islands' majestic "aborigines," a stately reminder of what Hawaiians had once been. Except for the Olympic gold medal swimmer,

Duke Kahanamoku, nearing forty-five, there were fewer and fewer pure examples of this once-great rapidly dwindling race. Reluctantly, Pono made her way to 'Iolani Palace on the appointed day.

Women rubbed her skin with aloe, coconut and jasmine so it glowed, brushed her hair until it shone like *pāhoehoe* cascading down her back. They dressed her in a white *holokū* with flowing *maile* leaves, and they stepped back. At the Governor's Reception, when she stood before President Roosevelt, all background motion ceased. Diplomats, island nobility, even the governor of Hawai'i stared. Her great height, her quiet dignity and beauty reminded them of what ancient Polynesians had been, fearless Vikings of the Pacific.

Pono bowed, shook hands warily, studied Roosevelt's handsome, tired face, his braced legs, then sat down at his feet, closed her eyes and dreamed. People in the Throne Room smiled, amused, but Roosevelt leaned forward, admiring the dreaming beauty. Then, unaccountably, she moaned, rocking back and forth. She hugged herself, beat her fists upon her chest, and wept. Alarmed Secret Service men surrounded Roosevelt; he pushed them back, curious, somewhat apprehensive. Pono rocked the longest time, sweat pouring down her arms. She woke, stood slowly, looked into his face and could not tell what she had seen.

But, to prove she was *kāhuna*, she raised her head and fairly shouted in clear tones.

"YOU WILL FIRESIDE-CHAT FOUR TERMS!"

Roosevelt guffawed. U.S. presidents weren't elected more than twice. Pono fell silent, and after a while she shook his hand, and left. Years later when Roosevelt set historical precedence, the only president in U.S. history to be elected to a third term, then a fourth, he would remember her. And he would wonder what else the Hawaiian beauty had dreamed, what she had kept from him.

"Exploding ships, running men on fire," she told Duke. "I smelled it. I tasted devastation."

She wondered how it would affect their lives. She thought of the years passing, the ebb and flow of her journeys back and forth, Honolulu to Moloka'i, living for that motion, everything else, her life, a blur. Would the devastation she envisioned really come? Or was it just an idle dream, flexing of her tired mind?

Duke thought her vision was a warning of coming catastrophe, volcanic eruption, earthquake. "We've taken too much from the land.

The land always takes back. I wish you would take our daughters home where they belong, they would be safer there."

Their daughters. She gave not much thought to them, sometimes confusing them, forgetting their names, absent-mindedly patting a head in passing, like a dog she must remember to feed. When the day came for the inter-island steamer to Kalaupapa, she left the girls with neighbors, strangers, anyone, piling them up like sacrifices offered to the world, throwing it off her scent while she lived for this man, this one obsession.

When is love too much? she wondered. *When is it not enough?* If she neglected the seed for the father, was it neglect? If she sacrificed part of their lives to enrich his, was it sacrifice?

Sometimes, watching his body erupt, more lesions, a clawed hand curling tighter, his handsome face thickening into something else, Pono lost hope, afraid the disease would someday eat his brain. It happened occasionally. She saw ghosts of humans round them, silent things suspended in final vegetation. It would be worse than seeing him dead. The wonder of him, the elegance and pride of him, the dignity he gave her, would be lost to her. There would be no one to listen, to give her back herself. She would be nothing. Racked by such thoughts, some nights she raced down to the sea, wanting to feel her skin change texture, feel her hands and legs withdraw into a bag of scales, a fin break through her back, feel her body torpedo the deep. Feel nothing, only speed.

He sensed her growing terror, imagined her struggling in the world without him. When she told him she was carrying his fourth child, Duke took steps. One day he sat her down, making her sign documents before a witness, an attorney. She gasped, her skin turned incandescent, she thought they were being married. While the man looked on, Duke held her hand, slowly guiding her in the writing of one word. P . . . O . . . N . . . O. She stared blankly while the attorney told her Duke's house, the plantation, three hundred acres of ancestral land, were now in her name. He gathered up the papers and departed.

"It all belongs to you," Duke said. "I've given you the land to protect you, insure you . . ."

"But you cannot marry me, give your children a name."

How often they had had this conversation. "Beloved, I can never marry you. The stigma. All over Kona District, people associate the Kealoha family with *ma'i Pākē*. Our daughters would be ostracized."

"You prefer to keep them bastards!"

"I prefer to think someday you'll find a proper husband. Someone who will give them a healthy, decent name. I'll never leave here, don't you understand? Even if they find a cure, by then I'll be too horrible to look upon. The land will give you dignity. Go home, please. Tang Pin is waiting."

She threw herself against a wall. "I'll kill this child. Destroy all of them!"

"Then you will be destroying me."

She couldn't fight him, couldn't resist him, obeyed him like a child. While the new one was still growing in her womb, she took the steamer from Honolulu to the Big Island and stood with Holo on her land overlooking Kona District and the sea. But she stood uneasily, waiting for strangers to attack her, stone-throwing crowds. Tang Pin came running from the porch of the big house now fallen into awful disrepair.

"Oh, Missus, no be afraid. Folks soon forget *ma'i Pākē*. They say soon find one cure." He lifted Holo in his arms. "Big for six! Can play with my son. Ten, very smart, no crazy like his mother." He saw alarm in Pono's eyes. "No worry! Mad wife die, I got new bride!"

"There are two more children now," she said, and pointed to her belly. "And one more on the way. I'll return with the others by and by." She knelt down, speaking softly to Holo. "Will you be good? Do you remember who Tang Pin is?"

Holo nodded gravely. She had survived six years with this woman. In six years, her mother had not killed her, so abandonment seemed fair. And Tang Pin seemed familiar. For years Pono had told her this man would give her love, *'ohana*, he would give her her history. Pono watched as she walked courageously toward Tang Pin's son. The boy handed her a present, a porcelain China doll. She stared at the little glass-eyed corpse, feeling repulsion, a desire to maim and, without hesitation, threw it to the ground, banging its head to splinters. Then she looked to her mother for approval. Pono gasped. Tang Pin's son retreated, but Holo soon dragged him off in search of mongoose, a palm to climb, coconuts to split.

The old house seemed to be disintegrating, little separated it from creeping foliage, the earth. Branches and vines grew through windows, animals roamed the halls. The LEPER sign was gone, but Tang Pin believed the house was haunted, explaining how each night something moaning climbed the stairs, slowly, as if exhausted, and slept in the master bed.

"Every day I air da sheets, remake da bed," he whispered. "Next morning, all messed up. Mirror fogged, like breath."

In Duke's study, photo albums rendered faceless generations. Termites had consumed whole genealogies. Years of mold had furred the walls so rooms seemed underwater; courting peacocks skittered on scatty floors, taking flight through paneless windows. At night they still sobbed in the trees like women. And on the lawn, flocks of ugly nesting birds, croaking frogs, sows wallowing in mud, and farther out, acres of forbidding, jungled coffee trees, and far across the island earthy ripples, Pele grumbling in her depths. And everywhere, the Big Island smell of volcanic sulfur.

Yet, how she wanted to be here, to have him here! She wanted to salvage it. Restore it for him. Food was plentiful, enough for them all. Mango, *pomelo*, avocado, papaya, starfruit, pomegranate. A small vegetable garden. And Tang Pin caught *'ahi, mahimahi* and bonito in the sea.

"Move back into the house," she told him. "Sweep one room each day. Wash, then polish. We will rebuild from inside out."

The last child took so much in being born, Pono thought it was a boy. But when the midwife said it was another girl, she pushed it viciously away. The old woman named her Mina, Sorrow, wet-nursed her, took her and the other girls home while Pono regained her senses. The woman wondered where the father was, maybe they all had different fathers. She wondered where the oldest girl was; maybe Pono had sold her. The old Hawaiian was afraid to ask, afraid Pono would look her to death.

In the autumn, when she and her three daughters stepped from the steamer onto the Big Island, Pono stood tall, refined, in a tailored, broadshouldered linen dress and tight, "toepinch" high heels, a wide-brimmed hat holding down hair gathered sedately in a bun. People stared because she was so lovely, her wild beauty staunched by such pragmatic clothes. Her well-dressed cubs leaned shyly back against her legs as Tang Pin pulled up waving in the rusty Buick, bird scat along its sorrowful grill. Holo jumped from the car and ran to her mother, as crowds slowed in the port, admiring her. Then someone recognized her. She felt eyes examining her brood, heard a voice, loud, unforgettable.

". . . *kamali'i o ma'i Pākē.*" Children of leprosy.

Perhaps she had never loved them as she did in that moment, would never again love them so passionately. She gathered Edita and Emmaline against her legs, held Mina to her ribs, put her hand over Holo's ears, daring the world until it looked away. She and her daughters were on the next boat back to Honolulu, Tang Pin weeping, bewildered, on the dock.

*   *   *

Four growing girls. Two suffocating rooms in Chinatown. All-night rattling of the Singer, sewing *cheongsams* for prostitutes. She thought she would go mad. She dried herb, bark and roots, sold them as cures, and juice of centipede for warts, and toad for arsenic. She dreamtold, but cash was slow, the Depression was in the streets. *Haole* sailors now thronged Chinatown, staring when she passed. Her girls needed milk and meat, she wondered if she could do it, wear a *cheongsam* and close her mind and do it. She sat in the dark, stroking her human-spine cane. The thought of what they wanted from her, what they had taken from her long ago, turned her eyes a brilliant red, her teeth grew into points, ripping a *cheongsam* to threads. Later she wept, tried to sew the pieces together, tried to pull herself together, hold herself intact.

One day Filipinos came, men she had hidden, and fed, and comforted on nights of such degrading loneliness they cried.

They handed her an envelope. "Yoah profits from da cockfights."

She had never bet on fights. They pushed the envelope at her. "Find one bettah place for live. So girls not grow up in da street. We come and see dem by and by."

She remembered years back, running from Kalihi Receiving Station, on the outskirts of Honolulu, a neighborhood of modest little houses, tiny yards, orchids flowering in cans.

"No sailors, no prostitutes," she told Duke. "Nearby a Catholic school."

She rented a small house in Kalihi, a swatch of yard for the girls, and neighbors she could trust. She bought them Buster Browns, white socks, good cotton underwear, and uniforms for Catholic school. Then, steeling herself, one day she walked down King Street toward Iwilei and Dole Cannery. Smell of syrupy pineapple in the air took her breath away, floating her remembrances of her first year in Honolulu at this same cannery.

Life is running backwards. What did I do wrong?

Carrying a lunch pail, rubber gloves, wearing a steely hair net, she joined waves of women flowing through iron gates into a mechanical landscape posted with armed guards. Haggard women approached, peeling off from peak-season twelve-hour shifts at racheting machines. Pono took one last breath and then was sucked inside.

Same locker room, same bango number pinned to her shirt. Over hair net, white cap, over powdered hands the suffocating rubber gloves, and passing through the Portal of Hell, they called it, into a giant warehouse of screaming machines. She was stationed high up on a platform, guiding ripe pines flooding in from trains, pushing them into a "Ginaca" machine that chewed them out of their skins, shelled and cored hundreds of them a minute, leaving smooth cylinders of yellow fruit ready to be trimmed.

Her back nearly breaking from the strain of bending over, feeding pines to the Ginaca, they moved her downstairs to the clash of metal teeth moving conveyor belts, connecting one belt to the next, so that pines moved in tandem across the width of the huge cannery. As naked pine cyclinders shuttled by, she grabbed one, twirled it in her hand, and with a sharp knife flicked out spots of rind "eyes," trimmed off bits of skin, replaced it on the belt and grabbed another. Hour after hour, day after day, she twirled and trimmed, twirled and trimmed until her hands were numb, arms raked with rash from dripping pine juice.

One day a forelady with a vague mustache walked her down the aisle from trimming machines to slicers. There they selected prime rounds emerging from machines and packed them in small cans. Women farther down the line selected rounds of lesser quality for larger cans. Broken slices went into tidbit cans, and badly broken bits were mashed to juice. Rounds came out of the machine clinging together, but the vibration of the belt shook them loose, so she could pick the sweetest and the yellowest. After a few days, Pono edged closer to the slicer, catching the pine as it shot from the mouth of the machine. Impatient, she reached higher and higher into the metal mouth.

One day the big Hawaiian forelady slapped her back. "You *pupule?* Want lose yoah hand?"

She dreamed of shark-fin soup, night after night, and woke up puzzled, distracted. One day, reaching into the mouth of the slicing machine, she felt her hand sing out. Pulling back, she looked down at her glove. A hole, a gaping mouth. Then blood frothed up like a flower. Women ran beside the conveyor belt, pointing, shrieking at something shuttling along on top of bloody pineapples. Screams echoed down the line from the choice-slice section, to tidbits, to crushed. She stood dumb, in shock, watching the squalid, dodging movements of hysterical women, until a forelady rushed at her, holding up her finger sliced off neatly at the second joint, waving it like a prize.

The ambulance, slow, sensuous hula of morphine. Three months Workmen's Compensation. Remembering her dreams, each night Pono ate shark-fin soup, the cartilage strengthening her bones and joints, healing, healing; she even imagined the little finger growing back. The stitches smoothed over, and, but for the missing digit, the hand healed perfectly, each finger articulating as before.

In three months of healing, she had "slow-time," time to look around. The next-door neighbors, a Chinese and his Filipino wife, were *lei* stringers, working for flower vendors who sat in front of smart Wakīkī hotels. Their trees and bushes, overhanging Pono's yard, bulged ginger, jasmine, frangipani, carnations, plumeria. At dawn, the wife took the two youngest girls, giving Pono time to tend Holo and Edita and send them off to school.

Singing softly, the woman joined her husband stringing *lei*, Pono's infant sleeping in her lap, while Emma dashed round gathering dew-drenched flowers from the grass. Pono watched the couple, pollinating each other with little deeds, endless conversation. She saw how life could be, one human brushing against the other each day, every day, refining one another, giving one another stature. She saw how in their small yard they had created an oasis, keeping the great risk of the world at bay. She envied them their smug and careful little life. She wished them dead.

Her own life was hazardous. Four growing girls, bills, sleepless nights, the one thing really important to her occurring in shadow. Some nights, she longed for Duke so badly she woke wounded all over, her body aching. Next day she would abuse the girls, slap or ignore them, make the three oldest eat in silence while she fed the infant with disdain. *Fatherless little bastards, wondering where he is. Who he is.* When they finally summoned up the nerve to ask, she told them their father worked the gold mines in Alaska.

"When will he come home, Mama?"

By and by.

And yet, they held her life together. Each child a strong thread in a worn sarong. Without them she would unravel.

Filipino "uncles" came visiting, bringing gifts of money for the girls, bringing sweets and storybooks, asking only for a little "kid-watching" time. Neighbors gossiped, suspecting they were the fathers of her daughters. She began discouraging their visits, refused their gifts, even though by now two girls were in private Catholic school. Four months from the day she lost her finger, Pono walked back into that awful smell, that screaming-machinery world. Women hugged her, cheering as she took her place on Warrior Row, where those with mutilated hands twirled and trimmed pines faster than anyone because they had less fingers to intrude. Some mornings, rising at four A.M., seeing the long twelve-hour stretch before her, she wondered, *How much longer can I take it?* She would take it for ten years.

There were moments, epiphanies. Some days, throwing off their uniforms and Buster Browns, the girls would roll in flower piles, then run to her as she dragged home from the cannery, frangipani in their hair, the smell so sweet it gave her instant headaches. But seeing them together, little, rollicking, barefoot *kānaka* like flowers wearing flowers, Pono staggered under the wealth of beauty she had failed to observe, what she and Duke had achieved. And for that day, her world was larger.

Some nights in white sleeping sarongs, they ran outside dancing under stars like little fireflies. Other nights they wept, heads in their pillows so she wouldn't hear, Holo missing Tang Pin, the only father she knew, Edita crying for her "uncles," missing their arms round her, smell of their pomade and tobacco. Emma, shy and pale, seemed to only stare, her face already exhausted in advance of time.

Loving them, covetting them, the childless neighbors, the *lei* stringers, spied and gossiped. "Poor little no-name buggahs. T'ink third one, Emma, be da one go bad. Look like fool-around type, sneaky eye."

"No. Edita, second one! She too much flirt."

"Wonder where da mot'er go when disappear for days."

"Maybe make extra money wid da sailors. She one good-lookin' *wahine*, but hard type. Real hard."

Sometimes she was so exhausted, on the boat to Kalaupapa she'd lean down at the rail and fall asleep, nearly falling in the sea. Duke half carried her to his small cottage where in his arms, she slept and slept. After ten or fourteen hours, she would wake weeping, wrung out at twenty-six. When she was calm they strolled beaches and lay up on the cliffs, watching sunsets, the gathering hordes.

"This is all I want," she said. "It seems so little to ask of life."

They had loved for ten years, and now in this decade of her hardship, these hazardous mothering years, Duke saw how decent she was, how noble. He knew his daughters only from snapshots, yet he suspected he loved them more than she did. She was not by nature maternal, her senses seemed tuned to something much more distant. Yet she endured, sacrificing youth, beauty, even body parts, to nourish, protect, educate his seed. His love for her quickened, deepened. And they were silent, and there was nothing more to say.

Her daughters moved cautiously through those scattered years, increasingly aware of her torn state, dark mysteries—where did she go each month? Fearing, yet loving her, sometimes a gesture from her was enough. Vague smile, a nod. But when they came too close, she turned away, and when they laughed, too loud, too gay, she pinned them down again. One look.

Holo turned ten, a quiet girl, always scribbling in her diary. One day she asked, "Mama, is Tang Pin my father?"

"No, foolish girl. He is *Pākē*."

"Then Tang Junior is not my brother?"

"No."

She went back to scribbling her secrets. Edita almost eight, turned her affections to the Chinese-Filipino neighbors who sang her "uncle" songs while stringing *lei*. Emma, seven, watched, and followed them around. Mina had no personality it seemed, just an appetite for love, for anyone who held her.

Some nights Holo heard Pono in her sleep, moaning, struggling with something awful. She wanted to wake her mother, comfort her. To do so was to perish. But one night Pono sat up in a sweat.

"Holo. What are you doing there? Come here." She gathered her close, looking at her face in darkness. "A dreadful thing is coming. I see it in my sleep." She showed her money hidden in a lacquered bowl. "If something happens to me, take the girls to Tang Pin on the Big Island. He will care for you."

"Mama! What do you see?"

"An old dream. I saw it when that President Roosevelt came to Honolulu." Exploding ships, running men on fire. Oil bubbling in tides.

She woke at dawn that Sunday, smell of burning flesh high in her nostrils. Wrapping the still-sleeping girls in blankets, she stole a neighbor's car and drove insanely, away from Kalihi, from the harbor of Pearl River. Following a red dirt road, she found her way to a deserted cove and just before eight o'clock, pushed her daughters into the sea.

"Swim!"

She did not know where they should swim to. She only knew they had to get away from land. Minutes later, she heard the planes, saw them approaching in formation.

"Dive!"

Like little seals, they dove, following their mother underwater. Surfacing only for air, she led them out toward the reef where it was deep and dangerous, knowing that beyond the reef was where their 'aumākua slept, and if they were going to die it should be in ancestral precincts. They dove again, this time so deep, they saw the ocean floor roll up like a carpet, saw the reef tremble like a building giving warning. She dragged them up again for air, let them take it in in gulps, then pulled them down again.

Down down where life was rhythmed by reflex she held her fingers out and they clasped hands floating in a circle squinting like embryos dreamily acknowledging each other in a giant womb and in that floatingtime a timeless time none of them hurt no one was damaged or frightened or alone they were just cells connected by a stroke of light by touch Pono holding Mina's hand and Mina holding Emma's and Emma grasping Edita's and her grasping Holo and they blended like the elements of color elements that somewhere in the grid of time would recede and rinse away and in this moment in this motherwomb flesh tendered watery and wrinkled so they looked wise they heard the clicking of the reef billions of cells building microscopic civilizations in its branches civilizations that would perish and be built again in time and perish and each of them even Mina the youngest seemed to smile understanding that things are as they are that things can be no other way they would never find that peace again not one of them they would never be that safe.

The ocean heaved again, raining down debris. Something human rippled the surface of their skin. They listened. Miles away in watery tombs, men screamed. At first the sounds were distant, then the ocean washed them near, and it was awful. The girls moved closer, frightened. Bursting for air, Pono dragged them to the surface, then dove again. And listened. Screams embalmed in sunken ships that would go on for days, and weeks, screams that would slowly fade to bleats, to nothing.

She shot to the surface and saw, far down the coast, the inferno of Pearl Harbor, huge flashes, devastating fireballs shooting up hundreds of feet, mushrooms of smoke boiling skyward. All the ocean seemed on fire, black drapes slowly drawn across exploding skies. Water around her daughters' shoulders spit and splattered and looking up, Pono saw two planes zigzagging in a deadly dogfight. One of them tumbled over and crashed out past the reef. Confused, terrified, she dragged the girls out of the water, heading straight at the oncoming plane. Nosing down in front of them, it dipped its wings, rising red sun on its fuselage. The pilot came so close, Pono saw him smile. He even waved.

She gathered the girls, pushing and shoving them up the beach into thick bushes. While they snuffled and screamed as if trying to climb inside her ribs, she squatted, hugging them to her, all of them, shielding them with her head and arms. Then, she closed her eyes. And saw.

A mama-san watering her plants looks up, sees spitfiring planes, and dies, blood sprinkling her orchids. A family in a car instantly incinerated. A child exploding in its mother's arms. Burning buildings, people leaping to their death. Charred corpses in a tofu factory. A saimin stand airborne, noodles raining down with limbs of seven high school athletes. A young boxer buried in the wreckage of a gym, his arms intact, legs never to be found. Bombed, machine gun strafed, shrapnel lodged in necks and hearts. A world of human jams and jellies. And in Pearl Harbor, battleships half submerged, pointing at the sky like smoldering fingers. And sailors, young sailors floating in their quiet tides.

She opened her eyes, saw more planes knock each other from the sky. In the hills behind her, an aerial torpedo hit a U.S. Air Force hangar holding a million rounds of machine gun ammunition. The earth shuddered and seemed to break in pieces. Somehow she crawled her daughters to the car, piling them in blankets on the floor. Then she accelerated up the highway, skidding like a madwoman. On the radio a fading voice, "McCoy ... the real McCoy ..." Wail of sirens, cars spinning, slamming into each other, humans in utter shock, not knowing where to hide.

A man waved from an ambulance, engine perforated with bomb splinters. "Queens Hospital. Need blood real bad!"

Hours later, Pono pushed her way inside the hospital. Corridors of flowing blood. Burn cases, mutilations in the thousands. A man squatted in a corner, cradling a human head like a dark cabbage. He cried out, begging someone to find the rest of his wife's body. Orderlies ran by ripping up hospital gowns for bandages. Surgeons, wearing rags across their mouths, operated in their underwear.

A nurse passed, carrying an amputation saw, eyes dead, her voice mechanical. "There is no more anesthesia." And everywhere, footprints and fingerprints in red.

By then, over a thousand civilians had lined up donating blood. Pono stood in line ten hours just to give one pint. Japanese arrived, offering blood, and money, each family dressed in black, the color worn when respect is due. A blind Hawaiian couple gave two pints, then stood in line to give again. In hospitals round the island, immigrant workers arrived, donating Chinese blood, and Filipino, blood of Puerto Rican and Korean. They came straight from their jobs, leaving donor beds stained with tractor oil, rust of machetes, filthy dust of sugarcane, red dirt of pine fields. They came, and they were welcomed.

Diplomats, rich *haole* corporate men and planters stood in line with cannery women, salesclerks, and servants. They wept openly, and held each other. Grief, the need to give. A pint of female blood contained more plasma than a man's. Word went out and women swarmed from every strata. High-born matrons, debutantes, waterfront prostitutes still wearing *cheongsams* Pono had made for them.

For days and weeks they volunteered, washing out bandages and tubing, throwing out body parts, painting "T" on foreheads of the wounded who received tetanus shots. Solemnly they folded uniforms of the dead, firemen, and policemen, men of the armed forces. They shared food and funeral clothes, hung denim blackout curtains for their neighbors, and painted over headlights of their cars. And for a time people drew together, forgetting race, religion, thinking only of each other and their precious islands. They would never be as vulnerable again, nor would they ever be as kind.

Not Mother Tongue

A WOMAN IN AN ALLEY near the waterfront. Pitch of nightly blackouts so complete she knows black marketeers only by their breath, the smell of Lucky Strikes. Transactions of the blind encoded by the senses. Her dollars slide across a calloused palm. He counts by feel the bills, places in her hand good-for-your-daughters nourishment, rusty blood-smell of something freshly killed—beef wrapped in ink-smelling newsprint. And then another weight, another packet, bitter-pungent smell that makes her sway, makes her mouth water, roasted beans of real kine coffee. Somewhere a skidding tire, shouts of military cops, more "Jap spies" taken for custodial detention. And she is running, a woman with a rubber face slung across her back.

They would be remembered as the gas-mask years. Government-issue worn by everyone, women, even infants. Rivers of cannery workers ebbing and flowing with rubber humpbacks. Some wore them hanging at their chests, like freak infants nursing. Even weddings: portraits of brides posed with gas masks tucked behind white gowns. And all the other accoutrements of war—martial law, curfews, fingerprinting, air raids, midnight arrests. Beaches barbed-wired, U.S. Army tanks surrounding 'Iolani Palace.

Japanese were spat upon, fired from their jobs. FBI teams arrived at midnight, took handcuffed neighbors off in trucks. At Sand Island Detention Center Japanese lived behind barbed wire in little tents, guarded round the clock. Some people hanged themselves in shame. A "Nip" caught with a shortwave radio in his orchid house was shot running down King Street in his pajamas.

Sugar and pineapple production were stepped up in those years, considered essential crops. After double shifts at the cannery, Pono swallowed nutmeg for false energy and labored as a volunteer, helped build air raid shelters, dig trenches in zigzag patterns to minimize casualties if bombs fell again. On weekends she helped inoculate hundreds of thousands against typhoid, diphtheria, smallpox, in case of epidemics. She made wreaths for graves of the dead.

She bought war bonds. And in return, a Red Cross supervisor let her make one phone call a month to Kalaupapa Missionary Hospital on Moloka'i. Travel was impossible. Japanese subs were shelling the outer islands. A U.S. naval station had been established "Topside" on Moloka'i, and patients down at Kalaupapa did their part, monitoring radio messages, scanning night skies for enemy bombers. Armed with nail-studded baseball bats and razor-sharp machetes, they patrolled the jungles and shoreline for infiltrators.

"Strange," Duke said, his voice ebbing and flowing through the ocean cables, "War has made us normal again, we feel important."

Watching local men go off to combat, Holo asked if her father was coming home to join them.

"He's already fighting somewhere," Pono said, and in a way it was so.

After six months, she discovered all inter-island calls were monitored by U.S. military intelligence. Everything she and Duke said had been heard by strangers; she went down on her knees, sick to her stomach. She paid two week's salary to be smuggled into Kalaupapa on a supply boat, then had to wait three months until the boat had space. They had one night together in 1942.

Holding each other, they talked for seven hours, while a radio played softly, "I'll Be Seeing You," and somewhere, someone sobbing, calling out a name. They talked about the shortages of meat, and butter, how Holo and Edita wrapped bandages and strung *lei* for wounded soldiers coming home. She told him how many more *Issei* and *Kibei* had been deported to mainland detention camps, and Buddhist and Shinto priests. And when her time was up, the supply boat ready to depart for Honolulu, Duke held his breath, then told her in one exhalation.

"We hear a new sulfone drug has been discovered, but precious little of it has reached us yet."

She grabbed him, begging. "What does it mean?"

". . . Maybe it will slow *ma'i Pākē*, even destroy it." It was so large a consideration, he said it casually.

She began praying to God again, still hoping if she prayed hard enough, she might learn to believe in him.

News came that, on the Big Island, the U.S. Army had turned the Ka'u Desert near Kilauea Crater into a training ground. Tanks crunched across volcano beds, graves of ancient warriors were obliterated by machine gun and mortar firing. There were rumblings from Pele. Flames shot from her fire pit at night. Then word came from Tang Pin that the Army had requisitioned the farm. Soldiers were billeted all over the house.

"One mess," he sobbed. "Evert'ing broken."

She began chanting, concentrating with all her might on each room in the house, each wall, each corridor, studying the very fibers in the wood, imagining *haole* soldiers with pale eyes, crude hands mauling Duke's genealogies. Touching his books. Their bed. After weeks of chanting, concentrating, word came again from Tang Pin. Strange things were happening. A young lieutenant broke his leg, walking in his sleep. The snapshot of a sergeant's wife wept blood. Men living in the house could not keep food down. Every night they heard a moaning, vapors clouded mirrors. After a year the Army evacuated the house, claiming it was "jinxed."

Pono silently rejoiced, and then she mourned. Tang Junior had enlisted, he was barely seventeen. When he was sent for basic training to Wisconsin, his father stopped eating, only a few rice grains a day, and when he was shipped out for combat in Italy, his father's heart stopped. When she told the girls, Holo walked outside and lay down with her face against the earth.

She had another night with Duke in spring 1943. Another, in the fall. Without visitors, patients were declining, dying of loneliness. Travel restrictions to Kalaupapa were eased somewhat but "due to the emergency," few visiting permits were issued. She bribed supply boat skippers whenever she could afford passage.

"You could be imprisoned," Duke warned.

"Small price to pay." Her fingers walked his face, feeling the thickness of the skin, trying to imagine it. She hadn't seen him in the light of day for three years. In the past two months he had begun the sulfone therapy. Patients were pessimistic; they had been through so many promises of cures.

"Is there improvement?" she asked. "Does it help?"

"The pain is less. There's hope." His dignity, his quiet acceptance which wasn't fatalism but a deep trust in life, made her feel greedy and ashamed.

The war droned on. In the cannery lunchroom women in white caps and aprons, arms raked and raw with pineapple rash, instructed each other on how to use brass knuckles, strangulation ropes, how to garrote the enemy if he returned. Under harsh neon lights, windows hung with blackout denim, big husky Hawaiians and delicate bird-boned Chinese showed each other how to knee a man between the legs, how to eviscerate with a small paring knife, how to break a windpipe with one karate chop.

In a corner, Japanese women sat alone, barely lifting their eyes. Sometimes, opening a lunch pail, they found live scorpions, a rat, human excrement. They never screamed, just stared, then closed their lunch pails quietly. One day a Japanese woman shoved her hand up into the pineapple slicing machine, and shoved and shoved. By the time they stopped the machine, the hand was unrecognizable, pulped flesh and crushed bones mangled past the wrist.

She held her hand out to workers, the non-Japanese, as supervisors carried her away. ""Bettah now? Huh? Dis *bettah* foah you?" And then she fainted.

The Andrew Sisters, "I'll Get By," the long, long nights, nights of praying, imagining Duke's healing. Nights of laundering her daughters' clothes, polishing their shoes. Damning them, yet proud. Honor students, each one, and someday they would go to university. She would find a way.

One day Holo stood before her in a prom gown, gas mask slung across her shoulder, a full-blown woman at sixteen. Pono stared, amazed. She looked at the others, hardly recognizing them. She looked in a mirror, she was thirty-five.

O Life, it was all before me. Then, somehow, it all got behind.

Humiliations, secret abominations, motherhood, the grinding years of work, the war. She had done it all alone, for him. Who else, if not for him? His hands could disintegrate, his feet could turn to claws, his bones could crumble in her palms, and she would still desire him. He had delved deep, chosen the best of what there was in her, and drawn it to the surface. Until Duke, Pono had not known who she was, how much she could be. He had taught her the verities of living, of the heart—honor, and pity and pride, compassion, sacrifice—lacking which a human life was doomed. All she had failed in was loving her children.

"She does things for us," Emma said. "She *must* love us."

Edita argued with her, turning bereaved and tedious whenever she discussed her mother. "She does them with resentment, even *hate*."

Holo knew her mother best, and when she spoke they listened. "It isn't hate. What Mama feels for us is love, but not exactly love, it's more . . . dangerous."

It wasn't something she could dredge up to the surface. When she thought of her mother, she thought of a hawk, tamed, brooding on a human wrist. After a while one forgot it was there, until you moved the wrong way, and it slashed you to pieces.

Victories, losses, the war went on and on, the only constant, the steady drizzle of mourners up in Punchbowl Cemetery, young dead soldiers coming home.

She dreamed of rivers of people, flesh melting from their bones. She dreamed it again and again. At first no one understood what happened in Hiroshima. Then, Nagasaki. Pictures smuggled out appeared in local papers: leveled cities, humans cindered into dust, shadows on walls where children had evaporated. They heard rumors of starving people in those cities, drinking broth made from hearts and livers of the dead. They were eating soil. In Kalihi, Japanese couples committed suicide out of grief. Their children carried paper lanterns to the sea, and soon small ribbons of softly glowing lights floated on the tide, returning spirits of the dead to the Buddhist paradise.

And then the war was over. It came like a silence, like held breath. First vague stupidity, disbelief. Then, jubilation. Bans were lifted, inter-island steamers sailed again. Pono felt such a fury of hope she gave off an odor of destruction. When she moved, her girls bent back like trees in hurricane.

"It's possible your father is finally coming home."

"Father."

A word they had always known, never felt, and so they had come to love the word because it named what was missing. Now she was threatening to fill that vacuum. They stepped back terrified, then went their quiet way, each girl trying to see herself through a father's eyes.

On that sulfone drug three years, ma'i Pākē *nearly arrested. So what if he's a little scarred, a little maimed—who will notice in the crowds of wounded soldiers coming home. A life is waiting. Now his girls can honor him. And maybe, after all, they will understand me.*

The inter-island steamer plied an ocean calm as glass. And she was a woman standing alone at the railing, lips moving so rapidly people thought she was praying.

She walked toward him down a beach, feeling herself enlarge, fattening up on courage, the will to move her feet.

And I will smile. Above all else. And I will accept.

Closing on him, she felt such terror, her shadow dropped behind her. Sun blinded her eyes, she moved by intuition. Nearing him, she heard the loud and raucous chattering of her teeth. And steeled herself, and looked.

Jesusyoubastard, Jesusyoubastard, why?

She had not seen him in broad daylight since 1941. She knew him only by his height. His face was the texture of boiled mud, hardened, bubbleblasted. The lips gone, as if they'd been sliced off. Scarred muscle tissues pulled all of his mouth to one side of his face. His nose bridge had finally collapsed.

"Beloved," he said softly. "This is what I have become."

He held his hands out, turning them palms up, then palms down. On one hand the fingers completely gone, the bone absorbed. A club. His arms were maps of lesion-scars, most of the muscles gone. He walked slowly, dragging one foot in a surgical boot.

Godyoucheat. Youcheat! I raised them, kept them all together, wasn't that enough?

Even in prayer, somehow she had resisted God by not believing. And God had paid her back.

She dragged her gaze across his face, picking out the good parts. His eyes still moderately clear, big, brown slanting, Polynesian eyes. And in them, deep within, a fierce, stubborn thing still ruffling its feathers, beating its wings. He was still the sum of everything that went before, of all that had made him. He was still the heart of things.

In that moment Pono saw that they would no longer be time-bound, that they were free to live in the future, the past, in fantasy. She understood with almost static serenity, that Duke would never leave this island. Nothing could save him now—not God, not science. His flesh had outpaced the medication, the damage could not be undone.

All those years, waiting for him to heal, to take him back into the world, she had been a woman preparing to live, not living. Now, she collapsed at his feet, mourning the not-lived years, mourning them like an orphan she must bury, and then burying them, her keening breaking the awful silence of that place. He gave her time, time to repudiate her dream, annihilate it. Gave her time to scrape around on her knees, biting up mouthfuls of sand. He gave her all the time she needed because that was what they had now. Time. Time congealed in changeless moments. Time to kill. Time that would be timeless. Even the mucus he spat up each day would quiver with time.

Finally, he lifted her to her feet. She dropped her head against his chest, exhausted. And she saw he was still the same, in that he demanded this of her: Dignity. Slowly, tenderly, he drew her to her full height.

"Beloved, how we walk out of this moment will determine how we remember it."

And she walked beside him feeling a strange and horrible happiness. For years, hope had battered at her. Like a drug, it had eaten away at her, ate her away from herself, left bone. Now, she took that bone, honing, honing, until it was sharp, a weapon. She would learn to aim it carefully. Each day would be the target. Duke took her arm, and carefully she matched his stride, and they were a couple walking the beach, struggling along in perverse magnificence.

After long nights engaged in pathetic monologues, she decided essential cold-heartedness was what was needed to tell them.

She gathered them together. "I'm afraid your father isn't coming home. I've learned he was killed in the war. I'm sorry." She wept, and it was easy. She was weeping for herself, not them.

One of them screamed, maybe the youngest. Edita plucked a gecko from the wall, and almost tenderly snapped its neck. The others faded like stains. She began to hear them moving round at night. A closing and opening of doors. Too numb to care, she felt a deep despondency consume her, she seemed to function less. One night she woke, someone outside moving past her room. She saw the movement every night for weeks, and then one evening she saw Edita crawling from her window.

She followed, not wanting to, compelled to. Neighborhoods became familiar, A'ala Park, Hotel Street, honky-tonk bars, houses of prostitution. Through a little door, and up the stairs, raucous crowds, fiery music jumping out at her. In din and smoke, Pono stood in shock, losing Edita for a while. Smell of cheap whiskey, someone sobbing in a microphone. Couples whirling past, like people dancing mambos on a carousel. Slender men with brutal faces, tight pants, barong Tagalog shirts, slick pomaded hair. Women made up like Egyptians, pompadour

hairdos, "toepinch" high heels, tight dresses following the curvature of
their behinds. The smell of brilliantine and sweat, damp powder, sour
armpits, the rotten fruit of stale perfumes. All the smells of desperation
and cheap dance halls. The men were Filipinos. The women were
anything.

A band behind the singer, frenzied strumming of guitars, bandurias,
their name emblazoned on the drums. VIBORA LUVIMINDA, the name of
the Filipino labor union which had given them better wages, better lives.
Many were citizens now, more assertive than the earlier generation.
They laughed, joked, stared brazenly at Pono. Smoke ebbed and flowed
like waves. Then she saw Edita.

She had changed her dress, remade herself. She looked ten years
older, professional and dangerous. Pono was so in shock, she didn't
move, she couldn't. Dark, voluptuous, disturbing, Edita slid round the
dance floor, moving her hips and shoulders like she was made for that
music, that life. Her partner spun her out, she flung her head back like
a movie star. He pulled her up against him, hard, so they seemed welded
together.

Too late, Pono thought, *it is too late. She has already chosen.* She pushed
through dancers, struggled out to the floor, as her daughter danced
groin-to-groin with this man, pelvises grinding, heads thrown back
ecstatically. Pono was the tallest, the biggest person in that room. She
lunged forward, picked her daughter up by her hair, held her high in
the air like dead game. People screamed. The dance partner, small and
wiry, seemed to be climbing Pono's shoulder.

She threw him off, screaming, "You *pilau* little *Flip*."

Music stopped, people froze. An odor permeated the crowd, the
smell of hate collecting round her. Edita whinnied, sobbing at her feet
where Pono dropped her. Her dance partner flicked his wrist; blue lights
from the ballroom chandelier reflected on his knife.

Pono looked at him and laughed. "You want her? Take her."

Edita struggled to her feet, thrusting her face into Pono's. "Yes! I
am his! I am carrying his child!"

She didn't even raise her voice. "You raving little slut." Then she
turned, pushing through the crowd.

Pushing her way blindly down the streets. *The lazy daughter, the
complaining one, always so yearning and vocal. I want! I want!* The one least
loved. The one let go of with such ease.

Holo tried to comfort her. "She isn't bad, Mama, she's just a taxi dancer not a prostitute. Don't you remember our 'uncles,' they were all Edita knew. She went down there looking for her father, for some kind of life."

"Don't speak to me of her. *Ever!*"

Holo didn't mention it again. She mentioned very little, seemed adrift in her own world. Then Pono found letters, piles of them ribboned and hidden in her underwear.

"Who is 'T'? What does he mean he dreams of holding you?"

Holo's face turned white, as if she had been internally punctured. "You read my letters?"

"I'm your mother. I have the right."

She was seventeen. For the first time in her life she had something of her own, something to protect. She turned on Pono, fearless.

"You have *nothing*. It's too late. You should have thought of motherhood when we were young."

Insane, she ripped up all of Holo's letters. "Tell me who he is!"

"All right, Mama." Her voice was deadly calm. "By and by you will know everything."

Four months later, Holo stood before her with a young man in a cheap suit, a war hero with a shattered shoulder. Holo seemed to be telling her that this was Tang Pin's son, Tang Junior. That she had loved him all these years, that he was using his G.I. Bill to go to accounting school, and that they had been married the night before. In Pono's eyes, her daughter seemed to enlarge and recede, so that her left cheek filled Pono's entire vision, then her face shrank to the size of a pin.

"*Pākē?* You have married a *Pākē?*" Ma'i Pākē. Stigma. Filth. Her oldest daughter, her pride, stoic witness to the years.

Later, Pono's memory would be that of a woman in a moving car, looking backwards—formless shadows, faint screams and flames rising up on either side of her in passing. Only months later would the images rinse clear: Pono attacking the young man, hammering at his damaged shoulder with her fists. Tang Junior trying to remind her who he was, who his father had been, how they had been loyal to Duke and his family's memory.

She heard nothing, saw nothing. "*Pākē! Pākē!*"

Holo and her husband running down the lane, Pono screaming at their heels. Then, the glowing blue pyre of Holo's clothes, books, high school honors—she would never graduate. Pono warming her hands at the flames, cursing her forever. Emma and Mina cowering in the arms of the neighbors, too frightened to come home. That night she poured salt all over herself, preserving Holo's memory, her betrayal, the way salt preserves a corpse. She banged on the door of the *lei* stringers.

"Give me back my girls." She took Emma's hand with her right, Mina's with her left. "You want kids, have your own. Dis friendship *pau*."

For days she stared at their dripping flowers overhanging her yard. One night after hours at the cannery, she started slapping wet mortar between ugly cement blocks, lifting them slowly, setting them evenly. She would work until one day the wall was higher than her head, blocking the *lei* stringers forever from her view. Night after night Mina cried for them. And Pono could hear them crying for her.

She knelt at Duke's feet, in abject despair. "I thought I had given our girls character, and conscience."

He stroked her head, thinking how one needed love to sustain those things.

After that, she kept her eye on Emma, pale-skinned, lovely, unpredictable. She seemed afraid of men, avoiding their eyes but moving round them in stops and starts, a victim's hesitation dance.

"You will graduate," Pono said. "You *must*. And go to university. To honor your father's memory."

She studied prodigiously, seemed to love books and music like her father. This pleased Pono, she gave her piano lessons, allowed her to visit the Listening Room, where for a small fee one could play classical records hour after hour.

Intent on Emma, Pono ignored the youngest one. One day when she was fourteen, Mina disappeared. A note in Pono's slipper. *"I hate you. You made me indecent."*

She read the note without sadness, without curiosity, read it almost without seeming to, without meaning to. She read it with a furtive poise, as if reading someone else's mail. Emma cried for weeks. Mina had been her favorite, the two of them united in a fundamental sadness, the two least wanted. Somehow she surmounted her resentment, tried to comfort Pono.

"She'll come back, Mama. She just wants attention."

"She'll come back ruined."

Emma thought how ruined they'd been all their lives. How they were born ruined. "We never wanted much. Just a little of your time."

"Time?" she whispered. "Ten, twelve hours at the cannery ... cooking ... ironing your Catholic uniforms at midnight. Shoes, bills ... four of you battering at me. No rest, running in my sleep."

"I know your life was hard, but sometimes we just needed to be held."

"You held each other."

"Oh, Mama . . ." She began to cry. "We were children. You never talked about our father. People said we had different fathers. Can you imagine what that's like. Kids called us *'ōpala manuahi*, bastard trash."

Pono gripped her arms, wanting to tell her she carried *ma'i Pākē* genes, that her father lived, a monster. She pulled herself together.

"Listen to me now. I know what people said, that I left you girls and went with men. And if I did? It was for you—food, clothes, Buster Browns. Your father didn't make much money. But he was a noble, learned man . . . oh, how he suffered."

Emma screamed, lost control and screamed for all the years. "Why couldn't we know him! Why didn't he come home!"

Pono flinched, seeing her own wildness in Emma. "In those days . . . there was no work here for locals. They went to Alaska to the mines. And then, the war."

"If we could have seen him! Even a photograph. We used to think he was a criminal, somewhere in hiding. You should have taken us to him. You deprived us of a father's love."

Something rose in her, just on the brink of fury. "What do you know of love! When you have survived without shelter, without speech or human dignity, when everything is scraped out of you because you honor something, won't let go of it . . . then you will deserve that word. It has to be earned."

"Why didn't *you* love us?"

"I did, Emma. I thought it was enough. Be glad for what you got. Some get much less."

But there were nights she stood looking down at empty beds. Nights when her hands flew to her face, remembering them dancing in their sleeping sarongs like little fireflies, clinging to each other in the dark. The beauty of each child. The shock, so late, of recognition.

Emma graduated with honors, and with a full scholarship entered the university in Manoa Valley. But there was little pride for Pono, one life could not make up for three. And Holo had been her favorite.

Loss seemed to deepen her conscience. She began to distinguish between lies that famished, and half-truths that nourished.

"Your father left me land on the Big Island. There's a house that's fallen down. That's where I sometimes go. One day I'll take you."

Emma seemed uninterested, caught up now in books, the bright and healthful quiet of deep thought.

The war had brought unionizing, better wages, fewer hours at the cannery. Pono felt suddenly less weighted, a plant pitched forward to the light. Still, sorrows ran deep, and guilt, and she began journeying back in her life trying to see where she had, in her feverish need for Duke, rejected parts of herself that would have made her a better mother, a more human being. She was over forty now, and maybe locating that former self would help her advance to the next phase of her life. She started swimming again, trying to retrieve the part of her cast aside for so many years, trying to fuse that cast-off self with the woman she had become.

Some days, stroking slowly, she saw fins moving in, listening to her heartbeat. They dove playfully, nudging her hip with their snouts, brushing along her back and shoulders, a gentle, sandpapery seduction. Pono swam with them a while, but only out of nostalgia. There would be time for dialogues, watery eons of shark-dreaming, her 'aumākua time. But for the present, she had to prove she was equal to this swift, disturbing human time. She had no appetite for blood, her jaw did not deform to snout.

Duke lived, or half lived, in perpetual grief for his lost daughters. But if their life could only be lived in fragments, that would be enough. Imagination was now the palette on which the life not lived, the life imagined, splashed, and breathed. Sometimes, lying on the cliffs above Kalaupapa, in the great choral fugue of nature, he and Pono studied colored plates of El Greco, Bonheur, Hiroshige's *One Hundred Views of Edo*. Or Duke read aloud, knowing she loved to project herself into characters and landscapes: to feel the fog of deserted floating palaces, the cold, damp napkins of Mann's winter Venice.

He read her Proust, cathedrals built in cork-lined rooms, until she fell asleep. And Gorki, abandoning romance for revolutionary drama of the slums. He read her his own verse: comical self-assessments, a secret vice, dreams of his lost daughters. In that way he kept her a thinker, a contemplator. Sometimes his voice would physically lift her, Pono would dance, dip and spin while he read on, swaying her broad, marbled, stretch-marked hips, long graceful torque of neck, then stand poised, an anchor in perfect arabesque. Only when he attempted to teach her to read did she withdraw, turn sullen. As if she distrusted printed words, could only accept strangers' thoughts if they were filtered through

Duke's amazing voice. And so life continued, endurably imperfect. They mourned, they imagined, they connected things with things.

One day, swimming on the north shore of Oʻahu, across the island from Honolulu, Pono looked up at U.S. bombers flying overhead. In town, new shiploads of American soldiers. People talked about Korea, calling it a "conflict," about Communist spies on the island ready to overthrow Democracy. She wondered where her daughters were. Would they be safe in another war. She swam to shallow waters, fought the undertow and dragged herself ashore. At that moment she heard something, a different sound, like the ocean clearing its throat. Picking up her towel, she watched small children playing in the surf.

A man stood up, gazing at the sea. "Strange da kine, too soon for changin' tide, neh?" The ocean was rapidly receding. The man called out again, "Hey, sometin' wrong da sea!"

Pono turned and saw a growing desert. Somewhere off Petropavlovsk the earth had quaked and cracked wide open, creating a towering *tsunami* heading straight for the Hawaiian Islands. In its first surge backward, the sea had left the ocean floor naked, acres of flapping, acrobatting fish, eels piled like fjords on reefs, giant octopi, astonished and exposed. People screamed, knowing what was coming. Livestock howled, and mongoose ran in squealing droves for upcountry shelter. The sky grew black and mothers swept their children from the surf, running toward high ground.

Then the ocean changed its mind, turned, and snapped back like a serpent. It approached in one awful wave, so loud it was silent, so massive it seemed to block the sky. Standing nearly eighty feet, it surged at several hundred miles an hour, obliterating the reef, approaching relentlessly. And it arrived, knocking houses flat, bearing cars, machinery swiftly inland. People grabbed for trees, telephone poles; the sound of humans crackling and frying.

Swept to the top of a construction crane floating like a prehistoric reptile, Pono watched the wave crash into a valley, taking bodies floating face-down. Hitting the point of the valley, the water began its recession, picking up ferocious speed. Railroad cars flew by like massive tankers. Buildings splintered, trucks broken up like toys. People reached out, looking operatic and doomed. Something floated near her, an Oriental boy. Face distorted like a rag, he screamed.

With no sense of it, Pono dived, grabbed the child as he swept by, and held him up to air. He screamed again, vomiting as she slid him onto her back, holding him with one hand, grabbing a tree limb with the other. Then she relaxed, let the ocean have its way, sweeping them miles out to sea. Years later the boy would swear they passed whales and dolphins, and sharks that pushed them up to air, kept them afloat with their snouts. He would swear Pono's skin turned gray, that her face changed shape, and that when his arms slid away from her neck, it was a fin he clung to.

Slowly the backwash exhausted itself, now everywhere debris. Bodies floated in and out. A human head, a fire truck. Bloated cattle upside down, a church, and somewhere a lone pig caterwauling. People who had watched the *tsunami* from the hills said they felt God, like glass, breaking through their foreheads. Children watching would never be young again; they had seen hundreds, a whole town disappear.

Pono spoke a half language, calming the child while she swam shoreward. There, delirium abounded, a small town lying on its side, kneelers plucking at corpses, trying to wake them. She staggered to shore, slid the boy from her back, and collapsed. Then the child gave way to terror, screaming for someone familiar. People approached, but not recognizing him as theirs, moved on. A short Japanese woman passed in a trance-state, then stood sobbing at the ocean. She seemed to be asking Why? Why?

The boy stretched out his arms to her, calling *"Tūtū! Tūtū!"*

The little woman turned. Pono looked into her face and felt a vague, eerie gleam of remembrance as the boy ran to her. Minutes later, holding him wrapped tight in a blanket, she bowed repeatedly, weeping, kissing Pono's hands, explaining he was her grandson, all she had. While she spoke, years slowly liquefied, images shivered. Pono remembered a prostitute named Miko, and her brave little girl who sat with her face to the wall.

"Run Run."

She stared at Pono, trying to remember, but all she could see was the undead child, and her mind called up a void.

"You know me?"

"Your mother was Miko."

"She dead. Everyt'ing dead but dis boy. How you know me?"

As if in response to her own question, she stepped back, looked Pono up and down. With almost mineral slowness, her expression changed, uncertainty, astonishment, clear joy.

"Pono! My *tita*! I search for you all my life. Now you come, save my child." She sobbed. With great, long honkings, she sat down and sobbed, pulling Pono down beside her so she seemed to be holding one small, and one very large, child. Hours later, in the heart of the broken town, she collected her meager life from a ramshackle room, then followed Pono home to Kalihi.

A *haole* stood in Pono's living room. A young U.S. Navy sailor, blond, blue-eyed, with a big, lopsided grin. Holding his hand, Emma carefully explained that they had met in the Listening Room, that he loved good music as she did. He had introduced her to Albinoni and Mussorgsky, composers she'd never heard of. They had spent the last few months meeting at the Listening Room, and they were in love. Emma wanted permission to become engaged before he shipped out to Korea.

Seeing Pono's face, Run Run picked up her child and backed out to the yard. It was the face of magisterial wrath, of all things destructive, it was the face of Satan.

"Not you," Pono whispered, staring at Emma.

Her voice seemed to come from the netherworld, slow and deep and hoarse, like someone damned.

"Not *you*. My last, my best daughter . . . You would go with . . . *haole*? You would be a . . . change-face? Do you know what they are? What they did to me?"

Emma held his hand tighter. The young sailor looked down. "Ma'am, we're not all bad."

"Emma. Take your hand away from him . . . or I will boil it for you."

"Mama, we want to be engaged. Do everything the right way. He's a good man. He wants me to meet his family on the mainland."

Pono rose, deadly calm. "Get him . . . out of here. Or I will kill him."

"He's going to Korea! He might die! Mama, please. We want to be engaged."

Pono moved to the kitchen. When she returned she was holding the glowing human-spine cane. She waved it in front of the sailor, began to tell its story, all of it, everything.

From the yard, Run Run heard Emma scream. She heard a chair being over-turned, saw the sailor rising to his feet, arm raised defensively. She heard the cracking impact of something hard against his head. He lifted the other arm. She heard the crack again. She saw him backing to the door, pulling Emma by her right arm, Pono waving a bloodied cane, pulling her back by her left.

Then Run Run heard what the girl called her, and she covered her grandson's ears.

Killer. She called her *Killer.* She called it over and over. She saw Pono drop the cane, saw her drop her daughter's arm. She saw Pono rear back as if thinking, contemplating the pale, lovely girl. Then she lunged, teeth ripping into her daughter's cheek. She saw the sailor's white face, white uniform, saw him running, half carrying the pale girl in the flowered dress, with the slashed cheek. She saw them diminishing, receding like a dream. She saw Pono standing alone, her daughter's blood scrawled across her lips.

Weeks later, Run Run was finally able to talk to her, to engage her. They sat in the dark, listening to her grandson's snores.

"When I fifteen," Run Run said, "Mama put me on da street. One customer knock me up. I have da child in same room where dey cleanin' fish-heads. I teach him what Mama teach me, turn face to da wall when I got customer. Life get real ugly. When my boy ten, I give up streets, learn cookin', moah bettah for yoah pride. When my boy eighteen, he bring home Toru, say it's his, da mama no want. Den he get shot selling drugs. Mot'er God take son, give me grandson. After many years, you find me, den lose your daughter. Mot'er God one strange *wahine.* Give wit' da right, take wit' da left."

After weeks spent in the backwash of rage and grief and silence, Pono took Run Run's hand.

"Teach me . . ." her voice was distant and broken, something crawling from a cave.

"Teach you what, *tita?* What you want to learn?"

". . . how to . . . live."

Run Run

EVERYT'ING I SAY NOT TRUE. *Who always need da truth? Sometime we just need stay sane. Dis part you bettah believe, foah shoah. Dis part fall from sleeve of truth like sweat. Pono one* wahine *widdout extra emotions. She love. Or hate. She also one* wahine *always doing what fear most—t'row herself in spots where can't always touch bottom.*

She learn to love Toru my grandson. Treat him like one big lazy cat, watch little flea playing on its paws. Afraid to touch, mash him like she mash her daughters. Sometime she look and look, just watch da day wash by.

"What you lookin' for?" I ask.

She still, like cobweb growin' from her mouth. One day she show me one black pearl, so big my eyes go bulge. And funny little book, she say made of jade.

"These were meant for Holo, my oldest," she say.

I t'ink dis Holo got untold stories bedded deep inside da skin. She her mama's witness all dose years. I t'ink what Pono waitin' for, she want Holo's shadow fall across her door again. She wait. And wait. Some days Pono disappear. Ot'er days she slowly wall up yard. Soon we livin' like two wāhine *in one coffin. Cement wall all way round dat Kalihi house.*

"Why we live like dis," I ask.

"Foah privacy," she say. "Foah save face."

Neighbors already seen too much. By and by, she talk. She tell me everyt'ing, it take her two years, tell me all. When she pau*, I know I her best friend. I also old woman, mourning foah her life.*

We walk down street, neighbors move aside, make room for her. Sometime keeds run up touch her, like need touch somet'ing one of a kine. Dey know she kahuna. *But here one funny t'ing. Pono got no power on herself. No magic foah change what life already given her. No can have Duke like normal man. Yeah, I know all about da kine. Maybe I love dis* kanaka, *too. He tragic.* Ma'i Pākē *keep Pono from happiness. But who know? Maybe dis a blessing.*

Happiness a funny t'ing, sometime rob you of compassion. Maybe we deeper when we hurt, neh? Lissen me. One day Pono come rollin' on da floor in pain. Later, find out in Kalaupapa, leper place, Duke got bad stomach sickness. One ot'er day, hot sunny day, no rain, Pono hair and clothes come soakin' wet! Find out big t'understorm at Kalaupapa, Duke catch real bad cold. Dis more den love, more den kahuna. *Maybe dis somet'ing make even Mot'er God sit down and t'ink.*

So I watch her, waitin' for dis daughter Holo come back home. She never come but nemmind. Mot'er God a funny wahine, *like I say, she send Pono somet'ing else instead. One day we come home find dis little t'ing wrapped up like one ham. Pono unwrap and scream. Ham got eyes and fingers, one note tied to wrist.*

"Her name is Rachel. Maybe you give her kine love I never got. Mina."

So. One daughter's vengeance now da whip on mama's back.

Dat's how we come travel to dis place, Big Island, two wāhine *and dere bastard keeds running from da world. Pono say moah bettah foah us. Big Island always been place of superstition, outcasts, rebels. Funny t'ing, we poor like dirt, first year everyt'ing is* pilau, *broken down, but dis where our happiness begin.*

I say, "Pono, try sell dat big, black pearl foah feed our keeds."

She no sell. Say Duke tell her moah bettah everybody own one t'ing dat's beautiful. Keep alive da soul. Now I see he one wise kanaka. *So, we work like slaves. Plant taro for sell* poi *factory. Plant sweet potato, daikon, cabbage, cucumbers, sell local grocers. Plant lichee, macadamia, anyt'ing, see what soil t'row back. Few dollars profit, we buy chickens, keep in coop under mango tree. Banana, papaya, mountain-apple tree grow wild. Plenty foah eat, save money. Pono say some day we grow da coffee bean again. Not Run Run, my hands come like pulp, small bleeding soldiers.*

I tell her, "My place da kitchen, I cook, you grow da fields."

By and by, she get one old man for gardenin'. After couple years she hire two.

One day I look round, peacocks squabbling in trees, bees in honeysuckle, dragonflies in ginger, chickens pecking in da dirt, radio playing, food huffing in da pot, keeds playin' on da floor. You know, I sit down, hold head and cry.

Pono shout, "What's wrong!"

I say, "Look! We happy! We two wāhine *got a life!"*

She laugh, tell me Duke say good she got a friend. She never had dis t'ing before. Pono mid-forties now. I five years behind.

I ask, "We old women now, neh?"

She say, "Maybe. Pretty soon."

I so happy. Old age time for respect. Now I say what on my mind. Even tell Mot'er God, "Listen, wahine, you take too much away from Pono, sometime you got no taste." But all da time, I touch da cross, so Mot'er God know where I stand.

I know I stubborn, not charmin' wahine. But who say friendship charmin'? I bully Pono, tell her hug da child. She lookin' frantic. I say, "Goin' lose Rachel like you lost da mama. Try show love." She try. I t'ink she try harder if dis be Holo's child.

Den one day Mot'er God tap me on da shoulder. I one sly wahine, get idea. Tell Pono old friend sick, I got take boat over Honolulu. She let me go. My brain so busy have to vomit out excitement on da boat, also too many waves. From boat I go down Chinatown, old neighborhood, dey know me on da streets. I see old customers, dey keed around wit' me, say I too old now for sell my body.

I laugh. "Listen, buggah, I got one life now you nevah dream."

Den I ask da Flips if hear of Edita, Pono's second girl. Got one kid now, maybe two. I ask and ask until my tongue hard like a doll's. Second day asking, one Flip lean close to me. I lie. Say Edita's mama very sick, asking for her.

He laugh. "Dis Pono one mean bitch. I know about. She t'row her daughters out. What you really want?"

Den I say da truth. Rachel abandoned by her mama, Mina, she all alone. Live in one big house, lots land. Pono growin' old. Be nice if Pono's daughters try bring dere keeds, Rachel's cousins, foah come see her, play wit' her.

Third day someone take me to Edita. She a woman now, live in tiny house, but clean. Her husband one young, handsome Flip, busboy in hotel, go refrigeration school at night, try be somebody. Edita very pretty, but years already growing on her hips, three babies now. Oldest, Vanya. When I say Pono's name, Edita cry. I hold her hand, cry too. T'ings our mamas done to us.

Den I say, "Look, she only human, got problems you cannot dream."

"She nevah explain t'ings," Edita say.

"Mama got explain?" I ask. "Giving birth not enough explanation?"

She laugh, look at her children. "Sometimes I like t'row dem away!"

But I see hurt, sharp hunger of her soul. I see it too late for Edita and Pono. But maybe not too late for daughter's daughter. Edita say maybe one day when Vanya older, let her visit Rachel on Big Island. Keeping blood apart not Hawaiian way. Dis how we come be pen pals, me and Edita. I no write so good, but not important. Fingers find da way. By and by, after one year, oldest daughter, Holo,

write me, find me through Edita. Holo want know for Rachel, what happen to
her mama. I so sorry, dis one t'ing Mot'er God never tell. Holo got kids, too,
oldest girl named Ming.

Two years pass, now Rachel five. One day Pono find out where my letters
from. How she find out, she one jealous wahine, want know who dese pen pals
be. Take my letters to da man who she sell taro. She look him in de eye, lock him
in da spell, say one word to him. "Read."

When she come home, she shove me. Hard. Won't listen what is said, what
is meant. She strike. My heart turn upside down. I grab clothes, grab Toru. He
fight me, want to stay. I look dis boy. He all I got. Da sum of what I am. I look
Pono, den say somet'ing very wise.

"One day you die, Pono. Duke die. Dis girl Rachel walk de earth one ghost.
No clan, no 'ohana. You keep her from her blood, and mad dogs gonna' gnaw
yoah bones. You gonna' rot in Hell." I leave.

Toru screamin' I drag him down da road. Rachel sobbing in da weeds. I hear
dis thundering, dese awful giant steps behind me. She grab me by da hair, I rearin'
up like rodeo horse, t'ink she tryin' kill me, bust me up. I try run. She slam fist
down my head. Me and Toru wake up in her lap like piglets in pilikua arms. She
huggin' us and little Rachel, lookin' scared. My head feel wet, so wet, her tears.
Sounds dat crack her chest like ax.

"No more," she sob, "no more."

My friend, my best friend. She finally see too much been subtracted from her
life. Maybe dis da day she start to look round, see time not standing still. What
gonna' happen, already happenin'. So, maybe dis why I been born, one bridge for
Pono's daughters, help dem make dere way back home. Finally, dey start to come,
each daughter. Dey come slow, like women walkin' into fire. At first Pono quiet,
like try be kind so dey come back bring dere keeds each summer foah dere cousin,
Rachel. But dis terrible old lion, she start swat dem daughters wit' her tongue.
Talk mean against dere husbands. Swat and swat until dey leave foah good. But,
you know, Mot'er God up dere, still take wit' her left, give wit' her right.

Rachel meet her many cousins, come close to t'ree of dem, Vanya, Jessamyn,
Ming. Dese t'ree love Rachel, come see her, stay and stay. Come back every summer,
like dey addicted to Big Island. What I t'ink is, dey addicted to Pono, like swimmers
addicted to da sea. Yeah, shoah, sea da mot'er of us all, but you no can tell,
sometime da bottom drop, suck swimmers down, grip de flesh till not'ing left but
bone.

Ka Po'e Hapa Hawai'i o Ka Honua Hou

Hybrids of the New World

Ka Hale o Nā Kīkepa Kea

House of White Sarongs

THEY COME BY PLANE TO THIS BLEAKEST and most desolate of places. They come returning to the woman who possesses them, whom they have never been able to let go of. Through the years, they come, arriving at the tiny airport of Keahole, an oasis, a green blink of palms in vast plains of lava, black mounds high as frozen cliffs. They slide into a taxi, and ride a highway snaking the dark forbidding landscape. Far off to the right, the sea, the brilliant sea, a blue suggestion hanging. And they are borne south and away, into the past. Each summer of their lives, they have lit down in this place—so bleak and scorched, early missionaries called it "Valley of Hell." And each summer, the lava, the black, smoldering land, has entered them a little more—becoming fixed in their vision, their memories. It has become their point of entry, and departure.

Now they see new wrinkles on the landscape, a giant yellow crane off in the distance gouging the lava, rearing back like a dinosaur. Ghettoes of concrete buildings, rental cars lined up in lots like dung beetles. A sprawling solar-energy lab far off to the left, white shriek against the black. The beginning of terrible sprawl: tract houses dotting the flanks of Hualālai, dormant volcano brooding in the sun.

Beside wrecked, oxidizing cars edging the road, the garish reds, purples, pinks of bougainvillea bushes, abundant, never-ending. And all across the land as far as the eye can see, messages, codes, entreaties spelled out in small, white pebbles stuck *in hard, pitted lava. HA'AHEO! . . . LŌKAHI! . . . KŌKUA 'OHANA! . . . MĀLAMA 'AINA! . . . HULI! HULI!*

After a time, the lava seems to part, a town sails forth Kailua, where tin-roofed shops shudder, overflown by giant jets, where tour buses spawn foreigners with video cameras, binoculars, sunglasses, like eager, monied, giant flies. Avoiding the town, they direct the driver up into the coffee-country hills of Kona District. Up, up two thousand feet, through little towns with "talk-song" names— Hōlualoa, Kainali'u, Kealakekua, Honaunau, Captain Cook. Slowly, the land becomes lush and green and mystic, the air cool, smell of cooking fires, guava, frangipani and soil, deep, rich soil.

The four of them stared silently as the taxi made its way up the old driveway lined with giant eucalypti. It was June, time of "Kona snow" white coffee blossoms washing the countryside with gardenia smell. The plantation was comparatively small, so planting, picking, sorting were all done by hand. In September when harvest was in full swing, flocks of Mexican, Micronesian, Filipino migrants would labor with baskets belted round their waists, picking ripe red coffee cherries, inside which was the jade-colored coffee bean.

Seeing the taxi sliding up the drive, workers in the fields yelled back and forth in Pidgin.

"Eh! Look, see. Pono girls come home!"

Up on the hill in the sprawling old house, Run Run cooked squabs full of ginger, garlic, lotus bulbs, black bean sauce on *aku, lomi* salmon, the girls' favorite dishes. While Run Run banged around, Marlboro sagging from her lips, Pono stood on the front *lānai*, heart banging so hard, her hair shivered. As the taxi drew nearer, she saw their faces turned her way, features growing clear.

There were other grandchildren, but these four—Rachel, Jess, Va-nya, Ming—were the ones who returned year after year down the decades of their lives, as if some swerving structure in their cells warped them forever backward to this lush, forbidding matriarch. Now she seemed to draw them up with her eyes. In a sweeping white *mu'umu'u*, long silver hair splashing her hips, her dark brown skin absorbed the light as if her power, her *mana*, forbade reflection. Stepping from the taxi, gazing at her, each woman felt fear bubble up, the girlish desire to please.

Pono studied them as they struggled with their luggage. Jess—

ruddy-skinned, in kahki jumpsuit, jungle boots, hair shorn like a recruit. Pono couldn't imagine that place where she lived, Manhattan. She had seen news reports, an island where people ate their pets, flung children from rooftops. And there was Vanya—intransigent, matronly, in tailored dress and "toepinch" shoes, trying to rein in her voluptuous looks. Rachel wore a simple dress, cardigan over her shoulders. But the dress was made of costly crimson Kyoto silk. Pono's eyes snagged on her face bare of makeup, leaving her beauty naked, therefore more startling. *Who does she fool?* Pono thought.

She turned lastly toward Ming, still sliding from the car. The shock. It had been a year since last she saw her. Now this daughter of her favorite daughter, Holo, looked suddenly aged, more sixty, than forty-five. Pono momentarily closed her eyes, keeping her balance. *She has stepped outside us, the constant pain.*

Now Run Run came screaming and chattering from the kitchen in her frayed, sun-bleached dress, rushing right past Pono.

"Ay, look, look, dey all come togedder! Who I goin' kiss first? Quick, come hug yoah aunty!"

They gathered round like feeding birds, while Run Run sobbed, embracing all of them, then each in turn.

"Mot'er God, look dis haircut! Jess look like one boy! Rachel, where yoah face? All naked like dat, shame! Vanya, Vanya, get out dem ugly, high-tone clothes . . ." Turning to Ming, she stepped back, her hand flew to her ribs.

"Ming, *Auwē*! You look too tired, make me cry."

Ming smiled, pale face benevolent and wise. Black hair pulled back severely in a bun, eyes blurred behind glasses, she seemed an aging academic—someone retired from discourse, from other humans. Run Run spun round, gazing at each of them, a wiry, little thing radiating all that was home, love, continuity. Above her on the *lānai*, their grand-mother's arms winged out in welcome, so she was momentarily poised like a statue. And it was as if the two women had been built there a century ago with the house and the coffee trees and the fields, as if they were carved out of the lava island itself, living ghosts haunting their genes, giving notice that they were home.

Then, as if she were the mother and Pono the child—unimaginably large, ferocious and moody—Run Run dragged the cousins up the steps like offerings, like dolls. They climbed slowly, gazing at Pono, her eyes unwavering, locking on each of them, searching out, dividing them, so each woman moved forward alone. Vanya held back as always and, perversely, Pono reached for her first, holding her distant, then hugging her.

"Vanya. You stay away too long." Though it had only been a year. More often than that was almost lethal, they were too much alike. Now, Pono pushed her gently away, her scent a sudden blow. She reeked of *haole*.

Ming came next, pale as a moth, melancholy eyes, frail little body. "Ming, oh, Ming." Pono hugged her the longest time.

Rachel thrust herself forward wanting it over, feeling Pono's fingers appraising the fabric of her dress as they embraced. Then Pono patted her back, dismissing her. Jess felt her grandmother's eyes devour her even before she let go of Rachel. Jess moved to her, whispering "*Tūtū!*" and Pono hugged her in silence. Most things that occurred between them would always be accomplished wordlessly, a choreography of looks.

Run Run danced round them pealing with laughter and relief, chattering nonsensically, leading them upstairs to separate rooms, joking, pinching cheeks, pinching bottoms.

"Jess, too thin! What dey feed you on da mainland? I gonna' stuff you wit *poi*. Good foah make you fat!"

Jess collapsed on the bed, hugging the old woman, loving her snaggled teeth going at crazy angles, her breath redolent of Marlboros.

Her voice went plaintive, she fought back tears. "Three years! She didn't even say she missed me."

Run Run turned quiet. "She miss you too much. Like miss yoah mot'er."

"No, she doesn't. She hates me. She never answers my letters."

"She yoah blood, yoah history. Someday maybe she explain you many t'ings."

"I'm forty, Run Run. I have a grown daughter. How long do I have to wait?"

Run Run laughed. "You got a choice? You wait. Like de others."

She kissed her cheek and left, moving on to Vanya's room, then Rachel's, Ming's—loving the life they brought to the big house, the crazy stirrings, loving their defiance, their fear, pigheadedness, instincts that connected them, all the silent rituals of blood. They were her little tribe of "many kine colors," skin different-hued but underneath, what she called "best kine blood, Hawaiian." Most of all she loved them, each one, for not seeing how much they resembled their grandmother.

Pono listened to them upstairs, chattering, gossiping, running in and out of rooms, then silence, their slow, stately descent downstairs. During dinner, she eyed them suspiciously, looking for change, but saw each woman had not deviated in her devotion to her, her fear of her, a fear she intentionally instilled. Someday when she was dead, they would know everything, and maybe they would hate her. Fear was the first step; she had taught them well.

Watching them bend over their plates, she saw how Vanya and Jess still ate voraciously, a way of avoiding her eyes. Rachel played with food, never seeming to actually eat. Now she sat toying with bamboo shoots, a pigeon heart, a beet, exclaiming over colors, how they mixed, bled, clashed.

Pono tapped her plate, "Run Run spent long hours on this meal. Fill the *'ōpū*, not the *maka*."

Run Run dashed in from the kitchen, covering the long mahogany table with more steaming dishes. "Vanya, tell us! You see kang'roo in Austraya?" She dashed out and returned, carrying a second bowl of rice. "Jess, how life in dat crazy Manhattan? It close to Cleveland? What da speed limit?" Her proliferation of questions, the same old questions, putting them at ease. "Rachel, what new t'ing Hiro bring you from Hong Kong? I like see dese treasures!"

Finally, she sat down with them, shoveling food between her great nicotine-stained teeth. Only then did Pono visibly relax. And in that magisterial repose, a signal: the other four relaxed, looked round the place, its windswept *lānai*. Only then did they glimpse the orchards, fields of "Kona snow" billowing out toward cliffs and far below the sea. Only then did they feel the ocean in water-haunted sunlight that lay across each room, making objects shiver. And only then did each woman feel impervious to the outside world, as the house closed round them.

So many sweet, dormant nights here, so many years, where childhood had faded into womanhood. Theirs were the fingerprints left on family albums, half-eaten photos of long-ago whalers and Tahitian beauties playing croquet with the king. Photos snapping and curling in corners where mucilage had dried, generations of photos until Pono. Then the albums had become something else, a world that mysteriously excluded men.

After dinner that night, Pono braided her hair in a long snake, pulled on high-top shoes and a big canvas jacket, left the house, and pulled up in her oxidizing Jeep.

"There's things I want you to see," she said, waving the women into the car. "Too much is happening, developments, controversy round the island."

She drove onto a paved road, then after a while, turned onto a long dirt road that led to a sacred wooded area outside Captain Cook, now threatened by Japanese and American developers.

"They want to raze this rain forest of old *koa* and monkeypod and *ohia* trees, build five power plants right over ancient, burial shrines."

The power plants would generate electricity that would be cabled over to the islands of Maui and Oʻahu, keeping empty high-rise office buildings lit all night. The sacred trees would be splintered into wood chips, burned to generate further electricity.

The women sat quietly, staring into mist-shrouded trees, a place where it was said "Night Marchers," ancient warrior ghosts, rested during the day. They heard faint murmurations. Jess felt bumps rise on her arms, saw Vanya lean forward, intent. They sat in utter silence, and after a while Pono backed up and turned around. As the Jeep rolled quietly away, something called after them.

"*'Ainaaaa . . . 'Ainaaa . . .*" The land. The land.

Pono drove back to the highway, kept to that course for a long, silent time, then after forty minutes or so, they entered the southern quarter of the Big Island called Kaʻu District. There she drove toward the southeast coast, an area of primeval cliffs and thunderous waves called Ka Lae, South Point. She turned off the igniton, staring at the cliffs.

"A huge spaceport being planned. Here on the first grounds of our ancestors!"

Vanya spoke up, already familiar with the plans. "The only area in the U.S., they say, where satellites can be launched into equatorial or polar orbits. Such a spaceport would deprive local fishermen of free access to the island's best fishing grounds. It would bring outsiders to fill technical jobs needed. Lifelong residents would lose their land."

They stood gazing along the coastline, site of earliest Polynesian landings almost two thousand years ago, site of ancient villages and fishing fleets, and sacred *heiau* still being excavated.

"Between here and Miloliʻi up the coast," Pono said, "they're building a nine-hundred-million-dollar Riviera Resort with marinas, the whole works. Chemicals, oil pollution, sewage. It will kill the fishing and the reef, impoverish all the *ole*-time net fisherman of these small coastal villages. I tell you it will kill off everything this side of the island."

She walked back slowly to the car; they followed close behind. "Why I'm telling you girls this . . . locals want me to join in the fight against its development. If I do, it will divide my workers, affect the coffee-harvesting season. *Haole* coffee distributors will blackball our plantation like before."

Later, back in the house, the women sat self-consciously, Pono eying each of them.

Finally, she cleared her throat. "Since you four will soon inherit this place, you need to make a decision on these things. I won't live forever."

The silence was palpable. They had never believed she would not live forever.

"*Tutu*," Ming said softly, "you have many good years . . ."

Pono waved her hand impatiently. "I have had today. This is all I know. And I am growing tired."

Alarmed, wanting to distract them, Vanya spoke up, explaining she had already offered her legal services to the coalition fighting the spacesport.

"What we have so far against spaceports is pretty impressive. We know that aluminum oxide poisoning is a by-product of solid rocket fuel during a launch. Alzheimer's disease is tied in with aluminum ingestion. We know clouds of polluting smoke from rocket launches inhaled by humans and animals are full of deadly toxins. A spaceport would conceivably destroy the ecosystem of the entire island. Pollutants will poison fish for miles around."

The others joined in, Jess offering medical opinions, Ming asking for the source of Vanya's information. With her granddaughters distracted, Pono sat back eyeing them, wondering who of them would really mourn her when she died, who really cared. Years yawned backwards and she saw herself warily welcoming her two oldest daughters, Holo and Edita, to the Big Island so their girls could meet Rachel. Then losing them again, alienating them, this time forever. And she learned how not loving, not having the love of one's children, diminishes the soul. Slowly, as her daughters' daughters returned summer after summer, she began in subtle ways to show them how they needed her, her wisdom, her mystery.

She instructed them in ocean ways. How eating certain seaweeds let them swim for hours without tiring. How to outsmart riptides by giving in. What shellfish were poisonous, and how to ride giant manta ray and dolphin. How to roll up in a ball when facing shark, how to tame shark, follow them to sleeping coves, and float beside them. And at what hour on a secret beach, the Pacific rolled in jewels from the

Orient. She tried to show them how women could do anything, and do it competently. How problems could be worked out if they ignored what people said and did what conscience required.

And always she reminded them, "Don't be drifters and dreamers. Don't get caught." Which the girls had interpreted as, "Don't be like your mothers." And so there had always been confusion in what she said, and what her granddaughters heard.

That night, hearing the squeak of bare feet on *koa* floors, she smiled, imagining them, full-blown women now, in white sleeping sarongs, running to each others' rooms. Ghosts of their girlhoods, like flames licking through the dark. She turned sideways on her pillow, imagining them huddled in one bed, still comparing their differences, their allegiances. Then she sighed, preparing herself for sleep.

Each night was a ritual now. Ingesting certain herbs that would clarify her dreams, Pono slept deeply and long, waiting for dreams to tell her how, and when, she would die. But dreams did not tell, they gave no clues. In sleep, she saw a corpse rocking on the ocean floor, but, as always, it was faceless. She jumped awake, suddenly terrified. *It is Duke's corpse. He is going to leave me behind.* She willed herself back into dreams, trying to see the face of the dead.

Restless, Jess walked barefoot through starlit coffee fields, her senses reaching out to the land, the land giving itself back to her in luxuriant gifts: smells, night sounds, damp soil underfoot, sea air detonating high in the roof of her mouth. Seeing the light in Vanya's window, she paused, watching her cousin's silhouette on the shade. She had always coveted Vanya's rich, dark skin. Not yellow, not caramel, but brown, the true golden-brown of Hawaiians. And she knew there had been years when Vanya envied her, hated her. *The walls of your white soul.* Making Jess feel bleached, useless as a root.

Tempestuous, always outspoken, this trip, Vanya was subdued. Lying with the others in their sleeping sarongs, she had said a strange thing. "She knows. She could smell *haole* on me. I absolutely reek." It came out of her so abruptly, so unexpectedly she got up and left the room.

Now, reflecting on Vanya, and Pono, and how Pono's beauty was duplicated in Vanya's face, her body, her gestures, Jess realized for the first time that this cousin, the one ever at odds with their grandmother, was probably the one most loved. *I used to think Ming was her favorite. But she's grown too private, too remote. Rachel is lost. And I am too haolefied, what my mother taught me, so we could survive in that other world, the one that killed her. It's Vanya, it was always Vanya.* She walked on through fields, heard dancing hoofs of a trotter, and saw someone approaching on horseback. It was Toru Sasaki, grandson of Run Run. They hadn't seen each other in several years.

From her window, Ming saw the figure on horseback slow down, cry out, slide from his saddle. She saw them embrace, spinning each other like brother and sister. She smiled, drew her shade. Reclining on an elbow, undoing the sash of her kimono, she arranged it round her comfortably, then reached for a pea-size wad of dark amber gum and her little bamboo pipe. Striking a match, she lit the pipe, dragging deeply, dreamily, repeating the gesture until she was stretched back completely, languorously, the pipe finished, in the bowl a tiny corpse.

"Toru," she whispered. "Forgive me."

Vanya

IT ISN'T LOVE. Maybe it isn't even lust. Maybe we just found a way to help each other sleep . . .

She brushes her long, wiry hair, sniffs her arms, her wrists.

. . . Three days since Darwin, still the haole *smell. Hit Tūtū like a blow. The bitch. When did she become my judge?*

She slides onto soft white fragrant sheets, air so damp and cool it leaves a sheen, like sweat. She remembers his sweat on her, all over her. She vows she will not fall asleep thinking of him.

. . . First time we made love, him unbuckling that gun strapped to his calf. Was that supposed to turn me on? Make me hot? And during the night, him rising soundlessly, buckling it back on, then lying down again, the thing cold like a reptile against my leg. Just before dawn this rough beast in me again, my dirty secret. Casting my lot once more with an outcast. Jesus, you think I would have learned. . . .

In that mild twilight of fatigue, waiting for sleep she forages backwards through the years.

. . . Sixteen, passing pigs sniffing coils of their own shit. Swinging my lunch pail toward Dole Cannery. Hating the life. Pineapple rash, hands slashed, sometimes screams, a woman's lopped-off finger. While up in Makiki Heights, rich whites using fingerbowls! Working that cannery for two summers saving for university. Christ, how I hated it, hated being mix-marriage mongrel. Hated seeing snot-nosed kids baubled with flies, mothers sucking warm cans of Primo. Smell of

pineapple still makes me sick . . . lunch pail full of sad same lunch—dried fish, riceballs, kimchi. *Rachel eloping, beginning her* waiwai *life with Hiro. Jess and Ming over on the Big Island lolling around like debutantes while I slaved at Dole . . .*

. . . Asking Mama, "Why can't Tūtū help with my tuition? She has that big house." Mama screaming, "You ask nothing from her. Nothing!" Me asking anyway. "She no got da money," Run Run says. "Fightin' keep dis place goin,' so can leave for you girls." Fuck it, then. Do it all alone, and doing it. Ten, twelve hours on assembly line, so tired can't sleep, can't stay awake. Tourists taking pictures, quaint island girls with lunch pails walking home to slums. Foreladies wonder why we spit in cans of pineapples going to the mainland . . .

. . . And entering university in Manoa Valley, frightened every day. What am I doing there, who do I think I am? Haole *students so well dressed, Orientals smarter. Silently swearing I will wear my fingers down, my eyes, I will die becoming something better. Smoothing out my English. Swallowing Pidgin, denying it, saving it for home, for "slang." This tongue I was born with, raised on, this part of my mouth demeaned, thrown out like garbage. Mama trying to keep up with me, ironing out her Pidgin, ironing other people's clothes. Papa telling her put down the iron, go to Dole, better wages at the cannery. She cringes. All her life the image of her mother's missing finger . . .*

. . . Papa coughing up in sunless rooms, small bones, frail ribs, propped before a black-and-white TV. His welfare checks, six-packs of Primo. He and friends ripping off hotel delivery trucks, selling their stash. Who could blame him? Five years refrigeration school, five years work, wife, children, to support. Then laid off, his heart. Six months, his heart improves. His job now filled by haole *from the mainland. Papa waits for job opening. Waits six years before he understands. No Flips wanted, still the bottom of the pile. He becomes a piece of furniture, propped in the living room before TV, prefiguration of an early grave . . .*

. . . University . . . this haole wahine *professor . . . a fondness for hugging me, which repulses me. Can't stand the idea of one of them touching me. Fish-belly skin, freckles, yellow teeth, their smell. And watching the news, violence on the mainland, a black boy charred, body parts dispersed. Sometimes in class, I'm the only dark-skin in a room of whites. I panic. Will I get out alive? Sometimes hating my Hawaiian mother, Filipino father. Sometimes hatred of myself. Men saying I'm beautiful who only want to fuck me. Maybe afterwards they will shit on me . . .*

Vanya tosses back and forth, memories jolting her awake, feeling the old resentments, the rage. And something else. The utter loneliness of those years.

. . . No one to talk to on campus, my slum friends thinking I've gone high-

tone, fancy-dancy. Can't even talk to "feminist" professors . . . the ones who see local women as "minority women," abstracts. Never ask us about our rage. How we manage to get through the day without killing. Where do we live, how do we eat? And breathe? Come on home, bitch. I will show you things. I begin to cultivate a who-can-I-knock-down-look. I begin to understand oppression . . .

. . . All those years a virgin, unaware of deep hunger between my hips. Until Ta'a Utu, handsome Samoan working his way through University, fire-dancing at the Moana. Me full of rum one night, getting up on stage, dancing shamelessly with him. Football scholarship, dark, muscled halfback with the gift of grace. Me burning when he swallowed fire . . . When did I first love him? When he entered me? When we woke in moonlight, his skin smelling of gasoline and cinnamon? His big hands holding my buttocks like loaves. No one had ever looked at me that way, treated me that way . . . deep, deep respect. For who I was, what I thought, my boundaries. "I will not go deeper inside you than you permit." Ta'a saying he would marry me after Stanford, graduate degree in engineering. Him telling me to go on, go on, be someone, apply for scholarships. And getting one . . . University of Chicago. Law! Neighbors laughing at my ambitions. Me laughing back. Yes. I will be a lawyer, crawl out of the maw chewing up our race. Mama weeping, Papa dumb. "How will you survive over there?" . . .

. . . BY WEARING IMAGINARY WHITE SKIN. By working part-time, full-time, anything. And getting off that Chicago plane terrified, so terrified. Knowing if I didn't freeze to death, the next three years would bleed me dry. And mainland classmates "nicing" me to death. "Where exactly is Hawai'i?" "What language do you people speak?" And townies with their bloodshot eyes, yelling from their pickups. "Hey, Nigger. Wetback. Bitch." Serving burgers at a fast-food. Switchboard operator. Two jobs, six days a week. Walking home at night, razor blades taped to my fingers. Scissors up my sleeves. Studying alone, eating-living-crying alone. Wanting so badly to make it, be adequate to my dreams . . .

Vanya sits up in the dark, weeping, remembering how in desperation she flew west and spent a weekend in a cheap Reno motel with Ta'a, both so homesick they looked pinched and old. His complaints of Stanford—racism, elitism, having to compete with men from Yale and Princeton. And Ta'a quitting Stanford in his second year. She shakes her head, remembering an eighteen-hour flight to Apia, Western Samoa, from Chicago. Their rendezvous. Their vows. And meeting his family, pure Samoans, proud, lighter-skinned than Vanya.

. . . And me with Flip blood. Jesus. His mother telling me in the softest voice, they had already chosen Ta'a's bride, daughter of a high chieftain. Ta'a weeping, explaining. "It is my father's wish. If I do not, I will be cast out from family, tribe." My swift departure. Calling Jess long-distance. Bypassing Honolulu, Chi-

cago, arriving drunk in New York City thirty hours later. Jess apprenticing as a vet, washing out acquarium tanks, tending convalescent animals. Polite disdain of the pale, blond Southerner she's dating. As if my skin were striped. And getting lost, picked up for loitering on Park Avenue. La-di-da doormen thinking I was cruising, a Harlem hooker, and calling cops. Jess standing in the precinct station red-faced. Cops apologizing while she screamed. "She's my cousin! She's studying law!" As if that changed the color of my skin . . .

. . . Two mix-marriage mongrels weeping in her bed, arms wrapped round each other like lost girls, wondering how we got there? Where were we? Who was I? And who was she? Me telling her that city would kill her. It would noise her to death. A year later Jess calling me long-distance. What the doctor did to her. O Jess! Jess! Maybe that was when I really loved her, when I saw how much she kept inside. (When we were young, how many times I hit her in the face, not very hard, not because I wanted to, only to satisfy the different colors of our skin) . . .

. . . So many times in those Chicago years, calling the Big Island, crying collect. Pono on the phone, voice deep, mean, but somehow kind. "How bad you want that law degree?" "Enough to kill for," I cry. "Then kill the fear. Be strong." Once, I thought I heard her say, "I am very proud." And finally, coming home, marrying Rigo, handsome Flip, secondary math teacher. Marrying because he admired me, would not compete with me. And because I had spent too many years alone.

She thinks back on the early years of practice, the struggle as a native. And a woman. Working for the Honolulu Legal Aid, fighting for native Hawaiian land rights, more jobs, more food stamps for low-income families. The senior partner of her firm expecting her to serve his coffee and doughnuts, asking her to dig up files while he studied her behind. Moving to another firm, working to improve prison conditions, and seeing so many of her childhood friends behind those bars, following the maze from juvenile hall to prison, life incarceration.

The years became a decade, Vanya's life dedicated to fighting for reforms. Fighting banks withdrawing business loans from Filipino barbershops in favor of more profitable Chinese restaurants. Fighting the stripping of Hawaiian students' scholarship funds in favor of brighter, more promising Orientals. The futility. Then Vanya and two colleagues struggling to incorporate a female law firm. Bank loans turned down seven times. Banks saying women didn't have the clout, would never attract clients. A bank officer, suave with tiepin and matching cuff links, staring at her breasts. Vanya staring at the scissors on his desk.

. . . (Five years passing, Ta'a Utu not fading from my dreams. Smell of cinnamon, even gasoline, leaving me breathless, inarticulate.) Late seventies . . .

Nationalist movement growing, Hawaiians wanting back their lands, their Mother Tongue. Thirty high schools and colleges voting to secede. "From what?" Mama asks. "From the United States, from desecration of our lands, economic slavery of our people." Papa sucking his Primo . . .

. . . Tense summers at Pono's, her coffee business thriving. Making us eat dinner by candlelight like haole! My cousins so manakā. Ming buried in academia, her books, her Bach. Rachel practicing the shamizen for Hiro, his little concubine. Me screaming, calling them names, wanting to snap them out of that bog of apathy. Pono looking like she wished me dead. Saying she was not a racist. Who was she kidding? Who ate at table with her besides Run Run? Not the little Puerto Rican girl who washed vegetables, not the Filipino housemaid, not the Filipino gardener. Not Ming's father. Not my own . . .

One night Vanya had gone to Ming, reminding her how their parents had slaved. Ming's Chinese father, Tang, a shattered-shoulder cook, her mother, Holo, ten years attendant in a women's prison, years she would not talk about, now a woman sewing other people's clothes. Vanya's father finished, her mother, Edita, eyes gone from all the years of spraying starch on other people's laundry. These women who had survived Pono, still sacrificing parts of themselves, their daughters, throwing them across the channel every summer so they would know their cousin, Rachel. Did Pono ever help them, even send them bags of gourmet coffee beans? No. Nothing.

Then one night Run Run had handed her a check. $1,000. "From yoah *tūtū,* and a little bit from me!" Stunned, Vanya asked, "For what?" Run Run had laughed. "Foah *Kokua Hawai'i* . . . Silly girl! T'ink we no care?" Vanya running to Pono, hugging her, and Pono turning away, collecting herself, turning back and looking Vanya in the eye. "Be strong. Dare everything." And Vanya feeling for the first time maybe this woman understood her. Even loved her.

. . . And all the while my boy, my keiki kāne, Hernando, growing up. Now at Punahou, private school. Wants to be a judge. So bright he skips two grades. But they discourage him from college preparatory courses, suggest auto mechanics, carpentry. Be a doorman, plumber, cop. I threaten to sue, pull him out of Punahou, put him in McKinley, public school with high scholastic standards. Competing with smart Orientals, he holds his own, my pride. And me traveling the South Pacific, networking with other native Nationalist women. Fiji, Tonga, Vanuatu, New Zealand, Australia. All fighting for same issues, equal wages, housing, education, recognition . . .

. . . One day in Auckland, this face stepping from a crowd. In suit and

briefcase, Ta'a Utu. We stumble into a shop, finger souvenirs while staring at each other. ". . . Never forgot you, Vanya . . . dream of you." Examining sheepskin jacket, jars of Waitaiki tongues. "I hope you're miserable. I hope your wife is bowlegged." Him laughing, and then tears. "I named my second daughter, Vanya, after you." Six nights together in that Auckland hotel, forgetting meetings, forgetting everything, describing our lives, the struggle, the bureaucrats. The man I married out of loneliness and gratitude. "He teaches math, gambles, watches 'The Love Boat' on TV. My son, Hernando, big, robust. Ten years old, looks like fifteen. Pure Polynesian-looking." Me lying there, wishing Hernando were Ta'a's son . . .

. . . And it begins, my monthly trips to Auckland, Ta'a meeting me. Five children, he will never leave his wife. "Then this will be enough," I say. My tongue burning, shaping itself to compromise, take crumbs from another woman's life. My body burning, knowing it moves and pleases, swallows, another woman's husband. Nothing can help me now. My cells are hooked, holding on, holding fast. I am a woman who holds fast. I think of Rachel and her unspeakable marriage. Alike, we are alike. Dumb, with a floating serenity of blind intent, loving out of all reason. Our drowning shadows waiting for our drowning . . .

. . . So makapō! *I don't see that drowning shadow waiting for my son. So driven by my loins, I let time go. And he is twelve, looking seventeen. That summer strange . . . typhoons, shark attacks, infants disappearing from their cribs. And natives swimming for Kaho'olawe, island of sacred Hawaiian* heiau, *protesting U.S. Navy bomb testing there, fifty years of blasting it with rockets. Hernando lies about his age, joins up with militants heading for the island to set up camp in protest, daring the Navy to bomb them. Hernando! Where was I? How did you slip away? Anchoring their boat in deep waters, swimming for shore, something dragged him down . . .*

Now she sobs in the dark, remembering. She was dozing peacefully on her *lānai*, dreaming of Ta'a Utu. Dreaming they could run away, leave it all behind. She remembers looking up. Rachel in a bright dress bringing her the news, a splashed palette moving through the leaves. She remembers her cells jostling each other, absorbing what Rachel is trying to say. In that moment they stepped out of time and entered a frame, a memory. That's what always comes back to her, that moment, the sheer peace before the splash between the leaves.

. . . After that couldn't talk to Rachel, couldn't look at her. Let her pay for everything, like it was her fault. Memorial, lū'au, *Hawaiian Nationalist spokesmen, several hundred people. Huge wreaths, endless ceremonies. Me screaming "Where is he? Where's the body? Who is pulling my leg?" My marriage goes, lost to grief.*

My skeleton alters, flesh lets go. Everything, even pubic hair turns white. Ming saying my body died for Hernando; what will regenerate is him reborn in me. What does she know, her vapid little life. She tries to preach that Buddhist crap— nothing is permanent, death is our natural condition. I bust her house up, throw furniture around, smash her Bach and Brahms . . .

. . . Flying to Ta'a, his horror at my face, a mask hung shapeless from my skull. He holds this sack, instantly old. He penetrates this hag. Using him like it was his fault, too, using him to fuck my way back to life, to sanity, slowly taking back the colorations. My hair growing black again, metabolism speeding up, flesh tightening. Then my drowning shadow surfacing above me. Ta'a's daughter, Vanya, struck with polio. "God's will," he sobs. "Our penance." Hernando gone, his daughter crippled. Me begging, "Give me another child." And Ta'a horrified, saying God will deliver us a freak. Now, he comes outside me, slowly kills me, lets go of me. One day, silently he walks away, leaves me screaming in a strange hotel, belly graffitied with dead sperm . . .

. . . the months, the years, humping myself into stupors with faceless men picked up in Auckland bars, beside airport carousels of locked leather. Slender Ethiopian, high buttocks like black tar. Korean drinking like an Irishman. Malaysian rubber king, brandy and Gitaines. An Indian with khas-smelling hair, impotent, describing cremation on the Ganges, ". . . mourners staying with the corpse until the head explodes." He only wants to suck my breasts. I hit him with my fists. "I'm not a bloody cow." Chaos, the meshing of my gears . . .

. . . Daring Pono, daring her to say one word. The stink of different nationalities on me. She's too distracted, grieving for Hernando, having loved him unnacountably, his robustness, his huge, godlike size. "He remind her someone," Run Run whispered. Her grief goes on and on, her looks so deadly, for three summers, Jess stays away. Jess and her mainland life, her own pale child, a daughter who betrayed her . . .

. . . Auwē! Our history . . . Tongueless women, eyes filled with ignorance of our own blood. I give Pono if-looks-could-kill stares, blame it all on her. What father was so rotten she couldn't tell our mothers who he was? And if she was a whore? If there were many fathers? TELL US! Too late for Jess's mother, dead, Rachel's disappeared. Ming's mama and mine, too damaged to care . . . and us, all those summers, little girls looking sideways for identity. Now grown women whose history rots beneath the layers of our skin . . .

. . . And in my rotting, meeting Simon Weir. I should have hawked and spat, walked away. His lips stretched tight, measuring the chances he would take with me. Eyes, intense blueness of burnt blades. Him circling me, my pulse fast, I can't wait to hate him. Outside that shabby hotel, flying foxes sleeping upside down in their own filth. Inside, creaking infinity of warped floorboards, ratty bed, oxidizing

springs, insects immolating themselves in the Rid-Ray. The place perfect. Combusti-
ble. Then he is in me, and he is nothing to me, a way to pass time between grief
and grief. And what is left for me, but mourning. Whoring. Lust a lunatic grinning
through a crowd.

She throws her arms out in the dark, and there is nothing.

. . . Hernando! I stand sonless all my days . . .

Ming

SHE WAKES, HER MOUTH SO VERY SOUR. She can feel the wolf approaching, her joints beginning to ache. Unless she can outrun it. Try. She lights another pipe, and counts back slowly, years of terrible fevers, arthritis, bone-weary fatigue. Hair loss, mouth sores, a crackling in the heart and lungs. And always, the butterfly rash across her nose and cheeks—a wolf's facial markings.

   . . . *One day they say my heart will fail. Or kidneys. System-ic lu-pus er-y-them-a-to-sus, enunciated slowly, like a mantra. Sometimes the wolf retreats, and I betray him with good health. The wrath when he returns. Dermatologists, rheumatologists, immunologists, their silly therapies—corticosteroids, antimalarials, immunosuppressants. Untamed, he comes and goes, my wolf. He is my sentence, the heavy bars before me. But I have something that unlocks those bars. He attacks, I deceive. How we abuse each other . . .*

   . . . *One day we will reach a truce, lie down together, join my father's ancestors: newborn girls whose mouths were stuffed with ash, soft-shouldered eunuchs beheaded for errors in calligraphy, courtesans with three-inch feet that ran to rot. Mistakes erased from the family genealogy. We will be fleetfooted, my wolf and I, dash through the afterlife without being bothered by stares . . .*

   . . . *Nineteen when it first struck. Papa trying to save me, bringing stews of garlic, cinnabar and rooster blood. Lungs of vermilion river frog, genitals of swans. Circling my room with* mi yao, *distracting evil spirits. Mama weeping, scouring my body like she did when I was small, looking for lesions on my skin. One night*

Pono standing at my bed, studying my delirium, arthritic limbs, looking at my skin like Mama. I knew what they were looking for. I have always known . . .

. . . Rachel, Vanya, Jess see me as mystical, a kind of martyr nailed to the crucifix of pain, humiliation. How can I explain to them how illness brings its twisted gifts. Privacy. And journeys. Dark hinterlands where creatures jibber, jeer and drool. My wolf visitations. My cousins mistake my silences for wisdom, my intuitions for magic. O dearest women, barefoot familiars of my youth! If I am magical it is only in the way rotting trees give off a kind of light . . .

. . . Maybe I was born exhausted, years of running in my mother's genes. I never learned to laugh. So quiet, people talked around me. In this way one learns. Father says I was a somber child, staring, contemplating. I remember him squatting in his vegetable patch—a garden so small he could hoe all corners of it from the center—crooning to me in my cradle. And Papa's "HAH! HAH! HAH!" at dawn, practicing Gong Fu in our little balding yard. In later years explaining it was good for his shoulder, shot in World War II. Growing up, I would wake, rest my head on the windowsill, see the sun coming up between his strong, yellow calves. Papa poised, a frozen warrior, the Mantis Walk, the Tiger Leap, the Cobra Coil—in his mind, vanquishing the enemy, the crack-shot German soldier. Even with his shattered shoulder, he could split giant summer squashes with two fingers. ZAP! . . .

. . . O Papa, I see you coming home from war, armed only with your dreams. To be someone, become someone, something more than stoop-work "coolie." Studying bookkeeping on the G.I. Bill, marrying an un-Chinese. But then, your shoulder refusing long hours turning into years, the physical endurance of hunching at a desk. O dreams! How they evaporated in the steam of kitchens wetly soothing, comforting your wounds. And you became a cook, floating in the fog of other people's meals . . .

In her half stupor, Ming didn't taste the tears brackish on her lips. She tasted stale rice, cold tea, the hard years when her father failed at bookkeeping, when he was learning to be *chef kine*, stealing salt and fish-heads from the restaurant for his family. Weeping, soaking his feet at night, while Ming massaged his shoulder, reciting her lessons. The years her mother worked as night attendant in the local women's prison, things her mother saw she never spoke of. Years her mother walked home, saving bus fare. For Ming, Ming's brothers, everything for them, their education.

. . . And Papa doing woman-chores for Mama . . . ear cleaning, toenail clipping, polishing our shoes. Some nights, shampooing my hair, drying it gently as if I were porcelain. And his fantastic stories! Tales of the Water Margin, stories of Gong Fu heroes, performing deeds like Robin Hood and his men of Sherwood

Forest. Sometimes, in a silly mood, Papa changed the endings or the beginnings. Sometimes Lu Zhishen, or Phony Monk, ended up a real monk, sometimes an emperor, a roasted dog. One day Papa bringing me a gift, a book of fairy tales. In this way, he led me to my Right World. Lives did not begin until I opened books, and when I closed them, lives were suspended, waiting for my eye, my finger on the page. The power! So I learned how Art does not betray . . .

. . . Other things he taught me: Pākē rituals of hospitality, sometimes lost to hapa-Pākē. How to hold chopsticks properly, palm up, never down. How to hold a bowl of rice, and tiny no-handle cups. Never to be late, too talkative. He taught me the un-Chinese. Father-affection. Father-love. Mama was loving, but only with her eyes, her silences. Held back by that invisible leash, her past. One day I opened Mama's lunch pail, threw her lunch out in the gutter. "Why can't you hug us, laugh with us, like Papa?" Why did brothers and I have to suffer for what Pono did to her. . . .

. . . "When angry do-say nothing," Papa instructed. "Before do-say something stupid, count to ten. If very angry, count to ten backwards. In Chinese." This was very hard, Papa very wise!

Mostly, I said nothing, growing up. A book-swallower, people thought I was bright, so I became bright. Even when marriage came, and children, I said mostly nothing, always living with the hermit's quirky grasp of words. Even now, the wolf years, books, music, thought, my consolation, that edge I count on when all the normal signs don't speak. The mind, the mind. Imagine, in one moment, you can see a hundred years!. . .

Sometimes Ming feels mild nostalgia for the early years, husband, Johnny, attentive, her children young, her body strong. Sundays in Chinatown, son and daughter carrying their Chinese singing parrot, Fong, to little tea shops where old men competed ruthlessly. Whose caged bird sang the brightest, the loudest. Chrysanthemum tea, shrimp dumplings, lotus-seed mooncakes. Her son and daughter laughing, small legs carrying them down streets where they guessed Chinese riddles printed on hanging paper lanterns.

. . . My little Pākē-kanaka. Life was most real for me when they were young, and still believed in magic. Johnny saying magic fit in with my meditative temperament. And then, my wolf returning, claiming me more often. My children frightened into strangers. The years. Haunted nights of sleeplessness, "white nights," when I turned to books. Johnny asking if his snores disturbed my reading, if he has left me enough space in our bed. Me thinking how one can read in the space of a coffin . . .

. . . I try gentle humor, telling him the concept of good health, normal life, bores me, the slow drip of the quotidian. "But you're still young," he says. "There's

so much life to live!" How can I speak of my exhaustion? When my wolf comes,
he consumes everything, even my excrement. Face haggard, eyes ringed like targets,
wolf mark spread across my face, spine bent, fingers swirling arthritically. Confront-
ing myself in mirrors, I cannot look, cannot turn away. When it hits me in full
stride, I ask Johnny to smother me, stab me in the heart. He weeps, measures out
my medication. And when the wolf softly pads away, what's left of me is ravened
from within. What now inhabits me? What stares out? A raw and wide-mouthed
nerve, begging, begging . . .

. . . "Expect nothing," the Buddha says. "Do not hope to attain. Go lightly
on the way." A sequin on the path, a sign. Pain can become another thing. Thus,
I turn to that bright sequin, Dragon Seed, buried in the smoked skin of my mind.
It leaves me aerial, embalmed. There is my Mongol in the Gobi, milking his singing
horse. Does he know that in the Gobi there are many types of water? Water that
lies two feet under sand. And water lying at a depth of one foot if one is positioned
near certain ancient dunes. Buri water is no good, it will kill you. And at certain
points of sun, if one stands in the length of one's own shadow, yen bur water can
be had, by scraping the sand ever so lightly. Once, the troops of K'ang-Hsi,
emperor of China, marched for forty-seven years without seeing a river or a stream,
surviving because they possessed water-wisdom and faith in their own shadows . . .

. . . I have faith in nothing now, lusted after by the wolf, addicted to the
Dragon. What are emotions, they chafe like uncured skins . . . O Toru! Only you
can understand and you have turned away. My knight, my mounted archer, who
first rode out to slay the Dragon, bringing me its seed. Before you, there was only
weak medication, my face stepped on by the will to die. Then you, home a hero
from the war, limping, damaged in so many ways.

In the dark, Ming sighs, remembering Toru home from Vietnam,
the two of them drawing together as damaged people do, him showing
her his blown-up foot, Ming explaining her wolf mark, butterfly rash
across the face, joints hugely swollen, her slowly curling spine. One day
after long hours of teaching, picking the dead man's hand of ignorance
off the faces of her students, Toru was waiting for her, waiting to lead
her down to Chinatown. She remembers sounds of honky-tonk saloons
and laughing bar-girls, singsong shouts of old men gambling at *mah-jongg*
and fan-tan. Midst hidden chimes, burning joss, smell of salt fish, ginger,
jook, she remembers ancient addicts clinging to tenement walls, like
starfish.

. . . I knew where we were going. I wanted to. A greasy alley, tiny man in
black pajamas opening the door. Face rigid, like a loaded pistol. Until he sees
Toru's wad of dollars. Leading us through steamy, crowded rooms, families brooding
over plates of food on oilcloth. Chopsticks poised, old woman waving, prawn

collapsed between her teeth. Sudden courtyard, then a slum of orchids. Long, dark room like a tunnel. Bunks, old mattresses against a wall. My knees collapsing, "I don't think I can." Toru's hand warm on my hip. "Try, Ming. It make everyt'ing kind." His voice odd, lungs already hungry, waiting . . .

. . . Oh, I remember . . . Sitting on a bunk, skin jumping off my face. Bamboo pipes, little oil lamps, brown gum like little playing marbles. Inhale, choke, inhale, get pipe going over flames. "Give me your hand," I beg, so afraid of dying. His hand warm and steady in mine. Then him lying beside me, someone somewhere moaning in their dreams. The gum all burned away, sweet smoke clotting my lungs. I want to be sick. Try to open my mouth. Form. The. Words. And cannot. So massively adrift. And somewhere . . . somewhere in the Gobi, a Mongol milks a singing horse. Caravans approach. Someone quietly removes my skin. "Toru!" His hand still in mine. I feel its weight. Could be a dog's paw, a grenade . . .

. . . How well they get to know us in that alley! My nausea slowly rinsing away. One night on those bunks, Toru coming at me, slick and amber. Bodies drugged, hijacked, indifferent as assassins. "I am a married woman." "Yes," he says, moving deep inside me. He promises we'll never grow addicted. If we respect Dragon Seed, it respects us. And yet, and yet . . . one day at school, in front of students, I moan. Feel like my lips are curling back. Filth, an appetite for filth. Turning away from my family, afraid my sour breath will convict me. Nothing helps. Not garlic, myrrh, not coriander . . .

. . . Now the little man in black pajamas greets us like family, eyes plump with the never-to-be-said: we are reaching the point where Dragon Seed ceases to be kind, the point at which its motionless speed addicts to you. Losing interest in other humans. Sitting like Ice Age artifacts, waiting for the hour of small gestures, lighting of a pipe. Still, somehow managing my family, classes, students, great spurts of academic passion. Term papers corrected overnight . . .

. . . One night, Toru quietly rolling up his sleeves. On his arms, snail track tattoos. "Oh, Toru." I touch the tracks, trying to erase them. "Ming," he says softly. "You not tired of this nineteenth-century shit? Dragon Seed small-time. Let me give you somet'ing make you soar, make you see da walls part." Backing away from him in horror, so terrified I even back away from Seed. The nights. My nerve ends begging, each nerve a gaping mouth. Nights when I cry for it, that smoke licking at my lungs. A feeling deeper than need, deeper than the human condition, like back-flipping through my soul. Going to Chinatown alone, smelling the smells. Walls hung with mildew. Mattresses of living yeast. Whose lips have touched this pipe? I cannot do it without Toru . . .

She sighs again, remembering how even the memory of clicking mah-jongg tiles in that alley made her retch. Or was she retching from the lack of it? Acupuncture, herbal cures, insomnia, gut-grinding weeks of what doctors called withdrawal. Turning her appetite back to books, the balm of Chopin, Albinoni. One syllable hacked from her lips. Seed. And missing Toru, him touching parts of her no man had ever known. Him doing things to her she didn't have a name for. Keeping her slick, circuits lit, terribly alert. In sleep, she wound herself round her husband, hungering for Toru. Or was the hunger a requiem for Seed, the mummy in the pipe?

    ... And then another flare-up, visitation of the wolf. This one so bad, neighbors hear me scream. Wrists and elbows, knees so swollen, I am a creature without joints. Pain. Pain that brings stupidity, grinds me into powder. Racking, racking. Jess in from the mainland sobbing over me. Rachel, Vanya, faces like crushed flowers. WATCH ME DIE. And one day Toru, sleeves rolled down, kissing my brow, leaving in my palm one small, solitary orb. Bringing one each day. Helping me light it, helping me drag it in. Pain deserting me. One night, like that! it goes. I run outside in circles, pull wings from a dozen fireflies, hang their bellies in my hair, a woman blinking off and on. The Dragon has consumed my wolf! ...

    ... After that, Toru is everywhere. I sleep and feel his breath, bite down on a pigeon heart and it is his. I feel his pulse in me. One day he is waiting, draws me down a path of crushed plumerias. "Ming, you miss me, neh? Want go to Chinatown? Old time's sake?" I would walk through fire. Same alley limned with bak choy, same little black pajama'ed man. Lying on the same bunks with pipes lit. Waiting for him to touch me. Him smiling, rolling up his sleeves, the same snail-track tattoos. "Why, Toru, why?" And he begins to tell ...

    ... One day in 'Nam, his unit had been ambushed outside Hoi An. For days he lay hidden in a paddy; maybe the rice mud helped, kept his shot-up foot from turning green. Every day, he said, he watched this little mama-san sitting in the sun, polishing her new metal legs. "She walk like Tin Man in Judy Garland movie! But oh, so proud." When the Army finally tracked him down and Medevac'ed him out, the escort bomber blew her legs and all of her away. And took her village, too. Old mama-san was Cong. Her face, those metal legs, kept leaking through his sedative and morphine. For weeks he couldn't close his eyes, just lay there in his foot-cast shrieking. An orderly took pity on him, shot him up with heavy stuff. The heaviest ...

    ... Maybe his tales from the paddies were tall tales. Maybe Toru had started smack on R&R, with some child-whore in Bangkok. Maybe he was priming me. "Next time your joints hurt, I'll take you where you don't feel not'ing!" His hand on me. "Ah, Ming, soft as dew on ginger." His warm fingers on my hip in a way that makes my hip, somehow, forever his. My circuits lit, terribly alert, his slick perfect entry ...

. . . After that he courts me, knowing lupus will return, a sickness like a dancer that waltzes off, masquerades, peeks from behind a fan. Eventually, Toru grows impatient, desperate to show me the void. I can't do it, can't make that leap from pipe to needle without the craven need. He grows more impatient, I can lose him in a minute. If lupus is my only hold on Toru, I tighten the embrace, start praying for another flare-up—hideously swollen joints, bone-weary fatigue, the wolf mark leaping on my face. I pray for so much pain I will beg him "Do it! With the needle! Hook me like a fish" . . .

. . . We wait, two people on a platform, looking down the track. O the perversity of my wolf! Biding his time. One night in Chinatown, Toru puts his hand on me, whispers in my hair. "Ah, Ming . . . it cost so much to live." I moan, drift back to dreams, cradling my pipe, inside it dark exhausted little mummy. Now, I imagine him that night, sliding from my bunk, dragging his small kit, dragging his extinction. Alcohol, lighter, spoon, cotton, rubber cord, syringe, an arsenal in moonlight. At dawn, I find him curled up like a child. He seems no bigger than my fist. Cold, so cold, his pulse so slow. I do the thing, forbidden thing . . .

. . . Panic. Finding little black-pajama'ed man, shaking him from sleep. "Emergency. My friend dying." Him cursing, telephoning, helping me drag Toru's body far from his greasy alley. Me writing Toru's name, address, attaching to his T-shirt, then holding him against my breast. "Live! Oh, live!" And waiting for the whining ambulance. Then running through a dawn limned with salt fish, ginger, jook. Running with my cowardice. Finding Papa in his little yard, still a Gong Fu warrior. Sun coming up between his calves, scrawny but still strong, Papa frozen in the Mantis Walk, Tiger Leap, the Cobra Coil. HAH! HAH! HAH! . . .

. . . Hospital corridors, Arctic white of nothingness. The nothingness of Toru's eyes. The months. Pono sworn to break his habit, even if it kills him. Run Run living on her knees, beseeching plaster saints with naked, moody little feet. The smell of Catholic priests, incense in her hair. In one year Toru's purged, his health oppressive. He lectures me, my mounted archer, who first slew the Dragon for me, bringing me its Seed. Now a preacher, proselytizer. I listen dreamily, leaving my body with him in conversation while in my mind another, younger man tiptoes through alleys bringing me my Seed. We nod politely, making the exchange. He never touches me. I never learn his name . . .

. . . Toru grows angry, "It will kill you. A slow and ugly death." I answer softly. "Uglier than lupus?" "I love you," he says. "For all time" . . .

. . . Time. That thing I no longer measure. Now time measures me. The wolf approaching with his yardstick. Racking. Racking. Then, his coy, perverse retreat. How many years now? Twenty? Twenty-five? The luxury of debilitating sickness: We are allowed to stop keeping track. Allowed to do the thing that's easiest, to

step back from the bleating stir of daily repetition. Allowed to not really live, as much as appear to. To circulate in silence, contemplation, so others can't hear the sly crushing of our bones, so they cannot see the thing with human fat dripping from its lips . . .

. . . Toru healed, his body purged of smack. No longer joined in addiction, we have lost our genealogy. Did I really love you? Mozart's piano concerti, Schumann's études, Bach's oboes. Euripedes, Saikaku, Lu Hsun. These I have loved. A word I could never apply to living humans, perhaps not even to my children. Vanya, Jess, Rachel—we are charged with something else, continuity, the voices in our blood. We are each other's conscience. But, you! Perhaps with you what I experienced was release. Blood-red drowning passion of release. Now I am old, and there is no release. There is only this triumvirate, me, my wolf, and Seed. But I remember. For a while with you, I was a woman without pain . . .

Toru . . . forgive . . .

Rachel

... VANYA NEXT DOOR SMELLING OF HAOLE, I can smell it through the wall. God, she carries it around like a trophy. And Ming smelling of her habit. Yet, I'm the one Pono judges. Eyes coming after me all these years. Fingers rubbing the fabric of my clothes, appraising, approximating. As if I'd stolen them! No one to turn to, to complain to. Jess's first trip home in three years, and she's silent, timid as a child. What has happened to her? How life has smoothed her sharp-edged tongue ...

... Once when we were ten ... me calling Jess "haole, fish-belly haole." The awful silence, then Jess screaming, screaming. "At least I know who my father is. At least I'm not illegitimate like you!" And running, mist from sea-coated coffee trees blanketing my skin. And hiding in the rocks all night, sea urchins sucking at my feet. Something like a cluster of wet rubies moving toward me, I still see its flaming eyes, horrible as that word ...

... Illegitimate. Knowing it. Had always known. Run Run hilahila everytime I asked. Saying my father had died in the war just before my birth. What war? I was born in 1952. Saying Mother died in childbirth, a broken heart. Lies, all lies. I had heard the whispers, the child who stood just outside the door. How I hated Jess, her truth-running mouth, her motherfather life ...

... Father. I didn't even know his name. Toshio, Run Run said, which I think had been her father's name. Staring at my mother's photograph, thinking, "Why, she was just a girl," praying for her dear, departed soul. Then, one day classmates jeering. "Your mother isn't dead. She ran away. She didn't want you."

Confronting Pono, Run Run. Their faces hanging, tired of the lie. . . . And understanding she was somewhere in the world. Unimaginable, to never know her, be without her, tomorrow, all my tomorrows . . .

. . . One day, I turned to Jess. "Yes. I am a bastard. There is nothing I can do." We were twelve, but for that moment she looked very old. Sobbing, begging my forgiveness . . . That day was our healing, our celebrational swim out beyond the reef, a thing forbidden. Out where the ocean floor dropped to nothingness . . . O how waves lifted us, sitting us on foam like birds! Then soaring, slamming us down. Jess smashed up against me in the deep, trying to hold me in our drowning . . . Hours later, Vanya finding us unconscious on the sand, Jess's wrist broken, still holding on to me . . . Maybe some acts of faith are stronger than forces of nature, having the power to keep us afloat . . . The miracle that day, not our survival, but that the rift between us had healed . . .

. . . Then one day Pono staring at me, leaving me paralyzed, the way small animals hypnotize themselves before the predator. What have I done? Run Run brushing my hair, polishing my skin with lemon and kukui oil. "She see you coming beautiful like yoah mama. Wonder what do wit' you." Do with me? Why not love me. Hold me in her arms. "She do love you, silly girl. More dan de ot'ers. Hard for her show dis kine affection. Too much choked out of her. Someday you know everyt'ing, Rachel. Hang yoah head in shock." I have always been in shock, eyes begging, so thirsty to be held. Ming saying Pono is shy, cannot show emotion. Okay for Ming. She's Pono's favorite. Or Vanya, dark and moody, Pono's carbon copy. I am nothing to her, a mistake . . .

. . . Ming's folks, Auntie Holo, Uncle Tang, poor but loving, enough love for me. I live for the times I visit them in Kalihi! Uncle Tang full of laughter, jokes, his wonderful gwai goo, his presents—kittens, baby owls. His frog-lip soups, sizzling chicken platters, so much smoke we wear napkins on our faces like outlaws! His double spatulas juggling mango and macadamia flapjacks. And even now, in old age, his Gong Fu exhibitions, two fingers splitting melons, ZAP! O laughter, innocence! O miracle of father-knowing . . .

Rachel stares at her image in a mirror, anoints her face with an unguent made of arsenic and human placenta. With delicate motions, her fingers stroke upward from neck to temple, the scent of the unguent at first alluring, then oppressive, overwhelming, as if something huge were standing in the shadows of the room, something with a vast, indomitable will. She squints, ignores the beauty of her face, sees only microscopic ditches, incipient wrinkles on the brow.

. . . I'm no longer a child, Hiro's child, the toy he dresses, undresses, attaches strange things to. I am becoming middle-aged, his nightmare. If I am old, then

he is ancient. Is sixty ancient for a man? When he looks forty? When he is virile as a goat? . . .

She drops her slip straps, studying teethmarks just below her nipple, talismans of his homecoming. Marks of his leavetaking reflected in her eyes, the whites sucked from them so they seemed smaller.

. . . Auwē, I was just a child, he was the father I'd been searching for. Sixteen, visiting Ming's folks. One night looking over a wall into the neighbor's yard . . . This man, naked, bathing with a garden hose. So blue and evil-looking, I had to know him. Knowing if I stayed with him, nothing in this world would ever hurt me . . . The moon full, he looked like living mold. Tattooed. All of him. Everything. And climbing the wall, walking up to him entranced. Did we speak, I don't remember. His tattooed penis rising, a snake dressed for a masquerade ball . . . Letting him take me right there, two lizards in wet grass. His skin changing colors in the moonlight, volcanoes on his back smoking, flowers on his shoulders blooming as if from radiation. Hiro. Twenty years older, handsome, thuggish, moving like a thoroughbred . . .

. . . And afterwards . . . there was no afterwards, only always . . . he wouldn't let me leave his side, dressed me, taught me how to eat and drink. Bombay Sapphire neat. One night, a diamond in the Sapphire. We eloped . . . Pono's wrath, disowning, abandoning me as my mother had. Run Run taking the ferry to Honolulu, confronting Hiro. Raising her fist at him, bowed legs shaking like Shoyu kegs. "I been like Rachel's mama, neh? She just a baby. You make her sad, I bust you up. Kill you good, foah shoah!" Hiro smiling, taking Run Run in his lap. "I cannot hurt her, Rachel owns my heart". . .

. . . He loves that I am so ready for passion, ready to take and take. And he takes me, his child, still growing, forming, without guile. I love his smell, gin, English cigarettes, contraband . . . Hiro fearing no one, but when he speaks of his father his face taking on the look of mourning. And maybe that is the beginning of something, discovering your protector, your lover, the one you journey with through great heat, he, too, has been discarded. He has been laid bare. And he begins to tell . . .

. . . When he was ten Hiro's father sent him from Honolulu home to Japan to be educated. Instead he became a gangster. In Kyoto he studied Kendo, "the way of the sword," and adopted the philosophy of Bushido: the way of the warrior, prepared to die at any moment, which is the only way to live . . . He believed the true Samurai had the heart of a criminal. At thirty-six, finally returning to Hawai'i. His father, seeing the tattoos, disowning him. The night before he leaves, bathing under that garden hose, Fate casting my eyes his way . . .

. . . And O the early years. Stepping outside the family, strolling the grounds of the Royal Hawaiian like tourists, dancing at the Halekūlani like bored peacocks!

People staring because we look like nothing else. The house he gives me in Kahala, overlooking the sea, neighborhood of long driveways, white-coated servants raking gravel, prize-winning koi. Meals eaten with Burmese imperial jade chopsticks. Even our own small grove of whispering, rare tortoiseshell bamboo . . .

. . . Hiro, my Yakuza, his business the "water trade"—liquor, prostitution, drugs—up and down the Asian coast, Malaysia, Hong Kong, Tokyo. His growing absences. When he is home, artists and buffoons swaggering in our gardens on Sunday afternoons. And gangsters . . . People I grow to hate, part of his world that takes him away from me. I compete with them in dangerous ways. Flirting, insulting, laughing at a Laotian drug czar's regrettable taste in Western clothes . . . Even koi in the pond surface, staring at each stranger like a thought in some very cold-blooded mind. Hiro's absences increasing through the years . . .

. . . I learn to beg, beseech. "Why do you stay away? Spend so much time in Hong Kong?" Sipping his Bombay Sapphire, his gaze raising my temperature, making me want to undress. "Because, Hong Kong leaves me alone." Years accumulate, making me needy, not letting him breathe . . . Hiro saying when he's with me, it's like he's poured into me, like something swallowed by an animal drinking. Says he wears his gun to protect himself from me. My beauty . . .

. . . Decade of twenties becoming thirties. My face remaining eerily young. The tyranny of rituals. Beauty tonics of crushed pearl. Bitter nightly drafts of Gyokuro, rarest of green Japanese teas, so precious one drinks it from thimbles. Baths of seaweed, ginseng, shark-liver oil. Masks of puréed buttermilk and brains. Then becoming forty . . . maybe my look of enduring youth is really the high color of terror, the games Hiro and I play, death/lust games with Fugu: the body's dizziness, its shock, making my blood rush to the surface. . . .

. . . Sometimes when he sleeps I want to smother him, join him on the other side. Maybe his absences are how we keep from killing each other. But when he's gone, my periods of squalor. Wrecking cars, running down peacocks. Throwing emeralds at the gulls. Gold-threaded silk kimonos slashed . . . Waiting, waiting for him. Ming says I should fill my days with works of charity, like other wealthy women. What does one say to other women? How does one sit? Besides, there is my origami, brush painting, calligraphy lessons, my ikebana, lessons on the shamisen, tea ceremony lessons . . . Fittings for my costumes, geisha wigs, impersonation wigs, of young girls, young boys, long red Mikado wig reaching to the floor. Our private theater, any, every fantasy . . .

. . . Then, I feel it with my loins, even my pupils enlarging. Back from another trip, he is home, on the lawn, approaching. White suit and tie, black gangster's shirt, long Mandarin fingers, sleek as a cat, eyes narrow as seeds . . . So aristocratic in his bearing, I have to look away. Hiro. Almost sixty, looking like a man of forty. Hair still black and slick as a croupier. Yellow face still handsome. My

breathlessness, my eagerness to love him, peel his clothes off expertly like skinning an animal . . .

. . . And always, he is affectionate, attentive. Precious gifts from the Orient, rubies, ancient museum-quality robes. And very private gifts . . . Harigata, hand-molded by a blind girl. Higozuki, of living wasps. And one anniversary, three pearls implanted in his foreskin, adding such gravelly shock and rapture. And sweet netsukes, graceful copulation of couples locked in jade . . . Handcuffs of braided, silkworm filaments, fear of tearing them from my wrists giving such intensity to pleasure. Games aging, childless, couples play. Me coming to him naked under Empress robes. His nipples wet with rare rice brandy. It trickles down his stomach, my tongue chasing. One long yellow icicle finger tracing my thigh, tracing endlessly, until I start to quiver, until my hair falls down . . .

. . . His "aviary" collection, the rarest pleasure sheaths. Feathered Bird of Paradise. Long-beaked Toucan. His "reptile" collection, Caped Chinese New Year Dragon. Handmade Lizard from Cambodia, great green fleshy crest . . . O dreamy, delicate task of outfitting Hiro, watching him grow more erect. Slipping the green-crested lizard over his member, slowly, solemnly, as if dressing a rare, prehistoric doll . . . Skin of the pleasure sheath astonishingly thin, thin as vapors, so I feel each contraction, feel his eyes narrow as blood drives through his heart. Him watching me electrified, bucking, cantering green crests. His childless child in endless rut . . .

. . . His aging child, shackled to her island. O the years. I dream of travel, journeying, of searching in the world. (Mother, come home, I forgive you, even though you were a slut.) I cannot. The fear of seeing Hiro—Singapore, Macao— laughing with young whores. Fear of finding the woman who threw me away. And throwing me away again. Brush painting, making sketches of her, wondering how she looks, if she remembers. Is she somewhere, sketching me? Does she know my name? Rachel, torn leaf on the ancestral tree. Half known, half suspected . . .

. . . The others say I'm a concubine, a slave. Living in fantasy. Is it so great a sin? Secrets? Deep secluded privacy? Vanya's life a spectacle. Divorce, death. Rage. Broadcasting her lust, the smell of strangers on her skin. Ming with her deadly secrets, her little pipes. Jess always running from us, keeping her distance. As if we were contagious . . . Yet, Pono's eyes are always after me: extravagance, my useless life. When did love, devotion, loyalty turn useless, extravagant? Maybe she's jealous, having never loved. Maybe Vanya's jealous, possessing only memories and grief . . .

. . . Run Run my only consolation. "Pono love you as a child. You don' remember how she rock you, sing you, hug you every hour?" Memory of eyes popping, lungs hurting, thinking she was trying to smother me. "Silly girl. That how much she love you. Feeling go through her heart like lightning. Frighten her, *so she step back . . ." They are always stepping back all of them. Why not give me a little credit, my fairness, generosity, always bearing gifts . . .*

. . . Buying Toru his first Arabian stallion after he kicked heroin, became a paniolo. And that whole year before, who was at his side? Even when he was too crazed to recognize me . . . Consulting with his doctors, sitting near his padded cell, listening to his screams. Who else came every single day. Christmas. Birthday. Days of hurricanes. Tsunami—waves rolling through the city, my driver deserting, leaving me in a floating car. Did I panic? Run for home? I dragged myself to high ground, then walked six miles in killer shoes . . . I know those hospital corridors by heart, awful, ammonia smell, swish of midnight mops. I know how many tiles in every hall . . .

. . . Just give me a little credit. Rachel, bearer of gifts. Early years of Ming's illness. Vanya, off with her Samoan. Who took their children in? . . . Sounds of young voices like chimes across the lawn, laughter in my lonely house. Days and months of playing at motherhood with other people's children. Not wanting my own, afraid of sharing Hiro . . . Then Ming's son and daughter suddenly adults, bored with Aunty Rachel. Vanya's son, my favorite, drowned. Shock, weeping servants. Even nature mourned. Gardens with no appetite for soil. The bamboo dead. Koi floating belly-up. Heart broken, my tongue stilled for weeks . . . Hiro rocking me, astonished at my grief. And really, whose loss was I mourning? Should I have had a child? I, who without Hiro, hardly breathed . . .

. . . Still Vanya comes, asking donations for this and this. Kōkua South Point. Kōkua sacred forests. Kōkua Literarcy Campaign. Kōkua the Sovereignty Movement. Scholarships. Educate our children. I give and give, feeling her continuing disdain. . . . Even Jess says my life is foolish, wasteful, not seeing how I count on her, on them, to stand by me, be loyal to my loyalty. Carrying Hiro's secret infidelities like corpses on my back, I become a keeper of accounts . . .

. . . Perfumes in his clothes, stains of many women. Tallying each scent. Shredding his silk robes, making funeral pyres of his hand-tailored shirts, shantung suits, even ostrich-skin slippers burning to black knots of leather . . . He laughs at me across the flames. My jealousy excites his passion. His kimono open, his penis blue and beckoning. When I am old, what will I leave behind? No deeds. No offspring. No meaning echo of my days. I will be despised. A concubine. A keeper of accounts . . .

Jess

SHE CIRCLES HER ROOM SLOWLY, an eerie sense of being watched. Assuming a somewhat aggressive stance, she flings wide a closet door, then another. Nothing. She searches through dresser drawers, only lavender sachets. She even looks under the big *hikie'e* in the corner covered with Batik. She imagines something damp brushing against her arm. Mosquito netting on the big four-poster trembles like skin. Jess stares, willing it still. She rummages in her duffel bag, unswivels the top of a bottle of Rémy Martin and pours a modest drink. She listens.

    ... *Why do I always get the haunted room? And these mosquito nets, as if we were living in Java. She never accepted that Hawai'i is not the tropics. It's north of the Equator* ...

She shakes the net a little, watches prismatic dust dance down in lamplight.

    ... *Human cells sloughed off down the decades. How many pounds are in this room? How many generations?* ...

She studies her reflection in an old bamboo-framed mirror. Jumpsuit, jungle trooper boots, so out of place here, but she likes the precision and suggested toughness they impart. And the cropped hair, the way it makes her eyes jump out alert, a certain mineral brilliance. Altogether, a paramilitary air. She circles the room again, avoiding the *lānai*, knowing what is out there, how it will get to her. After three years away, she feels she's established a sort of equilibrium, but knows she could lose it in a minute.

. . . As usual, she's given me the room farthest from the others. Why does she always do that? Keep me on the outside? . . .

She doesn't see it's the best room, a corner room, with almost a wraparound view of Kona District from the sprawling *lānai*. Far down on the right will be the glittering lights of the town of Kailua, ocean liners blinking in the harbor. To her left, the ghostly blue flanks of Mauna Loa. Down below, fringing the shoreline, swaying bamboo and palm groves, the City of Refuge in the distance. And before her, laid out like a gift, the sea, foam breaking its dark glass surface, a sickle of moon, stars bright as little suns. And somewhere out there in the dark, lava, whole deserts of it. It is all waiting, looming, so powerfully there.

At first Jess ignores it, too busy striking sparks, looking for the subtext, the accusation in everything. It will take days, slow hours, to relearn what she forgets each time she leaves this place—that this island, this lushness, is stern, tenacious, that the vast, invisible will, the mystery of nature so in abundance here, is what saves her from herself. That if she just leaves things alone, doesn't question, and accuse, there will be no need for answers, there will be no need for anything, everything will be all right. She feels the Rémy entering her blood, a semi-ease. She sighs, bends, unlaces her boots.

. . . Have I ever really left this place? Even when I leave I take it with me. In younger years, thinking Pono hated me. What she hated was my pre-life, what my mother did, marrying my father. Strange . . . I have no photograph of them together. Tonight, Pono staring at me as if she'd never seen me before. As if she has to learn me, after only three years. Sometimes in New York, I think I've imagined her. They're all a dream slipped sideways into my sleep. I wake terrified, bereft . . .

She slides off boots, pulls a framed snapshot from her duffel, a picture of her mother, Emma. Sometimes when she looks at her, Jess imagines she is now her mother waking from a coma, journeying out of a long intrusive sleep back to memory chains, to life, real life. The world racing just outside her skin.

. . . Seven, eight years old the first time Mother put me on that plane. So young I didn't know where I was going. Mother sobbing, Father holding her. How she must have wanted to come home, was dying to, something in her already dying. Her telling me I had to know my cousins, all the family I would ever have. Arriving terrified. So pale, so different from the others. One night, so desperate, so alone,

crawling into Pono's bed, thinking she would kill me, devour me. Finding Rachel there, and Vanya, Ming. We were all terrified! ...

... That huge bed where we slept against this snoring mountain. At first she just lay there, staring, like we were small pets she had to keep alive. Then drawing us to her large, warm breasts rising and falling, and us falling asleep, her heart thrumming against our heads, our lashes tangled in her hair. Tūtū ... Her scent oceanic, salty, ambrosial—seaweed, jasmine, wild plum. Her arms drawing us together. Little limbs entwined, shy hands creeping towards each other. In sleep, Vanya's brown arm thrown across my waist, feeling her breath, her pulse, the vital current. Me, whispering the word, trying to comprehend it. Cousin. And dreaming, turning, shifting, like small birds in formation. Summer unto summer, growing accustomed to our different hues, different temperaments. Less gaps and lapses. Trust. Finally, love ...

... Primitive draw of Run Run's kitchen, like fires in caves in the age when reptiles flew. Smells, grease, her snaggletoothed laughter, sucking mango seed while she hacked at fish, pigs, chickens, place looking like a cannibal's back yard. On the radio, Alfred Apaka, Hilo Hattie, "Hawai'i Calls," happy-sad Hawaiian songs. "Beyond the Reef," "Hanalai Bay." Four girls begging, "Tell us about our mothers! Are we like them? Were they smart and pretty?" Run Run seemed to hold so many keys. Our disappointment when she said, "I didn't know yoah mamas till dey was mamas too, bring you here foah meet yoah cuz, Rachel ... 'Cept foah you!" Run Run pointing at me. "I dere de day yoah mama bring home haole, say dey goin' marry. Auwē! She shoah one reckless, brave wahine!". ...

... After that, I began to think of my father as heroic. Marrying a reckless woman seemed such a daring thing. The life they lived, improvisation, drift, trying to fabricate some normalcy for me ... Tonight, sitting near Pono on the sofa, skidding toward her along the slope created by her weight, I wanted to grab her and tell her "They were happy! I remember laughter!" ... Mother going darker with the years, tea-colored, beautiful, hair black, electric. Father pale, blond, rangy in build, ethos of American Gothic in his long handsome face. A principled irony in the eyes ...

Jess places her mother's picture on a table, remembering her father, Vernon, growing ill. Learning to know him in a new silent form, face haggard, hair straggly like an aged revolutionary, hands grotesquely bloated, weeping sores, like rotting catcher's mitts. Months, years passing with the rise and fall of blood count, blood pressure, temperature. Radiation traveling him like a slow-paced virus. The hideous mouthpiece made of gold foil, so his inlays would stop radiating killer rays into his jawbone. With the mouthpiece, he became a monster.

She wonders why doctors bothered, so obvious he was dying. When he coughed, red lumps on white linen. Now she thinks of her handsome father dead of four types of cancer, and leukemia, in Bethesda Naval Hospital. She remembers doctors calling him heroic, and wonders if a man can be heroic for dying unintentionally. A man who, as a U.S. Navy sailor four decades earlier, had swept the decks of radiated battleships during Bomb testings in the Marshalls.

. . . *Mother drifting when he died, across oceans, into other hemispheres. To stop would have invalidated the penance she imposed on herself. Placeless woman, with no clan, drifting to confirm her placelessness. Then dying in the desert, all alone . . . Me traveling there to claim her ashes, longest, loneliest journey of my life, from which I am still returning. Ming says each journey conceals another journey within, that not every journey can be mapped. What does she know, she's never loved. Well, she has her secret; some secrets take the place of love. Maybe that's why she and Pono understand each other . . .*

In slow motion Jess removes her clothes, pulls a T-shirt from her duffel, pulls out other snapshots, her and her cousins waving from Pono's truck, cowgirls of different colors headed for a rodeo, bodies still sweet-scented, hairless, breastless.

. . . *Does childhood really happen? Do we imagine it? Everyone remembers something else. . . . Vanya saying I once packed my face with mud, trying to grow darker so she would love me. Brown, beautiful Vanya. Knowing exactly who she was. Yet there were times I'd catch her staring at my pale skin with a sort of . . . thirst. Each of us wanting something of the other. Sometimes in dreams becoming the other . . . Run Run saying we're all one thing, the sum of Pono . . .*

. . . *Anna said the same thing when she came that awful summer. Said we four cousins were like a drop of mercury, one splash shivering in clones. Scooped together we became one drop again, no seams, no shatter marks. Cold, clinical Anna, who seemed to burst from my womb with already formed opinions. . . . Bringing her here at sixteen. Introducing Pono, Run Run, Vanya, Rachel, Ming. HERE IS MY SKIN. THIS IS WHO I AM. Her diffidence, polite disdain. (Palomino hair, cold cream skin. So much like her father, so very much his child.) Her shock, her accusations, "You didn't tell me they were dark!" Summer of our fracturing. And when Benson and I divorced, Anna choosing to go with him. Tearing down genetic blocks, erasing my side of her history . . .*

. . . *Anna, now in pre-med, wanting to be a surgeon-of-the-open-heart-and-transplant-kind. Real medicine, she says, as opposed to what I do. Anna, who doesn't tell her Duke U. friends her mother is part native. Her friends would call Pono and Vanya "darkies." What would they call Ming and Rachel? "Slant-eyes?" . . . Marrying Benson, a Southerner, perhaps a way of resurrecting my father. Rewrite the script, make it work this time. Daddy, Daddy, I didn't know. Incessant*

*bleat of what we learn too late. Of what he dared in marrying my mother, taking
her home to Alabama . . .*

*. . . Imagining him at the front door of his father's house, puffing his chest
out, grinning and proud. He puts his arm around my mother, rings the bell.
(Didn't he know what was coming?) They're all assembled inside. Maybe there's
a cake, candles lit. WELCOME HOME THE HERO FROM THE WAR. Maybe
someone sits at a piano, fingers poised above the keys. A window curtain twitches.
My father rings and rings but no one ever answers. Finally, he and my mother
leave . . .*

*. . . The early fifties, Americans still weren't sure what Hawaiians were. Maybe
my father's folks thought they were like Nebraskans, or Canadians, white folks
from far away. Until someone inside the house looked out. Mother wasn't that
dark, but she was never white . . . What's always evoked here for me, not my
father's shame, not my mother's humiliation, not even the silence after he rings
the bell. What's evoked, always . . . the twitching of that curtain. They never went
south again, never returned to Hawai'i, both banished from their tribes. O Mother,
I saw your differentness, people calling you exotic, what they call those they tend
to stare at . . .*

Jess pours another shot of Rémy. How pale her hands are on
the glass! She swallows, shivers, fire flowers in her gut. She sits back
remembering a solitary childhood. Talking to trees, a blade of grass,
insects captured in her palm. Her first summers in Kona, hiding on
beaches, under *hau* trees whispering to geckos, mongoose, trying to
explain her situation. *Hapa.* Mix-blood. Half brown. Half white. Which
was really her? Hugging small living things, chattering to them, trying
to clear up the confusion, the ravel of her being.

*. . . And still preferring animals to humans, mostly. Their patience, quiet valor
in the face of death. The way they let me be. Poor Benson, thinking he was
marrying a clever woman, that I became a veterinarian surgeon for the money.
Thinking we would be a team, high-profile lawyer and his wife the social vet.
Until he understood my thing with animals. My need . . .*

*. . . Had I been darker, not yellow, caramel, gold, but rich, dark brown, I
would have lived different. Married different. Walked out in the world. Mars says
I've lived in silence: the mixed-blood anthem. Yet, all four of us are mix-blood.
Why does Pono treat me differently? "You white," Run Run says. "Skin dat stole
Hawai'i, took away our land, our queen. Also somet'ing in yoah tūtū's past. Make
her hate haole real bad." "Tell me," I beg her. She shakes her head. "Some
t'ings best forgotten." And wanting to run to Pono, hold her, share secrets,
mutilations. Tell me yours, I will tell you mine . . .*

* * *

. . . Me in stirrups, arms, legs strapped and buckled down . . . $1,000 prepaid to this doctor who will scrape out a mistake, seed planted in the throes of dying marriage. Needle in my arm, a sedative, then this doctor unzipping his pants, ugly, pink root waving and erect. Turning like a giant screw inside me. Rolling Stones full volume while I scream . . . Forcing Valium down my throat. Screams sighing into little bleats. His tongue insistent in my ear, telling me he's coming . . . coming. Then zipping up his pants. Hairy hands all business now, scraping, scraping out his sperm, my blood, departed husband's seed. And me, so new at this, thinking this is part of an abortion. They get to do this to you . . .

. . . Calling Vanya in Chicago, telling her, and telling her. Her voice turning lethal like a box of knives. Vanya flying east. I have to fight her, wrestle her, to keep her from burning down the doctor's house. Greasy pigment, smell of paint, painting under moonlight while the doctor slept. Next morning huge letters across his manicured green lawn. RAPIST. And how the word kept reappearing on his lawn, other women, other victims down the years. Women picketing his house, his office. Lawsuits, indictments. The man convicted, sentenced, put away. I never testify, carrying that rage for years. What happened to it? Maybe it became the dead husk of my marriage . . .

Jess rises now, circles the room, walks her hands along the walls, spreading her fingers, imagining them imprinted on ancient fingerprints. She wondered whose lives had been lived in that room, that house. How long ago? In what time? What is long, and what is time?

. . . Time, the thing we wave our dreams at, the way people in horror movies scare off vampires with crosses. Time, the thing we can't beat back . . . Yet, time is also what it takes to heal, what it takes for certain memory cells to die. That's what Vanya told me after my divorce . . . What I reminded her when her boy died . . . Hernando! And all I had were words. "I would give my life to bring him back." I would have done it in a minute. Not knowing how much I loved Vanya until we lost her that year. A cadaver, skin of ash, hair ghostly white. Eyes gone red, an awful red . . .

. . . Staying with her in Honolulu, afraid she'd kill herself alone. Flying her to Auckland to her lover, Ta'a Utu. And hearing them through that hotel wall . . . Vanya begging him for a child. Begging him to fuck her to death, to death, and meaning it. Me listening through the wall, their morbid, frenzied socketing . . . What Hernando's dying did, what it took from us . . . Run Run crazed, squatting in the kitchen waving her carving knife at God. And Pono full of sobbing rages, tearing everything apart. Plantation languishing, coffee harvest lost that

year . . . Pono pointing her rage at each of us. At me. And so I ran, putting three years between us . . .

. . . Maybe time doesn't heal. Maybe it doesn't even pass. We pass through time, and come out stunned, so rage, and memory, are blurred. Mings's letters arriving in New York, then Rachel's, even Run Run's, all saying the same thing . . . as if I wouldn't believe it from just one of them. Each letter corroborating the other two: Pono, the plantation, slowly reviving . . . Time I come back home. But Pono never writing me, never answering my letters. Not once in all my life . . . Sometimes her deep voice on the phone long-distance. Summoning. That deadliness that left our mothers frozen forever in roles of injured adolescents. Pono an obstacle they couldn't destroy, so they destroyed themselves instead . . .

. . . Now what will happen if she dies. Never made my peace with her. Or maybe it's made each time she calls me home. I come running, stand here with my luggage, a dog begging with its bowl. Pono greeting me with that look that shaves my spine. Hapa-haole. Half as good as the others. The message massed beneath her gaze, surrounding me like weather . . .

. . . Tonight her fierce, brown face in profile, my mother's more delicate profile layered, magnified. Then something new, she turned to me, studied me, took my hand and tapped it. Secret Morse of genealogy. Run Run says she wants me to come home. The wonder of it! . . . Later, Rachel saying something closer to truth. "She's growing old. Afraid she can't count on Ming and me. You and Vanya would know how to handle people, keep the farm going" . . .

. . . Vanya laughing. "Keep it going? Like to sell this termite palace, these acres of silly coffee trees. Donate the proceeds to Pūnana Leo, teach our kids their Mother Tongue." Vanya turning to me. "Anyway, Jess, you should come home. What kind of life is that, your daughter gone, spending your days and nights with broken animals". . . Not all days, Vanya, not all nights . . .

Jess slides another snapshot from her bag, a tense, rather handsome man in reading glasses. Dark, smooth Afro skin, short-cropped Afro hair, aggressive posture, almost a leaning forward, as if he had important things to tell and not much time. Intensity in the eyes, eyes that have seen too much, know too much, know it is too late. Mars, shaking his life at her like a brilliant bracelet, a lightning rod, a gourd. A life prodigiously brutal, shocking, and full of poetry and dreams. Mars, telling her his life would knock her down, telling her to go back to her blood, her people.

. . . It's not that simple, Mars. Sometimes blood can be so cruel, so damaging. And yet, what other road is there, except the one that leads us back. But, what is here . . . Ming frail, racked by that disease. Rachel shackled to her husband. Vanya lost. And me, still the haole, tapping on the pane. Life is wearing down

our edges, our defenses . . . Even Pono wearing down. I see hesitations, hints of
frailty, a life of loss—daughters, grandson—God only knows what else. O if we
could just forget. Maybe a little oblivion is what is needed to get by . . .

. . . That's what Toru said tonight, riding up through coffee fields, phantom
of my youth. Seeing him, I wept! Talking of our lives, me going off to college,
him going off to 'Nam. . . . Then a decade of his life lost to smack, living in the
dregs of Honolulu. Now a man who negotiates each day with caution. Thicker,
muscular, paniolo smell of pastures, horse sweat, cattle. Smell of mountains,
magic, our youth. Beloved Toru! How we learned to trust him with our lives . . .
Climbing thirty-foot palm trees swaying over cliffs, diving blind into deep rock
quarries. Swimming into coves of sleeping sharks. Running over lava still seething
just beneath the surface. He could have led us through fire. He was everything we
knew, everything we trusted . . .

. . . And when we thought he'd died in 'Nam, when he was MIA, how each
of us held him in our memory, breathing life into him, praying, talking to his
snapshots. Pono out there in the sea chanting, begging 'aumākua. "Let my
grandson live!" And he remembered us. Under triple canopy, watching his shattered
foot sizzle and shimmer with maggots, thinking he would lose it, lose his mind. "I
had deep memories of each of you." he said. "That's what kept me going. I was
the repository of your lives . . ."

Jess sighs, looks at the snapshots aligned on her table. Feeling the
weight and moment of blood, history, this house. So much converging
here. Maybe this is their last refuge, what keeps them all from madness.
Maybe this will be the genesis of their madness. Maybe they will eat
each other's corpses. She dozes in the chair, knowing she is cheating,
she hasn't yet stepped out on the *lānai.* Living in New York she has lost
touch with nature, the elements, has become forgetful, almost ignorant,
of them. Now she knows the moon is just outside, looming and actual.
And the sea, she hears the sea. And the silver, humming land. She is
suddenly fatigued, knowing the island will engulf her, she will lose
perspective, she will be beseiged. She throws herself across the bed,
plunges into sleep.

. . . Let it attend, it has always attended.

Toru

HE HAS WAITED FOR YEARS. Trained himself to wait. He has worked, slept, communed with other humans, but something in him sat apart, day after day, year after year, like a sniper, a roadside mendicant. He has waited for their return, all of them, for they are his key to the past, antiphonal and staggered youth. They are the landscape that fills in his blanks so he is more than just a man who's lost his edge.

Now he drives past *haole* tourists in linen shorts and nipple-bottomed shoes, girl-hipped men swinging golf irons. He sacrificed his youth so soft, favored men like these could spend their lives sinking graceful putts into rich, landscaped Bermuda grass. Toru gazes out at them with almost a sense of affection. *When you hate something for twenty years, you get to know it well.*

His jet-black hair, once braided down his back in filthy rawhide, is short, almost a municipal cut. His Asian face is handsome, almond eyes darting like quick fishes. But the crazy sizzle—the glittering, snapping, sightless gaze—of his drug years is gone. Now, his gaze is steady, dense as silt. At forty, here is a man whose body is lean and ready, legs slightly bowed, but built for endurance, long distances. Tall for a Japanese, his skin is tan, *paniolo* tan, except for the shrapnel scars—ruffles of gray fading to bad industrial brown on his back, gut, forearms.

The limp is hardly noticeable, unless he's stiff from hours on the range. Unlike many *paniolo*, Toru doesn't swagger in the saddle, sits straight, intent. His manner is quiet, unobtrusive, a man reined in by tension. Silence seems his natural state so that in crowds of other men—cowboys, vets—he seems held in equilibrium, not drifting too near, not apart. He is most at ease in fog-swept pastures of the Kohala Mountains, overseeing bawling herds, wrangling and branding calves, or just gazing down.

Down into the valleys of the Big Island, south to the pricey coastal resorts, golf fairways, new subdivisions eating up the view. Populated more and more by *malihini*—people retiring to Hawai'i from Japan, Europe, the U.S. mainland, people living beside Hawaiians, but overlooking them—the land was being stratified, obliterated, poor families slipping into the cracks.

Toru has heard the rhetoric for years: without industrial progress, more real estate development, Hawai'i would be depleted of its youth, would experience a brain-drain as local engineers and other professionals emigrated to Asia, the U.S. mainland. They emigrate anyway, seeing in Hawai'i the coming death of all sane harmonies. Locals left behind labor as manuals, construction men, cowboys, for which they are paid *no-pay* wages, working for foremen imported from the mainland.

At a Kamuela rodeo, Toru overhears two millionaire developers.

"*Bettah pay, bettah pay*, that's all I hear. You think higher wages will quiet these *kānaka?*"

"No. Erasing them will. Booze, drugs, fast cars."

Toru smiles bitterly. *This is what I fought for. Democracy.*

After the war, after years of solace as a needle in his veins, life had been a ghost town. Rehab—Pono stalking him, policing him down nights of nerve ends shrieking for a drop of "junk" leaking down his spine—then University of Boredom, then stasis, his degree a thing he mopped his brow with. Then finally hiring on as ranch hand. And wondering, still wondering, if this was all there was. Sometimes it seemed momentum alone compelled him through the years. Except for nights of stealth, nights when he took the thirty-minute flight over to Honolulu, stole into Ming's house, her bedroom, wanting to feel her breath on him, enveloping him.

(Her husband snoring prodigiously in another room, off in his orchid hothouse dreams) Toru stood quietly, studying Ming's arms flung wide in sleep, a human crucified. Some nights he just stood there, burying his face in her clothes. Some nights he lay down beside her, this woman loyal to her pipe. *What have I remained loyal to?* he wonders. *Not even my addiction.* In those early years, when he first led her down to Chinatown, nights when he was slick within her, he was sure they were the only living things. The rest of the world, well, that was done with mirrors.

Now, sometimes in sleep, she turned, opened her eyes and stared at him without seeing him. In the dark, behind those fractured eyes, he thought he saw the afterlife. Some nights he turned her body over, tenderly washing the flats of his hands down the slope of her back, birdlike spine, baby hips, all whittled down by Seed. Holding his face against her hips, he wept. Afterwards, he slipped quietly from her house and on the early morning plane back to the Big Island, Toru smelled his hands, the odor of hands that had caressed a corpse. *We love that which we corrupt.*

Some nights he dreamed of Ming, her lovely face shriveled into a hag, little mama-san sitting in the sun, polishing her new metal legs, then standing, goosestepping proudly. *Like Tin Man in Judy Garland movie!* Old mama-san, blown into stars of flesh, a human galaxy, outside Hoi An. Occasionally he thought of ending it, there seemed so little of real value left for him. Rubbing the stock of a hunting rifle, he thought how a simple bullet would ease him to the other side, help him get from here to there a little faster—like taking a jet.

But then there was the smell of new grass and fresh dung on the trades, of *maile* ripe for wreathing, his horse nuzzling him at feeding time, the bleak magnificence of snowcapped Mauna Kea at dawn, a bawling calf begging for its bottle, hoarse-throated songs and slack-key guitars of ancient *paniolo*, back porch music and Primo beer. And Toru would want to hang around a little longer, fall asleep on his feet in some Honoka'a tavern, jukebox a thumping heart warming his backside.

Now, seeing Jess after several years, he felt energized, as if suddenly bolted from lethargy. Ming and Rachel seemed frozen in time, dolls behind glass, but Jess and Vanya were women of the world, bursting in on him like Trojans. And more, they saw him as heroic, a *paniolo*, dear and dying breed. They could give him precision, help orchestrate his plan.

And yet, he thought, *what do they really know of me? Only what they read and hear, the glamour: trophies, medals, Toru bull-wrestling, bronc-taming, ro-deoing down the years.* They didn't know, could not imagine, the reality. Years of three A.M. reveilles, cleaning shit from stalls and water troughs, mending rusted barbed-wire fences with bare hands—who could afford gloves?—digging holes in frozen earth, dressed in denim jackets stuffed for warmth with newspapers. Knocking cows down at a dead run, dodging flailing hoofs on branding day. Horse-kicked, horse-bitten, thrown. Leg casts, penicillin shots. The horn of a bull entering your side.

And single men's dorms, fifteen to a one-room bunkhouse from the 1930s (tin roof oxidizing, flaking rust floating up his nostrils while he slept). That was the mid-1970s, people demonstrating across America for equal rights, equal pay, and here they owned you for three bucks an hour. Hundred-thousand-acre ranches owned by rich *haole* in Palm Springs, men who showed up twice a year in cashmere breeches, English riding boots.

Fourteen-fifteen years later, what did he have to show for it? Crew boss title, the glory jobs of roping, branding. Fifteen to sixteen thousand dollars a year with benefits. Insurance, low-rent housing belonging to the ranch—a house he shared with another bachelor, scruffy don't-want furniture, Rodeo doodads on the walls—discount meat supplies and milk, hunting privileges, free pasture. But what did he really *own*? A pickup truck, his horse. And if he left the job, all benefits would cease. He was indentured, like the rest of them. Except for the married *paniolo*, the ones living off of the ranchlands, two- and three-job men killing themselves to meet keep-you-down mortgages.

How could he share this with Jess and Vanya? How, he wondered, could he approach them, tell them about the guys now starting to agitate? Some had been born and raised down near the south point of the island in little fishing villages like Miloli'i, where ancient outrigger fishing canoes were still used and old fishing traditions were still observed, net-fishing, and hand-bait fishing. The villages were now threatened by that proposed $900 million Riviera Resort, which would destroy everything in the area. Yacht basins, berths accommodating huge seagoing ships, would pollute the waters, scare off or kill all sea-life, deprive old-timers of their only food and income.

Real estate agents were already cruising Miloli'i (a village so tiny and "quaint," signs were posted: NOTICE TO PIG OWNERS, ALL STRAY PIGS WILL BE SEIZED ON AND AFTER JUNE 30), offering outrageous prices for small parcels of land. Fishermen had shot the tires out from under chartered buses bringing in potential investors. But two locals had sold out and fled the island. Toru saw that as the beginning of the end. Fishermen giving in, selling out, becoming no-job, no-land people, pockets full of *haole* money which they would blow on fast cars, high-tone rents and booze. One day they would end up living in Honolulu's slums. The pattern kept repeating itself.

On weekends now, some *paniolo* drove down toward South Point, joining groups of local men blocking roads to outsiders. Across lava boulders along the roads, huge words were painted in stark white: KAPU! HAOLE . . . KEEP OUT OR DIE! Locals knew it wasn't enough. Federal officials on the island were too greedy, too much money had already passed hands. Something drastic needed to be done.

When Toru first heard the federal government wanted to make a spaceport of Ka Lae, he bowed his head. The landing place of the earliest Polynesians in the islands, Ka Lae was sacred, Hawai'i's Plymouth Rock. Southernmost point on the Big Island, it was only twenty or thirty miles from Miloli'i, and if developers had their way, within a decade the entire southern half of the Big Island would be obliterated.

Which is already happening here, he thought, looking down from the graze pastures of Kohala to the Big Island's west coast. It was lined with four-star deluxe resorts like the Halenani, House of Splendor, a rich man's ghetto of six low-rise towers connected by lagoons and bridges, guests ferried from shops to restaurants in motorboats, gondolas, even a train. A visual orgasm of Greek, Italian, Mayan, Chinese, Indonesian, Oceanic art and sculpture all strung together by marble halls connecting the towers.

The Halenani, where, for the amusement of guests, eight dolphins were imprisoned in a pond less than the size of an acre. Now and then a dolphin died, ciguatera, pollution from the motorboats, an infected human's hands, who knew? and more dolphins were shipped in. Each time Toru drove past the place, he thought of the dolphins at night, circling, hearing the clicking, squeals and chirps of their own kind calling to them from beyond lava walls too high to leap. The ocean, so tantalizingly close, so impossibly attainable.

One day, watching tinted-window limos turning at the entrance to the Halenani, limos driven by locals whose families could not afford a meal there, were not allowed to swim there, Toru experienced a kind of jolt, a mental spasm, raw vision of a plan. He began brooding, studying his friends, wondering who he could trust. Day after day he studied them, weeding out, discarding. And during that time, Pono had summoned her girls home.

Jess woke in an old *koa* four-poster, watching lace curtains dance in the trades. A *lei* of burnished *kukui* nuts hung on the wall, catching sunlight like dark mirrors. She sat up lazily, drawn by the smell of cooking fires sweet with bark of coconut and guava. The weeks since her arrival had slowly uncreated her. A general shedding, of shoes, mainland clothes for soft, faded house-sarongs, even a sloughing off of skin, pale outer layer going pink, then red, blistered patches peeling into tan, slow bronze.

She even shed her English, as island Pidgin slid from beneath her tongue where it seemed to have been simmering. "Good food," translated into " *'Ono loa!*" "You know what I mean," became "*You know da kine?*" Every day she shouted up the stairs to Vanya. "*Wiki wiki* for da beach!" Now, her every sentence seemed to end in "Yeaah." "It's goin' be one hot day, yeaah?"

And then the first Pacific submerging—mother-stroke of waves against her skin, not like the cold, metallic slaps of the Atlantic. And then descending—coral branches scraping shins and wrists, tattooing her with scabs. And then the nights, wrapped in odor of ripe guavas, rotting papaya, narcotic sizzle of ginger. The smell of *pomelo*, big as human heads, thunking to the ground.

Ah, *pomelos!* Like giant grapefruits stuffed with scent. Inside coarse yellow skin, white flesh thick as fillets smelling like gardenias. And under that, veiny grapefruit sections like big prawns containing globules green as peridots, and pink, like rose quartz. The wet, glittery green was sour, but the pink was sweet as sugar cubes. One could not stop sucking. The sour made you hungry for the sweet, which sent you back to the sour. Afterwards, after the strenuous ritual of peeling and eating one of these monstrosities, Jess would rub the flesh across her cheeks, feeling her face tighten. For days her hands and arms would smell of gardenias.

Sometimes she woke before dawn, leaned from her window, yanked a *pomelo* from the tree, and lay it on her pillow like the scented head of a lover, one that required nothing and would not wound her. She closed her eyes, caressed the fruit, its slightly oily, fragrant skin reminding her of Mars: bawling jazz bands, ambulance sirens, his long, black, graceful hands pushing her away, out of scrupulousness, out of anger. Mars telling her she was living wrong, wrong rhythms, wrong priorities, that her history was taking place without her. That he would not be in her life.

Some days, just cusping dawn, she glided down to the kitchen, joining Run Run. Like two grinning Aborigines, they squatted before the wood stove cupping hot bowls of fresh Kona coffee, each woman lost in glowing embers of a bark fire, fragrant woody smoke curling in their hair like dreams. One morning Run Run looked at her, juice of fresh mango dripping down her knuckles.

"You know, Jess, foah shoah, you real *kanaka kine*, not *high-tone haole kine*. Sometime I t'ink you more *da kine* dan all de ot'ers put togeddah. Swim foah hours in da sea, squat wit' me at dawn, eat wit' fingahs. And how you get dat look sometime, dat Pono-look, like you diggin' down, listenin' to da whisperin' in yoah blood!"

Jess shook her head. "Strange, yeaah? Me, the outsider. The one she likes least."

Run Run shouted at her. "No talk *pupule*! You more in dan out. It's de ot'ers worry me. Rachel like one wind-up doll for dat Hiro. Ming floatin' off and off, like she nevah be *pau* sick. And Vanya! When not doin' shame kine t'ing wit' strangahs, so busy wit' politics forget what she politicking foah! Foah us, local folks. For taro patches, one small plot for livin.'"

She stood, stirring a pot maliciously. "Know what she say me? She no like *poi*! Nevah did. She make me cry, make my old gums hurt. *Poi*! Dat like juice of mama's tee-tee. And—you ready?—she no like swim no moah. Say it boring, nevah did like. Mot'er God. Somet'ime I t'ink you don' come home foah good, Jess, we all goin' disappear. Not'ing left behind to show we evah been!"

Jess frowned, still disbelieving. "Pono gets nervous when I stay too long. I remind her of too much."

Run Run gently shook her arm. "Hold dat tongue . . . and lissen. We runnin' out of time. Pono *love* you. Because guess what? You a lot like her. Try read behind de eyes when lookin' in her face."

Later, gathering 'opihi on wet rocks, tossing live cowrie back into the sea, Jess replayed the conversation, trying to imagine Pono loving her, wanting her there permanently. Wanting any of them there. This hoarder of secrets, always keeping her granddaughters, the world, at bay. Yet, this was where Jess felt she belonged, she had always known it. Back in New York, she was clanless, no one to shield her, make claims on her. No one to comfort her when men—her husband, Mars—walked out because she was too dark, too light, too angry, too timid, not tough enough. She felt sterile and wasted in New York, her life seemed to have gone underground, a world of humid, artificially lit rooms, convalescing animals in cages. Only here, at home, did Jess feel alive, a sense of coming back to her self, as if from long banishment.

Here, it was possible to get very close to the actuality of things. The sea was the sea, lava was lava. One washed away the beaches, the other kept belching up more land. She woke at dawn and drank a cup of coffee, brewed from beans she had helped harvest one year. That season she had picked so long for so many hours so many weeks, her fingers split, her back creaked like a crone's, cherry basket hanging from her waist growing fuller and fuller, into a twenty-five-pound monster fetus that at day's end left her hiding, weeping in excruciating pain. But that was how it was done, you picked until baskets were full. You did not stop to empty half-baskets into burlap sacks.

When one had picked for that long, with that intensity, something happened, the coffee beans had become Jess's beans. The beans had somehow become *her*. Now, when she heard coffee beans dancing and popping in the roaster, when she smelled the pungent oil and mossy, sharp aroma as it perked, felt the first frisson when it slid across her tongue, and swallowing, feeling it jazzing her system awake, she remembered the winey smell of ripe coffee cherries, Filipinos, Mexicans, Micronesians humming or whistling as they picked, their earthy sweat, tobacco, their brilliantine. She remembered a hornet stinging her cheek, a big ponderous rat eyeing her between the trees. She *lived* the cup of coffee, drinking it was not something she did in passing.

And walking barefoot to the mailbox wormy feel of rotten *liliko'i* seeds squishing between her toes and driving to Kamagaki Market hoards of frangipani like dead butterflies stuck against her windshield and pulling lush tomatoes from red dirt shaking down ripe avocados for lunch watching Run Run slurp *one-fingah* poi and carrying *'ōpakapaka* home from fishing boats blood scrolling down her leg and lip-smacking *laulau* grease scootering round her wrist and reading by kerosene or candlelight in storms Benny Goodman on scratchy 78s or Ming downstairs on the piano Chopin études ghosting up and down the halls and watching a momcat go berserk eating a new litter leaving only the tiny heads and termites whispering in ancient volumes Thackeray Yeats "The Queen's Book" by Lili'uokalani and camphored linens damp perfumed sheets her cousins calling out in dreams.

Jess was not on vacation when she came home. She had to earn life minute by minute, pay attention to each thing, not cheat her senses. And she wondered if maybe in this attentiveness, one day she would find what she needed to live by, a code, a deep abiding conviction. *Maybe that's why we keep coming back, each of us. Trying to find the clue. Maybe Pono is the clue. Nothing else has ever terrified me so.*

While Jess stood brooding on the sand, her grandmother sat high above her on the cliffs, pulling up medicinal roots, herbal leaves, the healing *popolo, kukui, la'i.* It was noon, bringing gentle Kona rains; across the land coffee trees glittered like dark emeralds. Pono stood, watched her granddaughter's slender form jog down the beach in splashes.

A woman now, early forties, battling life on her own. Did I help her all these years? Give her enough clues on how to survive? I tried, God knows. In my keep-your-distance way, I tried. Pathetic, skinny little white thing when she first arrived, but she had Emma's eyes. I knew she could hurt me, outsmart me like her mother. Emma, scholar, lover of music, and the sea. She chose the white man's world, and died alone, of thirst. But I gave to her girl. What I had, what I could afford. Summer after summer.

She remembered the day she knew this seed of Emma could invade her and betray. It had happened at Hawaiian Mass, the Catholic Painted Church at Honaunau ... (Pono never entered a church, not since the years of God's desertion when she and Duke were hunted down. But she was fair, let Run Run take the girls to Mass and teach them her, Run Run's, version of religion. "God *not* da faddah, he just da spoiled moody child, but you got to go t'rough him to get to da real power, his mama, Mot'er God. She da real Almighty! She run da heavens alone. Original single parent. When somethin' bad happen, usually mean she let God try his hand, and he screw up plenny. You need somet'ing important, you go directly Mot'er God. Jesus, Mary, Joseph? Dey just small potatoes, part of da chorus, neh?")

Pono remembered this particular Sunday. Junior Girls Choir singing in Hawaiian, accompanied by locals playing gourds, shell trumpets, bamboo pipes, nose flutes. A special Mass commemorating King Kamehameha's birthday, when people came from miles around, crowding the little church, spilling out onto the lawns and down into the cemetery. Jess, eleven, not speaking Hawaiian, was still invited to join in Junior Girls Choir. During choir practice, Pono saw her little hands shake as she strained, trying to learn the ancient words. Pono began coaching her night after night, while the others slept. That Sunday, she had stood outside an open window of the church, waving her arms like a maestro, mouthing the Hawaiian words, filling Jess with confidence as her choir sang (led by those twin showoffs, Daisy and Pansy Freitas).

Mother God, how she opened up her lungs and sang! Mouth wide as a hungry young bird's, pronouncing every vowel, drowning out everyone.

Hemolele, Hemolele, Hemolele! Ke akua	Holy, Holy, Holy! Lord, God almighty!
mana loa! Ka lani a me ta honua, e ho-	Heaven and earth are filled with your
opiha me kou nani. Hosanna i ke ki'eki'e.	glory. Hosanna in the highest. Blessed is

Nani wale ke ali'i, o ka Iseraela, e hele mai	He of Israel who comes in the name of
ana, ma ka inoa o ka Haku. Hosana i ke	the Lord. Hosanna in the highest,
ki'eki'e, Hosana i ke ki'eki'e. Hosana i ke	Hosanna in the highest, Hosanna in the
ki'eki'e.	highest.

Seeing her grandmother out on the lawn, waving her arms, mouthing the words, not caring that the crowds looked on, thinking only of Jess, something deep inside the girl had answered. A light, an audible and pointed light, soared out of her with the warbling yearning of a dove, the resonance of a bell. She sang in someone else's voice, sang the ancient words so perfectly, so beautifully, snoring elders blinked awake and stood up in their pews. A mangy dog wandering the aisles whined softly, going down on its belly. Women wept, and Father Rodriguez—leaning forward in his chair—stared openmouthed and crossed himself. After Mass, tearful elders gathered round Jess, hugging her, telling Pono her granddaughter sang *Mai nei loko! Mai nei loko!* From the heart!

In that moment, Pono had turned her back on her, shunning Jess. For the rest of that summer, the girl retreated to the shadows in abject sadness, wondering what wrong she had done.

So proud of her! Like pride I remember having for her mother. She could hurt me, I saw it then. Hurt me like Emma. Well, half of her could hurt me. The other half, the haole *half, wasn't worth my spit.*

And yet, each of these girls was half of something else. Duke said she had to learn to accept this, that the true, original blood of their ancestors, the only one she recognized, was dying. Their granddaughters, Duke said, were hybrids of a new world. *Their* offspring were even more alien, Hawaiian blood blurred into quarters, someday eighths. A world Pono didn't want to know. Yet, now she was asking them to bring that alien, that mixed-mongrel world, home.

She thought of Toru then, so much a son. He would get an equal share of what she left behind. He could marry local, a girl with thick Hawaiian blood. He could run the farm, let the cousins share the profits but keep their tainted blood away. He could . . . she shook her head, defeated.

Toru, how could I ask such promises of you? At least you are alive. You get from day to day. It seems such an achievement. But dear boy, in your life, have you never loved? Will you never know that passion? To be swept away? This is why I mourn for you, your heart was left a shell. What can I do? What can your cousins do for you when I am gone? Your tūtū, Run Run . . . I see her pain, watching you live half a life. She goes down on her knees each day, because you are alive. And sane, not sucking the teat of heroin. But is it enough to live only for one's self?

Thinking of him, whose life she had saved twice, she saw a kind of solitary beauty in the image of people making their way alone, not weighted down with the emotions of another, nothing but the weight of their own flesh as burden. *What is it like, I wonder?* She who had always lived for another, had wound her life around the existence of this other, so that her life became a sentence, a mystery, a dream. *All I ever wanted was that one day we could walk out in the world. Now we are growing old in shadows, Duke and I. My dream has been so small.*

Late at night, Toru drove back and forth past the house of women, all the lights ablaze. And he felt whole because, within that place were people he could worry over, look after, long for, love. Finally, lights dimmed, the house went dark. Easing his truck up the gravelly drive beside the old place, a place he knew every inch of, by touch, by memory, he turned off the ignition, lit a cigarette. After a while he leaned back, dozing, as silver moonlight fell across his face. For the moment, he was safe. And they were safe. Everyone was home.

Nā Manawale'a

The Caring Hearts

THEY LOOKED FOR CLUES. In those first weeks of summer, each woman moved cautiously, watching Pono from a distance, glancing at her sideways over meals. What she was preparing them for, whatever onrushing, nameless event, would be related in her time, at her pace. They slid into routines, individual rhythms, each woman feeling a sense of breathlessness, of imminent reckoning, like something in a web.

Vanya flew back and forth to Honolulu, brooding over legal briefs on Native Land Rights, National Health Insurance, the fight for Hawaiian Sovereignty. With two associates covering for her, Jess had taken a sorely needed vacation from her practice in Manhattan. As days passed she seemed content to move at dream-pace, letting the hours, the days, rub up against her. Rachel spent her time staring at the phone, waiting for Hiro's nightly call from Hong Kong or Bangkok. Ming read, or seemed to, eyes aimless with a diligence. Some days she never left her room. Some days she moved in slow motion so her kimono sleeve dragged through the guava jam at breakfast.

Slowly, inevitably, they reverted back to island girls, chattering in Pidgin, beachcombing before dawn, dipping Saloon Pilot crackers in mango juice. Blank whiteness of summer noons drove them to bedrooms where shades were drawn, where they stretched out beside each other, gossiping. And they dozed, smelling the perfume of each other, sometimes dreaming of each other. Sometimes one would wake and watch the others in sleep, as if watching *over* them.

Afternoons bled into night, heat warping appetites. Run Run brought up trays of sliced papaya, melons, and stretched out on the floor beside them "talking story," family myths, histories, getting stories mixed up, different endings, different beginnings, until the dark brought coolness, and the cycle of sleep resumed. It seemed they slept for weeks.

Some nights—all of them drowsing in one of the giant four-posters built for a time when royalty had visited this house—they would sense her presence, even in their sleep. Waking, half rising, they would find Pono there, continuing a story she had left off at days earlier. Anecdotes about her field-workers, their lives. Modestly, she talked about children she now helped send to secondary school, to university.

One evening Run Run cried, "Tell about *Nā Manawale'a*, 'Da Caring Heart.' " Running down the hall, she returned with a huge inscribed *koa calabash*, awarded Pono by the mayor of Kona District. "Dis one great honor!"

They passed the bowl around, admiring it as Pono explained how the Hawai'i Island Food Bank worked to prevent the waste of food by receiving donations of surplus produce, and distributing it to the homeless and needy, a growing population on the Big Island. The Caring Heart *calabash* had been presented to Pono for outstanding contributions, and food donations from her farm, and for outstanding volunteerism on fund-raising drives. Discovering, too late, that the Food Bank was a project of the Social Ministry of the Catholic church, Pono had thrown the *calabash* out in the mud. Run Run now used it to mix gruel for ducks and pigs.

"Who care about *ole calabash*," she said. "Important t'ing is what yoah *tūtū* doin' for da poor." She pumped her pigeon chest out proudly. "You laugh yoahself to tears, see locals' eye pop when Pono drive up to dere house, askin' foah food donations foah da bank. See dis big *wahine*, famous *kahuna* standing on dere soil. Hah! Dey almost on dere knees, ready give everyt'ing. All dere food, dere house! So she don't *kahuna* dem, leave dem lyin' dead like empty rice sacks!" She hugged herself laughing. "One *kanaka*, I t'ink ready give his wife and keeds!"

Pono sat back in a scrolled teak chair, its cracked claw feet creaking with her weight. "So much easier to give. I detest asking, driving up and down the roads like beggars. I thought a check would do. But this one"—a finger jabbed at Run Run—"roped me in. Said I couldn't just give checks, other coffee planters would *'imi 'ōlelo*, say I was trying buy favors for our farm."

She paused, studying her granddaughters one by one, each woman big-eyed, over-eager, trying to read in her eyes how they should respond.

"Lot of public relations involved in coffee farming. You need diplomacy." She looked at Vanya. "It won't come naturally to you. Rachel or Jess could handle that end of it . . ."

They sat up suddenly alert, like women pulled by strings.

". . . unless you're planning to sell the place when I'm gone. You seem so silent on the matter. Have you forgotten the importance of owning land?"

Rachel cleared her throat, speaking softly. "It isn't that, *Tūtū*. It's just . . . we can't imagine you not here." She burst into tears, burying her face. "Don't make me think about it, please!"

Vanya looked at her distastefully, then turned to Pono. "I know you're thinking of our future. But isn't it a little premature . . ."

Pono snapped herself into a standing position. "You. Sometimes you're absolutely blind. Traipsing round the Pacific, woman of the world, solving everyone's dilemmas. But here"—Pono tapped her heart theatrically—"here at home, within yourself, you can't face the truth. I am *old*. My time is coming. Do any of you understand?"

They looked down at their hands like children. Somehow Jess found her voice. "There's so much we never understood. To think of you . . . dying. Leaving everything unsaid . . ." She turned her head away.

Pono seemed to grow, to dwarf the door she was suddenly moving toward. Her voice turned hard, coming back at them like blows. "You think knowing things will solve your private little griefs? You think I hold the key?"

She felt herself turn ugly, seeing them spread across the bed like bored odalisques, women who led lives of pleasure, luxury. Lives filled with human traffic. She stormed out of the room and down the hall.

". . . Grow up! Make your decisions and live with them. *That's* the key."

They sat in slow, respirating shock. "I thought," Vanya whispered, "it would be normal for once. Questions, answers, you know?"

Run Run sighed, shook her head. "You girls nevah understand. She no like questions. You got to wait. One day, maybe she tell you what 'n' what."

"Why, for once, don't you tell us?" Jess asked. "You know her history. Are you afraid?"

"Yeah," Run Run said, backing away. "I a true chicken. I tell you what I know, you girls age before my eyes. Not my place to tell . . . and what I know, sometime I no believe."

Vanya stood impatiently, flinging back her hair. "Same old mysterious crap. I'm flying back to Honolulu in the morning."

And now, as ever, frustrated by the scene with Pono, they turned on each other.

"And where from Honolulu?" Rachel smiled. "Darwin? Intrigues Down Under?"

Vanya turned, studying her long enough to make the others tense. "Don't ever . . . presume to criticize my life, you casualty. Without Hiro, you'd be cleaning people's houses."

Ming tried to intercede. "Please . . . don't . . ."

"At least I'm faithful to my husband," Rachel said.

"His eager prey."

"What are you faithful to?"

Vanya turned on her then, on all of them, rage flushing her cheeks, so she was beautiful, and dark and broken.

"The barricades! Wherever they are. Wherever our people have to go down on their knees. All those *kānaka*-putdown checkpoints, that keep us second-rate. That's what I work for, what I'm faithful to. While you lie around playing concubine." She looked at Jess. "And you, still catering to mainland *haole* whose pets eat better than our kids! And you . . ."

Turning to Ming, Vanya's words died on her lips. Her cousin looked so eerily frail, she wanted to take her in her arms.

She collapsed on the bed, shaking. "I hate her. I *hate* her. This is how she leaves us every time, snarling, ripping at each other."

Rachel stood in a superior way, gathering her sarong round her perfect breasts. "I don't care where you go, or who you're sleeping with. I just worry, Vanya . . . that you won't make it back. That one day you'll drift out of our lives for good. What would we be, any of us? I mean . . . without each other?"

Jess lay in her room alone, exhausted. *This is what Pono can do, what she is capable of. Tearing us apart. Is she, I wonder, jealous? Our lives, allegiances, so bound. We have always had each other. Who did she ever have, but Run Run?*

Late that night she woke feeling the house tremble, bottles on the dresser jumped. She turned on a lamp; everything in her room had shifted, pictures hung sideways on the wall. Jess cried out as her bed shook, the floor slanted violently and down in the valley someone screamed. Within minutes the house was astir. Radio reports said seismographs at the Volcano Observatory were dancing.

By dawn, two infants in Hilo had disappeared from their cribs. A fisherman had been taken at Kawaihae, snapped in two by a twelve-foot tiger shark. Random horrors that always presaged volcanic eruptions, as if the earth were purging its bowels of evil. A subterranean arm of Kīlauea Crater, Pu'u 'O'ō Vent, was surfacing again, threatening to swallow up more homes in the path of its flowing molten lava. By six A.M., the sky was obliterated, gritty clouds lowering across the island. In the distance Jess heard the *Wup! Wup! Wup!* of Coast Guard helicopters headed for the inundation areas. By seven, Toru was sitting in the driveway, gunning his motor.

Pono strode through the house, instructing everyone. "Pele has begun! Let's go, you folks." Looking pointedly at Vanya with her packed suitcase, her reservation on the early flight to Honolulu.

Within minutes, Pono was behind the wheel of her Jeep, Ming and Rachel beside her, holding fruits, ti leaves, fifths of gin. Pele, fiery Goddess of Volcanoes, was demanding offerings. Toru followed in his truck with Jess and Vanya, watching headlights of cars—tourists, locals, shamans—whipping across the landscape, headed for the lava-viewing area. By now, the whole island seemed hung with *vog*, volcanic ash and fog, and news reports said Pu'u 'O'ō Vent was shooting lava two thousand feet into the air. The island was giving birth again, more families were being evacuated.

During the ninety-minute drive south toward the Hot Zone, they were silent, feeling their metabolisms change. Like demarcated dreams, the land transformed from lush coffee and macadamia nut orchards to thin, emaciated woods, and then, within a few more miles, starkness— the black glittering moonscape of hardened lava. They passed little resurrected villages of Ho'okena and Ho'opuloa where black was absolute. To their left the slopes of Mauna Loa rose thirteen thousand feet. To their right, bleak reminders of Mauna Loa's great lava flows of 1919, 1926, 1950—flows that had cindered everything in their path, rain forests, fields, villages.

Pono gazed up at Mauna Loa, remembering another, later flow in the years when she and Run Run were struggling with the farm, nights when she felt so hopeless, so exhausted, she thought of torching the place, leaving nothing but ash. Then one dawn they had heard the rumblings, seen the smoke of Mauna Loa all the way from Captain Cook, and joined hundreds of locals rushing to the Hot Zone, watching as molten lava rushed down to the sea. *Vog* had been so thick the day was dark as night, the sky ghostly orange, a 1,500-foot lava fountain shooting upward, then flowing like an Oriental scroll.

Finally the lava had slowed, wind shifted, people watched, frightened, as ruby clouds moved in. Then cooled, red cinders filtered down, like delicate spices. Pono had moved close to Run Run, and they laughed, dancing in red showers. Then everyone had danced because that day Pele had been kind, had spared a village, no lives were taken. And in that dancing-time Pono had remembered her long-ago dream, that of a young girl, left alone in Chinatown. A dream of her and Run Run as old women, dancing in showers of cinnamon.

Seeing her cinnamon-dream come true had rekindled Pono's belief in her personal *mana*. She could still dream the future, maybe bend it to her will. It gave her strength to work the farm until it almost killed her, until she revived the coffee orchards, resurrected the long-abandoned house for Duke's someday-homecoming. Down the years, she had dreamed his homecoming with almost penitential rigor. But lately Pono's dream had deserted her. *Now I only dream of dying, my faceless corpse snuggled by eels. Why can't I see my face?. . . Why?* Skidding into a pothole, she swerved the Jeep and cursed.

Passing the Ka'u District, southernmost district of the island, bypassing the villages of Miloli'i, and Na'alehu, the old sugar towns of Pahala and Punalu'u, they entered Volcanoes National Park and the rumbling arm of Kilauea, Pu'u O'o Vent. Here was a region of ethereal, dripping rain forests, of primeval giant tree ferns. Then, with shocking abruptness, green gave way to another blasted, lava landscape of smoldering *pāhoehoe* and *'a'ā*.

Gas was heavy in the air. Steam clouds rose from fumaroles, drifting like disembodied spirits. Cars pulled off the road, passengers sick from sulfur dioxide. It was morning but seemed like coming night. They were within five miles of Pu'u 'Ō'ō Vent. As long lines of cars locomoted one behind the other, *vog* grew thicker, sounds louder, rumble and hiss of lava gushing from reservoirs beneath the earth.

Driving down the Chain of Craters Road, they passed giant pits from past eruptions, stretches of lava of varying ages frozen in their surge toward the sea. In the distance they saw fiery skies, even clouds glowed with the crimson reflection of liquid rock shooting thousands of feet into the air. In this otherworldly region, Pele, Volcano Goddess, reigned, her eerie presence everywhere. Hundreds of locals stood at the rim of the steaming, sulfur-streaked caldera of Kīlauea, inside which was the eerily quiet Halemaumau Pit where Pele lived. People chanted and prayed, asking her to spare another village, another school, a church. And in the distance, Puʻu ʻŌʻō spewed fresh lava.

Stepping from her Jeep, Pono pulled herself to her full height. Age had not whittled her spine; nearing eighty, she stood almost six feet two inches tall. Even to foreigners cataracting from tour buses, she was frightening, bewitching. Her stature, flowing hair, dark, handsome profile from another age, and finally her deep, black look, all seemed to say: BEWARE. A warning that magic was real, that this woman of mythic proportion demanded something of all who breathed her air.

Along the rim of Kīlauea, offerings of joss sticks, roast pigs, pyramids of fruit were piled beside fifths of gin and whiskey wrapped in ti leaves. Tourists aimed their cameras, inwardly scoffing, not knowing that within hours, a cloud would blanket the pit, bringing utter blackness, and when it lifted, the offerings would be gone. But not now, not yet. Pele liked to titillate and tease.

Now Pono stood at Kīlauea's rim, chanting, asking Pele to be merciful, calm the surging earth, gulp back down the molten lava. Chanting louder and louder, she looked out across the black desert of older inundations, cold, glittery *pāhoehoe*—fold upon fold like miles of elephant hide—and *aʻa*, the ragged, brittle chunks jutting up in peaks. Crowds stood back, watching the towering figure with blowing hair, calling to the pit. She seemed to chant forever so people fell into a standing trance. Then, overhead, clouds were suddenly flung down, and gray silty showers, leaving grit on people's eyelids and their lips. Pono swayed, seemed to float, the gownlike *muʻumuʻu* she was wearing flying out behind her. She chanted louder, flung a fifth of gin wrapped in ti leaf down into the pit. It didn't break, it didn't even seem to land. It disappeared.

And in that moment, Pono's hair lifted all about her as if by invisible hands. The clouds dissolved and she was a woman lit by colors—neon explosions from her eyes, breasts, joints. People screamed, terrified. When they looked up, Pono was enveloped in a rainbow, the other end of which arched and settled into Pele's dead, black center, Halemaumau Pit. A German tourist cursed as the lens of his camera shattered. A woman watched her Polaroid melt to black putty.

"Sleep, *Kaikuʻana*," Pono whispered. "You have done enough today."

She dropped her arms and walked away, past tourists who would remember her as a shaman seven feet tall, with glowing coals for eyes, a woman with hair of flowing lava, nails of lightning. They would remember her so fantastically, no one would believe them, and in time they would not believe themselves. Disbelieving, they would eventually forget. For such sacred chants, such secret rituals between Polynesians and their gods, were not meant for eyes of *malihini*.

She left the pit, the others following behind. Half a mile from Puʻu ʻŌʻō Vent, they stepped from their cars again, heat on their faces like an open furnace. Sulfur fumes were so thick, Jess felt she'd swallowed gravel; when she turned, her clothes seemed to burn her skin. Moving closer to the flow, she felt the soles of her shoes begin to melt. They were standing near cooling, encrusted lava, but its surface temperature was still over 200 degrees. A few feet beneath that surface, molten lava still flowed at degrees of 1,500.

From behind wooden barricades, crowds watched silently, handkerchiefed like bandits as, in the distance red fountains shot the sky, then waves of lava boiled down, igniting everything. On level ground, lava moved slowly, only a few feet an hour, bushes exploding into white skeletons. Like great dripping zombies, trees coated with ash trembled, twisted, then were buried, revealing the flow's great depth. Farther south, the roar of incandescent lava poured into the sea; at night these lava fountains would be visible for miles.

Moving away from intense heat that made it hard to swallow, Toru led the others half a mile away to a hardened lava flow that had buried eight miles of villages and forests. They felt the sting in their nostrils, or maybe the memory of things charred, histories erased. Jess shivered, trying to fathom that, twenty feet beneath them, where they stood, where they were walking, were neighborhood churches, graveyards, educational systems, movie houses, people's bedrooms. She kicked at the crumbling husk of what had been a cow, saw incinerated tractors, skulls of buses, frozen in their sinking. She closed her eyes, imagining people running from their homes, turning back for one more thing, a ring, a photograph.

Now there was only calm, dead calm, and dunes of hardened lava. Out where late-day mist was rolling in, lava was furred a funereal gray, and here and there families stood formally, or knelt, over what had been their homes. Park rangers moved quietly. And even the *Wup! Wup! Wup!* of choppers overhead seemed monitored down to a sorrowful sound, as if whipping out, in secret code, WE ARE SORRY . . . SORRY . . . SORRY . . .

Jess gazed across the land, bleak as a black Sahara. She moved away from the others, her body appearing suddenly older, like that of a woman struggling through sand, weak with a thirst that would be ultimate, attending to her final stare. Toru and the others watched her, for each time she came home, the lava drew her in. She spent hours hiking across charred black land, a woman in a netherworld of jagged dunes. Sometimes she walked for days and nights, nothing but beef jerky, a canteen of water, scorpions and centipedes. Lava deserts were treacherous, people got lost in the dark, lacerated by knife projections of 'a'ā. Thin surfaces that gave in to bottomless pits beneath.

"So foolish, what she does," Rachel whispered. "One misstep she's down. Broken leg, crushed ankle. Out there calling, nothing but the sea in front of her."

Stoned bikers and hippies were sometimes found wandering in circles for days. Locals said all one had to do was walk inland, keep the sea behind you, and you would come to the end of the lava desert. But knife-sharp 'a'ā shredded shoes in hours. One could go sunblind, become dehydrated. Infected bites blew up the body, causing fevers. One could begin to not care. One could die, people had. Jess chanced it every time, obssessed as a Bedouin musing on sands.

"Got something to do with guilt," Toru said. "Her mother, neh?"

"Guilt. Longing. Got something to do with all of us." Rachel shook her head, keeping an eye on Jess.

From a distance, Pono watched her too. *What is she thinking out there? What is she looking for?* She turned away, not wanting to recognize in Jess's stride, her mother, Emma.

It was evening, they had been on the lava all day.

"Come," Pono said. "We have honored Pele. She will do what she will do."

Joining lines of cars locomoting the highway back to Captain Cook, Toru stopped for Cokes, bags of barbecued pork rinds, and *Okonomi Mame*. Passing the bags back and forth between them, he idled the engine until Pono's Jeep was lost in the ruby-strung necklace of tail-lights far ahead.

"Want to show you gals something."

After eight or nine miles, he turned the truck off the highway at a sign for Pahala. Jess grinned, recognizing the old sugar plantation town, rows of flaking blue and yellow shacks, corrugated tin roofs, splintered steps of each house studded with zoris, oxidizing coffee cans sprouting orchids. Elderly Japanese and Filipinos leaning on their fences puffed cigars and waved, one man holding a vicious-looking fighting cock, its red comb ruffed, a boiled claw.

Toru made a sudden turn, then flew down a red dirt road, canyoned left and right by waving sugarcane. Jess suddenly recalled how, as teenagers drunk on Primo and 'ōkolehao, they had drag-raced down these roads, gunning motors, flatbeds whining side by side. Nights of cane-burning, it had seemed they were racing through a hell of boiling molasses, masked cane cutters running with their forks, little nightmare devils black against the fires.

Toru accelerated, racing them back to a time when they were innocent and whole, wrestling, bullying each other in the careless way of those who loved, not noticing how life was gaining, how much of what was innocent would be discarded. The women whooped and yelled, as tires spun and skidded, the truck bouncing them like melons. Then Toru turned onto a wooden bridge crossing into a sudden rain forest, an oasis out there in the cane. On a muddy path, he slowed, inching along.

"Oh, my God," Vanya laughed. "Jade Valley Monastery!"

They stopped before a large Oriental-looking building, its green-tiled, wing-edged roof like a great mythic bird about to fly. *Koa* bark walls, rosewood doors, stone lions grinning at the gates. All around, the ancient, penitential smell of incense. Broad steps were scalloped with the passage of monks, acolytes, meditating down the years. Toru pushed the door open, motioned them inside. Imprints of pews, statues, a seven-foot stone Buddha, all moved years ago to a new location. It was like an empty warehouse.

Vanya looked down at mummies of joss sticks gone to dust, flowers rotted into shadows. "Remember how we'd steal the offerings and neck behind the pews? Me and Chicky Gomez, French-kissing in the Buddha's lap!"

He played a flashlight across the room, sleeping bags, lanterns, *lauhala* mats piled neatly in a corner.

"People still coming on retreat?" Jess asked.

"Nah," Toru answered softly. "That's our gear. Me and the guys. Sometimes we come on weekends, you know ... sushi, Primo, poker ..."

"That's a long drive from Kohala."

". . . some of them were born round here, down South Point, Miloli'i way . . ."

Vanya looked at him steadily. "That what you guys talk about . . . problems at Miloli'i?"

"Why not? They're plenty pissed off. Ancient fishing grounds and so on, watching their parents shoved out by real estate bastards . . ."

"And what you gonna' do about it?" She felt herself slipping into Pidgin, which always made talk more intimate and real.

". . . Oh, different ideas . . . preventive measures . . ."

She strolled round, her voice echoing in the emptiness. "These guys all *paniolo*, from the ranch?"

Toru cleared his throat. "Some."

"Some. And . . . who the others?"

"Friends . . . from 'Nam."

Jess turned. That word, soft as a mantra, lethal as a blade. It seemed to resurrect the years they thought were buried. Months when Toru was MIA, when they thought him dead. And then the baggage he brought home, snail tracks on his arms. Needles suckling his veins. Years of seeing him a zombie, wishing 'Nam had killed him honorably. Lack of air suddenly made the place seem stifling. They stepped outside, watched the swoop of hoary bats hunting silently at dusk. Nearby, a thrush, laughing like a girl.

"You know," he said patiently, "lot of these guys still need a little help. Over twenty years now, we're still fighting for a fuckin' in-patient clinic, right here, biggest concentration of 'Nam vets in the islands. Guys with PTSD have to fly all the way to Tripler on O'ahu, or even the mainland."

Vanya answered carefully. "I thought Congress had approved funds for a vet center here."

Toru laughed. "Right. Two million dollars allocated. But first the 'fiscal studies,' VA approval, choosing of a site, architects, legal fees, administrative costs. Estimated year of ground-breaking . . . *1998!*"

They walked silently back to the truck. "Oh, well," he said, "just wanted you to see it again. You know, the memories. Boy, we were young!"

They sat still for a time, as if waiting for the truck to start itself.

"What were the arrows?" Jess asked. "Over the sleeping bags? I saw arrows and numbers on the walls."

He hesitated. ". . . Distances round the island. You know, here to there."

Vanya leaned forward. "Toru. What are you guys up to?"

He took a slug of Coke, held a barbecued pork rind against the dashboard light. "See those bumps? Those are the pores through which the pig used to sweat."

He crunched the rind, turned the ignition, the truck slid quietly down the path. "We're up to the same thing you are, cuz. Only . . . we're gonna' make it happen. Maybe we can make it happen together. You got all that credibility, people behind you, militant lawyers with *high-tone* degrees."

"Make what happen?"

He shifted gears impatiently. "Don't you remember that interview you gave the *Advertiser*. You said maybe the only way for Native Hawaiians to get back their lands was to kick some butt. Make the world sit up and take notice. It's happening all over the Pacific, people balking at the superpowers. You said . . ."

"I know what I said. It got me into trouble. And I was half joking . . ."

". . . said maybe we should bomb a military installation, a hotel. Hit them with guerilla forces."

Vanya shook her head. "It was just a way of getting media attention."

"Don't give me that, Vanya. You've been saying it for years, started people thinking maybe you were right. We tried everything else. Demonstrations, legislation, begging on our knees. They don't give a damn about Hawaiians, we're history. All I'm saying is . . . think about it. We're here every weekend, talking, planning."

"Toru." She stared at him, willing him to listen. "You don't attack your parent country. We're part of the United States, remember?"

"Right. Bought, sold, signed, sealed, delivered. Whoever asked us if we wanted statehood? If we even wanted to be a territory? Our history's based on theft. Our lands, our rights stolen out from under us. In ten years we'll be Disneyland."

She answered quietly. "In ten years we'll be a sovereign nation, we'll have our stolen lands back, have our own Hawaiian government again. That's what all the shouting's for. You want to blow all that? You're talking like an Arab. You want us to walk into the State Capitol waving Uzis."

His voice changed. Suddenly it was someone else's voice.

"Don't talk to me of sovereignty. They gave it to the American Indians and they're still dying out . . . poverty, alcoholism, prison. Let me tell you something, Vanya. Know why they're building that new State Veterans' Cemetery at Kānehoe? They're running out of room at Punchbowl. Kānehoe will have casket space for *seventy-five thousand* new veterans. Didn't you see the news last week? Projected cost, fifteen

million dollars. All for our boys in uniform, the expendables, underedu-
cated locals."

In the silence, Jess heard her heart pounding.

"Just think about what I said. You and Jess. You two are out there
in the world. You know what it takes. People want violence. Theater."

"You're crazy, Toru."

"Maybe. But, with you, or without you, we're goin' the limit. *Goin'
foah broke!*"

Silently, they watched the highway scroll under them. Toru lit a
cigarette, eased up on the gas, and talked about a friend, newly dead.
"A skinning knife across his jugular, wife and kids in the next room."

The man had just been sentenced to twenty years in prison no
possible parole, for possession of a sawed-off shotgun, and for growing
a tiny patch of marijuana in his yard.

"Eight little rows, just enough smoke for himself. And the gun, he
wasn't charged with threatening anyone. Just for possessing it. A one-
armed man, how many people could he kill? Everyone I know keeps a
gun. Judge said he wanted to make him an example. Imagine this guy,
Purple Heart, Bronze Medal, two tours in 'Nam. A wife, two kids. In
the year 2014, he'd be released a sixty-two-year-old ex-con. Wife gone,
kids grown, one arm . . ."

He shook his head, and Jess could see sweat beads on his lip.

". . . Twenty years in prison, twenty thousand dollars a year burden
on taxpayers, all told four hundred thousand plus. Money they could
use on health care for the aged, education for our kids, AIDS research.
Poor bastard. Well, he's okay now. At peace."

He wiped his eyes, cursing softly, drove on a while. "You know, I
love you, each one of you. You're family, all I've ever known. Please
understand. We're not nuts. We're just guys who went to war. Sometimes on weekends, playing poker, a little buzzed, someone remembers
and breaks down. I mean, we were *Orientals*, over there killing other
Orientals. Wiping out their families. You think about it, and everything
gets real concentrated, real narrowed down."

Jess watched the windshield go underwater as her eyes filled up and
spilled. She took his hand from the steering wheel, held it to her cheek.
"Toru. You never talked about it. We wanted to help you, wanted to
ask you about it. We were too afraid. . . . What was it like? I mean . . .
'Nam."

"Green," he said softly. ". . . Real green."

* * *

That night, Jess drove Vanya to Keahole Airport for the late flight to Honolulu. Standing at the boarding gate, she asked, "What did he mean, 'goin' for broke'?"

Exhausted, Vanya shrugged. "Old World War II expression. Island boys in combat overseas never quit, even when they were wounded, they just kept fightin, 'goin' foah broke' until they won. Or died."

She hugged her good-bye, then strode across the tarmac to the plane. At the foot of the boarding steps she turned, raised her arm, and seemed to freeze mid-wave. Jess waved back, frowning, for Vanya suddenly looked petrified, a clay woman fired in a kiln. Airport lights flicked back and forth across her face. Finally she came alive, mounting the steps slowly as if just regaining sight.

Winging homeward on the thirty-minute flight, Vanya leaned her head against the cold, hard pane. It had been years since she thought of what Toru did in 'Nam, what he became an expert at. But just then, at the foot of the boarding steps, it came back to her. *Demolitions.* In his letters home, he had called himself "The Dean of Demolitions."

The Wet
and the Dry

SHE STARED AT THE PITCH AND YAW of lolloping kangaroos in headlights as the bus to Darwin rattled along, frenzied agitation of a moving container carrying human bodies through a night. One thousand miles through the bone-dry heart of Australia's Outback to the continent's Top End, a grueling trip on the only paved road, the "bitumen," Stuart Highway.

Outside on the roof rack, spare tires bounced and thudded, jerrycans of emergency water rattled and slurped. Now and then the driver cursed, pulled over for a "road-train," semis with three attached trailers driven by truckies blind on amphetamines. Inside the bus, humidity was thick enough to bathe in, and the odors—rotting teeth, yeasty socks, white wild buff hunters scratching their filthy crotches.

A few German tourists smelling of hair spray and polyester, but for the most, the rest were Aborigines with their mysterious wild and earthy smell. And the sounds: hiss of doors opening at desert stops, of breaks whining as cattle strayed into the road, the suck of interrupted snores, a mouth organ bleating down the aisle. Vanya trembled with nausea, looked at the Outback sky, moon huge, stars so close she felt they could sizzle her brain. The idea of a civilized world outside her window seemed alien, something already expired. The bus took a slight turn, blinding *galahs* bursting from the bush, and for a moment headlights picked up dead cattle ballooned with gas, legs pointed upward.

Vanya leaned forward, querying the driver. "Is it the drought?"

"Nah," he said. "Heat just bloody boils their brains!"

Nothing but red dust, occasionally a riverbed, skeletons ringing a dry billabong. She dozed until the bus whined to a stop. An Aborigine got off in the middle, it seemed, of nowhere.

"Gone Walkabout," the driver volunteered. "On 'is way to Darwin, a new job, suddenly changed 'is mind. That's what they do, trek for weeks, months, no bloody destination. That's their way of thinking, mind you. Middle of a sentence, they drop everything . . . wander off to the Outback. Year or two later, you come across them, ask where in hell they've been. 'Gone Walkabout!' "

"How will he survive?" she asked.

"'Is wits! They can smell out water in the ground. Real genius for that. Snakes, kookaburra, hell, that's good tucker to a hungry bloke."

Near midnight they stopped at a pub for gas. Bodies creaked alive, staggered off and into the pub, parched for cold lagers. An Aborigine woman plunked down in the shadows beside the bus, pulling a Violet Crumbly from her pocket. Vanya moved close, trying to make conversation, but the woman yanked her hair over her face, went on with her silent munching.

A half-blood—half Aborigine, half white—stood in the doorway, his body half inside and half outside the pub, his inside arm holding a bottle of beer. Now and again, he stuck his head in, took a slug, then swung it back outside chatting with full-blood Aborigines.

The driver made light of it. "Owner won't serve full-bloods, but he compromises with half-bloods. Bloke's got a sense of humor, I'll give 'im that!"

The half-blood was wearing an Aborigine flag stuck in his knitted cap. He smiled, flirting with Vanya. "Where you from, Missus? Torres Straits?"

"Hawai'i."

"Oh, mahn, you a bloody Yank!"

"Hawaiian first. What's the flag?" Already knowing what it was, a reminder that the presence of whites in Australia was illegal. Aborigines had never signed a treaty, never ceded one square inch of their territories to foreigners. Like Hawaiians, their lands had been stolen out from under them, their numbers decimated by white man's diseases and superior weapons of death. Sovereignty and land rights were now hot issues, Aborigines marching and calling strikes.

A white buff hunter swaggered past the flag wearer. "You're livin' in the past, mate!"

The half-blood turned, eyes glittering. "Yeah, mahn, *my* past. You be careful it don't catch up wif' you."

Exhausted, Vanya sank back into her seat, closed her eyes, envisioning Darwin, hours ahead. Beery boomtown, time-warped city of the fifties perched on the northern tip of the continent. Australia's capital, Darwin existed between seasonal extremes, the Wet and the Dry, yielding up nothing but cattle and mining. After a while, she made her way to the toilet at the back of the bus. In the dark, sleeping faces like masks of the dead leapt up at her. She felt the earth moving under the wheels, wondered which way it was spinning on its axis. The bus was traveling at seventy miles an hour. *At what speed am I rushing to my destination backwards?*

She had flown from Honolulu to Brisbane for a conference on Pacific Women for Saving Island Environments. The week-long meetings had centered round the extensive mining taking place in Arnhem Land, the Kakadu Forest outside Darwin. Geologists hired by the Aboriginal Women's Environmental Watch Society had tested and proven that uranium and bauxite mining in the Kakadu was letting loose toxic waste. Acid was being dispersed, dust clouds blowing it all over the continent, leaving whole communities sick, children with mysterious lung infections.

Vanya had sat on a panel for hours, discussing how the toxic air would eventually meld with toxic clouds from other islands—copper and gold mining in Papua New Guinea, nickel mining in nearby New Caledonia, pollution and nuclear testing in Hawai'i, Micronesia, French Polynesia—eventually poisoning the air and the sea across the entire Pacific. The Women's Conference was attempting to draw up petitions against mining corporations operating in Arnhem Land, but a small faction of Aboriginal women lawyers had challenged the petitions.

A woman with a deep, pedogogical voice had stood up in the audience. "Mining's *income* for us, forty percent of Australia's exports. You rather we eat witchety grub and live on welfare?" She pointed her finger at Vanya. "What are you grousing about? You Hawaiians travel about crying for ecology and land rights, but you're the ones that bloody well sell out!"

She was referring to that morning's headlines in Australia's leading paper. Amid controversy on Hawai'i's Big Island over the proposed $900 million Riviera Resort, it had been discovered that two more Miloli'i elders had sold their beachfront land to foreign developers for $500,000 each.

Another woman had stood, challenging Vanya. "And what about those geothermal wells on your islands? By-products from them wells cause acid rain, killing rain forests." She turned round, addressing the audience. "Lord, I tired of outsiders coming, telling us how to do. The whole Pacific sliding down. Why can't we profit a bit like everyone else 'fore its too late."

A disembodied voice floated up from the audience, accent of a New Caledonian. "Why we listening to a Yank? We not American property!"

Vanya had jumped to her feet with no sense of it. "Yes, Hawaiians are American citizens. But you and I share the same ocean continent. We are all *Oceanians* first!" She raised her hands beseeching. "We're such small nations, our news gets pushed aside. We have to count on each other, keep each other from dying. You know how the rest of the world sees us? You know what the *London Times* calls the Pacific? 'An irradiated lake.' We're losing touch with the natural world, the mother-sea, our beginnings!"

The audience of almost five hundred women turned suddenly silent. Vanya inhaled, stepped to the edge of the stage, as if about to dive. "Sisters, I entreat you! Be iron-fisted! Commit yourself to our future, our children, and our children's children. Shout! Lobby! So they'll stop mining out your lands! Fight your husbands and sons seduced by white men's wages, wasted by his booze. I tell you, the future, our salvation, is in the . . . *Hands of Pacific women!*"

They rose to their feet, applause deafening. They clapped until it had a rhythmn, until Vanya bowed, heaved herself into the wings where they surrounded her. But later, in the milling of exited crowds, she heard the after-thoughts.

"Good. Very good to stay angry, keep our husbands from the mines—but, who then buy my children's milk? Pay for their schooling if husbands go on strike? Who going keep my kids from starving? Keep my husband from beating me when he wants meat we cannot afford?"

Vanya sat in her hotel room, defeated. *Easy for me to preach. Divorced. No mouths to feed. Mother God, what good am I doing?*

A follow-up conference took her from Brisbane to Alice Springs in the dead heart of Australia's Outback. There she listened to Aborigines challenge lawyers from mining corporations, contending the mines were on lands that had been stolen and they wanted them back. The mining lawyers shuffled their papers, got shouted down, seemed to vacillate between disdain and serious derangement. Exhausted, disillusioned, after four days, Vanya had left to meet Simon Weir. Flights out of Alice were booked for a week and, desperate, she'd caught the night bus to Darwin, the "beetle that crawled up the continent's backside," as locals described it, a grueling thousand-mile ride.

Now she half dozed, feeling him pulling her up the continent, unraveling her resolutions, weaving them into ambidextrous knots. Her spine creaked, imagining him touching her, leaving his mark. She moaned, saw herself a woman on a leash. *Leaping the length of my chain for him.*

He sat up in the dark, moved stealthily to the center of the room and listened. After a while he turned to a mirror, leaned close and, for the longest time, just stared. Finally, he eased back into bed. Vanya snored softly, some principle of light playing across her shoulder. Simon leaned over, watching her. The fact that she trusted him enough to sleep so deeply in his presence seemed to him a miracle.

Months back—already a year?—he had seen in her first glance that this woman would not be incorporated, not easily solved. Much about her was catastrophic, wayward and mean. Yet in odd moments everything fell away but a lyrical delicacy, the girlishness of a child. She was beautiful, but he was not after beauty. He had seen too much of it: delicate Thai whores with the clavicle and wristbones of birds, lush South Americans with porcelain skin, debutantes, prospectors, refugees.

But this one left him jittery, alert. That so impersonal and animalistic a dignity as hers should be allied with so poignantly human a sensibility was what drew him to his feet. Exactly why, he didn't know. Maybe he was tired of his life. Maybe he wanted the adventure to be over. He lay back, feeling her warmth along his side, remembering his youth. A boy in the Outback, eyelids creased with red dust, day-dreaming, waiting for the streamlined jet of his future to conjure itself in a blank and white-faced sky.

Well, he'd fulfilled that young boy's dreams. Seen it all, done it all. All the voyages he'd made, from which he had returned not quite intact. By the time he first encountered Vanya, he was down to the bare and rusty fixtures of living, begging the past for mercy, begging it to leave him alone. *The past, that twisted, tireless magician, pulling dead rabbits from a hat.*

In actuality, he had had no childhood to speak of, father a drinker, mother gone, dissolved into the Outback for the further unknown. Except for Aborigines who'd half raised him, he'd raised himself in the desert alone, running wild with the 'roos and *galahs*, growing into a man slightly sadistic and crude, ripe for the Army where he'd proven himself a warrior, a combat hero. Now, he slept, and the dreams began. Just before dawn in humid dark, Vanya woke, hearing his sobs full of a sorrow so distilled she needed to stop them.

"Simon." She shook him gently.

He jumped awake, astonished and angry. "Bloody malaria. Gets into my dreams." Seeing her there, smelling her, he was immediately erect.

And when it was over—the tangling of limbs, quick nips, long protracted moans, him steering her ankles like a wheelbarrow, her body responding wildly but her eyes closed, face side-turned as if sealed by a resolution to dismiss the whole scene—when it was over, they lay exhausted as penitents. Catching her breath, she arranged herself into a calm geometry, thinking how easily he possessed her, how relentlessly he reeled her in. Her breasts coated with sweat from his matted chest— ginger-colored sworls—his sperm leaking out of her, she felt such disgust she wanted to whip around and strike him. Strike him dead.

But something persisted in the soul of this white, rough beast beside her. Sometimes, watching the ugly way he dealt with inferiors, whites working under him, but the gentle way he dealt with Aborigines, and the solemn manner with which he talked about nature, the land, she suspected that deep in his being was an ineluctable hankering for maybe one moment he and another human could understand, a touching of minds, a down-deep nod in the cluttered chaos called living. She lay quiet while he dozed, something inside her tensing, already preparing herself for a journey that would leave him behind.

His hands a ruddy Outback burn, he deftly maneuvered the toylike chopper, so small it seemed homemade. Flying forty miles southeast of Darwin, Simon pushed forward on the joystick, as they ghosted over "the Kakadu." Spurred by the discovery of uranium within their lands, the almost seven-thousand-square-mile Kakadu National Park had been created as a sanctuary for its people, the Gagudju Aborigines. From the mining of uranium, they received and invested $2.2 million annually in royalties, each adult receiving $2,000 a year for life. Vanya looked down at rain forests, escarpments, towering waterfalls, parts of it still unexplored, so vivid, it seemed to reach up and tear at her eyes.

Forty thousand years ago, when Aborigines first set foot on Australia, crossing over from Asia, they had spread across this land of boulder canyons, eucalyptus woodlands and floodplains, and seeped down into the continent. It was sacred, mysterious land where crossovers still existed: platypus cavorting in large ponds, and in mudflats and mangroves, pop-eyed fish swam out of tidal creeks, climbed trees on leglike fins and peeped from branches like birds.

"Here, things are still coming ashore," Simon said. "Some things so strange and wild, they still haven't named them."

Yet on its fringes, Vanya could see inroads of mining companies—dump trucks, conveyor belts, huge ore-carrying transport ships.

"I know what you're thinking," he said. " 'Bloody mining devils!' Well, most of the leases are held by Yanks. And Japanese. Our own government's too timid, says this area's not fit to live in. Only local miners are pick-and-shovel boys eking out a bit of change."

He eased up on the throttle, shaking his fist. "This is *rich*, bloody *beautiful* country. Just need to develop it, is all. Create jobs for the blacks. Instead, they give it away on a plate. Outsiders are taking the minerals, true. But they're the only ones making improvements here."

"Improvements?" she said, incredulous.

"Proper schools for the kids, computers in classrooms. Hospitals, stores. Don't you see, without mines they'd still be beggars on welfare. A culture of poverty, drugs, blacks syringing themselves to death in public urinals. God in heaven, why they've even got community theaters. And art. Co-ops set up for locals to sell their 'Dreaming' paintings."

"Art." Vanya snorted. "A way to keep them distracted. Whites used the same system in Hawai'i. Give the 'natives' brushes and paints, keep them occupied. Art dealers buy up a canvas for a few hundred bucks, sell it on the mainland for thousands. Authentic *Primitif*, fruits of a dying race. Meanwhile, their stolen land's being weapons-tested and mined out from under them. Profits of billions. *Billions*."

Simon canted the chopper to the left like a lopsided dragonfly. The earth turned sideways, her stomach flipped, and the rain forest came at them at crazy angles. After a time of staring down at great gorges and plains where herds of wild buffs roamed, she sat back, determined. "Now, I want to see the mines."

Simon frowned. "I'll show you what I can. They catch me, I'm fired."

There were no real roads between the Kakadu Park and Darwin. For ten years, he'd flown for a helicopter service, bringing in foreigners wanting to view forty-thousand-year-old cave paintings deep in the forests. Now, he managed the company, and spent much of his time flying executives into the mines.

By some miracle of maneuvering, he put the helicopter down on a patch of grass. When the rotors were still, when it was quiet, he spoke. "Vanya. Who are you doing this for? Abos? You'll never get to know them. You're native, but not *their* native. You'll always be 'outside' to them."

She didn't respond.

"You're using them, aren't you?" he said. "Shoring up your glamour campaign to save the Pacific. For what? The whole planet's gone to hell in a basket. And what are you giving Abos in return? Their land? Their history?"

"Simon." The sound of it, the feel of his name on her tongue was hard. Metallic. She experienced again, that almost palpable loathing for him, for herself for being with him. Her words came out in bites. "You cannot . . . grasp it, can you? With your white . . . supremacist mentality, your colonialist history of . . ."

"Bloody crap. My great-grandfather came here in shackles. A simple Irish farmer who'd cursed Mother England after a couple of stouts. Died in his excrement, chained to a wall."

"A convict background doesn't make you less white."

He shook his head slowly. "God, it's absolutely daunting. Tough as nails, but you've got the perspective of a child."

"Look, I'm being paid to gather facts. I have reports to write, I have . . ."

"That the only reason you're here?" It seemed such a desperate question, he looked away.

"I can't face any other reason. How do you think I feel when I wake up beside you. You're working for *them*." She shook her head. "Jesus Christ, haven't you seen enough destruction. If mining corporations keep moving in, one day there'll be no more land, no schools, no need for computers. When the earth's mined out, these rivers and creeks poisoned with acid rain, when people are killing their neighbors for fresh water, Aborigines will be the first people to die of thirst, corraled in some parched hole." She sat back, sighing. "I know whites aren't all bad. Some of you feel guilt, give time and money, stand up in Parliament arguing for blacks . . ."

"You don't know a damned thing. I grew up with Abos, changed blood with 'em, went through their gory initiations into manhood. I love them in a way you'll never understand, maybe more than you feel for your own. The day they fence them in, I'll be on the inside."

"And how . . ." she spoke carefully, ". . . do your Abo brothers feel about you being in the Reserves, *Captain* Weir? What do they say about you flying into Papua New Guinea every other weekend, shooting native 'rebels' for rioting against your gold and copper mines, which are on their ancestral lands?"

"You bitch . . ." She could only have known that if she read his mail.

"The letter was open on your desk."

He thought of all he could say then, that the Australian Army went in to train the local police, that the Aussies had not taken part in the shootings. That he had in fact risked his life, a spear glancing off his shoulder, squatting in villages, trying to reason with elders who wanted huge payments for their lands. He could go further back, tell her about a day in a village north of Pnom Penh, when troops were pulling out.

(A half-bombed hamlet of medieval filth, open sewage forming estuaries in the mud . . . villagers in rags reeking of fish sauce, hugging corpses of children lately strafed. And him, Simon, trying to express some human emotion, giving a legless boy his watch . . . And the boy, hands ground down almost to bone dragging his torso around, overjoyed, a look of wonderment in his eyes . . . The boy's head darting back and forth, desperate to give Simon something in return. Finally, jubilantly, offering his eight-year-old sister.)

He could have told her that. And the aftermath, years of looking for that boy in his sleep, looking for the brother and sister, whole, unwhored, winnowing rice in their father's field. He could have told her of the years after 'Nam as a mercenary, a junkie hooked on coups. He sat there thinking of all the truths he could tell, but that was something he only told when he was alone.

"That's what first attracted you, sweetheart. Remember? You said I looked like an exterminator."

She winced, then silently climbed out of the chopper.

The $375 million complex had been built for mining uranium and bauxite. Not only was it mined and shipped, but a huge plant had been built to produce a million tons a year of alumina, the floury white powder from which aluminum was made. The head of operations gave them a quick tour, accepting Vanya as Simon's native girlfriend "in the bush for a thrill." Passing front-end loaders filling fifty-ton dump trucks, he took them into a mineshaft where shin-scraped miners picked away, dumping ore in trollied barrows.

Then he showed them how ore was crushed, fed onto a belt-conveyor system twenty miles long, carrying it to ships at the end of a deepwater dock. One of the longest conveyors in the world. They followed the route to the aluminum plant, complex chemical operations whose seepage flowed into nearby creeks. When she'd had enough, Simon took her to one of the Aborigine settlements, built by the mining company.

Elders and youngbloods gathered round, patted his shoulder, shook his hand. With their damp, loamy smell, soft droning voices, they peered at Vanya from under cantilevered brows. In the distance, children dangled lizards by the tail while bashful clan women sang softly, carrying bush tucker home—turtles, freshwater prawns, wild honey, snails.

She saw instantly how materialism had entered their lives. Mining royalties brought radios, electric saws, rifles, secondhand pickups. Men sat back, blowing smoke dreamily, while their neighbors bent over bark paintings which the co-ops would sell. They painted casually, a stroke or two, then lay back and snored. Living on royalties, they painted now for relaxation, for "fun." Vanya glanced round at broken radios, broken battery-run shavers, cast-out clothes. Royalties had cancelled certain needs, like washing and mending things. Laxness had become another form of welfare.

Simon led her to an elder sitting outside a *wurlie*, a shelter of bark and twigs, which Aborigines prefered to prefab houses the mining corporation had given them. She bowed reverently, studying the pitch-black skin, huge paunch, his hair and beard glowing white. Waving his walking stick at his dog and pet baby wallaby, unexpectedly the elder spoke.

"Yeah, money been good, give us time to think, fish, hunt for crocs, snakes, goannas. We skilled hunters, spear a buffalo skull at a hundred feet. Good for us to sit about, singing songs of the 'Dreaming,' teach young boys clan totems, prepare dem for secrets of initiations . . ."

He hesitated, firelight reflecting off his cataracts.

"Go on," Simon said, nodding toward Vanya. "She's all right, Digger, I give you my word."

Tossing his luminous mane, he continued. ". . . Sometimes I curse da mine. Want the white man *out*. Widdout royalties, we have to do more dan talk and sing. Have to fight and hunt and build and paint in bloody earnest. Dey turning us into layabouts, slowly drugging us . . . helping us die out."

He looked at Simon, his big body steaming with the fervor of his words. "Not many left, Simon, not even two percent of da country's population. City blacks becoming whitefella' losing dere culture, dying of drink. Kids go to university, learn to think white, marry Asians, Europeans. We losin' our grip. Families broken. Dat what gave us grip."

He kicked away a bark painting, waiting for pickup by the co-op. "Garbage. That not our real "Dreaming" paintings. You think we share real thing with whites!" Handing round plastic cups of tea, he studied Vanya. "Where you from, Missus? Torres Straits?"

She shook her head, smiling. "I'm dark enough, aren't I? I'm Hawaiian."

"Yank."

She sighed, "Yeah. Yank."

"Dat's okay, you with Simon. Trustworthy bloke."

Embarrassed, Simon let himself be dragged off by a child in search of witchetty grub. From behind a clump of stringybark trees, Vanya heard men playing instruments used in initiation rites, the sharp clack of clap-sticks, the deep snore of the trumpetlike didgeridoo. Digger looked up, half whistled, half whined. That quick, a hawk screamed down in a rapture of bronze, took something from his hand.

"All dis earth my mates," Digger boomed. "Eagles, plants, 'roo. I tell you da name of t'ree hundred things you never even seen."

He had a disturbing physical glow, great liquid eyes threatening to drip in the heat of the fire. Leaning over, he gave her a bit of *pitjuri*, slightly narcotic tobacco, and they chewed silently, time seeming to snag on the point of his stick embering in the flames. Dropping the baby wallaby in her lap, he cuddled his mangy dog, and they sat in a scene out of prehistory. Slowly, he began to yarn, telling her of sacred sites, secret "Dreaming" places, where his ancestors had sung up the land. Her tongue grew numb, Vanya looked down shocked as the wallaby nuzzled against her chest; she was not a woman small living things were drawn to. Digger asked what she did out in the world, and when she said she practiced law, he laughed, pouring a handful of dirt into the wind.

"Dat what laws become! You got to make somet'ing lasting. Pretty missus like you. Got to make somet'ing of flesh!"

She cuddled the wallaby, a dog-faced child with huge feet. "I had a son. He died."

Hearing the words, she was struck by the staying power of pain, its almost palpable presence. Yet, talking about the pain of losing Hernando seemed to make it easier, kept her from feeling it. She talked quietly, unceasingly, and when she finished, Digger's cheeks were wet. He dropped his chin to his chest, praying for the boy. When he finally sat up, his voice seemed to resonate beyond the measure of their conversation, engulfing her like some furious force of nature.

"Lay de pain down. Leave it here wif me. Pick up yer *rage*. Rage give you courage."

As she and Simon left Digger sang out after them, stabbing the air with his walking stick. "Who dreamed de land? Who sing about it? *We! We de land!*"

His house in Darwin was Spartan and bleak. Worn sheepskin rugs. Bare walls. Cheap vinyl chairs that clung to her skin, making a tearing sound when she stood. His "base," Simon called it, and she thought how men living alone never called it "home."

He opened cold beers, wiped the calligraphy of dead flies off a counter. "I thought you'd stay a bit longer this trip."

"I will next time," she lied. "Look, I want to apologize for reading your mail."

"Don't dwell on it. I'll say this much, though. You don't know me, Vanya."

"I know what you were."

"And that fits right into your pattern, does it? Sleeping with men you loathe, men you have nothing in common with, so as not to clutter up your life. There's a word for that . . ." He bit off the rest of it, rubbed his forehead wearily. "Sorry. It's been so long since I cared, I hardly know what I'm saying."

She stood. "I'll miss my plane."

"Sit down, please. I've something to say." He paused and everything he'd planned to say drained out of him. ". . . I've never been account-able." He stopped, started again. "I know you'll never compromise yourself, but there's a part of you needs looking after." He got up feeling a complete ass and paced the room.

"Simon. Don't."

"Why 'don't'? We've gotten too close, have we? Bit more than your usual one-night stand?"

She seemed to lunge, slapped him viciously across the face, then flinched, anticipating his reaction.

He cupped his jaw, working it back and forth. "Now I slap you. We work up our lust, then fall in bed and go at it. The old cliché?" His face blotched red, melting into the auburn mustache and auburn hair so he seemed to be wearing an awful ginger-colored mask.

She thought of her boy then, and how he had died. And she thought of the old man telling her to pick up her rage.

"I *hate* you! I hate everything you are, and ever were. I hate that I've slept with you. I hate myself. I hate . . ." She couldn't seem to stop.

He didn't touch her, didn't even move close. "Listen to me, I've not much to offer. Health-wise I'm probably pushing eighty. Malaria. Touch of Agent Orange from 'Nam. Leaves you sterile, crook in the gut. I look in the mirror and see the face of a man who will never father a child."

She shook her head, not wanting to hear it.

". . . But I could teach you things about the land. How to find freshwater mussels under reeds, show you crocodiles that are playful and harmless, and what weeds make teas that cure tropical ulcers. I'd teach you what grasses are poison, and where water is always found near casuarinas. I'd take you to places where billygoat plums are big as my fist, and where black-lip oysters will nourish you with iodine. I'd teach you what grapes cure the bite of deaf adders. And which crayfish-squeals draw sharks. I'd show you were to find edible worms inside the bark of mangrove trees, where to find bush bananas, and the right season for wild honey called Sugar Bag. I'd show you how to mend jerrycan cracks with resin of spinifex, and how to make shelters from banana leaves. The best time for eating abdomen of green ants, and how to eat the larva from their nests."

He went on, like a man under hypnosis.

"And oh . . . I'd teach you secret seasons, the ones between the Wet and Dry that only Abos know. Like, when certin lilies flower, you'll know barramundi will be swimming in schools eager for bait. And when bark peels from certain trees, you'd know crocodiles are spawning, and what beaches will be full of their buried eggs. I'd even teach you to smell a 'soak,' water lying far below the most parched and barren earth. I'd teach you how to smell coming rains, and coming dust storms. You'd learn to listen. You'd see how smart nature is. Vanya, you'd be amazed."

She was weeping, and he came to the end of it.

"I have given this considerable thought . . . I would even die for you, if you required such a marvel."

Even at Darwin Airport, he didn't touch her, didn't move too close.

Her skin turned dark, she looked old and severe, a woman consigning herself to the extreme verge of austerity.

"Simon . . . I won't be back."

He looked down, thoughtfully. "You want this over?"

"Yes."

He pulled her close, in slow motion. "Then, it's over, sweetheart. But I promise you . . . it's not finished."

He let her go, across the tarmac to the waiting plane, sun on her shoulders throwing her shadow ahead of her.

Gaman Suru, Ganbaru

To Endure and to Persevere

HIS CAR IN THE DRIVEWAY, chauffeur leaning on the hood. He was already somewhere in the house, moving toward her.

Rachel swept down the stairs, half running, no thoughts of composure. "Hiro, are you home? Is it you?"

And through the dark, cool, marble corridors, she heard his deep, resounding, "*Hai!*" Profoundly male, something between a whisper and a bark, such a drilling sound, she felt an absolute frisson. And he was there, sleek, composed, impeccably dressed. Handsome face the color of lemon drops sucked to transparency, unmarked hands like slender yellow icicles, except for the missing digit of one finger showing membership in the *Yakuza*.

She stood very still, defeating the need to touch him, to test the reality of him. In that moment, almost imperceptibly, he measured her, appraised her. Flawless, porcelain face, Oriental fineness of bone, rounded breasts and hips of a Hawaiian. Her hair was black thick as tar, her eyes an odd green like spoiled bronze. Just now her cheeks were flushed, and she was beautiful, still full of grace and fire. She would never be a closed-face, quiet-feet wife, she would always excite him. He would always come back to her.

"It's you," she said, as if expecting someone else.

He threw back his head and laughed, laughter that resounded through the house, as if it were more than his body could accommodate.

Only Rachel made him laugh, the laughter of relief, of being home. Yet, even in that moment, he seemed intrepid, never quite exposed. And leading him upstairs, undressing him, slowly soaping and rinsing, and massage-bathing him, his body tattooed from neck to ankles, she saw nothing had changed, not one inch of him. Time had blended the bright reds, yellows, greens of his tattoos into a steely lustrous, gleaming blue, alive, beautiful in steam. There were years she had hated that skin, cool, reptilian shield between Hiro and the world, manifestation of his inner life, emotions she would never know. Once in the early years, she asked why he had tattooed his entire body.

He had brooded for a while, then answered. "I wanted to be a warrior." The pain was so debilitating, only one of two hundred men ever completed full-body tattooing. "Or, perhaps I wanted to replicate what I was not sure the world contained—beauty, legend, virtue."

"Or," she said, "perhaps you wanted to die." He had explained how the life span of those fully tattooed was shorter than average, too little free skin left to "breathe."

Now Rachel knelt beside the tub, disrobing, only a towel round her, so that leaning toward him, shoulders hunched, rich black hair winging out on either side of her, she seemed a butterfly throbbing outside its cocoon. Drowsily, he studied her moist shoulders, thinking how, later, in the throes of sex, her body would gape and steam. He smiled, kissed her fingers one by one as she ran the handcloth over him. Only with her did he relax, become courtly and shy.

"How is your circulation?" she asked.

"Good," he grunted. "Except in cold and damp."

He bent his head like a child so she could scrub his neck, and in that moment he seemed vulnerable. Sixty years old, physique of an athlete in his forties, but life was gaining. She heard a slight wheezing when he bent. As she gently massaged, Rachel studied his back, the dragon, fiercest part of his body-art that only she had intimate knowledge of. Hiro knew it only from mirrors, photographs.

As a young bride, the thing had terrified her. Then she learned to embrace it, caress it in the act of love, a monster that drew strength from each bizarre creature that formed it. Hog-nosed viper with horns of a bull, the brilliant razor-sharp scales of a koi, four ripping talons of a hawk, whiskers of the clever catfish, shoulders and haunches of hellish fire. As he moved in the tub, the dragon leapt, majestic, mythical, grotesque.

"Where have you been?" she asked. "Macao? Singapore? Entertain me!"

"Ah, Rachel," he sighed. "Each year there is . . . more to see, less to learn. A sad thing, that you have never traveled further than your impulse. There are wonders I could show you . . ."

Yes, she thought. *Whores laughing at me behind drapes of your plush brothels. Addicts leering from your drug dens. Never! I'd rather wait here by the sea where everything is pure and private. Even our sex under pale silk sheets, like making love in the interior of an eyelid . . .*

". . . I would show you the Squid Men of Kowloon, criminals hiding in giant underground pipes, bodies blue-black from washing ink from squid for the fisheries, never seeing daylight. And, I would show you the Flour Ghosts, Chinese refugees living in the catacombs of temples, earning income by making noodles. Whole rooms white with flour, floors, ceilings, walls. Year after year they knead and shape their noodles. Hair, eyes, clothes, thick with flour, layering their skin, moldering in their lungs. Until they die of suffocation . . ."

She rubbed *kukui* oil into his shoulders.

". . . And I would show you beauty, the golden Wats of Bangkok. Rivers of saffron-robed monks strolling in twos through flame trees. And white moons riding Chinese junks on Victoria Harbor. How I have wanted to show you humanity! Teach you to ignore the general, to search for the particular."

Sometimes she thought, yes, she would walk out into the world beside him. If, first, she could tattoo his face. Brand him with a delta like the Greeks. Stamp his forehead like the Roman gladiators. MINE. Often, listening to him, his life, this man who led a dozen lives, Rachel felt unused, unlived, she felt like stabbing him. Now he bent a little, wheezed again. She sat back, imagining a time when Hiro would be old, soft-skinned, soft-mannered, almost frail, except for his tattooed penis, blue, swaggering masquerader. She reached for him between his legs.

Gently, so gently, she fondled him, feeling three distinct masses in the foreskin and penile skin. He sighed. Genuine pearls, perfectly round, sturdy, firm. Implanted for her coital pleasure. They caused him no discomfort, actually embellished the configuration of his already embellished penis, and in coitus they delayed his orgasm, giving her more pleasure, for longer periods. Now it rose between his legs and Hiro followed, rising from the tub, lifting her in his arms so they seemed borne on the steam of the bath to the bed, with no sense of having made the journey.

And sweet delays O small titillations . . . stroking her stomach ever so lightly with a delicate fan of hummingbird feathers, stroking until her rosy skin shivered, seemed to reach up to the fan. And then slow journeying—Hiro's fingers opening a lacquered box, inside a sleek and shining ant, silk thread tied round its midriff, lured into Rachel's ear by a daub of sweet rice honey.

And her eyes swinging back and forth in almost-terror as the ant began its journey how many humans Hiro asked perceived the erogeny of the inner ear and Rachel's jerks goose bumps starting at the back of the neck creeping over the face and scalp sweat darting along the shoulders trickling down the arms that visual shiver up the spine then chills enveloping her body as the ant writhed in some thickening canal tugged gently backwards now and then by Hiro's finger on the thread then creeping on foraging brushing tiny hairs that triggered tiny nerve cells that traveled to her brain O pleasurepain and Rachel yipping feeling drunk off-balance little feelers footsteps scratching scratching echoing as it fought suffocation in some oily seedy jungle gasping struggling in little death-throes and Rachel freezing pleasurepain and Hiro penetrating heaving on her in her Rachel feeling the groping sliding O surprise pearls being polished by the pushing pulling of his skin the rhythm honing polishing their luster bright reflections like a heat refracting light from sea-translucent layers gems glowing in her turning Hiro iridescent moans her moans her leapings silk thread lost in tangled hair something dying in her skull tiny corpse sneezing out of her tomorrow and she was and she was and she was coming coming coming leaping bucking up the air and Hiro thrilled so thrilled at how she lit up in her coming took flight withdrew from him into her eyes right at the height of pleasure withdrew foiled him coming like a solitary comer in the precinct of her own alone coming in a way that led him pushed him thrust him over some brink of terrible onrushing he was diving leaping crashing growing old yes old in his coming his fatigued ejaculation like pearls in foreskin he would they would grow soft grow old wear down by rubbing toxins body acids heat. *We are subject to decay.*

They woke at dusk, exhausted, his dry sperm tarried on her thighs. Far in the distance the glitter of Waikīkī, lights profiling giant ocean liners, winkings of small freighters waving fractionally against the tide. Across the *lānai* breezes blew them "Malaguena" from an orchestra in some hotel. Rachel sighed, lay her arm across his chest, while his long, yellow fingers gently brushed her nipples. And she thought how theater, costumes, little tricks gave their lovemaking the aspect of piety. Yet there was nothing pious in it, it was fantasy, escape, what people did to beat back fear, beat back waves of lonely respiration.

"Does it mean we've lost desire for each other? That we can't make love without these ... accessories?" In the early years, they hadn't needed props, only each other.

"No." His voice was gruff and tender. "It means only that we are children, after all. We need a little make-believe."

"At our age? When love should be enough?"

"Even now, Rachel. Especially now. Love. Lust. Different but ... somehow not inseparable, not indistinguishable. They imitate each other. Imagine loving me, without desiring me."

"I have," she said. "When we're old and there's only remembering."

He half sat up and smiled. "You're very self-conscious these days."

This was something new, for she had always shown a lack of curiosity about people and things, perhaps out of fear of arousing people's curiosity about her. But lately, Rachel seemed restless, full of questions, sloughing off her usual elusiveness. He noticed a disturbance in her eyes, a luster, as if in her mind slumbering things had wakened and sat up. She seemed to want to turn life this way and that, examine it, make pronouncements. It detracted from her air of innocence, that girlishness he found so charming, so in need of possessing.

Yet, who possesses whom? he wondered.

Away from her, he could still feel her hold on him. Sometimes he went to other women without wanting to, without needing to, but needing to push her back so he could breathe. Rachel's beauty was extreme, her love morbidly stern, all-encompassing, her passion the lust of every child-whore he had ever craved. She was what charged him, relaxed him, drew a blind over the ugly world he knew. She was all that would be left when he lost track of life's meaning. She was behind him, beside him, pulling his strings like a puppet.

He glanced at her and she was quiet, still troubled, still pondering, and it disturbed him. He knew her perversities, her waywardness, knew that in subtle ways, by sheer will, remarkable agility, she could destroy him, destroy his desire for her. Which would destroy everything.

"Be careful," he said softly. "You're becoming unadorned, very ... down to earth."

She stood up slowly from the bed, wrapped a kimono round her shoulders. "Perhaps it's age. One begins to look at things. Is it unattractive?"

"It can be dangerous. I know there are regrets. No children, no grandchildren, laughing in this house. A house without echoes. My fault, I suppose. You were enough pleasure, enough child for me."

She remembered the years of staring at her cousins—manifestly pregnant—with disgust, the notion of a parasite living in her womb a horror.

"I'm no victim, Hiro. I chose my fate. We lived as we were meant to. My only regret has been losing you, continually losing you. I have never been enough. And, why? I wonder why?"

Gracefully, he slid into a robe. "Rachel, Rachel. Why question everything? There's not always a reason. Life is not that logical. Perhaps I am evil. Perhaps you're a sorcerer. Perhaps we're just children lost at sea."

She sat in her bath, studying runic marks on her breasts, stomach, thighs, Hiro's teeth seeking refuge in her skin.

. . . *His mother died when he was six. He couldn't stop crying, this boy, this child, crying for days. His father rowed him out beyond the reef and threw him in and rowed away. He was a man when he reached shore* . . .

That was his life, all the youth he had before he was sent away to Japan, defying his father, becoming a *Yakuza*, member of the criminal underworld. She thought of the nights she toyed with cutting her wrists. Of hanging herself in the bamboo grove. Her Mercedes over a cliff. Nights, and months, and years of his comings and goings. *And yet he says I never leave him, am always with him, keeping after him. Perhaps my steady gaze rides the eyeball of every whore he penetrates in his pleasure-palaces on the Ginza, the backstreet gutters of his water trade!*

In the past two years, she had rounded forty, and the centrifugal force of that rounding, impelling her out away from the center of things, of her ego for instance, gave her an odd, a new perspective. She began to see how Hiro had dominated her all these years toward an end almost impossible to grasp, the desire to desire beyond satisfaction. He had driven her to excite herself for someone else, someone unseen who watched them. Someday Hiro would die and she would be left naked and craving, recorded in the blinking eye of something cold, unknown. Something, perhaps, outside the species.

Then, one night it came to her that all these years the thing unknown, the faceless voyeur, was her husband. He had watched her, kept her at bay, so she would never have enough of him, never know him entirely. In that way she would never outgrow him, never grow bored with him. He would be her sickness, obsession, her judge and executioner. She would want him unto death. She thought of him now in the gentlest way, felt ignoble before him. He was suffering. He had always suffered.

At dinner, he scowled at the dishes—beef fillets in cream and brandy, buttery squash, Pouilly Fumé in crystal.

He called softly to the cook, "Take it away. Bring plates of bean curd, cuttlefish. Crack seed. And sake."

Rachel laughed. "You want Run Run kine food!"

Hiro shook his head. "This Western, early death food. I see it on faces everywhere, capillaries, apoplectic cheeks."

While they ate, he looked round the room at urns, porcelains, ancient bronzes, and seemed to discard them with his gaze. *How strange objects look when we no longer want them. When we are freed from the thingness of things.*

He dabbed at his dish with no appetite. "Tomorrow, our dinner of *Fugu Akirame*! And now . . . is it playing time?"

In the candle-lit playing room, subtle incense of clove and sandalwood, he watched as Rachel's shapely arms grew from her silk kimono of indigo splash pattern. Hair done up in the peach-cleft style, head slightly inclined, her fingers stroked the *shamizen* so delicately the sounds evoked the haunting notes of a young soprano drifting in a barren world, searching for her lover.

Three strings of catgut, the surface and underside of cat skin, body shaped and with the sound reminiscent of a banjo, the ancient *shamizen* could—in the hands of an amateur—be played in a way that injured: twanging, dissonant sad squalls. Or the sounds could be transporting, ethereal. The song Rachel played subsided into six low notes, repeated over and over, lighter and lighter, like wasps circling, higher and higher, the young soprano finding her lover wounded and dying from stag wounds, their souls transported above the temporal world.

Rachel bowed, began a new song. Leaning down, she concentrated then began plucking sounds out of nature, sounds of a place of extremes. And as she played, Hiro understood she was playing the sounds of the Big Island. First flowing sounds, like contours of volcanoes that had shaped most of the island—Mauna Kea, Mauna Loa, Hualālai. Then sounds of molten lava erupting from open fissures. Destruction. Black, arid deserts, heat, sound of distant steam plumes rising from new volcanic vents, bubbling below the surface, looking for its next outlet, its next eruption.

Then plucking softly, dreamily, she drifted into valleys of the Big Island, bamboo forests, royal palms, hurricanes of butterflies in fields of vanda orchids. One by one, sounds of island animals issued from the rasping strings, neighing horses, calling steers, the squeak of mongoose, grunting and charging of wild boar. Mynahs mating, geckos chittering in guava trees. She plucked out this world, her world, with closed eyes, her perfect face glowing, hands dissociated from her body, carrying out a will of their own as she drew sounds of the island's eerie *mana*, drawn from the presence of sacred sites, temples and burial grounds.

Then Rachel drew out sacred sounds of the hula, the ancient narrative dance designed to enhance the meaning of *mele*, singing-chants containing legends, genealogies, the history of Hawaiians. It was the sound of dancers accompanied on gourd drums, of *kāne* and *wāhine* in *malo* and *kīkepa*, wearing dog-tooth anklets, sacred fern and feather crowns. This was not the cheap, flirtatious hula danced for tourists. These were sounds of warriors, movements quick and bold, movements of the hands, not hips, dancers who didn't smile, who danced to honor ancients, or call down death on enemies.

Then from the strings of the *shamizen* came the rhythm of a single drum, insistent chanting of a voice, deep, haunting, untranslatable, the sting and hurt of history. So often, it seemed, Hiro had forgotten Rachel's native blood. There was so much of him in her—culture, gestures, taste—he chose to think of her as his creation, pure-blood Japanese. Now, he saw her Hawaiian side draw closer to the surface.

Beads of sweat shone on her brow, even her neck perspired with the effort of her playing, the physical love she felt for that island manifested in her skin, her expression, her hands upon the strings. All of those heartrending sounds on three strings! It seemed a miracle. It made him weep a little. And, maybe Hiro wept because he saw how much she loved that place, how she belonged there. The Big Island was her history, blood she loved was there. And he had left her alone too many years.

Late that night she talked, as if she needed to hear it to understand it. "Something is happening. Pono thinks she's dying. These *kahuna* dreams. She takes her mysterious trips more often. I've thought of following her, but she would kill me, strike me dead . . ."

"She is old," Hiro said. "Allow her her precious secrets."

"I'm scared, Hiro, *maka'u* for all of us! Vanya's throwing herself away on strangers. Toru talking about killing *haole* developers. And Jess . . . I think she wants to come home. She's such a *kanaka*, real island girl. But 'come home to what?' she asks. Everything is falling down."

"And how is Ming?" His voice was especially gentle, knowing she was ill.

Rachel wept and clung to him. "Ming! She's becoming transparent. I swear, I can see right through her. What will happen? What will I do?"

He held her, hugged her like a child. "You were the orphan. You had to invent yourself, create a life from nothing."

"Like you," she whispered.

"Yes. Perhaps, like me. It gives one endurance, perseverance. You, my Rachel, will survive. You will be amazed."

Flowers tossed and brooded in the trades, splashed palettes on the lawn. Wasps hummed like airborne samurai; now and then a hornet snorting down. They stood beside the pond, feeding Hiro's prize koi, Hiro monkish and benign in kimono and slippers. He moved with care along the stepping-stones traversing the pond, and when he bent, she saw he was going bald. His hair had been black and thick, and now the skull shone through. Three koi surfaced, scales brilliant in the sun.

"The bravest of fish," Hiro said. "When caught, they await the knife calmly, without flinching."

He knelt slowly, clearing the surface of the pond with chopsticks, delicately extracting a leaf, the feather of a bird, gestures serene as a lama. Through the years she had learned that he spoke mostly by implication. She had to look for the echo, not the sound, the shadow not the light, but in this instance he spoke unequivocally.

"I have taught you many things. Now you must learn patience."

"Why?"

"It outlasts greed. Life will come at you when I am gone. You will need patience to outwit it."

"Don't talk like that. Life will be over when you are gone." She took up a pair of chopsticks, endeavoring to help him clear the pond, stabbing at the water ruthlessly. Her jeweled hairpin fell into the water, immediately swallowed by a large, robust koi.

"You!" she shouted, chasing the koi round the pond, kimono skirt held up between her legs like a diaper.

Hiro sat down laughing, rocking back and forth. A half-tame peacock skittered by, pursuing Rachel as she pursued the koi, the bird fan-tailed, screeching like a witch. Alarmed, Rachel kicked off her *getas*, running barefoot from the thing. Kori-Kori, the gardener, bounded over from a jasmine bush, attacking the peacock with a rake while it lunged after Rachel, Rachel screaming, running round and round the pond. The koi who had swallowed her hairpin, swam in circles, head just above the water as if observing everything. Hiro lay back helpless, tears streaming down his face.

Later, composed, they sat in their little teahouse facing the ocean, sipping green tea. And this man, who had always used language as a means of exclusion rather than expression, began to talk.

"What the world knows of me is mythical. But you, ah, you, dear Rachel. You make me laugh and weep. Say and do."

She smiled, somewhat shy. "Why now, Hiro? Why do you tell me so much now?"

"Because. It is time."

In that fugitive instant, her ribs creaked, she felt her heart shudder. She wondered if he were dying, his life shortened by the tattoos, too little free skin left to breathe. She closed her eyes, seeing him a boy of sixteen, when he had begun the tattoos, finally reaching completion at twenty-six. She saw him hour by hour, inch by inch, braving the insertion of black nara ink that turned blue when perforating live flesh, and the deadly Indian Red ink that glowed brown beneath the surface of the skin making a tattoo shine, and slowly poisoning the body.

She thought of this man with no childhood to speak of, and how the tattooist's needle was perhaps the first thing to pierce his unfeeling and unfelt existence. She knew the whores from Bangkok and Hong Kong and Macao meant nothing to him. Perhaps she meant nothing to him. Perhaps his deepest love had been for his *sensei*, the tattooist, penetrating him for ten years.

He's dying. He knows it in his skin. "Hiro! Are you in pain?"

He smiled, reached for her hand. "No. It's not as interesting as pain. More a . . . premonition." He lied because it was important, lies allowed him to defy reality, the truth. "Forgive me, dear. Words are such a nuisance."

"No!" she cried. "I've waited almost thirty years for you to talk. How else can we know each other."

He sighed, poured more tea. "Does one ever really know the other? Do we know ourselves? We live in doubt. And vanity. And in the end we go to silence."

He looked so beautiful and stoic then, in the shape of his head, the grace of his bones, long mandarin fingers holding a tiny porcelain cup. But the exalted elegance of him was marred by the brutal blues of his chest mounting the open V of his kimono, blue wrists leaking from his sleeves, the missing digit of a finger.

"All we can do is add a little grace and beauty to our moments."
He looked at his watch. "And now, is it time for calligraphy?"

He watched again the grace of her, the shape of her extended arm
as she began the ritual of calligraphy, one of silence, patience, precision.
Dressed in a black robe, black hair twisted up from her neck, Rachel
knelt before a black-lacquered table, the only large object in an eight-
tatami room. Her hands were folded in her lap, eyes fixed on the floor
in a prescriptural, almost meditative, trance.

From a small box, she produced the *sumi* stick, coal black, looking
like a hunk of resin several inches long. Beside it, a smooth slatelike
inkstone troughed at one end into which she poured a dash of water.
Moistening the end of the resin stick she began to rub it against the
inkstone with steady rhythms, lubricating the stone with water. Slowly,
the surface of the inkstone began dissolving under the pressure of the
stick. Mixing with the inkstone, the water gradually thickened, a miniature bubbling, becoming the thick black ink called *sumi*. This was the
ritual of *Sumi o suru*. A practiced writer knew the consistency of *sumi*
was right when one's heart quieted, when one's pulse slowed down.

Laying the *sumi* stick aside, Rachel placed a length of felt on the
table, arranged a sheet of ricepaper on top, weighting it with an ancient
bronze. Everything in the room was black, her robe, her hair, the
lacquered table, the case, the felt, the stick, the stone. Only the ricepaper
was white. Hiro breathed in deeply, something touched his spine.

She opened a case, producing a large *ofude*, a brush, and slowly
dipped it into the *sumi*, kneading the tip until it was moist, becoming
soft. Arm outstretched, for an instant, she held the brush poised over
the ricepaper, then swooped it down like a sword. Rich, lugubrious,
medallioned black loomed suddenly, even as her hand passed on. Arm
stroking, flourishing, she wrote on and on like someone in a trance, as
if tracing shapes already sleeping in the paper, waiting to be born.

Lines restrained, slender as arrows, then loud, bold, reverberating
like a shot. Then runic slaps as the brush turned in its own wet spoors,
sighing down into the vertical. Stuttering loops, obtuse twists, then the
brush barely breathing on the paper, skimming it, then . . . emptiness.
White suddenly blooming in empty space between black characters,
producing form, negative form, so valued by masters of the *shodo*, the
Superior Way of Writing.

Rachel sat back, exhausted. He heard her heart pounding. She laid
down the brush, studied the characters in silence. He sat beside her,
studying her composition, a love letter written in *kanji*, common Chinese

characters. Immediately he saw the change. She had practiced daily for eight years, and there was a period when her writing possessed great delicacy and flourish in the pressure of her brush, rhythm of her hand, the quiet of her heart. It gave promise that one day she might approach Celestial Consistency, which was what *shodo* demanded.

Now he saw that her writing was bolder but less beautiful, the speed and pressure of handling the brush was more obvious, less abstract. There were decorative junctures, almost academic twists in the structure of her characters, but these were not aesthetic to the learned eye. And in the white of spaces, there was no sound, nothing bloomed. He saw she would never embark on *shodo*, the Superior Way of Writing, she would always be engaged in *shuji*, the mere Practice of Letters. She had turned down another road, she was moving in her own direction. He saw she had no conscious knowledge of it, no real control of it. In her mind, she would always be waiting for him in their house overlooking the sea.

Now, it was early evening. The hour of fantasy and legend, and still the hours far ahead, dinner of Fugu Akirame, their death/lust exercise. But first. The young perfumed prince dancing for Hiro in glittering, caparisoned crimson robe. Coy, at first flirting from behind a fan, then suddenly the face, smiling, dead, a look of cruel eroticism. The boy-prince swooning for him, falling naked in the open robe, lifelike *harigata* erect between his legs, his boy-groin slowly grinding, pumping, waiting.

Hiro knelt, touched the boy between the legs, fingers sticky with *liliko'i*, so they were like suction disks on the hands of river frogs. The *harigata* waved, enticing him. Then Hiro fell upon the boy, wrestling with him, cursing him, his silent ugly, laughing face. He pinched the cheeks maliciously, the mask slipped sideways from the back of her head, Rachel on her hands and knees, flesh-like penis strapped to the base of her spine. Righting the mask, Hiro plunged into the freakish boy, gripping the *harigata* like a pommel. Wrapping his arms round its back, he held Rachel's breasts, his inexhaustible boy-girl, needing only to be turned like something on a spit.

And later, in near darkness, Rachel dressed as a *bonze*, a monk sworn to chastity, in cape and stocking cap, Hiro in wig and robes, a harlot of Yoshiwara, Capital of Sin, playing with the *bonze*, seducing him, forcing him to stare at forbidden *Shunga*, erotic prints of Hokusai, Utamaro, from the Edo period. (Samurais ravaging young boys. Courtesans riding giant phalluses. A wrinkled death-face entering a virgin in her sleep. A woman penetrated by a dog, her brother, a priest. A giant tongue, a cleft.) They studied the prints silently, molesting each other, working themselves to fever pitch. And at that pitch, Rachel ready, almost begging to receive him, they abruptly stopped. He let his swollen member settle in his lap, and they were left with inner frenzy.

They took that frenzy to a room of candlelight and linens where they would play the quietest, most exquisite game, a game that took them to the very brink. A chef appeared, uniformed and businesslike. He smiled, bowed, displayed on a platter, a *fugu*, a puffer fish, intact, benign-looking. Hiro studied it, touched, sniffed, then nodded. The chef repaired to the kitchen, humming quietly, knife licking this way and that, deftly removing the deadly poisonous skin and organs of the *fugu*. With the sweet, light taste of raw *mahimahi*, the *fugu*, if inefficiently prepared, brought death, prolonged and agonizing.

Skin and organs of the fish were filled with tetrodotoxin more lethal than cyanide. A sliver of it, no more than the size of a firefly wing, could kill twenty people. This night, the chef prepared the fish raw, arranged elaborately as small white petals on a platter, duplicating delicate petals of the centerpeice, a rare albino orchid. Twice a year he came, and twice a year they played the deadly game of *Fugu Akirame*, Resignation without Despair. For one must be resigned once the petal was devoured.

They dined. The terror on their lips, the tingling. This was a special chef Hiro flew in from Kowloon, one schooled in the sly art of dressing *fugu*, leaving just enough poison in the fish for diners' lips to thrill, to tingle. In certain streets of certain cities—Tokyo, Kyoto, Hong Kong, right here in Honolulu—there were certain tiny restaurants where people played with chance, lay their lives in soft knowing hands of chefs who, for large sums of money, left more and more toxin in the *fugu* they prepared. Until lips surpassed the tingling stage, began to shiver, until teeth chattered, the body going into shock.

Sometimes one bite was lethal, death almost instantaneous. More often, death came slowly, numbness in one limb, one digit at a time. In this way, in those tiny restaurants, in dark pockets of certain cities, *fugu* devotees had time to argue, even as they died. That death existed. It did not exist. That life prevailed, or it did not. That everything was based on chance, the toxin in one bite. Westerners were not invited to partake of *fugu*. They were too self-conscious about death.

And they dined, Hiro and Rachel, eating one small sliver at a time, barely enough to hold between their chopsticks. Lifting tiny petals to their lips, they felt lips stiffen, tingle, felt the tongue draw back. They chewed delicately, waiting until nerve ends calmed, until their bodies would accept. And in that silence, the room was filled with the galloping of their hearts, a gut rumbling, cringing. They swallowed ever so slowly, occasionally laying down their chopsticks, staring at each other until their pulses slowed, hair on their arms lay down.

And while they paused in their exquisite game, Hiro related his first *"fugu*-death," his initiation at nineteen into the *Yakuza*. He spoke softly, pausing now and then, like a fortune-teller in an Oriental dream.

"First a swooning, dizziness, numbness of mouth and lips. I remember I had trouble breathing. Men around the table went on eating, one or two cast a glance my way, thinking I was joking, pretending. My lips turned blue, they said. I had cramps like a woman. And then this crawling itchiness, like maggots hatching in my skin. I turned my head and vomited behind the table. The others went on eating. I was dying, and they were finishing a meal. You see, I had taken too big a bite, too much poison all at once, to prove I was a man! . . .

". . . I fell back in my chair, slid down a little, and it was like watching a movie on a screen. I was paralyzed, head to toe, yet saw, heard, felt everything going on around me. I couldn't move an eyelash. I had no pulse. Then these gangsters realized I had died! . . . They hoisted me into a car, drove far out into the country, this hovel of a town outside Kyoto. The man holding on to me had a scar on his temple, small and blue. It was all I saw in front of me, and I thought if I could just hold on to it with my eyes, I wouldn't die. It was just a scar, but it became so blue, so pure, and beautiful, it took my breath away. I didn't mind dying then . . .

". . . After many hours, the car stopped. They wrapped me in a blanket, carried my body to a half-dug grave. I understood they were going to bury me, and yet I had not died. I tried to scream, to move, I was paralyzed. They put me in a box, closed the box, continued digging. I could hear them, smell the earth, three of them, still digging, cursing me for having died . . . And then, my limbs came back to life, a burning, thawing-out sensation. I opened the box, sat up, and asked for a cigarette. I saw what I have never seen again . . ."

Now Hiro laughed softly. "*Yakuza* on their knees, screaming for mercy. They thought I had come back from the dead. I suppose I had, neh?"

In slow motion, in flickering candlelight, he and Rachel took up their chopsticks again, selected a petal, hearts pounding, hands trembling slightly, so tiny *fugu* petals seemed to flutter to their lips.

We grow older. She thought. *Life is more precious. And still we play these games.*

He saw her look. "Think of it. Life reduces us to patterns. Right now we are outside the pattern."

Suddenly, her whole body shook and ran with sweat. She was momentarily blinded, her system shot with adrenaline, fighting the minute particles of toxin inside her. Her teeth chattered, she could no longer concentrate. She gripped the table edge with both hands.

Hiro leaned forward, perspiring profusely. "Use this moment. Use it. Remember how you never felt so alive ... bowels trembling, nerve ends shrieking ... as when you put the *fugu* to your lips. Freeze the terror. Step back. Observe. And know."

After terrible moments, her vision cleared, her teeth stopped clacking, she was drenched and totally exhausted.

"Why do I need this knowledge?" she whispered. "What is it for?"

"When you know what you can stand, you'll never compromise yourself."

"Hiro, I'm your wife. Not a *Yakuza*."

"This was not learned as *Yakuza*," he said softly, "this was learned in ten years of needles piercing every day."

That night, his green-crested pleasure sheath within her, Rachel bucked and moaned, loving him as if she were dying. Yet he felt part of her stand aside, coolly observing. He moved slower then, more rhythmically, making the cool, observing side of her lose its balance, pulling her so close, so tight, his hands on her back felt each vertebrae in her spine.

And he whispered in her hair. "How much I've loved you. No one else. And I will always love you."

"And ... you will always hurt me, always go away."

Just then he came in her, and came in truth.

"Yes!"

Later, feeling her soft, sad snores against his chest, he wondered if in time she would grow fastidious, detesting men. For, what in this world would be new to her? He had taught her everything. She had an air now, a posture that revealed an inner poise. She would never compromise.

You are my river of clear skin, flowing on your own. I want to wake you, ask your forgiveness. For everything. He sighed, looked out the window at the sky. *In the end, all we can do is forgive ourselves.*

'Imi 'Ike

To Seek, to Search, to Understand

"I CONFESS," Duke said, "to remembering."

"No! We promised. To not look back, not mourn what could have been." Pono rubbed the fingerless club that had once been his hand, *koali* oil giving it the smoothness and glow of an old artifact.

"Ah, Beloved, what is the difference? Memory. Dreams. At this age it's much the same." He had long ago given up the destructive, repercussive ritual of longing that in younger years had almost driven him insane.

Now he lay his head against her breast, his thick hair hammered by sun into shimmering white waves. "I was remembering peacocks skittering on polished floors. You wore a Paris gown. We waltzed . . ."

Pono softly chided him, like a young girl with indomitable unregret. "Stop being an old man who sits at a window! There is much to discuss." She waved newspapers in front of him. "Shark attacks. Filthy geothermal plants. The Miloli'i mess . . ."

He sighed as she wrapped his hands in soft cotton gloves, placed an old sunhat on his head, and moved behind his wheelchair.

". . . but first, fresh air, the sea. Nature always makes you lusty!"

Canting back his massive head, he laughed, slid on sunglasses, tilted his hat like a gigolo. Tourists transferring from a tiny plane to a sight-seeing bus, saw them in the distance. A giant woman, hair a thick gray shawl, moving with mythic heft and grace along a grassy knoll facing the sea. In the wheelchair before her, a wide-shouldered, big-chested man, profile reminiscent of old prints of Polynesian royalty.

"Are *they* lepers?" Tourists asked.

The driver of the Damien Tours bus hit the brakes and turned, addressing passengers. "We *all* victims of Hansen's disease, what you folks call . . . 'lepers.' "

The strangers looked vastly disappointed. "But, you look so healthy. We thought . . ."

"Dat you'd see apes, minus dere ears and noses. You want take pictures of t'ings in cages, neh?" He shook his head. "Sorry. We got not'ing to show you but buildings, churches, graves. And some spit holes in da floor. You want go back to da plane?"

In the silence, he eased onto the main road, heading toward Philomena Church, the oldest constructed church at Kalaupapa, intact with its expectoration holes in wooden floors. Until the tourist plane lifted off again, most patients stayed home behind drawn shades.

As the bus passed, Pono pointed at it with her cane. "Sugar's in a bad mood today. Those *haole* won't see much."

"Last month he got letters from two grandchildren." Duke said. "So joyful, he gave a group of Swedes the Super Tour!"

They laughed. The Super Tour: old abandoned cottages, artificial arms and legs still hanging in closets. And the artifact shop: eating spoons whose handles curled around a fist, for those whose fingers had worn down to knuckles. And the abandoned hospital: operating tables with arm and leg restraints for patients on whom experiments had been performed without anesthesia. And pointed wooden sticks in jars, with which opium-soaked swabs had numbed nasal passages so tissue could be extracted for testing, a method that left patients addicts, and slowly broke down the bridge of the nose. The grislier, the better, tourists loved it.

Now that leprosy was no longer communicable thanks to sulfone pills, there were only two dozen patients left at Kalaupapa, too old or scarred to live out in the world. Proceeds from the tours benefited them, and some nights, they gathered at Rea's Bar, drank beers and invented new "horrors" for the tourists. The Mongoose Radical Cure, a jar of mongoose eyes, which in the old days patients had been "forced to swallow." Old rusty fire extinguishers, which had been "chained round the necks" of those with artificial limbs, cheap flammable wooden limbs that "sometimes ignited, turning patients into fireballs."

Then there was Duke's favorite ruse—three pet dogs that went berserk when their owner whistled through his teeth. On Super-Super Tour days, the owner corraled them in his basement, whistled up "Amazing Grace" while the tour bus circled round the block, the driver explaining that the bestial howlings issuing from the house were patients who for years had been injected with wild boar blood, a medical experiment gone awry. Asked to see the howling mutations, the driver shuddered, drove away.

Pono braked Duke's Amigo wheelchair on a grassy knoll, flung out a blanket, and helped him to the ground, spreading lunch and papers beside him.

Duke groaned, staring at headlines of the *Honolulu Advertiser*. "MILOLI'I ELDERS ON THE BIG ISLAND SELL OUT TO DEVELOPERS."

"One of them will die separated from his manhood." Pono had already seen his legs mangled in the engine of a brand-new powerboat. "There will be other deaths, before they build this cursed resort . . ."

"Have you dreamed again?" he asked.

"Yes. Confusing dreams." Drinking cups of *noni* tea at night, she was still trying to see her face as she lay dying. But dreams gave her only this blurred, anonymous corpse. Then, lately she had envisioned people running, bodies cartwheeling across moonlit glass. "I wake with the smell of something bitter in my nose."

He looked at her, knowing what she saw would in some form or other, come to pass. "And have you seen me in your dreams, Beloved?"

She stretched across the blanket, lay her hand upon his cheek. "Why dream you, when I have you here? And we have had the best, the most luxurious of lives. We have traveled round the world, heard many languages. Lived in many climates. Perhaps lived with our senses more than most humans dare."

He had steeped her thoroughly in life, in history, through decades of reading to her. They had traveled with Marco Polo, fought with Napoleon, ridden with Alexander the Great. They had witnessed beheadings, investitures, assassinations. They had drowned in northern seas off Finland, and starved, exploring the Antarctic. She understood what freezing was, the sense of sinking barefoot in deep snow, blue and solitary particles that fell in whispers, she could count the crystals in a flake.

". . . And tonight," Duke said. "We will fly into the future. I will read you H. G. Wells." He pulled her close, so close they lay like youngsters in a gale. "Ah, Pono, except for this solitary peninsula, and this hellish tomb of a body I inhabit, we have lived like swashbucklers!

Seen more than most people can imagine. We have had the time. I wonder . . . if a life lived only in the mind is any less intense? If all the senses are engaged what is lost, but fact?"

They wandered in and out of daydreams, as if oblivious to the beauty around them. He had been in that place so long they ceased to see it, it was in them now. Just-thrown fishing nets hovering like jeweled skin across the sea. Lush green peninsula washed a blinding gold, sun turning it into an emperor's slipper. And massive cliffs, like robes of purple chinoiserie, the emperor's shoulders hunched round them. And nearby, the old dance pavilion washed with waves, a broken diamond.

(Yes, they had danced after years of blackouts. Victory Dances of the postwar forties. Victory over leprosy, the sulfone cure that, for many, came too late. Sometimes, sitting near the cracked and crumbling pavilion, wind blew them the memory of saxophones, mandolins, concertinas, plaintive steel guitars, voices singing softly in falsetto. And sometimes Duke thought he saw ghosts still whirling, couples spinning round the floor, withered legs, broken arches, useless hands giving them unique, undaunted rhythms, articulations of perhaps a newer, better race.)

"Now, back to business." Pono sat up, pointing to a headline Run Run had circled. "What about this fellow?"

A fifteen-foot shark had killed a local woman swimming in known breeding waters, a resting place for 'aumākua manō. The Department of Land and Natural Resources had hired professional shark hunters who slung bloody bait across the bay, then sat in boats with loaded rifles. Hawaiian activists had massed together, threatening to kill the shark hunters. Even the media was taking sides. Locals had come to Pono, asking for advice.

"What can they do?" Duke's voice was angry. "Kill every shark they see? Murder all our ancestors? Manō respect us, they do not come ashore. They swim and breed in their own waters, leaving our waters alone. Why can't we respect them?" He read the article quickly. "That wahine was pupule. She swam in Shark Bay on a dare, knowing it's kapu." He paused. "Tell them for every shark they kill, we will take a hunter."

Pono smiled, for this was how she had instructed the angry activists. Eye for an eye, the way of their ancestors.

"Now." She pointed to another article. "More geothermal refugees."

The explosion of a geothermal well ninety miles from Captain Cook had caused a steam eruption of noxious hydrogen sulfide that spewed all over the small community of Puna. Locals had fought the building of the $100 million Israeli-owned project, because of dangerous air pollutants. Now the air smelled like rotten eggs, children couldn't keep food down, elders suffered from respiratory ailments. People in neighboring communities were sick from fish caught in the waters near the plant. Milk and beef cows were lying feet-up in comas. Even as they demanded shutdown of the Puna Geothermal Project, locals were being forcefully evacuated by the Hawaiian Civil Defense.

Duke slammed his fist to the ground. "Do our people have to die before they shut these plants down? Or are they being used as guinea pigs? Now that they're sick, they tell them they have to permanently relocate, rip up roots, their lives!"

"They refuse," Pono said. "They will not become nomads like the 'lava refugees' who lost their homes to Pele. Homes no one would insure."

"Tell them," he said, "to stand and *fight*. Fight until those plants are all dismantled. Get the media behind them. Vanya has connections."

He struck the ground again. "Israelis. My God! As if they didn't know about extermination."

She felt his fury, his frustration, knowing he was thinking of all the lepers through the years, imprisoned, experimented on, abandoned. Wiped from their family genealogies. She thought how there were many forms of extermination.

He shuffled through the stack of papers and his cheeks were wet. "They're rinsing us from history. All we can do is fight, until the end. That's what our children must remember. We fought valiantly, honorably, until the end."

After a while he pulled himself together. "Tell me about our girls. How is Ming? The illness, has it progressed?"

"It comes and goes, this lupus. She is often in pain. Little appetite . . ."

He was silent, afraid to ask.

Pono took his hand. "No, it is not your illness. There is no *ma'i Pākē* in her blood."

Yet there were nights while Ming slept, when Pono still pulled back the sheets, searching her skin, telltale signs, sly suppurations. Forty years had not distilled the fear.

"She takes her medication. She endures. That's all one can do with this disease." She didn't tell him the rest, Ming's little pipe, days of drifting, leaving all of them behind.

"And the others? How are they?" he asked.

They think I'm old and near-sighted. That I don't see what they've become.

A whore. An addict. A concubine. And one whose pale skin slaps my face. And yet, each time she saw them turning up the drive, tremulous and fearful—like young nuns rushing toward that which terrified them, toward rumors of the fibrillating heart of God—something in her surged, something noble trying to articulate.

"They're coming home slowly," she said. Perhaps saying it would make it so. "Not understanding their past makes the voyage very hard. Duke, why can't we finally tell them the truth?"

"Truth is temporary."

"But one day we'll be gone. They'll be women without history."

His voice was harsh, ungiving. "I'm part of the past they will have to fill in with conjecture."

"Not telling is a form of lying. Your daughters never knew you. Now, another generation, and still the lie persists. How can meeting your granddaughters hurt you?"

"Pono. I will not leave a legacy of horror."

"It's so unfair. You deny me even *my* history."

"Yes. Lepers are selfish, too."

"I will die asking this one thing of you. I will never stop."

In his stubborn silence, she studied his face, thinking how the years had taken pity on him. Leprosy, so pronounced in outward manifestations years ago, had with the sulfone drugs, almost entirely left the surface of his face. What was left were indentations, keloids, pits, a dearth of bone about the nose and cheeks. His mouth twisted sideways somewhat. But hideous suppurations, the bloated "lion look" was gone. Between the scars and pits, his skin was dark and smooth again, the face still somehow handsome, one could see what he had been as a healthy young man. Yet, with the visible retreat, came the advance to his interior, ravages of the years of experimental drugs, which had damaged his kidneys, lungs, the heart.

She thought how much easier life could have been had she been able to tell her granddaughters the truth. *They might have forgiven all the years. They might have loved me.* She knew that sometimes when she slept, they stood outside her door, waiting, hoping that in her dreams she might call out. And they would know everything.

"I have this fear," Duke said. "This racking, blinding terror, that you will let them see me in my coffin." He took her hand, pressed it to his heart. His body shook. "My granddaughters looking down. This broken, pitted horror peering up at them through satin ripples. Oh, Beloved, promise me!"

She had a vision then, so sudden, she thought her ribs had splintered. Duke, charioting the foam, lapped by cold, moon-spattered waves. She caught her breath, drew his face to hers. Her fingers ran in panic over his features like fingers on a flute.

"No one but *'aumākua* will gaze upon us then. For I will be beside you."

Jess moved as stealthily as a cat burglar, fingers drifting over brushes, combs, picture frames, an 'ukulele Pono sometimes played softly in her room. Gone for almost a week now, off on one of her ghostly, monthly errands, she would return the way she always returned, veiled in a grand, soft silence no one could penetrate. This woman, silent for so many decades no longer harbored her secret, it harbored her.

"Where does she go? Who does she see?" Jess asked.

Run Run had stood at the kitchen stove, holding in her hand what looked like someone's brain. "How many years you ask dat question? How many years I tell you no need know everyt'ing . . ."

"She has the nerve to ask us to come home. What home? This mausoleum of riddles. Jesus, I hate it!"

"Hate a big word, Jess. Take more muscle dan you got. You one brave *wahine* when Pono not here, screaming round, demanding dis and dis. When you gonna' learn to wait?"

"I've been waiting all my life." Her voice turned soft. "It seems that's all I've ever done."

Now, she stumbled in the dark, smelling Pono's perfume, the way it pervaded the house even when she was gone. A scent that had always troubled Jess, hint of bergamot and vetiver, warm Eastern mosses. She opened the bottle, put it to her nose, was struck as if from a blow. She sat down unsteadily, remembering her mother in silk slips like peachskin aged to transparency. Ancient, delicate kimonos. Oriental shawls. A certain scent hanging in her hair.

Jacarandas tumbled across the *lānai*, moonlight turning them into cool, blue throats of infants. *Mother. Did you have a childhood? Did she allow you one?* She tried to imagine her a girl, mothered by someone like Pono, so powerful she called down eagles, chanted giant squid in from the sea, a woman whose glance brought wild boars to their knees. She pictured Pono gazing at four unwanted daughters, her malice like broken glass on which they had to kneel.

Each pregnancy must have been like a powerful gun kicking back, its shout reverberating, lingering for years. Until one by one each daughter revolted, each in her own way. Why had she bothered birthing them? Why not rip them from her womb? She had the power. Her grandmother was not a woman who lived life as a victim, chained by circumstance. Sitting in that room, it occurred to Jess for the first time that at some point, Pono must have had a plan, some definite design.

Our mothers weren't accidents. She wanted them! But then, what in her life had gone monstrously awry?

Her head began to throb, as it always did when she tried to understand the past, know what it wanted from her, what she would have to pay. The door opened, a blade of light sliced the dark. Jess felt such terror she went momentarily blind. In that second even the house seemed to hold its breath. She heard plants sigh, something moist turned into dust. *She will crunch my bones like chicken parts.*

"She find you in here, in her room, she break you up good." Run Run spoke softly, crossing the floor.

Jess moaned with relief, threw her arms round her, weeping. "She wears my mother's perfume. Why? Who *was* my mother? Who am I? It's killing me!"

"Maybe you got it wrong, *keiki*. Maybe all dese yeahs yoah Mama wore *Pono's* perfume. Don't dat tell you somet'ing?" Run Run stroked her head and crooned. "Lissen me. I make one promise, neh? If Pono never say, and die before I do, one day I tell you t'ings. So life stop killing you. Maybe den, you let your mama rest in peace."

Jess saw her mother's face then, sinking, blurring into sand. And she saw herself sliding her hands beneath that face, lifting it up to air, as if lifting her own reflection from a pool.

Pono returned, sat with them, not seeing them, ate meals without tasting, even held conversations, her voice distant, almost formal, as if coming from another age. And dreamily she floated down the halls, brooding for hours in front of bookshelves in the study, a room she left untouched, stale tobacco smells, fingerprinted glasses furred with mold, crumbling antimacassars on dusty chairs. She sat in those chairs, open books on her lap, not reading, just staring, as if studying the way the words seemed to comfort the page. Some nights she stood over Jess or Ming while they slept, touching a foot, a head, with so much feeling. Some nights she sat with Run Run, weeping until she fell asleep, exhausted.

After a few days, she snapped back into the present, striding through coffee orchards, whacking at bushes with her ugly cane, consulting with the foreman about weather, distribution of fertilizers, pesticides, asking after the health and punctuality of workers. Herself again, she lectured the women at dinner, bullied them. When would they commit themselves? Did they want the farm? Did they understand the importance of owning land?

Land. Land. Jess thought. *What we need is our history, a legitimate past.* She dropped her head, exhausted, unable to meet Pono's gaze.

Pono turned to her, feeling her withdrawal. "You could probably do the most here, Jess. Your knowledge of animals, nature. Of course, someone needs to oversee the staff. Rachel would be good for that. Where is Rachel?"

Run Run cleared her throat. "Honolulu. Hiro come home foah few days."

She rode right over it, never having acknowledged him.

"... and Vanya for the legal end, tax abatements, so on ..." She pressed a drift of linen to her lips, then placed it on the table. "Or do I delude myself? Maybe we should just put the whole place up for sale?"

Only Ming had the nerve to say it. "Why do you keep pushing this, *Tūtū*? You're in perfect health."

Pono stared at her indignantly. "Do you know what *old age* is? I will tell you. On rare days, when you wake up with no pain ... you think you're already dead."

They laughed then, even Pono laughed.

"You're stronger than all of us," Jess said.

"I'm no longer strong, dear. Just determined."

"How can we take over?" Jess complained. "A house we don't even know is legally hers. What's its history? How did she acquire it? Don't you want to know?" She lay in Ming's room, avoiding her cousin's eyes now permanently ringed in blue, her face a pale gray moth's. Even her hair was thinning, becoming the memory of hair.

"Ah, Jess." Ming stared down at her small, arthritic fingers, the way they seemed to curl and nod. "Too much knowledge makes one desperate. What do you really want to know?"

"... What makes her tick. That's what." She sat up, looked at Ming straight on. "Sometimes I think you know. I see our history racing just behind your eyes. Your mother was firstborn. She must remember things. Things she never told her sisters ..."

Ming shook her head, spoke softly. "You feel responsible for your mother's death, don't you? Because she died alone. You saw her for one minute in a morgue, then they cremated her. It happened too fast. Do you know that sometimes you refer to her as if she isn't dead, just traveling? You were never given time to break down in the presence of her corpse. We need these rituals, Jess dear. Now you think solving Pono's past will be the proper gesture, a rite of mourning for your mother."

Jess sat motionless, in shock. After a while she found her voice. "Yes, I'm guilty of what you said. But maybe guilt, like love, is a way of keeping her alive so I can understand her. How else can I understand myself? How can I accomplish any of this without understanding Pono? Look at us, this not knowing in our lives. It ruined our mothers. It's warping us." Her voice grew louder. "I'm tired of feeling I'm not this, I'm not that, so I'm not worth a damn. If I'm not worth a damn, I want to know why! I want to know who screwed up."

"Cousin. Leave it alone. Move on to the next stage, not the past."

Ming suddenly sat up, coughing, a horrible rattling sound like parts of her were shaking loose. Jess smelled the blood before Ming spat it out, a pinkish quivering on the sheet.

Ming covered it instantly with her hand. ". . . A tissue, please. And now," she whispered, "I need to be alone."

The hour of little gestures. The lighting of a pipe.

"No!" Jess wanted to drag the pipe out from under the bed, confront her with it. Did she think they didn't know? "That filth . . . can't you see you're mortgaging your future?"

She pulled Jess close, her breath hideous. "I *have* no future. I'm shrinking. My spine is bent. When I sit down my feet no longer touch the floor."

The feet themselves seemed shrunken, a footbinder's dream, as if she could walk in shoes the size of teacups.

She pushed Jess gently away. "Now, please. Get out."

Jess lay in bed shaking. Overwhelmed by this sick, doomed tribe she was part of. She wanted to pack, run, get clear of this place of sleeplessness, conspiracies and whisperings, and pain. In that moment she wanted to break all ties to this scraping, lacerating nightmare-link of family handcuffed to her wrist. She pictured the woman in the next room clutching a pipe, a small mummy cindering within, its scant drip secreting into her, her sighs staining the walls around her. Jess heard a rat squeal down in the guava trees, imagined the mongoose clamping down, gleaming teeth, slick lunar fur.

This is no place for me. I'll get up and go away forever.

She half sat up but, feeling drugged, fell back, one foot raised in flight. Dreams blew her visions of Pono's rough, man-working hands, rememberance of how, when Jess was young, she saw Pono kill and clean a wild boar quicker than a man, cutting out the liver, eating it still steaming from the beast. Seeing Jess, she had turned with the bloody, dripping thing, offering her a bite. A test. Jess had bitten off a chunk, held the thing between her teeth, her stomach churning, legs wobbling as if coming unscrewed.

She had stood there chewing slowly, staring at her grandmother, thinking *I will not throw up. I will show her*. Workers had laughed, waiting for her to spit out the bloody mass. She chewed and chewed. And when they saw she had swallowed it, field-workers cheered, swung her through the air. That night, all night Pono held Jess in her lap, while workers strummed 'ukulele and sang before a fire. Only hours later in her bed did Jess remove the hunk of meat stored inside her cheek.

Now she woke. Or thought she woke. The sound of someone weeping. She put her ear against Ming's wall, only silence. But emanating through the wall, a smell sourish and feral, smell of a room with awful secrets. Wrapping her sleeping sarong tighter, Jess moved slowly down the hall. Downstairs, beside the kitchen a dim light shone from Run Run's room. Jess moved fast thinking she was ill, then froze before the open door. Run Run in a rocking chair, wet-faced and rocking slowly, Pono sprawled weeping on the floor beside her, head and arms in Run Run's lap. All around lay photo albums, snapshots of their mothers through the years, and of the granddaughters posed self-consciously with Pono. Photos of women, mostly women, husbands and sons peripheral, blurring off to crumbled edges where mucilage had dried.

Jess stood paralyzed. *I have never seen her cry*. It was like looking at the very fiber of a soul.

Lifting her head, Pono stared unseeing. "He forbids me. He will not let me *tell*." She dropped her head again, shoulders, all of her—the massive beauty of this strange forbidding human—shaking, shuddering, like a child.

Running, stumbling through the halls, Jess felt she had swallowed a small, deadly animal, that it was lodged somewhere in her ribs, attacking her, gnawing its way out through her heart. She closed her door, leaned against it, terribly alert.

Something else is in this house. "He." She said, "He."

Someone had a grip on Pono. She was hostage to some past. It meant she was human, frail, not always in control. Jess slid to the floor, amazed, wondering if all these years, Pono's demands on them were really needs disguised. "Her girls"—the only thing between her and the intrusive, outside world. Jess thought of the raw hunk of boar liver she could not swallow as a child. *Maybe all these years we were Pono's shield, the cheek within which she stored something she could not digest, yet could not tell.*

She watched the easing of night, sly coming of dawn, and hung her head exhausted, thinking of her grandmother, the rest of the women in this house, each one such a raw, unique event, they seemed a miracle. Their frailties, conspiracies, their private deaths. *There is so little left. We must not brutalize each other.*

Later, from deep within the creaking house, she heard sweet native voices, Ann and Abe Dudoit singing in soft falsetto "*Ke Kali Nei Au*," the classic "Hawaiian Wedding Song." She pictured Pono lying on her bed, listening, wrung out from the night. She pictured Ming, too, holding her small pipe, cuddling it like a doll. Soon she would wake, fill it again, until the pellet glowed, became another cindered mummy. She would come to breakfast calm, her gestures slowed, pain a dog sleeping at her feet.

She lay back in bed, trying to see Ming in a new, a sympathetic, light. What was addiction, anyway? Another form of sleep. There had always been about her an innate lawlessness. Vanya was angrier, full of rhetoric, all knife-flash, no blood. But Ming was always the quiet anarchist. Jess thought with great sadness how much she loved her, how none of them could ever understand her pain. How that pain kept her in a state of grace, and how her addiction sustained that grace, waltzing her further and further outside the zone of other humans.

She thought of Rachel then, and how in the past month she had surprised Jess, showing a certain toughness and diplomacy regarding Ming.

"I've seen her every day for over twenty years," she said. "I've watched what lupus does, the slow, inevitable, cellular deterioration. That's what the doctors call it . . . cellular . . . deterioration. Do you know how many people go insane?"

Jess argued with her. "She should get into therapy, get psychological help. Or ask for stronger medication."

Rachel had spun round so swiftly, Jess expected to be struck. "You!

You come home on vacation with your round-trip air tickets. You sit here and judge. You and Vanya, with your busy lives, checking in now and then, like we're just another port."

She smiled then, her face so perfect it seemed to produce a glare. "I know what you both think of me. A paper doll, a toy, something Hiro dresses, undresses, plays with, puts aside. You have no idea what marriage is, what it takes. Yours lasted what, Jess? Eight years? Ten? I have been with one man . . . over . . . twenty-five years!"

She turned away then, not wanting Jess to see the weight of things. "When we were kids, I loved you. I still do. But life has intervened. There's been no one to listen, no confessor. Only Ming. And I am here for her."

"I only meant," Jess said, "therapy might give some quality to her life, so I wouldn't feel we're losing her to that unspeakable stuff. Everyone's in therapy in this day and age . . ."

"What's the day? What's the age? Wake up, Jess. Our cousin's dying."

Jess's shock was absolute. In the ensuing days, she saw a part of Rachel she had never known, resilience, a way of handling Ming, of letting Ming retain authority and dignity as the eldest cousin.

"Of course Pono knows," Rachel said. "It's killing her. But what is a little addiction, compared to what it could be. Ming racked and mindless, like something on a plate."

At meals, she tenderly lifted Ming's kimono sleeve from the guava jam, finished sentences when she got lost. At night she drifted in and out of Ming's room like a rubber-soled nurse, her perfect face tacked on as a joke.

"She's been like my child," Rachel said. "A wise, old child, who teaches you the verities."

"Like what?" Jess asked.

"That there isn't much we can change. That each of us has our dirty little secret, our addiction. That we can only attend to that which we can attend to." She paused, studied Jess. "You'd understand Ming's needs if you came home more often. You've been dying to come home for years. Why do you hold back?"

I'll end up like my mother. A sacrifice. Instead, she said other things. "Well, there's my daughter . . . my practice . . ."

"Your daughter's gone. Your practice should be here. We need you, Jess."

Now, exhausted, still fighting sleep, Jess drew cool sheets across her chest. *"He."* Who is *"He"?* The word flickered, a flame that momentarily scorched the nostrils. Then pure fatigue turned everything to dreams.

Next day the house was very still, as if the women therein could not rouse themselves from sleep. Ming smoked and dreamed. Pono played old records, strummed her 'ukulele, wept alone. Run Run cooked a meal, left the dishes covered, and dozed off in her rocker. In early evening, Jess sat up, something whistling through the riggings of her nerves. Disoriented, not knowing if it was dawn or dusk, not sure of the day, the hour, she groped her way down the hall towards the shrill ringing of a phone.

She lifted the receiver, talked a while, listened, inhaled deeply, and responded. Then slowly, dreamily, she groped her way back to her room and sat in a chair, facing the sea. Cautiously, in slow motion, she lifted a hand-mirror to her face, astounded, thinking how simple life was, how all the mysteries, riddles, the trick figures hidden in dreams, were often merely one's reflection. And she thought how things that seemed to happen by chance were long ago seeded in one's subconscious, how thought was incipient action.

That night at dinner, she looked round the table, not quite sure of her expression, if she looked happy, or confused.

"One of my associates at the clinic called today. I've been talking about leaving New York for years . . . they want to buy out my share of the practice."

The table was silent, hands poised over plates. Ming smiled, nodding and nodding. Run Run twisted her napkin in her lap, trying to contain herself, big yellow teeth snaggling her grin.

Then Pono spoke, voice deep, contained. "Go back next month. Close your house, put your life in order. Be back here October for coffee harvesting."

"Here?" Jess said.

"Here!" She banged her cane for emphasis. "Home. Where you belong."

Ke One Haena

Barking Sands

PLANE TRAVEL DID THAT TO HER. She would feel the metallic chill, close her eyes, and be standing again in a desert morgue looking at her mother's feet. She leaned back in her seat on the flight bound for New York City, remembering her mother's letters describing how Tuareg women had stained the soles of her feet with indigo dye, in miniature desert scenes of palm trees and figures in robes. The morgue attendant with murky, submarine eyes, had studied Jess while she studied her mother's feet, as if she were planning to steal a part of her lower body.

... *Tattoos had turned her soles soft blues and greens of bruises ... little palm trees, swaying men. The attendant pointing repeatedly to her face, while I leaned closer to her feet. I had an image of that face, carried it with me. How she looked in death had nothing to do with it. My hand on her cold shoulder, wanting to sink my teeth into the curve of that shoulder out of grief. Morgue attendant sliding her away. My hand seeming to enlarge, a lobster's fighting claw. I wanted her back, wanted to know her ...*

... *A morgue in Tamanrasset, Algerian oasis town dead-center in the Sahara. Three and a half million square miles of sand. Mother, for Godsake, why?* ...

Jess sighed, pulled an airline blanket tight around her shoulders. In half sleep she remembered the tiny airport outside Tamanrasset, tarmac landing strip, bronze-colored men in tunics, camel pants. One of them approaching. She remembered eyes of an Oriental slant, cheekbones broad and high, hands long and graceful like leather cured in sun. He

had the air of an impoverished prince swathed in faded blue head wrap
and billowing blue tunic. Under a pollen of dust, his feet had a greenish
cast like old seamed jade, arches carved, beautifully high. Rassi ould
Mahmould ould Sheddadi. He had been her mother's lover for two years.

*. . . And then that drive through desert in his oxidizing van. Nothing, only
spindly acacias, camel skeletons, abandoned cars of foreigners who had disappeared.
Why had they left their cars? Were they searching for water? Rassi shaking his
head, saying it was something else. "La Baptême de la Solitude. Often, they feel
. . . they are called" . . .*

Then, Tamanrasset. Tourists in virulently colored Western clothes
looking cheap beside blue-robed Tuaregs, so lordlike in their stride. A
single paved street, dirt alleys radiating off in all directions, concrete
dwellings behind mud walls. Inside one wall lay swaddled infants, flies
lining their eyes like sequins. A woman in black robes had smiled shyly
from a doorway.

*. . . That dwelling, a place built of concrete blocks the size of a single-car
garage. Mother's home for two years . . . living there with Rassi, his wives, five
children, Mother supporting all of them. When she first wrote of her "oasis" I
pictured courtyards, trickling fountains . . . a mosque-like house with onion domes.
Mother perfumed, draped in robes, servants in gauzy trousers . . .*

Jess had stepped inside that dwelling and half learned what she had
never learned, yet knew so well. It was never happiness her mother
sought, but something else. Forgiveness, perhaps. The place had been
immaculate, like a Vermeer, bare except for sleeping rugs, blankets, a
tray and tea glasses. And a clue to a life she would never know: smoke
of cindered desert branch mixed with odor of goat and camel.

*. . . Rassi showing me her paintings, one canvas repeated and repeated: palm
trees, swaying natives, an ocean looming and endless. Mother's life spent painting
the wished-for innocence of childhood in the Pacific . . . Rassi's wives staring at
me, robes half drawn across their faces like confessional curtains between us. Pale,
boy-hipped, face nondescript, brown hair shorn like a recruit. How could I, they
must have wondered, have been her daughter? People had always wondered. Even
I had wondered . . .*

And then a two-day camel ride deeper into the Sahara, to Assekrem,
religious retreat, where her mother had spent many hours. "This man,"
she told Rassi, ". . . this seer my mother confided in, I want to meet
him."

Blinding sands, stones cracking in the sun. Rassi with his soft, elastic
tread, tending fires, brewing tea. And frigid nights, the moon massive,
close enough to freeze her cheek. And heat, oppressive sense of carrion:

flesh of the newly dead withering on bone stalks, great pickets of camel ribs, once a human skull inside a half-buried suitcase.

. . . How had she survived there? So close to death, maybe the automatic response was to fight back, to live. Until one got past wanting to . . .

Jean-Marie, part hermit/priest, part seer and medicine man for the Tuaregs. His hermitage in the Hoggar Mountains was two stone huts just beneath a sandstone mountain top. A wiry old man with rather sad, juridical eyes, he had ceremoniously poured green tea, then led Jess to a tiny chapel in one of the huts where her mother often meditated.

. . . Sitting there facing the altar, letting the room work on me. Wanting to feel her presence, feeling nothing . . .

For a moment, Jess had thought she smelled Mitsouko, the perfume her mother wore for years. It came and went, quick syllable, profit of a wish. She had dropped her head, recalling fragments of her mother's letters.

. . . We tend to wash piecemeal with basins and rags at the points d'eau, keeping clean, and on the move. . . .

. . . You ask if I'm lonely. The desert has nothing to do with loneliness. Its more a solution. Here, everything counts. The smallest word, gesture has enormous power. It redeems, leaves you pure like a child. . . .

Jess had pictured her then, swimming into the dunes, giving in to the undertow. The thought of it filled her with such grief she wanted to rip the chapel apart with her teeth. What good had praying done her mother? She had died alone, mouth gaping sand. Later Jess stood with the hermit sage, looking out over the desert, the sandstone Hoggars recalling dreamlike and misty extinct volcanoes.

"We did not discuss religion," he said. "Much of her time was spent here on the terrace, brooding." He waved his hand at thousands of miles, empty beyond sensing. "Your mother came because she loved the view. It reminded her of the Pacific, to which she could never return."

Jess had thought he was trying to trick her, hide from her that her mother had become a zealot, a convert, perhaps she had gained clairvoyance, something he would not share.

He continued, as if talking to a child. "You are searching for a solution to something you imagine as irreducible about your mother. She was not that complicated. Your father died, you were beginning your own life, travel was her way of mourning. As for her paintings, I think her greatest work of art was herself. All in all, she had managed. She survived."

"Can't you tell me any more?" Jess had practically begged him. "I need to understand why she died. I have to live with this . . ."

He sighed, gave what he could. "Her death was not intentional. Nor was it accidental. She walked too far into the dunes without water. Fasting had become a habit. Or a test. That is all, my child."

She left the hermitage empty-handed, no answers, no clues. In Tamanrasset, she had given her mother's clothes to Rassi's wives, then slid her canvases into cardboard cylinders. At the airstrip, Rassi stood beside her, radiant with the unsaid. She suspected he had loved her mother very much. Beyond her lush beauty and generosity, she had possessed an innocence like an invisible shield nature had placed around her. Rassi would have protected her, defended that shield to the death. They embraced, then he stood waving, immaculate against the sands.

On the small plane out of Tamanrasset, Jess's hand had slid up and down the cardboard cylinders, remembering how her father had referred to her mother's painting as a "hobby," not as a way of belittling her talent, as much as a way of keeping her attention focused on him. That night she lay on her bed in a hotel in Algiers, a leather box on her stomach.

. . . Her ashes. The weight of it. Picking the box up, walking around thinking, "This is my mother." Remembering her raw moods, tearing off jewelry and clothes, yelling at my father, how they were placeless, without family or blood, how they lived like Gypsies, and how would their child be normal? . . . My fear that she wouldn't know how to stop tearing things, that she would begin tearing at her skin . . . Then, her gentle, dreamy moods bringing me relief, hoping the good moods would outlast the bad and she wouldn't go insane . . .

With a sense of fatigue, Jess had opened a box of old snapshots, her mother and father. Her mother, a child, held in Pono's lap. Her mother holding Jess. She studied the pictures, then opened one of her mother's journals.

. . . this snapshot of me rollicking in mud of taro patches, Mama dark, stately, watching. And chasing mongoose across lava shelves, and running, running to her, from her. Then running forever with Vernon, pale and blond . . . running from the horror, what she told . . .

. . . like that snapshot in Vernon's trunk. His father in Decatur, Alabama, 1921. Wearing a white robe, funny cone-shaped hood. Behind him other

men in robes and hoods, and masks with eyeholes. Peekaboo. I could smell the kerosene, hear the crackling wood, the flaming cross. That night, afraid to lie down beside him, locking myself in another room, falling asleep on my feet like a horse . . .

. . . This snapshot has always puzzled me. Emperor Hirohito and his wife, walking their palace grounds, their dog beside them, leaping and yapping in the sun. Two days before Hiroshima. I never understood that dog. Didn't he know what was coming? Aren't animals intuitive? Each time I see this photo I think of Vernon taking me home to meet his folks in Alabama. Didn't he know what was coming? . . . A doorbell ringing, curtain twitching, his folks looking through a window at my skin. How long we rang that bell! And no one ever answered . . .

. . . couldn't go forward, couldn't go back. Life lived on the point of a pin. Thank God Jess's skin is pale like his. Life will not test her every day. Strangers won't stare . . .

. . . the years . . . and every summer Jess comes back from Kona deeply tanned, Hawaiian working its way out from the blood. Something registering in Vernon's eyes, until her skin fades again, the paleness of an Anglo . . .

. . . Then Vernon's skin becoming something else, ballooning like layers of mushrooms. Loss of thirty pounds. He remembers sweeping decks of U.S. Naval ships in the Marshalls in the '50s. They were testing Atom bombs. He remembers rash, vomitting, and then it went away . . .

Jess imagined all the sailors coming home, young boys who had joked around while standing ankle-deep in radioactive dust. Sailors entering civilian life, internal organs glowing, something lurid in the bone. Somewhere old Naval ships in watery graves like poisoned, irradiated whales.

. . . What do I tell our child? Her father is irradiated. Maybe it is in her genes. All I can do is send her away. Back, and back to Kona. When he dies, where will I belong? . . .

When Jess's father finally died, her mother cut herself adrift, moving through the Mediterranean—Malta, Cyprus, Crete. Islands, always islands, trying to re-create her childhood in the Pacific. Eventually, she grew weary, finding a certain peace in an oasis floating in the oceans of the Sahara. In the end, that metaphor sufficed.

Jess had lain all night in that hotel in Algiers, reading her mother's journals, weeping until she felt bled out. It was dawn when she rose from a bed reliefed in used tissues, a colony of small, damp mummies. She leaned against the window, smelling creosote and bait from the docks, hearing cocks crow from the roofs of the Casbah, watching a street merchant whose cart had tipped chase oranges down a cobbled street toward the leaping light of the sea.

Morning had burst upon her senses, and Jess thought of her mother as a child, skin embossed with mist of rain forests dense with mynah and wild boar. Then she saw her mother older, tea-colored and beautiful—broad cheeks, full lips, hair dark, electric—riding bareback on a beach of coral fragments that, washed by waves, made a barking sound like dogs. And in the background, Pono stately, aloof, beckoning to her. Then her mother banished from the world of her origins, and how, with desperate bursts of color on canvas, she spent her life re-creating that world. She thought how her mother's life had been set on a course many years ago, a course neither time, nor place, nor age could change. Maybe her death was more than accident, or intention. Maybe it was, in a final sense, a pledge of accountability.

Cocks crowed again, a cruise ship in the harbor gave a Wagnerian blast, and Jess knew it was time to go. Watching the merchant chase oranges into the sea, diminishing like a figure swimming into the dunes, she had hugged the box with her mother's ashes. She would take her home to her ocean origins, back to her beach of barking sands. Her mother would roam coral canyons with 'aumākua, "talk story" with the ghosts of her blood.

That summer, Pono turned away when Jess arrived with her mother's remains. But Jess saw her mourning at night in the ocean, diving under and under, drinking her daughter's ashes. Her mother had always said the sea was the Hawaiian's nourishment and escape. For Jess it became like an amniotic fluid that kept her alive in the months of grief that followed. *I didn't want to remember, wanted only to swim.* She found peace in the drug-like stroking day after day, night after night along the Pacific shores, swimming with the intensity of a starving woman wallowing in food. Feeling nothing but the suck and pull of the tide, she swam for miles with the agility and speed of a racer, day after day, week after week.

Sometimes, feeling the grind of aching muscles, she rolled over on her back, paralleling sharks dreaming off in the distance. Sometimes she was shocked to see stars and a partial moon. The day had passed and Jess had consumed nothing but air. *Sometimes at night the canoe, Vanya and Rachel coming after me.* She lost flesh and looked starved, her tongue and lips cracked. For weeks, Pono kept her from the sea. But when her mouth healed she plunged in again, deep down into boulevards of perpetual forgetting, streets she could navigate blind.

One day, feeling her arms spin in their sockets, pulling the ocean behind her, Jess looked down at the ocean floor, seeing forests of staghorn coral like ivory branches glowing through the blue. Her mother had described this coral, the feeling of flying over preserves of running reindeer. And in that moment, Jess felt airborne, beneath her herds of pounding hooves. She began to feel her mother inhabited her, that she was seeing the world with two pairs of eyes. She was living for two.

Swimming became so much a part of her body, her interior, Jess began to swim without the ocean. She swam in her dreams, and the dreams became constant. Sometimes she woke with stiff arms, exhausted. Returning to Manhattan, she swam through her days while bent over broken animals, swam through the city, stroking through crowds, the ocean so indelibly imprinted on her, she carried it within her, giving her movements a certain grace. Perhaps this unreal quality, this fluid transluence, was what drew the man named Mars.

That year Jess had begun wearing what she thought of as urban guerilla clothes. At a certain age, living alone in Manhattan, women tended to tighten up. You moved at top speed, hands on your holster, so to speak. You slept with your eyes open. It was a city of quick swerves, where the race was to avoid waking up in your own blood. A city where laconic rich of marmoreal pallor peeked out from French windows on the park. And in the park, tribal sounds, drums, rituals, now and then a clutch of fur, a dog's head. Even a human sacrifice.

After fifteen years in the city, Jess had begun to draw in, her world circumscribed by five or six blocks. Or, maybe, she thought, the city was shrinking. Her house and clinic were on a quiet street in Greenwich Village, not far from where there had once been beautiful young men cruising in bars where they danced, fought, made love in back rooms. Now the streets were quiet, the young men gone, or going, rampantly, and in degrees. They limped down the streets together, weak, and wary, and proud, and dying.

She wanted to say to them, "We are completely in your power." Because youth and beauty and valor suddenly erased leave a place impoverished.

And in some warped corner of her head, Jess envied them, these young men, nursing each other, mourning each other, some even dying in twos. Who would nurse her in this town? Who would mourn her? Since her divorce she had had random lovers, affairs that sieved from lack of trying. Friends left the city in droves, exhausted by death, decay and violence. Now no one claimed her time. She was of interest to no one except, maybe, her daughter, Anna, in college down south near her father.

Then one day two years earlier, Jess had stood watching thousands of marathon runners locomote across bridges, through city streets, like herds of wildlife on the Serengeti. She watched for hours, thinking how after ten miles the body starts feeding on itself, and after twenty, it starts eating the muscles and heart. Running seemed something else in this city, not a sport, but a form of panic. Later, strolling downtown to the Village, Jess had stood before the Flatiron Building in coming dusk, its great angled structure lit up like the prow of an ocean liner sailing into port. It seemed to be bearing down on her like ships they had watched as girls in Honolulu swaying in to Aloha Tower from Hong Kong and Singapore. She stood there, feeling little paw-strokes of homesickness, knowing night would bring the full assault. Then she crossed the street, heedless to the swerving ambulance.

The driver saw a boy-haired woman with a dreamy gait, gliding against the light. In the stretcher behind him, a homeless man was bleeding to death, a technician yelling, ". . . this dude's going, BP's dropping ninety over sixty-eight . . . we're losing him . . ."

Radio crackling, oxygen cylinders wildly rocking, the driver hit the brakes, throwing the technician to his knees. He thought he hit the brakes, the ambulance kept moving. Jess turned, something bearing down on her. She woke with rain pattering her cheeks.

"Miss, can you hear me? Jesus, can you hear me?" His voice was deep, angry, eyes floaty behind thick glasses. His sweat poured down on her. "Blink your eyes. Miss, can you blink your eyes?"

She blinked slowly. "It's all right. I'm a physician."

"I don't give a damn what you are. You walked against the light."

Someone probed her arms and legs. She flexed her fingers. "Really, I think I'm okay."

He leaned close, gently lifted one of her lids, peered at her with a light. Unaccountably, Jess reached up and touched his face. A crowd gathered like a small herd at feeding time. The technician pushed them back as Jess stood, shaky but alert. She couldn't seem to let go of the stranger's arm.

"Okay," he said. "Let's get you to Saint Vincent's, get some X rays."

The dead man was covered with a sheet, the technician beside him on the radio. The driver was tall, Afro-American, all elbows and wrists, his bones so close to the surface he looked slightly undernourished. But there was a tenseness of muscles in his face, a resoluteness that spoke of someone sustained by nerves. He waited with her for the lab reports, and when she said she was a a veterinarian, he laughed.

"Animals? Jesus, whole neighborhoods dying of hunger, you're playing around with people's pets."

Mars Scoville, who had hoped to become an orthopedic surgeon. Someone had sponsored him, someone had died, his scholarship fell through. With his mother ill, his younger brothers hungry, he had dropped out of college, taking jobs that went nowhere. For the last ten years he had driven an ambulance for Emergency Medical Services in the city.

"But I'm still a contender, I've still got dreams."

Now he was trying to fund a Volunteer Ambulance Corps in Harlem, his off-hours filled with walking his neighborhood drumming up cash donations. He had outfitted an old van as a makeshift ambulance, and on weekends he and several medical technicians listened in on police and EMS radio scanners, responding to calls in Harlem on their own, sometimes arriving ten or twenty minutes before the regular ambulance, and often saving lives.

He asked Jess a hundred questions about medical procedures, the difference between human blood counts and animals, differences in blood pressure, body temperatures, the quickest way to cauterize a wound, sterilize a puncture. The quickest emetics for food poisoning. He stood silent as she showed him through her clinic on the first floor of her small townhouse. Carpeted foyer, expensively furnished waiting room, receptionist, assistants in white coats. Examining room, surgery room, a room full of pampered animals in roomy cages.

Mars shook his head, laughing. "We got families uptown so hungry . . . you know what they'd call these silly, little pets? Meat. They'd call them meat."

She offered him a drink, and spent the next few hours trying to justify her practice, her income, the nights she volunteered, tending the poor and homeless, nights she put in at an AIDS hospice. She talked about the psychology of medicine and compassion, healing and charity. While she chattered on nervously, he stared at her, his gaze on her face like the cold, flat side of a knife.

"You're what we call a twenty-minute do-gooder," he said. "You people . . . when you're finished with your so-many-hours-a-week volunteer work, you wash your hands, comb your hair, and go to cocktails in your townhouses, your designer penthouses. I hate that kinda' shit. It means the poor and the homeless and the dying are only visible at your convenience. The rest of your life we just seem to . . . Golly! . . . disappear."

Jess had studied him intently. "I volunteer every single night and every weekend. I don't deserve your disdain."

He answered quietly and thoughtfully. "Guess what I'm saying is you got to live it, to understand it. Be poor, to *know* poor. Sounds like your life has been kinda' soft, Jess. You tell me your people in Hawai'i are dying out, they're being wiped out. Why not go home and fight for them? Your history is taking place without you."

He found he had to control his anger when talking to her as a white. Yet he was drawn to her native side, her longing for family, her confusion about her skin. In turn, she sometimes found Mars childlike, the way those driven with a purity of purpose—who plunge straight on, looking neither left or right—seem vulnerable and childlike. Other times Jess felt if she touched him, she ran the risk of being burned. He was angry, the angriest man she'd ever known, and that rage shone out of him with a strange and terrifying beauty.

The first time they made love, he took her ruthlessly and quickly, thinking that was what she wanted. In time, he slowed, made love to her tenderly, patiently, with regard for her pleasure, sweat turning his dark shoulders to epaulets of light, their bodies thrumming and matched in a wordless Morse of understanding. Still, he was resentful, hating her privilege, her lack of struggle, her seeming complacency about the injustices, the indecencies of life. He pulled away from her, then, missing her, came back, so that she was never sure of him, of his feelings.

Yet, for two years Mars performed a kind of exorcism over her loneliness, the pain of her self-exile from the islands. When Jess looked back, that time with him would be a time when the city became more threatening, more intelligible and real, than it had ever been for her. She saw the horror of real poverty, children stunted by starvation, teenagers strung out on needles. It would be a remembrance of weekends spent answering emergency calls in Harlem, of sleeping in shifts in the van, eating meals from paper plates while IV bottles clanged against her head. The smell of deep-fried food and blood. Weekends without bathing, living like guerillas speeding through war zones.

When the van finally broke down, Jess donated funds for a real ambulance, and seeing his dream coming to fruition, Mars now envisioned half a dozen Volunteer Ambulances in Harlem, even a headquarters office. Jess's presence, her pale skin, caused tension, but her medical background was invaluable.

"We can learn from her," Mars told his crews. "Shortcuts, save more lives."

She helped teach new volunteers "triage," a series of vital-signs checks in the ambulance which saved time when they got to the hospital. She helped train Harlem youngsters as a youth corps whose members attended first-aid classes. Some kids were excited by the training, talked about becoming medics, heart surgeons.

"Maybe one of them will make it," Mars said. "And, definitely, my boy."

His son lived with his ex-wife in Philadelphia, an athlete and top student who wanted to be a pediatrician. "He walks the line. I told him he ever slipped up, I'd kill him myself, before the drugs did." He softened when he talked about his son, so Jess forgot about his anger, the rage that seemed to propel him, hold him to his vision.

One night in Harlem, a sixteen-year-old boy was jumped by a gang, shot through the ear, beaten with lead pipes. Blood poured so copiously from his head and chest, he seemed to be floating in a pool. Jess applied a neck brace, helped lift him onto the backboard, then the stretcher, holding the oxygen mask to his face.

"Breathe in deeply, son! Breathe in . . ."

His pulse was gone before they reached the hospital. Afterwards, sitting in the parking lot, she dropped her face and sobbed. "Why? How can they do this to each other?"

"How?" Mars looked at her, disgusted. "You know what it's like to be born into a system that says you're shit, that wears you down year after year till you've got no self-esteem? You *despise* yourself, can't wait to mortify your own flesh, wipe out your race." He shook his head. "Naw, you'll never understand. Half of you is white, the other half is running scared." He pushed open the ambulance door and walked away.

Jess sat there shaking, trying to understand.

After a while the black technician spoke up gently from the rear.

"Listen to me, Jess. I know your intentions are good. But man, it's like
. . . we're those broken cats and dogs in your clinic. You want to set
our bones, stitch our wounds, make us better. You can't *do* that unless
you know what makes us tick. You got to have blood knowledge, our
history, our gospel. You got to know where it hurts."

"I love Mars."

He moved up close, so his face was just behind her head.

"No, baby. You don't even know him. You're looking for something
you think Mars can give you, a . . . a key, a solution." He drove her
home and reached across, opening her door. "I'm sorry, Jess. But like I
said, you ain't us. Whoever your people are, we ain't them."

Now, riding in from Kennedy Airport, all she could think of was
Mars, what she had to tell him, her decisions, her moves. Then she
remembered he wouldn't be there anymore, and life outside the taxi
turned one-dimensional, instantly flat. In her house, she ignored the
reception room and clinic, went straight upstairs, flicked on a tape Mars
had left behind, John Coltrane's *Ascension*.

She buried her face in Mars's shirt, his smell like the music—wild,
tart, ironic—a beautiful smell of church socials and outings, of gospel-
rock and liquor and laughter, and slave ships and lynchings and killings,
and runnings, and grief and poetry and jazz. The smell of someone ahead
of her in vision, in rage, in demanding and rejoicing in the force of life,
of life itself. The smell of a man whose stride she couldn't match.

The days, mechanical days. Consultations with attorneys, associates
buying out her practice. Meetings with real estate agents, clients, her
staff.

"The house sale will take months, I know," she told her attorney.
"But I want the papers for the business transferral drawn up as fast
as possible. I want to be home next month for the start of coffee
harvesting."

They were sitting in her office at the clinic, Jess toying with a pair
of scissors. The man was a native New Yorker, a shrewd and costly
lawyer.

"This move is insane," he said. "I totally advise against it. You're
giving up a thriving practice, a six-figure income, to move to a place
where plumbers go on honeymoons. Jess, what will you do with your
brain?"

With not much thought she reached across and cut his tie in half.

And then, a flight to Durham, North Carolina, sitting with her daughter in a restaurant near Duke University. The girl was lovely, green eyes, palomino hair, skin of an almost milky transparency. Jess watched a blue vein pulsing in her neck. *This is what I have accomplished. Though she's no longer mine.*

She saw her daughter seldom enough to see her with a perspective which was not totally distorted by sorrow or regret. So, as the years passed, she saw her each time in the light of an accelerated personal conflagration. That pleased Jess, she felt her daughter needed a little grief, a little humility. And yet . . . seeing hints of her mother's features in the girl's, her breathing changed, something hurt, like breathing through the wounded lungs of a bird. Sometimes Jess was guilty of the faint and singular hope that she would find her daughter ugly, abandoned, waiting for Jess to come and save her.

She recalled a day in the city when they were still a family, before she and her husband began to compete for Anna. Before Jess began to know she would lose the competition. She was out shopping that day and suddenly saw them coming down the street together, laughing. *This is what they look like when I'm not there*, she thought. *I have stumbled on the life they lead without me.* Seeing her, their movements had changed, their expressions, they drew together almost instinctively. She didn't sleep that night. The next morning it hurt to rise, to face a marriage of false claims, and a daughter who had deserted her.

What had been in her husband an almost forgiving permission, allowing Jess to throw herself into her practice, keep long hours, become a success, now became something else—apathy, cold and absolute. She stood on agitated subways rushing close, so close windows seemed to brush against each other. Through one of them a trembling, fleeting moray eye, her own reflection sucked into the black. Once visible as half a couple, she would now evaporate. In the year preceding her divorce, she walked slightly lopsided, like a woman with two legs who remembered having three. And after the divorce, when Anna chose to go with her father, to live with him, Jess wasn't shocked. By then, she lacked awe for anything.

". . . so I have decided to go home to Hawai'i. I wanted to discuss it with you."

Now Anna looked frightened, defensive. "You're deserting me."

Jess smiled sadly. "We haven't seen each other in two years. You don't even visit at Christmas."

"Daddy gets depressed at Christmas." She looked down, a college junior, but looking just now adolescent. "Sometimes, I don't understand why you two married. I mean, he's so Southern, you're so . . . different."

"We loved each other for a while."

Anna shook her head. "That's not what he says. He says you married him out of perversity, that you wanted to fix up your parents' marriage in your head, make it perfect this time. He says he didn't even really know you."

"He means he didn't want to know. My family, my background. The native side. He never went home with me. Never saw Hawai'i. It was like he loved half of me, my father's white, Southern half, so the other half didn't exist. He put off meeting my mother for three years after we eloped. And, Anna, she was beautiful. Don't you remember?"

"I remember she was dark." She began to cry. "I have this blood in me, right? One-fourth Hawaiian. Suppose I have a child some day."

"Yes . . ."

"And it's dark, like a Puerto Rican, or a Mexican. How do I explain that to my husband?"

"Perhaps you should tell him what you are *before* you marry. People usually do."

"Suppose he's Southern like Daddy? I couldn't."

They were silent, letting the insult of the remark reverberate.

Then Jess stood up. "Anna, do you know what you are? You're a racist, a woman ashamed of her blood. God help you. I won't bother you again. If you need me, you know where I am."

"Why now?" Anna looked up at her, demanding. "You're all set up. You could have a summer home, travel round the world. Why are you throwing it all away, just to go back to those dopey islands?"

Jess leaned down, hit the table with her fist. "Listen to me. I love you. But you are shallow and cruel. Some of that is my fault. I should have given you more of a sense of identity. Of pride. All those summers I left you with your father, I should have taken you home with me, *forced* you to get to know Hawai'i. I hope you grow up, Anna. Your world is ugly and narrow."

They walked together, yet apart, out toward a taxi stand.

"I'm sorry. I love you, too," Anna said. "I guess I just take after Daddy."

Her leavetaking was easy, because she didn't know her daughter felt the lack of her immediately. She didn't know, couldn't imagine, that when she left for the Pacific, Anna would feel something involuntary, something inside of her diminish.

* * *

At night, Jess walked the streets of Manhattan, seeing it as a great ocean liner slowly sinking, straining to hoist itself upright while its chandeliers still glowed. Crumbling bridges. Splintering ramparts of glass and chrome. Caravans of human rags traversing worn spice routes of garbage bins. When she had first arrived, Manhattan seemed frightening, blatant and raw. Now it seemed only weary and wise.

She thought back on how she and the city had matured together, Manhattan in the face of the Italian grocer Jess chatted down the years, whose face slowly changed to Korean, while her face just got older. She felt great affection for the place, a giant *souk* where she had pitched a tent, selling her talents, the ability to conjure animals well. She would miss it because she had never been faithful to it, and so it had never quite accepted her. Yet, it had been a refuge, a sanctuary. It let her hide.

One evening, returning home, she stepped into the dark and paused, feeling a subtle change in her surroundings, a new form brush-stroked into the environment. She stood very still.

"I heard you're leaving." Mars got up from a chair, jiggling a set of keys. "I wanted to return these, and say . . . Aw, Christ . . ."

He crossed the room, took her in his arms, the beautiful and sudden smell of him, the feel of him, striking her like blows. Jess hung her head, and wept.

"I know, baby, I know." His voice was deep and calm. "But don't you see, it never could have worked. Besides, you'd already started your journey home when I met you. Maybe you didn't know it, but you had."

"I knew it, Mars," she whispered. "It's just . . . sometimes people pass through our lives, and we don't want to let them go because . . . who knows if we'll ever feel that way again? You woke me up, made me take full measure of myself. And I love you. I always will."

He sat back down, pulling her into his lap like a child.

"Love. That word means so many things. When you're on the street, fighting for your life, it could mean a dime. A pair of shoes. It could mean someone not pissing on you while you sleep." He pressed her head against his shoulder. "I know I'm gonna' miss you. That's a kind of love. And I know I'm proud of you. You got a grip on things now. That's a second kind of love. I know I used you. Maybe we used each other, but I think we did it decently. That's love, too. We didn't do too bad, girl."

They sat all night, holding each other, talking, conjuring their dreams. At dawn she stood at a window, watching him go.

* * *

For days she trailed strangers through her house, moving men built
like commandos. One night she stood in empty rooms, the clinic stripped
to bare walls, equipment, everything gone. And she felt the final exhalations of the years—animals panting quietly in humid rooms, the argot
of incisions, exorcisms. Her cheek against cold bars of a cage. Now she
felt a turning, felt herself rotating into position for the next phase.

She was standing in the dark, just standing, when the phone rang.
Hearing Rachel's voice, her body temperature changed. Jess thought of
that night at Pono's, listening to Ming's breathing through the walls, of
finally seeing Ming's addiction as just another way to sleep. She even
recalled the fungus smell of her cousin's breath, as Rachel told her Ming
was dying.

Ka 'Ano 'Ano Mo'o

Dragon Seed

HER WOLF WAS CONSTANT NOW, he prowled inside her, pain a personal myth and remembrance etched in scars along the bone. The butterfly rash now descended from her face to shoulders and chest, so her breasts seemed stung with ragged bites. Her eyes looked prehistoric, obsidian crawfish lit from within. One night she was so racked, so far beyond human expression, Ming put the Dragon Seed aside, started drinking laudanum in her tea. Rachel watched, holding the teacup when Ming's hands shook, knowing laudanum was the last resort. After this there was only the begging for mercy.

"How disgusting you must find me," she whispered.

"No." Rachel kissed her cheeks and little hands. "Remember what you said? We each have our addiction."

"Such a complex, Western word," she said softly, "for such a simple act. As normal as breathing." Knowing her addiction was more than that, a shrieking need, final leap over the battering reef of choice.

One day, watching her will to live slowly leak away, Rachel called Vanya in Honolulu, and Jess in New York. She took Ming's hand, asking if there was something special she desired, music she wanted to hear.

"Everything has been heard," Ming said.

Rachel asked another thing. "Cousin, do you pray?"

"For what? Health? Understanding? How useless prayer is when your senses have closed down. You no longer want to think, read Yeats or Proust, hear Bach, or even the shouts of children playing . . . It comes with such clarity, the sudden *lack* of want. Yes, I pray. That the Dragon will outrun my wolf."

She was beginning to talk in riddles, so that Rachel went away perplexed. Pono came, mostly at night when Ming was drugged. She stood over her, weeping, remembering her as a young girl, her laughter like moonlight on water, a thousand dimes tossed. Some nights she heard Rachel crying in the next room, full of a sorrow so distilled, Pono wiped it from her mind. But one night she woke drenched in sweat, glowing like an icon. In her dreams she had finally seen the face of the corpse, elusive for so long. "Ming!"

The house suddenly bulged with people, Ming's husband, parents, children, flying in from Honolulu. Then they flew away. She had no wish to see them, to see anyone but Pono, her cousins, and Run Run who battered through the house cursing God, trying to feed Ming back to life, preparing *laulau*, pigeons stuffed with lotus bulbs, meals no one could bear to gaze upon.

All Ming seemed to do was drift, watching water-haunted sunlight play on walls, cross-currents of rays and shadows glancing off her *lānai*. Gulleys beneath her eyes intensified in blue, as if she were being constantly slapped in sleep. She had no appetite, all she hungered for was Seed.

"As you know," Rachel said one night, "my husband traffics in the poppy, though he has never let me have the pipe. What is it like, I wonder?"

Ming spoke with the slow authority of a connoisseur. "It makes everything kind."

Rachel frowned. "It kills all sensations. How can you say it's kind?"

"Ah, Rachel, don't you see? Kindness is like fear, having less to do with human emotions than with a certain . . . distribution of chemicals in the body. Did you know, if a spider drinks the tears of someone terrified, the spider will go mad, satanic designs appear in its web . . ."

Rachel turned to Vanya. "She doesn't make sense. She sounds *lōlō*!"

"She's dying," Vanya said. "She doesn't have to make sense."

Drifting days, need of only drops and puffs. Sometimes she cheated, put extra drops of laudanum in her tea which made her eerily alert, her brain a fertile pit inside a decomposing fruit.

One night she woke, found Pono hovering at her side. "I saw him, *Tūtū*. Grandfather Duke."

Pono lunged forward as if struck from behind.

"Years back. One day I took the boat to Moloka'i, the leper settlement. I watched him from a distance for hours, fishing by the sea. Such a big, handsome head! I felt so proud. In all my life I never wanted so much to touch someone, take his hand. Then I took the boat back . . ." She smiled dreamily. "Did you think my father could forget his childhood here? This house . . . the rumors . . . stories of the . . . bounty hunters?"

Pono collapsed beside the bed and wailed. "I used you! Used all of you to hide my fate!"

Ming half sat up, grabbing her arm. "Do this. Do this one thing. Let them know him before he dies. Grandfather is our link, our history."

Pono gazed upon this slowly ebbing human, issue of her blood. In that moment, Ming's face shone as if her skull were an hourglass through which Pono watched sand shift, charting her living seconds. She crawled into bed, took Ming in her massive arms like a little cheeping bird. "Yes," she whispered. "Yes."

Vanya met Jess at Keahole Airport in the Jeep, driving the highway like a maniac, ripping through intersections hurling profanities. Jess gripped the seat as they ascended up, up into the coffee hills of Kona District, little "talk-song" towns, Hōlualoa, Kainali'u, Kealakekua, Captain Cook. Cool air gnawed her cheeks like little teeth, and she was not afraid, would not be afraid until it was over, because she could not imagine Ming dying. For now it was only spectacle, her cousin drugged, incessantly drugged, something to be watched in stages.

"She won't die," she said. "Ming would find dying too absolute."

Hunched over the steering wheel, Vanya momentarily lost control as if something were wrenching the course of her life from her hands. Gripping the wheel again, she whipped her head round at Jess. "You blind, egotistical, *haole*."

Entering Ming's room, Jess froze. A pervasive odor of mortal exhaustion, doomed flesh and bone. Nothing moved. Then something turned its head and looked at her, a mildewed gaze. Her cousin was lying in a rust-mottled kimono, and there was little left of her. For the first time, Jess saw the total massacre, saw how a human body could become a battlefield.

Lupus, like a terrible flame, had scorched Ming's solar plexus, her joints, marrow, cells, sluicing through her arms and legs, her kidney, spleen, deforming her spine, frying her hands into claws. And yet, each drop and puff of Seed fought back, impaling that flame, a head on a pike. Ming smiled dully, and Jess understood that, for the moment, Seed was in ascendency. Even the *memory* of pain was blurred.

But, O! the price. Less than two months ago when Jess had departed, Ming's pain had momentarily abated, her lovely features resurfacing like an ancient coin from the Orient, elegant ciphers in relief. Now she stood stunned by the change. Ming's face was frightful, nothing left but eyes on stalks, her mouth uncertain as the rash accrued. Her hair was a prodigy of white spiders. Trapped in that awful grotto of bone, she seemed the living larva of the dead.

She cried out in horror. "Ming! What happened? I was gone such a short time . . ."

Her voice seemed to issue from an ancient crone locked in chains in the dark and damp. "Who can measure time? Time measures me." With great effort, she held out her arms. "Am I too hideous to embrace?"

Jess flung herself upon her, gathering up her sour bones. There was so little left, she could almost feel something spread its wings, lift Ming in a final glide. "Oh, God," she sobbed. "Don't leave me!"

Ming pushed her back a little. "Be still, and listen. I left you years ago. You and Rachel, and Vanya . . . my existence is already your existence. Don't you see . . . in time you will forget if you are remembering me, or if you *are* me."

Jess tried to speak. Ming raised her hand, and drew her closer, slowly and with great fatigue.

"*Milimili* Jess, have you ever understood your name? The strap fastened round the leg of a hawk. Jess. The thing that restrains the falcon." She slumped, exhausted.

Jess lay her gently on the pillow, kissed her face, and it was cold, like *'ahi* hooked in deep December when seas went gray with hurricanes. She held Ming's hands until it was dark, grief crackling within her. Ming, the vital current, the strength that flowed through all of them. With her as their shield, they had formed a weapon against the world, wielding their way through anything. What would become of them? A tapestry unraveling, a composition breaking down.

On her last night, Jess knew it was the last, she could smell it, Ming motioned them close from where they all stood sobbing in the doorway.

"Promise me . . ." she croaked, ". . . look after Toru. I have loved him more than he can know. Jess, stay here at home where you belong."

Jess wept, nodding like a child.

"Now, remember. First will come the sadness, then an understanding . . ."

Wearily she reached up, hugging them in turn.

". . . Gradually you will feel that I am here still, that I inhabit you . . . and you will bring me back to life. Each of you will even begin to use my gestures. Your expressions will be my expressions. Whatever of me was wise and gentle, I leave with you."

Her voice grew thin, a woman passing through a mirror.

"I will be the conscience whispering in your genes . . ."

In slow motion, she waved them away. And as they closed the door behind them, Ming sighed, reaching for the laudanum.

For a year she had hoarded drops, slowly filling up a four-ounce bottle. Now she held its dark contents to the light, then took the bottle in her mouth.

Her hands caressed it sucking it as if she would engorge it make it throb its sloping shoulders exciting her ravenous to feel its contents flowering in her belly nerve ends gaping like discarded mouths her groin alive wanting it like a woman wants the act of love wanted to be full in every rancid cavity she writhed and hardly removing the bottle from her mouth pulled off the rubber stopper sucked the slender thing again like she would swallow it whole felt the first big spurt bitter burn the message in the bottle felt the contents flow and sucked and sucked felt it sluicing in her down her now *she* was the message in the bottle something coming at her someone running he was coming slick and amber she was coming circuits lit terribly alert. *Toru.*

All that night, wailing echoed through the house, Pono shrieking, yanking Ming's big toe, trying to bring her back from death. In the kitchen Run Run squatted, cursing, waving her carving knife at God. In the morning, Run Run stood in the driveway, waving the knife at a Catholic priest crossing himself as he drove away. He had entered Ming's room, seen the pipe and empty bottles, and fled, refusing her Last Rites because of her appetite for filth.

Ho'omana'o . . .

Remember . . . Remember . . . Remember . . .

UP IN KOHALA, TORU STUMBLED ACROSS A PASTURE, whistling in his horse. Leaving a dark wake in silver grass, the great black stallion floated forward, whinnying affection. Toru rode his hand along its back, buried his head in its mane and wept so hard the horse danced off, alarmed. Blindly, he flung himself face-down against the earth.

Ming. How we traveled deep in Seed, how we parted the walls! Once more, he walked with her, took her by the hand to Chinatown, taught her how to smoke, to find that place in the Gobi where a Mongol milked a singing horse. Taught her to receive him, slick and amber, to love things she didn't have a name for. *And then deserting her for smack, journey I could only take alone . . . Pono snatching me back, long rehabilitating climb. And finding Ming again, lost to what I had instilled in her. A craving.*

After a long time, he clutched a handful of tall grass, seemed to suck the oxygen from it and finally stood, empty of everything save all the urgent chronicles he and Ming had never shared and should have, all the lustful, panting dialogues that give humans history, something to recollect. *Paniolo* straddling a fence watched at a distance as Toru approached a pine tree thick as his waist. He stood before the tree, apologized, and hit it, attacking it because he didn't know how he could bear to go on living.

He could live without her everyday presence, perhaps, live without forbidden nights of stroking her drugged and childlike body. But how could he live without existing in her conscious mind, her thoughts of him his only definition. He hit the side of the tree again with the edge of his open palm, a sharp karate chop. Numbness, then fire up his aching limb.

He rubbed his hand against his chaps, then whacked the tree again, the impact rolling his eyeballs back. Men approached warily as he embraced the tree, trying get his balance, embraced and groaned as if about to penetrate, to mate, his hair now needled, elbows full of bark. He groaned again, as if ejaculating, as if he would, with this tree, create a thing whose blood was green. He whacked the tree again. It shuddered.

"Hey, *brah*," someone yelled. "Yoah karate not so good. Gonna' broke yoah hand."

He hit and hit the tree, the impact resounding in the woods. His hand split, squirting blood, he noticed bone. A crew boss rode up shouting, reining in a piebald with a quirky trot. The pine tree listed, began to creak and whine. This sad, blind, grieving human, whacking! whacking! even as the tree went down. Alarmed, doves suddenly shot the sky, soaring like white sheets of music. He looked up, thought of Ming, her love of Telemann and Bach, and pointed with that hand, splintered bone, shredded flesh bursting from his skin like atoms. He felt nothing, his pain deeper than human tissue. The shock of feeling nothing smote him, and he fainted.

What stood for years between Toru and his past was now erased. He sat up in the dark, propelled by blinding flashbacks, children floating face-down in green paddies, tanks sprouting human heads. Dismemberment, evisceration, taking a human being down to its very marrow. *Funny, the enemy looks like me.* GIs circling a naked girl, hands kneading testicles. The tale behind the valor. Ming was the only one he told it to. Even pronouncing the word ... 'Nam ... was like lifting a corner of some awful veil, glimpsing a final horror. Now he was there again, other times, other places. He walked on tiptoe, waiting for ambush, feeling for trip mines in the dark. He woke with nostrils singed from the smell of phosphorous grenades. He tried to snap out of it. Nothing signified, all hopes gone. It was a world with new definition for what it now denied him: Ming.

He grew tired of remembering, tired of running, of standing still. He thought of dying, cleverly and fast. But something pressed against him, something backed by rage, enough to keep him going. His wounded arm was in a cast, he walked it like a friend, hiking into valleys, across far fields. He sat on cliffs overlooking the Pacific, in lashing rain and blinding sun, unmoving, unseeing. Weeks passed, grief held, yet it was generous, making room for something else. One day he looked around, feeling stretched and cured like hide left out in weather. *What was all the suffering for? It must have been for something. Someone stole twenty years from me. What happened to it? How can I get it back?*

He thought of Ming, how she used to tell him, "Find the thing that keeps you angry."

Maybe, he had a mission, a pathetically small task on the grand scale of living, but for now it was implicit and would do.

He stood on the sand at dusk, while muscled paddlers took Ming's remains out beyond the reef. Up and down torchlit beaches drums throbbed, *kāhuna* chanted, while Pono stood majestically, scattering ashes from the canoe. Arms lifted high, she stared into the depths, calling, calling, and slowly, one by one, and two by two, *'aumākua manō*, shark ancestors appeared. Random iridescence of Ming's ashes on their snouts, they circled round and round, rubbing mournfully against the drifting hull. And there were crowds, students, friends, so many who had never really known her, only knew about her pain. They lined the beaches, clefts in sand. The night was isolate.

Pono came ashore, poured something in his hand. "My granddaughter, who felt many things for you."

Toru stared down at his palm, holding the woman he had loved. With consummate grace, he flung his hand out, casting her ashes into the waves.

"E Pūpūkahi." We are one.

Jess, Vanya, Rachel gathered near. Tall, muscular, wiry, smelling of sweat, grass, steer and saddle, and mountains and myth, this man, vessel of their youth, looked terribly injured, old. In the violent, static smack-years after he came home from war, Ming had been his solace, his confessor. And after? in between? before? he had been to her, for her, what none of them were sure of. Young and dreamy suitor? Procurer? Lover? Past all reasoning, he and Ming had retreated together into a place unspeakable, impregnable. Toru had known her best of all.

They attended him, waiting for some utterance, some pronouncement that would give everything, her death, this day, a grace and clarity.

He looked round, wanting to tell them they were silly, mediocre, because they knew nothing of pain, real pain. Ming had been a soldier. She understood combat. Together they had traveled far. Journeys that would shock. He said nothing.

After a while, he rolled his Stetson in his hands, set it on his head and walked away. Passing Vanya, he paused, seemed to fling his face at hers so that their eyes connected, and held. He nodded slowly, pushed his Stetson back from his forehead and walked on.

That night, in Pono's house, Vanya snapped out of sleep. Tension like electricity ran through her. As if answering a summons, she pulled her sleeping sarong around her, made her way downstairs. Toru's truck idled in the driveway.

"The monastery . . . tomorrow afternoon."

". . . for what?" she asked.

He inhaled, flicked a butt across the lawn. "Don't act stupid, Vanya. You want in on this, or not?" Before she could respond, he shifted gears, eased back down the drive.

All night he studied the play of moonlight on walls, insects skittering across bare floors, snores of men in sleeping bags. *Bivouac, is what it's like, half sleep, cold sweats, waiting for dawn and combat.* Only it wasn't combat, they were still in the talking stage. Nearby, a stray cat woke, licked its private parts. Moonlight shifted. The outline of the long-gone Buddha seemed to sparkle on the wall, reminding him of Bangkok, saffron robes of virgin monks, glittering Wats. Tongue of a girl-whore engorging him, his journey into smack. He shifted, dug deeper into his sleeping bag, remembering Morse code from combat training, tapping out on his chest, BORN TO DIE, tapping tapping until sleep took him down.

Driving up that afternoon, Vanya heard the din before she reached the dirt turn-off to the monastery. She drove slowly through slums of frangipani sticking to the tires, through chandeliers of bees drunk on honeysuckle, and dragonflies in ginger. The music was so deafening, she swerved into a bush, crushing blue flowers like tiny feet.

It was angry music, clearing her brain like a shot. Music that brought back years of deadly newscasts—monks in fierce self-immolation, Diem, napalm, My Lai. And she felt the weight of those years pass through her. Someone had pushed a button, and all the boys, in all the graves at Punchbowl Cemetery came to life, marching in formation. The music grew louder, uglier.

The lunatic is in the hall / the lunatics are in my hall / the paper holds their folded faces to the floor / and every day the paperboy brings more . . . [©]

It seemed as if speakers were everywhere.

. . . the lunatic is in my head / the lunatic is in my head / you raise the blade, you make the change / you rearrange me til I'm sane / You lock the door, and throw away the key / There's someone in my head, but it's not me . . . [©]

Music gathering the day into a mad geometry. Music of the Apocalypse, of men whose young lives had burned away as light passed through them, leaving them without belief in normal things.

Toru stood in the doorway like something smoking, about to ignite. He waved with that oversize, dirty cast, making his arm look like a gray lobster's claw. When he hugged her, she felt his muscles hum, so jazzed up, it seemed all the things that could have been, were now cut loose within him.

"Turn that awful music down." She watched men, like maturing larva, crawl out of sleeping bags. "What is this? What war games are you playing?"

His words came out mean and brittle, like they'd been saved for twenty years. "The games are over. We're calling in the debts."

She sat for hours with men who were vets, and some who were not. Some were just angry locals, watching their island go to the highest bidders: resort developers, marina designers, spaceport advocates. And as she listened, looking over diagrams, manuals on hand bombs, Vanya saw her sense of logic leap from a high window.

"What is there to lose?" they asked. "They talk of sovereignty, but we have nothing. There is nowhere left to even cry."

They talked all afternoon, an exchange in which outrage was the currency. All they had to do was organize. She had a vision then, of the need in her for vengeance, payback. After all the years, it gave her life a point. All the years of working for law firms, doing "piecework" as a female attorney. The years of courting the media, the speeches, years of shouting for her people. Theater, mere theater.

I'm over forty, and I have not made a difference.

She listened and listened. Hawaiians were tired of feigning subservience, tired of false modesty. A *hapa-Pākē* described the alkali shrouding his village from a leaking geothermal well. His face was sickly and sallow, he showed her Polaroids of his children with stomach ailments. They looked embalmed. Others listened silently, held in the equilibrium of waste and loss, the dying of their island, of all the islands:

Irreversible pollution of coral gardens at Kāneohe. Stockpiling of nuclear weapons at Waikele. Radiation of productive fishing grounds at Pu'uloa by nuclear submarines. A proposed rail transit system on O'ahu, that would devastate the tiny island's fragile volcanic foundations, traumatizing Hawai'i's entire ecological system. And the hideous and dangerous H-3 Freeway under construction, costing $1.2 billion federal dollars. While high schools crumbled. Day-care centers went to rust. While college scholarships for native locals disappeared. While unemployment, alcoholism, crime, suicides soared among Hawaiians.

"No more exploitation," someone said. "One hundred years we been enslaved. Dey stole de throne from out our queen. Sovereignty too late, an empty word. Now time foah payback."

"People might die," Vanya warned.

"So? We take death by surprise."

"What about your wives and children? Your elders?"

"Hey! Vanya! You forget? All Hawaiians warriors! Try wait, you see how dey been ready!"

She pictured them on every island, massing, marching, fighting for their land. Remembering the old Aborigine, Digger, in the Kakadu, she felt she was setting a course then, sighting down the barrel of her life. She sat back, watched men brood over maps, blueprints for revolution.

Yes. There is obligation. Rage must be expressed.

And it began, spreading among locals from village to village, passing through walls like molecules. It was only a matter of organizing, determination, and being ready to die. Throughout each island they began to meet, doormen and busboys, and doctors, teachers, and maids, Hawaiians tired of living on their knees. They formulated plans, drummed up cash donations. They studied maps, sewed banners together, frightened, but resolved. December 7, 1991, fiftieth anniversary of Japan's attack on Pearl Harbor, was the occasion on which they would begin.

Nothing stopped them. Tourists jeered, the military shoved them back, roping them off. Dignitaries, survivors of Pearl Harbor, families of Pearl Harbor's dead, drove past them, shocked, uncomprehending. A human chain of thousands, they lined the highway outside Honolulu, leading to Pearl Harbor Naval Base, the Arizona Memorial Center. No chanting, no demonstrating, just the silent, thoughtful gaze of people who remembered. Above their heads broad white canvas banners were stitched end to end, one continuous, awful artery lettered in black, mourning the casualties of war, of invasions, of forced annexations, calling the U.S. government into account.

Hearing sirens in the distance—the motorcade bringing in the president of the United States—they raised their arms higher, banners bursting into white battalions as far as the eye could see. His limousine approached, flanked by motorcycled military escorts. Cameramen, the international press ran alongside his motorcade, romancing his profile as he passed—cosmetic smile, eyes entirely unseeing—hand waving gently like a wand. MPs leaned inside the ropes, viciously elbowing back the bannered crowds. And they were silent, arms stiff below the fluttering white, their gaze unflinching, as the president of the United States rode by.

And what passed through him down the miles? Recognition? The ghosts and gallops of invasion, domination? Or through his tinted windows, was there only blur, a passing whiteness, on which black forms accrued:

REMEMBER BAGHDAD . . . REMEMBER PANAMA . . . REMEMBER NIC-
ARAGUA . . . REMEMBER GUATEMALA . . . REMEMBER THE FALKLANDS
. . . REMEMBER ARGENTINA . . . REMEMBER EL SALVADOR . . . REMEM-
BER LIBYA . . . REMEMBER MY LAI . . . REMEMBER CAMBODIA . . . RE-
MEMBER LAOS . . . REMEMBER KENT STATE . . . REMEMBER
MONTGOMERY, ALABAMA . . . REMEMBER MISSISSIPPI . . . REMEMBER
THE BAY OF PIGS . . . REMEMBER MICRONESIA . . . REMEMBER BIKINI
. . . REMEMBER HIROSHIMA . . . REMEMBER NAGASAKI . . . REMEMBER
ALAMAGORDA . . . REMEMBER MANZANAR . . . REMEMBER TULE LAKE
. . . REMEMBER THE 442ND . . . REMEMBER THE HILO MASSACRE . . .
REMEMBER LILI'UOKALANI . . . REMEMBER . . . REMEMBER . . . REMEM-
BER . . .

And finally, when the president stood weeping on the U.S.S. *Arizona* Memorial, hand across his heart like an opera tenor, asking the world to "Remember Pearl Harbor," his brothers-in-arms of fifty years ago—1,200 young men wounded when Japan attacked, 2,400 still lying in this watery grave—people wept, the eyes of the world were cast down.

The world was not allowed to see the rest, highway miles of bodies gaudy with sweat, holding glowing banners. It didn't see the miles of locals weeping hard and long for their own Pearl Harbor victims—locals accidentally killed, burned, mutilated by American military antiaircraft in the chaos following Japan's attack. Locals wept, too, for young *haole* sailors entombed in the *Arizona*, and for local boys of Guadalcanal and Anzio, Korea, 'Nam, the traumatized in vets' hospitals, the graves in Punchbowl Cemetery, the living dead, the druggies, the outcasts.

And when the U.S. president left Pearl Harbor, traveling in reverse, the banners were still floating high, the words reflected on his tinted windows. REMEMBER . . . REMEMBER . . . REMEMBER . . . As he approached, Rachel, trembling violently, grasped Vanya's hand raising their banner higher, and Jess stood beside them clutching Toru's hand, the four of them a run of colors, composite of the crowds: fair, amber, tan, mahogany. For a moment, the president glanced out, pale eyes appraising: a subminority, a people tentative, easily ignored.

Behind his motorcade, men in plain cars, dressed in cryptic coloration, drove slowly by, videotaping the crowds. And still they held the banners high, glaring at the cameras, belligerently pointing to their T-shirts . . . MĀLAMA 'AINA . . . ALOHA 'OHANA . . . refusing to hide their faces, to turn away.

The day had passed, palms clattered under cool, respirating breezes. Fog came, soothing aching wrists. Some folks could not drop their arms. Elbows seemed frozen, fingers welded to their banners. Then, with a long gigantic sigh, wind brought the banners dancing down. Exhausted, people rolled them up, embraced, shook hands, and shuffled homeward in night's obscurity.

Yet something audible, like footsteps, walked softly in the dark beside them—the unemployed, the homeless, families living in cardboard containers, in blue yurt-like tents of A'ala Park's new ghetto. And what they heard resounding softly in the air—what seemed to drift like ash among them, even sifting through their dreams—was one simple word, a sound. Children woke from sleep, eerily alert, couples sat up like covert, nocturnal listeners. And what they seemed to hear floating in the alleys, the guttered streets, the tenements of cardboard boxes, what seemed to illuminate the small blue tents of A'ala, was that one word. *HULI*. Revolution.

Elders shivered, remembering the word from other centuries, memory chains linking back to warrior days. For, in the word was something sacred, ancestral, nearly forgotten: valor. People fell back into sleep. Morning would bring the usual vicissitudes of trying to survive. But later, days, maybe weeks, in the intuition of an instant, the word returned, floating up in conversation. *HULI.* It was with them now. It permeated, filled the vacuum of their lives.

He Mōhai o Nā Maka

An Offering of Eyes

PONO LEANED ON HER CANE OF HUMAN SPINE, fighting a terror she could hardly bear. She paced her room, eyes unnaturally bright, shoulders exhausted from holding herself erect. Downstairs Run Run pattered round, filling rooms with armloads of plumeria, heliconia, orchids, torch ginger, Bird of Paradise. Whenever she was frightened, she made the house a jungle. Now there was cursing from the kitchen, Run Run plucking notoriously at a chicken, then viciously kneading *poi*. Suddenly she appeared upstairs, scratched and mauled by Ula, the mongoose, whom she had accidentally set on fire.

"You!" she wailed, pointing at Pono. "After all dese years, you don't even give dah comfort of yoah arms! I lost Ming, too. Dat girl my almost favorite."

Pono turned, crossed the room, hugging her passionately. "Oh, Run Run. *Kalahala!* Touch is still such a novelty, it scares me."

Run Run nestled in her massive arms, wiped her nose, and sighed. "Dere t'ings you gotta learn fast, Pono. Life starting to subtract from us."

She looked through the window, down through the coffee orchards to the sea. "My heart has been hard. I have been mean. But daring. Do you think they will have pity on me?"

"Who can tell?" Run Run said. "You never taught dem pity. All you can do now is break dah future to dem gently."

"... and the past."

Run Run stared at her. "What you gonna' do?"

Pono shuddered, leaning close, as if looking for a place to hide. She thought of her granddaughters, her daughters' scars, healed in different colors.

"There are women locked in my womb forever, the memory of their birth. All I can do now is liberate the fruit of *their* wombs. And it may be too late."

For a moment, the house, the land around them fell silent, as if all life had stopped with Ming. And Pono tried to imagine this land, this place without her girls, without the beating of their hearts animating everything. Water would cease to flow, birds and flowers vanish, crops, all life, would abdicate.

"Mot'er God," Run Run whispered. "Why you wait so long? Why now, after so many years?"

"Because I'm old, the senses are becoming dull, the pain is bearable. Or ... maybe I am doing it for vanity."

"Yeah, you plenty vain, *tita*. But if you do dis t'ing, is not for you, not for Duke, or Ming. You do it for *kahe koko*, flow of blood, for *kahe 'aumakua*, flow of ancestors. Dese t'ings you gonna tell dem been waiting all dese years. Written by yoah mot'er's mot'er's mot'er's hand. Dese girls been livin' empty-handed in da world. Now you gonna' give dem dere destiny."

She felt suddenly dangerous, highly explosive. She was going to bring her life to words, cast it from her lips. And everything would change.

"Run Run, help me! Something deep inside is passing through a wall!"

Run Run crossed herself, stretched her arms round her, held her like a child. In that room, in all those ancient rooms, they could feel dread massing, like weather.

They sat back, listening as Pono's old Buick with the sorrowful grill wheezed and shrieked, Pono's foreman driving them in from the airport, taking the long way home. The old laboring Māmalahoa Highway curved up and up through Hōlualoa, Kainali'u, Kealakekua, that archipelago of vowels, old coffee towns, the fruity, winey smell of coffee cherries, rusty little tin-roof shacks under regal monkeypods.

Jess rolled down the window, smelling the sweet scent of a Kona evening drifting upcountry, jungle, sea, and fertile soil, mixed with charcoal fires of guava stumps and coconut-husk bark. Something tugged at her, a ticking in the ribs, a premonition. She felt chilled, wanted to keep traveling, to fall asleep in the safety of the moving car.

Passing through Kainali'u, they saw Kimura's Fabric Store, Mrs. Kimura sweeping off the sidewalk. She squinted at the passing car, and waved. Jess turned to Rachel and Vanya who smiled, remembering the years. Tiny Mrs. Kimura flitting among her fabrics like a butterfly, face popping out of bolts of cotton, silk, batik, while Pono brooded over price.

"You like dis floral pattern? Moah bettah dis color foah you, neh?"

Hours, whole afternoons, lost among the designs—parrots, orchids, garish colors, then cool pastels. While Pono and Mrs. Kimura gossiped, the girls collapsed on hardwood floors with Coca-Colas, leaned their heads against glass counters wherein dust glowed on ancient Tootsie Rolls and bags of *Okonomi Mame*. Next door, a damaged phonograph played songs from *West Side Story*, the slapping time-step, shuffle-ball-change of pounding feet at Damron Academy of Dance.

Now, Jess looked longingly behind, watching it all recede, as Vanya asked the foreman if Pono and Run Run had seen them with their banners on TV.

He shook his head. "Nobody see. Real tragic. One small paragraph in dah papah."

Toru turned round from the front seat. "I told you. They gonna ignore us until there's fireworks."

Jess felt that ticking in the ribs again, vague uneasiness, like something was waiting for them at the house. She leaned forward, nudging the driver. "Let's stop at Manago's. It's pork chop night."

The foreman grinned and shook his head. "You girls *pau* wastin' time. Make me come lose my job. Anyway . . ." He glanced back from the steering wheel. "Somet'ing up wit' yoah *tūtū*. When I left da house she dressed up . . . real formal kine."

Glances darting back and forth, they hugged themselves, dug into individual corners.

She stood on the porch as they stepped from the car, then leaning heavily on her cane, turned her back and went inside. They entered slowly, feeling again the fluid, shivering air along the corridors, the haunted sunlight of each room. Place of childhood, refuge from a world that would corrupt them. Yet, returning, they felt doubly corrupted by what each room withheld.

She didn't come to dinner. They hardly noticed for their eyes were glued to Run Run, dressed as they had never seen her. Gray hair upswept, held with small jade combs, rouged cheeks giving her the look of rampant health. She had painted on delicate black eyebrows, and smelled of jasmine. Like little ivory roots, her arms protruded from a pale blue satin *cheongsam* flowered with yellow chrysanthemums. She seemed full of tremor, eerie and fragile.

"Run Run?" Vanya sounded scared. "Why are you dressed like that? What's happening?" The others only stared.

She shook her head over her plate, making a tsk! tsk! sound. And yet she didn't eat. No one ate. The food stared back at them. It was so still, they heard the suctioning sounds, tiny fingers and toes, of geckos on the ceiling. Jess looked up, seeing a miniature blue heart beating through green skin.

Finally, Run Run picked up a fork, brought food to her lips. "Eat." She whispered. "Chew slowly, as always."

Rachel's voice erupted with the falsetto of an old man's. "This is how she operates. Theater! Mystery! Using Run Run as a prop. Calling us home, then ignoring us. Ming is dead. The only constant in my life is gone." She stood up, throwing down her napkin. "I'm going back to Honolulu."

"*Sit!*" Run Run spoke with such authority, she had to look behind her, as if someone else had shouted.

After a while she cleared their plates, hardly touched, and brought out sliced mangoes, papayas and kiwi in bowls carpeted with jacarandas. Pinks, oranges, greens, purples—jagged, too-bright colors. They just stared.

Then she brought out ginger tea, and bottles of plum wine. "Drink," she said. "Unshock dah blood."

As she spoke, Pono opened double doors leading to the living room, so seldom used. She was dressed in a velvet *holokū* the purple-black of barking-deer lips. Her hair was wound round her head like a crown, like royalty. Shimmering dust rose in the room behind her, giving her an aura.

"Bring wine and glasses, please. And things to make you comfortable. Pillows, fans."

A peacock skittered down the hall, stopped in the doorway, then slowly, majestically, unfolded its great tail, turquoise eyes beholding them. In the wide doorway, it preened, then turned, facing Pono.

Her hand went to her heart, she gasped. . . . *I confess to remembering*

... Duke had lain his head against her breast ... *Peacocks skittering on polished floors ... You wore a Paris gown. We waltzed ...*

Her granddaughters faced her in a semi-circle of old chairs spilling out musty kapok. Run Run dispensed wine in little glasses, and when she stopped, she chose a chair next to Pono, so they seemed a team, facing the others.

She has chosen sides, Jess thought. *We're on our own.*

"I made Ming a promise when she died ..." Pono began. "That is only a small part of why I want to talk to you."

Their faces were turned up to hers, and in their features she discerned their mothers, rich centripetal eddies of defenselessness and sadness near the eyes. A potential hardness, too, the ease with which they could succumb to hate and malice.

"I will talk and talk for hours. And when I finish, you will be other women. Perhaps, you will have no eyes for me."

She watched Vanya's skin grow darker, that deep, native tone which surfaced when she was angry or scared. Vanya hugged her arms round her waist defensively, her blouse trembling with her pulse.

Pono began. "... My life, much of it, has been lived in shadow ..."

She shook her head, looked at Run Run whose eyes were downcast.

She began again. "... A mother has an obligation to her daughters. To pass on everything they need to survive." For an instant, Pono saw her daughters in those long, gone-forever years, girls in starched, blue uniforms, white socks, Buster Browns. She passed her hand across her face.

"... I failed my daughters. I was silent in ten thousand tongues. In this way, I slaughtered them."

They looked up dumb, too terrified to move.

"Ming's mother, Holo, my oldest, knew many things. She had seen too much. I numbed her into silence. I took her mouth."

She gazed at Vanya. "I was afraid of your mother, Edita. She was spirited, demanding love. I made her keep her distance. I froze her heart."

She turned slightly, looked down at Jess.

Jess nodded. "I know. My mother ran off with a *haole*."

"Emma. I struck her away with terror."

Rachel stood, as if to run, but no message was transmitted from brain to limbs. She dropped back into the chair.

"My youngest daughter, Mina ... I made her rubbish."

There was the slightest sound, a sob, then heavy breathing, as if the room were full of panting dogs. After a while, one by one, they looked at her again, shocked stares jelling into pools of light. She didn't know what they could see: how lamplight flickered on her face, pulling out the grief, all the daughterless decades, the blood-women whose absences from her, and from each other, distributed themselves across her life like daily crucifixions.

"Many people hate and fear me. Some say I am *kahuna*, half shark, that fins sprout from my back in water. They say Ula, the mongoose is my husband, who I bewitched into giving me this farm. That I cursed him, made him a rodent that lives on other rodents. Some say I have prehistoric lusts, that I mate with octopi, that the sting of large scorpions excites me. They say I have *kahuna'ed* Run Run into slavery, that I keep her near so I appear beautiful in comparison. None of this is true. My great sin has been ambition. I have been deliberately harsh with you, so you would develop the ability to survive."

She poured a glass of wine, watched how it shook, how before she got it to her lips the glass became half empty. She sat down, feeling dusk's cool air eat perspiration pouring down her neck. She fanned herself, dipped a handkerchief in water, wiped her brow. Run Run was sitting on the floor now, hugging her knees, like a young *lei* stringer, a flower-girl beneath Aloha Tower, when people still took pleasure cruises in the fifties.

Pono continued. ". . . I have never offered consolation. Because of this, you have learned to depend only on each other, to trust each other. Not just with your lives, but with the memory of each other. With each other's reputation. Yes, you criticize, resent each other, and much *hukihuki*. But I have seen how you defend each other, too. Apart, you suffer, you long for each other. Together, you are little girls, even now, even now. And oh! I have envied you. I know you will hold Ming forever in your hearts, I already see her in your postures, your gestures. You are the repository of each other's lives. You accomplished this without me. I am proud of you."

"You? Proud?" Vanya asked. "Why should we believe you?"

"Because you are courageous."

She stood, circled the room, held on to the back of the chair like she would faint.

"Now. I am going to tell you a story. When I finish . . . you will know who you are."

For reasons they could not discern, Run Run began to cry. She was no longer the feisty, lovable, irascible old cook, Pono's sidekick, the one who held the keys. In spite of her wrinkles, her spine bent from seventy-five hard years, her yellow horse teeth and ginger-root feet, she seemed to regress before them, into a younger and younger version of herself. Slowly, they would see that, as Pono "talked-story," she was telling Run Run's history, too.

And she began:

". . . In each life, there is someone waiting to come to our rescue. I believe it now. I didn't know it when I first beheld this stranger, charioting the waves on what I thought was a long hard corpse. A wave-sliding board. He saw me, knew I belonged to him, but knew I did not know it yet. I was injured, and so he took me home, nursed me, and waited patiently. Until I discovered I belonged to him, discovered it for myself. . . .

". . . His name was . . . Duke. Duke Kealoha. He lived in a house of porcelain and linen, a driveway umbrella'ed with giant ironwoods and eucalyptus. It was, and is, this house, where you grew into womanhood. I used to think he watched you in your sleep, watched over you. And when you flew down corridors at night, in your sleeping sarongs, like little candles flickering, he stood outside the house, walked the driveway, shouting the Night Marchers away. Asking even his ancestor ghosts to tread softly, not frighten you . . .

". . . Until him, my life was a half-life. He taught me everything, how to dress, he even brushed my hair, rubbbed kukui *oil into my hands, harsh from years of plantation living. He ordered clothes for me from Paris, and Hong Kong. I had suede gloves and shoes to match. And he was cultured, imported art, records, books from London and Japan. He showed me maps, explained the world to me, and other languages. He read to me, and taught me writing, though some things didn't take. We stayed alone, and people gossiped, for we were young and arrogant, blessed with good looks, and eager for the future . . .*

". . . His family had descended from royalty. He taught me their history, going all the way back to a curing doctor who served Kamehameha the Great. I taught him about Mathys Coenradtsen, the Dutch whaler who married a Tahitian, daughter of a great chief from Papeete. These were our ancestors, your kū-puna . . .

". . . Mostly he tried to instruct me about the coffee plantation. About soil, rainfall, ideal altitudes. Fertilizer, and planting. And picking and processing. It seemed very complicated. I was young and bored, so we went back to books, the

phonograph, dancing to the latest songs from Europe and New York, pretending we were on a luxury liner crossing the Atlantic . . .

". . . And, in time, I understood why we stayed alone, what happened to his family, a sickness in their blood. Those relatives who had not caught it fled. By then, you see, the plantation had a bad name, a stigma. Hale make. People said Duke was contagious, his workers would spread the sickness to the town. It was, of course . . . ma'i Pākē. Eventually, a spot grew on his arm. Little by little, his coffee workers ran away, all except Tang Pin, father of Ming's father. And, in time, the bounty hunters came . . .

". . . And there were months of hiding, Waipi'o Valley, living like rodents in the bush. Sometimes it was paradise, all of nature enfolding us. Sometimes it was the face of death. One wrong step would pitch you down a cliff. Some nights we slipped down to the valley floor, into the ocean, and thereby lived on fish for days. Some weeks all we ate was root. There were others with the sickness hiding in the valley. We shared when we could. Sometimes we found charred human bones. Kōkua families had burned their dead in hiding. Some nights we heard screams, bounty hunters capturing the hidden. Duke's sickness spread, his skin ran with it . . .

". . . I was seventeen. We hid in the valley for over a year. And one day looking in a stream, I saw a hag, I had grown very old. Duke said I was still beautiful, though starved-looking. His condition grew worse, much worse. Probably he would have died in that jungle, nature can be vicious. But one night, after all those months that bound us together for all time, one night they found us. We woke already trussed up by the bounty hunters . . .

". . . And we were led out of the valley. And, you know . . . people mourned him. In the villages, they wept. On the docks, as our boat pulled away, they went down on their knees. He had been to them the finest example of the human progression of the Hawaiian race, all that encompassed dignity and valor and fairness. When they took him away, people said a lion had got up and left the land . . ."

She was quiet for a while, looking through the window at the night. She felt magisterial ease, a gradual deflating, like a giant sponge wringing itself dry of what it had gathered in a lifetime. Emotions would come to her this night, and sweeping grief, but just now she saw how spoken words—this orderly, almost fairy-tale accounting—gave her access to a world that had remained invisible, therefore not real, until the telling. She looked at her granddaughters, and they had changed somewhat, in their faces sorrow, wide-eyed calm. Their bodies now were flung in attitudes of listening. She went on.

". . . I began to live then in a state of exemption. I stood apart from time. And I lived with guilt, cursing God, damning him for my perfect health. You see, I had wanted the sickness, craved ma'i Pākē *so I could ever be with Duke. Alone, running, living like a wild thing, I felt life winding up inside me in ever-increasing circles of dread. I was a woman without currency, stealing food from poor farmers, killing their chickens with bare hands. I stole their tools, entering each day with an ax. Then one day under a* hau *tree, a shawl of yellow petals settled on my shoulders like soft lightning. In my womb, something stirred, Duke's child . . .*

". . . I birthed her in a bamboo grove, on grass thick and warm as just-baked loaves. I made my way back to Duke's farm, but people were terrified of ma'i Pākē. *They knew it was his child, and stoned me. So I ran. I named that first child, Ming's mother, Holo. For she was born running. For several years we lived on a sugar plantation. There, things were cut out of me, my soul. It was filthy work, and dangerous. Workers were trying to unionize, and some of them were killed. I thought Duke was dead by then. Most people with the sickness didn't last. They had taken him to the colony on Moloka'i, the place called Kalaupapa. A union organizer helped me trace him. Yes! He was alive . . ."*

She faltered, remembering. For a while her voice was stilled.

". . . And so, I found him. And then, again, I lost him. I could not live at Kalaupapa. I was not ma'i Pākē. *I was immune. I moved to Honolulu, to Chinatown, sewing clothes for street girls and plantation workers. And, often as I could, I stowed away to Moloka'i on the steamer, and stayed with Duke at Kalaupapa. The Depression of the thirties came, no one could afford new clothes . . .*

". . . I sat on street corners, telling people's fortunes through my dreams. I was not kahuna, *in that I didn't know long sacred chants and rituals. But, yes, I had the gift of dream-seeing, prophesying. I had been born with* mana. *If I was* kahuna, *it was as* kahuna na. *Guardian of something. The secret I guarded was that of Duke, my life. Filipinos were my best customers, delicate, lonely men who lived on dreams. I hid Filipino strikers fighting for fair wages and conditions. You see, the ILWU had crossed the sea . . ."*

She looked at Vanya. "You would have been proud of me."

". . . Years passed, there was another daughter, then another, and another. Duke gave the farm to me, but it had fallen down. Nothing could be grown without money and workers. Tang Pin lived there with his wife and son, overseeing no one, looking after it for me. Because I had been kind, Filipino strikers helped

me rent a tiny house in Kalihi, so your mothers wouldn't grow up near the whores and dens of Chinatown. The only decent work was at the cannery. It wasn't so bad. Losing fingers was so common then it was almost like a Purple Heart. And it was income. And money came in from the Filipinos. They had no families, and loved my little girls, took care of them when I went to Kalaupapa . . .

". . . I worked hard, providing for my daughters. Uniforms, Catholic school. But I was not a good mother. I made them afraid to even laugh in front of me. They walked on tiptoe through their lives. Then World War II, and everything, the islands, changed. Your mothers grew up fast. One day I was thirty-five. Then they dropped the Bomb, the war was over. And one by one, your mothers ran, married, disappeared. Who could blame them. I never showed them love . . . I had hardly touched them . . ."

Pono hesitated, reached out her hand to Run Run who wept softly now.

". . . One day a tsunami swept Run Run back into my life. She was struggling, trying to raise her grandson alone. Her son had died. The mother disappeared. Run Run saved me, saved what was left of me. She gave me something I had never known, friendship, love of another woman. We grew to be like sisters. One day we found you, Rachel, at my door. We brought you and Toru here, to the Big Island, and tried to make a go of the plantation. Those were the years! Planting, pruning, picking, meditating on improvements in the soil. But, you know, the land took hold of us the way it does . . .

". . . Resurrecting coffee trees grown wild in the orchards. Throwing out the bad. Carrying little boxes of new coffee plants from nurseries, setting them in rows of holes in wet ground, making sure they were shaded by the sun. All stoop work, killing work, at night we couldn't straighten up, walked round like little crones. We did it all ourselves those first years. Three, four years until new trees came into bearing. So many died. Drought, weeds, rats, disease . . .

". . . And, oh! the picking season. That noon sun in Kona, like white fire and gray dust. And sap from coffee cherries sticky as resin, mean, it slit the skin of our fingers. And the winey, cherry pulp of the outer layer before you got to the bean, that too-sweet fruity smell that made you drunk and sick. And sweat, the grimey, ginger-colored sweat glued to your body. Some years the endless miles of coffee fields exhausted me. That line of vision, nothing but a nightmare green. Some years I prayed for death, it seemed a needed recreation. We didn't die. We didn't stop once in ten years . . .

". . . And there was beauty! Clouds of coffee flowers like gardenia in spring, what you know as 'Kona snow.' The mist and rainy season. Then fields ripe with

berries. Pickers coming in their trucks! And picking all night, torches lighting up
cobwebs on coffee trees, dark shining, laughing faces. And, raking beans in sunlight,
drying them on the hoshidana. And donkeys carrying burlap sacks of beans,
braying like nightingales! And at night, the coffee mills glowing like hung jewels
out on a hillside. Clackety old machines hulling the beans, grading, sorting. The
excitement of wagons, trucks, horses all loaded up, on their way from mills to
waterfront, shipping our beans to Honolulu! . . .

". . . Year after year we labored, and then we prospered. Sometimes now, old
as I am, I find myself out there, still picking. I look round at workers, Mexicans,
Micronesians, Filipinos working for me, an old Hawaiian. And something flows
through my heart for all those sweaty faces, the ones for whom stoop-work is still
a way of life. I pay them better wages than anyone, provide health insurance for
their families, send their kids to college. Yes, somehow, I learned to be kind.
Sometimes I want to tell workers about the man who gave me this land. I don't,
of course. I can only till the soil, keeping it alive, keeping it a memorial to
him . . .

". . . And when I pass this land to you, I am passing you his legacy. Duke
Kealoha. We shared a life, a magnificent tapestry made up of scraps. When you're
only allowed the scraps, life burns deep into your soul, every word, every curve of
light you see, is a sacrament. He was my life. The father of your mothers. I broke
all the laws, risked everything, health, prison, dodging submarine torpedoes going
to him in the war. He was my destination. He is still my destination. Where I go
each month . . ."

She fell silent, they were all silent, struck dumb and witless.

Then Jess looked up at her, confused. "Where you go . . . you mean
his grave, at Kalaupapa? When did Grandfather die?"

Run Run rocked herself, sobbing loudly on the floor.

"Die?" Pono whispered. Then her voice grew strong. "Don't you
understand? He lives! He is who you are."

Something issued from Rachel, a high-pitched scream. Beside her,
Vanya trembled violently, covering her mouth with her hands.

Pono wept then. Shorn, naked of all pretense, she dropped her head
and wept. "He *lives!*"

And they were a tribe, rich with sobs, great inhalations, a turning
in the blood. They stood, slowly streaming forward, each and each.
Hearing them, she raised her hands before her face, as if they were
coming to hit her. And they bent forward, gathering her up, she who
was so broken, and so daring, gathering in a rush of limbs.

Kupuna Kāne

Grandfather

HE SAT ON THE OLD DANCE PAVILION now cracked and weather-mauled with years, behind him mist-shrouded jungle, great humpbacked cliffs that hid him from the world. Slowly he whirred round and round in his Amigo, so the seabeachjunglecliff became a lazy blur. When he stopped whirling, he faced the cemetery, miles of headstones shimmering in sun, the warriors of Kalaupapa.

He shook his head, clicking off his small, transistor radio. Newscasts of Pearl Harbor's fiftieth anniversary ceremonies had brought back memories of the war years, patients volunteering for all-night watch up on the cliffs, nerves thrilling, hearts jackhammering as they searched with binoculars for surfacing Japanese subs, enemy planes landing on the beaches. And they had sacrificed: Food rationed, gasoline, even medical supplies. Clothes made from rags, tobacco from ti leaves. Those with fingers sat all day, rolling bandages which were then fumigated and shipped to hospitals. Those with eyes collected tin and scraps. But all in all, World War II had not come to Kalaupapa, as if the enemy knew better.

Then, soldiers coming home from war, parades, families wreathing them in *lei*. These were things the patients of Kalaupapa had to imagine. Maybe, some of them said, the whole war had been imagined! Nonetheless, they celebrated V-J Day, *lū'au*, church choirs singing, and victory dances here, on this pavilion, patients playing piano, 'uke and bass, and drums, high sweet notes of trumpet, tenor sax. Lipless, fingerless musicians improvising, playing valiantly off-key.

And O! the dancers dancing, some just shuffling mutilated feet, clutching a partner, denying the terror outside the moment. Soldier boys were coming home, but most folks here would never see their homes again. Their sickness would outlive them. Patients like Johnny, the Tango Eel, frail, self-possessed, hair slicked back like a movie star, cigarette dangling at an oblique angle to his elegant mustache. Legs long and slender, buttocks tight, he had moved like a whip across the floor. Even though he coughed blood, and they could hear his tissues tearing, women fought to partner him, to couple with his fierce, ecstatic hum.

And Lomi, whose face was massacred, cheeks eerie craters, mouth a gaping maw. But when she danced the hula!—movements of her hips and thighs, long arms undulating like courting water snakes—men moaned, eyes oily with desire. There were worse: some looking like old ruins, crumbling foundations gone to moss. Some just torsos left, some with limbs like giant vegetables.

But there was beauty, too! Balmy nights, Southern Cross mirrored on the ocean, the universe of stars, the songs, "Sweet Lorraine," "Toot Toot Tootsie, Good-bye," "The Sheik of Araby." Wilhelmina Lono, propped up on canes, singing "I'll Get By" like an angel. Crimson paper lanterns swinging dancers in and out of shadow. The scent of frangipani, and jasmine *eau*. Throat-scalding kiss of rum and Coca-Cola, the dazzle of an earring. Nights when wild deer drifted down from the jungle, noses black as truffles, ears pricked, eyes gleaming through bamboo.

There were nights Duke had moved round the floor with partners, authoritative and superb. But most nights he had sat and thought of Pono and, watching the crucible of dancers, sometimes it seemed to him as if the pavilion had become an airy, floating, Oriental tomb, wherein all the necessities for the afterlife had been laid out for the soon-departed: music, food, clothes, perfumes, even large pets. And they danced on, with grace and destination, as if speeding up their imminent departure.

Now he canted back his head, looked at the sky and thought about the long-lost past, and memory and truth, and how remembering was easier than believing. Memory was selective, weeding out horror. The horror of the very young who, mercifully, died young. Of men with faces like matinee idols expiring in galloping rot. And glamour girls whose families had sent them boxes of cosmetics. Girls who would die without profiles, noses gone, and chins. Thousands, so many thousands, each one horribly unique, as if individuated by mad sculptors, the idiosyncratic limb, hand foreshortened into knuckles, blasted feet, elephantine earlobes. Flesh like suppurating ornaments, lipless smile, eye sockets like scorched fat.

Street girls and debutantes and matrons. Teachers and beachboys and farmers. Beggars and the very rich. Some expiring swiftly. Others, who knew why? lasting twenty, forty, even sixty, seventy years. The decades weighed on them. Some patients had been intellectuals, knowing Greek and Latin. Some were students of Chopin, Brahms, playing their records over and over, listening, listening and weeping, because Art could enrich but not cure. Could not return them to the world of normal humans.

And yet, we lived with dignity. Perhaps we lived more vividly than they.

Who could match the passion of KimChee, Hawaiian-Korean, who had long declared her love for Duke. Dancing with him, she felt his chest, his arms, knew he was *konakona*.

"I hear you fathful to dat witch, Pono. But I wait for you, Duke, for when she *pau* wit' you."

Blind, eyes just empty, weeping sockets, a tattered wild woman, one hand always on her hip-holstered gun. Whether a man wanted her or not, KimChee would drag him out on the dance floor, her loafing bulk thrust against his frame, point her gun at him and rip his shirt off. (Who knew if it was loaded?) Dancing wasn't the kick it was for others unless she could feel somebody chest to chest, feel their hips and knees knocking hers. Sometimes she grabbed a blind man, the two of them lurching and banging round like barrels in a ship's hull. Or she'd find someone with a shriveled leg who'd pump her back and forth across the dance floor like wildly off-beat metronomes. KimChee didn't care. What she loved was music, motion, the pumping of another heart.

There were patients who could only watch, limbs so hugely bloated and disfigured, they were barely ambulatory, had to be carted and wagoned to the pavilion. There they would sit or half lie, crutches and canes beside them, their breathing loud and raspy. But some nights! some nights the songs rinsed away a little of the pain, intoxicating them. They would half stand, propped against each other laughing, and they would sway, waving their canes and crutches, like elephants rocking the tusks of their dead.

Dancers would cheer them, and dance on, dancing with all their hearts, as if the pavilion were a palette on which they wrung out all the beauty left in them, all the colors of grief and desire and madness that stained, splashed down. And they danced. Until music ran into exhaustion and night washed away. And in the dimness of near-dawn, midst sweaty, shredded clothes and lost shoes, they'd scavenge looks, tilt their heads a little closer to each other, run their listening down each other's breathing. Hoping. Hoping that this life had been a long, bad dream and they were finally awakening. Tenderly attentive, they touched their faces, and each other's, deep longing in their mesh to heal, to be healed, to tumble perfect back into the world. But what they felt and heard was only fraying, shredding and decay. A sweetish odor in the flesh, a tearing in the lungs. Some would laugh, turn giddy at their own lush wreckage, seeing their reflections in their partners' eyes.

While fatigued musicians packed away their songsheets, dancers' voices quavered, turning staticky, the fevered rush to pull apart, lie down in rooms without mirrors and sob themselves to sleep. Lovers who had been coupling on the beach dragged home and drew their curtains, men exhausted with the rush of sperm. And in the next room, women douched, splashing out that sperm. Blood that had driven their thighs now drove the brain. No children of *ma'i Pākē*, death was in the egg.

In the mid-1940s sulfone drugs brought a kind of cure for leprosy. But those already ravaged had no cure. Cratered faces, caved-in bodies, weak kidneys, lungs and hearts from years of medical experiments. Many chose to stay at Kalaupapa, having been too long outside the outside world. The staring gasps of strangers would be another kind of slaughter.

The orchestra shrank to a small band. And so, the band played on. Dance steps changed from Jitterbug to Cha-cha, then something painful called the Twist. Valiantly, they Cha-cha'ed, improvised a gentle hybrid called the Hula-Twist. Their numbers dwindled, large cracks began to mar the dance floor of the pavilion. Banyan roots erupted a whole corner of cement. The columns shifted slightly, seemed to list. And when they grew too old to dance, patients came to reminisce, sat beside the dance pavilion in their wheelchairs and laughed, remembering.

". . . Jitterbug Thaddeus, dancing till his shoes squished like galoshes, full of sweat. Jesusmaryjoseph!"

". . . And KimChee, dat blind, wild t'ing, aiming from da hip . . . *Auwē*! Life been long widdout dem."

The pavilion encapsulated for them what they had been allowed to know of youth, and grace, and dreams. And some nights, even love, the animal warmth of someone holding them, breathing with them, and into them. Life seemed to gain, subtracting more and more—friends, health, even memory. Some old-timers forgot their friends, forgot the long-lost spangled nights of dancing. But now and then, something out there near the beach, a columned structure, drew their gaze. And they would smile, not quite remembering. And yet remembering. A sobbing clarinet. Sequins winking on a dress. Moonlight on a young man moving like a matador. Couples spinning, aerial and haughty.

I'm the Sheik of Araby / Your love belongs to me / At night when you're asleep / Into your tent I'll creep . . .

Duke smiled, dropped his head against his chest, and dozed.

Her tension seemed to hold them together. When she was still, they froze. When she resumed motion, they seemed to breathe again. Mostly they gave her eager, frightened smiles, this woman, this majestic, loving, yet still intimidating mother of their mothers, who had, finally, rendered unto them their history.

She reached forward, tapped Toru's shoulder. "You driving like you're *pupule*."

Toru slowed the old Buick, glanced round the car at Vanya beside him, Jess and Rachel in the back, on either side of Pono, their hands all joined to hers like little girls.

He grinned. "Hey, I feel real *ikaika*! Finally gonna be another man in the house!"

"He is an old man," Pono said. "And what I am about to do may kill him. You should come with us, Toru. You're like a grandson to both of us."

Toru shook his head. "Not my place. I'll be waiting with the foreman, make sure everything's ready, workers clean, the orchards . . ."

Pono sighed as he wheeled onto Highway 19 for Keahole Airport. "The orchards . . . the land . . . yes! the land." She looked round at the others, each woman dressed carefully as if for church. "I hope all I've told you in these two days is not in vain. Freedom depends on possession of land. I can't impress that upon you enough."

"But, you have," Jess said quietly. "It all means something now. The house, the plantation . . ."

"Now? Only now, because you suddenly have a flesh-and-blood *kupuna kāne*?" Pono shifted in her seat, facing Jess, her old-fashioned picture hat blocking out the light. "How is it, Jess? You know so much. And yet you are naive. You think land means only trees and soil."

She pointed her finger at each granddaughter. "You and you and you. You are marching, fighting for our people, but while you look the other way, *haole* are creeping up your *holokū*!"

"What do you mean?" Vanya asked.

"In Kona they say my granddaughters are too 'high-tone' to tend the farm, that when I die, you'll sell it to the highest bidder."

Rachel shook her head. "Silly gossip."

"Not gossip! The foreman has been approached by real estate agents, whose clients, *haole*, want the farm. Disgusting dilettantes who own grape orchards in California, rich snakes who want to preen and pose as coffee growers in Hawai'i. They don't even wait until I'm dead. Local growers, rich competitors like the Sugai family, would love to own my orchards, consolidate it into theirs. But they would never sneak up while my back is turned. Only *haole* . . ."

"What did the foreman tell them?" Jess asked.

Toru laughed out loud. "Zakaria started carrying his Remington, the one he's always polishing. The last real estate agent who came sniffing round asking if Pono needed money, Zakaria flipped his business card in the air and shot it into dust."

Laughter in the car, then they turned serious again.

"This man, your grandfather, I have died for him many times. Waited more than sixty years! Mother God, you girls are just rounding forty, and still don't know what love is." She stared from a window, wiped her eyes. "But he is not why you should love the farm, not why you must kneel down on the soil, keep breathing life into it, nourish it."

She paused, leaned back and fanned herself, then took a long, deep breath. "No one in history has ever respected those who did not own their *own* land. Do you know why, for a hundred years Hawaiians have been despised, kept in bondage, looked upon as only half-human by the whites? *Because our kings gave away our lands.* The *haole* charmed them, missionaries, merchants, beguiling the royals who traded our precious land for their books, their written Bible, their trinkets. Yes, the written word is powerful, but kings can make mistakes. And so, we paid. You girls know all this, but I am leading up to something."

Toru slowed, listening, knowing it was important.

"The land doesn't belong to us, you see. We belong to the land. So it ever was, even when we lived under a feudal system, long before the *haole* came. But this the *haole* cannot see. They use our land to adorn themselves. And so adorned, they delude themselves that they're superior. Hawaiians who are stupid and greedy, sell their honor with their land for easy money, then find whites laugh at them, think of them as low, lazy, without culture. For who would sell their land on these small, precious islands? And when they have our land, they teach us nothing by example, only to despise ourselves, take handouts, mortify our flesh with booze, the needle."

She hesitated, looked at Toru, then continued. "But—and this is my point—*haole* are becoming a minority in the world. So severe a minority they begin to look like souvenirs. They're threatened, out-smarted by Afro-Americans, out-manufactured and out-bid by Japanese, hated in most of Central and South America . . ."

Vanya looked at her in shock. "*Tūtū*, I never heard you sound so . . . informed."

"What do you think your grandfather and I have done for sixty years, just bill and coo? He is very learned, speaks three languages. He follows the news, discusses it with me, beats issues into my brain. He believes, and I agree, it is very late for white America. They're frightened, looking for new victims, so they have turned back to the Pacific, preying on *old* victims, small island nations like Micronesians, and, yes, even Hawaiians. We are the little men who aren't really there. You see, they don't fear us, because we are *too small to be assessed*. All they have to do is keep us in our place. They do that by buying up our land."

As Toru approached the airport she sat up, imperiously arranged her dress and hat. "I'm exhausting myself. What I am saying is: sell the land, you sell your souls, you will damn yourselves to slavery, and keep the whites in power."

Inside the terminal at Keahole, they sat waiting to board, watching husky Hawaiians load luggage onto baggage ramps. Arriving tourists smiled at their dark, muscled bodies, handsome, full-featured faces, the ease with which they lifted things of bulk and weight. Departing tourists took snapshots of them.

"That's how they see us," Pono whispered. "Porters, servants. Hula dancers, clowns. They never see us as we are, complex, ambiguous, inspired humans."

"Not all *haole* see us that way . . ." Jess argued.

Vanya stared at her. "Yes, *all. Haole* and every foreigner who comes here put us in one of two categories: The malignant stereotype of the vicious, drunken, do-nothing *kānaka* and their loose-hipped, whoring *wāhine.* Or, the benign stereotype of the childlike, tourist-loving, bare-foot, *aloha*-spirit natives."

They fell quiet then, hearing the boarding call for the thirty-minute flight to Moloka'i. As they droned over the Pacific, over the saddle-shaped island of Maui, Pono clasped her hands, cold and hard as ice cubes, watching her granddaughters staring from the windows, terrified. At Moloka'i, a smaller plane took them down the cliffs to Kalaupapa. And on this short ten-minute flight, they huddled near Pono, clutching her arms.

Time, she thought. *I have had so much time. But never time for pity. Mother God! Have pity on me now. I have spat upon a lifelong vow.*

Her breathing became a panting, because she wanted it to happen fast, be over. The landing strip, shocked look of patients who knew her, had witnessed her furtive, solitary visits down the decades, girls following behind her, short walk along the beach to the pavilion, to where he sat each day near clattering palms, the surf. His head turning. Cool indentures of his eyes. Then, slow comprehension.

He had been dreaming of his family, his mother and father, sisters, cousins, diseased, deserted, buried down the years. Only Duke left, in ruins. In the dream, he stared up at shadows all around him, the cliffs of Kalaupapa like huge columns of lost and wasted years. They moved in close, engulfing him, so that he lay, a human shell, watching them tumble down and bury him.

He woke with a shout, rubbed the chill from his arms, and saw the day was beautiful, air sharp and clear, the sun relentless. In the distance, teeming jungle, and far above, polished mosaics of cliffs, his cliffs, familiar, safe, benign. He sat back, marveling at nature's intelligence. Wind blew, and grasses bent. Rain pattered down, and flowers yawned their thirsty throats. Evening fell, and buds closed. Even the air seemed intelligent, changing its temperature with the time of day. He felt immensely wealthy. Interior things were breaking down, lungs, and heart, but he was still in possession of his five senses.

Then reluctantly, he went back to his dream. And he thought how a family could not live if it did not evolve, how it would exhaust itself, come to the end of its curve. How the living family needed the guidance of the dead, that Mother Tongue whispering ever in the genes.

But no one guided me. My family died in shame and silence, here, hidden from the world. But for Pono, our blood would have died with me. Our name. Our history. Gone. Without a footprint. Who would know that I had even passed this way? Now I am growing weak. What will become of her? Milimili Pono . . .

Thinking of her, he spun round and round in his chair again. Only his stubbornness and bad temper kept doctors from declaring Duke bedridden. Instead, they gently humored him, imagining one day a nurse would find him expired in his wheelchair on the dance pavilion. In the evenings, they brought him dinner trays with legs that balanced over his lap, so he seemed to be sitting under a bridge piled high with bland foods, pens, books, newspapers, most of which he ignored. All he wanted now was to sit out on the pavilion, to reminisce, hold Pono's hand, behold her wondrous face.

She seemed his only sustenance. Her touch still energized him. He loved her so intensely, still, when she was gone, her mouth remained on his mouth, her hand in his hand, hot like a wound. And some nights he would press his hand, imprinted with the heat of her hand, against his body, his member, unamazed when it became erect.

Everything breaks down but desire. And because we're old, doctors try to shame that out of us. Young punks! Lose one's youth, and doctors take it as axiomatic that you've lost your mind, your balls.

He chuckled, sighed, thought of Pono's luscious breasts, giving way to gravity, but still beautiful, hips still embraceable. Only Polynesian women could still incite desire in old age—their slow grace, fluidness in hands and hips, a certain golden tone of skin, and laughter, sly laughter—rendered them ageless, disturbing. And Pono was even more exceptional, had always been a beauty, taller than most men, mysterious and proud.

He leaned back, thinking of their youth—Pono just a frightened, slender girl when he had found her. But he had found her in another form, fin just diminishing, disappearing, sandpaper skin fading from mottled gray to golden. *Shark, the genesis, the destination, of our souls. It only enhanced her in my eyes. That's why she loved me. I was not afraid.*

"Pono," he whispered. ". . . who came to me from the sea."

He sat up startled, for she *was* approaching him, the sun against her, so that she seemed a faceless silhouette, coming closer, rising from the sea. He shook his head, sure he was dreaming.

"Pono. Is it you?"

"Yes, Beloved." She stood stark-still, feeling everything suspended, frozen in place—horses in pasture, confetti of gulls against the cliffs. Even the sea behind her seemed to hold its breath.

His face lit up with happiness. He spread his arms. "Is it time? Third week of the month? Oh, my darling. Come close."

She moved mechanically in slow motion. But, up close, she was shocked by changes wrought since last she had seen him, barely a month ago. Among the twisted scars and wrinkles, his big face was still handsome; wild Mephistophelian eyebrows gave him a look of mischief. But cataracts had thickened so now he had a gaze almost cloudy and benign. Bones from his big shoulders had stepped forward, so flesh hung from his upper arms. His posture had changed. He slumped in his wheelchair now, a tired child.

She rushed forward, hugged his head against her breasts. "Duke, what has happened?"

He shook his head and sighed. "No appetite." Then tapped his heart. "Sometimes there's pain. But seeing you, smelling your perfume, still makes the pulse race. Feel!" He pressed her hand to his chest, then looked at her again. "You're all dressed up. Where have you been?"

Self-consciously, she removed her picture hat. Took off her Sunday "toepinch" shoes and sat at his feet, looking round the old pavilion as if trying to memorize it. Out in the waves, a lone canoer rowed slowly toward the Orient.

"Duke . . . oh, Duke." Her voice was like a child's, small and begging.

"You grieve, I know, for Ming. And I grieve, too. Daughters I have never seen, Emma, Mina, gone. Edita, Holo, silent, unforgiving. Now *their* daughters going . . . life subtracting one by one. And I have only photographs." He paused. "I have lived my life in shadow. I have kept you in the dark with me. And yet this life we dreamed, this life we improvised, has been richer, deeper than any I could have imagined. Please, don't be sad, Beloved. Here, lean on me. Tell me all the news, where you have been."

She moved closer, dropped her head against his knee. He could feel her body tremble like something combustible. He reached down, removed her hairpins, tenderly undoing the long luxuriant coil of gray hair wrapped round her head. It hung, a thick shawl, billowing about her. She looked up at him like a blind girl, eyes flying round helplessly.

But when she spoke her voice was cool and neutral. "I have . . . broken a vow. A sacred vow between us. When I tell you, you might hate me. Cast me away."

He leaned back, vertebrae exploring the crooks and deviations in the wheelchair. As she continued, he grew still, as still as he had ever been.

"For years, two generations, you and I denied our blood, our daughters and their daughters. We rendered them invisible, moving like ghosts through all their days. You and I are fading, Duke, our bodies, our vision. 'Aumākua will soon take us by the hand. But there is in me now, an obligation, a white furnace. It burns so bright, it melts away all fear. It is the need, the moral need, to mingle blood with blood, touch flesh to flesh. I have broken my vow to you, in order to keep a vow to Ming."

She took his hands, held them to her breast, weeping softly. "Oh, Duke. We have so little time. There isn't time for pride."

His voice seemed to come from another dimension. "Pono. What are you saying? What is it?"

She saw them in the distance, hovering on the beach behind him, and realized for the first time that they were all in white. They huddled close, then moved apart, like virgins, nurses, acolytes.

"Mother God, help me!" she whispered. "I have brought them here to Kalaupapa. Your daughters' daughters. They have come to meet you."

And all across the settlement, across that lone peninsula, they heard his scream. The tortured scream of shame, indignity. The scream of generations. Of people mutilated, cast out of the world. It was a cry for mercy, a cry of rage. A cry for all the voiceless victims lying in their graves. It was a wish to run, to die.

Duke struggled to his feet, insane. He thrust his hands out, pushing her away, took one step forward, then another. He swayed, feeling meager strength desert him, staggered backwards, collapsed in his Amigo, hid his face and wept. Deep within him something rolled into a ball, trying to shrink, to hide.

Half blind. Ears twisted like green peppers. One hand clawed. One hand gone. Toeless feet. Legs cratered nightmares. Scarred. Twisted. Humped and wrinkled like an ape. I am what normal people pay to look at.

They came up the slope, a surge of white that paused, unsure. They studied him, what they could see—shirt soft and faded as old dollar bills, broad shoulders of a man once built like an athlete, handsome head of white hair ruffled by the trades. He was sobbing, face down in his hands. Pono knelt before him, whispering, whispering. Finally, she raised her head, nodding for them to come closer.

They floated forward, silently. And then they stood behind him, panting like young animals who'd run themselves out. He sensed something, sat up gasping and tried to wipe his face. Then, painfully he turned his head and stared, a wide-eyed calm like something cornered. They didn't gasp, didn't look away. They held his gaze, each one, looking deep beyond the scars, the mutilation, looking deep within at who he was, and who they were. They smiled, holding out their arms.

"Grandfather."

And it seemed as if the cliffs around him parted, finally releasing his life to him. Watching them surround him, fall on him like children, wreathing him in *lei*, Pono stepped back. In that moment, he belonged to them.

No crowds greeted him. In Kona District there were no parades. He came home as he wished, anonymous, a stranger in a wheelchair. But seeing the old Buick at the airport, the one he bought for Pono in the twenties, the same dents where she had banged it with a hammer, he wept behind his sunglasses. And meeting Toru, embracing him, his only "grandson," he wept again. And driving through old coffee towns, past ancient tin shacks, the old Aloha and Kainali'u theaters, smelling upcountry smells of coffee cherries, charcoal smoke and frangipani— riding backward through the landscape of his youth—Duke was very still.

Then sliding down Napo'opo'o Road, he saw far below Kealakekua Bay glittering blue and jade, and all around coffee orchards, and macadamia nut orchards, rows of avocado and papaya, outrageous colored flowers, all of nature rioting, a tapestry before him. And turning into the driveway, and seeing on the hill, the house, the same old rockers on the *lānai*, he let out a long, low cry.

Field-workers and yard-workers, neighbors and mill hands, lined the long driveway carpeted with flowers, a carpet so thick the car skidded a little. They stood quietly and bowed their heads. They had not come to stare. Many wept for friends and family, victims of *ma'i Pākē*, hunted down, banished to that place where they had perished. And when his car had passed on up the drive, people went back to their homes and sat in quiet rooms, remembering. And for that day, all the coffee towns of Kona were silent. Mills were shut. No dogs barked. Even doves in the guava trees were still.

Run Run stood on the *lānai* in real shoes, a new dress, so neat she looked like someone else. Hair netted, nails trimmed, face rice-powdered. And she was utterly composed. When they carried him from the car, she walked beside him, touching his wheelchair repeatedly, like something she was familiar with and dearly loved. They set him down in the living room, and he squinted at the sunlight, asking them to pull the shade.

Then he looked at Run Run. "I hope I don't scare you . . ."

She shook her head, ready for anything. Self-consciously, he removed his sunglasses, then looked up at her.

She hesitated, then ran to him, covering his face with sloppy kisses. "Look dis face! Look dis face! You still one handsome devil!" Tears streaming, she stood back, trying to regain composure. "Now. What I gonna' call you? Sir? Lord a dah manah?"

He laughed, drew her to him with his good hand. "I am Duke. Now. What you going to feed me, *tita iki*?"

For weeks, they sat beside him day and night, beside his Amigo, beside his bed, curled up at his feet on the *lānai* as he lifted his face to the trades. They touched him constantly, kissed his cheeks, wept into his hand, needing to feel him to confirm the reality of him. For the first time in years, Jess didn't hear the ocean, didn't miss the suck and pull of tides, arms whirling in her sockets. Vanya lost all need for motion, everything, all legal work on hold. Rachel could not be without him, sat outside his door when he was sleeping.

In the following months, they told him all about their lives, their work, their travels. And it was as if the man had journeyed all his life, knowing languages, history, art, up-to-date on politics, the madness of the world. He asked Jess about the homeless population in New York, about the Guggenheim Museum, about her work as a vet. He discussed with Vanya malpractice suits, the struggle of Hawaiians to establish sovereignty. He queried her on New Zealand Maoris, the Aborigines of Australia, fighting, like Hawaiians, to gain back stolen lands.

"You girls seem astounded," he said, "that I am up on things. Sixty years of reading papers, listening to the news, I am a tome of information!" He took Pono's hand. "As for local scandals, your *tūtū* kept me up-to-date!"

He teased her, regaling the women with memories of Pono as a young girl. Her secret healing herbs, her addiction to the sea. "Always out beyond the reef with giant octopi and dolphin. How she loved storms! When there was thunder, I had to tie her down." He looked at Jess. "You have this ocean-love in common."

He told them of Pono's boredom in the kitchen, always begging Duke to take her to Manago Hotel for "good kine pork chops." How she had learned to love champagne, and waltzing. He showed Toru how he had made swim goggles for her carved from sturdy *hau* branch, how to make fishhooks from sea urchin spine, and how lava made good squid-lures.

Seasons changed as day after day they wheeled him through the house, room to room, filled with old *koa*, monkeypod, teak furniture all carved by hand. Sometimes he would drift, remembering sunlight trembling on a silken dress, his mother at a window. Lip-prints left on old Venetian goblets. Tradewinds turning pages of his father's books. Sometimes he pulled volumes from library shelves, pages crumbling in his hands.

"Termite fodder. The fate of genealogies." He sighed. "Well. You girls will carry on. Blood continues in the life of the soil. And you have given life to this old house."

"No, Grandfather," Rachel said. "It's you. Workers in the orchards say the house seems to vibrate now that you are home."

And it was so. The place echoed with his deep baritone laughter. After so many years as the brooding backdrop of the plantation, the house now seemed to step forward, the white center, the pivot of all these lives, repository of all the years of toil and rancour and longing. Walls seemed to glow as his strong male scent wafted through each room. Even the sound of him urinating in the john—copious, percussive—rang through the house, his whistling as he flushed, like that of a young boy piping down the halls, keeping the place astir.

At night the women gathered on the *lānai* beneath his window just to hear his loud, protracted snores. And in the mornings, they sat breathless, waiting for the loud thump of his feet hitting the floor as Pono helped him from their bed. And then, the ceremonial huff and strain of his slow descent downstairs to breakfast, the cousins lined up waiting at the doorway as he kissed them each and took his place at the head of the table. And the quiet solemn moment before eating, moment of thanks to Mother God, not for food, but life, this miracle. And then the sweet ballet of shared blood sharing bread.

One night, Duke saw Vanya and Toru talking in another room. Later, he called her to him.

"You are very talented, my child. And beautiful. Much like your *tūtū*."

She snuggled close to him on the *hikie'e*, loving his scent, peculiar mint odor of medication and the sharp clean smell of salt, of a man who had lived for years beside the sea.

"*Mahalo*, Grandfather. Run Run, too, says I favor her. But she and I . . ."

"I know." He patted her arm, kissed her forehead. "She talked for years. I listened. You are so much alike. She saw her stubbornness in you, knew she would never quite control you. Each of you disturb her, because each of you carry different traits that are all part of her."

Vanya joked. "You mean she recognizes how impossible she is!"

Duke laughed. "Ah, the energy it takes to love such a woman. A man must be half mad." Then he turned serious. "Vanya. I know you and Toru are involved in . . . many things important to our people. Things that may be dangerous. I applaud this. I admire you. But I suggest one thing. Before you do something irreversible, ask yourself how can you best serve Hawaiians. Working with other legal experts, representing organized reform groups? Or joining up with renegades, angry activists impatient with the system?"

She started to respond. He raised his hand. "I only ask that when you are alone you look in a mirror. Examine what you see. Ask yourself what is your true motive. Maybe you need something louder than the system. Maybe violence is really what our people need. We have never been that good at words. We have only had a written language for two hundred years. But, think, *keiki*, only think. What you do will be irreversible."

She wrapped her arms round his scarred and mottled neck.

"I have known for years what my mission is. You see, Grandfather, I have nothing left to lose. My boy . . . he looked like you. A carbon copy . . ."

Duke nodded, stretched and unstretched the crippled fingers of his hand. "When Hernando died, I screamed like a woman. For years I mourned, kissing his photograph until there was nothing left. Dust, damp with tears. Loss seems to be our legacy. Grief. And loss."

"He died believing in something," she said. "Even so young, he had ideals. His friends say he was murdered. That the U.S. Navy wanted to make an example of people fighting their bomb-testing on Kaho'olawe."

"Don't live with that thought in your heart, Vanya."

"But, he was an excellent swimmer, better than any of the others. And the sea was calm that night. The shore was rocky, so they anchored their boat at a distance and were swimming to the beach. They say something pulled him down. He fought it. It wasn't a shark, there would have been blood. He would have screamed. There were Navy boats around that night, frogmen waiting for protestors. It was random, Hernando just happened to be the one they caught."

Duke moaned, knowing what she said could be true.

"Now the Navy is returning Kaho'olawe to our people, so perhaps my son died for good cause. But please understand, Grandfather. I cannot digest this anger. Whatever I do, I have nothing left to lose."

Several nights later, Toru pulled up in the driveway, called Vanya to his truck, and handed her an envelope.

"That has to get to Honolulu. Someone wants it up front."

She looked inside, a certified check for $10,000.

"Something's brewing with her," Rachel said.

Jess shook her head. "She has work obligations. Everytime Vanya ignores you, you think she's expressing hate."

"I know she loves me. She just can't get inside me. It disturbs her." She stroked the moist flesh of a mango as if it were something conscious and undressed. "*Tūtū*'s life now revolves around Grandfather. She leaves Vanya alone. Vanya doesn't have to defend herself, so she has more time to torture me."

Jess felt something tearing loose in her. "Rachel, stop it, stop it! Whenever Hiro's trips turn into long, extended journeys, you go *pupule*. Look what's happened to us. We have Grandfather now. We have pride, knowing who we are. Hiro was your refuge, you don't need a refuge anymore. You were his plaything. You're *not* that anymore. You're a woman over forty. How can you put up with a husband who deserts you, and deserts you?"

Rachel turned her perfect face to her, and in the sunlight Jess saw little crow's-feet gathering.

"Yes," Rachel said. "Look at me in sunlight. Little cobwebs edging the eyes, a thinning in the lips. I have a mole growing hair. Who else would want me now? Have you never learned, Jess, the comfort of ... habit? Addiction? Ming understood so perfectly."

She drifted from the room and closed the door. Five minutes later, she returned. "I've slept beside him, smelling scents of other women. He slumbers in my thighs, calling out their names. Children, really. I've seen their photographs. I begin to feel motherly, concerned. Are they healthy? Does he pay them well? Tell me, Jess, is that age? A lessening of desire as hair lengthens in the mole? Or have I found morality?"

Jess caught her breath; Rachel had never talked so confessionally. Her voice turned soft as she replied. "All I know, cousin, is that you're missing out on life. The one Hiro built for you is a decoy."

She stood still, thinking. "Perhaps. Perhaps. Grandfather says I must learn to close the five doors of desire. I must memorize the blending of the elements of incense."

She drifted from the room again, and Jess sat back thinking how all those years she had believed Ming was the enigmatic one, the mystery. Ming was ill and found escape. There was no mystery. It was Rachel all the time, the riddle, the wavering equation, impossible to fathom.

Dog That Travels
the Rough Seas

SHE STARED AT THE CORPSE OF A CAT floating down the Ala Wai Canal. A
haole approached in ribald-colored cycle shorts, a baseball cap, and zoris.

He stood so close, his breath blew on her cheek. "What's the magic
word?"

She turned and walked away.

He ran after her. "Just kidding. I forgot what I'm supposed to say."
He shoved a package at her. "Here. It's shatter-proof. You got the
check?"

Vanya hesitated. "Are you Toru's . . . connection?"

He looked around, nervous. "Time is money. Where's the check?"

She handed him an envelope.

Now she sat in her house in Honolulu, staring at the package. First
step away from the known perimeter. Several more steps, and things
would be irreversible. She thought of her son, Hernando. Would she be
doing this if he were alive? Or was it temperament? Was she a woman
who would always go against the wind? She sat there brooding for a
long time, then something moved, something alien in her landscape.
Looking across the room at a mirror on the wall, she saw her reflection,
and that of a man sitting in a nearby chair.

He stood slowly, switched on a lamp, his face gaunt, hard, paleness accentuating the auburn mustache and hair. He faced her as if curiously empty of emotion, his manner quiet, almost courtly.

"Simon. What are you doing here?"

"Let's say my life took a turn without my knowledge."

She switched on another lamp. He hadn't shaved, his beard was pushing out, orange spikes that made her think of sparks from axes on a whetstone.

"What do you want?"

"Look, Vanya. I didn't mean to . . . coming here like this, I suppose I'm out of line. I just don't seem to belong where I come from anymore."

"You don't belong here, either."

"I belong with you." His voice changed, verging on belligerence. "And don't give me that bit about animal lust. It's something else. Something in you I don't have. Something that, when I'm with you, makes me feel a bit of all right. Christ, I don't know. I've missed you."

She walked into the kitchen, flicked a switch, filled a kettle with water. "There's no room in my life for you. If you need healing, find a nurse." She turned on the stove, keeping her back to him. "Find a woman who'll mother you, screw you all the way back to your youth in the Outback. That's what you want. Innocence. It's what we all want."

"You can stand there, saying you feel nothing for me, haven't thought of me one second? After what we had?"

She slammed the kettle down and faced him. "You . . . do . . . not . . . belong . . . here. I don't want you here!"

"Because I'm *haole*? The face of the oppressor? Because I was, as you say, a hired gun? Or is it that you can't stand how good I make you feel?"

Something happened to her face, it seemed to pulse with rage. "Listen closely. I have seen my grandfather, a man I didn't know existed. I've sat for days with my arms wrapped round him. He's a leper, crippled, scarred. Banished, hidden away for . . . *sixty years*. They hid them all away, thousands upon thousands, until they died. Slowly and horribly. Oh, its curable now, no longer contagious, they've given it a pretty name, Hansen's disease, as if someone *donated* it. It's robbed us of family for almost two hundred years. Outsiders brought us that disease. And syphilis. Smallpox. In return, they stole our land. And *still* take our land. You're an outsider. I don't want you in my life." She paused, caught her breath. "Anyway, times are a-changing, as they say. There's going to be a little payback."

He backed into the living room, sat down in a chair. "What do you mean 'payback'? That's not a word in your legal lexicon."

"I'm not speaking as an attorney."

"No. You sound more like a . . . mobster. A terrorist."

She came and stood before him. "There are certain instances when terrorism is imperative."

"Vanya, what are you up to? Nothing you do will be as effective as what you can do for your people through the legal system. You're a role model for Hawaiians. You're what they can achieve. Don't fuck it up, don't demoralize them."

"Simon, I've worked for years and look at me. I still represent people who are faceless, landless. We *have* no moral agenda."

"Sounds like someone's gotten to you. You're not thinking clearly."

"Thought's a luxury."

"Look. Hawaiians are a small, small group. In ten, twenty years, you'll be almost totally assimilated. You know that. And most of them welcome progress. Fast cars, fast food, VCRs. So, what is it you're fighting for? What do you really want?"

"We want back our *land*. We want back our *seas*. We want to be visible. We want tomorrow like today. We don't want foreigners telling us what we *want*."

He reached out touching the hem of her dress. "You know, you're like those Amazons who cut off their breasts to better bend their bows. You want to live life on the jagged edge. I promise you, there are better ways to handle grief. Ways that would make your son proud."

"Don't mention him. Get out. Get out!"

He stood, respectful, keeping a distance. "I'm not going anywhere. You see, I've burned all my bridges. Chucked the heli job, told them where to stuff it. Gave all my gear to Digger in the Kakadu. I'm a dog traveling the rough seas. You're the end of the road for me. Use me, Vanya. I want to be in your life."

"You mean you want to fuck me."

"No! Not just. I mean, I want to be beside you. I want to be the one who listens. Maybe if someone takes the time to listen, you won't throw yourself away. Forget the color of my skin. Use me. Let me keep grief from taking one more bite out of you."

She turned away, exhausted, saw the package on the table and moved toward it instinctively, half stumbling. Simon picked it up, started to hand it to her.

"Get away from that!" she screamed. "Don't touch it."

Her voice alerted him. Gently, he shook the box, then sniffed. "Jesus
. . . Christ."

"Put it down, Simon. Please."

"You silly, silly bitch. What have you gotten into? I know cordite
when I smell it. Who's assembling this stuff?"

She sat down, absolutely silent.

"Talk to me!"

". . . Locals who work with explosives in construction and demoli-
tion. And vets . . ."

He shook his head, laughing softly. "Hardhats. And dropouts."

"My cousin, Toru, was a bomb expert in 'Nam."

"Toru, the ex-junkie." He shook his head again. "Vanya. 'Nam was
twenty years ago. Don't you see, these guys are amateurs, they probably
remember just enough to blow themselves to pieces."

"It's too late now."

"What are they planning to bomb?"

"I can't tell you. I don't trust you. How do I know you're not
working for them? How do I know the military didn't send you here?
That's what you're expert at, spying. And killing."

He hung his head. "I know how costly trust is. I know what betrayal
is. Can't you forgive someone their past? I beg you, trust me."

"I hate that word, it's sentimental and dangerous."

"So is love. If you can't trust someone who loves you, who will you
trust? Now, tell me. What are they planning to bomb?"

She looked down, shook her head. "Hotels, mostly . . ."

"When?"

"January, the Centennial. The Hundred Year Memorial to Queen
Lili'uokalani. In 1893, U.S. Marines came in with fixed bayonets. Whites
forced our queen from her throne. They stole our kingdom. We were
illegally annexed."

"I know the history. Be grateful it wasn't the French. Or the bloody
Dutch." He looked at her for a long time. "Sweetheart. Don't do this."

"Too late. Too many people involved. Groups on every island planning, selecting sites."

"How many *haole* do you plan to kill to make your point?"

"None. We just want to make a statement. Let the world know we
exist."

"Oh, dear girl. You are so naive." He sat back in the chair, closed
his eyes as if praying. "I thought I left all this behind."

"You have no place in this," she said. "This is not your business."

"Listen to me." He leaned forward, his face all frontal like a cat. "I was in Laos, Cambodia, as deep as you could get. The Falklands, Nicaragua, Argentina. They jetted us around like celebrities. Gave us fancy names. Elite Corps. Encounter Strategists. International military death-squads is what we were. We had a special appetite, you see, a craving, for guerillas, terrorists. We would stalk them, annihilate them. It was an art. Vanya, once you get involved, the day you fire that first bullet, pull that first grenade pin, you're a fugitive. You'll spend your life running, cops, soldiers, always on your trail. They'll follow you for years. They will sniff your excrement, run you down like dogs. Have you thought of that?"

She looked at him in shock.

"Everyone who knows you will be hounded, under constant surveillance. Your friends, family, your *grandparents*. Anyone who ever spoke to you. A local priest, a field-worker. They'll lose their jobs. Some will disappear. What will happen to their kids? Who will feed them? And, for what? Ego? Your picture in the news? Sure, people will march, call you a hero, a martyr. But nothing will change. Your cause is lost. It was lost the day you started trading with the white man. Bombs will accomplish nothing. Maybe kill a few tourists. And you will live a life of running."

She was silent, her face looked strange and bloodless. After a while she answered. "I've exhausted every other way. For almost twenty years I've tried. All that's left is this. I won't back down."

His eyes grew dark, he listened to a kettle screaming in another room. She turned it off, came back and paced the room, highly agitated. He stood up, reached for her hand, turning it over and over in his, her golden-brown skin making his look larval.

"I know you're not in love with me. Maybe one day. But part of you trusts part of me, don't deny it. What I'm saying is, if this is what you choose . . . I choose to go with you. I'll work beside you, teach your people what I know about explosives, assembling, detonating."

"They won't trust you. They won't accept you."

"Then, make them!" He rubbed his hand across his face. "Christ, I'm exhausted, been up three nights tracking you. It's late. I've taken a room at the Ilikai. I think I've given you enough to dwell on." Timidly, he kissed her cheek. "I'll see you in the morning, Vanya."

She held him back by his arm. "I need to know why. Why did you really come here? Why are you offering to help me?"

He looked at her, the dark, lush beauty of this woman, a principled anger in the eyes. He could smell her scent, even smell the change in her temperature. "You still don't get it, do you?"

When he left, she paced the living room again, still agitated. Then she touched the chair he sat in, as if touch would process the experience of his really having been there. A simple chair, upright, accommodating. He was gone, and if he never returned, that was all she had, a chair he sat in.

In bed, she tossed and turned, remembering his ginger hair brushing her shoulders, how it disturbed, then aroused her. She put her hand between her legs, touching, touching until she was very moist. Then driving, outdistancing herself, but when she had come and come again, and lay exhausted, she still wanted him. She moaned, sat up, leaning at a window, wondering if sex was just the body screaming of its will to live. Flowers pelted down, poinciana, pīkake, trees bent praying in the wind. *What has happened, that I can no longer pray?*

The phone rang very late, and it was Simon. "There was something on the news. Federal agents just busted marijuana growers over on the Big Island, vicinity of Hilo. You know, of course, the FBI has opened up a branch there?"

"I've heard rumors."

"Well, it may fit in with something I got on the military pipeline before I left Darwin. Outside Kailua there's a shop, sells Army-Navy surplus, you know, tents, boots, fatigues. Word is, it's a front for Army Intelligence." He paused. "You get my drift?"

"Not exactly."

"They're stepping up surveillance, Vanya. Too much happening on the Big Island, proposed spaceport, huge resorts, too many angry locals. Now, they've got both sides of the island covered, Hilo, and Kailua." He paused, thinking. "Actually, I'd be careful about conversations on the phone."

She hung up slowly, thinking of Simon, how he could help her, the possibility that he might really care for her. She turned her back to such possibilities, fell asleep reciting her long list of reasons not to trust him.

Ka Hale o Ka ʻIli

House of Skin

RACHEL LAY BACK ON A CHAISE, sunlight dappling her hand which held her grandfather's hand. He dozed beside her in his wheelchair, newspaper drifting from his lap. Beyond him, Pono sprawled, snoring softly in the porch-swing, hair flowing down to the *lānai*. It billowed softly in the trades. Her beauty seemed to have stepped forward in the months since they brought Duke home. Lying there, head flung back, her cheeks were smooth, as if all the wrinkles had been ironed out. She looked like a young, native girl on a Sunday porch beside her lover.

A peacock strutted by, pecking at the ground, doves warbled in the guavas, and Rachel was struck by the brilliance of the day, feeling drugged from the sweet heaviness of pīkake and frangipani. She gazed at her grandparents, their faces played upon by light and shadow. In sleep, Pono's foot was touching Duke's foot, in turn his hand was held by Rachel's. Blood humming through each other, blending into one another. A breathing, dreaming tribe. She knew such perfect joy then, such completeness, the moment seemed a sacrament.

Yet Pono's movements, even in the past few weeks, had slowed, as if all the days of all the decades of summoning the superhuman strength that kept her life, her land, her secret intact, had finally taken their toll. Duke was home, she was allowed to rest.

Rachel sat up as if a bell had clanged inside her. She could feel each moment's passing, like electric shocks, knowing she could never re-create this wholeness, this magic, with anything of equal weight. She would have to learn the lesson every day: that, sometimes, all that will define a person—instill within them dignity and purpose—all the human answers, are frozen in a few moments, a few days, and all the days to come are just a looking back. She closed her eyes, stroked Duke's hand, tears drifted down her cheeks. *This is my childhood. It has come so very late. But, it has come.*

Later, when Run Run stepped outside, she found the three of them so deep in sleep—side by side, hands, feet touching—they looked like the newly dead.

She crossed herself, shook Rachel awake. "Da phone . . . somet'ing wrong wit' Hiro."

Rachel listened, could make no sense of it. Her cook, Fumiko, hated the phone, all "ring-ring, yak-yak," she complained. When messages were left, she wrote nothing down, remembered only key words. "Hiro . . . hurt . . . coming home." Puzzled, Rachel slowly climbed the stairs to pack.

While the driver slid her bags into a taxi, she sat with her head on Duke's shoulder. "I was so young when we married, so in need. I thought I had found my father, that being with Hiro would protect me from the world."

Duke spoke softly, caressing her hair. "Has he taught you wisdom?"

Pono grunted. "Taught her the ways of lowlife, *mizu-shobai!*"

Duke frowned at her. "Tsssk! Learn charity in your old age, woman."

"He taught me . . ." Rachel paused, giving it consideration. He had taught her to explore the many secret passages of lust, had taught her nuance, illusion, veiled suggestion. But he had also taught her to be sly, how to foil and disarm the world. He had taught her there was nothing more accurate than silence.

". . . He taught me how to listen to a person's voice, their implications, to look for the echo, not the sound. The shadow, not the light. Yes, Grandfather, he has taught me wisdom. And humility."

"These are important things, things a father would have taught you. Be grateful to your husband. There are many kinds of love." He turned to Pono. "Have you nothing to say to our child who is going to her injured husband?"

Pono looked away, smoothed her dress, looked back at Rachel. "Each night of my long life, your mother's feet have run across my heart.

Each day, your beauty, your generosity to others, leaves wet tracks on
my vision. Come here, *keiki*."

Pono held her then, like she would never let her go, this cub, this
orphaned one. "My bones will rock with pride for you, through all
eternity." She hugged her with such ferocity, Rachel wondered if her
grandmother had loved her most of all.

A taxi in the driveway of her house. A strange man standing on her
lawn. From the back, she thought it was Hiro, hair slick, ebony-dark,
slender waist, shoulder blades like drake's wings pushing through his
tailored suit. He turned, and he was young, he was no one she had ever
seen. Approaching her slowly, he bowed. Alarmed, somewhat confused,
Rachel motioned him through French doors into the living room.

He looked round at wealth displayed so subtly it could be missed
by the unknowing. But Hiro had trained him well. A soft austerity in
simple silk-covered couches and chairs. In an otherwise empty corner,
a solitary Menji vase, museum-quality. An ancient, nine-foot scroll embossed with gold-leaf characters hung from a wall.

"Ming dynasty," he said softly, looking at the scroll, his English
halting, but correct.

Rachel waited, as the cook served tea in tall glasses with jade straws,
cookies shaped like lotuses. She studied him before she spoke. No more
than thirty, extremely fine-boned like a bird, which gave him natural
elegance. Face flat, cheekbones wide, the amber skin of an Indo-Chinese.

"Where is my husband? What has happened to him? Who are you?"

He looked at her, puzzled. "I understood you had received the
message. From the U.S. Embassy."

She shook her head. "I know nothing. They never reached me. My
cook called, told me Hiro was hurt, and coming home."

The young man dropped his face in his hands, began to sob. "Master
. . . is dead!"

Rachel stared at him, his dark head reflecting iridescence of a
sunbeam. Hiro was due. He'd soon be home, roaming the house calling
out "*Hai!*" Even if he was dead, he'd soon be home.

When her voice came it was husky, almost male. "What did you
say?"

"Master is dead!"

"Don't use that word in my house. Stand up, please. Your name."

He struggled to his feet, still weeping. "Ban Somporn Chantai."

"Tell me what has happened."

He wiped his face, blew his nose delicately. "Master . . . Mr. Hiro was shot, in a gambling den in Chiang Mai." He began to weep again.

She couldn't move. It seemed wrong to move. She suddenly felt exhausted. She wanted to lie down on the floor. "Who . . . shot him?"

He looked up, frightened. "Gangsters from Burma, now called My-anmar. He was moving into their gum trade."

"Gum?"

"Poppy."

Opium. Heroin. She passed her hand over her eyes, thinking of Ming. "Where is my husband's body?"

"Honolulu Airport. You must have a mortuary sign for its release."

She always thought she would die when Hiro died. She would die without him. Yet, here was her heart beating along inside her ribs. *Maybe hearts are nearsighted*, she thought. *Maybe it thinks the man before me is Hiro, a younger Hiro.* He wasn't dead. Not yet. Even if he was. His death would come slowly, emerging in her shrieks at some dark hour when she accepted it. Her hands fell into pieces in her lap, yet her voice was calm, unnaturally calm.

"What is your role in all of this? Be honest. I will investigate you, anyway."

His eyes, so dark and earnest, filled her with inquietude. He seemed so fragile, so defenseless, she wondered how he came to know someone like Hiro.

"I was . . . some years ago, he came to my village near Chiang Mai, several hours north of Bangkok. He was scouting for young girls for his pleasure houses. I have . . . I had . . . three sisters, and he wanted them."

"How old?"

"Kim was thirteen. My father sold her. The others, eight and nine, were beauties. Mr. Hiro offered much money. My mother said too young, said she would kill herself. So, he took the oldest. And me. I was twenty then. Had been to Pali Introductory School in Bangkok, studying to be a teacher, but was called home when my father fell ill with tuberculosis."

Hiro's death—if he was dead—his life leading to his death, began to be an odyssey spiralling into other odysseys.

"What did my husband train you for?"

He looked down, then looked across the room. "At first, I was going to be one of his boys. The ones he dressed as girls."

She closed her eyes, at first she thought she had fainted. *How can I bear this? How can I bear myself?* She remembered all the nights Hiro had dressed her as a boy, bound her in delicate braided silk handcuffs, entered her stealthily, as he would a boy. Calling her boy-names.

"But I am clever," Ban continued. "I began to tell him stories, myths, our lives, our village. It was like Scheherazade—night after night I talked. He began to see how bright I was, see me in a different way. He took me out of girl-clothes, began to train me as an adjutant. He began to call me Son, the son he said he never had."

She gasped. *The child I never gave him. How could I? That was not what I was for. I was another kind of child, in endless rut. Who is that weeping? Yes, it could be me.*

"Oh, please don't cry!" he begged.

Rachel calmed herself, motioned for him to continue.

"He was good to me," Ban said. "And patient. But something happened to my sister, Kim. He put her in a pleasure house for sailors, gangsters. Men were very cruel because she was not beautiful. One day she hanged herself. She was my favorite and I ran away. Mr. Hiro found me, and promised me a better life. He gave me more responsibility, ordering his clothes and jewelry, dealing with doctors and examinations for the girls, while quietly learning the business-side of things. Shipments, delays, distributors. Yet, in my heart always the desire to finish my education, be someone respectable."

"And how did you get his body out of Thailand?"

"Paying the authorities, police, consulates, even people at the U.S. Embassy. No one wants to be involved. You see, he had done things for the U.S. during the Korean War, and Vietnam."

"Things?"

"Well, passing information. His connections through the water trade. In return, he said, no one interfered with his businesses. They turned their heads, gave him an open passport, anywhere he wished to go. But now . . ."

"Now he is of no use to them. And where did you get the money to pay off these people?"

"I have a modest bank account in Hong Kong."

"Yes. You are clever, Ban. And now you want a show of gratitude from me. Perhaps a large check?"

He leaned forward, clasping his hands as if in prayer. "I have something else in mind, though I fear it may shock you."

She sat back, wondering what more he could tell her, what more he could do to her. He had already made her different; she was no longer a woman waiting. There was no one to wait for.

He saw Rachel's apprehension. "Please. I am not an opportunist. Someday I am going back to school. I shall be a doctor. Yes, that sounds artificial and cliché, what every grasping Thai says. 'I want to help my people.' But, I am going to succeed. So, I must keep my conscience clean."

"What is it you are asking me?"

He looked round the room, and outside toward the spacious lawns, koi splashing in the pond, the gardener, the long, wide swimming pool. "You are not poor."

"Obviously." She crossed her slender legs with considerable composure. Yet her head swam. She felt extremely weak, knowing when she digested what this Ban had told her, she would shriek, her body would revolt.

". . . so you must have many connections. Immigration, the Board of Health. People who would help you."

A vision surfaced, Hiro in a box. She stood up almost screaming. "Please! Get on with it."

"I will give you all I own, all of my savings. I will start again from scratch, if you will only help them, sponsor them. You would save their lives."

She looked at him, confused. "Who? Who is so important to you?"

"My sisters! Men working for your husband, they have already bought them from my father. Only thirteen and twelve, they are already in a brothel. No rules, customers don't care. Only filthy signs that read CUSTOMERS REQUESTED TO WEAR CONDOMS. Men laugh! Our neighbor's daughter, they threw her out of the brothel when she grew too big. She came home begging with her newborn, both of them infected with AIDS virus."

Rachel sat very still. He was presenting her with too much reality.

"I don't know where to turn. My visa here is only for two weeks. I know no one else outside of Thailand."

"What do you mean 'sponsor'?" she asked.

"Buy my sisters. Anyone can buy them, men, women. Bring them here to Honolulu, give them work as servants, yard-girls, anything." He wept again, his fist hitting his knee repeatedly. "They are my life, my connection to this earth. They are beaten because I have made them promise to refuse men who will not wear condoms. They sit behind glass windows on a stage. Customers select them like a piece of fruit.

In six months, one month, one night! the wrong man will come, they will surely catch the virus. It's a terrible epidemic in my country, did you know?"

She could not believe what she was hearing, what he was asking her to do. "You want me to travel to Chiang Mai, to buy your sisters from these thugs?"

"Yes! If I were rich, I would buy them, take them far away."

"Why are you asking me?"

He looked at Rachel for a long time. "Because it is the moral thing. I have met others like you, wives whose husbands trade in girls, and boys, and drugs. The wives profess ignorance, pretend their husbands are international financiers, yacht and soy investors. But in their eyes I read guilt, terrible self-hatred."

Rachel pointed her finger at him. "My husband paid you with profits made from young girls. How could you accept it?"

"I worked for him to save my sisters. Now I am asking *you* to save them."

She stared at him, astonished. "I've never laid eyes on you before. How dare you come here, asking such a thing. Besides, I've never left these islands. I know nothing of the world."

"Yes," he said. "Living here in Paradise. No one starving, no one desperate . . ." His voice turned dreamy, as if in a trance. "Have you ever loved someone enough to take their life? I have thought of killing my sisters, so they would die clean. It would be fast, painless. Of course, I would then kill myself. Life is not so precious. Life is very dirty."

He seemed a young boy then, battered, lost. She wanted to touch his head like a mother.

"You are my last hope," Ban said. "Someone with power."

She had never thought of herself as powerful. She had only possessed the power of her beauty. A beautiful child. Hiro's child. One of Hiro's many children. *You filth. You fornicator. Pederast. You trafficker in slaves.*

"Ban, you say my husband is dead. I must be alone with this. If it's true, there are things I must do. There's a guest house here across the lawn. Kori-Kori will attend you. Go and rest for now."

"Please. Think of my sisters. They will be lost. So many of them lost."

Rachel watched Kori-Kori lead him to the guest house, then walked unsteadily into the kitchen. "Hiro . . . is dead." Like a paper doll she folded in slow motion to the floor.

She woke to Fumiko screaming, splashing thimbles of gin down her throat. Rachel gagged, threw the bottle of Bombay Sapphire against the wall, welcoming the shatter.

"Stop it! Or I will slap you." She said it in such a different way, cold, authoritative and controlled, Fumiko immediately stopped screaming.

She drifted in a dream from room to room. So much wasted wealth. She opened closets full of dresses in dozens, evening clothes, shoes arranged by color, by heel height. Some clothes she had never even worn. She entered Hiro's room, a monochrome of gray. So many suits he had had a wall removed and built a carousel, matching shoes beneath each suit. She tried to feel grief, tried to justify his sick and seamy life. She closed her eyes, and saw children posed behind glass windows on which were posted small fly-speckled signs. CUSTOMERS REQUESTED TO WEAR CONDOMS.

She sat by a window, full of dark speculations which turned to sober intricacies, rage tempered by sane reason. She returned to Hiro's room. On an old teak pedestal, under a crystal bell jar was an object he had highly prized. A perfect, pure white porcelain bowl from the Yi dynasty. It was serenely round, rounder than anything she had ever seen, so perfect that, leaning close, she felt it correct the shape of her eyes. The bowl had always instilled in her envy, malice; its perfection was what Hiro had wanted her to be. His child-bride, personified in this small, empty vessel.

She removed the jar, picked up the bowl, walked into his bathroom, walls and floor tiled in the flecked green marble of Renaissance palazzos. She fondled the bowl, such fine porcelain she could see her hand through it, could see blood pulsing in the blue veins in her hand. Watching her reflection in a mirror, she let the Yi bowl slip through her fingers, the sound on marble tiles mere tinkling that echoed and echoed, like temple chimes in ancient dreams. She shook her shoes free of slivers, turned, and left the room.

First, she placed a call to a Dr. Seko at Tokyo University. A man Hiro had consulted on numerous purchases: an antique yak fan from the court of K'ang-hsi, emperor of China, a preserved bound foot, hard and tiny as an inkwell, from the Manchu dynasty. Hiro had paid him handsome consultation fees, had endowed his pathology department in Seko's name, thereby giving the man enormous status. He was also celebrated in his field as one with hands of surgical dexterity.

Hearing her voice he gasped, made weeping sounds. He had already learned of Hiro's death.

"Yes," she said. "A tragedy." Then she told him what she wanted. "I will pay you anything. I know your expertise in such an art."

"Are you quite sure?" he asked. "It is such an extreme . . ."

"It would be the handsomest memorial to my husband."

Still he seemed to hesitate.

"It should not take more than a week to accomplish the first step?" she said. "You will have everything at your disposal, a car and driver. I will arrange a suite for you at the Royal Hawaiian. Anything you need or desire. Anything."

Finally, he agreed to come to Honolulu.

Next, she called Shiroshi's Mortuary and Crematorium in downtown Honolulu. The owner was *Yakuza*, a man Hiro had set up in business thirty years ago when he needed to dispose of small-time thugs. Mr. Shiroshi cursed the Burmese druglords who had killed his friend, promising revenge.

"Yes, tragic," Rachel said flicking paint from her fingernails. "Of course it's fitting that you handle the ceremony of final leavetaking."

"Honored. I am deeply honored."

"There will be certain tasks first. A Dr. Seko is arriving from Tokyo in two days. He will explain. I think he will need perhaps a week before the final ceremonies, a room at your establishment in which to work."

"To . . . work?"

He was silent while she explained the purpose of Seko's visit. After considering, Shiroshi sounded overjoyed, exhilarated.

"Yes. Fitting! Proper! We will send a car now for the body."

Lastly, she called Hiro's attorney. The man had not heard of his death, and when she told him, something happened in his throat, he sounded terrified. "What has to be done? Who has taken over?"

She knew he owed Hiro nearly $60,000 in gambling debts. "Don't worry, Lee. No one will come for you. I'll erase you from the ledger. But do not gamble anymore."

The silence was protracted; he was choking with relief. "Anything. Anything I can do."

"Call our accountants. Find out how much I'm worth. In liquid assets."

"Not on the phone, Rachel. I'll see you first thing in the morning."

"No. Tonight."

Several hours later, he sat across from her. "It seems last year he divested himself of huge blocks of stocks in his portfolio here in Honolulu. Investing in businesses in Hong Kong, Bangkok—the water trade. Profits of that whole empire—gambling casinos, liquor, pornography, the rest—are in banks in Tokyo, under corporate names. You'll never be able to touch them, Rachel. But really, would you want to?"

"No. Please go on."

He looked down at a page of figures. "His personal holdings here, securities, gold certificates, real estate . . ." He looked at her, apologetic. "I'm sorry. If he hadn't sold those stocks, there would be much, much more."

"Lee. Just tell me what I'm worth."

He glanced at the statements again. "You're his sole heir, of course." Then he wrote a figure on a piece of paper.

That night Rachel lay in bed, looking round the room as if she were a stranger. She shook her head from side to side, sat up, flung herself down again. *What was I doing when they shot him? The moment when his body felt the impact of the bullet. His tattoos—did they change color when he died? Will I have the energy to suffer if all of this is true?* Suddenly she shrieked, and could not stop. She was finally free of him; she was totally alone. Now she could go out in the world; she was paralyzed. She was widowed and rich; she was orphaned and damned. She shrieked again, the sound so frightful the young man, Ban, heard her from the guest house. He shivered, bowed his head, imagining her wrenched with shame and grief, not knowing the genesis of that grief was the terror of a child abandoned by her father, her lover, her judge and executioner.

Long before dawn, when it was still dark, Rachel rose, the crumpled paper in her hand drifting to the rug. She wrapped herself in Hiro's old kimono, embroidered silk of midnight blue, and softly, half-blindly, stumbled out across the lawn, lying down beside the pond, dropping her hand in the water. They swirled round, sighing, nipping gently at her fingers as she stroked them, his flower-patterned koi, the bravest of fish, who, when captured, face the knife without flinching. She lay there feeling tradewinds brush her cheeks, watching the ocean's skin take on a sunrise blush.

In her bedroom, a piece of paper shivered in the breeze so the figures seemed to resonate: "$27,000,000."

Toru arrived with Jess and Vanya, each puzzled by Rachel's lack of grief. No emotion whatsoever. Immaculate in black, she seemed serene, or drugged, a woman moving on a trolley. The wake was long, politicians, tycoons, museum curators, people Hiro had boosted through the years, each one indebted to him. Then there were the faceless ones, the men nobody knew. *Yakuza.* One hand kept inside their pockets, hiding the missing digit of a finger, they stood silent, expensively dressed.

Mr. Shiroshi bowed and bowed, unctuous, overeager. There was no window in the coffin, Hiro's face could not be seen. Instead, a large photograph of him had been placed on the wall above, on a sort of hanging altar arrangement. Directly beneath on a shelf, propitiatory offerings, uncooked riceballs, fruit, incense. Flowers surrounded the coffin. Crowds filed past, shook Rachel's hand. Some shook it too vociferously, Hiro's death unweighting them. There was no funeral ceremony. She made a large contribution to the Buddhist temple priests, preferring a memorial service in the future.

Behind Shiroshi's Mortuary was the crematorium, where guests were handed sticks of incense by attendants, which did not dilute the pervasive odor of charred human flesh. There was a period of ten minutes or so during which Rachel stood alone in a room with his coffin, saying farewell. An old Filipino cleaning woman opened the door and entered. Hearing murmuring, she started to back out, but curiosity held her. She moved closer and what she saw would haunt her dreams for years.

A beautiful woman dressed in black, leaning on an open coffin like a sailor leaning at a bar. She seemed to be laughing softly, joking with whoever lay within. The cleaning woman paused. People did strange things here: some buried their pets in king-sized coffins all decked out in baby clothes. One couple was married here, in coffins! Who was the beautiful woman laughing with? The old woman edged closer.

Hair stood straight up on her arms. She screamed, and screaming, fled the room, dropping her rags and pail, fled the mortuary, fled across a parking lot, and fell to her knees on gravel. Crossing herself repeatedly, trying to understand what she had seen. The beautiful woman leaning over, joking with what looked like a giant, skinned animal. What had once been pink flesh and sheer, glistening, yellow fat, had turned gray, shiny-hard and hideous. Yes, a giant skinned animal, surely not a human in that coffin.

Hiro's closed coffin was rolled out, Rachel walking soberly beside it. A small man in overalls standing before what looked like an elevator, shouted theatrically, "The moment of final leavetaking!" With no further ado, he pressed a button, which opened the door to the furnace. The coffin rolled forward, flames roared up, the doors closed behind. During cremation and final preparation of the ashes, the mourners were led to a room with tables laid out in damask linen, porcelain china, and crystal.

"He would have wanted it this way." Rachel said, as waiters served Dom Perignon, Beluga caviar.

People drank and ate copiously during the cooling of the ashes. Two hours later they ambled leisurely back to the main hall of the crematorium. There they were ushered into a room where Hiro's remains had been placed upon a tray. The heap of bone and ash was rusty colored, large fragments sticking up like coral. Beside the tray, stood a large jade urn and very large chopsticks.

Each guest stepped forward, gingerly transferring a piece of Hiro from tray to urn. A fragment of skull was so unwieldy Jess dropped it repeatedly, thinking she would faint each time it slipped through her chopsticks. Rachel finally came to her aid, picked up the fragment with her fingers, nonchalantly dropped it in the urn. When the last deposition had been made, the urn was sealed. Guests quietly departed as Rachel dutifully shook hands.

The last man she spoke to was Dr. Seko from Tokyo. "A beautiful job," she said. "Very . . . clean."

"It has been an honor. It will be a work of art." He took her aside. "Forgive me for this boldness, but your husband was a brilliant strategist, he did not make mistakes. I think he chose the bullet. You see, he was already dying, slowly suffocating. The tattoos. Ink toxins in his blood accumulating in the lungs, a common thing with full-body art. We discussed this many times. I understand he had prepared you."

"Yes," she said. "Though I should have listened more attentively."

He looked down at his slender hands as if they were jeweled. "Death is most beautiful when swift. In the end that's all that is remembered, how we die." He patted her arm. "As you saw, the bullet entered the base of the skull and lodged there. The rest of him was not disturbed. Curing will take a matter of months."

"As long as you need, Dr. Seko. Patience was something Hiro taught me." She shook his hand, watched him walk away, a *sensei* of decortication.

Later, at the house she poured small cups of sake for Toru and the others.

"How do you feel?" Vanya asked, still waiting for some show of grief, a little theater.

"Don't rush it, Vanya. Grief will come in its time." She sat back, speaking modestly. "Of course, Hiro left me everything."

"Including a new houseboy?" Toru gazed through the windows at a young man brooding by the pond.

"Ban. He worked for Hiro. I've extended his visa here. I'm thinking of helping him."

Toru smiled. "And what will he do for you?"

Her face grew pale. "My feelings are maternal. Hiro regarded him as a son, the child we never had. You see, I have desires now beyond the physical, desires that are . . ."

They sat forward, suddenly intrigued. Jess asked her in the softest voice. "Cousin, what is it you desire?"

"To learn." She saw their skepticism. "Did you think Hiro's death would stop my progress in life? I want to know about things. The thingness of things. I want to make up for all the years I . . ." She waved those thoughts aside for now. "As I said, Hiro left me wealthy. I want to do something for the family, for each of you. Tell me, what do you need?"

Jess shook her head, she couldn't think of anything.

"Come. There must be something I can give you!"

Vanya studied Rachel, as if measuring her. She glanced at Toru, and finally spoke.

"Bombs," she said. "More bombs."

Hiamoe Loa

Eternal Sleep

"SNAP OUT OF IT, JESS. This is revolution, not a bad mood."

Jess slowly shook her head. "Revolution is the overthrow, or renunciation, of one political organization for another. What's happening here isn't organized. It's chaos."

They were sitting on the beach, stumbling through that featureless zone of two humans trying to understand each other.

"This is America, Vanya. You can't . . ."

"Don't tell me I can't *this*, can't *that*. The politics of retreat are finished. You've seen what's happening in the Pacific."

Jess had to agree. Living here now, she saw in the papers and on TV tragedies that never reached mainland America.

"Look what's happened in the past ten years," Vanya said. "Assassinations in Palau, military coups in Fiji. Armored tanks, the killing of schoolchildren in New Caledonia. Perhaps it was all accelerated by the French bombing of the peace ship, *Rainbow Warrior*, in '85, killing that Canadian photographer. The point is, on a smaller scale, upheavals across the Pacific mirror what's going on around the world. Island nations are fighting back. Terrorism is now our Mother Tongue."

"How much good can you do?" Jess asked. "It's theater, bad theater. Blowing up hotels won't give Hawaiians back our land. Only sovereignty will."

"Jess. Listen to me. Achieving sovereignty will take eight to ten years. After that, bureaucratic paper-shuffling here and in Washington will take *another* ten years. Our people will still be waiting for their lands twenty-thirty years from now. Meanwhile our kids and elders will be dying from respiratory problems, from polluted milk and water, from drugs and booze. We've got to show the world we've had enough. This isn't protest anymore. It's war."

Jess looked at her like she was mad. "A dozen radicals pitting yourselves against billion-dollar business interests and the U.S. military. It's not war. It's suicide."

Vanya's lovely face turned dark, anger pulsing just beneath the skin. "Do you think I want to die? I want to live. I want to make a difference. I'm so tired of talking, pleading, compromising."

"Can't I change your mind? Can't I?" Jess threw her arms around her, rocking her. "For God's sake, we're nearing middle age. We have Grandfather now. Can't we be a family for a while?"

"Family." Vanya pulled back, studying her. "I used to hate you, because you could walk out in the world and fit. I'd stand in elevators, sit in classrooms full of *haole*, wondering if I'd get out of there alive. Do you know what that's like? That fear? The feeling you're no good because you're dark? No. You'll never know." She laughed, half joking. "You're only part-time dark."

Jess rubbed her wrists, remembering restraints on her arms and legs when the abortionist did what he did to her all those years ago which were just a moment ago because it never faded, never went away.

"White skin doesn't save you, not if you're a woman. I was never any safer in the world than you."

"Maybe that's all I'm fighting for," Vanya said softly. "A place where we can feel safe. I know we're doomed, dying out. Maybe I just need to show that we failed honorably."

"What about Pono and Grandfather? What you're planning to do will kill them."

"They know."

Jess looked at her in total disbelief.

"Accept it, Jess. Just accept it. Why do you have to *understand* everything?"

Jess was quiet then, looking at the sea, perceiving how it had its own dark rituals, creating, uncreating, tiny organisms dead in froth, others born in phosphorescence.

"Then . . . what can I do to help you?" she said. "I'll do anything you ask. I swear."

"Take care of them."

They gazed down the beach at their grandparents, mooning on a blanket like young lovers. Pono suddenly stood, galloping down the beach after Duke's Amigo as waves carried it into the surf. Duke rolled on his side, laughing uproariously, his handsome, broken face aglow.

Jess spent her days and nights with them, every hour they could give her. And everything Duke said seemed to define her, things she had never known, yet knew.

"I never thought my mother loved me. That made her very interesting to me."

"She loved you," Duke said. "But, maybe you were not enough. From what you say, she lived a life of penance. One can die of longing for a place. I know."

Things Jess confessed were said for Pono, too, giving her back parts of her daughter, Emma. "Mother was beautiful, and very sensitive. She was an artist, she painted, that's why she traveled so."

"She was the smart one, could have been anything." Pono shook her head sadly.

"She wanted me to be a surgeon, not a vet," Jess said. "She felt you were only a doctor if you dug down into the heart and liver, the real mortality of a human. Maybe I passed that on to Anna."

"I would have chosen . . . pathology," Pono said.

Duke teased her affectionately. "So you could raise the dead."

Jess tried to imagine her grandmother, *kahuna* of fluorescent corridors, charioting the high of sleep deprivation, wearing surgical scrubs, a beeper at her waist. She pictured her holding up a human brain, the delicate filigree and convolutions of a curdlike mass floating in her open palm. She pictured Pono talking that brain back to life outside its diseased body, jumpstarting the heart of another body that needed a healthy brain. She could do such things. Jess had seen her raise a field-worker with a crushed skull, transfer birth pains from wife to husband. She had cured a cancered pancreas by concentrating on the woman's urine. She had paralyzed a wife-beater by standing barefoot on his spit.

"Your life has been incredible enough," Jess said. "And I don't know the half of it."

Pono's expression turned cold, almost ferocious. "And never will."

"This *wahine*." Duke patted her knee. "Everything I know of her is only sometimes true! After sixty years I only know a part of her. That is shocking. And exciting." He winked at Jess. "Remember everything she's taught you, *keiki*. This woman is all that is superior."

Sitting at her feet, Jess moved closer to Pono, playing with a tattered *lauhala* fan on Pono's lap.

"That's what Mother said when she sent me here each summer. 'Pono will terrify you, but she will teach you how to keep from drowning.' " Suddenly she dropped her head. "She loved the sea! I never understood why she ended in the desert."

Duke shook his head. "Sometimes, child, we die in metaphor."

"My father loved her, but he never felt she was white enough. He used to lie, tell people she was only one-eighth Hawaiian. One day, in front of company I asked him what the other seven-eighths were. He made me leave the room. You see, he was panicking, she seemed to get darker as she got older . . ."

"So will you," Pono said. "The blood steps forth."

Duke straightened in his chair, threw his shoulders back. "You're also *haole*, Jess. Never forget that. You're hybrids, all of you. You're what the future is."

"That future scares people. My daughter, Anna, for instance. She thinks of me as 'part-dark' as they say down south." Jess shook her head, extremely sad. "Sometimes I wonder when love is too much? When is it not enough? I only know not loving leaves one poor. I gave her everything, trying to compensate for what she saw as my shortcoming. Or maybe, I was making up for what my mother didn't, couldn't, give— warmth, companionship."

"Things I never gave her," Pono said. She seemed to go into a trance. "She will come one day, your daughter, Anna. She will sit with you and ask about your blood, our history."

Jess grabbed her round the knees. "Oh, *Tūtū*, did you see this in a dream? How do you know?"

"Common sense. Mothers are the last riddle, the worst horror, the only consolation." *Mama handing me a pouch of pearls. "Leave. Go out in the world! We fear you. Your kahuna powers." Mama, I forgive you. I am loved, and whole.*

Thinking of her daughter, Jess covered her eyes and wept a little. Duke stroked her head, knowing she was the one Pono worried over most. The one least sure, lacking the unsettling confidence, the obstinate drive of Vanya, the beauty and indefatigable vanity of Rachel. Yet he suspected Jess was the one with physical genius. In spite of her slender build, she was the strongest of them all, with the durability of a balanced weight. He imagined, if necessary, she could be cruel, alarmingly so, to protect what was precious to her. There was so much of Pono in this one, they seemed to meld together, both having the rusty scent of ocean about them.

"Listen to me, *keiki*," he said. "Forget your daughter for a while. She will come in her time. Concentrate on yourself, for you have experienced upheaval and heartache, and changed your life round completely. You are retracing your mother's life, walking in her footsteps. This takes great energy and *koa*. But you have been moving much too fast, leaving parts of yourself behind. In your daughter, your marriage, in this man you mentioned, Mars."

Jess winced at his name. As if in response, Duke winced, rubbed his chest, as if something small had kicked him in the ribs.

"You must slow down, Jess, so that those parts of you may catch up. You must not brood, or your other selves will have no eagerness to join you. Look round, remember things you have forgotten. Names of flowers, birds. Learn new things. And when you have done that, shout out loud, 'LOOK! I HAVE LEARNED SOMETHING I NEVER KNEW BEFORE!' Remember the delight you felt as a child? This will make your other selves want to join you. It will make you whole again."

"And," Pono said, "you must spend more time in the sea. Eating from it, drinking from it. You have to let the sea know you are home so that it will begin to welcome you again. Seawater is still the best tonic, best cleanser. Three tall glasses every day. Once it is running in your veins, you will never drown, for you will have lost the fear of drowning. You will *become* the sea. One thing more, eat squid, plenty squid, good for muscle, brain. But no octopus, they are your cousins, very intelligent. And never, never shark."

At another period in her life, Jess might have laughed. Now she had re-entered an ancient realm surrounded by, therefore empowered by, the sea. She would respect its laws, abide by its legends. She understood Pono was passing on to her a legacy, part of which was Hawaiian respect for myth.

She recalled one summer as a girl, hunting octopus with tough kids from down Kainali'u way. They wanted to show her and Vanya how to tear octopus brains out with her teeth. Jess had watched as a lure attracted an octopus who attached itself, slowly climbing her leg, gently clutching her, its suckers leaving small white circles on her skin. She remembered something childlike, human, in the desperation of those slender arms wrapping round her so tightly, as if asking for protection.

Black eyes blinking steadily at her, Jess stared back, seeing such intelligence and intuition, her eyes filled with tears. She didn't want to rip its brains out. She wanted to hug the thing, and take it home.

She had surfaced in shallow water with the octopus wrapped round her leg. Yipping and shouting, the toughies started swimming toward her, spear guns raised. Slowly and deliberately, Jess bared her slender skinning knife, waving it at them, threatening to slice their cheeks off. Vanya swam over, stood beside her, cursing the toughies as they dispersed down the beach, calling Jess *pilau, hapa pupule*, waving their spear guns like commandos. She and Vanya had stood in the shallows, stroking the octopus's head like a puppy, calling it "dear thing," stroking until its suckers slowly loosened. With one of its arms, it patted Jess's leg repeatedly, almost affectionately, then floated off into the deep.

Now, Jess looked at her grandparents in the soft light of the room, and the room in the house and the house in the world in all the universe was liquid balm, a pool, and she had been dropped in the center.

"I am where I belong," she said. "Here, where you are, your voices together, talking, arguing. It means my mother didn't drop down from a star. It means no one was an orphan, that *Tūtū* had a life, a real life, all these years." She paused. "Why don't you two get married?"

Pono laughed so hard, her hair fell down from its pins. "I tried for years to snare him, give your mothers a name. He was too shamed. Afraid they would find out who he was. Now he wants to walk me down the aisle. Let him suffer!"

Duke shook his head. "She is my everlasting penance."

Pono holds him at night between her thighs, still amazed at his passion, his drive, loving him for the parchment sketch that remains, faint rubbing of the lust that was. Later, after he has ejaculated, shuddering and sighing like a child, there is sleep, a tortured sleep, his staggered-whistle inhalations, then exhalations, long, slow knives.

Duke sat up wheezing, eyes bulging, for the third night in a row. Weeks back, a doctor had examined him, found his heartbeat alarming, and tried to admit him to the hospital. He refused.

"Promise me, Beloved. You won't deliver me to them. I have died innumerably in institutions."

Pono promised him. And one night she woke up with a start. In a dream she saw two corpses, two familiar faces. She sat all night, holding his hand, knowing *way-finding* time was drawing near. The next night she walked from room to room, weeping, touching the faces of her granddaughters, remembering the years she had examined them in sleep, looking for telltale signs, sly suppurations of *maʻi Pākē*. She sat talking with Run Run all of one day, holding her while the old cook rocked herself and sobbed. One afternoon, Pono called Toru and walked him through the orchards, discussing coffee planting, fertilizing, picking, grading.

"You have always been my boy. Don't let this go to dust."

And she walked Jess up and down the beach, discussing her field-workers, their needs. One day she took Jess by the shoulders, looked her in the eye. "You will step into my shadow. You will fit."

Jess stopped dead in her tracks.

"Yes. You. The true *kanaka*, struggling all these years to get back to your blood. Did you think I was blind?"

Jess shook her head. "I thought you merely tolerated me. I never thought you loved me."

Pono brushed her words away, there wasn't time. "Now you must help the others, keep this family intact. Rachel needs to find herself, a task to verify her life; she is stronger than she knows. And you must force discipline on Vanya. Her cause is good, but she must stay within the legal system, not become a she-dog war-slut, living underground. What will that accomplish? And she has been in sluthood for too many years."

Jess stepped back, shock vibrating into fury. She stared at this woman who had scaled life with her teeth through sixty years of heart-break, mutilation, loss. And yet. For sixty years she had not been alone. Someone in a sad, cursed place had pledged himself to her. Through more than half a century, someone had loved her, had lived his life for her. They had had forbidden times.

What does she know, Jess thought, *of utter, total lovelessness? Of being faceless in the world? Of standing alone in middle age, totally exposed. She has had everything. We have had nothing.*

In that moment Pono pulled herself up to her full, epic height. Not seeing her pain and terror, seeing her only as superior and smug, Jess lashed out at her.

"Sailors, lepers, opium, spies ... with such a family history, how could we be anything but *sluts*?" She turned her back, walked away, and dove into a wave.

Those were her last words to Pono.

That night when there was nothing left, when Duke's chest pain was so intense, he couldn't lie down, couldn't sit, Pono knew it was time. While the house slept, she wheeled him to the car, lifted him slowly and clumsily into the old Buick, covered him with blankets, and eased down the driveway. He seemed half conscious during the drive, leaning against her shoulder like a child. She drove on Māmalahoa Highway for a while, past Captain Cook, Kealakekua, Kainaliʻu, Hōlua-hoa, driving back through their past, life lived in reverse. Finally she turned onto Highway 19, heading north toward the Kohala Coast. An hour later, as they approached the port town of Kawaihae, Pono took a sharp left onto a barely visible dirt road.

Duke sat up, fully conscious, eerily alert, pointing to a huge temple on a grassy promontory hovering over them.

"Puʻukohola!" He cried.

Puʻukohola Heiau. One of the most sacred of all temples, place of worship for Kamehameha I, The Lonely One, greatest of all Hawaiian kings. Also sacrificial temple for his enemies. Halfway down the hill was a smaller temple, Mailikini where commoners—artisans and soldiers— worshiped in times of war. Both temples overlooked a large body of water, Shark Bay, which, out beyond the reef, emptied into the sea. It was said, in ancient times Kamehameha I, would race from the temple to the bay, swim out, and call up his ʻaumākua manō, play and wrestle with them. Now the sacred bay was quiet, sharks dreaming in caves beneath the reef. Even Puʻukohola temple was quiet, no sleepless gods about.

"Where are we going?" Duke asked, his voice harsh with pain.

Pono drove the car under kiawe trees, where she had instructed Toru to leave a big, handmade canoe. She pulled the wheelchair from the car, lifted Duke out with almost superhuman strength and settled him in the chair. Muscles straining, she pushed the Amigo through the sand, until water lapped Duke's feet. Then she dragged the canoe from under trees out into the shallows.

He smiled, finally understanding. "Life has been full. Now we are going home."

"Yes," she said. "The way ancestors came. Crossing the same tracks that cannot be detected, but will be clear to those who know the way."

He was soaked by the time she settled him in the canoe, a blanket wrapped round him. She flung her head back, looked at the stars, lips moving rapidly, then heaved the canoe farther out. When it was deep, when waves lapped her breasts, she climbed in and started paddling. And all the while she chanted, softly at first, then chanting into shouts that bounded back in echoes. Suddenly, flames leapt up from Pu'ukohola Heaiu, a jagged bolt of lightning streaked the sky, searing their faces, stunning them. For a while they lay unconscious.

In that time, Pono saw them waiting, beckoning to her. "Ming!" she cried out. "We are coming. Emma! Mina! Wait, my daughters. Wait!"

And in her crying out, dream-seeing visions of the future came: Rachel, sitting on *tatami* mats, dressed in somber gray kimono, instructing foreign-looking girls in the Japanese tea ceremony. Then, the sound of bombs across the islands, Vanya stumbling through jungles, hunted like prey.

Pono shouted, last-wishing for this headstrong daughter of her daughter. "Run, Vanya! Run for all your days!"

She woke chanting, voices from Pu'ukohola Heaiu chanting back. Fires from the temple turned the night to day. She rose, pointing to the outlines of the heads, ancient chieftains in a row, attendants carrying *kahili*, tabu sticks, images held aloft on long poles. The walls of the *heaiu* were now lined with living dieties. *Kāhuna* in white tapa cloth held their staffs out to Pono, loudly chanting prayers. Chiefs rose from their seats on the row of stones along the outside platform of the temple, wearing crested helmets, patterned cloaks of red and yellow feathers. Now *kāhuna* chanted out her name, a sound that echoed all across the night.

Pono flung her arms out, chanting back, her hair a great cape floating about her.

"YES! I AM PONO! THIS IS MY HUSBAND DUKE WHO HAS SERVED YOU IN GREAT PAIN. WE ARE TIRED! WE ARE GOING HOME TO 'AUMĀKUA. WHATEVER *MANA* YOU HAVE GIVEN ME WAS NOT ABUSED. I LIVED FAIRLY. MY HEART IS PURE!"

In that moment, the earth shuddered, huge waves stood up on their sides, the temple belched great flames, turning the sky a circus of exploding fireballs. Instantly, the dieties faded, disappeared, and there were only flames. Their canoe had been swept into deep waters and, turning to Duke, holding him, Pono saw the temple fires reflected in the golden, glowing eyes of *niuhi*, huge, white sacred sharks who ate only the flesh of *kāhuna* and those of royal blood. They swam about the boat in lazy, graceful circles.

"Beloved," Pono said, "we are going to that deep, forever place. In eternal meditation, we will rock side by side, you and I, with our *'aumākua*. Now and then we will be touched by shafts of light which will be granddaughter-thoughts commemorating us. Through them our history will continue to grow, like hair upon the dead."

"Pono," he whispered, wrapping his tired arms round her waist, kissing her mouth, deeply, passionately. Then he took her face in both hands. "Think of it! There will be no time to rot."

They lay back like lovers, waves washing over them. Then *niuhi* ghosted in. Golden eyes. And fins.

Nā Kaikamāhine o Moaʻe

Daughters of the Tradewinds

THEY FOUND RUN RUN SQUATTING in Pono's room, staring at the huge four-poster bed, ominous for what it no longer contained. They couldn't budge her, couldn't make her speak.

"Where are Pono and Grandfather?" Vanya shook her almost viciously. "What's wrong with you?"

Jess thought she'd had a stroke. Her eyes weren't focusing. "Call Dr. Nori." She knelt in front of Run Run, peered into her eyes and took her pulse.

"No need foah doctor," Run Run whispered. "I like boiled peanut. Den maybe tell you what and what . . ."

Vanya brought her boiled peanuts in a bowl, then crossed her arms and sat impatient on the bed.

Run Run erupted, screaming at her. "Nevah yoah *ʻōkole* touch no moah dat bed!"

She went back to her concentration on one peanut, worrying it with her tongue like a parrot. Still, she wouldn't talk until they brought Toru. He entered the house quietly, looking neither left nor right. He climbed the stairs to Pono's room, stood very still, staring at Run Run.

"Pono and Grandfather have been gone all morning." Jess nodded toward Run Run. "She won't talk. Just sits there."

Toru knelt beside her, took her in his arms, whispering softly in Japanese. Softly, she answered.

He dropped his head, stifling a sob. *"Gomen nasai! Gomen nasai!"*

Run Run brushed her fingers through his hair and sighed. She motioned the others closer, until they were sitting on the floor around her. In the silence, they heard workers joking in the orchards down below.

"Basho-Gara," Run Run said. *"Basho-Gara."*

"Jesus Christ, speak English," Vanya cried. "Where *are* they?"

Toru sat up straight, looked at each of them. "It means . . . behavior in keeping with the circumstances. I think Pono and Grandfather Duke . . . are dead."

There was such silence, such shaking of heads. A disbelieving. And then a terrible keening resounding through the house, wafting through the windows, a sound like old Greek women dressed in black, in mourning. The need to stand, stroke the linens on the bed, press their faces to the pillows. The need to shake Toru, abuse him, make him understand they did not understand.

He looked at Jess. "You saw it coming, you said you could smell it, that ammonia smell of failing kidneys. You said you could see his heart failing in the blueness of his fingernails."

She nodded, dumbfounded. "I thought there was time, that *Tūtū* would get him to the hospital. My God, where are they?"

He sobbed it out. "Shark Bay! She said when it was time, when there was no more time, they would go. One night they would paddle home to *'aumākua.*"

Rachel knelt forward, banged her head against the floor repeatedly. She had seen the Buick after midnight, easing down the driveway. Now she made screaming, barking sounds, trying to articulate. *The moon was full. I thought they were going for a drive.* She could say nothing sensical.

"How do you know? How!" Vanya shook Toru violently, her face an ugly mask.

He grabbed her arms, like a man about to kiss her. "I helped them. She told me where to hide the canoe, under the kiawes, below Pu'ukohola. I went there every morning. This morning it was gone. The Buick was there."

Vanya hit him in the face with all her might, then threw herself upon him, sobbing. Their escalating screams took wing, wafted through the windows, rendering workers silent down below. Toru hugged Vanya until she calmed down. Then he sat down in a chair, took Run Run in his arms and rocked her like a child. They gathered round him in shock, in aspirating disbelief.

". . . they wanted to *make* together," he said. "Is it such a terrible desire? They were over eighty. The world kept them apart for over sixty years. The shock of being in a hospital, another institution, after six decades of it, would have killed Grandfather. They would have died apart. Can you imagine?"

Jess wept softly, holding Pono's robe to her face.

"Somehow she got him into the canoe. Then she must have paddled out." He wiped his eyes. "And then they slept."

"Maybe they're still out there," Rachel cried. "Lost at sea. Oh, Mother God. Let them be alive."

"Rachel, how can you?" Toru asked. "Isn't it better that they go in privacy and peace."

She sobbed out loud. "I wanted to tell them I have plans, to accomplish an important thing. I wanted her to be proud of me."

Vanya's voice was ugly. "Of course she was proud of you. You take after her. Everything she did was *desperate*." She stumbled, blind and brokenhearted, from the room.

Within hours, all of Kona knew. The grieving in the house was taken up by keening in the fields, and then the little towns. By evening, people lined the driveway and Napo'opo'o Road all the way down to Kealakekua Bay. There, crowds stood holding torches. Chanting went on all night, *kāhuna* spanking the waves with ti leaves as canoers paddled boatloads of flower *lei* out to the deep, calling out to *'aumākua manō*, asking them to guide Duke and Pono home.

Locals thought they had set out on their way-finding voyage from Kealakekua's shores, that they were sleeping in the waters of this bay. Only Toru and the others knew their grandparents had departed from Shark Bay, an hour north of here.

"Better this way," Toru said. "Let Shark Bay be left in peace, no crowds, no ceremonials. And anyway, it's all the same. They've gone home to the Mother Sea."

Through days and nights, they roamed the house like phantoms, disbelieving she was gone, waiting for her scent, her gaze, her sudden presence overwhelming them, turning them infantile. Vanya denied her grief, went on with late night rendezvous with locals, with boats carrying crates of dynamite making drops off Punalu'u, not far from Jade Valley Monastery. Rachel locked herself in her room, alternately sobbing and brooding over a crumbling sepia snapshot, her mother as a girl. Now the mother-link was dead, the girl was set adrift.

Jess's pain was articulated in the way she clung to Run Run like a child. "I insulted her, insulted our ancestors, told her we would end up *sluts*. Those were my last words to her. My God, I want to die."

Run Run shook her head. "No, *keiki*, you want *live*. Lissen me, you be strong, neh? My sistah gone. I no want live widdout my sistah. I need someone be strong, help me find out what Mot'er God plannin' foah me. No reason keep me goin' widdout plan." She wept a little. "Pono give me pride, importance, dignity. You know da kine?"

Jess hugged herself and rocked. "I want her back. I won't know how to live without her."

Night after night, she drove to Shark Bay, calling out to Pono. Her grief did not subside. Even after weeks, then months, it was so raw, so wrenching, Jess seemed to lose touch with herself, did not know how to move her body, amazed when her body moved on its own. In a daze, she crisscrossed the coffee belt, threading her way in and out of Captain Cook, Kainali'u, Hōlualoha, birthing lambs, saving cows from milk-fever death with intravenous calcium. She slogged through barn muck, taking blood samples from squealing hogs, scrubbing her rubber boots with lye soap to avoid spreading disease, then driving Pono's old truck to Shark Bay, smelling of manure, feed dust, and livestock.

Her practice was now far different than it had been in Manhattan, work she now recalled as moribund and bloodless. Here it was dirty, physical, sometimes scary. A convulsing piglet showed symptoms of a sickness that could wipe out a farmer's entire operation. A feverish steer could infect a herd of hundreds. Some calls were routine: shots, births, a mare needing her teeth filed, a rabbit with a rheumy eye. Some were challenging—a llama in Kohala needing cataracts removed, a quarter horse's deep depression after being gelded. Jess refused to perform the gelding operation but afterwards, through days and nights she sat with the huge beast, soothing it slowly back to, if not joy, then well-adjusted melancholia.

One night at Kealakekua Veterinary Clinic where she was now an associate, Jess sat at a microscope, checking a rooster's blood sample for parasite eggs. She made notations, closed the file, nearly paralyzed with exhuastion, so fatigued she did not feel the weight of grief, felt only the constellation of moments, small but brilliant incidents that had made up this day, its odd caprices and impulses. A newborn calf's blood and stench, its blind nuzzling of her chest, looking for a teat. The burst heart of an overworked sheepdog, dying on pillows like a rajah. The sobbing of the *hapa* who had driven it too hard.

That night her fatigue-trance drove her not to Shark Bay, but directly home. And though, in Jess's dreams the wild sea drubbed and hummed

on empty beaches, beating like a fateful drum, and though in sleep she
called out for Pono, she woke knowing grief was moving over, making
room for other things.

Squatting before the kitchen stove with Run Run, she described
blind fatigue that drove her home the night before. "I never got to Shark
Bay. I forgot to mourn."

"*Mono no aware,*" Run Run whispered. *The impermanence of things.*
Even grief.

The attorney was slender as a girl, delicately handsome in spite of
an astounding overbite. His grandfather had been one of the Filipino
unionizers who befriended Pono in Chinatown in the 1930s. She had
financed this man's way through Stanford Law School. He read the will,
looking at each of them in turn. The house, coffee orchards, the land
beyond, nearly three hundred acres, had been split four ways, Ming's
share going to Toru. Her children, now professionals in California,
wanted nothing to do with the place. Neither did Ming's parents. Ten
acres overlooking the bay at the south end of the property had been set
aside for Run Run.

"True?" she said sadly. "Now I a landowner?"

The others smiled, knowing, with Pono's help, she had been buying
up small plots of land for years. Nothing as prime, though, as this ten
acres overlooking the sea.

She immediately signed the land over to Toru. "Give him somet'ing
worry over."

The next morning, Rachel flew over to Honolulu. Two days later
she flew back, handing Jess a sheaf of documents.

"Power of attorney. If anything happens to me, everything I own
goes to you, Toru and Vanya."

Jess looked at her steadily. "Why would anything happen to you?"

She chose her words carefully. "I'm going, Jess. Out. Into the world."

"What?"

"I want to see if I can stand it."

Jess moved close, took her by the shoulders. "I need you, Rachel.
Pono's gone. Ming. Vanya's turning into someone else. You have to help
me carry on."

Rachel sat her down and they were face to face. "Listen to me. All
your life you've been trying to get home. You made it, Jess."

"What has that got to do with . . ."

"All my life I've wanted to grow up, break out. I was too terrified. I knew the world would show me how useless my life was. You see, I couldn't violate the order of self-imprisonment I'd chosen. Now I can."

"But, where are you going? How will you know how to talk to people?"

She explained about Ban and his sisters. About going to Thailand. "I want to sponsor them, bring them here. It won't take long. Hiro had connections everywhere, Immigration, Board of Health, the U.S. Embassy, people who in return for a few favors, would like me to erase them from his files. The girls will live with me in Kahala, go to school, one day university. In summers they can work here in the orchards, a healthy environment . . ."

Jess stared at her in utter shock. "How can you do this? Why do you want to?"

"Money is a strange thing, Jess. It helps you find out who you are. A part of you sits back and watches, waiting to see what you'll do when there are no limits. Hiro left me millions, as you know, profits from his water trade: drugs, gambling, prostitution. I've already given a good deal away. Scholarship-funds for local kids, and so on. Now I want to help these girls, and others. If they're sick, infected with the AIDS virus, I'll give them first-rate medical attention. I know it will take time. You see, time is what I have."

"My God," Jess whispered. "I can't believe this."

Rachel smiled. "You know, all my life I dreamed one day I'd find my mother working the streets in some place like Hong Kong. I'd bring her back to Honolulu, take care of her. Maybe helping young girls is a way of doing that." Her voice broke. ". . . Of bringing Mother home."

Jess studied her as if memorizing her, this cousin Siamated to her in the search for mothers they would never know. How had it come to this? Each woman flung out blindly into space, whirling alone on her own trajectory. She blamed it on Pono. The years with her had left them perilous, extreme, women balanced on the jagged edge. Conversely, Jess saw how her grandmother had indemnified them against that which was false, fleeting, or detestable. Now she hugged Rachel telling her she loved her.

"I don't have the right to try to talk you out of this, though it sounds insane. But, knowing you, it will somehow deviate into good sense. Will you just *please* be careful. I don't want to lose you."

Rachel smiled. "I was always careful. I was the one picking up the pieces in this family. No one ever noticed."

Jess stood, sounding suddenly harsh, determined. "Before you go, help me talk to Vanya. I don't want to lose her either."

They sat in the living room of the big house, Toru beside Vanya, Rachel and Jess facing them like opponents. Run Run banged and clattered in the kitchen, peacocks shrieked outside, and at first they were silent, trying to marshal their arguments, their declarations. Jess wanted to say things that would save their lives, but she didn't know what the words were.

Vanya broke the silence. "This is going to be a waste of time."

"I hope not," Jess said. "I just need to understand what you people are trying to prove."

"That we're not dead meat. That we won't back quietly into history."

"Can't you do it without . . ."

"It's too late," Toru said. "Don't you read the papers? Every environmentalist in the islands is behind this movement. They're pushing for boycotts, storming the governor's mansion. They've had enough."

"Great," Jess said. "That means they'll carry posters with your pictures when you're in federal prison."

Vanya leaned forward. "Jess, I love you. Even though we haven't always understood each other. But now our trains are definitely on different tracks. You're carrying on Tūtū's tradition, the farm, the coffee business. We need that, without land we're slaves. But, someone has to fight for preservation of that land. Don't you understand?"

Jess pointed a finger at her, almost shouting.

"This is what I understand. When environmentalists go up against billion-dollar businesses, business . . . always . . . wins. I can't think what these industries are doing to our air, our reefs and soil. But they didn't steal the land, Vanya. Someone—a farmer, or rancher, or Boards of Trusts—someone local *sold* that land. When you're flinging bombs round the island, how many of these people will support you?"

"Enough. Toru feels the same."

"I don't believe that," Jess said softly. "He already fought his war, several times."

Toru looked at each of them, looked down, rubbed his damaged hand. It had healed as well as it would heal, fingers stiff, tendons permanently scarred. His voice was deep and resonant.

"I signed a treaty with my government when I went to 'Nam. I would fight for them, maybe die for them. But if I survived, I could come home and live in peace. Somebody screwed me. I signed a *bad treaty*. All the politicians and developers and scientists who defend democracy, they don't give a . . . shit about the environment." His voice grew softer. "This island's all I've got, the only place that means anything at all."

"You might have to die for it."

"Dying's nothing. It's not enough."

In the kitchen, Run Run was suddenly still.

"We're dying anyway," Vanya said. "We were lost when we were born because we're Polynesians, intelligent, competitive, vain. We coveted things *haole* owned. They gave us progress, we gave them land. What I can't understand is, why nature has to pay."

"When has nature not paid?" Rachel asked. "What I want to know is why we, this family, have to pay. We're practically extinct. Why do you have to jeopardize your lives? Do you despise us so?"

Vanya did a slow turn, staring at her. "Miss Big Bucks. Have you forgotten you donated money to this cause?"

"I thought you were just going to blow a fishing yacht, make a statement." Rachel shook her head. "How stupid of me, Vanya. I forgot you're Major League. You have to dynamite hotels, make headlines, though people might be killed."

Toru shrugged, with a resignation that made no threats and bided its time. "BORN TO KILL. BORN TO DIE. That's what they trained me for."

Jess studied him, feeling immense sadness. *Yes. Maybe he is tired of living.*

They argued relentlessly through dinner, name-calling, attacking each other like wild dogs. And as they debated into the night Jess saw her argument was lost. Vanya's "revolution" no longer sounded like a moralistic move. It had become for her a drug.

Defeated, feeling all was lost, Jess lunged at Vanya in a desperate, tawdry move. "It seems to me, the villains in all of this, the ones raping our lands, are foreigners. Mostly Japanese and *haole*. Right?"

Vanya nodded, weary of the game.

"Yet you are importing a foreigner to fight beside our people. You're gambling all your shipments, your plans, your campaigns on this . . . *haole*. How do you know he's not a plant, someone working for the military?"

Toru glanced round the table, his eyes coming to rest on Vanya. "What the hell is she talking about?"

"Simon Weir," Jess said. "Ex-Green Beret, or whatever they call them in Australia." Vanya looked at her with such profound hate, Jess felt her stomach contract. "Sorry, cousin, I listened in on the extension."

Run Run suddenly appeared, ignoring everyone but Vanya.

Banging round in the kitchen, kicking Ula, the mongoose, from underfoot, it had come to her what she was being saved for, what Mother God had in mind. It had come with such startling clarity that, standing in the doorway, Run Run seemed to glow.

Now, she beckoned Vanya. "Come. I need talk wit' you."

Still in shock, Vanya rose, drifted from the room, leaving the others facing Toru.

"Simon Weir. Her lover," Rachel said softly. "She's bringing in the enemy. How does that make you feel?"

Toru pushed his chair back, looked from one to the other. "I never thought you'd sink to being cunts." Quietly he left the house.

In her room, Run Run threaded her rosary through her fingers. She touched the feet of Jesus hanging bored and crucified on the wall, and in a show of divided allegiance, rubbed the head of a Lotus-positioned Buddha. Then she snapped off her ancient Philco shaped like a miniature jukebox.

"Sit, I want show you somet'ing."

Easing herself into a creaky, monkeypod chair, Vanya was struck by half a dozen bottles of medicinals for leaking bladders, for arthritis, for sleeplessness. She looked up in shock, as if realizing for the first time that Run Run—this deeply loved fixture in their lives—was old. Pono's death had aged her twice as much. Her room had the melancholy smell of tired flesh, a woman on the brink of giving up.

"Oh, Run Run," she cried, throwing her arms round the old woman. "Whatever happens, remember not to hate me. Remember me the way you loved me best, when I was young."

Run Run pulled away. "*Keiki*, I nevah love you moah dan now. You *pupule* I t'ink, but still got principle. But I goin' curse you if you no do what I say. I goin' curse you to *death*. Now. Shut up. Close mouth. Look de eye."

Vanya stared at what she was pointing to. In her hand, Run Run held an object the size of a grape. A perfect sphere, reflecting light from such depths, it seemed to pulsate from black to deepest blue.

"My God."

"One rare South Seas pearl," Run Run whispered. "Dis from your *tūtū*. She been given dis from her mot'er, her mot'er's mot'er, and back and back. One time plenty moah, dis da last one left. Pono gave me, say when I die, I give it one of you. But, I no wait to die. Got too many t'ings to do. I choose you, *keiki*. I give dis to you."

Vanya shook her head, "I can't. It looks too valuable!"

"Is valuable. I took to one jeweler." Run Run's eyes grew wide. "He almost cry. Say dis pearl worth over, you believe it? T'ree hundred t'ousand dollahs. Foah dis kine perfection, dis kine size. No moah dis kine pearl, he say. He try buy from me." She paused. "Vanya. I make one deal wit' you. Dis pearl yours . . . if you gimme back my boy."

Vanya looked at her without comprehension, as if she were speaking another language.

"I want Toru to live, dig soil wit' his hands. Have family, be a man. He already die. In da war. And in da years wit' heroin. NO DIE NO MOAH! You understan'?"

Vanya shook her head. "Run Run, I can't change his mind. He's too involved in this thing now."

"You dig his coffin, girl, I goin' hate you, wish you dead. Don't take dis boy from me! He what I live for. Pono gone, you girls grown, not'ing left foah me. Mot'er God take him from me twice, den twice give him back. I no can pray no more askin' for anot'er favor. Now, I askin' you, Vanya, give him back to me. Here!" She threw the pearl in Vanya's lap. "Buy all da bombs and soldiers dat you need. Leave my boy foah me."

Vanya pleaded with her. "How could I explain this to him? How could I convince him . . ."

Run Run grabbed her by the arm, dragged her to the window. Down below, fireflies swarmed in winking clouds, lighting up the orchards. The moon sickled through a stand of guavas, its light falling on pale tapestries of frangipani whose haunting scent seemed to stun the land.

"Look dere. Look hard!" She shook her. "Dat's land you see, precious land. Some of it now Toru's. What he worked for, dreamed all his life. Pono love him, she give him his dream. Dat land waitin' foah him run his fingahs t'rough da soil. Seedlings waitin' him to plant dem so dey grow. Lumber singin' to him, you no hear it singin'? 'Come build a house and live.'"

Her eyes spilled, her wrinkled cheeks were wet. ". . . And coffee cherries squeezin' ripe foah him, and pick, and pulp, and weigh. Dis what Hawaiians live for, die for. Land! He pay foah it wit' twenty years. Vanya, ain't dat what you fightin' foah, so we can have da land. Oh, give my boy a chance. You got to let him live!"

Vanya sighed, slid her arms round her, held her tight, a way of asking to be held. She looked out across the fields humming with a universe of insects, minerals and soil, a universe that gave Hawaiians breath. She thought of Pono then, what she had taught them, drilled into them. Land, pride of ownership, earth enriching blood.

She slumped, feeling very tired. "Keep the pearl. Just tell me what you want. And how you want to do it."

Run Run pressed the pearl into her hand, then sat Vanya down, and talked, and planned.

Finally she covered her face with sloppy kisses. "Take time, take time. Be clevah, so he no get suspicious. Now, I gonna' pray foah you. Ask Mot'er God watch over you."

She was cool, almost formal as Toru eased his truck down the drive.

"Why didn't you tell me about your boyfriend?"

"I didn't invite him, Toru."

"Then, why is he in Honolulu?"

"Our thing was over. He flew in to try to change my mind. He was sitting in my living room when I walked in with that first delivery, the box of cordite."

"Jesus Christ."

"He worked out most of it himself. There wasn't much I had to tell him. It's happening in Australia, too. Aborigines fed up, demonstrating, strikes."

"And now he wants to join up with us," Toru said softly. "Get down with the *kānaka* and the *'coolies.'* "

"He asked to, yes."

"Why? He could give a shit about Hawaiians."

"He gives a shit about me."

His fist hit the steering wheel. "Don't you get it? He's the *enemy*."

"He's not. He's just . . . *haole*."

"Don't bring that sucker here. Understand?"

"I didn't say I would."

"But you didn't tell him to get lost, go back to Australia."

"He's an expert, Toru. There are only three of you who know what they're doing with firearms and explosives. One of you could get hurt, change your mind, drop out."

"I mean it, Vanya."

His headlights picked out a small group of men fixing a tire at an intersection.

Toru pulled up, yelled out the window. "Eh! Howzit?"

Someone leaned into his window. "Cool, *brah*. Delivery right on time. Thirty rifles in the trunk."

"Well, get it the hell off the highway," Toru yelled. "A cop could pull up anytime."

"Hey, *brah*, relax. That's a *real* flat tire."

Vanya watched him saunter away, a little too loose, too nonchalant. "Is he high, or something?"

"Maybe."

"Great. He's one of your explosives guys."

Toru shifted gears, and slowly pulled away. "He's fine. I saw him level a hamlet in 'Nam with damp gunpowder and a stick of Juicy Fruit."

"That was twenty years ago. Twenty years of smoking dope."

He looked over at Vanya. "Your *haole* doesn't dope?"

"Of course not."

"Right. He just fucks our *wāhine*."

Keaumiki

Quick Hands

THE MEETING HAD GONE on until after midnight. Exhausted, Vanya pulled into the driveway. It was nearing the Christmas season, America had a new, young president-elect, and locals were distracted, wanting to postpone nationalist activities until after the holidays and the presidential inauguration ceremonies. Vanya had found this unconscionable.

"Why should we care what happens on the mainland? Mainland America has never helped us. January seventeen is a crucial date. A hundred years ago our queen was deposed, our lands stolen from us while the U.S. president looked the other way. After Christmas will be too late to begin to organize and execute our plans."

A *hapa*-Japanese had challenged her. "But we like have Christmas, too. *Kamali'i* no remember Lili'uokalani. Dey only care 'bout Santa Claus. Why we have deprive dem?"

It went on and on. Vanya saw that old Hawaiian sense of *pa'ani* creeping in, love of play, of good times.

"This is why we're fading into history," she argued. "I'm discussing revolution, and you're worried about Santa Claus."

A big Hawaiian jumped up, pointed his finger at her. "Who dese islands for, if not for our children? If I gonna blow myself up, I gonna give my keeds good Christmas first!"

People were still applauding him when Vanya left.

Now she killed the engine, slid from the car. A hand gripped her arm, and she spun around.

"Simon. What are you doing here."

He looked different in moonlight, features harder to define. "I'm tired of waiting, Vanya."

"How dare you come to this house! I didn't send for you."

He pulled her into the shadows. "Listen. I've been playing tourist long enough. Sitting on the beach in Waikīkī for weeks. Except when you check in on the phone to pick my brain . . ."

"They don't want you here."

"I'm here."

"You must leave. Please."

He drew her deep into the orchard, moonlight flickering on tall grasses where he sat her down. "Talk to me. Tell me what's going on."

In that moment, the weight of everything defeated her. Her voice began to crack. "My grandparents . . . dead . . . they paddled out to sea . . ."

"I know, sweetheart. You told me."

She wept and Simon drew her to him. "We had so little time, it isn't fair. Everything's disintegrating. Rachel's leaving home, I think she's lost her mind. I promised Run Run . . . Toru's out of this. My God, he started this whole thing, now I've got to drop him. People backing down. They want to postpone everything. Suddenly, I'm out there all alone."

"No. You're not." He kissed her hair, kissed her forehead. It was the first time he had really touched her since Darwin, months ago. He could feel his muscles tense like little parachutes. "I'm here. I'm not going anywhere."

She felt his teeth nipping at her face, her neck, like little tusks. She felt her blood hum, heartbeat quickening, felt her pores expand.

"Don't . . ."

"Don't tell me don't. Use me, sweetheart."

He seemed to enfold her, then unfold her, wanting everything— her plasma, spleen, the lining of her mouth—every living part of her. He went slowly, as if plotting each one of the millions of cells that made up this woman. She moaned, stretched back on the grass, still fighting the tricks and feats of her body, how nerve ends gaped like little mouths, how skin felt chilled then heated, how tiny vessels flowed and ebbed in arteries and veins, making way for him.

He opened her shirt, cried out softly at her breasts in moonlight.

Full, golden, nipples hard, casting their own small shadows. He cupped each breast, fingers twirling the nipples so she whined softly. He buried his head between those breasts, wanting to weep, to hide.

"I don't want this," she lied, turning her body away from him, arms over face, cheek against soil. He studied the outline of her shoulders, her thighs, the full voluptuous length of her.

"Yes. You do." He wrapped his arms round her from the back, gathered her to him.

She felt his long, ginger-colored lashes on her neck, felt his breath in little puffs, his hands stroking her ever so lightly like a large cat he was beginning to calm.

She turned back to him, staring at his face. "It won't mean anything."

He took her nipple in his mouth, moon behind him aureoling his reddish hair. She felt the charge, electric, lift her in the groin, and pulled his head down closer, wanting her whole breast in his mouth, him sucking like a greedy child. His hands moved then, as if brushing water from her stomach and her thighs. Vanya sighed, turned one leg slightly outward.

He ran his hand along her thigh, feeling muscles tighten. Then he stopped, lifted her head, and kissed her eyes, her cheeks, put his lips on hers, long, tender greeting, hello, then lips pressing harder, teeth clicking against teeth. Her mouth yawned wide sucking in his tongue so forcefully he felt the corrugated roof. Deft movements, her underthings flung white against the night.

Simon reared back, pulled off his shirt, the pelted chest came slowly down. His hand between her legs, fingers winding in her hair, probing with slow, curious dexterity. *The wet, the waiting wet.* Fingers gently spreading her sex, he arched down and kissed her there. Vanya moaned, flung back her head. His tongue shot out, thrust into her, and then— surprise—he took her clitoris between his teeth, gently, O, so gently, and nibbled on that nest of nerves, shocking, electrifying, her.

She cried out as his tongue drove in again, and out and in, establishing a rhythm. He felt her engagement, watched her buck and kick, legs cycling the air. Her hands gripped his head; his tongue pushed deeper, an implement, a primer. Rhythms riding rhythms, snorting like a mare, she rose and reached for him.

"In me . . . you in me."

Zipper rattling, pants jamming round his ankles, kicking everything off, he watched her take his hardness in her hand, guiding him, guiding Simon in.

"Like this?" he cried. "Like this?"

She barked aloud, his slow and stuttering entry. She bit the shoulder of this pale beast working up a rhythm, assassin assassin assassin. He would break her down cell by cell and she would help him, she would wring him dry.

And they were running yes she ran him so his eyes bled sweat back sprung wet like sequins everything was concentrated in his spine small bullets of brain matter blasting through each cushioned vertebrae down into his cock down down he would run her they would run and they were running turning O the length of her and his saliva furrowing her back and O the way she loved it he loved watching how she loved it lifting up her rump to him and humping no not in the butt dark delicate alley too-tight winking place but the vagina the somehow better angle him piling falling driving into as far as he could go and loving her loving it and going like two homeless dogs yelping throats parched chins straining upward giving it all up everything and mouths slack eyes screwed shut then staring blind defenseless spasms of the terribly insane her losing sight losing everything lost in specific concentration of this moist socketing hard force of him locked and bolted in the intuition and the proof her boiling muscle quickening impoundment of her senses glimpsing for a second some pure definition quickly swamped in winey fruit smell cherries soil orchards both of them diminishing vanishing remnants of a frail ferocious dream.

The moon lit up their bodies, splotched red and yellow from squashed ripe and rotting coffee cherries. It stuck all over them like glue. The fragrance singed their nostrils, sticky and cloying, clots of earth on cheeks and breasts. Earth-smell like semen. He was still in her, and she was semen-full.

In front of Jade Valley Monastery, men in jungle fatigues stood up with rifles, suddenly alert.

Toru approached the car, looked in the window. "I said no way, Vanya." He looked over at Simon. "This place *kapu, haole*. You savvy?"

Simon smiled. "You sound like a bloody Apache, mate."

"I'm getting out of the car," Vanya said. "Unless you're planning to shoot us."

Toru slammed his body against the door. "No way! Now get the fuck out of here."

She sighed, looked through the windshield, looked back at him. "Do you think I'd risk it if I weren't sure of him? Listen to me. You're supposed to have guards posted three miles down the road. They should have stopped me, asked what I'm doing with this *haole*."

Toru frowned. "What happen?"

"Know what I found? Half-empty case of Primo, one guy snoring, the other two slobbering over *Playboy* magazine." She pushed her way out of the car. "We're putting our lives in the hands of *lōlōs*, and you fight me for bringing in an expert."

"Expert at *panipani* maybe."

The others laughed and shifted their rifles.

Vanya spun round pointing a handgun at him. "Don't *ever* . . . belittle me like that again." She threw the gun and two rifles on the ground before him. "We took them from your 'security' boys. They don't deserve guns."

"What do you mean you took?"

Simon stepped easily from the car. "Let's say we . . . liberated them. You boys should brush up on karate, you're in drastic shape."

A huge, husky Hawaiian-Portuguese approached, and tried to take him from behind, arm slamming like a club. Simon dodged instinctively, twisted, and did something with his fist against the man's windpipe. He went down like a baby.

Simon shook his head. "Close, but no cigar." He looked round at the others, big locals, innately strong, but stomachs soft and paunchy. "Anyone?"

They saw he was physically superior, muscular and wiry, not an ounce of extra fat. No one moved. Then Simon turned to Toru. It was a good physical match, and Toru was so obviously full of hate, Simon suspected this one might be able to take him, maybe take him all the way.

Vanya stepped between them. "Give him a chance, Toru. We've got half a dozen qualified men. The rest, what are they? farmers, construction crews, gas attendants. We've got whole villages organizing, yelling *Huli*! But they're people with families. They don't want to throw bombs. They just want parades."

Toru looked at the others, they shrugged. He kicked the dirt, motioned Vanya and Simon inside. Sleeping bags, empty take-out cartons, maps, diagrams on walls. Toru led them to a blanket spread out on the floor.

"So, a *haole* wants to join up with *kānaka*?"

Simon sat forward, looking earnest. "Something like that."

"You want to help blow hotels?"

"I think I can be of service."

"You believe in our cause, right? *Hah!*"

"Let me make it easy for you, mate." He leaned so close, Toru felt his breath. "Your cause is hopeless. No, I don't believe in it. I don't believe in much of anything. I'm here because of her. And if I have to blow something up to prove myself to her, I'll do it."

"Tell him what you know, Simon."

"I know nothing for sure. I don't trust anyone, nor should you. If any of you lads are shopping for fatigues, I'd say avoid that Army surplus shop in Kailua. Same goes for anyone over Hilo way. This operation is so sloppy, anyone could infiltrate. What's in the corner?"

Toru hesitated. "Ammo, explosives. The works."

Simon walked to the back of the monastary, and lifted sheets of waterproofed tarpaulin.

"Jesus wept. You've got a bloody arsenal here. I thought you only planned to blow a few hotels, maybe a plant."

"Ain't gonna stop with just hotels," Toru said. "We got a large agenda."

Simon turned to him, disgusted. "I've never seen anything so . . ." He took Toru aside, trying to control himself. "Someone drops a cigarette, you'll blow this part of the island off the map. Break it up, man. Cache it, miles apart. You saw combat. Forget the drill?"

Toru clenched his fists, looking at dozens of crates. "There's a problem. Movement, transportation. The only men I trust are in this room."

"You have whole villages behind you."

"Not with this. Besides, tell him, Vanya."

She looked down, embarrassed. "Locals are asking us to wait."

"Until . . . ?"

"After the holidays."

Simon threw his hands up, and walked out to the car.

Driving him to his motel near Captain Cook, she felt his deep disdain, a professional soldier confronted with amateurs.

"I told you we need help."

"Vanya, Vanya, this is a joke. A very sad, expensive joke.

"If I do this, I'm giving up my practice, maybe my freedom. It's not a joke."

He passed his hands across his eyes. "No. It's not. It's a metaphor. For every egotistical, ill-timed, laughable, abominably amateur, farcical, anarchical plot that ever failed. You *cannot* go through with this."

She pulled up in front of the motel, looking straight ahead. "I'm going through with it. Alone."

He sighed, stared at his hands. His voice was old, resigned. "Right. Just tell me what you want to do. And we will do it."

Jess stood in her doorway, hesitant. "Vanya? Are you okay?"

She covered a sheaf of papers, maps, diagrams. "Come in."

Affectionately, Jess put her arm round her shoulder. "I hardly see you anymore. Where do you go?"

"Oh, meetings."

"He's here isn't he? Your friend."

"He's come to help us, Jess."

"Are you in love with him?"

She shook her head, half smiling. "Such a funny word. It means so many things. Or nothing. I would say we're sexually in thrall."

Jess pulled back from her. "Your old cliché, reducing everything to . . ."

"Lust. Curiosity in heat." She crossed her feet up on the desk, assuming the air of a philosopher. "Let me tell you something, Jess. Except for blood ties, tribal connections, what people think of as love is a coma, a trusted dog at your feet. But lust, real driving lust is something else. It . . . I don't know, it challenges you, distorts the brain. You don't court it, it comes when your back is turned. Think of a lion tamer. And every time it roars, you back up, flick the whip, daring it to leap. It's mental, completely mental."

"Right," Jess said. "The whip is control. Even in the throes, you're still flicking the whip." She studied her, trying to fathom her. "If you don't love this Simon, then you're using him."

"That's what people do. It's not a dirty word. We use people to learn, progress. We compare ourselves as humans, see how we stack up, then try to make improvements. Didn't you use your friend in New York?"

She flinched, still missing Mars. "He helped me understand what was important to me, that my history here was taking place without me. I never used him. I loved him."

"Or was it lust? His big, shimmering black body . . ."

"Shut up, Vanya. Just shut up. I loved him, and I respected him, I even respected his rage."

"You were scamming, Jess. You don't possess that kind of temperament, you wouldn't blow things up. You're a healer, remember? You came home looking for the past, some tropical Utopia. You romanticized us, now you feel betrayed."

Jess hugged herself while Vanya fired all her guns. "I will only feel betrayed if you and Toru die or go to prison. This won't be a family anymore. It will be just me and Rachel, struggling with this place."

Vanya smiled. "You can do it, Jess. I was never meant to run a farm." She suddenly laughed, disdainful. "Rachel and her little harem harvesting the fields. God, what a joke. We're fighting for our lands, she's going off to rescue prostitutes in Thailand."

"She financed half your explosives shipments with money made from prostitutes. How does that make you feel?"

Vanya dropped her feet to the floor, seriously considering the question. "It makes me very glad Hiro's dead. Look, I understand she needs to launder all that wealth, little do-good errands for her conscience. But why not stay home, take care of *our* prostitutes? This Thai scheme . . . she asked me what a visa was. She doesn't even own a passport."

"She does now." Jess folded her arms. "Give her credit, will you? She's going out into the world alone. Think of it!"

Vanya's expression changed, she suddenly looked pained. "Stubborn, frivolous, crazy bitch. She can't even read a map. Suppose something happens to her? I won't be there to help her. Jess, don't let her go."

"I can't stop her. I can't stop you. No one could stop Ming. *Tūtū* once said she needed *keaumiki* to raise us, keep us in line. We inherited her stubborn streak, it's like the Hapsburg lip. I don't have that gift of *keaumiki*. We're flying apart, Vanya."

She sat thinking, patting Jess's arm almost absentmindedly. "When was the last time you saw Waipi'o Jimi?"

"Years ago. Five? Ten? The last time we went hiking."

"I want you to call him, Jess. Take a note to him. I can't be seen up there for several reasons. I won't involve you any more than this."

Jess nodded. "Only, promise me after the Centennial you'll get out of this for good."

"We'll see."

The next day Jess drove up to the northwestern tip of the island, up past Shark Bay and Pu'ukohola Heiau, past the deep waters of Kawaihae, and the dreaming little sugar towns of Hawi and Kapa'au, where air was cooler, diamond sharp and clear. She arrived at a spot of lush tropical gulches, waterfalls soaring three thousand feet from jungle cliffs down to black lava beaches. Below her lay a jungle floor almost two miles wide, twisting back into itself for seven miles.

Mysterious Waipi'o Valley, the Valley of Ancient Kings—Umi, Liloa. Here in 1780, Kamehameha I received his war god, Kukailimoku, from reigning chiefs, and here he was singled out as future ruler, the Great One. Here in 1791, he and Kaheiki engaged in the first naval battle in Hawaiian history using *kepuwahaulaula*, cannon, the red-mouthed gun.

Waipi'o was the home of ancient Hawaiian settlers numbering in the thousands, place of mass human sacrifices, burial caves laced with bones untouched for centuries. Down the years it had become a sanctuary for priests, *kāhuna*, refuge for rebels, outcasts, victims of *ma'i Pākē*. Except for old renegades still tending taro farms, few people lived in the valley now. Those who came, left soon with tales of Night Marchers clubbing them in sleep, angry *menehune* who pushed branches through their cheeks, and blue-faced dogs who danced on hind legs like *wāhine*.

Jess parked her car at Lookout Point, frequented by tourists. There were mudslide paths for sturdy hikers willing to struggle through jungle brush down to black sand beaches fronting the valley. Most tourists were content to stand beside their cars, snapping photos of the lushness far below. After half an hour, Jess heard a horse whinny. Someone cursed softly, urging it up the mountain path. She smiled as the old man's dark, leathery face appeared. He waved, dismounted, tied his horse to a tree.

They sat in sunlight, sucking Kona oranges, while he read Vanya's note. Waipi'o Jimi had lived in the valley all his life, descendant of Royalists-turned-guerillas who, a hundred years ago when America dethroned their queen, sought sanctuary in the valley after kidnapping five U.S. Marines, relieving them of uniforms and arms, tying them naked to palm trees on Honolulu's main street. Sixty years ago, his 'ohana had helped Duke and Pono when they were running for their lives.

"Can you tell me what it says, Jimi?"

He folded the note, shook his head. "Vanya say no. See, *keiki*, she want you stay safe, for run da farm. You girls da bosses now. Somet'ing happen you, farm be *pau*."

"Will you help her?"

He smiled, baring big purple gums. "I go foah broke foah Vanya. Any *keiki* of Pono, I cut my heart out for. Look my horse, handsome, neh? Pono give me, years ago. She give me five horses. I say Pono, 'nuff! 'nuff! I no want no ranch! She nevah forget me. I six years old when bounty hunters chase her and Duke here to Waipi'o. Some weeks we got no food foah dem, 'cept taro. Dey live like wild dogs in da bush. You know, even when she starvin' look like scarecrow, she most beautiful *wahine* I ever seen."

He wiped his eyes, studied Jess. "You got a little bit her face, da nose, da chin. God bless you, *keiki*. Go home take care da farm."

She stood and hugged him. "What should I tell Vanya?"

"Yes. Say her Waipi'o Jimi say yes."

Dressed like a tourist in Bermuda shorts, tortoise sunglasses, Simon Weir studied a brochure and frowned. "Twelve restaurants. Ten bars. Two full-size discotheques. Six free-form swimming pools. Six tennis courts, including a nine-hundred-seat stadium. Golf, racquetball, squash. Health spa. Thirty-seven boutiques. Three thousand guest rooms, each with bidet. All under one roof. 'THE MOST FANTASTIC RESORT ON EARTH.'" He looked across the table at Vanya. "God, it's a bloody circus."

She read off other "amenities" offered by the Halenani Resort. "Besides the health spa, they offer a 'Holotropic Breathing' workshop. Also workshops with 'Life Enhancement Consultants.' Here's a weekend seminar led by a 'Cranial-Sacral Therapist,' a Dr. Rebirth, held in the Temple of Love." She looked at him, spoke softly. "Can you believe this crap."

They sat at one of one of the hotel's posh outdoor cafés, this one overlooking a pond surrounded by tall lava stone walls, where hotel guests, under supervision, fed and played with eight imprisoned bottlenosed dolphins.

"They advertise the dolphins as part of a 'Marine Life Fund,' kept here for the 'Advancement of Marine Education, Conservation and Research,'" Vanya said. "I contacted two of the marine biologists from Stanford University listed on their Board of Research. They're qualified researchers all right. The hotel pays them for the use of their names, but neither of them has ever set foot on this island."

In a corner cage affair, bars kept four of the dolphins from the other four.

"That's to discipline them," Simon said. "The waiter said sometimes they get depressed, and won't perform. They're kept in the cage for a penalty period, like delinquents. Meanwhile three dolphins have already died in here. They blame it on ciguatera."

Vanya gazed at the intelligent, graceful mammals leaping in the pathetically small pond.

"What about public sentiment?" he asked. "I should think locals would be up in arms."

"When they first brought in the dolphins, locals demonstrated in front of the hotel, on the highway, in town; they wrote letters to the governor demanding their release. No response. When dolphins started dying, a group of *kānaka* tried to set the others free. Came in by sea, used slings trying to lift them over those lava walls. A disaster. They went to prison. Now this place is crawling with security."

Simon glanced round the bar and adjoining pool, picking them out easily. Clothes, posture, casual, but bodies a little too fit, eyes a little too quick behind sunglasses.

"Who's your 'in' here?" he asked.

"Gardeners. Chambermaids. All locals. The head of maintenance has access to the infrastructure, plumbing, pipelines, sewage units."

As they strolled round, taking snapshots of Vanya in tennis whites, the hotel grounds strategically behind her, Simon shook his head, disbelieving the layout of this $400 million mega-resort. The two-hundred-acre complex had once been nothing but a bleak lava desert fronting the Pacific. Tons of sand were hauled in, thousands of tropical plants, palm trees, acres of roll-out lawns. Now, half a dozen man-made ponds and grottoes were separated from large lagoons by islets boasting Oriental statuary and even smaller "contemplation pools," connected one to the other by myriad arched bridges.

Big-engined pleasure boats with uniformed "captains" cruised canals, ferrying guests to one of six suite towers. Guides bellowed out approaching towers through bullhorns. On an elevated monorail, a high-tech "torpedo" train circumnavigated the entire resort. Eerily juxtaposed against swaying palms, ancient volcanoes in the distance, the thing screeched in at designated "stations," then snorted out again. Most guests pointedly avoided it. At night, shrieking through the hotel's sound-and-light show, it seemed a ghost train rumbling round and round, abandoned toy of a giant, moody child.

Strolling through the lobby, an architect's wet dream of a twenty-first-century Polynesian palace, they climbed a monumental staircase with huge towering columns, which gave out onto a panoramic view of a lagoon, beyond that a simulated beach—sand imported from another island—and, finally, the sea.

"Talk about urban blight," Simon whispered. "Whole place should be leveled."

"Where would you start?"

"Right here. At night." He looked at the grandiose roof and columns overhead, the empty staircase behind them. "Least amount of human traffic. Far from shops and restaurants. I'd also like to blow that fucking silly train. Too risky, though. Has to be something stationary."

"How long would it take, once a bomb is planted?"

He looked at her steadily. "As long as you like. Any *way* you like. Timer. Climate-activated. Do it dry, do it wet. Voice-activated. Even code. I can sing 'Waltzing Matilda' ten miles away. On the second chorus, it would blow."

They shot another roll of film, then strolled back toward the parking lot, observing security cameras positioned in the lobby, outside the hotel entrance, in bushes leading to the tennis courts.

"Crucial part is the plant," he said. "It has to be staff, someone low-profile we can trust."

Vanya nodded. "There's an old gardener here named Kito. Loves flowers, hates *haole*. A decorated infantryman in Korea."

"Let's hope he still remembers explosives."

In late afternoon, they stood in Kailua Town overlooking the bay, watching Santa arrive by submarine, escorted by a flotilla of Christmas-lit boats. All through the town, in towns throughout the island, glitter lights were wound round trunks of palm trees. Bands marched in the streets playing "Mele Kalikimaka," and in King Kamehameha Hotel a children's choir sang "Joy to the World," and "Drummer Boy," in Hawaiian.

"Christmas in the islands." Simon smiled. "Rather innocent, and touching."

"What's it like at home, in the Kakadu?" she asked.

"Oh, I sit round campfires with the boys, eating witchetty grub and talking 'Dreamtime.' "

"Do you miss it, Simon?"

"Not yet. Though, I aim to go back. After we serve our prison terms, I figure you and I can retire there. Pen our memoirs in the bush."

Driving north up into the hill towns, they saw coffee shacks adorned with gold and silver garlands, cardboard Nativity scenes blinked off and on. In the town of Kainali'u, a flatbed truck roared past them in the back of which staggered a half-naked man in red Santa hat, red rubber boots and grass skirt. He was clutching a bottle of whiskey in one hand and in the other what looked like a rifle. The driver pulled over, got out and flagged them down, slightly drunk.

He leaned down in her window. "Vanya! Lissen, we did one numbah-one job tonight! Stashed plenny crates in one hidin' place no one evah goin' find. Like one giant bunkah!"

Simon threw open his door, staring at the reeling Santa on the truck. "Say, mate, tell me that's not an assault rifle that silly fucker's waving."

"Oh, sheeet!" The driver ran back toward the truck as Santa flung the bottle in the air, aimed the rifle, and shot. A telephone pole cracked and tilted, wires sagging.

Before the drunk could aim again, Simon was on the truck beside him, squeezing his windpipe with thumb and forefinger. Santa dropped the assault rifle, seeming to fall asleep on his feet. Simon kicked his legs out from under him, grabbed the rifle, and jumped down, throwing the husky driver against the truck. He seemed to question him, then waved him on. The truck roared off as he climbed back into the car, running his hands down the rifle barrel.

"Should have shot the bleeder. Shot them both. Said they liberated the rifle from the cache so they could target practice. Target practice!"

Later, lying beside him in his bed, she could still feel his tension. She tried to apologize but it came out defensive.

"I'm sorry, Simon, sorry they don't have the ethos of a crack commando unit!"

"Its a right mess I can tell you. Be a miracle if we don't end up behind bars."

"You can pull out anytime."

He turned to her. "No. I can't. Leave it to your *kānaka* boys, they'll blow themselves to pieces. If you'd just let me work alone, I could do it with my eyes closed."

She sat up chilled, rubbing her arms. "You could do it in your sleep, I bet."

"It takes a certain amount of gall. One must be swift, detached. No apprehension. One should not even perspire."

"God, how you relish it. You're still an assassin in your heart."

He pulled away from her, so stunned his voice turned soft. "No. I'm not. It came with basic military training, something I was schooled in, became expert in. One day I discovered I was addicted to the drill. Bait, Pursue, Exterminate. I started fearing for my sanity."

He took her hand, sick with remembering. "In Central America, I saw a friend hose down a family while they were still wiping sleep from their eyes. He didn't know why; they weren't insurgents. It was like his gun had become his brain, dictating every move. When he was finished, I looked down at three generations, sweet-faced people, even children, in slippers and robes. I saw what we were, what we'd become. I wasted him, my best friend. Everything I had, I poured into his stomach. Then, I walked out of that country and out of that life. For years there was this large fatigue, a kind of gutlessness, lack of stomach for any kind of confrontation. I have retained that gutlessness."

"Then why are you here?"

He pulled her closer. "I said I'd do what it takes to prove myself. I wouldn't choose to do this, but now I see I might save your life. You cannot put bombs in the hands of irresponsible drunken blokes, even if it *is* their cause." He smoothed her hair back like a child. "I'm not an assassin, sweetheart. I'm just a man, trying to save someone I value."

Much later, a sudden absence in the bed beside her woke her. Simon sat by a window, energetically scratching his arm and neck.

"What is it?" she asked.

"This bloody crud . . ."

She lit a lamp and stood beside him, seeing on his arm a pimply red rash, and interspersed among the rash odd, small, white patches. She closed her eyes, steadying herself. "How long have you had this."

"Comes and goes. Now it's on the neck."

She looked closely at his neck, red and raw in small areas. "Simon, do you know your earlobe is swollen?"

"Not surprised."

She sat down on the bed, speaking carefully. "Have you seen a doctor?"

"At least half a dozen."

"What do they say?"

He hesitated. "Say it's the 'crud.' Pills take care of it, somewhat."

Something swept her, she wanted to be ill. "What do you mean . . . 'crud'?"

He looked out the window, looked back at her. "Effects of Agent Orange. Carcinogen. We were overexposed in 'Nam, Cambodia. I told you I wasn't much of a bargain. Health-wise I'm a liability." He scratched again. "Thought the pills were taking. Now this silly rash has started up again."

"Your sores, they look like what my grandfather had."

"Right. Patches, bloating. I've seen leprosy amongst the Abos. This crud's similar. Sometimes, hits internal organs, central nervous system. Vets go blind. Their kids are freaks, a son born without an anus." He sighed. "Not to worry sweetheart, it's not contagious."

She reached up gingerly and touched his arm. "Simon, you have to see another doctor."

"After our 'sound-and-light' show, I promise."

She turned off the lamp, drew him to bed. In the silence, she could feel his vulnerability, almost hear it. She took him in her arms, wanting to hold him, to comfort him. At first he seemed shy, as if she would be disgusted with his flesh, newly patched, cells cantankerous. Then he relaxed, buried his head between her breasts, and slept.

In the deepest hour of night, he woke to her mouth on him, tongue skiing unbroken rhythmns, sparking plumes of shock and color in his brain. She sucked slowly, taking all of him, as much as she could, until her jawbone creaked. She lifted her head, their eyes met, dazed and blistered. Then, her mouth went diligently back to him, tuning him, turning his shoulders silvery with sweat until, like metal poured, he came. And coming, the wet slapping of his thighs against her cheeks, he sang out in an argot, sad and lonely, all his own.

While he snored softly, Vanya touched the rash on his neck and arms, thinking of her grandfather, Duke. Then, carefully, almost reverently, she wrapped her arms round Simon and held him in fatigued tenderness, a dawning wonderment.

Paukū Manawa

A Portion of Time

FLIES MOONED SEDULOUSLY OVER HER FACE, her cheeks sticky with sap, arms itchy and aching. The basket belted round her waist sagged with the weight of coffee cherries. Jess felt the pressure like a twenty-pound fetus weighing on her groin. She knelt, unbuckling the basket, relieving the terrible strain on her back. A Filipino worker helped her pour the cherries into a large burlap sack, then she collapsed, hung her head between her legs.

"Good fun, eh?" The man laughed. "You do good job, boss-lady. Today fill hundred-pound sack all by yoah self, foah shoah!"

She groaned, studied her cracked fingers, filthy nails. *Forty years of this.* Tutu, *how did you survive?*

Rachel pushed through trees, emptied her own basket, collapsed beside her in the grass. Even in long-sleeved shirt, bandanna, sun hat, flies had gotten to her, and mosquitoes, welting her left cheek. Her face was mottled, nose red with too much sun. The air they breathed was thick with juice from coffee cherries that had in it the weight of the land, vicissitudes of the weather, even the dust and sweat of pickers. Dumb with fatigue, they gazed at the road ahead, loaders hoisting hundred-pound sacks of cherries onto flatbeds headed for the mills.

The mills themselves had always been a mystery to Jess, barn-like structures full of dust, men masked like bandits throwing sacks around. Then weeks back, Kona District had celebrated its Annual Coffee Festival—cherry-picking contests, beauty pageants, parades. The Kona Coffee Council paid tribute to Pono and her forty years in the business and afterwards, a young coffee grower, Lee Sugai, had invited Jess to tour his family's mills. "Come," he said. "See how we process your beans."

Run Run took her aside. "You watch out dem Sugai folks! Want sweet-talk you, buy yoah land. Maybe dat sly son want marry you, den no pay foah yoah land!"

Jess laughed. "He's already married, Run Run."

She and Rachel visited Sugai's cherry mill, seeing firsthand how coffee beans were processed. Transported from the fields, sacks of coffee cherries were poured into clacking pulping machines, which removed the red fruit skin. Then they were soaked in water, removing the fleshy mucilage. Beans were then rinsed, and sun-dried for several days, until their "parchment," a thin, golden skin, was brittle, cracked, ready to be removed.

After drying, beans were transported to the Green Mill and sent through hullers removing the parchment, then polishing the jade-colored beans. Graded by size and shape, gravity-separated and density-graded by a vibrating air table, the green beans were then inspected for size, color, taste, and number of defects per pound. Finally, they were hand-sorted, ready to be roasted, and bagged.

"It's not an easy business," Lee Sugai explained. "But something is happening, young people are turning it around."

Pure Kona coffee was now in demand, competing with the best French gourmet brands. The business was attracting entrepreneurs from the mainland, trying to edge out local growers.

"I'll help you anyway I can," Lee said. "Just, please, don't sell your land to outsiders." He stood looking out across the fields, breathing in the air. "We own a few hundred acres in California. You know, I can take it or leave it. It's not the same, not 'aina."

He was the only third-generation coffee farmer on the island, his family having entered it eighty years ago. One of the few remaining coffee families who owned and operated their own land and mills, Lee and his father now competed successfully with big distributors like AMFAC. After graduate school, the son had moved to the mainland, spent six years as an aerospace engineer, but he missed the islands, missed the smells and climate of Kona. He came home, studied coffee processing and roasting, business and marketing, while still hand-picking cherries with his eighty-nine-year-old grandparents. Over the years the

Sugais had succeeded in expanding their brand name to markets in the mainland United States, Europe, and Asia.

Jess suspected Lee was curious, perhaps in admiration of her, too. Like him she had left another life to come home to the land. He was gracious, his wife was attractive, they offered her their friendship and advice, which made Jess all the more determined to work the farm, keep it thriving. Still, she was fearful of so much responsibility, so many workers depending on her for income.

"Suppose there's a drought? An earthquake? Suppose I lose my nerve!"

"I keep telling you you're not alone," Rachel assured her. "You've got me and Toru. We grew up in these orchards, remember? Even as kids, we'd get drunk on fermented coffee cherries, and workers would find us hanging in the trees. They taught us to smoke tobacco made from coffee leaves. And, often as I could, I'd follow Pono, a little shadow, touching every leaf she touched. This farm is my *kumu*, Jess. My origins, my home."

"I thought your house in Kahala . . ."

"Hiro's showplace, built to intimidate his enemies. I always wanted to be here."

They trudged toward the big house, wiping their cheeks with rags.

"I used to think you were selfish, not wanting kids. Now I see you were busy raising Hiro."

"In the beginning, I was *his* child. But then . . . I suppose I always had that nurturing instinct, though I denied it. You have it, too. Ming did not. Vanya, I don't know."

"She loved her son."

"But the responsibility of motherhood never engaged her. The boy was a stabilizer, a sedative. In infancy, he slowed her down. But, she was already flying across the Pacific, making the rounds of conferences, when he was still a child. He was alone too much. If Vanya had paid attention, he wouldn't have been swimming to Kaho'olawe. He was trying to ape his mother, be committed to a cause."

Jess shook her head. "She's still a ricocheting arrow looking for a target. I wonder if she's ever really loved."

Rachel recalled the Samoan, Ta'a Utu. "She would have married him. I always wondered why he cast her out."

Jess remembered taking Vanya to Ta'a Utu after her son died. She remembered lying in a hotel room, hearing them through a wall. "He didn't cast her out, he was running for his life."

"What can we do to save her, Jess? What does she need?"

"Something . . ." She answered slowly, trying to understand fully the implication of what she said. ". . . that will shock her into kindness."

Thousands of poinsettia bushes set the roads aflame, while Christmas lights blinked off and on across the island. Strapping locals side-stepped into traffic, Christmas trees roped across their backs, and seven grass-skirted Santas flew by in a fire truck, answering alarms. A TV station broadcast the icy, blue slopes of Mauna Kea, fourteen thousand feet up, where a giant, solitary snowman held a banner. "JOY TO DA WORLD . . . YOU CAN READ DIS, YOAH PLANE TOO DAMN CLOSE!"

As Jess passed Kamagakai Market, one of her field-workers yelled, "'Ey, Boss-lady! *Mele Kalikimaka!*"

It was Christmas Eve. The sounds and odors swept her when she walked into the house. KCCN broadcasting Christmas carols played on old-time 'ukulele Run Run crooning over pans of *laulau* cats wearing silver bells batting hunks of squid Toru smelling wonderfully of horse grass cattle strumming his old Kamaka 'uke singing softly in falsetto in the oven pork simmering and splashing a turkey mummified with stuffing and from a pail fish smell of *lomi* salmon Ula whining and drooling the smell of melting chocolate roasting chestnuts mixed with smell of soy sauce tripe pig's cheeks purple *poi* sitting morbidly in bowls and sheets of pastries shaped like little bladders duck-sauce oyster kimchi apple pie assaulted drunk her senses all askew Jess stepped outside the kitchen damp-earth smell of coconut-husk fires blowing up the hill.

They sat at dinner discussing fertilizing, pruning, rat control, a new kind of roaster for coffee beans.

Run Run waved her fork at them. "You folks don' know real kine work, when evert'ing done by hand. Old days, Pono and me so poor, roasted beans in *wok* . . ."

She paused, hearing Vanya's car in the driveway. "Late for dinna'! Gonna' knock dat *wahine* down."

Her passage through the house was strange. No slamming doors, no yelling out in greeting. She entered the dining room quietly, almost stealthily, waiting until he caught up with her.

"This is Simon Weir. I asked him home to dinner."

No one moved. No one seemed able.

Run Run stared, then flew to her feet. "Girl, why you come late Christmas Eve!" She pulled out a chair for Simon. "Come! Come! We got plenny. You got good appetite?" She started filling up a plate. "Vanya, introduce who and who."

Toru abruptly stood and left the room. Run Run ignored him until Simon's plate was full and conversation going, then she stormed into the kitchen.

"You. What you doin'?"

"Fuckin' *haole*. Some kind nerve!"

"Get in dinin' room." She picked up the carving knife.

"Hell with you. I'm not sitting at the same table. Just because she *panipani* him, why we have to share our food."

Run Run grabbed his arm, spun him around. "Why you care? What he done to you?"

"He's *haole*. *Pilau!*"

She pushed him up against the wall. "Lissen me. You no moah do-nothin' own-nothin' *kanaka*. You a landowner now. Dis man come, you *lele koke* like one street Flip. Toru, you gonna change. Else I skin dat tongue."

"What do you want? Want me kiss *haole* feet?"

She slapped his cheek, but gently. "I want you show *hanohano* manners. Act like gran'son of Pono. Like man wit' land beneat' his feet. Dis *haole*, what he own? He rich?"

"He's nothing. He left Australia for her. Can you believe? *Vanya*, and a *haole*?"

"So he not'ing. Den treat him like you treat stray dog. Kind. Wit' dignity, like yoah grandfat'er Duke. You gotta learn dis, boy, befoah I die."

Jess studied Simon sideways. His directness, his blatant manliness, made eye contact a challenge. He seemed all wire and taut muscle, an almost vicious fastidiousness in his clipped nasal speech. Yet he was trying, she could see he was trying, everything in him struggling to relax. She wished Vanya would take his hand. She wished . . . she was blown out of her cloud of thought as the table exploded in laughter.

"Say again? Ooh, funny dat . . ." Run Run filled his plate to the brim a second time.

"Well, you see," he explained, "we thought it was a drink. Kept ordering it in every bar. Bourbon Dwarf, mate. Give us a round of Bourbon Dwarfs. They kept serving us cups of java! Turns out, it's a type of bloody coffee bean in Central America."

"Where dat? . . . Central America?" she asked.

Simon drew an imaginary map for her.

"Plenny far from Austraya. What you doin' dere?"

"Hmmm, buying livestock." Changing the subject, he turned to Toru. "And, how does it feel to own a decent bit of land?"

Toru looked at Run Run. She stared him down. "I feel I deserve it. That's what we're fighting for."

"Fair enough," Simon said. "But you're not Hawaiian. That's who the land rightfully belongs to, doesn't it?"

Something came over Toru, a confidence that left him calm. "I was born here, that makes me Hawaiian. I fought this country's war. They didn't ask me, they told me to. For fifteen years I've humped up north for a wealthy *haole* rancher. My broken bones, my blood, are in his soil. Know what I got to show for it? A horse that was a gift from Rachel. I don't even own the shack I live in. You see, I deserve ten acres, because I killed for it. I slaved for it, in a system that wants to keep us slaves."

Simon answered thoughtfully. "Can't argue with that, mate. I know the drill by heart."

Vanya shifted in her chair, and took his hand under the table. The gesture, so welcomed, touched Jess, and she smiled. Then something eclipsed her reaction, in fact, jolted her to her very bowels. As Simon talked, turning his head, she noticed his flushed, slightly swollen earlobe. Below it, small patch of whitish skin. As Run Run gouged the stomach of a trout enmeshed in seaweed, something in Jess cracked open like a rib.

They entered slowly, crowding the little Painted Church at Honaunau for midnight mass. From somewhere they heard the sound of weeping. A young priest, Father Florin, welcomed everyone, then *mahalo*'ed Krash Kiwaha for donating his time and heavy machinery clearing the cemetery of old guava and mango trees whose fruit kept splashing the tombstones. He explained that Hualani Amarino was crying because someone had "borrowed" her *pahu hula* and it was Christmas and would they give it back.

Then he raised his hands. The choir upstairs began Handel's "Messiah" in Hawaiian, the aging showoff twins, Daisy and Pansy Freitas, still outsinging everyone. The congregation chimed in, modestly at first, people joining hands. Jess sang softly, feeling the vital current pass from hand to hand, Rachel on her right, Vanya on her left, beyond that, Run Run, Toru, even Simon Weir. She sang for Ming, Grandfather, Pono, feeling their breath, their pulse, within. She sang for her daughter, Anna, who didn't need her, for her mother, Emma, dead of thirst, for Rachel's mother lost so young. She sang, and singing, wept a little because it was Christmas, because the congregation was singing terribly off-key. Because she was not alone.

A memory closed in, Junior Girls Choir singing in Hawaiian, in this very church, Jess eleven, terrified. Pono outside on the grass, waving through a window, pulling out of Jess a light, a soaring, so that her voice, her singing brought people to their feet. She would always see Pono through that window, arms waving like a maestro, head inclined, inspiring her, giving her equilibrium.

Young Father Florin seemed to have fallen into a trance, eyes wide, his body collapsed in a chair. Jess suspected locals had given him too much Christmas 'ōkolehao. The choir just sang on and on, "Joy to the World" carrying them to operatic heights, so that wooden columns supporting the balcony seemed to creak and sway. And in the singing congregation, dark faces shone with the candor of glass, people sitting, stood, and people standing moved into the aisles, arms outstretched toward their neighbors.

Candles along the walls cast people in giant shadows, so that in front of them, Jess saw her cousins thrown down in radiance, their lengthened shadows prodigious and bold. She felt the heat of bodies, vibrations of the pouring out of song, the dagger-tip point of the present moment, everything, in searing clarity. And in that warm, pulsating crowd, a chill came over her, a blueness brushed her bones.

In that moment, she stopped singing, even her breathing was stilled. She was suddenly swept with visions, clear as pictures on a screen. Rachel on a train moving through Malaysia.

Milimili Jess,
    I am traveling up the peninsula toward Chiang Mai. It is beautiful and strange. The people tiny-boned like birds. They wave from their paddies. The smell of sewage everywhere, and jasmine. I drink bottled water. There is a rice-bird in the sun.

Then, Jess had another vision. Vanya, running through green fire.

'A'a Me Pāhoehoe

The Rough and
the Smooth (Lava)

RADIO, TV BROADCASTS, ENERGIZED THEM hour after hour. For weeks now, there had been the call to march, demonstrate, join sit-ins, moratoriums, observing the Centennial of Queen Lili'uokalani forced from her throne, the lands stolen from the people on January 17, 1893. Now, Christmas festivities were interrupted by crowds of Hawaiians already holding all-night vigils in front of the Royal Mausoleum in Honolulu. 'Iolani Palace was swathed in black, and during Commemoration Week, the United States flag would be removed from the state capitol and all government buildings. Only the Hawaiian flag would fly.

In every town of every island, thousands marched, demanding return of their lands, financial reparations for the past one hundred years, Hawaiian sovereignty making them a separate Native Hawaiian nation. Locals were calling the 1990s the Decade of Decision: they were prepared to march right into the twenty-first century. They were 'onipa'a.

Certain groups of wealthy haole laughed, calling Hawaiians lazy do-nothings, seeing their all-night vigils as a form of entertainment, their demonstrations a joke. This would pass, haole said, and Hawaiians would go back to their Primo beers and 'ukulele.

Then, a man wearing a black hood with eyeholes appeared on TV. "Wake up, haole. This revolution been going on for years. You know how many airline stewards piss in your drinks? Restaurant chefs wipe their armpits with your steaks. How come your pets are missing? How many *haole* tourists mugged? How many sailors disappeared?"

A reporter interviewing him said this was harassment, not revolution.

The man nodded. "Yeah, we know this is small-time, so we gonna' step it up. Now we entering the big-time, our Libyan brothers teaching us the fine art of . . . *plastiques*. Hey, *brah*! Welcome to the war zone!" He made the *Shaka* sign, waving his thumb and little finger in greeting.

The reporter was arrested for refusing to divluge the man's identity.

Hearing of the newscast, Simon shook his head. "Just what we need. A bloody publicist."

They were sitting at Jade Valley Monastery, going over plans, bombs set to go off simultaneously at a hotel and a geothermal plant. Men argued with Simon, wanting the bombs to go off on the exact date of the overthrow of their monarchy.

"Listen carefully," he said. "Bombs went off yesterday in a bowling alley near Kaneohe Air Force Base. *Kānaka* left their calling card. *'HO'OMA-NA'O LILI'UOKALANI.'* By January 17, things will be popping on every island. Police, the National Guard are already tripling forces. Security will soon be so tight you won't be able to get near a hotel."

"He's right," Vanya said. "There's been so much coverage, everyone from here to Botswana knows it's our Centennial and what was done to us. Sympathetic groups are faxing messages from round the world. One came yesterday from Northern Ireland. Another from Latvia."

"It's got to be soon, very soon," Simon said. "I figure early morning, New Year's Day. National hangover. Most people still in bed. You're not out to kill. You just want to make a statement. Right?"

He was tense and it gave his nasal voice an edge, an arrogance that put locals on the defensive.

"What you sayin'? We gotta stay sober, sittin' in dis dump on New Year's Eve?"

"You want a revolution . . . or a fucking *lū'au?*" He stood up, knocking men aside.

Vanya stood beside him in the dark, staring at the sky.

"The funny thing, the absolutely hilarious thing," he said, "is that I volunteered for this."

"You're still the enemy, Simon. It's clever men like you that stole our lands."

"All due respect, sweetheart, doesn't take much cleverness. Well, that's a bit unfair. These men are smart, they're tough and angry. But, something holds them back. Goes back to your *ali'i* days, kings, chiefs, that whole caste system, someone over them, always telling them what to do." He paused. "And what about Toru? Still doesn't know he's out, does he?"

She shook her head. "He'd kill me."

In the distance they heard rumblings. Pu'u O'o Vent of Kilauea was flowing off and on again, boiling along new paths, burning small forests. At night cars drove up and down Volcanoes National Park, hoping to see Pu'u O'o spew its fireworks in moonlight.

"We've got two nights left," Simon said. "The night before we'll transport the bombs to holding sheds, each group moving closer to their target. One heads up the west coast toward the Halekūnani Hotel. One up the east coast toward the geothermal plant at Puna. Then they sit tight in those sheds all night."

"You didn't tell them that just now."

"I don't want them all together. Men going into combat have an odor. Smells like flesh burning; adrenaline sizzling through the veins. You get a group like that squeezed in one place, invariably one of them blows. I've seen it time and again. They can't swallow, can't spit. Someone coughs, they go berserk, start shooting guns off."

She tilted her head, looked up at him. "How are you feeling?"

"I'm fine, sweetheart. Just plowing on."

"After this . . ."

"After this, I'm taking you on holiday. Denpensar. Find a bungalow with real curtains. Lie in hammocks sipping drinks."

She laughed disdainfully. "Holiday. That sounds so . . ."

"Watered down?" He studied her. "Vanya, do you absolutely need to grab each day by the throat? Don't you ever want to sit quiet, see what life blows your way?"

She tried to imagine it, a quiet, settled life, and it was like seeing herself buried neck-down in wet sand, some huge obscenity sprawled beside her licking her face.

"Is Simon on medication?" Jess asked.

"For what?"

"Vanya. I'm a physician, remember?"

She looked down, frightened. "He says its from Agent Orange in the war."

Jess closed her eyes. "Dioxin. Without medication it destroys the human organism. Liver, central nervous system. The skin. I looked at him and thought of . . ."

". . . Grandfather. He says it's similar, Jess. He's not sure the medication's working. As soon as we finish our project, I'm taking him to a specialist in Honolulu."

Jess looked down at her hands and they were shaking. "Vanya. You can't go through with this. You *can't*."

"It's too late."

Jess took her by the shoulders. "Something's happening. Ever since Pono died, I have these dreams, visions . . ."

Vanya shook her off. "We're all spooked. It's in the air. People are thinking. Really thinking."

"It's more than that. I'm frightened."

"Don't you think I'm scared? I'm terrified. You have to hold up your end, take care of the farm. It's why you came home. Don't you understand, Jess. You were called."

She hesitated, then pulled from a pouch the large black pearl, glowing and precious and rare. "Take this, Pono left it for us. It was our great-great-great-grandmother's. Sell it if you have to, to keep the farm going."

Jess held it in her hand, the beauty, the weight of it a sudden burden. Looking close, she was made dizzy by a hundred human images leaping at her from its blue-black depths, or was it light refracting? She felt momentary fright, felt intense heat from the pearl threatening to scald her nerves to a climax.

She pushed it back at Vanya. "I could never sell it."

"Jess, we haven't time for sentiment!"

She placed it in its pouch, placed the pouch in Vanya's palm. "Keep it, keep it with you. Grandfather said we should each own something small and beautiful, remember? Later, we'll decide."

Vanya embraced her, feeling they were girls again. They held each other silently, held and seemed beheld in shafts of sunlight going dim and dusty, like messages from a god who had begun to vacillate. In that moment Vanya galvanized herself into exclaiming what was truth.

"I love you, Jess. I always did. You've got to hold our world together. So much of it has slipped away."

Then exclaiming what she wished were truth.

"And I promise, when this is over, no more bombs. I'll go back to a safe bureaucratic life. I'll help out on the farm. We'll be a family."

Jess watched her leave the room reluctantly, hand brushing old *koa* chairs, a warped teak desk, her passage dignified and melancholy, as if she wanted to pick things up, hold them to her breast.

All day Run Run's face was flushed, her movements quick, irregular.

Toru sat in the kitchen braiding a rawhide bullwhip, watching her. "What's wrong with you? Slow down, slow down."

"What for, slow down." She moved close, stroked his sleek, handsome head. "Pono always say slow-motion vulgar."

He put the whip down, studied his calloused hands. He finished a quart of guava juice straight from the carton, then spoke in half Pidgin, his boyhood argot.

"*Tūtū*. I never tell you this, why, because I know you know. But, sometimes, good to hear."

"What. What." She raced round, flinging fresh squid, ink splashing up her arms.

"Everything I do, for you. To make you proud. You understand?"

She closed her eyes, crossing herself. *Grandson. Forgive me what I gotta do.*

"Okay! Okay!" She tossed a bag in his lap. "Good kine crack seed." She pushed him toward the kitchen door. "Now, out da way, till I *pau* makin' suppah."

At dinner, Jess kept her head down, unable to make eye contact with anyone. At the same time she wanted to stand up and shout at them.

Vanya. Love! Be brave. It will make your life a richer thing. Forget bombs and revolutions. We're here for such a short while. Toru, turn around. Look! Your youth is passing. Stop aiming at yourself, you're not the target. Life is the target. Live!

Slumped over her plate, she felt her shoulders hunch. Rachel had departed days ago. If these two left Jess would be alone. Middle-aged-alone. Since Pono's death, Jess felt youth had closed and locked a door, a shot and rusted bolt. She saw it in her mirror, as if someone had draped older skin across her face in sleep. *Funny, it happened when I wasn't looking, and yet I was looking. It was so subtle, the way day becomes night in a plane.*

Throughout the meal, Run Run rattled back and forth table to kitchen, hand clutching her apron pocket. She seemed unable to sit down. Now she cleared dishes and carried in a tray of finely etched shot glasses.

"Yoah *tūtū*'s crystal, time you use. Everybody going out tomorrow night, we celebrate New Year's Eve now!"

Simon sniffed at his little glass. "Smells like first-rate brandy."

"Good kine," Run Run said. "Friends bring when Duke come home from Kalaupapa."

They lifted their shot glasses, " *'Ōkole Maluna!*" threw back the brandy.

Run Run circled the table, instantly refilling their glasses. *"Hau'oli Makahiki Hou!"*

This time she didn't drink. She just stood tense, holding her glass while the others threw theirs back. Toru swallowed, smacked his lips, and motioned for another. Then his expression changed; he squinted, as if trying to focus underwater. He grunted twice, and tried to stand. His head rolled, he fell face-forward on the table.

"Mot'er God." Run Run wept as she picked his head up, looking at the others. "Okay. You help me tie 'im up, den everybody *pau*, I do da rest."

Simon stared at her, then Vanya, then it all fell into place. "Right. Now, how do you plan to keep him out for thirty-six hours?"

Run Run pulled a bottle from her pocket. "Knockout drop. He wake up too soon, I give him moah. Keep 'im out for weeks, if got to."

The four of them struggled, dragging him upstairs to Pono's big four-poster.

"Why this room?" Jess asked. "We've kept it clean, untouched."

The old woman wept bitterly, as they tied Toru's wrists criss-crossed in front of him, rolled his body in a sheet, bound the sheets tightly with rope.

"He sleep wit' smell of Duke and Pono, by and by dey enter his dreams. Dey hold him like a child, speak wise. Maybe he wake up kind. No *ho'omake* me for what I done."

Early New Year's Eve, Vanya watched men leave the monastery, gym bags cradled in their arms. Carefully, as if the bags held infants, they placed them in their cars. Two cars carrying bombs, and two escort cars. One car and escort would head up the west coast, spend the night in a deserted garage outside Kailua. At five A.M. New Year's morning, they would make the forty-minute drive up the coast to the Halenani Hotel, where Kito, the gardener, would be waiting. Another car would head up the east coast, hole up in a deserted airplane hangar, and at the same time tomorrow morning, drive to nearby Puna, where a contact would be waiting near the geothermal plant. Simon, Vanya and a driver were in the escort car headed east to Puna.

Now Simon looked round the monastery, stripped bare of everything, even walls washed clean of fingerprints.

"This is it, then," he said. "I shouldn't come back if I were you. They'll be looking in every niche, bringing in dogs. You get caught back here, they'll smell it in your hair, your clothes. A trace of explosives powder, those Dobermans ejaculate." He shook hands. "All the best. You're a good bunch of mates even if you despise me!"

Vanya hugged each man, wanting in her heart to cry.

"Kōkua Hawai'i!" she whispered. *"Huli!"*

"Aloha 'Aina! Huli!"

They drove without headlights through the woods until they reached the paved road. One by one, they hit their lights, accelerating softly, each car keeping distance from the next. Three miles down the road, a big flatbed lumbered toward them, its single headlight a bouncing eye.

Simon flicked on his two-way radio. "Eeeasy, boys, eeeeasy. Just a sugar truck."

"How do you know?" his driver asked.

He flicked off the radio. "I don't. You play the odds."

The truck passed, swerving slightly. They drove on quietly for several miles until they reached Highway 11. The first two cars turned right, headed west toward Captain Cook and farther on, Kailua. Simon's car turned left following the lead car up the east coast. After ten minutes, he rolled down the window, eyeing traffic, people driving into Volcanoes National Park hoping Pu'u 'O'ō Vent would be active that night. The park was open round the clock, and people drove in at all hours, heading down toward the sea, watching for volcanic fireworks.

Another ten minutes passed. The driver, a wiry Hawaiian-Chinese named Lloyd, looked at Vanya in the rear-view.

"So, Vanya, what happened to Toru? He plenny sick?"

"Plenty," she lied. "Food poisoning. He'll catch up with us if he can."

Simon scratched the rash beneath his ear, turned on his radio. "Simon here. Carl, how's the west coast contingent?"

The radio squawked, a husky voice came through. "A-OK! Light traffic. Boys ahead are fine."

He turned off his radio, leaned back, and felt his metabolism change.

Overhead, the sudden *Wup! Wup! Wup!* of helicopters. He spun round, looking at Vanya; she saw panic in his eyes.

"Park rangers, Simon. Keeping a night-watch on Puʻu ʻŌʻō Vent."

He looked up, saw their outlines circling like locusts, zooming far, then close. *Wup! Wup!* One of them seemed to hover directly over the car. Simon felt his wrists sprout sweat, smelled the jungles of 'Nam and Laos, excrement on punji sticks. His skin trembled all over, like something ill-fitting he had borrowed for this journey. A journey that was side-tracking, veering dangerously.

"Suppose they're not rangers. Suppose we're being tracked . . . that truck back at the monastery, too coincidental."

"Then why didn't they arrest us?"

"Maybe they don't know who they're looking for. Maybe they just got the tip." He turned on his radio. "Carl? How you boys doing? Anything behind you?"

Carl's voice again, crackling, distant. "Nothing, man. All clear."

They drove in silence, except for the chopper that seemed to be keeping pace with them. Simon cursed as the lead car suddenly braked and pulled over, signaling them.

He was out of his car before it even stopped. "What's up?"

"Spooky, man. Why dat buggah followin' us?" The driver of the lead car studied the chopper, then he pointed down the road. "Somet'ing wrong, Simon. Pile up. Look like accident maybe."

Simon moved ahead of him, eyes straining in the dark. He walked on for several minutes, stood very still, then came back half running.

"Bloody roadblock."

He slid into his car, clicked on the radio. "Simon here. Carl, listen. Where are you boys approximately? What town?"

"Hey! Not far from my folks," Carl squawked. "Six, seven miles down da road, turn-off for Miloliʻi. Five-mile roller-coaster road take you right down da sea. Paradise, man!"

Simon's voice turned clipped and harsh. "Listen carefully. Signal the car in front of you. I want you both to turn off at Miloliʻi. Got that? Both cars. *Turn off at Miloliʻi.*"

". . . What's happenin,' man?"

"Get rid of your cars, hide them."

"But . . ."

"It's *your* village. Borrow other cars. Tomorrow morning, everything according to plan."

"Simon, what da fuck . . . ?"

"They're on to something. There's a chopper cruising us. They've set up a roadblock. Maybe that truck from the monastery is tracking you. If we lose touch, hear me, *if we lose touch*, you boys are on your own."

He turned off the radio, sat there thinking. "We've got to ditch these cars."

"You're panicking," Vanya cried. "Those choppers are park rangers."

Overhead, the chopper seemed to momentarily veer off, heading toward the roadblock.

"Shut up, Vanya." Simon turned to Lloyd. "If we head into the park, we're cornered, right? There's no where to go except the sea."

"Right."

"They wouldn't expect us to do that."

"Who is 'they'?"

"Dunno. That's what bothers me." He turned on a flashlight, studied a map. "Tell those boys ahead what's happening. Leave nothing in their car."

Lloyd stared at him, confused. "Dey'll find da cars."

"Right. And assume we outsmarted them, finessed their roadblock in pickups."

"But, where are we going?" Vanya asked.

"We're going to hitch-hike, sweetheart, into Volcanoes Park. Join the crowds ogling the lava flows."

Three men got out of the car ahead, one of them cradling the gym bag. In the dark, Simon explained things quickly, relieving them of the bag.

"Break up in twos. We'll meet down at Kamoamoa Beach, fast as you can get there."

One of them hit the hood of the car with his fist. "Okay foah ditch da cars, but I no like dis park idea. Moah bettah we stay on da highway, hitchhike *past* da park. Keep going in original direction."

Simon clicked his teeth impatiently. "Listen, mate. That's a road-block ahead. Maybe they're only spot-checking. On the other hand, maybe they're waiting for us. Which of you wants to chance it, and get caught with this damned gym bag? You've got two assembled bombs in here with the nitroglycerine content equal to ten sticks of dynamite apiece."

Vanya stepped forward. "Simon. What do we do once we get to the beach?"

He looked at his map again. "Trust me."

One of the men half smiled, took the others aside. "Smart buggah! I t'ink he got a boat waiting near da beach. Take us right along da coast, near Puna way."

They dispersed along the highway, sticking out their thumbs. Within ten minutes a couple picked up Simon and Vanya.

"Not so good tonight," the young man said. "Hasn't flowed all day. Mostly you just see a red glow in the sky where the caldera is bubbling."

Simon leaned forward, making conversation. "How long does that lava take to harden?"

The young man shrugged. "Hours. Days. Depends on what's happening under the surface."

Exhausted, Vanya drifted beyond the range of their voices. When she woke, they were winding down the Chain of Craters Road, headed to the sea, passing huge, dead craters from past eruptions. The moon was full and in the distance they could see waves of frozen lava distinct against each other, more recent black flows shouldering older gray surfaces. Then they smelled gaseous, sulfur air, and in their headlights, saw the landscape change to a forbidding black moonscape. *Vog* turned the air thick, a cindery veil in the headlights' scan. The driver's wife ooh'ed and ahh'ed as the land turned spooky, cars ahead of them invisible.

Simon rolled his window down, and the woman fairly squealed. "No! Night Marchers are everywhere. They reach in, rip off your cheek! One time they spun our car in circles, tore out the windshield. We were carrying pork sandwiches. They hate pig, you know."

He and Vanya sat back, staring at the bag between his feet. After almost an hour, they reached Kamoamoa. A mile of glittering black sand, the beach had been created three years earlier by the fury of boiling lava burying forests, rushing to cold seas. Exploding underwater like fireworks, the lava had fractured into tiny particles blown skyward, that were then thrown back to land. Now Simon stared at this stretch of sand brilliant as black diamonds.

Momentarily forgetting the danger they were facing, Vanya scooped up a handful of black sand. "Exploded viscera of this island, it's freeze-dried blood. It's very fertile. Unfortunately, it also buries towns." She shook her head. "Either developers get us, or nature does. Well, Simon, what now?"

He scanned the sky, choppers hovering under clouds. One of them zoomed in, tilting and swaying in the dark, and it was like looking up at the outline of a thought, one's state of mind embodied. Then he remembered how dawn would strike a sudden blow, rendering them both visible. He sank down on the sand immensely fatigued, as if understanding for the first time his lack, his human lack, even as a strategist.

"I don't know sweetheart. I've got to get my bearings."

Singly, and in twos, the others appeared, half jogging across the sand.

Simon stood, addressing them apologetically. "Bit short on options, mates. Any ideas?"

They stared at him, disbelieving, then backed away, arguing among themselves.

One of them finally returned, his big chest heaving as he faced Simon. "No boat, right? No nothin'. Dis fuckin' insane. We goin' back da highway. Hitchhike Miloli'i, help de ot'er guys. No more takin' orders from one bullshit *haole*!" Three of them turned and walked away.

Lloyd crossed his arms and studied Simon, then disappeared in the dark. After a few minutes he returned. "Simon. Da phones work . . ."

"What phones?"

"Pay phones behind da rest rooms."

"Right. Who shall we call? The National Guard?"

Lloyd hesitated. "Dis one long shot but . . . I got *calabash* cousins, ovah Puna way. Maybe dey come get us in one boat."

Simon leapt up, grabbed him by the arm. "Christ, man. Try! Try!" He shoved change at Lloyd, dragged him to the phones, Vanya running alongside them.

She and Simon sat on the sand as coins dropped down a slot. And they waited. A voice whispering. After a while the phone was replaced in its receiver. Then, minutes later, the phone ringing, ringing! like a squalling newborn in the dark. Lloyd's voice whispering again, imploring. Then silence, as if he'd disappeared. The soft collision of Vanya's hand in Simon's, the inability to speak. Lloyd climbing out of the darkness round them.

"Simon . . . not possible with boat, currents plenny mean at night, sweep us out foah good."

Simon thought a moment. "What about this bag? Could they pick it up? Get it to that plant by morning?"

Lloyd sounded embarrassed, but somehow not defeated. "I asked. Cousins say forget it. No roadblock with no gym bag. Cops maybe lookin' for dem, too." He moved closer. "But listen, dey say maybe can help us. Can be waitin' for us with a car."

Vanya stood up with a jolt. "Where?"

He cleared his throat. "Ot'er side da lava."

"My God," she whispered. "They want us to walk it."

"Walk . . . the . . . lava." Simon shook his head confused, his brain cells jostling, settling into a new pattern. "How far? How many miles from this end to the other, over those buried towns?"

"Eight maybe."

"Has it been done?"

Vanya hesitated. "That kid on TV, did it on a bet. Took him just under seven hours."

"No miracle," Lloyd said. "Last week friends walk two miles along da shore, lava plenty hard dere."

"It's dangerous," she warned. "People fall in crevasses, break legs. You think you're on solid rock but it's boiling lava below. Even on hard surfaces, it can erupt beneath your feet."

"We've got no choice," Simon said.

Lloyd jiggled change in his pocket. "So? Okay?"

"Okay."

He slipped back into the dark. The sound of coins dropping in the metal slot, the murmuration. Lloyd came running back.

"Cousins say, 'Can do'!"

Simon checked his watch. "Almost nine now. Seven hours will put us across at about four A.M. The guy at the geothermal plant . . ." He scanned a blueprint of the plant grounds, an X marked where the fence had been cut. ". . . be waiting there at six A.M. Says that's when guards change shifts, shoot the breeze. Give him a chance to slip in, plant the bombs, slip out. They should go off some time near seven."

They left the beach then, walking the road beside cars moving slower and slower, approaching the spot where molten lava first flowed across the park road in 1986, cutting it off, continuing to the sea. Now hardened lava, rippled like hills of elephant-skin ten and twenty feet high, covered the road for over eight miles, following the shoreline. Where the black edge of asphalt disappeared beneath lava, locals and tourists parked their cars, sat on mats and blankets, looking up at Pu'u 'Ō'ō Vent, wondering if there would be eruptions tonight. Here and there little fires flared, brief as candles, but there were no big flows.

"This end has had six years to harden," Vanya said, as they began the arduous hike. "Right now we're on solid rock, but see the steam snoring out of that hole? It means somewhere in the depths, things are heating up again."

They moved slowly, surrounded by flickering flashlights, people laughing, joking, the full moon making it almost light as day. Simon had the sense of walking across a black ocean that, half a mile out to his right, soared into black cathedral cliffs, then crashed down to the real sea. Now the sea was calm; blinking ships studding the horizon.

The moon seemed close enough to stun, and Lloyd called out behind them. "Man, so bright you can *run* across dis stuff. No need foah flashlight."

They continued on, like people riding waves, undulating mounds of smooth *pāhoehoe*, then sudden ditches filled with jagged *ʻaʻā*. Here and there, orange flags warned of heavy fumes, sudden crevasses, places where the surface thinned like eggshells. There was a pervasive sulfur smell, but the air was clear of *vog*. Now and then, up on the mountain, things exploded into flames, *ohia* trees, abandoned houses, then died out like stars. Here below, only occasional pinpoints of light, tourists tripping across the lava. Vanya stumbled, nearly going down. She caught herself, stood still, taking stock of her nerves. The night was cool, December cool, yet she felt feverish.

She heard a sudden groan, and spun around, the spin leaving her so dizzy, lava seemed to twist and writhe, a great snake she had awakened.

"Lloyd?" She flashed her light, moved back in his direction. Simon leaned over him stupidly, and Vanya thought how little use one man can ever be to another, really.

"Ahh, man, look dis stuff," Lloyd cried. He was on his knees, trying to free a foot that seemed buried in the rock. "So thin went right t'rough da surface! Sneaky, yeaah?"

A couple approached in neon cycle suits, miners headlamps and pink kneepads. They shone their lights on Lloyd.

"Need help, dude?"

He struggled, freed his foot, and yelled at them. "Get the fuck off our island, '*dudes*'! Dis ain't Club Med. People's homes are buried underneath yoah *haole* feet!"

They swaggered on, shiny and vulgar.

A cloud sailed in, bringing total darkness so that things seemed to unexist. In that moment there was no conscious order, only morose ticking of the distant sea. Simon went into a time spin, his body dissolving in an almost mystical state of nothingness. This was the hour he dreaded most, when the enemy was close. He knew the Vietcong by their breath, the smell of fish fermenting in their guts.

"Vanya . . ."

"I'm here."

He spun back to the present. "What's that godawful smell?"

She shone her flashlight on a pile of rotting fish the sea had flung up in a storm. Clouds dissolved, the moon shone through, they moved slowly on, like high plains drifters, cautious, squint-eyed, surveying uncharted, unpeopled land. They were more than a mile out on the lava now, leaving crowds behind. Suddenly a forest of huge, twisted steel girders loomed up at the sky, eerie and forbidding.

"The Park's Visitor Center." Vanya played her light across the awful skeletons. "Lava flow of '89 took that. A million dollars. Gone."

They moved on, over a now-buried, but once heavily populated subdivision, Royal Gardens, beyond that, little buried towns, refuge of old-timers who had lived the old-time ways. The moon moved closer, and it was like walking across silver. Crevasses appeared, large enough to swallow human bodies. They skirted holes, creeping along in half-squats. Here and there, hard lava stood up, gruesome and confused, like futuristic buildings half-built and half-collapsed.

The burned-orange metal of a school bus protruded its full length, like something prehistoric floating in a lake. Stark totems of charred, denuded palms rose stoically, but in their midst, a tiny island of young, green palms bent and squeaked like infants. Molten lava had mysteriously forked round them.

Vanya knelt at a patch of ground beneath a palm. "Simon, look!"

He saw where her light was trained. In the midst of hunks of lava, charred branches, earth, there was actual movement, ants, tiny bugs.

"You see," she whispered. "Life prevails."

They pushed on, three miles, four, the landscape changing from smooth *pāhoehoe* hills to treacherous ditches and ravines. They were entering the heart of the destruction, where lava had flowed the deepest with greatest surge and fury. They moved cautiously, stopping, backing up when earth beneath them creaked, the sound like bacon crackling. It meant the surface was flaky and thin. Sometimes on their knees, they tested ground ahead with their hands, then carefully placed their feet there. Sometimes, they stood still, panting.

Now, they stood at the very core of volcanic destruction. Since 1983, two-thousand-degree rivers of torrential molten lava had swallowed everything here in their paths. Sometimes flowing easterly, sometimes westerly, lava had consumed highways, cemeteries, sacred *heiau*, churches, homes, whole towns.

"We are standing," Vanya said, "on genealogies."

She moved reluctantly feeling flashes of history beneath her feet, generations of fishermen dragging in nets mending them by torchlight farmers plowing modest fields wives tending supper-fires sweat pearling mahogany shoulders bent heads at table shared blood sharing food births burials graduation-*lū'au* dancing and the slap of feet clicking of *mah-jongg* tiles against the sizzz! of Primo drunk from cans and 'ukulele mandolins harmonicas whining down the years crazy shadows dipping acrobating on tent walls men gambling fighting-cocks killing with a kind of grandness and smells red earth torch ginger fresh dung the yeastiness of earth.

Kalapana. This is a village I remember being a girl in. She shivered, memories so close to the surface she seemed to hear voices below her. She smelled their food.

"We ate here one day," she whispered. "Sushi and Cokes. Pono was taking us to see the old Lava Tree Park down the highway. She bought fresh anthuriums and *ohelo* berry jam from the sushi man. I think I'm standing right over his store. Do you hear him, hear his kids' voices?"

Lloyd moved close, looked into her face. "Vanya. No more sound 'cept us. You hearin' heat ghosts."

He and Simon flanked her so they advanced across the lava like a careful wedge. She could not seem to separate what they were carrying in the gym bag from what had already happened here. They were moving across destruction, to destruction. They were *delivering* the destruction. Something rode her plasma, overtaking her. Guilt. Maybe loss of courage. *What am I doing? This is what they want. They want Hawaiians to self-destruct.* She looked seaward, toward huge cracks in lava cliffs, like water-parted hair. She felt thirst, great thirst. Her feet hurt, her lungs hurt, she ran deeper into herself.

Suddenly the earth shook, the sky exploded, Vanya was flung face-down. Simon threw himself across her protectively, gym bag in one hand, the Walther in his other, waving slowly, left and right.

Lloyd looked up at the sky. "Oh sheet, man, New Year's Eve!"

A living circus of careening lights, giant pinwheels, starbursts. A screaming green that grew into a palm tree, took up the entire sky, then sagged, melting into what looked like awful mouthwash. Catherine wheels, Roman candles, rockets in twenty colors, it went on and on, dwarfing the small embers of Pu'u 'Ō'ō Vent that occasionally burped flames. Then, the largest, loudest fireworks, an American flag, reds, whites and blues, stars and stripes laid out across the universe it seemed, saluting the new president-elect. Its sound was deafening, it made the night bright as noon and in that moment, Simon looked across the black, forbidding land.

"What the devil . . . ?"

The lava was carpeted with what looked like air crash victims, humans sprawled like the dead, others sitting, kneeling. Within arm's reach of Simon an elderly couple got up from their knees, embarrassed. Before them was a little altar, joss sticks and a Buddha. Simon stared at them, astonished.

Vanya whispered, pulling him away. "Leave them. Leave them."

"Dey prayin ovah dere house," Lloyd said. "T'ings dey left behind."

"In the middle of this blackness?" Simon asked. "How would they know where . . .?"

"Dey know."

Incredulous, Simon switched on his flashlight, swung it in an arc. Across the landscape, dozens of faces looked up, then looked away. He quickly switched it off.

"Lava refugees," Vanya said. "They come and sit for hours, even nap. They dream they're watering their lawns, tending their orchids. I've seen old men out here with wheelbarrows of fertilizer. They bring flowers to their cemeteries. They lie on blankets, the wife crochets, they talk about roofing, a water heater, a new car. One man had saved two years to buy an indoor toilet. He used it once before the lava came. Most of them weren't insured. Companies refused them, they were too close to volcano country."

They could hear murmurings across the rock, people mourning their ghost village, their buried lives. Clouds bunkered down, the night went black, and they moved on. Finding solid ground, Simon lowered the gym bag, turned to relieve himself, and tumbled down and down. In Vanya's flashlight scan, he looked like a sacrifice at the bottom of a charred pit, a shallow ditch of jagged 'a'ā.

Slowly, laboriously, he climbed back out, shirt sleeve shredded, his arm full of lacerations. "It's nothing, few scratches."

He picked up the bag, opened it, and checked. Timers, bomb cases, initiating charges, explosives, fittings, everything intact, nearly assembled, only the timers needing to be set. He pulled out a canteen, took a swig of water, offered it to Vanya. She drank greedily, passing it to Lloyd.

While they rested Lloyd ripped off the bottom of his T-shirt in a circle, wrapping it round Simon's arm. "You bleedin' plenny, man. Watch out, da heat ghosts don' get you. Dey like *haole* blood."

Simon slapped his back. "Let's move."

Hours passed. And miles. Exhaustion had set in; they could hear each other's breathing, hear their pounding hearts. Their eyes itched from dehydrated sockets, their nostrils burned from sulfur. There was the sense of limbs like giant sausage-skins weighted with wet sand. They pushed on until eventually, by some subtle change, the sense of going downhill, they knew they had passed the deepest part of the lava. A slow leveling was the sign that they had left the buried villages behind, left them to their mourners—shadows still occasionally weaving past, like stragglers in the evening *passagiata* of small Italian towns.

"Look." Vanya's flashlight picked out trees far in the distance. "As we get closer, the lava will become level with the ground, where the flow slowed and finally stopped."

It was almost three A.M. In another hour they were near the trees, palms swaying and rustling in moonlight.

"No more flashlights," Simon said.

They heard a truck somewhere on a highway. They heard the barking of a dog.

"What about your cousins?" Simon whispered.

"Dey dere, foah shoah," Lloyd said. "All I gotta' do is signal."

"Listen now. We must be very prudent. We have to go under the assumption that each step we take is a potential ambush."

Lloyd pointed toward the stand of trees. "We get close to end of lava, we move into dat grove. Where highway starts again, is like big parking lot where church was. Dey moved da church when lava started comin'. My cousins waitin' dere. I guarantee."

Ho'auhuli

Revolution, to Overthrow

THE SMELL OF TREES AFTER EIGHT HOURS, pure air entering their pores. They flung themselves face-down in grass, momentarily stunned by the runneling off of adrenaline. The sky had changed, a lessening dark, confusion in the light. After a few minutes, Lloyd rose, moved deeper into the trees. They followed at a distance. A hundred yards ahead, the parking lot seemed to float under a lone streetlight. Half a dozen trucks and cars.

Lloyd squatted, took several deep breaths, stretched back his neck and let loose with an awful keening sound, hellish and occult, so blood-chilling Vanya felt atavistic hairs ride the back of her neck. Simon counted the ripples down his spine, feeling as if someone were probing his eyeballs with needles. He thought of human sacrifices, black masses, cannibals.

"Jesus," he whispered, "that's the most disgusting, foul and filthy sound I've ever heard."

"I thought you knew jungles," she said. "That's the sound of wild boars mating."

Lloyd waited, made the hellish sounds again. An engine started, a second engine coughed. Two cars made a lazy circle round the parking lot, aiming their headlights at the trees, and blinking several times. Cautiously Lloyd stood, and whistled. Someone whistled back. He waved Simon and Vanya forward, and they were running, flinging themselves into the cars, speeding off before they'd even closed the doors. Miles down the road the cars turned right, then left, and right again, pulling up before a shack.

Inside, two men hugged Lloyd, slapped him on the back. "Eh, cousin, *howzit!*"

Then they stood back, studying Simon. They were locals, but there was something deadly and alien about them.

Simon sized them up immediately. "Where'd you boys train?"

"U.S. Navy. S.E.A.L.S."

He grinned. "I probably coordinated with you boys in 'Nam."

One of them stepped forward, a wiry, muscular Hawaiian-Chinese. "We're not boys. You're not coordinating with us now."

He turned back to Lloyd. "You've got two hours till oh-six-hundred. The plants are nine miles down the road. Once you hit them, you're moving targets."

He looked at Simon again. "So. What's your interest in this? Got a hard-on for Eskimos? Navajos? Hawaiians?"

Simon glanced at Vanya, endeavoring to keep calm.

"I like Australians," the man said. "Dumb. But tough. Only, why can't you suckers stay away from our women?"

"Now look, mate . . ."

"You look. We're doing Lloyd a favor, he's *'ohana*. One favor, that's it. This is *our* territory. We have our own agenda."

Very casually, he took the gym bag from between Simon's feet, looked inside at the bombs, the intricate wirings.

"Hmmm. Not bad. Just enough to soften up those plants for us."

He stood up, took Lloyd by the arm. "So. You make your contact, then you leave this district. Drive real fast. And take care, cousin, neh?"

He hugged him like a brother, then left with the others, all piling into one car, leaving a nondescript Hyundai behind. Outside, clouds lowered, the morning cool and overcast. The three of them sat quiet in the empty shack, like coma victims, seeing nothing, hearing nothing, so exhausted, they neither spoke nor moved. After a while, Simon stepped outside, relieved himself, stroked the gym bag like a pet, then sat down again.

Vanya studied him, with no sense of seeing, for she was looking inward. *Mine has been a life of running. And why, I wonder, why? What is in the distance that will heal me?* She dropped her head, saw Pono running through time, shattering the years like glass, a woman of heat and light, scathed, nearly broken, but running on, sizzling through the clear paralysis of mediocre lives. *Tūtū! Where are you now? I need you. Something is pointed at me. Something is gaining.*

Casting about, trying to focus on something, her gaze fell again on Simon, his swollen ear, neck red with rash, and her grandfather's voice came back to her. *Think. Only think. What you do will be irreversible.*

"Simon!"

He lifted his head, alarmed.

"I'm going to die," she whispered. "Death, it feels so close."

He came and sat beside her and she saw his eyes were wet. Rapidly, he blinked them dry. "It's all right, sweetheart. No one's going to die, we're just delivering a gym bag."

"What's wrong," she asked. "Why are you sad?"

". . . I was thinking of those folks out there, those villages, all the lives beneath the lava. I was wondering how nature, which is all we know of God, can be so damned cruel, so mindless!" He wiped his eyes again, and put his arm round her, a way of comforting himself.

"I don't know the answer, Simon. Who can know? The earth came first. This place was born of lava. It flows, and it abides. Maybe that's why we worship the sea, it's the only thing that stops the lava."

"Then why do folks stay on?"

"The land is in us now. They say this was a sacred island, not meant to be inhabited, only worshiped from a distance. Ancestors breached those sacred laws, and devastation came. Walls of flowing, boiling lava. Thousands died, or lost their minds. Survivors had no memory. They stayed. The land took hold."

He leaned his head against the wall.

"Once near the 'Nam/Laos border, I saw the Mekong River rise up like a filthy monster, taking in the country in one gulp. It swallowed paddies, villages, took cattle, entire forests. Afterward, there was nothing, just miles of mud that hardened in the sun. For weeks, families squatted over what had been their shacks, just staring at the mud. Except when we dropped shells on them, they forgot about the war. I asked a local scout why these people settled so close to the Mekong, right in its flood-path, knowing every year, generation after generation, their houses would be taken, villages obliterated. He turned to me, this skinny little bloke, and said, 'We must allow the river.' "

Simon shook his head. "There's a saying over there: 'Beware of logic.' "

"We believe that, too." She spoke slowly, thoughtfully. "Logic is a *haole* concept, we've always been suspicious of it. That's why we still follow the mystics. I think I chose the field of law and logic out of pure perversity."

He pulled her head gently to his shoulder, favoring his wounded arm. "You're not perverse, Vanya. You're a woman with an almost palpable need to offer herself up to life. Though life will never measure up to you."

As they talked he saw her life as it had been, would be: a blind leap repeated and repeated, the taut line of her trajectory lingering on his retina.

As if reading his mind, she said, "I'm sorry I'm not another kind of woman, that I dragged you into this. You don't belong here. Like Toru, you've already fought your wars."

"Don't go all metaphysical on me, sweetheart. No, I wouldn't have chosen this. But I'll tell you something most men can't admit—being a soldier is much easier than being a man. Now get some sleep, it's almost time."

She closed her eyes, then looked up again. "Simon. That roadblock was for us. They're tracking us, aren't they?"

"They're tracking something. Or maybe not. I've lost touch with intuition."

At six A.M., they stood and stretched, and moved outside. Lloyd, eerily alert, took the wheel of the car and they drove slowly down a road still empty of traffic. It took them through small towns which residents had been forced to evacuate. Drillers at a nearby geothermal well had hit a hot spot at 3,500 feet causing an eruption of hydrogen sulfide steam. Backup systems to prevent the blowout failed; hydrogen sulfide emissions poured down on villages, even on fishermen at sea. The second such blowout in a year, it left locals with respiratory ailments, nausea, infants unable to digest food. Developers of the $100 million plant refused to close down the wells, and families who had lived there for generations now faced forced relocation.

Vanya rolled down her window, gagging. "Gas still in the air. Smells like rotten eggs."

"One more blowout," Lloyd said, "maybe folks begin to die. Why dey do dis to us? Why?"

"Because we're *pau*," she said softly. "Vanishing like the Cheyenne and the Sioux."

Fifteen minutes later, they passed the turnoff where the geothermal plant was located. Signs identifying the plant had been removed.

"Couple miles down dat road," Lloyd said, "is fences, triple barbed-wire. Guards patrol." He looked at his watch. "Soon time." Then he turned the car around and swung right at the turnoff, driving slowly. "You look for funny tree, look like sideswiped by car. Dat where we turn into da field."

"In broad daylight?"

"Guards changing now. No pay attention. T'ink only be trouble at night."

Of many trees along the road, they spotted one whose bark was stripped and ragged, raw green skin shining through. Lloyd swerved, whipped into a field, tall grasses burying the car as it moved forward.

Vanya closed her eyes and they were girls again. Adolescents running through vast fields of sugarcane, limbs bare against razor-tooth-edged grasses, pricked so many times their arms and legs ran red. She saw them chasing terrified workers through the fields as if they, the blood-red girls, were cane-ghosts, couriers of death. She kept her head down, not wanting to be in this moment. She wanted to step over it, throw bombs, not deliver them. Not be resigned to courier, accomplice in the back seat of a car. It seemed so ignoble, so second-rate.

Lloyd drove straight on until they saw the fence. He slowed, stuck his head out, made a funny chirp-chirp sound. Twelve feet ahead, a bush parted, a man in guard uniform lay on his stomach. Simon and Vanya opened their doors, slid to the ground, crawling, pushing the bag before them. The "guard" thrust bushes aside, showing a large hole cut through the triple barbed-wire fence. For a second he and Simon whispered, the gym bag between them, then he pushed it through the fence, and squirmed in after it.

By the time they reached the car, Lloyd had executed a quiet U-turn. Then they were moving again, tall whispering grass caressing metal as they passed. Slumped behind the two men, Vanya felt enormous pressure in her bladder, tension in her so palpable, she felt her brain cleave to the roof of her skull. At any moment, her eyes would explode, squirting adrenaline.

Simon checked his watch. "All right. How do we get clear of here?"

"Back to parkin' lot where we come off da lava," Lloyd said softly. "Dere we pick up Route 130 take us up Hilo way. Moah bettah we take long way home, coast road 'round de island."

Simon leaned forward, fiddled with the radio. "Almost six-thirty. If those boys made it up to Halenani Hotel, something should be happening soon." There was nothing, only static. Eyes flying left and right, he snapped the radio off.

Overhead trees were coming to life, thousands of mynahs in loud oration. In a field, a boy galloping lopsided on an albino mule. Adagio of young priests rounding the corner of a church, holding down their skirts like girls. Merchants opening their road stands, fruit like clustered jewels. Black cat loping down the highway, a thoroughbred trotter. Gray stain of a dead mongoose on asphalt. They sensed these things, saw them, heard them, in unsullied rawness of new morning—yet they saw, heard nothing, their minds absorbed with fleeing.

Simon's left arm hurt, he felt deep cuts pulsing, blood dripping through rag. "Christ, I must have banged it." He thought of the man lying in the grass, waiting for the bag. "Would he squeal? If he got caught?"

Lloyd looked at him, cursed softly. "Man, you piss me off. I wonda' why Vanya wit' someone like you."

Simon shook his head. "Sorry, Lloyd. You're all right. You saved our butts last night."

"Bullshit. You t'ink we like blowin' up our homeland? In old days, we fight for honor, now we fightin' to survive. Dat Navy guy, my cousin, real intelligent, should be professor kine, role model for our kids. Look Vanya, draggin' bombs, when should be in courtroom makin' high-tone speeches. Don' patronize me, man."

They drove in silence, passing a bakery, smell of morning coffee, *malasadas*.

"I gotta take a leak, or die," Lloyd said.

He pulled into the parking lot already crowded with tour buses come to view destruction. People milled round, changing shoes, checking water jugs, guides bracing to take them across the lava. Lloyd headed for the trees. Simon and Vanya stepped from the car, stretching their limbs like children. He cursed as blood escaped the filthy bandage, running down his arm. Bending to wipe it on his pants, he noticed a *haole* in aloha shirt eyeing him. The man moved from the crowd and, almost casually, approached.

"Fishing?" He grinned and pointed at Simon's arm.

"Yeah," Simon said. "Damned moray eel. Nothing serious."

As the man continued to advance, Simon picked up the scent of Old Spice. His hair crew cut, his face smooth shaven, all edge and clarity. He knew the type. He glanced at the man's waist, where his aloha shirt, worn outside his pants, covered bulk, possibly a handgun. Intuitively, without the slightest eyeball movement, Simon knew there were two of them. Then he saw the second man, tall ambler in a dream, moving in slowly from the left. He almost felt sorry for them, wanted to tell them no one wore aloha shirts these days, except cashiers and tourists.

Some subliminal change in him, a sudden inhalation, registered with Lloyd and Vanya. They slid back into the car.

"Live here?" One of them asked carefully.

"Maybe." Simon smiled, a mean smile. "What are you boys up to?"

The shorter man waved nonchalantly toward the crowds. "Oh, lava."

"Well." He moved toward the car. "Take it slow, mates."

The tall one moved forward. "Say, mind if we ask a few questions . . . ?"

Simon's expression changed. "Who in hell are *you*?"

The man reached toward his pocket, or maybe he was reaching for his gun. In that moment the other man bent down, looking in the car. Simon's knee shot upward, connecting with a crotch. His elbow shot out, slamming into the other's jaw. Lloyd gunned out of the parking lot, car door swinging back and forth like a damaged wing.

In the back seat, Vanya lunged at him. "You fool! They were just tourists."

"Shut up." He twisted round beside her, scanning the rear window. His gun was in his hand, his face looked awful.

"That's all we need!" she cried. "We were doing fine, just fine."

Lloyd half turned from the steering wheel. "Vanya, dey wasn't tourists. I seen dere guns."

She stared, dropped her face in her hands.

"Bleeders were too curious." Simon tucked his gun back inside his pants. His arm throbbed. His head. The woman beside him was frightened. He loved her, and had not taken care of her. "Sweetheart, I know those men, that type."

"Who are they?"

"Intelligence. Narc boys. Whatever. Those bombs could blow any minute, and we're standing there passing the time of day with Feds!"

They drove in silence until they heard, somewhere in the distance, a series of explosions. Lloyd hit the brakes involuntarily, then speeded up.

Vanya moaned, bent forward rocking. "I need a rest room. Bad."

They pulled behind an ancient diner, used the rest rooms, picked up food and coffee. At 7:20 Lloyd came back from a pay phone, his face absolutely white.

"Dey blew, man. Dey blew. All hell break loose!"

Simon dropped his head, exhaling loudly.

"My cousin tell me get north of Hilo quick. He goin' underground foah now. No can call him anymore."

He drove fast, coffee jazzing up his veins. At the intersection for Hilo Airport they counted four squad cars spreading out behind them stopping traffic on both sides of the highway. The light turned red. They stared straight ahead, and prayed until the light turned green.

Lloyd swung down Banyan Drive, past smart hotels on Hilo Bay. "We follow de bay till it become Highway 19 North. Den we home free. Foah now."

They cruised along for ten or fifteen minutes, then unaccountably Lloyd braked, pulling over to the curb.

"What are you . . . ?"

He studied his rearview, put his hand up to silence them. Three cars behind him, a slate-gray Honda pulled over to the curb. He waited several minutes, pulled into traffic again. The Honda followed, keeping several cars behind. Very casually, Lloyd turned down a quiet street. He'd driven half a block when the Honda turned into the street behind him. He accelerated, made a quick right, shooting a Stop sign. The Honda speeded up, and shot the sign.

"Simon. Somebody tailin' us." He sped down narrow streets of Chinatown, making random lefts and rights. "Try look see who."

Thrown side to side, Simon steadied himself and looked behind them, pulling out his gun.

"Those clowns from the parking lot!"

Lloyd ran a red light, cursing. A woman screamed and seemed to throw small children in the air, a bag of Oriental dolls. Trapped behind a sanitation truck, the Honda lost them. The long, low blare of horns.

"We can't go north," Simon said. "They might have radioed ahead."

Vanya sat forward. "We can't backtrack. There's no way out but Saddle Road."

Lloyd hit the brakes, coming to a full stop. "No way. Moah bettah go to jail."

"It's our only chance."

He threw up his hands. "Nobody drive it. Fog, rain. *Kapu!* Dey lift our car up, put us down in hell!"

Simon stared at him as if he'd lost his senses. "What's he babbling about? What is it?"

She shook her head. "Saddle Road . . . shortcut across the island that skirts the slopes of Mauna Kea. Scientists stay at the observatories at the top."

Lloyd shouted at her. "Nobody drive it! Even scientists take helicopters to da top."

Vanya sighed. "It's the Night Marchers. He's afraid."

"Ghosts? Is that what he's afraid of?" Simon jumped from the back seat, yanked Lloyd's door open, shoved him over, and took the wheel. "Now, just direct me to this damned Saddle Road."

Following her directions, he accelerated through residential streets of Hilo that quickly became outskirts, then chilly, damp brush country. The road so far was paved and decent, but the landscape on either side turned gray as if covered with wet fungus.

"Lava flow," Vanya explained. "From the 1800s. Nothing grew back. They say the area's cursed."

It wasn't the rich black lava of the night before. Beneath gray suedelike growth on scant vegetation there were only solidified rivers of more gray. The air cooled noticeably as they began to climb. The road deteriorated, asphalt crumbling to potholes. Lloyd sat shaking, his head hanging, refusing to look out the window.

Simon glanced at him. "A grown man afraid of bloody ghosts!" He reared back as a large hunk of lava hit the hood. And then another. "What the . . . where did that come from!"

Lloyd screamed and covered his face as Vanya leaned forward, gripping Simon's shoulder. "That's what he meant. They don't want us here. It's their place."

A ball of gray filth seemed to whirl in from the left, splintering Simon's window. He struggled as the car swerved and teetered on its side, then hit the brakes and stopped dead still. Picking glass from his lap, he flung open the door and stood there yelling.

"You bleeders think I'm afraid of you!" Waving his gun at the foggy void. "I come from Abo, the Kakadu! We invented the spirit world. We invented *you*!" He waved the gun again and there was only silence.

It grew colder, as if they were entering autumn. Fog settled on the windshield like wet hair. Hitting a massive pothole, the car skidded. Simon cursed, spun the wheel, kept going. A solitary tree of gray fungus rose against the landscape like a dripping phantom and, through the splintered pane, the smell of decay, as if something hideous were sitting beside them, wrapping its arms round them. Lloyd whimpered, hid his face with his shirt. They crept along with almost no visibility. Rain came down, pelting them, an awful sulfur smell.

Simon slowed, hearing the wind, was it the wind? a moaning, almost a weeping sound, then shrieks, subhuman shrieks. His headlights picked up patches of fog shaped like moving humans. They spun away, ran forward, threw themselves against the car.

Lloyd cried, "Oh, Jesus, Mary, Joseph . . ."

"Godawful, bloody island," Simon shouted. "Why do you people stay? I mean, what is here worth *saving?*"

He was aware by Vanya's silence how that remark had cut. And he thought of her side of the island, the Kona side. Soft showers draping steep-sided valleys, drifting through banana and papaya groves, then turning into hard legs of rain that marched down to the sea and were resurrected as rainbows, like bright spent but implacable warriors climbing up the hills toward home, and flooded taro patches iridescent in sun, and lotus fields like heads of newborns, and smoke of poignant little cooking fires coming up the hills, and dusk, a certain moment when everything turned into fiction, him startled like he was startled now, remembering the first night she brought him to the house, roads gleaming sacrificial-red from coffee cherries, and coming up the drive, smell of fertilizer, soil, coffee, ginger, guava, flowers exploding all about in Gypsy-colors, the house so white, so old, so definite, enfolding this high-strung mournful feverish clan.

. . . What is it like I wonder to be so connected? Is it what I feel for that massive bulge in the Outback, Uluru? And mobs of rose-breasted galahs dragging their colors up the geometry of the rock, and how I feel when staring in the distance at pitch and yaw of lolloping kangaroos, and out beyond Perth an azure sea, and then that moment sun going, all of nature, everything rinsed into amethyst, improbable color, pure fiction, maybe everything is fiction . . .

"Simon!" She grabbed his shoulder from behind, waking him from a half-sleep.

"No one can drive in this soup," he muttered.

"That's how it takes you," she said. "The fog swallows everything. People, cars just disappear. We have to stay awake."

She looked at Lloyd snoring softly, and seeing his head relaxed and drooped, she felt unutterable exhaustion, trying to remember when last she had slept.

"About two more miles, there's a hunting cabin. We'll rest an hour, and start again. No one could follow us out here."

The place was dismal, a one-room shelter of damp wood, no windows, no door, no electricity, a corpse of something in the fireplace. A wooden box nailed to the wall with crumbling, yellowed forms asked hunters to list what game they had killed. BOAR. SOW. FERAL RAM. FERAL EWE. FERAL BILLY. And what game birds. QUAIL. PHEASANT. TURKEY. DOVE.

Amazed that they were still alive, Lloyd seemed to come to his senses. Gathering rags and sticks from a corner, he lit a match, sat huddling at the fire. "Can't stay here long, too cold. Simon, how de arm?"

He frowned, unwrapped the bloody bandage. Skin on his forearm all lacerated, above the elbow two large gashes. It hurt, but not as much as it should have.

"You know why no infection?" Lloyd said, looking pleased. "*Kukui* oil, good medicine for skin. *Kānaka* rub on dere bellies, rub everywhere. Bandage from my T-shirt full of it!"

"Thanks, mate." Simon clenched, unclenched the hand of the injured arm. "Bit stiff, and it's my shooting arm." He slid the Walther from under his shirt, checked the magazine, snapped it shut as Vanya knelt, wrapping his wound with a strip of her shirt.

"Now rest," she said. "One hour, then we go."

The men curled up on their sides. She lay facing them and closed her eyes, images dancing behind her eyelids. All-night flight across black lava. Figures like air-crash victims flung across the land. Fireworks. Explosions. Two strangers in a car, pursuing. *Bombs blew. And what did they accomplish? Will it make a difference? How many more before we make a difference?* As soon as she heard them snoring, she sat up cautiously, taking the gun from Simon. Then she slid into a corner, and propped herself against the wall.

Now, she let sleep come, there was nothing left to fight it. But it was the sleep of a woman with something lethal in her lap, like sleeping with a puff adder, so that an inner eye remained alert. In her half-sleep she drooled, the weight in her hand becoming the weight of food she was carrying to her mouth. She smelled *laulau* and twice-fried rice. *Poi.* And squid. She could taste the squid, hear oil popping in the skillet. She woke, heard something crunching on gravel, like things deep-frying. Rain. Again, she slept, dreams ebbing and flowing, like figures passing through a door.

One of the figures bent over Simon with a gun. "Easy. Slow . . . and . . . easy. Put your hands above your head. Now, turn over on your stomach." He leaned down, frisking him.

The other one waved his gun in Lloyd's face, his hand between Lloyd's legs. Locating a hunting knife, the man started withdrawing it from a slender sheath sewn in the inner thigh of Lloyd's jeans. Lloyd grunted, did something funny with his leg, the *haole* tumbled back. In that instant, Simon rolled away from the other.

"Don't do it," the man yelled. "I'll shoot!"

Simon kept rolling toward the doorway. The man half squatted, aiming with both hands. Walls reverberated with the shot. A piece of doorway splintered and he aimed again.

Later, she would think it was his posture that repulsed her, lethal, premeditated. Vanya stood and sighed, lifted both arms, her finger on the trigger, squeezing, squeezing in the rueful certainty that this act made everything irreversible. Her arms exploded in their sockets. Deaf, she was flung against the wall. The cabin lit up with the shot, and in the brightness, he spun, surprised, dismayed, trying to speak, but some vital element within was breaking down. He seemed to kneel, looked at his gun, then up at Vanya, his lips lax, eyes blank, expression fading like bright colors of a hooked fish.

Simon came up behind him, tipped him over with his foot. He fell forward, the back of his aloha shirt petalled out and crimson.

Across the room, his partner sprawled, Lloyd spread-eagled over him, gun in one hand, knife in the other.

The man stared at Vanya, disbelieving. "Lady, you just shot an agent of . . ."

Lloyd struck him in the face with the gun, then pushed the barrel up his nose, speaking quietly. "Now it yoah turn. *Haole*."

Simon crossed the room in long strides, took the gun from Lloyd, and dragged the man to his feet. "Your lucky day. We're going to let you live." He shoved him outside, pushed him into the trunk of the Hyundai. "You start yelling, even dare to think of it, they'll find your entrails down the road."

The man folded himself into the trunk, holding his bleeding face. Inside the cabin, no one moved. The man on the floor seemed to be sleeping. Very carefully, Simon took the gun from Vanya and held her by the hand.

"Simon." Lloyd seemed half angry, half in shock. "Why you let de ot'er live? He bring da cops . . ."

"He *is* the cops. If I waited one more minute, you'd have wasted him."

"Dat's right. Look dis one, he try shoot you."

Simon shook his head. "Lloyd, listen to me. You've still got a chance to get out of this without killing somebody. Once you do that, take that step . . ."

He gazed at Vanya, standing next to him and yet a long way away from him. She was suddenly a long way away from everything. He moved to the body, bent down to touch it.

"He dead," Lloyd whispered. "Real dead. What we do now?"

"We run. Alone. It's bad for you to be with us."

"No, man. I stick it out wit' you. Find some place to hide."

Vanya murmured something.

"What, sweetheart?"

Her voice was very small. "Waipi'o . . ."

"Yeah," Lloyd cried. "Da valley. Jungles, caves, plenny old-timers help us. Outsiders *kapu*. Not even U.S. Army find us."

"All right, then get us there." Simon looked out the door. "We take their car, then you ditch it, chuck it in the sea. Then get back to your boys."

"But, Simon . . ."

"Don't worry, that bloke could never make you in a lineup. The cabin was dim. You'd be just another *kanaka*."

Lloyd shook his head defiantly, and Simon grabbed him.

"Don't you get it? It's all over for her. We're fugitives now."

Lloyd glanced at Vanya and what was on her face so chilled him, he began to understand. He started the engine as Simon slid into the back with her, not talking, knowing the futility of words to one in shock. He put his arm round her and she looked at him with an expression he had never seen in another human. He had only seen it in wild animals at full gallop. Then her eyes changed; all of a sudden the idea that he existed here beside her entered her mind. He pulled her head against his shoulder, held her tight.

Geography had formed him, the Outback, space so limitless it left some men insatiable for human commerce, left others silent, perverse. That perversity simmered for years within him, so Simon found himself outside society, committed to nothing and no one except a fraternity of assassins. One day, in an ecstasy of betrayal, retaining the right not to belong, not to be accountable, he abandoned that fraternity, became again a man outside everything.

He rode the years alone, and there was nothing. He searched for an Absolute, some force, some thing that would not incorporate, not easily be solved. He went back to the Aborigines, the mystics, who knew where they were going. But years had intervened, now they scraped their sticks across the land and slowly died. Simon went his way again, and saw her.

There was her telling posture, proud, and when she turned to him, something broken in the eyes. That so impersonal and animalistic a dignity should be allied with so poignantly human a sensitivity, stilled him. His first thought was not possession of her, but rather, *She will teach me something. She is my apprenticeship.* Now they were running side by side, and he ran with the reconcilable knowledge that here was something he would not betray. He would save her by going under with her.

Very subtlely, the land changed as they moved west. A lessening of that gray fungus pelting everything, a few more trees, sunshot fog, a coming green. Still, the air was damp and cold, the road hellish, hairpin turns, potholes. Lloyd twisted his head left and right, looking for Night Marchers, but he no longer flinched when hunks of lava hit the car, whirling as if thrown. Having witnessed how totally a bullet could eradicate a human—how swiftly it stopped all the inner sluicings and murmurations—the moody spirits of this landscape seemed harmless, all knife-flash and no blood.

"Simon," he said, "maybe I come visit you when t'ings cool down. Old-timers in Waipi'o guarding bunch our crates. Whooo, what a bitch dat was, sliding guns, explosives, down da mud at night." He studied him in the rearview. "What you folks goin' do? Live dere forevah? Vanya real *kalaima* now, foah shoah."

"We'll take it slow." He gazed down at her. "Very slow indeed."

She stirred, dug down in her pocket, poured from a small pouch a perfect sphere, a large, glittering black pearl. She stared, as if willing it to speak, then held it up against her cheek.

"Waipi'o?" she whispered.

"We're on our way."

"Then . . . what happens . . . ?"

"Nothing, sweetheart. Everything has happened."

'Awa

The Tea for Curing Grief

RAGGED PLUMES OF STUTTERED SPEECH held between clenched teeth. He struggled like something being born, hands moving erratically, one scratching, one knitting. The bed seemed draped in billowing white skin and underneath therein, the mummy coming back to life. They braced themselves, ignoring the odor, fetid, something just short of serious disease.

For fifty-four hours Run Run had sat there with a loaded gun. Twice he had moaned, swimming to the surface, and twice she had tried giving him more knockout drops. Trussed, bound in winding sheet, only one-quarter conscious, he did not, could not, swallow.

She pleaded with Jess. "Do it. Wit' da needle." And she watched. *Mot'er God, I nevah t'ought I see again a needle goin' in his arm.*

Jess was professional and calm. A beautiful decorum in the way she held the needle to the light, then pierced him. Afterward she stood alone and sobbed, imagining his junkie years, Toru hooked, like a fish.

Now the awful, prodigious resurrection. ". . . water . . ."

Jess lifted the mosquito net, and then his head, bringing a cup to his mouth. He drank slowly, eyes traveling her face.

". . . feel awful . . . what happened . . . ?"

She looked across the room.

"Tell him!" Run Run said. "Wha' can he do but kill me."

He twisted, looked down at his body, the fouled sheet, burn of ropes round his wrists. He thrashed wildly, tossing his head side to side, the movement freeing odors, urine, worse.

"... get me out ... of this ..."

The shock. Residue of drugs. He fell back into sleep.

"I smell like shit." Now he was fully awake.

Run Run and Jess approached the bed, silently threw back the net. Both looking very old, they came at him with scissors.

"What time is it?"

"Amost midnight."

"What day?"

"January first."

His face blue-gray, frenzied in defeat. He sobbed. They snipped and snipped. Sheets, pads, mattress, everything would have to be burned.

Arms freed, he tried to grab Run Run by the throat. "I'll kill you, filthy bitch!"

"Yeah," she seemed exhausted. "First you bathe. Den you can beat me to deat'."

They sat him up slowly, then Jess ran his bath, her expression strange, a curious lack of emotion. Toru sat sobbing in the tub, cursing them while Run Run soaped him down. Then shakily, he stood, showering, rinsing all of it, all the unlived, medicated hours, down the drain.

She wrapped him in a towel, sat him in a chair. "Try wait. I bring you food. You get up yet, you gonna faint."

He lashed out at her with his foot. "Why? Why? People were counting on me ..." He dropped his head and cried again, somewhat dopey and confused.

She came back with a tray of food. Toru grabbed it and slid down to the floor, eating with his hands like a mendicant.

"You're never gonna see me again. Never! You made me look like a coward."

Silently, Run Run bent to take the tray, her lack of expression infuriating him.

He threw the tray across the hall, and slapped her face. "Are you deaf? You have made me a *girl!*"

She staggered back, slid herself along the wall. Something was wrong with her, no response, no emotion whatsoever.

Jess called up the stairs. "Run Run, the news again."

She looked at Toru. "Yeah. I deserve yoah hate. But first, come look da TV, so you know."

Television cameras scanned wreckage of a storage building, housing drilling equipment for a geothermal plant in Puna District. Bomb damage to the plant itself was negligible.

Then, the face of a reporter broadcasting from another location. "In a perhaps-related incident, a bomb blast here at the Halenani Resort Complex early this morning was responsible for the destruction of a swimwear boutique and the loss of a staff member's hand. Another bomb, a dud, was found inside the office of Dr. Rebirth, a so-called Cranial-Sacral Therapist who offers seminars in what the hotel calls its Polynesian Temple of Love. Scrawled across the walls was the message: HERE IS OUR KINE LOVE TO YOU. *HULI*!"

The complex had been evacuated while bomb crews combed the grounds.

Toru cursed as hotel spokesmen aired their views on local "terrorists." Then a well-known newscaster appeared on-screen. Jess and Run Run moved together, holding each other.

". . . an update of the evening news. Richard Flanner, an agent of the Federal Bureau of Investigation, based here in Hilo, was shot to death today by what police are describing as a female member of a probable terrorist group. The man's partner, Fred Moriarity, eyewitness to the shooting, said Flanner was shot in cold blood at a hunting cabin on Saddle Road early this morning. Unaccountably, the group set Moriarity free. He described the female suspect as dark-skinned, locallooking, accompanied by a local-looking male, and a tall Caucasian with a red mustache, sounding Australian. The man appeared wounded in his left arm . . ."

In disbelief, Toru turned. By their dead faces, he knew they had heard the news earlier.

". . . blood found on the grass where terrorists entered the Puna plant matched blood found on the door of the car abandoned by the fugitives on Saddle Road. When last seen, the female suspect was wearing khaki pants and jacket, black T-shirt, black running shoes. The men were wearing blue jeans, T-shirts and jackets. They are believed to have fled in the FBI agents' car, a light blue Honda. They are armed and dangerous. Anyone with information regarding the whereabouts of this group, or of their affiliates, is asked to call this station. Your calls will be treated as confidential . . ."

Run Run's head was bowed. "She a runnin' dog now dat will haunt my ashes." Her voice broke and she sobbed.

He staggered out to the *lānai*, fell to his knees, stretched his arms across the filigree railing, and hung like a big, damaged spider. The days lost, the hours, the drug still licking at his nerve ends, the dreamlike nightmare of it all. It was another year, and everything was gone.

"VANYAAAA!" His cry echoed out across the lawn, down through the fields, went brooding in the trees. Two running dogs stopped and listened. He folded, weeping like a woman. Jess came and knelt beside him.

"I should have been there. It wouldn't have happened!"

"Toru. She didn't want you there."

"Why?" He beat the floor of the *lānai*.

"She wanted you to stay and help me with the land. She was afraid your life would pass unlived." She wrapped her arms round him, rocking him, trying not to let him hear how she was broken down inside. "She was afraid if you started down that road with her, there would be no way back."

"But this was *my* plan. How could she double-cross me?"

Jess shook him a little, and it hurt, the motion hurt, as if her bones were giving up. "Don't you see, she was trying to point the way."

"Vanya. Oh, Vanya . . . what are we gonna do?"

"I don't know. How can we know." She rocked him, rocked herself, dropped her head and prayed. For what, she didn't know; all she knew was that she desperately needed a point of focus.

He lay injured in her arms calling Vanya's name, so it became like the beat of a metronome inside an empty skull. After a time, Jess cocked her head and listened. The crunch of gravel, slow silhouettes of bodies accumulating. Pinpoint lights flickered up the road, people carrying tiny candles inside small paper lanterns. Very quietly, they filled the drive, moved across the lawn, closer to the house. The night was cool, some wore headscarves, bulky vests, and boots, like Mongols slipping from their yurts at milking time, whistling up their mares. She saw the moon on faces. There was weeping.

"Toru. They've come to be with us."

Little packets, discharges of soft artillery like small birds, flew up from their hands, landing softly on the *lānai*.

Jess held one to her nose, inhaling. "'*Awa*. For rinsing grief."

And then their words flew up in whispers.

"*Mālama 'Āina!*"

"*Kōkua Hawai'i!*"

"*Aloha 'Ohana!*"

"*Imua . . . Imua . . . Imua . . .*"

Run Run crept outside, leaned over the railing, threw down her sobs like coins. "Pray! Pray for her! Vanya my granddaughta' too!"

Jess gathered Run Run's old birdbones in her arms, and rocked her.

Looking at the faces staring up at them, folks crying, praying, needing to be there, Jess called out. "Come, come inside. We are all *'ohana.*"

They came and they came. They stood along the walls, and sat on floors and filled the kitchen and the living room, silently chewing, pounding the *'awa* root, straining it through water. From huge bowls, Jess ladled it into cups. They held their cups in weather-beaten hands, and when their cups were empty they held each other, drawing strength from the old Hawaiian way of hugging, staining each other's skin with tears. Some stretched out and slept, lining the floors, touching each other's hand or foot, their blood, their *pumehana*, deep belief in *E pupukahi* the bridge over which they traversed these awful hours.

Pre-dawn colors sliding in, workers quietly dispersed, heading for the fields. The warmth of bodies filling up the empty house had strengthened her. Jess stood feeling immensely worn but durable. She would endure. Whatever was coming, she would not break, and she knew they were coming. She woke Toru and Run Run, made strong coffee, sat them down and drilled.

"Be civil, helpful. We must appear shocked, confused. But don't . . . break . . . down. We've got to be *kanaka*-strong."

Toru leaned forward. "What if they ask . . ."

"*LIE.* Lie through your teeth. No matter what. Even if they punch you up. We know nothing of her activities. They'll question us separately. Threaten us. Threaten the workers. Maybe arrest us. *LIE.* We know nothing. Nothing."

They came up the drive. Squad cars, cars full of military types, and others. CIA. FBI. DEA. Jess was impervious as a wall. Toru watched her, amazed; her voice seemed changed, her body. He didn't even know parts of her. They came and came, day after day. They sat for hours, interrogating, searching the house, the sheds, the fields.

They showed videotapes of Vanya demonstrating at Pearl Harbor.

"REMEMBER . . . REMEMBER . . . REMEMBER."

"That's you beside her, right? Harassing the president of the United States."

"Yes," Jess said. "Me, my cousins, and our friends. People from all the islands. We were not harassing, it was very orderly. No arrests."

"Wasn't your purpose there to embarrass the president?"

"No. It was to remind him of people round the world who've suffered, not just the victims of Pearl Harbor."

They showed her tapes of Vanya demonstrating in the streets, leading Hawaiians marching for sovereignty, demanding back lands stolen from the people. They showed newscasts of her cursing construction crews for desecrating ancient *heiau*. News clippings quoting her as saying "Terrorism is the new Mother Tongue." If Hawaiians couldn't have access to all beaches, she had recommended beaches be blown up, and so should most of the luxury hotels where locals were allowed only as maintenance crews. FBI agent Moriarity had identified her as the woman who shot and killed his partner.

"There must be a mistake," Jess lied. "She never touched a gun."

"The man she's traveling with, the *haole*, you never saw or heard of him?"

"No, never. I don't believe the woman is my cousin."

"Then, where is your cousin?"

"Traveling, possibly. We don't always keep up with her."

They started in on Toru every day at dawn. His dropout years, the decade of heroin. They asked about his friends, who he spent his time with. He named old *paniolo* up in Kohala, men with no teeth. They asked of his whereabouts the day of the bombings and the shooting. A local physician lied, saying he had paid a house call, diagnosed it food poisoning, left Toru in Jess's hands. A local pharmacist showed them his records, a prescription Jess had had filled. Toru showed them the bed where he lay ill for almost three days, the odor still strong, offensive. His ranch bosses vouched for him, a good worker, no police record, now a small landowner, wanting to be left alone.

They questioned Run Run, who answered them in sobs and shrugs, barely comprehending. A local cop talked to her in Pidgin, coaxing her. She clasped her coral rosary beads, pinned a picture of the Virgin to her dress, crossed herself repeatedly. Impatient, the cop threatened her, threatened to make it hard on Toru, jeopardize his job. She threw herself upon her knees muttering incomprehensibly.

Mot'er God, get dis prick out my room befoah I slap him good. Imagine! One local boy, dis cop, workin' for haole devils. He t'ink I one pupule ol' wahine.

Hah! I like put wela chili peppah in his food. He sheet, his ʻōkole so hot, maybe he come blind! Now, please, get him out my room.

Still they came, prowling, questioning, looking for a clue. And when investigators went away, they wrote notes to each other, read them, burned them instantly.

"THE PHONE IS BUGGED, THE HOUSE. WE HAVE TO LEARN TO LIVE WITH THIS."

"WE'RE UNDER 24-HOUR SURVEILLANCE, DON'T DO ANYTHING STUPID."

"I KNOW WHERE SHE IS."

"IF YOU TRY TO REACH HER, YOU'LL THROW HER LIFE AWAY. ONE DAY SHE'LL SEND A MESSAGE, SOMETHING."

"THEY COULD GET A BOAT. HE COULD TAKE HER TO AUSTRALIA."

"SHE'LL DO WHAT SHE WILL DO."

"A LOT OF ARMS ARE CACHED IN WAIPIʻO. I THINK SHE'LL CARRY ON."

"TORU, NEVER, NEVER PUT SUCH THINGS IN WRITING. STORE UP WHAT YOU HAVE TO SAY. WE'LL WALK THE FIELDS EACH EVENING. HAVE YOU FORGIVEN ME AND RUN RUN?"

"NEVER."

Jess was immensely relieved. Anger, bitterness was better than guilt. Guilt led to grief, passivity. She and Run Run worked to harass him, keep his blood up.

He woke at dawn on weekdays, driving up to the ranch at Kohala, roping, branding, checking calves. Weekends he came home exhausted, tried to sleep and forget. Run Run banged around at five A.M., waking him, dragging him to church. For months, she had an eye on someone, a young, husky niece of Daisy and Pansy Freitas. Like them she was a choir showoff, voice awful but, by God, it carried. A student at the local university extension, she wanted to be a high school teacher.

Run Run studied her. *Smart. Good brain. And she got sturdy shoulders, hips. Body can handle one stubborn, wayward man. Knock him into shape. Look how she stroke her little brotʻer's head. Good girl, likes* kamaliʻi. *Maybe like have couple of her own.*

She pointed the young woman out to Toru. "See dat *wahine*? Not'ing but trouble. Showoff, wild, break her mot'er's heart. She like tease men. Go swimmin' in da nude! One day I seen her near de orchard. I say her, get off dis land! One da workers like go dancin' wit' her. I say him, you dance wit' dat cheap, vain *wahine*, you finished here. I no can look at her. She got evil smile."

Her name was Lena. Golden brown Hawaiian-Filipino. She wore a flower in her hair, and walked right past him, proud. He turned his face away, watching without watching.

One day an Army helicopter spotted a woman bathing in a stream in Waipi'o Valley. Squads of soldiers went in. It leaked into the news, and Toru sat before the TV scribbling a note:

"I HAVE TO GO AND HELP HER. I CAN'T JUST SIT HERE LIKE A GIRL."

Run Run burned the note, and dragged him to the fields.

"Look out, boy! Hand dat feed you now slap you to yoah senses. You try go to her, I shoot you in da leg, I swear. Not foah you. Foah Vanya! You lead dem right to her. Dat's what dey waitin' foah."

"This is killing me," he cried. "I'm so ashamed, I want to die."

"I know you shame." Her voice turned gentle. "I shame, too. But, you no want to die. Else why you bot'er cryin'? You nevah cry foah twenty years. Now you cry. Foah Ming, Pono, Grandfat'er, everyt'ing. See, *keiki*, cryin' like washin' clothes, come clean. When finished cryin' den a new beginnin', not same old, tired end. Cry good! Cry hard! Den *pau*, stand up like a man."

She put her hands on his shoulders, crooning, "Toru, you want help Vanya? You got ten acres good, good land. Build somet'ing permanent. Foah her."

She thought up tasks for him, feigning illness so he stayed home, helped cook, feed the workers, helped Jess oversee the picking, bagging, weighing of coffee cherries. He sat with Lee Sugai discussing fertilizers, new roasting methods. At night Run Run and Jess huffed beneath the moon, smashing large rocks against the rotting, sagging porch steps leading to the kitchen. Then they complained to him how everything was falling down. For weeks they listened to him cursing while he rebuilt the steps, then rebuilt the porch, his face eased and softened because his body was busy.

Sometimes when he and Jess were in the fields, he backslid, talked about Jade Valley Monastery, wanting to round up the boys who were lying low.

"We started something, we have to keep up the momentum."

"You didn't start it. It started years ago. It's doing fine without you."

A large earth-moving crane at a golf resort development had been blown up that week.

"What are you saying, Jess? You're saying Vanya killed someone so I could retire?"

"I'm saying you've given enough. Maybe your job now is to take care of what we're fighting for."

"'Āina. 'Āina. That's all you think about."

She turned on him, impatient. "I know you miss combat, the thrill of *mano a mano*. But look. They're blowing things up, yet nothing's changing for Hawaiians. Developers just bring in more cranes, rebuild the geothermal plants. Your strategy is wrong. No one's thinking straight. That's an individual process, not something you do in a mob. Toru, you can't figure out who you are and what you believe, and what you personally want to do, if people around you are throwing bombs. Tell me, maybe I'm slow, how does blowing up hotels advance our people?"

He looked at her dead on. "I thought you supported Vanya."

"Vanya lives by different rules. You've always known that."

"Then, what are you telling me to do?"

"Build a house, have a family, educate your kids. You're smart. You could have been a lawyer like Vanya. Maybe one of your kids will be that."

Very casually, she glanced across the orchard, and up a hill, across Napo'opo'o Road. Something glinted in the sun, reflection on binoculars maybe. They walked on silently, and Jess thought how in a way, Vanya *had* retired Toru. Knowing he was under surveillance kept his friends from trying to make contact, kept him exempt from anything subversive.

One day Jess came running to her room, dragged Run Run from her quilting. They stood together at a kitchen window. In the distance two figures on horseback, Toru and the young woman, Lena. They were near the south end of the land, and seemed to ride in long, lazy ever-widening circles, as he showed her the size of his ten acres. Then they leapt a fence, cantering down the road.

She spurred her horse into a sudden gallop, golden, husky she was, and golden the horse, and the golden dust they sent up in clouds, their yipping voices as she challenged him to catch up and keep up with her, and they ran hard together past fields of fermenting guava hanging in the trees and eucalyptus and ripe *liliko'i*, and running fowl and frangipani milky in the air and roots throwing out lichen, mold, humus, smells like the ocean after rain, gold dust making the ocean golden, and the day was golden, and Run Run clapped her hands and pledged herself to Mother God.

When he came home she was whacking chicken parts, kicking viciously at Ula.

"What you doin' wit' dat cheap *wahine*? She ugly, first of all. Body got no front, no back. Secondly, she phony. Talk dem high-tone words. No can talk Hawaiian kine."

For weeks he sat at dinner, dreamy and distracted. One night he pushed back his plate decisively. "I'm thinking of cutting back my hours at the ranch. It's hard to concentrate, spooks up there in unmarked cars, trying to look like cowboys. They sit there waiting for me to . . . I don't know what."

Silently he wrote the letter *W* in the air. They were waiting for him to try to make contact with Vanya in Waipi'o Valley. Army squads that went in had come out with nothing but scorpion stings, wounds from two wild boar attacks, and ringing in their ears, a ringing so incessant they were sent "stateside" for medical attention.

"Anyway," Toru continued, "It's good for workers' morale to see me here more often, taking an interest in things."

Run Run kept her eyes down, feigning apathy, hands clutching her knees under the table.

He was at a crossroads, an end and a beginning. He would never make his peace with life—the war, theft of his innocence, Run Run's betrayal, Vanya's sacrifice for him, yes, he would always feel it was for him, a bullet entering another human, the shot that took her out of time, maybe that had been for him, his lost years—but now there were nights they saw him down on his ten acres, walking round, or just sitting, strumming softly on his 'uke. He began to wake before dawn, taking each day by surprise. He began to clear his land.

One day they saw him sitting on a stool, stripped to the waist, bent over a water bucket. Lena, the golden, husky young woman, ceremoniously washed his hair, humming and singing as she scrubbed, as if she were currying a horse. His head was lathered into a white turban, her arms looked hung with frost. She poured water on his head, filled the bucket from a hose, and slowly poured again. When Toru's hair was rinsed, she towel-fluffed it dry until it shone black as wet tar. Solemnly, he closed his eyes and she combed his hair in place, trimmed a little at the neck, then stepped back, admiring his Oriental head, his beauty.

Then almost stealthily, she picked up the hose, aimed it full force, and he was a man exploding—hair, face, everything blown to pieces. He shouted, chased her down the hill, both wet and gleaming, bodies turning violet, terra-cotta, as they ran in and out of shadows of un-barbered trees. He caught her round the waist and they stood still, silhouettes against the land, a frail nobility of aspect and address.

* * *

'Awa entered their systems, swam in their veins like blood, packets of it left each night in little pyramids, workers saying without saying *E pūpūkahi*. It didn't seem to help. Sleepless, terribly alone, at night Jess pored over old photo albums, as if the stained and sepia and termite-pocked faces could tell her Pono's secret, how to follow in the footsteps of the ancients, how to go on. She studied a snapshot of her mother, Emma, then one of her daughter, Anna, wondering if she had lost her daughter because she, Jess, came from a family of women who were, themselves, so lost. Then one night she saw herself, a dream Pono was dreaming in the deep. She heard Pono's voice.

"YOU ARE ENTERING MIDDLE LIFE. NEED LESS. DESIRE LESS. MOST THINGS, AFTER ALL, ARE NOT WORTHWHILE. WITHDRAW FROM THEM. TAKE JOY IN STRUGGLING WITH THE LAND. BE TRUE TO BLOOD. ALWAYS FACE THE SEA."

She woke with a start, dragged her bed across the floor so it faced the ocean. Remembering her dream of Vanya running in green fire, now Jess dreamed of her melting into the soft eye of the jungle, full of her absolute vision. And she dreamed of Rachel, on a ferry, crossing from an island, Hong Kong, to Kowloon on the mainland. A woman alone, on the edge of a continent. She knew within a few days a postcard would arrive from Kowloon.

It came to Jess then that she had inherited part of Pono's gift, not the full, lush, burdensome gift of *kahuna*, of life-giving and life-taking, but the smaller gift of dream-seeing, of real-imaginings. She thought of the days prior to Rachel's departure for Thailand, her calm, her purity of purpose. Jess had flown over to Honolulu to see her off, and each thing she had dreamed would happen, happened.

Arriving in a cab, she had stood in Rachel's driveway, struck by the grounds, the house, everything manicured, paradoxical and lush, compared to Pono's sprawling, scrappy, termite-riddled farm. Then Rachel came at her across the lawn at an odd, maniacal tilt, sweeping Jess in circles.

"I have a surprise!" Ceremoniously, she had led Jess across the lawn. There was a teahouse beyond the fish pond, an ornate, winged-roof structure set off by itself. Rachel drew her in that direction.

"Wait a few minutes, then knock." She had disappeared inside.

The sun was slipping, shooting boulevards into the sea. On the beach below, birds attacked each other instead of courting, and fish seemed to be swimming in lopsided circles. Finally, Jess knocked, removed her shoes and entered the teahouse, dim, and smelling of cedar. *Tatami* mats covered the floor, the only furnishing a low, black, lacquered table with a tea service, where Rachel knelt, virginal in a white kimono. Her hair was in the *geisha* style and, like a *geisha* girl, she bowed her head, seemingly shy.

Jess moved forward, enchanted, and knelt facing her, smelling jasmine tea. There was a window beside them, looking out on the ocean. There was nothing else in the room.

"But . . . what is the surprise?"

Rachel seemed to fall into a state of deep meditation, and Jess sat back confused. The sun shifted, light flooded the room. Suddenly the wall behind Rachel resonated. A fierce red dragon was locked in mortal combat with a human warrior, both of them struggling under glass. What was mounted under the glass was large, life-size, and oddly shaped, remotely resembling a mounted deerksin.

The dragon seemed to gather strength each time the light shifted, so its eagle talons lengthened, its great scales glittered, and the goblin nose breathed flames. Above the head of the warrior, maple leaves fell, suggesting mortality. And lower, where the thing angled out in the shape of flattened thighs, blue carp with long eyelashes swam upstream trying to spawn.

Rachel lifted her head, her eyes fixed in a weird, exalted stare. "He was already dying when they killed him. Suffocation from the tattoos."

Sharp teeth clamped down on Jess's brain, she felt momentarily blinded. Then she rose unsteadily, and moved to the wall. The thing leapt out like a firmament, garish, blinding, but then up close, the elegance of fine calligraphy. She stared at the wonders of Hiro's skin, resplendently blue.

On each buttock, swords sliced through bursting red peonies, and yellow warrior lion-dogs barked at his shoulders. Thick green serpents encircled his arms, and around his calves Buddhist prayers curled diagonally. This childless man, who had had no childhood to speak of, had carried, tattooed on his belly, a perfectly etched, fat, laughing, little boy riding a whiskered catfish.

"After almost thirty years," Rachel whispered, "I deserved to keep something of him, didn't I? *Didn't I?*"

Finally, she possessed Hiro completely, by possessing his armor against the world. Jess thought of a large, defenseless, skinned rabbit-like being roaming the afterlife, and reached out toward the glass, and fainted.

Two days later at Honolulu Airport, Rachel seemed already gone, head turned, gazing at some far destination.

"There's a stopover in Hong Kong. Is that near Russia?"

"It's very far."

She threw her arms round Jess, clinging for a moment. "Isn't it strange. I don't know what is near, and what is far!"

"Rachel." Jess's voice shook, she struggled, pulled herself together. "Do what you need to do. Don't do more. Don't put yourself in danger."

"Ban is waiting. He will be beside me like a son."

They stood very still, and Jess felt they were bathed in light, invisible, immune, to others. Time burned in their nostrils. Then they heard the boarding call, a disembodied voice like God, summoning. Rachel moved quickly with long strides, waved at the entrance to the accordion passageway, then seemed to fling herself into a new dimension.

Some nights Jess lay in the dark, groaning, trying to force her dreams. *Where is Rachel now? Is Vanya hurt? Wounded?* Nothing. Dreams arrived in their time. One day a call came, a voice young and somewhat breathless.

"Mother? Men were here, asking Daddy about you. Are you all right?" Anna's voice verged on hysteria.

No, I'm not all right. You deserted me. I'm over forty. I'm alone.

"I'm fine. There's been a little trouble, a mistake. Things will blow over."

"They said somebody died!"

"People do. My grandmother died. And my grandfather. My cousin, Ming."

"Oh, God, I'm sorry. What are you doing there alone?"

"I'm living, Anna. I run a coffee farm. *This* is my home now."

"Will you ever come back east? I mean, to visit?"

"Probably not. But you are always welcome here."

"Right now I . . ."

"Someday, when you're ready."

"Daddy sends his best. He was worried, too."

She stumbled through the house, remembering her ex-husband, how toward the end of their marriage everything became a sign for her, that he hated her, or just disliked her. If she wore yellow, he preferred brown. She wore gray, he said she looked bloodless. She dressed in black, he wanted red. She stopped dressing, stopped functioning, stood in her marriage unclaimed. Yet, he was a good father, a provider. He had pressed Anna to make that call.

Sensing her terror, her isolation, the huge task she had undertaken with the farm, one day Run Run took her arm, and walked her through Pono's room, into a deep closet. In a box were all of Jess's letters through the years, the decades.

Jess fell to her knees, burying her arms in them. "But she never answered! Never. Not one."

Run Run sighed. "You nevah know dis but yoah *tūtū* . . . she no could read or write."

Jess sat back, looked at her in shock.

"I da one read newspapahs, lettahs to her. I sign checks, everyt'ing. Duke taken away befoah he teach her. By and by, she nevah wanna learn."

Jess moaned, trying to absorb so much she never understood. "I used to wonder . . . I never saw her write things down."

"You de only one wrote lettahs, Jess. She learn anot'er life from you. Real excitin' foah her, give her knowledge, dignity, like Duke give her. She grateful. Love you very much."

They sat for hours, rereading Jess's letters, Run Run imitating Pono, the way her chest pumped out while Run Run read passages describing Jess's clinic, her veterinary practice, even surgery. The way she strode back and forth whacking things viciously with her cane, when Run Run read letters describing Jess's failing marriage, the abdication of her husband and child.

"She live t'rough you," Run Run said. "You all da t'ings she wanted for yoah mot'er. Now she inside you. You got to live foah her. You da one, Jess. You."

In a trance, she let Run Run walk her through the fields, this new knowledge delivering her into a dreamlike state so she moved without realizing she was moving. Pono had respected her, had valued her. She listened while Run Run reminded her of all the lives connected to her, through her: Anna, and Rachel, Vanya, Toru. Workers in the field, neighbors bringing her their wounded pets, those who came and simply stood beside her. The Sugai family, other coffee farmers bringing *'awa*. Their children who held her hand and took her on heroic walks. It was all a turning wheel, Jess the hub as Pono had been. Run Run repeated and repeated this until Jess started to believe it, began to find the pattern, connect the dots, make sense.

"Even yoah ex-husband connected in dere somewhere," Run Run said. "Widdout him, you nevah have dat child. Look, maybe even dese cop-jerks connected to yoah wheel. Not so bad have someone spyin' all da time. Make you more conscious what you do. Each t'ing come moah important."

They were still watched, would always be watched: passing cars, a figure on a hill, light glancing off binoculars.

"Just remember, Jess. All a wheel, you da hub. Pono say me dat. She see it in you years ago. Say you quiet, steady, *akamai*. Just like yoah mama."

Mother, lost somewhere in the grid of time.

One night Jess woke up in the sea. How she got there from her bed, she didn't know. She stroked for hours, moon baubling her shoulders. She swam like a racer, arms spinning in her sockets, swam like a starving creature for whom the sea was food. *Just like my mother, and* Tūtū. *A race of swimmers, ocean in our genes. Now they're dead, rumored to be dead. But where is proof? Mother! Pono! Nothing left to touch, to look upon. Nothing left to mourn.*

She stopped stroking, hung sobbing in the sea, a human buoy. And all around, they took shape behind the waves, listening to her heartbeat. She cried so hard, she didn't feel their gathering. And when the ocean towed her down, each and each, they gently nudged her up to air. Jess felt nothing, only fatigue. Weary of crying, of swimming, she wanted sleep. In the morning, she would believe she dreamed it, the midnight swim, rough/raspy feel against her skin, a sense of being lifted from the deep, pushed toward home and shallow waters. Yet, her hair was tacky from the sea, and in her arms and legs a tingling, as if they had brushed against sandpaper.

After that, no one could keep her from the ocean. It took her in again, purging, strengthening. She sat on beaches eating seaweed, dragged home prawns and mussels for cleaning. She deep-dived, watching clever *he'e* outsmart moray eels. Sometimes a *he'e* wrapped its tentacles round her leg, emphatically clinging. Jess would drag it to the shallows, stroking its arms, patting its head until the arms fluttered out, a Hindu dancer, and gracefully it floated off. She developed muscles, her back and legs grew strong. Run Run saw the difference, the subtle heft.

"Just like yoah *tūtū*," she said. "By and by you start to sleep less. Swim moah and moah. Swimmin' become foah you anot'er form of sleep."

Hele Loa

To Go, With No Hope of Returning

NOW SHE LIVED BY OLDER LAWS. A slow and ancient pace. Absorbing each day like a sponge, swallowing, becoming nature, flora, bark. When they sat very still they saw birds so archaic, so unknown, they had no names for them. And then the rampant undergrowth—vines, mangroves—the hidden life where ancient ghosts reposed. They learned to think like animals, eat anything, roots, vegetation. Some things they killed were so small, with so little flesh, they ate the viscera.

There were wild goat, boar, deer, but she had come to hate the slaughter of such things. In their first month, Vanya's month of little stutterings, speech and senses slowly resurrecting, they killed a boar out of sheer hunger. But in the carcass of that thing lay sadness, an echoing reproach. Each kill now seemed to contribute to the death of this wild and sacred valley. When helicopters flew in too low, birds dropped dead of fright. One day old-timers brought the news, $20,000 on her head.

"Time to be off," Simon said. "Boat could get us out at night, a little cruiser to Tarawa, the Solomons, on down to Darwin."

She shook her head. "Once we start moving, we're predictable, they'll track us. Anyway, my place is here. As long as I'm around it makes folks think. Maybe some of the things they think are important will begin to look kind of stupid."

"You mean, they might find bombs more appealing than Primo and VCRs."

"I mean, Simon, they might begin to think of pride."

One day a bush parted, a soldier pointed a rifle at her. Vanya smiled, thinking *This is the one who will kill me.* Simon came up behind him, clapped his ears with simultaneous blows of his outstretched palms. The man went down and out.

"Learned that from the Abos." He picked up the rifle, slung it across his shoulders. "He'll wake with ringing in his ears, won't remember seeing you, won't recall a thing."

He taught the trick to old-timers. They crept up behind soldiers, clapped them hard on both ears. Soldiers reeled, collapsed, and woke up witless, rifleless. He taught Vanya how to hunt small game with bow and arrow fashioned from bamboo and gut. He found leaves to drink as tea that repelled mosquitoes, scorpions, and he found sweet little dream-inducing mussels under reeds in streams. He speared guava, papaya and giant *pomelos*, made her fruit salads with strange little berries that snapped in her teeth like hard bubbles.

"Antiseptic. Swill it round, saves on toothpaste."

She chewed and *snap! snap! snapped!* each small explosion bringing laughter.

"I never thought I . . ."

". . . would laugh in the wilds with a broken-down *haole.*"

His skin was tanned and leathery now, red hair and mustache dark with bark oil and *kukui*, extending to a beard kept neatly trimmed. She began to forget his *haole*ness, except when he was naked. Somehow the pale color mattered less. He was becoming someone she trusted, a man who would face death beside her with great calm. As they sank deeper into that place, threading slowly into rich, green tapestry, it seemed even their coloring turned green, brown with an old bronze overcast.

Their odors were less human. They had begun to absorb the fragrance of flowers, vegetation, humid smell of soil. She felt a slow shedding, of backgrounds, philosophies, even of the sense of time. All they had was each given moment. Some days she felt free of everything, but memory. The Walther, manifest and deadly, bucking in her hands. Her shoulders blown to incandescent pain. A stranger spinning, kneeling, as if she were a priest. Simon calmly taking her hand, walking away with her, forever, from any kind of normal life. Some days she was caring, tender, marveling at his perverse vagary in loving her. Other days, the jagged edge was there.

"Look at us, assassins fucking."

Some nights she saw the *mo'o* raise its head, the moon reflected in one eye, and it was time to run—the dangerous thing—miles down to the black sand beach, the valley mouth. She had to touch—not streams, not rivers—but the real thing, ocean, that old catastrophe from whence she came. Had to hear Pono's watervoice humming in her blood. Locals went first, lined the beaches and treeline, watching for soldiers, infiltrators. Then Vanya and Simon ran low and smooth like mongoose, waited for moon-sucking clouds and, in the temporary black, darted headfirst into full-moon crashing surf.

He knew if not for that, waves pounding her pounding heart, the mothersound connecting her, she might go off, reach out to Jess, or Toru, give herself away. He envied her that blood connection, that *'aumākua* love so deep, she would risk everything, her life. Nights when the surf was calm, locals moving in the background, watching over them, she and Simon walked the shallows with nets, then sat with flashlights, little fish glowing, bubbling and singing, entertaining them.

Weke, Tang, Spanish dancer, Puffer, Moorish Idol. One night a spotted cowfish sat in her palm. Vanya held it to her ear, listening to its high beeps like a child crying. She stroked its side, kissed its little lips, and gently carried it back to the sea. Some days they sat high atop the cliffs in tight, hidden caves overhung with vines, watching far out in the ocean, whales soar and plunge, piping out their songs. Sometimes at sunset they saw schools of shark come home from hunting, swimming in formation, fins high like distant sails. Watching them, one day with no sense of it, she wept. He held her and she wept.

"Rachel thought I hated her. I'll never see her again. And Jess, always wanting my dark skin! How can I live without them? How can I go on?"

"Talk to me," he said. "Talk away the grief."

She told about the early years, girlhood, the house of white sarongs. Pono's tyranny, her devotion, legends surrounding her, the mystery. And Run Run who kept them all from dying, from killing each other. Laughter, she remembered laughter. And the scent of each other changing, girls sliding into women. Then, slow abdication, Rachel first, one by one the others.

"Not abdication, really, just life. Marriage, children. Divorce. Death."

She talked for hours, until she slept. And when she woke, she talked again. "Pono did that, woke us, talked to us for hours, like patients, prisoners. Then we would sleep for days and nights. Four of us in one big bed, sleeping and waking exhausted, and sleeping again. Maybe it was all a sleep, a long, long dream."

She talked about meeting her grandfather, Duke, and that sense of looking at the world differently because they were now safe. They had a history, a link. And she told about Pono and Duke at Shark Bay, their final sleep.

"The whole district mourned. I never understood it when she was alive. She was like royalty. She had endowed scholarships, sent kids off to the mainland to law school and medical school. She never helped us, there wasn't money then. And I think she wanted us to be like her, tough, doing it alone, grabbing life with our teeth. I thought I hated her for years. Then I discovered her.

"She wanted so much for her daughters, slaved in canneries, lost a finger, sending them to Catholic school. And, because they were her daughters, they rebelled. Then we came along. Third-generation rebels. But there was Ming, a teacher, Jess, a doctor, me a lawyer. And Rachel, unspeakably beautiful and kind. Sometimes when Pono looked at us, I saw it in her eyes. Humility. Deep pride.

"One night Toru, Run Run, all of us went into their room. It was still full of them, Pono's perfume, Grandfather's minty medication, and that stale, almost rodent smell of *ma'i Pākē* he could never shake. We stood in that room, and what they had shared swept over us, because all they had for sixty years were dreams.

"They had traveled round the world in their imaginations. Grandfather read her all of Marco Polo's travels. They went to Persia, Manchuria. He read her all of Keats, Flaubert; they lived in France, and Russia. She knew these places, Simon. She talked so knowledgeably, we thought she *had* traveled the world. Music, politics, he taught her everything. They believed. They made each moment the purest essence of what life could be.

"Grandfather wasn't sure he believed in Fate. He couldn't say they'd been destined for each other. But they had found each other and never let go. They were true. Grandfather said he believed that's what love was. Enduring. Fanatically. Beyond reason. I think love replaced their need for religion. If they had been religious, maybe they wouldn't have loved so deeply . . ."

Another day had passed while Vanya talked and, seeing the pull of moonrise on the feathers of an owl, Simon dropped his head and slept.

And she continued talking, sometimes her words shrinking to the embryo of words, deciphering, reconstructing her life on the basis of sounds. She talked until the years, the memories were exhausted, then she lay down in their cave and slept, like a woman who had spent days stalking mammoths.

This time when they woke, Waipiʻo Jimi had left them *poi*, fresh seaweed and *ʻōpakapaka*. They ate slowly, theatrically, with total concentration, the way people eat when there is nothing else to do. When they were full, they gazed seaward again, and Simon talked about his great respect for sharks, Great Whites that owned certain waters off Australia, different species he had seen traveling round the world, the most vicious being off Central and South America.

"What is it like, that part of the world," she asked. "I only know the Asian coast, and the Pacific."

And he began to talk, Mexico, Guatemala, El Salvador, the windswept beauty of Argentina's pampas, lush viselike jungles of the Orinoco. She listened attentively, questioning customs, politics, the people. He knew Cuba, South Africa, the Seychelles, and slowly Vanya entered his world, became knowledgeable about distant religions, and climates.

She talked about books he had never read, music he didn't understand. He described foods she had never heard of, animals she could not imagine, the difference between sand in the Gobi and sand in the Sahara. He taught her similarity of words from Peru and Somalia, Ulan Bator and Holland. Eventually, Vanya began to think she had seen these worlds, had traveled through them. And as they talked, their worlds slowy intertwined, so it seemed they had traveled great distances together.

One day Waipiʻo Jimi brought fresh-baked *laulau* succulent with grease, Maui onions like apples, the sweetest in the world. They sat chewing them with raw Hawaiian salt and Primo beer. Jimi watched Vanya, relieved, for each time he came, she looked more human, less like a ghost. He saw how she was coming back to life, her body robust, energetic, straining like five dogs on a leash.

"A little news," he said softly.

Her eyes grew wide, she sat very still.

"Toru got one girlfriend, look plenny serious. He mapping out his land, goin' build one house. Slowly, he doin' everyt'ing slowly."

Vanya closed her eyes, held her hands against her heart. "And Run Run?"

"Old. Plenny old. I t'ink she die a little for you."

"And Rachel? Any word?"

"Dat *wahine* on strange kine errand. People say she goin' bring back Hiro's children."

"And Jess? The house?"

His shook his head. "Strange t'ing. She not a big *wahine* like Pono, neh? But people say Jess start *look* like Pono, stand tall, important. Dark now, like *kama'āina*, maybe little thickah round da waist. She even drive dat truck like Pono. Maniac! Strangest t'ing. Cousin o' my cousin . . . *calabash* kine . . . he work ovah Sugai Mill. Do pulpin'. He say when dat *wahine*, Jess, come round, he t'ink he go *pupule*, say she even *smell* like Pono now. And what you t'ink? She walk wit' Pono's cane sometime. Dat devil-lookin' cane. Oooh, spooky, no?"

Vanya hung her head. "And do they ever talk of me?"

"What you t'ink, Vanya? You v'hat dey live foah. Dey dyin' in dat house, tryin' find out how you are. But smart. Dey wait. I hear Toru and Jess sit in field and cry plenny. Dey love you, Vanya. No have to see you foah love you. Dey love you fifty years, forevah. Jess, she oldah in da face from grief. Happen plenny fast."

Simon studied Jimi, puzzled. "Have you actually talked to them?"

He shook his head, "I no go from dis valley."

"Then how do you know these things?"

Jimi laughed. "Hey, *brah*, you no understan' Hawaiian kine, one big *'ohana*. Cousin got cousin who got cousin . . . you know da kine? We got spies who watch da spies, like whatchoo call it? One big daisy chain!"

"If I could get a message," Vanya said, "that I'm okay, that I miss them . . ."

Jimi's body tensed. "Dat what Feds waitin' for. Den dey know you here, foah shoah. Right now dey confused. *Haole* been here, flashin' money, lots money, ask old-timers, taro farmers, have dey seen you? Folks say dey seen not'ing. One spy t'ink he see you go out on fishin' boat, go away forevah. See, dey don't even know foah shoah you still in de islands. One note, one written word, Vanya, you gonna bring plenny troops in here wit' bazookas, gas bombs. Maybe dey find where all dem ammo crates is buried. You gonna hurt lotta' folks been protectin' you. But, one day, *keiki* . . . I tell you when da time is right."

He stood, looked down at Simon for a moment, then left. Next day when Vanya went down to a stream, Jimi was waiting.

"Simon no look so good."

She flinched. "His arm is healed, just those few scars."

"Not talkin' bout de arm. Why you no tell me he *ma'i Pākē*."

"It isn't!"

"Somet'in' plenny similah, sores on neck, one big ear, dat glaze in de eye."

She sat down on the grass and wept, then pulled herself together. "It's from Agent Orange in the war, Jimi. Some of our boys came home with it, too. He's got this medication, but it's not strong enough. He needs to see a doctor." She looked up at him. "What can I do?"

"I seen dis stuff before, same like *ma'i Pākē*. It spread, be plenny bad foah him. Den he don' care if live or die. I try see one *kahuna* foah you, get special herb. Next time, I goin' bring back *noni* and chili peppah, plenny seawater foah clean da blood."

He put his arms round her, held her like a child. "Vanya, you got be strong. Like yoah *tūtū*, Pono. When she and Duke runnin' in dis jungle, bounty hunters closin' in, she tell my fat'er she *kill* foah Duke, die foah him. Only t'ing kept dem goin' was dat *wahine*'s will."

She breathed in carefully, smelled, had smelled, denied that smell for weeks, stale rodential odor on Simon of her grandfather's sickness. Things feeding on, snuffing out Simon's nerve ends, rot settling in. Sometimes he slept long hours, and she hunted alone, returning victorious with small kills, her hours away from him making their hours together more meaningful.

"You love me, Vanya. Say it."

She shook her head.

"Then why did you let me run with you? Why am I here?"

She looked into raveling mists, heard manic growth, dripping green, the jungle's ancient songs. "You're what's left."

His laugh was hoarse. "God almighty, my liver's crook, my ear looks like an udder, crud's climbing my legs. You'd better hurry up, and *love* what's left!"

She laughed, pulled him to her chest, and rocked him like a child. A comprehension then, that this was permanent. She would be with him, no matter what. He was the pain she had been assigned.

"When we first met, you terrified me. One of those men formed before the human race acquired a conscience. You looked like you could eat a human heart. If need be, you could eat your own heart. Now . . . you terrify me more."

"Because you love me." He shook her arm gently. "Say it, stop giving me a hard time."

"I'm not giving you anything. What you get, you'll have to earn."

Badgering, laughing back and forth, they lapsed into a kind of ease, acceptance. He was very ill, she was hunted, they were so enmeshed in horror they stepped back, eyed it with conspicuous detachment. One day he coughed up sputum, a new and a small pronouncement: he was carrying in his body, not life, but a disease whose final birth would be his death. He became feverish, his coughing escalated. Vanya dreamed she was holding his lung stretched taut at the end of a string. Walking it like a balloon. It floated, bounced along through trees, and then collapsed. What happened to the body? Where was the corpse? At night his hands and legs shook with a kind of palsy, his vision momentarily went. Sweat parted his hair in swatches and she bathed his face.

"I want to love you," he said. "Make love to you. Are you afraid?"

Suddenly she felt virginal and shy. "I've been afraid all my life, Simon. I just can't express it, that's all."

"Until I'm laid out like a corpse, I'll look after you."

She tried for humor, she always tried for humor now. "Funny, no? I join the revolution and end up a nurse."

"You didn't join it, sweetheart, you hijacked it."

Weeks passed, another month. Some days were bad, some days better. One night he spat up something large and dark, a rancid cluster. He flung it off into the bush.

"Jesus. I never thought dying would be so hard. It's like a bloody profession."

She washed his mouth and hands. He reached for her, held her gently by the waist. "Say it," he pleaded. "You love me."

She would not say it; it seemed that's what he lived for now. Once she said it, he would die.

Phantoms circled them, becoming shadows that fleshed out into human bodies. Three locals running, university students who had helped blow up another plant.

"We came to join you, Vanya."

She sat with them, spoke softly. "Join me? Do you know how my days are spent? The man with me is dying."

They reared back, then relaxed. This was a new generation, for them death had the dark stain of a magnet, drawing revolutionaries, choosing one or two at random.

"We will help you," they said, "carry medication and supplies. In return, you can tell us what to do, how to organize these valley people. They trust you."

"What do you mean 'organize'?"

"Militarize."

"And, why?"

"Sovereignty will take years. Some of our elders have waited sixty, seventy years for return of their lands. They'll die before they see it. And what will be left for the rest of us? Nothing. Everything has been defiled. Only here is pure. Waipi'o. As it was in Kamehameha's time. We will defend it to the last."

"Defend it? From what?" She leaned forward, confused.

One of the young men shook his head. "You didn't hear? They already got surveyors up round these cliffs. Japanese developers have bought land surrounding this valley. They're planning huge resort complexes built all the way round Waipi'o. They'll pollute our streams, kill off our wildlife, flush their excrement into our seas."

Vanya looked down for a long time. After a while she straightened up. "Go to where the crates are buried, dozens of them. I will give you the map. Take inventory. Bring me the lists."

"And then?"

"Then I will begin to help you organize the valley. There are not so many left. They are old, but still warriors."

"Don't worry, Vanya. Many are coming here to join us from outside. Soon as they heard of plans for Waipi'o's desecration, people started marching in the streets."

She looked out across the valley. "It will be taken, you know. By and by they will defeat us, wear us down. But that is not important."

They left quietly, and she stood still, breathing in the fragrant air.

Simon struggled from his cot, and leaned against a tree. "I heard every word."

"And you think I'm a fool. That I should run away with you, turn my back forever."

"No. I don't think that anymore. I've given up thought. Come here, sweetheart. I can't make it that far."

They sat together hand in hand, looking through the tangled jungle, out across the haunted, beautiful and fragile land.

"I've come to love it," he said. "It's like the Kakadu. You'll save it for a while. Developers will back off until the press is bored. But bit by bit, they'll hack it to pieces. They'll bury you."

"It doesn't matter, Simon. It only matters that we tried, that we fought honorably for what was left."

That night while she slept he studied her face in moonlight, a beautiful face, full of a woundedness to which she refused to capitulate. And limning that beauty, the look of a child, innocent, loving him without knowing it. Knowledge of it would bring her despair. He would not ask for love again.

Imua

To Press On, to Go Forward

SPRING CAME, AND SOAKING RAINS. The land burst into "Kona snow," white coffee blossoms smelling like gardenias, leaving locals reeling with their scent. Summer and the growing season, the never-ending cycle. Planting of new coffee trees, rejuvenating old trees, irrigating, weeding, pruning with sickles and light axes, all before harvesting season in late fall. In small greenhouses, Jess tended coffee seedlings in earthern pots. In two years they would be transferred to the soil. Some workers tended macadamia crops, avocado and papaya trees, enough to make a profit if the coffee yield that year were less than "bumper" crop.

In June when warm trades came, Rachel brought her girls from Honolulu. They were beautiful and shy with the golden, rainy skin of Thais, bones delicate as birds, but unexpected strength in their backs and thighs. And there was wariness, remembrance of that other life, the one she had erased them from, still cantering beside them. At first they clung to her, afraid they had been brought there to be sold to field-workers. Trust would be slow in coming.

Then, one day they laughed. Run Run made them laugh. They taught her a Thai word, *ling ling*, little monkey. She taught them *tūtū*, grandmother. They became her *linglings*, she became their *tootoot*. Toru gently hoisted them onto his horse, slowly trotting them in circles. He taught them how to play his 'ukulele. Jess peeled *pomelos* for them, braided flowers in their hair. Then they ran back to Rachel, holding her hands, counting her fingers, as if the act prevented her from forever disappearing. At dusk, she sat with them on the *lānai*, teaching them English, and they in turn instructed her in Thai, graceful words of patience, of acceptance.

"*Mai Pen Rai.*" It's all right. It doesn't matter.

When she stumbled on a phrase, they laughed, tinkling sounds running up and down the scale like intermission chimes in theaters. Jess watched them through a window, tradewinds rustling their hair, black, glossy heads shining against gentian fields behind them.

"Moah bettah teach dem t'ings to survive," Run Run said. "All dis chat-chat waste of time."

Jess smiled. "Why can't she waste a little time? What else is it for?"

Rachel had bobbed her hair to a short, efficient pageboy, stopped designing her lips with rouge. She had cut her long nails to the quick and now walked at something of a ruthless pace. It was a source of humor to Jess because even in her mid-forties, with little threatening crow's-feet and "hair lenghthening in the mole," Rachel was still so lovely, her features still so perfect, people stopped and turned. And as Jess seemed to have appropriated so much of Pono—compelled by some extreme degree of aggressiveness to push everything aside that wasn't necessary and worth the trouble—Rachel seemed to acquire traits reminding them of Vanya. No longer languid, mysterious and fraught, she made quick decisions, then acted on them, rode them to the ground. In rare pensive moments, she had the air of being twice as quiet that energetic humans have when they are still.

Jess shook her head. "She's like another person. It's uncanny."

Run Run glanced at Jess's proud stance, the human-spine cane always at her side like a scabbard. Run Run's only regret was that she could never tell Jess the history of that cane, what was imbedded in the polished wood, the vertebral bumpiness that made it somewhat crooked. Even after Pono's death, promises were kept. Now Jess yelled when workers turned lazy, cursed when she felt the urge, walked about whacking the cane, shameless as a crow.

"We all changin'," Run Run said. "All comin' pickled into whatchoo call it? . . . eccentricity!"

At certain hours of certain days the three of them sat in the kitchen, making up little packets—money, medication—that were light and traveled fast. They were passed to a worker in the field, from him to his cousin, from cousin to cousin and then from *paniolo* to local surfers who slid down muddy jungle paths to surf the black sand beaches of

Waipiʻo. Surfers passed the packets on to taro farmers, who muled them into the valley to Waipiʻo Jimi, who finally reached Vanya. But Jess never knew the final destination of those packets. No word ever came.

"I'd pay anything," Rachel said. "A chopper could lift them out of there at night. Get them to a seaplane. Australia. Singapore. Anywhere she wants to go."

Jess shook her head. "She's doing it her way. And in her time . . ." She didn't mean to say the other thing, didn't know she said it until she looked at Rachel's face. ". . . if she's still alive."

Saying it, she walked out on the lawn and vomitted.

Ban came from Thailand, and spent weeks on the farm with his sisters. They were like three children who had been badly tortured, then released, allowed to walk away and live. Sometimes they stood very still, the three of them, as if listening, waiting to be sucked backwards into that past life. Sometimes the older girl jumped from her bed, stood panting in Rachel's room in blackness, until her form emerged. She moved close, listened to her breathing, touched her face. Comforted, the girl went back to bed.

"I've sent him to medical school. He's going to be a surgeon." Proud, maternal, Rachel watched Ban stroll in sunlight, slender and graceful as a woman. "He's helping me bring out more girls."

"Where do you get the nerve?" Jess asked. "You're dealing with criminals."

Rachel leaned forward, trying to explain. "It's strange. You offer people enough money, they become almost . . . genteel. Besides, these men know who I am. They know Ban was Hiro's 'son.' "

They walked the fields arm in arm, Jess with a sense of weight lifted, burdens shared, a sense of Rachel's strength. She understood part of that strength came from Rachel's sudden wealth. Money now gave her mobility and speed—she cut through the trivial, the time-devouring, sliced right to the heart of what she needed.

"Never underestimate money," she said. "It gives a woman privacy, insulates you from the daily dross. You don't have to be anybody's darling. You get to choose your company. Or choose to be an outcast. And, yes, it gives you power. People listen."

Now when she wasn't with her girls, she spent time in Honolulu meeting with officials coffined in dark rooms, men from Immigration, the Health Department, the U.S. Embassy, eliciting their assistance in helping her bring more young girls out of Chiang Mai.

One day, just back from Honolulu, she called Jess to her room. In her hand was a tiny book, a diary with gold covers. Inside were pages of almost-transparent lengths of jade thin as eyelids, to which were attached sepia silk parchments embossed with delicate spidery inscriptions in gold lettering. The diary of an Empress from the Ming dynasty, almost five hundred years old, on certain pages the golden ghosts of empress fingerprints.

"Do you recognize it, Jess?"

She shook her head, then leaned closer. And it came stealthily, a memory of the two of them, nine or ten, sliding into Pono's room consumed with curiosity. Rifling through her things, they had found the diary with a faded inscription on the back. Now Jess turned it over. "Volume I. For Kelonikoa, from Rostov Anadyr, 1873." Another untellable mystery from Pono's past.

"One day," Rachel said, "after she brought Grandfather home, I remembered the diary, and asked about it. Pono told me Kelonikoa, our great-great-great grandmother, was a renowned Tahitian beauty, that this was a gift from a Russian who had loved her. But she was married to our one-eyed ancestor, Mathys Coenradtsen."

Rachel put her hand to her temple as if to ward off pain.

"The evening of that last night, the night I saw their car go down the drive, Pono brought me the diary, said it was for us. To sell if we needed to. In those days that followed, I forgot about it. It's been here all this time."

They studied the Empress's journal.

"I wonder what she wrote," Rachel whispered. "What the words mean."

Jess hesitated, and when she spoke her voice seemed to come from long distances, across the years, the generations.

"Perhaps she wrote that life is really lived through dreams and intuitions, not fate and circumstance. That the love most longed for actually exists, elsewhere, on another plane."

Jess thought of Duke and Pono, how they had lived life on the grandest scale in their imaginings. And she thought of her mother, and Rachel's, one barely known, one never glimpsed. Her eyes filled and her cheeks were wet.

"I know." Rachel sighed. "I still look for her in every wrinkled face. I've looked for her so long, in a way I've *become* my mother. As you became yours, Jess. In coming home, you brought her home. They've earned the right to peace."

In September, when school began, Rachel took her girls back to the house in Kahala, outside Honolulu. On weekends they sat quietly while she schooled them in calligraphy, wanting them to learn certain graces Hiro had instilled in her. And sometimes they sat in the teahouse in kimonos, Rachel instructing them in the traditional tea ceremony. Behind her on the wall, the sun beheld an eerie landscape under glass, like a spread-out mounted deerskin. It glowed, the blue of old tattoos.

Now, there were new rumors. People organizing in Waipi'o Valley. Skirmishes with troops of soldiers. Shots exchanged. Guerillas dragged their dead back into the jungle, so they couldn't be identified. Across the Big Island, folks whispered of a woman shot through the head. If it was Vanya, Jess suspected they would never know. The underground had to keep her name alive, what she symbolized. She and Toru sat on beaches, rocking back and forth, the pounding surf muffling their broken sobs.

One day Run Run stumbled in the kitchen, grabbing her chest. Jess thought it was her heart, that she had heard of Vanya's death. Run Run shook her head, staring with eyes that seemed half shaded with tiny shells of mother-of-pearl.

"No can see no moah. Eyes all comin' murky. Ah, *keiki*, maybe I goin' blind foah all my sins."

During the cataract operation of Run Run's left eye, Toru paced the clinic corridor, trembling like a child. They brought her home bandaged like a blind thing, and he held her head while Jess administered drops of medication. A month later, after the operation on her right eye, Jess held her head while Toru administered the drops.

"What dis mean?" Run Run asked softly. "Maybe you forgive me for tie you up, keep you from bombin' t'ings?"

"I never forgive," he answered just as softly, patting her cheek like a dear thing.

Now Run Run was like a child, dashing all about, discovering things. "Colors, ooh, many colors. T'ings I not seen foah yeahs! Ooh, look da pots shinin' in da sun. Look da frangipani! Jess, you goin' gray!"

She calmed down, turning serious. She looked across the fields.

"Life been long, Jess. It come at me in blows. I look my left eye, see me and Pono sacrificin' youth, blood, to dis earth, dese orchards. Den I look my right eye, see you and Toru plantin', weedin', harvestin'. Like you washin' our faces, trimmin' our hair, keepin' our blood fresh in da soil."

She sighed, pumped out her chest. "You see da place I sit each day, watchin' Toru build his house? Dat spot on da hill look down his ten acres? I like be buried dere. Right dere! So I watch dat boy for all eternity, drive him *pupule*."

Run Run moved slower now, saying less, eating less. Each day, she sat in her little niche atop a hill that rolled down to orchards, then the sea, grinning, holding her knees like a girl, watching the son of her dead son, building, going on. Jess knew one day by and by they'd find her there, head bowed, washed by rain, cured by sun, hardened to a little icon.

One stormy, sleepless night she found Toru in Vanya's bedroom, reverently touching her things. "*Tūtū*'s dying. Vanya's probably dead. We're disappearing, Jess."

Viciously, she whacked at his foot with her walking cane.

"Are you a man? Build your house! Plant your seed! Get on with living."

She didn't tell him she had dreamed. A corpse. A faceless corpse. Now her nights seemed haunted. One day soon, Run Run would be gone, Toru would marry, maybe Rachel would disappear in some estuary of the Mekong, rescuing her Chiang Mai girls. She suddenly didn't care about the wheel Run Run had envisioned, of which she, Jess, was the hub, the center of so many lives. The wheel was flying apart, everyone was abdicating. She moved about with a surety of purpose, instructing workers with kinetic calm, but in the evenings she sat alone, feeling larval and exposed.

When Lee Sugai introduced her to attractive men, men of ethics, reverence for the land, Jess panicked, felt she wasn't ready. She thought of Pono and Duke and how for sixty years their love had been based on some enigmatic will to believe in the impossible: that someday they would walk together out into the world. Their story meant miracles existed, it meant that conceivably, in some future time, someone—perhaps a little weathered, a little creased, but of large interior resources—would walk her way with momentous inevitability. Jess would be waiting, watching for clues. If he didn't come, she would track him down.

She called Rachel in Honolulu, needing to shore up her resolve.

"I want a life of human exchange. I don't want years of empty nights filled with trivia . . ."

Rachel sighed. "There's a lot to be said for trivia. And, what is night, really, but release from all those weird combinations it takes to get

through a day. The important half of life is just beginning, Jess! We have
to be discriminating about who we allow into our nights." She paused,
seemed to drift, thinking of Hiro. "As for love, who can survive more
than one great passion? Who would want to."

"Did you really love him, Rachel?"

"There were things between us . . . diabolical, unspeakable. But Hiro
shielded me from life, kept me from throwing myself away. He kept me
from dying, there were times I didn't care." She closed her eyes. "Yes,
he was evil. It's possible to love, with the greatest love, that which is
evil. When I first saw him I knew if I stayed with him, nothing could
ever hurt me."

"Then, what you really wanted was protection."

"No! I wanted to be used, used up, forever, over and over. I've lost
the taste for such delirium."

Jess wondered if she was right. Most people sought a blindingly
passionate, transcending love, the one impossible and tragic. At the same
time they wanted a less perfect, more prosaic love, one that got them
through the day-to-day. She brooded over this, wondering if it was age,
or just fatigue that took away large appetites, left us desiring a life
predictable and kind. Was wanting less the first step down the road to
dying, or to wisdom? Pono had said NEED LESS, DESIRE LESS, MOST THINGS
AFTER ALL, ARE NOT WORTHWHILE. But, surely physical affection, human
companionship, were worth while. Happiness had to depend on more
than just 'āina that threatened to break her back, and 'ohana that kept
deserting her.

"I keep forgetting we're Pono's girls. Maybe we're not supposed to
be happy."

"Then we'll *pretend* to be," Rachel said. "We'll make it a habit, no
matter what."

That's all we can do, Jess thought. *Live in readiness for whatever comes.*

There was so much to dwell on, as first she didn't notice the boy
hanging round the fields. He was nine or ten, and some days after school,
he stood with his bookbag on his shoulders, eating shave-ice, joking with
field-workers. He came round so often, he became part of the landscape.
Then she forgot him completely, because she dreamed again, a faceless
corpse, and woke up screaming for Vanya.

She drove again to Shark Bay and sat on beaches calling out to Pono,
to her 'aumākua, asking for strength, asking not to be abandoned. One

morning, after sitting there all night, she saw them parked between tour buses at the base of Pu'ukohola Heiau. They were still watching her. They would always watch.

And still the young boy came, seeming to integrate himself with workers and people round the house. One day, sitting at Shark Bay, Jess thought she saw him fishing out on the jetty. She dismissed him, caught up in her life—still making house calls birthing calves, vaccinating steers, taking blood samples from a dozen sows, then the punishing hours of harvesting sometimes straight on through the night.

Every morning she strode up and down the fields, yelling to workers, whacking bushes with Pono's cane. And every evening she stood on the loading platform with the foreman counting hundred-pound sacks of coffee cherries. In her fatigue she discovered that leaning on the cane sometimes brought great relief, as if some surging balm were flowing upward, as if another back were taking on her burdens.

One day, Lena came, golden, lovely, but very troubled. "I am so confused! Toru is no help."

"Be patient," Jess said. "He's sad because Run Run is getting old."

Lena shook her head. "Not just that. It's Toru's life, this family. No fathers, too many mothers . . . so mixed up, I cannot understand it. How will I tell our children what was what? And who was who?" She went away, despondent.

Jess gazed after her and thought, *I have been a selfish* wahine, *thinking only of me. Forgetting all the* kamali'i *who will come behind us.*

In five years she would be fifty. One day, her child, Anna, would have a child. What could Jess give that child, and Toru's children? Their children's children? What would be more valuable than genealogy. She could do that for them, begin the backward journey. Their heirs would have the wealth of history to aim at life, when life aimed at them. She sat down with pen and paper. Where to start? There was still so much she didn't know. What was truth, conjecture? What was purely myth?

Did their ancestor Kelonikoa really try to swim home to Tahiti? Had her one-eyed husband Mathys really been a cannibal? Had their children really been stone-eaters, defending Queen Lili'uokalani? Had Pono really hypnotized wild boar, turned deer into the bark of trees? Did she really resurrect the dead? Had Grandfather Duke really lived outside the world for sixty years? Did he really suffer as a human guinea pig? Did lepers really tango? Had Vanya's son merely drowned, or was he really murdered? Was Hiro really tattooed head to toe? Had he really been *Yakuza?* Or just a greedy thug? Had Ming really died from lupus? Or had she died from Dragon Seed? Was Vanya an idealistic revolutionary? Or had she just been born to self-destruct? So much had happened in their lives—or had it? Maybe they were all bit players lost in the knotted fringes of illusion. Even imagining their history was exhausting. Jess put aside the pen and paper.

Guerillas were still active in Waipiʻo. Surveying crews were shot at near the cliffs surrounding the valley; across the island, bombs still wrecked golf courses and marinas. But now people seemed to be turning their attention to something more important. Sovereignty. Maybe it would happen in this decade. Certainly, it would happen. Forces were gathering. It was under congressional consideration. It was in the air.

Jess sat at Shark Bay imagining the day they raised the Hawaiian flag again, resurrecting an independent Native Hawaiian nation, with its own separate government, by and for its own Native Peoples. She wondered who she would share that flag-raising moment with. Would she be alone. Christmas approaching now, she wondered how she would get through the holidays. There would only be a house of ghosts.

One evening at Shark Bay she thought she saw the young boy playing on the sand, the same boy who had hung round her fields. She had not seen him for weeks, and now something was wrong with his face. He had a terrible infection, his nose puffed out like a *kukui*. Ignoring the signs "WARNING SHARKS IN THESE WATERS," he seemed to moon along, strolling at the water's edge. She wondered where he came from, why she kept seeing him, what was wrong with him.

She eased closer. "Where are you from? Your folks live near by?"

He smiled, nodding yes.

"How come I see you at my farm?"

"Go to school near dere. Got ʻohana dere. School not so good here. I come home to Kawaihae for *Kalikimaka*, see parents, brothers, sisters." He spoke in half Pidgin, half proper English, as if he were vacillating.

"What's wrong with your face? Infection?"

He nodded, looked carefully up the hill behind them.

"Have you seen a doctor?"

He nodded again, his movements slow, self-conscious. Jess sat on the sand puzzled, watching him. Then she was swept back to her own thoughts.

Casually and very slowly, the boy approached and sat beside her. "Dose pretty girls work your fields in summer? Your daughters?"

She smiled. "Sort of. Well, my cousin Rachel's *hānai* daughters."

"Oh." He pushed sand between his toes. "You got children?"

It was hard to answer. "A daughter. Far away."

"Sad she not wit' you," he said softly.

"She'll come by and by. I saw it in a dream."

He seemed to move closer. He kept his head down, screwing his face like he was working up an awful sneeze. Then he snorted, so awful a sound, Jess turned away.

"Look," he whispered. "Please!"

She turned back to him, and gasped. His nose, mysteriously deflated, looked suddenly normal, uninfected. Jess squinted, looked at him more closely, then pulled back. He was nudging her outer thigh with his hand, his fist. She looked down. The fist opened, and in his small, sandy, pink and humid palm lay something gleaming, shot with colors like electric pulses. A large, perfect black pearl. She screamed.

He closed his fist. "No! Please. No scream. Man on hill is watching from a car."

Tears coursed her cheeks, she couldn't stop, just sat there shaking, silently sobbing. He took her hand under her skirt, placed therein the pearl. Jess clutched it as if it were a human heart. As long as she clutched it, it would beat. Then she remembered her dreams of a faceless corpse.

"Vanya!"

The boy casually looked up the hill, then stood lazily, throwing shells as if he were bored. After a while, he sat down again. They looked out at the sea.

"Is she alive?"

He nodded.

". . . Wounded?"

He shook his head no.

"Does she need me?"

"No." He spoke rapidly now, lips hardly moving. "I watch your place long time, send message back da valley you okay. One day *haole* pick me up, search bookbag, clothes, even underwear! Think I carrying message. My papa say bettah stop before dey catch me. But word come Vanya going crazy if not reach you by *Kalikimaka*. I no can carry written message. So dat's why da pearl, proof to you she still alive. Papa say put up da nose. Look like something contagious, like *ma'i Pākē*. Cops search me, I tell them got real bad infection. They no touch my face. Clever, neh?"

Her heart pounded so violently, she felt her hair shiver. Skin stood up on her neck and arms.

"Vanya! Oh, Vanya . . ." Then she remembered Simon Weir. "Do you know what happened to the *haole*? The man who was with her?"

The boy turned and looked at her. His eyes were sad. He raked a stick across the sand, drawing a cross.

"He dreamin' now in soil of Waipi'o."

Jess cried again, her head still, but her body shaking. Vanya had hinted at Simon's past and now Jess thought, *Maybe death for him wasn't the end of life. Maybe it was the end of guilt.* After a while the sobbing subsided to a deeper place. When her eyes cleared, when she was calm, the boy said one more thing.

"She send one word for you." Very casually he raked the stick across the sand again.

IMUA. Go forward! Press on!

It was as if he had raked a coal across her brain, the word imbedded there forever. After a while he strolled back to the water. She sat very still, so full of the moment, she could not move, did not know what the next move was. Time passed, it was the hour of tides, the ocean seemed to moan. Then, by a play of light, Jess saw countless images spring up before her in the waves, the light like a well chain drawing up not water, but faces, all, each of them, faces from other eras, and those more recent, their history more beautiful in remembering. She spoke their names, Kelonikoa, and Emmaline, and Lili, Pono, Duke, and Emma, Mina, Hernando, Ming, even Hiro, lives still attached and flowing, in myths, dreams, imaginings. Lives permanent because someone, Jess, was there to pass them on.

From the water's edge the boy waved, pointing to an old woman far in the distance, casting her fishing net. The net flew up and spread out of her hands, a bird opening its wings. Jess wondered why she was there, net-casting in dangerous shark waters. The old woman worked patiently and slowly with her net, drawing it in, untwisting and unfolding. Then she cast it out again, leaping, billowing, the four corners stretched, the center slack, like a great suspended awning. It hung in the air a long time, an eternity.

The old woman raised her arms, praising her mastery, the *haiku* of net-casting. She clasped her breast, then raised her arms again, as if flinging her heart up to join the net, still floating beyond the pull of gravity, of logic. Then the old woman turned her head and gazed at Jess. Their look held, steadfast, for the longest time. Jess felt such sudden peace, she closed her eyes, and for a while she dozed. When she looked again, the net had fallen to the water, floating now like moving skin. The old woman had disappeared. But one single fin huge, dark and brilliant, bladed toward the horizon.

"PONO!"

They were all out there watching, assembled, in formation, in ancient dialogues. She was not abandoned, she would never be alone. As long as they lived, she lived. She looked down at the sand. Wind had blown it clean. And yet the simple, potent word remained.

IMUA.

It hovered in the air round her, a sound of spirits soaring, a sound ringing and pure. A sound that echoed ancestral beliefs that would flow on forever, beyond the measure of human life. Beyond the measure of time.

Slowly, as in a trance, Jess drew from her bag a pen and sheet of paper. She would start with the story she knew best. Pono and Grandfather. She would work her way backward. What she did not know, they would tell her. They would come from other eras, other generations, each and each, they would come to her in dreams. She clutched the black pearl in her hand, rubbing it like a heart she had to keep beating. She felt its warmth reflected in her palm. Her pen was poised.

And she began:

"*. . . Peacocks skittered on polished floors . . . He was dark, and tall and noble . . . She was dark and beautiful . . . She wore a Paris gown . . . they waltzed. Soon they would be running through green fire . . .*"

IMUA

Glossary

'A'Ā (ah-ah) . . . Sharp, rough hunks of lava

'AHI (ah-hee) . . . Tunafish

'ĀINA (ein-ah) . . . Land, earth

AKAMAI (ah-kah-my) . . . Smart, clever

AKU (ah-koo) . . . Skipjack tuna

ALI'I (ah-lee-ee) . . . Noble, royal, former kings and queens

ALOHA (ah-lo-hah) . . . Love, mercy, greetings

ALOHA 'OHANA (o-hah-nah) . . . Love for the family

ANIANI (ah-nee-ah-nee) . . . Mirror

'AUMAKUA (ow-mah-ku-ah) . . . Family or personal god (Plural: 'AU-MĀKUA)

AUWĒ (ow-we) . . . Alas!

'AWA (ah-vah) . . . Slightly narcotic tea from kava root

BRAH (bra) . . . Pidgin-English for "brother"

CALABASH (cal-a-bash) . . . Mixing bowl. Also people not blood-related, but "family" because they eat from the same bowl.

DA KINE (da-kine) ... Pidgin-English for "the kind"

E PŪPŪKAHI (ay-poo-poo-kah-hee) ... We are one

FLIP (flip) ... Slang for Filipino

HAʻAHEO (hah-ah-he-o) ... Pride

HALE MAKE (hah-le-mah-ke) ... House of death

HALENANI (hah-le-na-ne) ... House of Splendor

HĀNĀI (ha-ni) ... Foster child, adopted child

HANA MAKE (hah-nah-mah-ke) ... Killer, thing of destruction

HANOHANO (hah-no-hah-no) ... Dignified

HAOLE (how-lee) ... White, Caucasian, foreigner

HAOLEFIED (how-lee-fied) ... Made white

HAPA (hah-pah) ... Of mixed blood

HAPA HAOLE (hah-pah-how-lee) ... Half white, half Hawaiian

HAPA-PĀKĒ (hah-pah-pah-ke) ... Half Chinese

HĀPUʻU (hah-poo-oo) ... Medicinal tree fern

HAUʻOLI MAKAHIKI HOU (hey-oo-lee-mah-kah-he-ke-ho) ... Happy New Year

HAWAIʻI PONOʻI (hah-vy-ee-po-no-ee) ... Hawaii's own people

HEʻE (hey-ey) ... Octopus

HEIAU (hey-ee-ow) ... Ancestral temple of worship

HIKIEʻE (hee-kee-e) ... Large movable Hawaiian couch

HILAHILA (hee-la-hee-la) ... Bashful, shy, embarrassed

HŌHĒ (ho-he) ... Coward

HOLOKŪ (ho-lo-koo) ... Long formal dress with train

HOʻOMAKE (ho-o-mah-ke) ... To kill

HOʻOMANAʻO (ho-o-mah-nah-o) ... Remember, commemorate

HOWZIT (how-zit) ... Pidgin-English, Hi! How are things?

HUHŪ (hoo-hoo) ... Angry

HUKIHUKI (hoo-kee-hoo-kee) ... Disagree, quarrel

HUKILAU (hoo-kee-lau) ... fish with a seine, fishing feast

HULI (hoo-lee) ... Short for *hoʻauhuli*, revolution, to overthrow

IKAIKA (ee-kah-ee-kah) ... Psychologically strong, powerful

IKI (ee-kee) . . . Little

'ILI'ILI (ee-lee-ee-lee) . . . Stone

'IMI 'ŌLELO (ee-me-o-lay-lo) . . . Slander

I MUA (ee-moo-ah) . . . Go forward! Press on! Spoken as one word

KAHIKO (kah-hee-ko) . . . Old, ancient person (Plural: KĀHIKO)

KAHUNA (kah-hoo-nah) . . . Prophet, seer, priest (Plural: KĀHUNA)

KAIKU'ANA (ki-koo-ah-nah) . . . Sister, formal

KALAHALA (kah-la-hah-la) . . . To forgive

KALAIMA (kah-leem-a) . . . Criminal

KALIKIMAKA (kah-lee-kee-mah-ka) . . . Christmas

KĀLUA (kah-loo-ah) . . . Bake in ground oven

KAMA'ĀINA (kah-mah-ein-ah) . . . Old-timer, native-born

KAMALI'I (kah-mah-lee-ee) . . . Children, plural of *child*

KANAKA (kah-nak-ah) . . . Slang, for Hawaiian (Plural: KĀNAKA)

KĀNE (kah-ne) . . . Man

KAPU (kah-poo) . . . Forbidden, taboo

KEIKI (kee-kee) . . . Child

KEIKI KĀNE (kee-kee-kah-ne) . . . Boy, male child

KEIKI MANUAHI (kee-kee-mah-noo-ah-hee) . . . Illegitimate child

KĪKEPA (kee-ke-pah) . . . Sarong, also *pa'u*

KINIPŌPŌ (kee-nee-po-po) . . . Baseball

KOA (ko-ah) . . . Fearlessness, also a type of Hawaiian wood

KOALI (ko-ah-lee) . . . Kind of morning glory

KŌKUA (ko-koo-ah) . . . Helper, assistant

KŌKUA 'OHANA (ko-koo-ah-o-hah-nah) . . . Help the family

KONAKONA (ko-nah-ko-nah) . . . Strong, muscled

KUKUI (koo-koo-ee) . . . Candlenut used for oil, cooking, jewelry

KUMU (koo-moo) . . . Base, foundation, beginnings

KUPUNA (koo-poo-nah) . . . Ancestor, grandparent (Plural: KŪPUNA)

KUPUNA KĀNE (koo-poo-nah-kah-ne) . . . (Formal) grandfather

KUPUNA WAHINE (koo-poo-nah-va-hee-ne) . . . (Formal) grandmother

LĀNAI (lah-ny) . . . Porch, veranda, balcony

LANI (lah-nee) . . . Sky, heaven, highborn

LĀʻĪ (lah-ee) . . . Ti leaf

LAULAU (lau-lau) . . . Meat wrapped in steamed ti leaf, banana leaf

LEI (lay) . . . Flowered necklace, wreath for the neck

LELE KOKE (le-le-ko-ke) . . . Quick to fight

LEPOLEPO (lepo-lepo) . . . Filthy, contaminated

LILIKOʻI (lee-lee-koy) . . . Passion fruit, the juice

LOKAHI (lo-kah-ee) . . . Unity, agreement

LOKO ʻINO (lo-ko-ee-no) . . . Evil

LŌLŌ (lo-lo) . . . Feeble-minded

LOMI (lo-mee) . . . Pressed raw salmon, tomato, and onion

LŪʻAU (loo-ow) . . . Hawaiian feast

LUNA (loo-nah) . . . Foreman

MAHALO (mah-hah-lo) . . . Thank you

MAHIMAHI (mah-hee-mah-hee) . . . Sweet dorado fish

MAILE (my-le) . . . Native twining shrub for *lei*

MAʻI PĀKĒ (my-pah-kee) . . . Leprosy (literally, Chinese sickness)

MAKA (mah-kah) . . . Eye

MĀKAʻI (mah-kah-ee) . . . Police

MAKAPŌ (mah-kah-po) . . . Blind

MAKAʻU (mah-kah-oo) . . . Afraid

MAKAʻU WALE (mah-kah-oo-wah-lee) . . . Coward

MAKE (mah-ke) . . . To die

MAKIKA (mah-kee-kah) . . . Mosquito

MALIHINI (mah-lee-hee-nee) . . . Newcomer to the islands

MĀLAMA ʻAINA (mah-lah-mah-ein-ah) . . . Preserve, care for, the land

MALO (mah-lo) . . . Loincloth worn by men

MANA (mah-nah) . . . Divine power

MANAKĀ (mah-nah-ka) . . . Boring

MANA PĀLUA (mah-nah-pah-loo-ah) . . . Doubly endowed with divine power

MANŌ (mah-no) . . . Shark

MANŌ 'AUMĀKUA (mah-no-ow-mah-koo-ah) . . . Shark ancestors

MEA HUNA (me-ah-hoo-nah) . . . Possessor of a secret

MELE KALIKIMAKA (may-lay-kah-lee-kee-mak-ah) . . . Merry Christmas

MENEHUNE (mee-nee-hoo-nee) . . . Legendary race of small people

MIKANELE (me-kah-ne-le) . . . Missionary

MILIMILI (mee-lee-mee-lee) . . . Dearest, beloved

MIMI (mee-mee) . . . Urine

MOAMAHI (mo-ah-mah-ee) . . . Fighting bird

MO'O (mo-o) . . . Lizard, dragon, reptile

MU'UMU'U (moo-oo-moo-oo) . . . Long, shapeless Mother Hubbard dress

NĀ MANAWALE'A (na-mah-nah-way-lee-ah) . . . The caring hearts

NELE (ne-le) . . . Lacking, without

NIU (nee-oo) . . . Coconut

NONI (naw-nee) . . . Medicinal roots and fruit of mulberry tree

NUI LOA (noo-ee-lo-ah) . . . With very much (love, thanks)

'OHANA (o-hah-nah) . . . Family, extended family

'ŌKOLE (o-ko-le) . . . Behind, the buttocks

'ŌKOLEHAO (o-ko-le-how) . . . Liquor from fermented rice, pineapple

'ŌKOLE MALUNA (o-ko-lee-mah-loo-nah) . . . Bottom's up! A drinking toast

'OLE (oh-le) . . . Nothingness

OLE KINE (ol-kine) . . . Pidgin-English for old-fashioned

ONE-FINGAH POI (one-fing-ah-poy) . . . Pidgin-English, *poi* thick enough to scoop with one finger

ONE MIMIKI (own-ee-mee-mee-ke) . . . Quicksand

'ONIPA'A (oh-nee-pah-ah) . . . Steadfast, determined

'ONO (oh-no) . . . Good, delicious

'ŌPAE (oh-pay-ee) . . . Prawns

'ŌPAKAPAKA (oh-pah-ka-pah-ka) . . . Snapper

'ŌPIHI (oh-pee-hee) . . . Limpet

'ŌPŪ (oh-poo) . . . Belly, stomach

PA'A (pah-ah) . . . Strong, firm, solid.

PĀHOEHOE (pah-hoy-hoy) . . . Smooth, unbroken lava

PAHU HULA (pah-hoo-hoo-lah) . . . Hula drum

PĀKĒ KANAKA (pah-ke-kah-nak-ah) . . . Chinese-Hawaiian (slang)

PANIOLO (pan-ee-o-lo) . . . Hawaiian cowboy, derived from *Español*

PANIPANI (pah-nee-pah-nee) . . . Sexual intercourse (vulgar, slang)

PAU (pow) . . . Finished

PAU HANA (pow-hah-nah) . . . Finished work

PAU MANŌ (pow-mah-no) . . . Eaten by shark

PELE (pe-le) . . . Goddess of volcanoes, of fire

PĪKAKE (pee-kah-kee) . . . Jasmine

PILAU (pee-lau) . . . Rotten, contaminated

PILIKUA (pee-lee-koo-ah) . . . Powerful, from manual labor

POI (poy) . . . Pudding of taro root

POMELO (po-me-lo) . . . Hawaiian grapefruit

PONO (po-no) . . . Goodness, morality, excellence

PŌPOLO (po-po-lo) . . . Nightshade plant

PRIMO (pree-mo) . . . Brand of beer

PUA KALA (poo-ah-ka-la) . . . Prickly poppy, juice of which is narcotic

PŪ'ALI (poo-ah-lee) . . . Warrior

PUMEHANA (poo-me-hah-nah) . . . Warmth, affection

PŪNANA LEO (poo-nah-nah-le-o) . . . The Language Nest, Hawaiian-language immersion preschool program.

PUPULE (poo-poo-le) . . . Crazy

PUPULE HAPA (poo-poo-lee-hah-pah) . . . Crazy mixed-blood

PU'U 'O'Ō (poo-oo-o-o) . . . Leaping, bleeding peak

SHAKA (sha-kah) . . . Greeting by wriggling little finger and thumb

SOAH (so-ah) . . . Pidgin-English, sore

TITA (tee-ta) . . . Sister (informal)

TŪTŪ (too-too) . . . Grandmother (informal)

'UKULELE (oo-koo-le-le) . . . Hawaiian guitar, literally "leaping flea"

VOG (vog) . . . Volcanic ash and fog mixed

WAIWAI (why-ee-why-ee) . . . Rich, wealth

WAHINE (va-hee-nee) . . . Woman (Plural: WĀHINE)

WELA (we-lah) . . . Hot, fiery

WIKIWIKI (wee-kee-wee-kee) . . . Hurry, quick!

Japanese-English Glossary

FUGU . . . Poisonous puffer fish

GAMAN SURU . . . To endure

GANBARU . . . To presevere

GETA . . . Clogs

GOMEN NASAI . . . I am sorry

HAI (hi) . . . Yes!

HARIGATA . . . Artificial penis

HIGOZUKI . . . Cage put between the legs

HOSHIDANA . . . Sun-drying roof for coffee beans

ISSEI . . . First-generation Japanese, immigrant to United States

KIBEI . . . Japanese-American born in Hawai'i

KOI . . . Carp fish

MIZU SHOBAI . . . The low life, underworld

OKONOMI MAME . . . Rice and nut snacks

SAIMIN . . . Type of noodle soup

SENSEI . . . Master teacher

SHODO . . . Superior art of writing

SHOYU . . . Soy sauce

TABI . . . Toed socks (often of rubber for fishing on rocks)

TATAMI . . . Rush mats

TSUNAMI . . . Tidal wave

YAKUZA . . . Japanese Mafia

YUKATA . . . short jacket

Chinese-English Glossary

BAIJIU ... Rice liquor

CHEONGSAM ... Mandarin-collared, form-fitting dress

DIM SUM ... Assorted steamed or fried dumplings

GWAI GOO ... Ghost stories

KOWTOW ... Bow in a servile way

MI YAO ... Stupefying powder

Personal Acknowledgments

Mahalo 'a nui to the people whose assistance, love and faith made writing this novel possible.

On the U.S. mainland: Kaye Burnett and Morris Shaxon, Peter Dee and Ed Nemeth, Kimiko Hahn and Ted Hanna, Camille Hykes, Edith Konecky, Florence Ladd and Bill Harris, Richard Miller, Joyce and John McGinnis, Nancy Nordhoff, Elizabeth Nunez-Harrell, Tillie Olsen, Kathrin Perutz, Patricia Powell and Teresa Langle, Alix Kates Shulman and Scott York, Mary TallMountain. And my mainland family, Mary and Braxton B. Davenport, Anita Bergin, Braxton R. Davenport, Denise Davenport, and Pauline Kreitz.

In the South Pacific: Peau Lomu, Momata, and Suliana Fifita, Vava'u, Tonga; Peter Kafcaloudis, Brisbane, Australia; Jeanette and Sanele Mageo, Pago Pago, American Samoa; Papu and Alofa Va'ai, Savai'i, Western Samoa; Captain John Sloane, Papua New Guinea; and Buffer Joe and Jim Jim, singing their *Dreaming* through Arnhem Land.

In Honolulu: Marie Hara, and Esther Kiki Mo'okini.

On the Big Island of Hawai'i: Lana and Lorenzo Aduca of Honaunau; Gus and Flo Becklund of Kailua; Paul Gomes of Kapa'au; Jill Olsen, Kona Historical Society; Fusao Sugai and Lee Sugai of Sugai Kona Coffee, Kealakekua; Luke and Ron of the Ocean View Inn, Kailua; the Manago family of Captain Cook.

Special *alohas* to my *'ohana* in Honolulu for guidance and assistance in tracing our family genealogy: Lucille and Daniel True Houghtailing, Jr., Helene and Calvin Bailey, Hazel Stone, Evelyn and Richard Liu, Pearly and George Kam, Jr., Leinaala and Arthur Kam, Rosemond Aho, Teddy and Mary Houghtailing, Raenette Ing, Aileen Rodriques, George Stone, Vernon Stone, Marshell and Richard Raymond, Dannette and Bill Gardner, Kathleen Viela, Pat and Clifford Everett, Carrie and Sonny Chang.

And to Uncle George Ayau Kam, Sr., ninety-three years old, husband of Minnie Kelomika for sixty-eight years. A love story.

E Pūpūkahi

Author's Note

While some of the characters in this book are based on historical figures, and while many of the areas described—such as Kalaupapa on the island of Moloka'i, and Waipi'o Valley on the Big Island—exist, this is a work of fiction. Portraits of the characters who appear in it are fictional, as are some of the events.

Conversely, it is important to stress that the overthrow of our queen, Lili'uokalani, in 1893, by forces seeking an American alliance, and the illegal annexation of the Hawaiian Islands by the U.S. government in 1898, is documented fact. The tragic history of leprosy in Hawai'i, and the development of the Kalaupapa Settlement on Moloka'i, is historically accurate.

I would like to thank the staff of the Bernice Pauahi Bishop Museum Library, the staff of the Hawaiian State Archives and staff members of the Hawaiian Historical Society Library for allowing me to pore over old documents and photographs. Thanks, too, to Beverly Fujita and Janice Otaguro for supplying back issues of *Honolulu* magazine. And thanks to the staff of the New York State Archives at Albany.

Many books were important to me in my research. Some of them are: *Kumulipo, the Hawaiian Hymn of Creation*, reinterpreted by Rubellite Ka-wena Johnson; *Hawai'i's Story by Hawai'i's Queen*, by Queen Lili'uokalani;

The Betrayal of Lili'uokalani, by Helena G. Allen, back copies of *Bamboo Ridge, the Hawai'i Writer's Quarterly*, edited by Eric Chock and Darrell Lum, *All I Asking for Is My Body*, by Milton Murayama, *Na Paniolo o Hawai'i*, edited by Lynn Martin, *Ma'i Ho'oka'Awale, the Separating Sickness*, edited by Ted Gugelyk and Milton Bloombaum, and *"Moolelo Hawai'i"* (Hawaiian Antiquities), by David Malo, translated by Nathaniel Emerson.

Waimea Summer, by John Dominis Holt, is a beautiful novel dealing with the problem of ethnic identity, the importance of our cultural and spiritual heritage. *Mahele O Maui*, a novel by Lynn Kalama Nakkim, investigates the old Hawaiian agricultural way of life and its threatened extinction.

Other books that influenced me are: the writings of Lu Hsun, especially *Na Han, (Call to Arms), A Dream of Red Mansions*, by Tsao Hsueh-chin and Kao Ngo, *The Pillow Book of Sei Shonagon, The Life of an Amorous Woman*, by Ihara Saikaku, the writings of Kenzaburo Oe, especially *A Personal Matter*. Also *Masks*, by Fumiko Enchi, *Silence*, by Shusaku Endo, *Memoirs of Hadrian*, and *The Dark Brain of Piranesi* by Marguerite Yourcenar, whose meditations on the life of the mind, the imagination, continue to influence me.

For the scene where Pono is first transformed into a shark I am indebted to Kobo Abe's short excerpt, "Then I dozed Off a Number of Times," from his novel *The Box Man*.

The scene where different types of water in the Gobi are discussed, though not direct quotes, echoes a journal entry in the book *Emperor of China, Self-Portrait of Kang-Hsi*, translated and edited by Jonathan D. Spence.

Acknowledgment is made to the following for permission to reprint previously published material:

The Richmond Organization: Excerpt from "Brain Damage," by Roger Waters. TRO Copyright © 1973 by Hampshire House Publishing Corp., New York, NY. Used by permission.

Excerpt from "The Sheik of Araby," by Ted Snyder, used by permission of the Jerry Vogel Music Co., Inc.

DUTTON **PLUME**

COMPELLING NOVELS

☐ **SINGING SONGS by Meg Tilly.** Written by the acclaimed actress, this novel explores how one family lives, centerless, caught in a flux of emotion and violence that touches and transforms each of its members. It is the masterful realization of a young girl's journey to adulthood in a chaotic, abusive, and fragmented world— an affirmation of a child's ability to use her judgment and imagination alone to light her way. "A triumph . . . absolutely believable, completely irresistible."
—*Chicago Sun-Times* (271657—$9.95)

☐ **THE BOOK OF REUBEN by Tabitha King.** Reuben Styles has spent his entire life in Nodd's Ridge, Maine trying to do the right thing according to the standard American success story. While nothing turns out as he expects, his incredible spirit and strength keep him struggling to become the man he envisioned. Capturing the searing, gritty reality of small-town America of the '50s, '60s, and '70s, this stunning, deeply involving novel touches a common nerve and casts a light on our own lives. (937668—$22.95)

☐ **RIVER OF SKY by Karen Harper.** This magnificent epic of the American frontier brings to vivid life one woman's stirring quest for fortune and happiness. This is Kate Craig's story—one of rousing adventure and heartbreaking struggle, of wild-fire passion and a wondrous love, as strong and deep as the river itself. It will sweep you into an America long gone by. (938222—$21.95)

☐ **MIAMI: A SAGA by Evelyn Wilde Mayerson.** Spanning a hundred years of challenge and change, this breathtaking panorama of Miami, Florida traces the tragedies and triumphs of five families—from the hardy homesteaders of the post-Civil War era to their descendants who bravely battle the devastation left by hurricane Andrew in 1992. (936467—$22.95)

Prices slightly higher in Canada.

Visa and Mastercard holders can order Plume, Meridian, and Dutton books by calling
1-800-253-6476.
They are also available at your local bookstore. Allow 4-6 weeks for delivery.
This offer is subject to change without notice.